It was time to fill the trousers again.

Or drown.

'Life is hope,' said Drake.

And manoeuvred himself off his trousers, meaning to slip them behind him to catch another load of air. But he was so weak that, as the last of that air-support left him, he slipped beneath the waves, losing his grip on the trousers. Which sank.

Drake sank.

Grabbing for the surface.

Something rose up beside him. He seized it. He found himself brought to the surface. By a shark. Too exhausted to scream, he lay there in the sea, lay with his cheek against the water-smooth flank of the shark, his arm over its great smooth back.

Then remembered that sharks are not smooth, for their skin has more teeth than their jaws. So this must be a dolphin, yes, he had heard of such, that accounted for the whistling and all, it was a dolphin, life answering to life just as the legends claimed. And Drake, unable to help himself, wept.

And heard someone hail him:

'Ahoy there! You with the fish!'

Also by Hugh Cook

THE WIZARDS AND THE WARRIORS
THE WORDSMITHS AND THE WARGUILD
THE WOMEN AND THE WARLORDS

and published by Corgi Books

THE WALRUS AND THE WARWOLF

Hugh Cook

CORGI BOOKS

THE WALRUS AND THE WARWOLF
A CORGI BOOK   0 552   13327 2

Originally published in Great Britain by Colin Smythe Limited

PRINTING HISTORY

Colin Smythe edition published 1988
Corgi edition published 1988

This book is set in Times

Corgi Books are published by Transworld Publishers Ltd., 61-63
Uxbridge Road, Ealing, London W5 5SA, in Australia by Transworld
Publishers (Australia) Pty. Ltd., 15-23 Helles Avenue, Moorebank,
NSW 2170, and in New Zealand by Transworld Publishers (N.Z.) Ltd.,
Cnr. Moselle and Waipareira Avenues, Henderson, Auckland.

Printed and bound in Great Britain by
Cox & Wyman Ltd., Reading, Berks.

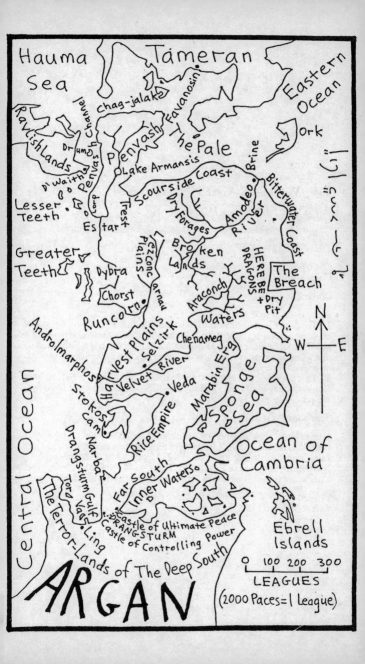

Hok

Stokos

Cam

Central
Ocean

N
W — E

0 20 40 60 80 100
Leagues

Narba

Drangsturm
Gulf

Tor

Provincial
Endergeneer

Burntos

Va

Ko

Quanat

Ling

DRANGSTURM

Castle of
Controlling
Power

Nidbelzik &
Torameer

Inner
Waters

1

Iron: metal made on Stokos by smelting the local hematite, a blood-red ore containing 70 parts in 100 of iron.

Steel: iron alloyed with carbon. Made on Stokos by baking iron with charcoal in a sealed pot kept at red heat for eight days, then melting the 'blister steel' thus produced in covered crucibles, skimming off the slag.

Firelight steel: fabric of the masterswords of Stokos; consists of interwoven layers of high carbon and low carbon steel; represents the height of the swordsmith's art.

Drake Douay had his sixteenth birthday two months before the start of the year Khmar 17. That night he celebrated by getting:
  (a) laid;
  (b) drunk;
  (c) into an enormous amount of trouble.
  At midnight he was trapped in a cul-de-sac by four coal miners, two dogs and an angry butcher's boy, all of them out for his blood.
  However, Drake was a practised survivor. He escaped with nothing worse than bruised ribs, a broken toe, and a nick in his left ear where a dagger had scratched him in the skirmish.
  Shortly afterwards, he stood outside the temple of the Demon Hagon, beating his fists against his naked chest and howling like a werewolf. Guards gave chase, but Drake lost them in the twisting back-streets of Cam. After

that, he was so tired he decided it was time for bed. But, to his surprise, he found the door of Hardhammer Forge barred against him.

'Wake up, Muck, you grouty old octopus!' bawled Drake.

But got no response, which was scarcely surprising, since Gouda Muck was nine-parts deaf and slept as soundly as a drunken crocodile quietly digesting a bellyful of plague-bloated rats.

Drake threw stones on the roof, then shouted, sang and howled, until one of the neighbours opened an attic window and threw a cat at him. Whereupon Drake decided on a tactical withdrawal.

Come dawn, he crawled out from underneath the boat where he had slept away the last of the night, yawned, grinned, stretched, hawked, then spat.

'Ahoy there!' called someone in very bad Galish.

Who was it?

A coal miner? The butcher's boy? The ruffian he had knocked out after last night's gambling quarrel?

It was none of the above, but a man rowing ashore from an evil-looking barque anchored out in the harbour of Cam. The ship's sails were furled, but, even so, Drake could see they were black.

'Ahoy yourself!' called Drake. 'What ship are you from?'

'Never mind the ship,' said the man, bringing the boat alongside some waterfront steps.

'Do you want a woman?' said Drake. 'I can get you one cheap.'

The stranger did not answer immediately, but secured the dinghy to a bollard with a painter, then came scrambling up the steps. He was an ill-favoured fellow with coarse foreign features, a thick neck, a barrel chest, rough-cut black hair and a shaggy black beard.

'Who be you?' he said.

'Narda Narkin,' said Drake Douay, answering at random.

10

Some mighty queer people came into Cam from time to time, so it was only common sense for Drake to reserve his true name.

'Pleased to meet you then, Narda Narkin,' said the stranger. 'I be Atsimo Andranovory. I search for three men. Rumour has them in Cam.'

'Their names?' said Drake.

'Whale Mike, Ish Ulpin and Bucks Cat.'

'I know them well,' said Drake, who had never heard of them, but thought himself unlikely to profit by confessing ignorance. 'I can direct you to their very door – for a price. What's it worth?'

'As much as the air between your lips,' said Atsimo Andranovory, putting a hand to the hilt of the cutlass he wore at his belt.

Drake glanced around. The waterfront was deserted. His bargaining position was poor.

'Take the street which leads from the southern end of the waterfront,' said Drake, pointing. 'Take the third turning on the left then the second on the right, and it's the third house along.'

'Thank you kindly,' said Andranovory.

And, with perfect faith in these directions, set off. Whereupon Drake turned in the opposite direction, whistling a jaunty tune as he made for Hardhammer Forge.

It was going to be another fine day. The air was cool, calm and clean. The sky was an enormous ascension of blue, flaunting banners of white cloud. Drake was happy, despite fatigue and headache. He was young, he was strong – and everything was going his way.

On reaching the forge, Drake was dismayed by an enormous heap of dusty black coal which had been delivered the previous evening. It would have to be put in sacks then stacked in the cellar. That was apprentice work, hence Drake's work.

'Such is life,' said Drake.

And slipped inside.

Hands in pockets, he leaned against a wall, looking

11

around as if he owned the place. He breathed in heat and coal dust, and smirked. He was sixteen. He knew it all. He was ready for the world.

'What are you doing here?' yelled Gouda Muck.

'Why, I work here, don't I?' said Drake.

'Work!' screamed old man Muck. 'That's a joke! You've never done a day's decent work in your life. You're such an ugly little runt you couldn't work if you wanted to!'

Drake was unhurt by the word 'ugly'. If there was such a thing as male beauty, then he, with his athlete's build and perfect muscle definition, was beautiful – and he knew it. But 'runt' – now that stung. For Drake was fearfully close to being short, which was disastrous on Stokos, where the fashion was to be as tall as possible.

To annoy Muck, Drake made no answer, but simply whistled the lilting tune of that ditty which starts as follows:

Two whores and a sheepdog were tupping one day
When a cat and a virgin came dancing that way.

'Stop whistling!' shouted Muck. 'You should be ashamed of yourself. You look like a walking rubbish heap.'

Muck was exaggerating. But, in truth, Drake Douay was not a pretty sight. Or a pretty smell, either. Unwashed, largely unslept and decidedly dishevelled. Shirtless. Blood, dirt, paint, rust and tomato sauce splattered across his torso. Dried blood in his blond hair. Breath like a brewery.

'How did you get in such a state?' said Muck. 'Look at yourself!'

'Can't,' said Drake. 'Got no mirror.'

'Just as well,' said Muck. 'You'd frighten any self-respecting mirror to death.'

'Mirrors can be frightened?' said Drake. 'This sounds like experience speaking!'

At that, Muck picked up a beautiful chunk of specular

iron with a hand which was old, gnarled, freckled with liver spots, and cunning with long experience. Muck heaved the rock at his apprentice. Drake ducked. The missile hit the wall, shattering into 376 pieces. Each fragment was made of crystallized hematite: for such is the nature of specular iron.

'Man, don't do that,' said Drake. 'This ducking business makes my head hurt.'

'Then cease your cheek,' said Muck, picking up a sword which he brandished so wildly that Drake feared for his head. 'Tell me – what's this?'

Even inside the forge, the weapon glittered like an eagle's eye. It was a mastersword made of firelight steel. And not just any old mastersword, either, but the masterwork Muck had made many dusty years ago to win entry to the swordsmith's guild.

'That?' said Drake, sneering at the blade. 'That's a giant's toothpick or a splinter of last month's moon, for all I know.'

'It's a sword! And where should you be? At sword!'

'Oh? Is it Temple Day again?'

'Yes,' said Muck, with satisfaction.

On these occasions, which happened every tenth day, everything at the temple of Hagon was half-price.

'What say,' said Drake. 'You set me free for the day. Just this once.'

'No!' said Gouda Muck, who delighted in forcing his apprentices to labour extra hard on Temple Day.

'You're wrong to deny me religion,' said Drake.

'I know you've got a sister in the temple,' said Muck, putting down his mastersword. 'I can't see you suffering too much denial. Why, I can smell a woman on you now!'

'That's not a woman,' said Drake promptly. 'That's a dog!'

'Then she's a dog with very poor taste,' said Muck, not caring whether Drake's claim was literal or metaphorical.

'Graf begrik,' muttered Drake.

'What was that?' said Muck sharply, suspecting –

correctly – that Drake had just said something lewd.

'I said where's Dragon's Tooth?' said Drake, scanning the sword rack, which held second-rate blades suitable for apprentice use.

'Yot's got it.'

'Oh, but that's my favourite!'

'Don't worry, you've no monsters to kill today,' said Muck, with a heavy attempt at sarcasm.

'No monsters?' said Drake. 'Only because you're off-limits!'

Muck swung at him with a poker. But Drake, who had expected as much, ducked. And Muck's boot caught Drake hard near the base of his spine. The blow with the poker had been only a feint.

'Ow!' said Drake. 'That hurt!'

'It was meant to,' said Muck, picking up a strange sword which Drake had never seen before. 'Here, take this. It's just come in. It's from Pribble's estate, in payment of a debt he owed me.'

The strange sword was big and heavy, but Drake had the muscles to handle the weight. The blade balanced nicely.

'Mind you Investigate it before use!' said Muck.

'That I will,' said Drake, and, naked blade resting lightly on his shoulder, strolled out of the forge.

'Move yourself!' shouted Muck. 'You haven't got all day!'

So Drake got the hustle on, at least until he was round the corner.

Drake swung his sword. Liberated from the gloom of the forge, it glittered in the daylight. He danced on the cobblestones between two rows of whitewashed buildings, stabbing at ghosts with his vorpal blade.

What should he call it?

'Warwolf', perhaps.

That was scarcely original, as many fabled swords and heroes bore that name. But Drake had the temperament of a craftsman rather than that of an artist; he preferred utility to originality any day of the year.

'I name thee Warwolf,' he said. 'Too long hast thou lingered amidst dust and debts. Thou shouldst have had ruler like me beforehand.'

Then, whistling, he began to Investigate the brave sword Warwolf.

By using it.

First he tried to lop the head off a stray cat – but it was too quick for him. Then he slashed a branch off a stunted little tree trying to grow in a big streetside stone pot. That was reckless, since all potted trees in Cam were under the protection of King Tor. But it was still early morning, so few people were about in the streets to bear witness.

Rounding another corner, Drake was startled to be confronted by a watermelon stand. A massive, old, unpainted stand of weathered grey wood, heaped high with watermelons. This fearsome apparition made Drake entirely forget about his hangover.

'Not a watermelon stand!' he gasped. 'Nay! Say not! But no! It is! My eyes fail! My blood turns to water!'

But, regardless of failing eyes and watery blood, Drake stood his ground. And challenged his fell foe.

'Stand aside!' he said. 'Aside, I say! Or it shall go ill with you.'

The watermelon stand, undaunted by this threat, made no effort to get out of his way. Drake knew his peril. For, truly, in all the annals of heroism and romance, there is no account of any man ever daring battle with a watermelon stand and living to tell the tale.

'Die, hell-fiend!' gritted Drake.

And hewed like a hero. *Thwap*! The nearest watermelon fell dead at his feet.

'Shalt fear the dreaded Drake Douay hereafter,' snarled he, menacing a particularly big brute of a watermelon.

The monster's skin was a thick, tough, alien green, stippled with patterns of sunlight yellow. A challenge indeed! But Drake the Doughty stabbed with a strength against which even the strongest armour could not avail.

He wounded his enemy.

15

Ichor dripped from the wound.

Drake stabbed again – for, as is well known, the watermelon has neither heart nor liver, nor any other vital organ, and thus is seldom killed by a single stab wound.

'What's this?' said Drake. 'It will not die! Could it be that I am face to face with an immortal?'

He drew his sword back, intending to strike the most awesome blow imaginable.

At that moment, the watermelon seller came roaring out of a nearby tavern, screaming threats and abuse. Drake snatched up half a watermelon and sprinted away with this trophy. He went flying up a side-street, which was steep, narrow and radically kinked.

Drake tore round one corner then whipped round another. The street steep, still rising. Another corner. He saw a fully laden coal cart waiting uphill. He dug in his heels for a final burst of speed. Gaining the coal cart, he kicked the chocks away from its wheels.

Panting harshly, Drake stood watching as the cart went rumbling downhill. Lumps of coal jumped for freedom as the cart jolted over the cobblestones. It was gaining speed.

'Look out below!' screamed Drake. 'Runaway cart!'

Then the cart hit a kink in the street. It smashed into a wall. The wall shattered. The cart burst asunder. Coal dust exploded into the air. The wall collapsed. Until that moment, it had been supporting a roof. A landslide of sky-blue tiles slithered from the roof and shattered in the street.

'Oh, great stuff, great stuff!' said Drake, trying to pant and laugh at the same time.

He would have clapped his hands for joy and delight – only that would have meant dropping both sword and watermelon.

'Zooma floragin!' screamed a manic figure, bursting out of the building which the cart had wrecked. 'Thamana lok!'

'That's not polite,' muttered Drake.

And, indeed, it was not polite at all – it was low and filthy gutter language.

As the demented figure gave chase, Drake fled.

Once he had lost his pursuer, Drake munched down the juicy pink flesh of the watermelon, then strolled along with a mouthful of pips, spitting them out one at a time. Which took skill, but he had been practising for as long as he could remember (and stealing watermelons for that long, too).

Splip! Stlip!

Watermelon seeds flew, with considerable accuracy, through every open window he passed.

That was fun.

But, all too soon, he arrived at the sword field, which was not a field at all, but a dusty courtyard where, usually, three dozen apprentices would have been practising sword.

'Bugger,' said Drake.

The sun was getting up. The excitement of the coal cart crash had worn off. His legs were tired, his boots heavy. He was remembering his headache. It felt bad. How had he ever forgotten it? A wave of weariness rolled over him. He wanted to be in bed. But his bed was in the loft over the forge, so Muck would know exactly where to find him if he tried skiving off. Holding his sword by the pommel, Drake entered the sword field, letting the blade's point trail behind him in the dust.

Today there was nobody present but an instructor, and Sully Yot. All the other apprentices had been released by their masters so they could enjoy the delights of Temple Day.

'Ah, there you are, young Dreldragon!' said the instructor. Then, seeing what Drake was doing: 'Get that sword out of the dust before I shove it up your arse! Get your arse over here! Get working!'

'Hey, man,' said Drake. 'Give us a break, why don't you? How about you come to the temple with us? I'll buy you a beer, man. A woman, even. Muck will never know different.'

In reply, the instructor booted Drake in the backside, then set him to work with Yot, making the pair of them practise a two-man kata.

The swordsmiths' guild believed apprentices should

17

learn weapon skills, the better to be able to make a decent killing blade. But they allowed no rough-and-tumble play with wasters.

As the instructor was fond of saying: 'We are not teaching you how to brawl it out on a battlefield, but to learn how weight, length and balance dictate utility.'

Nevertheless, sword training was deadly serious, done with bare blades and no protection. A single mistake could wound, mutilate or kill. However, though dangerous, it could almost have been mistaken for a kind of dance – for it was strictly a no-contact affair. Every thrust, fake, step, jump and counter was pre-arranged.

Drake, after years of this, was thoroughly bored with the rituals of the one-man, two-man and multiple-encounter katas. He longed to make steel chime with steel. But, when Yot struck and Drake parried, both halted their blades the instant before contact. For, if ever edge met edge, a sword might be notched, bent, or even broken.

'I need a drink,' said Drake, after the first kata.

'Booze is the last thing you need,' said the instructor.

'I didn't meant liquor, I mean water.'

'Why would you be needing that? Because you've got the dry horrors, I suppose. And whose fault is that? You young kids! You shouldn't be allowed to drink.'

'Liquor is holy,' said Drake. 'The High Priest says so.'

'Steel is also holy.'

'Who said that?' demanded Drake.

'I did!' said the instructor.

And kick-started his recalcitrant student.

Drake felt as if he was breathing a mixture of thorns and ashes. As the sun lifted itself above the wall of the sword field, his head began to throb. Yot – lanky, wart-faced, a vapid smile on his lips – was just dancing through the motions, holding his sword lightly, loosely, as if its hilt were a little girl's hand. How come Yot had all that height, when he had no decent use for it?

Round and round they went, their shadows scuffling in

18

the dust. And suddenly Drake could stand it no longer, and, with an almighty sweep, brought the flat of his blade crashing into the flat of Dragon's Tooth, knocking that sword right out of Yot's hand.

'Gaaa!' screamed Drake.

Hacking at his disarmed enemy.

He tried to halt his blade as it reached Yot's skin. But, despite all Drake's skill, Yot got a cut on the side of his neck. It was tiny – no more than a boy would get from scratching away a pimple. But Yot touched it, then, seeing blood on his fingers, fainted clean away. Yot had never liked the sight of blood – especially his own.

'Dogs, pox and buggeration!' said the instructor. 'Get out of my sight!'

'As you wish,' said Drake.

And strode toward the exit, weapon in hand.

'Hey!' said the instructor. 'Come back! You've left something behind!'

'What, Yot? He'll come on his own two feet once he gets his wits back.'

'No, ninny. This!'

And the instructor held up for Drake's inspection a strange little bit of hooked iron which he had fished out of the dust.

'What's that?' said Drake.

'It's a letter, you illiterate son of an octopus. The letter Àçøwæ, in fact.'

'Well where did that come from?'

'Out of your sword, moron. Look!'

And, looking, Drake saw an indentation in the flat of his sword which precisely matched the shape of the bit of iron which the instructor alleged was the letter Àçøwæ.

'Look closely,' said the instructor. 'There's other iron letters in the steel. See? They spell out a word. A foreign word, yes, in one of the languages of Provincial Endergeneer. I won't tax your brain by making you learn it. But I'll tell you what it means. It means "think before using"!'

And, having warned Drake that he would be taking the

19

matter up with Gouda Muck, the instructor bid him good day.

Back at the forge, Muck was furious.

'Well, I wasn't to know,' said Drake. 'I didn't even know there were iron-bits there to start with.'

'I told you to Investigate!' said Muck. 'Haven't you learnt anything?'

'As much as I've been taught,' said Drake.

Muck stared at him, speechless, face saying:

'¿¡!?'

Once Muck had recovered his voice, he used it to baste his apprentice nicely, then gave him a lecture on iron inlay.

'It sounds right fancy stuff,' said Drake. 'But how come we never do it here?'

'Because the best steel needs no adornment,' said Muck. 'Watch close. I'll show you how to replace this missing iron letter. We'll start from scratch.'

And Muck showed Drake how to make a new letter by twisting bits of iron wire together. Then, with the blade white-hot, the cold iron was hammered into place.

'Now,' said Muck. 'We take the blade to welding heat and do just a little extra hammering to make sure the iron inlay stays there for a lifetime. What's welding heat, boy?'

'Don't know,' said Drake.

'It's about a thousand degrees on the Saglag Scale, where zero is the temperature at which shlug freezes, and fifty is the temperature at which that thixotropic fluid known as dikle suddenly trembles into fluid. What does thixotropic mean, boy?'

'It means the heat at which tilps jiffle,' said Drake.

Which was obscene, and uncalled for, and untrue to boot, and earned him a slap around the ears, that stung.

But it was a mere flea-bite compared to the beating he got the next day, after Gouda Muck had heard from the sword field instructor (whose truths conflicted somewhat with the tale Drake had brought back to the forge), from a man who sold watermelons, and from the Protector of the Royal Trees.

After the beating, Drake, somewhat tearful, confronted Muck.

'All you do is kick me and hit me,' said Drake.

'Well, what else can I do?' said Muck. 'You won't listen, you won't learn, you won't do as you're told.'

'You could teach me how to make swords,' said Drake. 'That's what I'm here for. I've been here four years, and what have you taught me? Levil Norkin is only fifteen, and he made his first sword a year ago.'

'Then maybe he'll finish up as a swordsmith,' said Gouda Muck.

'You mean I won't?' said Drake in dismay.

'You don't get to be a swordsmith by spending your apprenticeship boozing, fighting, wenching and gambling,' said Muck. 'Have you never thought of that?'

Drake made no reply.

'Well?' said Muck.

'I never got much encouragement,' said Drake.

'It's your life, not mine,' said Muck. 'You're not a child! Your life is what you make it.'

'Do I—'

'Do you still have a chance? You may have. A slim chance, mind! But a chance, all the same. It really depends what you want out of life. Do you want to be a swordsmith? Or do you want to go back and live as your parents do?'

Drake thought of his parents and the life they lived, cutting coal out of the cliffs, gathering seaweed, fishing off the Wrecking Rocks. No, that was not what he wanted. Not at all.

'I . . . I love steel,' said Drake, in a slow and sober voice. 'There's . . . there's a special light about steel. It shines. I like—'

'Spare me the poetry!' said Muck. 'I'll tell you what. If you promise to work hard, really hard, I'll let you start your first sword tomorrow.'

'Really?' said Drake.

'When did I ever speak in jest?' said Muck.

'Done!' said Drake. 'It's a bargain!'

'Right,' said Muck. 'Now hustle off, or you'll be late for your theory class.'

As Drake sped away to his theory class, he exulted. So he was going to start on the real stuff at last! After all these years of sweeping, shovelling, pumping the bellows, grinding, sharpening and patching. He was going to be a real swordsmith, and make his own blade.

Wow!

'Great stuff!' said Drake. 'Great stuff!'

And then, in two more years he would be a swordsmith himself, with apprentices of his own to beat about the ears.

Or so he thought.

In practice, it did not prove that easy.

For, half-way through his theory class, guards burst into the classroom.

'Dreldragon Drakedon Douay,' said their leader. 'Where are you?'

'Here,' said Drake.

'You're under arrest.'

'Arrest?' said Drake. 'Whatever for?'

'Don't ask questions. Come with us!'

And Drake was marched through the streets of Cam to the Iron Palace, where he was thrown into a cell, and told he would stand trial before King Tor in the morning.

'What have I done wrong?' wailed Drake.

'Boy, don't ask me,' said his gaoler. 'But unless you've been very, very good of late, you can expect to get your head chopped off tomorrow. The king's lately been in the worst of tempers imaginable.'

Which was bad news indeed. For King Tor was an ogre – and the temper of an ogre is never the sweetest of things at the best of times.

2

Name: Parry Iklemass Tinklebeth Terrorjaw Tor. (NB: by law, none may address the king by any of his three first names, on pain of death.)

Birthplace: Cam.

Occupation: king.

Status: absolute ruler of Stokos.

Description: an ogre twice man-height; width almost equal to height; elephant-style ears; tusks jutting downwards from upper jaw; age 54; hair black; eyes blue; six fingers on each hand; grey skin patterned like that of a crocodile.

Residence: the Iron Palace of Cam.

When night came, Drake hunched up in a corner of his cell and tried to get to sleep. It was almost impossible. The darkness echoed with the crash of great doors, the tramp of iron-shod boots, the garbled intercourse of coarse voices, occasional screams and the racket of hyena-flavoured laughter.

Sitting in darkness, breathing an ineffable jail-stench in which the reek of blocked drains predominated, Drake imagined he heard rats moving in his cell on razor-clawed feet. He thought he heard them sharpening their teeth against the cold tombstone-sized slabs of the floor. At last he fell asleep and dreamed – briefly – of the sword he would make with the help of Gouda Muck.

He woke to find things crawling over his face. He beat at them, knocking them into the dark. Spiders? Cockroaches? Something went whirling round his cell with a staccato clitter-clatter of wings.

'Grief,' muttered Drake.

And found himself unable to regain the realms of sleep.

When morning came, the gaoler served breakfast, which was a jug of water and a bowl of fish chowder.

'What happens now?' said Drake.

'Now? Why, your trial starts shortly.'

'Good,' said Drake.

He was glad, for a prompt trial meant he would soon be out of here. Excellent! He was in a hurry to return to Hardhammer Forge. He wanted to get down to work, yes, to start on his first sword. Surely King Tor would let him go. What had he done wrong? Nothing serious.

Drake thought Tor might even give him some compensation for false arrest and wrongful imprisonment.

Yes.

'Rise and shine,' said the gaoler, interrupting Drake's calculations of probable compensation. 'We're going to the Iron Hall.'

Shortly Drake was shown into the Iron Hall of the Iron Palace. He had never been in a building so large, or so full of noise and people. Once there, sitting on a hard wooden bench, watching King Tor administer justice, Drake swiftly began to change his mind about his prospects.

The ruler of Stokos seemed to take law and life very seriously indeed.

Again and again Tor cried:

'Off with his head!'

It seemed to be the king's favourite punishment.

Pleas for mercy did no good. Neither did grovelling. One particularly abject petitioner crawled to the throne and started licking the king's clawed feet. The snivelling fool was promptly kicked to death for his cowardice.

'Be bold,' muttered Drake to Drake.

'What did you say?' demanded a guard.

24

'I said, funny how there's so much iron in this place,' said Drake.

'Oh,' said the guard. 'That's easy enough explained. Things human-built tend to break when an ogre gets hold of them. The king's always complaining about how fragile everything is.'

'Oh,' said Drake, eyeing the king.

Who sat on a throne of black iron. Wearing leather trousers and a leather jacket, both studded with iron. Refreshments on an iron table beside him: live frogs in a huge bowl of cast iron. Blood in a chalice of wrought iron. A heap of mules' eyes on a plate of pig iron. At his feet, a gryphon.

'What,' said Drake, 'am I charged with?'

'You expect a bill of particulars?' said the guard, with a laugh. 'We're not so stupid. If you knew what you were charged with, you'd be inventing lies and fantasizing alibis right now. Wouldn't you?'

'I'd be doing no such thing,' said Drake, indignantly. 'I'm a humble, law-abiding apprentice. And very religious into the bargain.'

'We'll see about that,' said the guard. 'Your case is next.'

Upon which King Tor pronounced sentence on his latest victim:

'Cut off the top of his head then feed him his own brains.'

Drake shivered.

And an orderly shouted:

'Dreldragon Drakedon Douay! Be upstanding! Advance to receive justice!'

Drake got to his feet and strode forward with as much of a swagger as he could manage. His body was alive with frantic pulses. His heart was asking for out. His arsehole was quivering. His knees trembled.

He halted, ten paces in front of the king. Set his feet shoulder-width apart. And tensed the muscles in his legs, to keep them from shaking. He eyed the king's gryphon

25

uneasily. The brute appeared to be asleep, its purple wings folded against its tawny lionskin body. On its great hooked eagle's beak was what looked suspiciously like dried blood.

'What have you been doing wrong?' said Tor, in a buffalo-built voice.

'Man,' said Drake, in a loud voice which rang against stone and against iron, 'you're real hot on wrong. How about some right for a change? If it pleases your majesty – and even if it doesn't – I've done a good bit right in my time. Yes. Good work at the forge. Good work with steel. Good work at sword, too.'

King Tor snorted.

'Don't snort so quick!' said Drake. 'It's logic, isn't it? Right should mean as much as wrong. But here you only talk of wrong, wrong, wrong, wrong. All about error. Well, I say this. Maybe I killed a couple of watermelons. Maybe I took a little twig off a tree – sorry about that, your ugliness, but it'll live. Anyway, those are only little wrongs. The great rights of my life should cancel them out altogether.'

'You're talking nonsense,' said King Tor.

'Not so!' exclaimed Drake. 'Man, you should set up a court of rights as well as a court of wrongs. I volunteer for trial in such a court. I guarantee I'd walk away with reward rather than punishment. Stands to reason, doesn't it? If wrongs deserve punishment, rights deserve rewards. And in my case, rights outweigh wrongs by nine thousand to one.'

Tor laughed. Even at ten paces, Drake was assailed by royal halitosis. Tor's breath stank like a heap of guts which has sat for twenty-four days in a midden pit. Drake did his best not to flinch.

'Let's see, little mannikin,' said King Tor. 'Let's see exactly what you're charged with. Bring in the witnesses!'

While Drake was still suppressing his indignation about being called a mannikin, the witnesses trouped in. And a long line they made. They began to give evidence.

There was the watermelon seller.

There was the Protector of the Royal Trees.

There was the owner of a certain coal cart.

There was the owner of a certain house which had been wrecked by a certain coal cart.

There was the father of a girl of fourteen whom Drake had deflowered on his birthday.

There was the owner of a certain boat which was somewhat the worse for wear as a consequence of Drake's birthday celebrations.

There was—

But why go on? It is a long list, and the recital of such a list would not increase the world's wisdom, and might well give the unwise certain ideas they would be better off not having.

Once the witnesses had finished, King Tor said:

'What have you got to say for yourself?'

'What have I got to say for myself?' said Drake. 'Why, that I'd like to marry your daughter. For I'm just the man, as the witnesses have proved. Yea. For I am strong, brave, determined, resolute in decision, ruthless in action, swift, cunning, subtle as a serpent, fit, healthy, and the boldest cocksman who ever stalked the streets of Cam.'

'Do your talents excuse you from obedience to the law?' said King Tor, in something which sounded fearfully like anger.

'Man,' said Drake. 'There's no excuse needed. Those petty little quibbling pranks hardly rate a slap on the hand, far less the greater punishments. Why, they're all but boyish larks of one kind or another.

'And I'll have you know this. That girl wasn't much of a virgin, she'd had her father and brother before me.

'As for the other things, why, most of them weren't my fault either. They were the fault of the way the world's built. It's a right flimsy place, your majesty, not built to take the strain of hard-living men like you and me. Why, if that cart had been built proper, it would never have ruptured when it hit that wall. That wall wasn't built well, either, or it would have stopped the cart. And that boat wasn't up to much, either.

27

'All in all, if you must talk punishment, I think you could let me get away with all this for no more than a slap on the hand.'

King Tor sat in thought.

He drank a draught of blood. Good stuff! He burped, and wiped his lips. He plucked a frog from the snack-bowl and munched it down. Ah! Great eating!

'Well,' said King Tor. 'We were all young once.'

Drake waited.

The king drank some more blood.

A little dripped from his lips to his leather trousers.

'You're right,' said King Tor. 'Those were but boyish pranks. So I'll let you off lightly. We'll have you birched in public today. You spend tonight buried to the neck in the public dungheap. Towards morning, we'll put you on a boat. Three leagues from shore, you'll be thrown overboard. That is my justice!'

Drake knew he had got a good deal. But he could not resist the impulse to push his luck.

'Man,' said Drake, 'my offer for your daughter still holds good.'

Tor sat in silence, staring at Drake. Then:

'You have a very high opinion of yourself,' said Tor.

'I'm a man's man, man,' said Drake, wishing he had kept quiet.

Tor considered. There was, for once, something close to silence in the Iron Hall. Everyone assembled wanted to hear the king's judgment. Would this boy get to marry Hilda, the king's daughter? Or would he be torn to pieces on the spot for his impudence?

'You hold yourself nicely enough,' said Tor, slowly. 'But substance may differ from appearance. That three-league swim from sea to shore should tell us rather more about you. If . . . if you can make it back to my palace before sunset, then you're the man to marry my daughter.'

'Why, that's right handsome of you,' said Drake. 'It's a deal.'

And they shook on it. As Tor's six-fingered hand closed on Drake's, the ogre squeezed. Just slightly. Drake winced, and squeezed back.

'Good muscles there,' said Tor, approvingly. 'Good luck!'

'Thought of the fair visage of your daughter will sustain me, sire,' said Drake gravely.

Tor laughed, released Drake and clapped his hands.

'Take him away!' said Tor.

So Drake was taken out and birched in public, getting the standard twenty lashes. And it's no good pretending it didn't hurt, because it did. Worse than the pain was the publicity – for, as Drake was well aware, Sully Yot was amongst those watching.

Then Drake was planted in the dung heap, naked, up to his neck in ordure. And it's no good pretending that was comfortable – it was the worst night he'd had in his life. But for a fresh breeze coming in off the sea, he would have perished that night by reason of the fumes from the dung.

Towards dawn, Drake experienced something very close to despair. He felt shattered. He doubted that he could swim even as far as a sick snail could crawl while a hungry man was gulping down a very small piece of bread and jam, let alone three leagues. Three leagues! That was six thousand paces!

Still, he had to try.

The sun was rising when Drake was dug out of the dung heap. First off, he was thrown into the harbour. The shock of the water revived him somewhat; he found he could swim, and swim quite well. Once he was clean – more or less – he was allowed to climb out of the harbour.

A considerable crowd had gathered to see the young man who had set himself up as a contender for the throne of Stokos. As someone threw a blanket over his shoulders, Drake gazed around at the mob. Why, he must be famous!

'Good morning, young Drake,' said a familiar voice.

It was Gouda Muck.

'Hi,' said Drake. 'Come to watch the fun, have you? Why couldn't you stay back at the forge torturing rats with a red-hot poker?'

'Don't be like that,' said Muck. 'I've brought you a present.'

And so he had – a pair of new trousers and a thick jersey of greasy wool. Drake was startled.

'Why,' said Drake. 'Why, this – I—'

'Thank me by surviving,' said Muck, clapping a hard and horny hand onto his shoulder. 'You're a good lad, really. I know that.'

Such presents and such praise were the very last thing Drake had expected to get on that particular morning. His heart was gladdened; he felt almost human again.

'Morning, young sprogling,' said a rough but cheery voice.

It was Drake's uncle, Oleg Douay. And what had he brought with him? Why, breakfast!

Bacon, yes, and devilled kidneys, and bread greasy with fat. Drake scrambled into his new clothes then ate with a will, feeding warmth, strength and energy into his belly. Three leagues? No problem! He could do it lying on his back.

'That breakfast will see you drowned with cramp,' said an anonymous pessimist.

'Not me,' said Drake, carelessly, and downed another kidney. 'What's that other package? Something else for me?'

'Some new boots,' said Oleg Douay. 'But I won't hand them over yet. I'll be waiting when you make it back to shore. I expect you to dine with me this evening.'

'With pleasure,' said Drake.

'Five shangles says you can't swim the three leagues wearing the boots,' said a voice.

It was Sully Yot, half-hidden amongst the crowd.

'Done!' said Drake. Then, to his uncle: 'Give me the boots.' Reluctantly, his uncle handed them over.

'This isn't wise,' said Oleg. 'Those boots will drown you.'

'Not me,' said Drake, determined to win five shangles off Sully Yot.

Five shangles! Why, that was a week's wages. With five shangles, he could be drunk for two and a half days without a moment's sobriety.

Then Drake remembered that his days of boozing, gambling and wenching were over. He was a serious sword-smith now, soon to settle down to the job of making his first blade. Well . . . once he'd made that weapon, surely a little celebration would be in order.

Yes. Surely.

'I'll be here myself when you get to shore,' said Yot, 'to make sure you're still wearing the boots. So no cheating!'

'I'll be wearing the boots all right,' said Drake. 'I'll keep them on if only for the pleasure of kicking you.'

Then Drake was shown to the canary-yellow dinghy in which he would be rowed out to sea. The boat, he was told, was the *Walrus*. Unbeknownst to Drake, her owner had named her thus because he had once sailed on a pirate ship captained by a water-thief of that name.

Drake was introduced to the crew.

There were three of them. Ish Ulpin (owner of the *Walrus*) and Bucks Cat were both human. The third, Whale Mike, was mostly ogre; he was twice man-height. But, unlike King Tor, he was of fairly slim build – his shoulders were no wider than a man's outstretched arms. He wore tarpaulin overalls and a great big leather apron with a huge pocket in the front.

The rowing boat – a big wide strongbuilt thing which would usually have had a crew of ten – settled noticeably as Whale Mike stepped into it. Drake dreaded to think what he weighed.

'Well, gentlemen,' said Drake. 'It looks like a good day for it. Shall we be setting to sea?'

He stepped into the boat. Ish Ulpin took the tiller; Whale Mike and Bucks Cat began to row. Men on ships in the harbour cheered or jeered according to their nature.

Then, as the *Walrus* passed by the bow of an ill-favoured barque with furled black sails, a man leaned over the railing and cried:

'Hey, boys! That's the pup I told you about! The one who gave me the wrong directions!'

Looking up, Drake saw the man on the ship was Atsimo Andranovory.

'Belt him round the earhole for me!' cried Andranovory.

Whereupon Ish Ulpin did just that.

'Hit him again!' said Andranovory.

'No, that not fair,' said Whale Mike. Then, raising his voice so Andranovory could hear: 'You want hit boy, you know where to find him! You swim out after us if that what you want!'

Andranovory answered in curses.

Soon, he was out of earshot. The dinghy left the protection of the harbour and began to rock uncomfortably on the swells. Drake started feeling uneasy.

Or, to be precise, queasy.

All that bacon fat in his belly was getting distinctly uneasy about this adventure.

'You not happy stomach?' said Whale Mike. 'Here, you get this good, she put you right.'

And Whale Mike handed Drake a small stone bottle. What was in it, Drake didn't ask. He simply swigged. It was bitter. It burnt. At first, he felt worse than ever. Then his stomach settled, and seasickness threatened no more as the *Walrus* rowed out into the open sea.

3

Ish Ulpin: a lean, pale man with a thin, mirthless mouth. He is given to great anger; he loves to kill. Once was a gladiator in Chi 'ash-lan; later, sailed with the Orfus pirates of the Greater Teeth. Now works for King Tor as executioner and torturer, but is not averse to a little private enterprise on the side. In anyone's language, this man is dangerous.

Bucks Cat: a tall man with a wrestler's build; black hair; ebony skin; a knife-scar grinning on his throat. Born on Island Talsh in Sponge Sea. After capture in slaving raid, worked for many years in a quarry in the Ashun Mountains. Led slave revolt which took three years to suppress; spent five years on Greater Teeth before settling on Stokos.

Whale Mike: an ogre built as tall as King Tor. Has a trace of human ancestry (ogres can breed with humans, as wolves can with dogs) as evidenced by a face showing what is almost a standard human configuration. Small eyes of incontrovertible imbecility; cheeks bulging as if a full-moon resides within each; sallow yellow skin. He has no ears, only holes in the side of his head where ears should be. (His hearing, even so, is acute.)

His past is unspeakable.

The day was bright; the sun glittered on the sea and glinted from the blue and green tiled rooves of Cam. The clouds were few, white and very high. Drake felt strangely tranquil as he watched the whitewashed buildings of Cam

33

receding into the distance. Three leagues was a long way to swim. But he had every confidence of success. In fact, he felt he had energy to spare. By way of showing off, he offered to row.

'You not row, man,' said Whale Mike. 'You sleep.'

'I don't need to sleep,' said Drake. 'I know what's best for me.'

'You like kitten,' said Whale Mike. 'Eyes not open yet. You not know which way up.'

'It doesn't matter what he knows,' said Ish Ulpin, with a laugh which suggested no humour. 'It'll all be over soon enough in any case.'

'What?' said Drake. 'You think I'm going to drown or something?'

'Shut up,' said Bucks Cat.

'You make nice sleep,' said Whale Mike. 'That always good thing. Not much sleep in water. That not so?'

Drake hated to take advice from anything which looked so stupid, but, in the end, he made himself as comfortable as he could and closed his eyes. And slept, right enough. Dreaming of munched frogs and dripping blood. After a while, he woke to hear someone – Ish Ulpin, by the sound of it – talking about Andranovory.

'We should have taken old Andranovory's offer,' said Ish Ulpin. 'It's our chance to get back to the Greaters.'

'Yes,' said Bucks Cat.

'You really want go back there?' said Whale Mike. 'I not like that. We happy here, that not so? In Greaters, nobody trust anybody. That not nice.'

'Who cares about nice?' said Ish Ulpin. 'I care about money.'

And Drake thought: *Well, and so do we all*.

Then drifted off to sleep again. Waking considerably later. What had woken him? A gull, yes, the harsh cry of a gull. Lament of the ages. He sat up, blinked. His eyes hot, red, sore. Infected from the dung heap? Maybe. The boat rocked. His arse was sore. His back was sore. A boat was no place to sleep.

34

'Hey,' said Drake. 'Where are we?'

He looked for the shore. It was a fair way distant. Well, to be exact: an unfair way distant. The whitewashed buildings with their roofs of blue and green tiles were shrunk by distance to the size of flecks of paint.

'This is more than three leagues!' said Drake.

And promptly leaped overboard. The sea was so wet! So big! So dark! Drake was most unhappy about it. But he was even less happy when Ish Ulpin picked up a harpoon and threatened him.

'Back in the boat, boy,' said Ish Ulpin. 'Get in, or I spear you.'

'What is this?' said Drake.

'Don't argue,' said Ish Ulpin. 'Get in!'

Drake paddled back to the boat. Whale Mike hauled him aboard, then took his turn at the tiller. Buck Cat and Ish Ulpin continued rowing.

'Hey, man,' said Drake uneasily. 'Three leagues is but six thousand paces. We're that far from shore already, I'll swear to it.'

He got no answer. He felt stupid, sitting there dripping wet, so stripped himself naked, wrung out his clothes then put them back on. Leaving his boots off. Those lovely new boots had felt dangerously heavy when he had been swimming in the sea. He bitterly regretted making his bet with Sully Yot, because it was clear enough now that he was going to lose his five shangles. Yes, and Yot would never let him forget it.

'Hey, boys,' said Drake, 'row me most of the way back in and I'll let you have three shangles. That's one each. That's a lot of money.'

Bucks Cat laughed, and pulled on his oars with a will.

'You're going too far!' said Drake.

'And we'll go further yet before you jump,' said Ish Ulpin, sunlight glinting on his fine white teeth as he smiled.

Smiled without humour.

'What is this?' said Drake. 'Vigilante justice or something?'

35

'Exactly,' said Ish Ulpin.

'I'm a citizen!' shouted Drake. 'A very religious boy! Just a boy, a tender-hearted boy. I want to work hard and worship, to learn obedience under the law, yes, learn my lessons, pay my taxes, reform, be good. Why are you doing this to me?'

'Certain merchants have paid us to,' said Ish Ulpin. 'Aye, and paid well, too. Nice work for easy money.'

'Merchants?' said Drake. 'Who? The guy with the watermelon stand? Or that man with the daughter?'

'None of those,' said Ish Ulpin. 'Nay. Men of more importance. Men who fear to see a fool named Dreldragon marry King Tor's daughter.'

'What?' said Drake. 'They're in lust with her?'

'Nay. But they fear a fool like you as king. You marry her tomorrow, the king could be dead the next day. He's old enough to die.'

'He might last another thirty years,' said Drake.

'And might not,' said Ish Ulpin. 'The people who pay us want no risks.'

'You can't do this!' howled Drake.

But got no reaction. Until Whale Mike said:

'He only boy, you know. We long way out. He not get back. This far enough, yes?'

'You always were soft in the head,' said Bucks Cat. 'I've swum further than this myself. He might do the same himself.'

'Unless we put a harpoon through him,' said Ish Ulpin. 'How about it?'

'Yes,' said Bucks Cat.

'Oh no,' said Whale Mike. 'That cruel. We not do that. We give him maybe just little chance. That nice, give some joker chance.'

'Was it you who gave Jon Arabin a chance?' said Ish Ulpin.

'What you talking about?' said Whale Mike.

'When Slagger Mulps had him thrown overboard with all that iron tied to his feet,' said Ish Ulpin. 'You did the knots for the iron, didn't you?'

Whale Mike's big foolish face split in a grin.

'Oh yes,' he said. 'Good knots, eh? Jon, he smart fellow. He get those knots undone real nice. I make knots so he have little chance. No much. But he come up all right. That good fun. Old Walrus, he real pissed off. Good stuff. Jon blow kiss, that cracked me up, that real funny.'

'So that's why the Warwolf survived,' said Bucks Cat. 'Because Mike was in one of his funny moods.'

'I had a sword called Warwolf,' said Drake. 'Who's the Warwolf you're talking about?'

'You shut up,' said Ish Ulpin. 'We've heard enough out of you.'

'Yes,' said Bucks Cat. 'Keep your mouth shut, or we'll tie the anchor to your feet before we throw you over. I'll do the knots myself. They won't come undone if I do them!'

Drake, seeing the threat was serious, kept quiet thereafter. He counted what gulls he saw. There were not many of them. How far did gulls fly from shore? Some, he had heard, lived eternally at sea, never touching ground from one year to the next. He looked at his toes. Wriggled them. There were little ginger hairs growing on his toes. That was funny, that his head-hair should be blond yet his toe-hair ginger.

Knowing he might be close to death, he started to review his life.

What did he see?

Mostly, lost opportunities. Women never laid, foes never beaten, fruit never stolen. Well, if he got out of this, the world would see a change in Drake Douay. Yes. No more Mr Nice Guy! He'd go for what he wanted, yes, ruthlessly, yielding to nothing. Life was short, so: grab while the grabbing's good.

While Drake was thinking thus, the crewmen rowed on. Bucks Cat put a line out and trolled for fish, with some success. As each fish was hauled aboard, it was cut up then eaten raw. Drake was horrified.

'This good,' said Whale Mike, throwing Drake a lump of fish. 'Eat!'

'No,' said Drake. 'Raw fish is poison. Everyone knows that.'

'I eat, I not hurt,' said Whale Mike.

'You're not human,' said Drake.

'Oh, I human enough,' said Whale Mike complacently. 'Come on, you try. That way find things out.'

'So it is,' said Drake, remembering what he had been taught in his theory classes about the experimental method.

But, even so, he was most reluctant to eat something which almost all of Stokos regarded as deadly poison. Finally, compelled by hunger, he tried some of the fish. It was not bad at all. And he got no harm from it.

'Well,' said Drake, 'they do say that travel broadens the mind.'

He was starting to feel quite comfortable in the boat. He had managed to convince himself that the crewmen would never force him into the sea. No, they were just indulging in a rather cruel joke. Sooner or later, they would admit as much. Then everyone on the brave boat *Walrus* would have a good laugh, and they would turn and row for shore. Once there, the crewmen might buy Drake a beer by way of apology. A beer? Two beers, minimum! They might buy him a woman, as well. Then Drake would go home and get a good night's sleep. And, bright and early in the morning, he would start on his first sword.

With such thoughts, Drake comforted himself. Until, toward sunset, when only a line of distant clouds marked the position of the shore, Ish Ulpin gave an order:

'Ease oars!'

The *Walrus* wallowed in the greasy swells. What lay beneath the sea's surface? Immense depths of dark, of cold, of drifting seaweed and hunting sharks.

'Sorry about this,' said Whale Mike.

'You mean . . .' said Drake. 'You mean you're really—'

'Did you think we were joking?' said Ish Ulpin. 'Jump!'

'Yes,' said Bucks Cat. 'Before we cut your lips off.'

'This isn't fair!' said Drake. 'I never did anything to hurt you.'

'You lied to one of our friends,' said Ish Ulpin. 'You gave Atsimo Andranovory duff directions. Aye. You met him on the waterfront and—'

'But that's ridiculous!' said Drake. 'You can't kill me just because of that!'

'Ish Ulpin joking,' said Whale Mike. 'We not kill you because of that. We kill you because that our job. You better leave now.'

'Yes,' said Bucks Cat, jabbing at Drake with a harpoon. 'Leave now, if you want to leave with your liver.'

Bucks jabbed again. And Drake jumped. The oarsmen turned the good boat *Walrus* around and started rowing for the shore.

'This is a joke,' said Drake, swimming after them. 'It is a joke, isn't it? It could be, you know. I'll hold no grudge. I'll swear to you. Everything I own. My flesh, my body.'

'Keep your distance,' said Ish Ulpin, snatching the harpoon from Bucks Cat.

Ish Ulpin was ready to kill. Yes. It was no joke.

Drake trod water, floundering around in the swell and the slop. He swore. He wailed in despair. Then he shouted:

'It's too late now!' he screamed. 'Too late for me to get to the palace by sunset! So I'll never marry the king's daughter! Your merchants have got what they want! They're safe! You've earnt your money! I'll never be king! Pick me up, for love of your mother!'

'I've no love for my mother,' called Ish Ulpin. 'In fact, I strangled the bitch to celebrate my fourteenth birthday.'

And on rowed the boat.

Bucks Cat, holding the tiller, reclined like a lady of leisure. He trailed his free hand over the side, so water played around his fingers. He was safe. He was earning good money for this murder. He was happy. And he was letting Drake know just how good he felt.

Whereupon Drake was filled with seething anger, with outrage, with implacable hatred. He would not drown! He would live! He would get to shore then murder those boatmen, one by one! Hang them! Jugulate them! Smash them to pulp then jump up and down on their splattered bowels!

Drake forced himself out of his trousers. He lay on his back, kicking his feet to keep himself afloat. He knotted each trouser-leg at the ankle. Then held the trousers by the waistband, so the legs dangled limply in the water. Then, treading water, he brought the trousers sweeping in a sudden arc toward the sea.

Air shot into the trouser-legs. The waistband, widened to a circle by the inrush of air, hit the sea. Drake forced it down. The trouser-legs stuck up into the air. Drake laid himself across the crotch of the trousers, trapping the waistband beneath him.

He was now afloat on his trousers. Bit by bit, the air would surely leak out, but by repeating his trick he could refill them. He looked a right daft lunatic, floating on his trousers with his naked arse shimmering in the seas of sunset. But he would live, unless he died of cold, or was eaten by sharks, or was set upon by giant seabirds, or—

Yes, probably he would die.

'But I'm not dead yet,' said Drake.

And floated.

All grim determination.

Darkness came, bringing a night longer than all the wormholes that ever were, longer than every bit of spaghetti which has ever been made since the dawn of time.

Drake fell asleep often, experiencing just a flash of dreamtime hallucination before waking again to the cold everwash of the sea. The greasy wool which protected his torso helped keep him alive. But for the warmth of wool, Drake would have been dead long before dawn.

By the time dawn approached there was no

determination left. Only a boy of sixteen, alone, lonely, exhausted almost beyond endurance, cold to the bone, nine parts dead, skin wrinkled by the sea.

'It's lighter,' said Drake. 'A new day . . .'

Life is hope.

The east was grey. Then sullen red. Then ginger. Then up came the sun, as bright and cheerful as ever. Blue shone the sky. Blue sky. White clouds.

'It is a good day to die,' said Drake, since that was the kind of thing heroes were supposed to say.

Maybe heroes convinced heroes. But Drake failed to convince Drake. As far as he could tell, no day was a good day to die.

But it didn't look like he had much choice in the matter, for, by the bright happy sunlight, he saw a fin sliding through the sea. An evil fin. Sleek. Cold. Polished as a knife. Then out from the water came a sleek and polished head, which whistled at him in a high and alien language.

'I see,' said Drake. 'A whistling shark. Well, nice to be eaten by a novelty, I suppose.'

The brute rolled on its side, then dived. Going under. Drake drew his knees to his belly. Where was it? Where was it?

'Show yourself, bugger-breath!' he snarled.

And the monster did. It came out of the sea. It leaped right out of the water, described a fantastic arc, then plunged beneath the waves again. Then surfaced. Grinning. Yes! Its vicious beak of a mouth was grinning at him! There was no mistaking that expression. What next? Laughing, no doubt.

The smiling shark began to circle. The swells lifted Drake up then dropped him down. His trousers were almost empty of air: he was getting lower and lower in the water.

'Come on, shark!' said Drake. 'Make an end of it, you ugly bugger!'

But the shark just circled, chirruping now and then. Another joined it. Two of them, then. No, three!

41

'A dinner party, is it?' said Drake. 'Man, sorry to show up for dinner with a bare arse.'

It was time to fill the trousers again.

Or drown.

'Life is hope,' said Drake.

And manoeuvred himself off his trousers, meaning to slip them behind him to catch another load of air. But he was so weak that, as the last of that air-support left him, he slipped beneath the waves, losing his grip on the trousers. Which sank.

Drake sank.

Grabbing for the surface.

Something rose up beside him. He seized it. He found himself brought to the surface. By a shark. Too exhausted to scream, he lay there in the sea, lay with his cheek against the water-smooth flank of the shark, his arm over its great smooth back.

Then remembered that sharks are not smooth, for their skin has more teeth than their jaws. So this must be a dolphin, yes, he had heard of such, that accounted for the whistling and all, it was a dolphin, life answering to life just as the legends claimed. And Drake, unable to help himself, wept.

And heard someone hail him:

'Ahoy there! You with the fish!'

Now the dolphin is no fish, for its blood is warm, and, what's more, mother dolphins give birth to their young in a fashion close to human, then suckle their babies on milk. But Drake knew well enough that the voice was speaking to him.

'So it's true,' he said. 'The dead begin to speak to you as you die. Well, who'd have thought it?'

Then the voice called again. Turning his head, Drake saw a ship on the sea behind him. If he had looked around earlier, he would have seen it much sooner.

'Investigate,' said Drake. 'That's what I should have done.'

Then the dolphin submerged, leaving him floundering

in the swell. But hope gave him strength, and he kept himself afloat until the ship came alongside. It was a xebec with sails of the palest lilac, a hull painted gold and topsides of silver. It looked like something out of a dream.

Looking up, Drake saw a woman looking down. She was tall. She was luxurious. Her hair was red, her skin also; her mouth was broad, her breasts high-lofted.

'Are you all right?' she said anxiously, in Galish tinged with a foreign accent.

Drake floated there, gazing up at her. What a mouth! What a nose! What beautiful body-lines! Suddenly he remembered all the good resolutions he had made in the face of death: Go for what you want! Yield to nothing! Grab while the grabbing's good!

Well, then . . .

'Will you marry me?' said Drake.

'What?' said the woman, her face showing alarm.

'Marry me! I'm in love!'

'You're crazy,' she said.

Drake lacked the strength to protest. He floated, his hair – beautifully clean by now – floating around him in the easy seas. Then a capture net scooped him from the water, and he was hauled aboard like a bit of dead meat.

Shortly, he was lying on hard boards with a coarse woollen blanket draped over his nakedness. The tall red woman was bending over him, feeding him sips of water.

'Careful, now,' she said, supporting his head. 'Not all at once!'

He seized her hand, and kissed it.

'Marry me,' he said.

'I'll learn you a rather hard lesson, if you talk on so foolish,' she said, a note of warning in her voice.

She was, he judged, about four years older than him, and a good head taller. He was in lust with her. Strenuously in lust. Or, to be more exact: he liked what he saw, and his ego compelled him to imagine that he had strength enough for lust, even after the trauma of his deep-sea survival exercise. It was that same ego which compelled him to pursue his suit:

43

'Tell me,' said Drake, 'tell me at least your name.'

'Zanya,' she said. 'Zanya Kliedervaust, lately of the temple of the Orgy God on the Ebrells.'

'The Orgy God?' said Drake. 'That sounds like my kind of deity.'

'Mayhap,' said Zanya. 'But I have renounced the temple. Also the flesh it worships. I seek a higher calling. That I hope to find on Stokos.'

At that moment, they were interrupted by a tall, well-built man with violet eyes and purple skin. He wore a purple robe; heavy golden ear-rings dangled beside his cheeks.

'Zanya,' he said. *'Faa n'koto afa dree takaloka tee?'*

'Gaa n'moto seki seki,' answered Zanya. *'Ka ta funofoonu ti.'*

'Who are you?' said Drake, staring up at the big purple man.

'He speaks no Galish,' said Zanya. 'But his name is Oronoko. He's a prince from one of the provinces of Parengarenga.'

'Yakoto,' said Prince Oronoko, smiling as he put a hand to his heart. *'N'mo k'nozo Oronoko. Ka nafu-nafu.'*

'Is this your boyfriend?' said Drake.

'He's a pilgrim,' said Zanya. 'He came to the Ebrells in a quest for purity. We've been questing together ever since.'

'I see,' said Drake. 'Questing for long enough to share a language between you.'

'Oh, I've known the speaking of Frangoni for years,' said Zanya. 'It's a language common enough on the Ebrells.'

Drake wanted to question her further, but first he had to deal with the ship's captain, a lean, anxious man who came bustling along the deck, peered at Drake with some misgivings, then asked, in a high-pitched voice scarcely half a tone away from hysteria:

'How came you to be in the water? What evil put you there? Witchcraft, perhaps?'

'Nay, man,' said Drake, improvising. 'I was on my uncle's fishing boat. Then up came a kraken! Ah, a brute of

44

a thing it was! Terrible with tentacles. It drowned the boat. Ate all but me.'

His eyes were bright, his voice frenzied.

'Say no more,' said the captain, his fears of the occult apparently appeased. 'Leisure back, boy. Rest. Sleep. We'll land in Stokos soon enough. That will be the time for you to make a settlement with your grief.'

All the way back to Stokos, Drake's resolution hardened. His flesh, for the moment, was too weak to harden with his resolution. But there was no doubt about it. He could have, would have, must have this big beautiful red-skinned Ebrell bitch.

But he was to be disappointed.

For, on reaching Stokos, Zanya quit the ship swiftly, in company with Oronoko, without even bothering to learn Drake's name.

'Must follow,' muttered Drake to Drake.

And he gave chase.

But he had scarce taken a dozen steps when the ground snatched itself from under his feet and a sheet of stifling black tar rolled across the surface of the sun.

When Drake recovered consciousness, he found himself lying on a truckle-bed in the room which housed the skull collection which was the pride and joy of his uncle, Oleg Douay. When Drake called out, his uncle came to his bedside.

'What happened?' said Drake.

'Why, the sea gods saved you, that's what happened,' said Oleg. 'I prayed to them mightily. My faith, as you see, is justified.'

'No,' said Drake. 'I mean down at the waterfront. What happened there?'

'You fainted, or so report would have it. Nothing to be ashamed of. After what you've been through, it's a wonder you could walk from the ship on your own two legs. Rest.'

'Man,' said Drake, 'a woman came off that ship. She—'

'Never you mind about women!' said Oleg. 'There'll be plenty of time for that later.'

Shortly, Drake had a visitor: it was Sully Yot.

'Five shangles,' said Yot, sticking out his hand.

'Man!' said Drake. 'That's a fine form of greeting!'

'Pay up!' said Yot, obviously delighting in his triumph.

It occurred to Drake that, if the mischances of fate ever reduced him to slavery, then Yot was the very last person he would want as a master.

'Man, I'll pay all right, but only if you can find a woman for me.'

And Drake proceeded to name and describe Zanya Kliedervaust. By diligent inquiry, Yot found she had taken work in the leper colony on the outskirts of town. Drake paid over the five shangles, though the news gave him little joy.

He dared not venture to the leprosarium. For ordinary leprosy is terrible, but in that colony they had something worse still – blue lepers, who suffered outbreaks of blue sores, then great septic ulcers, then a black rot which consumed the eyes, Then a terrible variant of gangrene which broke out all over and finished them. They generally took two long, slow years to die, from the time the first blue sores erupted on their skin.

Love conquers all?

Maybe.

But Drake was not in love – he was in lust. And lust alone was not sufficient to compel him inside a leper colony.

'Woe is me!' cried Drake.

Then remembered that life did, after all, have some compensations. For he was about to start work on his first sword, was he not? That happy thought gave him the strength to rise from his bed after only three days of recuperation.

But, on proceeding to Hardhammer Forge, Drake found his hopes of making a sword of his own were not yet to be fulfilled. Gouda Muck had received a special order from King Tor for five blades of firelight steel. Muck was working flat out; he lacked the time to supervise apprentice work.

'But you promised!' said Drake.

'Wait till these blades are done,' said Muck. 'I'll be no use as a teacher if Tor chops my head off, will I?'

Drake had to concede the logic of that.

'How long before you're finished?' he asked.

'How long is a piece of string?' said Muck. 'What have you done about those men who threw you overboard? Have you reported them?'

'Not yet,' said Drake.

'Then I suggest you get on with it,' said Muck, who loved justice as much as any other man. 'Today. Off you go!'

'But I'm supposed to go to theory class this afternoon.'

'Do you care?'

'I do,' said Drake, with both truth and determination. 'I've decided to go all out for what I want. And what I want is to be a swordsmith, yes, the very best swordsmith on Stokos.'

'I'm impressed,' said Muck, who wasn't, but thought such an attitude deserved encouragement. 'Right. Go to theory class this afternoon, then tomorrow morning make your report.'

That night, Drake dreamed of the horrifying tortures which would claim Ish Ulpin, Bucks Cat and Whale Mike once King Tor was persuaded to punish them. He woke early, and, after a quick breakfast, hurried off to the Iron Palace to make his report.

4

Place: Stokos, a deeply indented island in Gulf of Veda off western coast of continent of Argan.

Area: by Court Cartographer's reckoning, about 4,750 vlests (some 12,000 square leagues).

Population: 123,045 according to the taxcount of Tor 5.

Ruler: King Tor (an ogre of noble birth).

Capital: the seaport of Cam (pop. 53,000).

Religion: worship of the demon Hagon.

Language: Kerzen, Arham and Ligin (all native to Stokos); also Galish (lingua franca of Cam, where all three native tongues meet and compete).

Literacy: 27 per cent.

Life expectancy: 53 years.

Economy: mining; fishing; banking, import-export; steel production: metalwork (particularly weapons).

Lust mixes but poorly with justice.

By the time Drake's pursuit of Zanya had been stalled by the discovery that his lover was working in a leper colony, the boatmen who had tried to murder Drake had fled Cam. Indeed, they had fled Stokos, for the wrath of King Tor would be terrible if he learned they had exceeded his instructions.

He did learn – for, obedient to Muck's instructions, Drake went and told him. And his wrath was indeed terrible.

'By royal decree,' said King Tor, in a voice which woke the gryphon sleeping at his feet, 'Bucks Cat, Ish Ulpin and Whale Mike are to be executed immediately if they ever again set foot on Stokos. Thus will justice be fulfilled.'

'Well,' said Drake, 'now we've done with justice, how about marrying me off to your daughter?'

'You failed the challenge I set you,' said King Tor. 'You failed to get back to my palace by sunset.'

'Be reasonable!' said Drake. 'I never had a chance! Anyway, I survived perils worse than anything you had in mind – as you've heard. That proves I've got a lot going for me.'

'This is true,' said King Tor, munching on a frog. 'But perhaps I was a little hasty to offer my daughter so casually. Come back in two years, when you finish your apprenticeship. We'll decide then.'

Well. That was better than a poke in the eye with a blunt stick. Two years from now, he might be Prince Drake. No, probably the title would be more formal: Prince Dreldragon. Lord Dreldragon, maybe? Either way, it had a nice ring to it.

Meanwhile, there was still Zanya. Now was the time to chase her. If she became Drake's lover, she could still be his concubine when he married Tor's daughter. But Zanya was working with lepers! What if she got the disease herself? Drake thought about it. Lust confused his intellectual processes, such as they were: he decided Zanya was far, far too beautiful ever to get leprosy.

'She's too high-class for such a low-class disease,' he declared.

Then dared himself as far as the rough-and-ready paling which marked the perimeter of the leper colony.

He did not see Zanya Kliedervaust, but, through generous gaps in the fence, he did see diseased corpses writhing on a huge pyre. A big purple-skinned man wearing

49

nothing but a loin-cloth was heaping fresh wood on the fire. It was Prince Oronoko, who had been with Zanya on the xebec. Drake was so jealous he wanted to spit.

Imagine! A stinking foreigner enjoying the company of the fair Zanya Kliedervaust. Her company? Oh, she had been slick enough with her weird-rare talk about purity, but Drake could guess what pleasures she shared with her uitlander prince. Oronoko's muscles, oiled with sweat, glistened in the hot sun. Drake wondered how he would fare against Oronoko in a fight.

'Hey! You!' cried Drake. 'Where are you keeping Zanya?'

Oronoko did not seem to hear. Belatedly, Drake remembered that the foreigner spoke no Galish. He spoke some kind of alien gibberish instead.

Purple-skinned Oronoko threw one last load of wood on the fire then went away, perhaps to get some more bodies. The flames hungered noisily. Stray bits of bamboo burst asunder in the heart of the blaze. Drake felt the heat of the fire amplifying the heat of the sun. A corpse, compelled by the inferno, sat up, its arms warping amidst the smoke in a parody of agony.

Then a shift of the wind sent smoke plunging in Drake's direction. Before he could flee, he was enveloped in thick choking smoke, in the stench of burning hair and charring flesh. He scrambled away, cursing, coughing, spluttering, eyes watering. He was stricken with terror. What if the smoke had contaminated him? What if he had caught leprosy from that filthy disposal fire?

He was no longer so sure that it would be safe to bed the fair Zanya Kliedervaust.

But he could not get her out of his mind.

Ten days after his ordeal at sea, Drake decided to discuss his problem with his sister.

'I'm in love,' he said.

'Then demonstrate it,' she said tartly. 'Lean on your elbows! Stop dribbling!'

'I'm not in love with you, stupid,' said Drake.

50

'Watch your language,' said his sister, with danger in her voice, 'or I'll spit in your eye!'

And Drake thought; *Women! They're so emotional!*

'Well,' said his sister, shortly afterwards, 'who are you in love with?'

'A woman from Ebrell,' said Drake, dreamily, staring up at the ceiling. 'Red skin, red hair . . . she's gorgeous.'

'Is she a good lay?'

'I haven't been able to find out,' said Drake. And he explained.

'This is a hopeless case,' said his sister. 'You'd better see a pox doctor.'

'For what?'

'For a cure for love. We've got a pox doctor working in the temple now. He's quite nice.'

'Is he good in bed?' said Drake.

'He's a wizard, stupid. They don't go in for that kind of stuff.'

'Oh,' said Drake. 'Somehow . . . somehow I don't think a pox doctor would help me.'

But, that night, he endured grim dreams of blue leprosy. He dreamed of Zanya, of her body studded with blue sores, just as King Tor's leather clothing was studded with iron. He dreamed of Zanya suffering long, slow months of decay, eventually becoming ulcerated, blind, gangrenous. Then dead. He woke in a sweat.

And, that very morning, he fronted up to the temple for an interview with their pox doctor, who was a wizard of the order of Nin, one of the weakest of the eight orders of wizards. His name was Miphon. The temple of Hagon, hoping to end an unpleasant outbreak of gonorrhoea, had lately imported him to Stokos to advise on sexual hygiene. Miphon had given much valuable advice with respect to the use of condoms, and was almost ready to leave the island.

On being admitted to Miphon's presence, Drake saw the wizard was fairly old – maybe aged about thirty. He wore businesslike leathers and a broad-brimmed hat

51

which sported a single feather. Being nervous, Drake started the interview by being rude.

'Why are your eyes green?' he said.

Miphon was unsurprised by this brusque demand for information. Guessing at Drake's unease, Miphon made allowances for it.

'My eyes are green,' said he, 'because I am descended from the elven folk. My great-grandfather was of the People.'

So he spoke. But, as the Book of Wisdom puts it: 'Much is spoken, but little is truthed.' Drake, who knew as much, took Miphon's claim with a grain of salt.

'I see from your face that you disbelieve me,' said Miphon. 'But I can prove myself. Thanks to my elven ancestry, I am fay. I can read minds. I can tell who you are, what you are, and what you want.'

'Tell, then,' said Drake, disbelieving.

'You are Drake Douay, a swordsmith's apprentice,' said Miphon. 'You love the fair Zanya Kliedervaust, who resides in the leprosarium on the outskirts of this town of Cam.'

Drake had never had his mind read before.

He was shocked. Startled. Stunned. Awed.

'My . . . my lord,' said Drake. 'I . . . I did not mean to be rude. I have never met an elven lord before. It was – the clothes confused me. I thought great people to dress greatly. Man, if you dressed with more style you'd get much more respect.'

'The leathers serve,' said Miphon. 'Would you seek to embellish wisdom with gaudy silks and golden baubles? Do the postures of fashion improve veracity?'

'Embellish?' said Drake. 'Veracity?'

He had learnt a great many very long words and complicated ideas in his theory classes, but there were still enormous gaps in his education.

'To embellish is to decorate,' said Miphon patiently. 'Veracity is another word for truth.'

'Great is the wisdom of the elven lords!' said Drake.

'I did not say that I was an elf,' said Miphon, 'only that I am of elven descent. Not all of the powers of the People are mine. Only some.'

Actually, there is less magic in the world than most folk think, and certainly less magic than Miphon claimed. For – regardless of the truth or otherwise of his claim to elven descent – the wizard Miphon was most certainly not fay. He was not telepathic. (Well, he could read the minds of rocks, stones and the lesser animals – such as the mole, phoenix, basilisk, badger, rat, mouse, dragon, gryphon, rabbit, cow and codfish – but such skill is of very little practical use.)

So how did he know about Drake?

Simple.

Drake's sister had already seen Miphon to brief him in depth regarding her brother's name, appearance and mission.

'Have no fear,' said Miphon, 'for I will do you no harm, even though I am mighty in power. Instead, I will tell you how to resolve your problem.'

'You will cure me of love?' said Drake.

'Yes,' said Miphon, handing Drake a little tablet. 'Dissolve this in water to make a philtre which is a certain cure for love. Drink the philtre by the light of a full moon. Turn round widershins. Kneel down. Kiss the ground three times, each time saying the name of the woman you love. Then work as hard as you can for the next thirty days, doing every task your master sets you – or twice as much, if possible. That will cure you of love, for certain.'

'Does the moon have to be full?' said Drake.

'Oh yes,' said Miphon. 'For this magic is animated by the power of the moon herself. Only by the full moon can such power be conjured.'

Drake was very impressed.

This was great magic indeed!

In truth, the tablet contained nothing but a little salt and sugar. But Miphon, who was a great believer in the power of the placebo, had found he could cure a truly staggering

53

range of conditions with such little tablets.

'Happy?' said Miphon.

'Well . . . if you can give me this kind of pill . . . why not a philtre to make the lady love me?'

'If you must have the lady,' said Miphon, 'then woo her. Pledge your love with poetry and flowers. Visit her daily. Let her know the sincerity of your devotions. Speak to her prettily, and persist. To destroy is easier than to create. Magic can destroy your love easily – but cannot create love for you in her.'

'It's all very well to talk of wooing,' said Drake. 'But how can I? She's in the leper colony. It's death to enter – particularly with that blue leprosy on the loose.'

'Leprosy is hard to catch,' said Miphon. 'As for blue leprosy – that's a different disease entirely. A kind of pox, only to be caught when man lies with woman. It's slow to develop, sometimes taking years to appear. That's why the nature of the disease is seldom properly understood.'

'I see,' said Drake.

'Trust me,' said Miphon. 'If you visit the leper colony, you'll likely come away unscathed. Yes, even if you visit a hundred times. Do you have any other questions?'

'Only this,' said Drake. 'Do wizards pork women? Or do they go for men?'

Miphon refused to be upset by this rudeness.

'We limit every indulgence,' said Miphon gravely. 'We must, because of the demands of the Balance.'

'What is this Balance?' said Drake.

'Many have asked,' said Miphon, 'but few have been answered. You know your future now. You have magic to cure you of love, if you wish. If not – then woo the lady.'

And with that, Drake had to be content.

That very evening, Miphon quit Stokos on a dirty, wallowing brig taking coal from Cam to Narba. The next morning, Drake was discussing the wizard with his sister, and saying what a marvellous mind-reading elf he was, when she broke into peals of laughter.

'He's no elf!' she said. 'There's no such thing as elves.'

'Then how did he know who I was?' said Drake. 'How did he know what I wanted?'

'How do you think?' said she.

Drake put his mind to it.

And, since his mind had been rigorously trained in logic (and rhetoric, debate, analysis, and half a dozen other useless things besides) he soon came up with an answer which was claw-sharp and correct.

'Well,' said Drake, 'so that wizard was at least three-parts sham. So what about his tablet? What about his advice?'

'The answer to the tablet is easy,' said his sister. 'See what an alchemist makes of it.'

So Drake went looking for an alchemist. He should have known better. After all, as part of his apprenticeship theory he had already learnt that there is no truth in alchemy, astrology, poetry, politics, paternity or weather forecasts. But Drake was young – and there is much the young can only learn the hard way.

Drake found an alchemist soon enough: a muttering, gnomish old man named Villet Vate, who had a dark narrow shop which he shared with moths, woodlice and a multitude of spiders.

'Come in, come in!' said Vate.

And Drake entered the shop; breathed its mysterious atmosphere of menthol, cajuput oil, cloves and camphor; breathed dust as well, and sneezed; gazed, open-mouthed, at mysterious stills, alembics and antique devices of unknown function.

'What's . . . what's this?' he said, touching a huge contraption of strangely-wrought metal.

'Ah, that,' said Vate, rubbing his hands together. 'That's a telescope. Very ancient, very ancient. All the best things are old.'

'A telescope?'

'A device for looking on the faces of the stars,' said Vate. 'I can't quite make it work yet. But I'll get there, I'll get there.'

(He was over-optimistic, for what he thought was a telescope was in fact an electron microscope. And the device with which he hoped to transmute lead to gold was a zymometer. And his latest purchase – a curious metal sphere washed out of the sea by a storm – was not the magical treasure chest he imagined it was, but a bomb powerful enough to blow Stokos right off the map.)

'And what's . . . what's this?' said Drake, pointing to a very intricate device of interlocking wheels, arcs, crescents, levers and slides.

'That?' said Vate. 'Ah, that's an astrolabe. It tells sun, moon, tide and time. It's elven work. Very ancient. Very rare. But for sale, if you've gold sufficient.'

'No thanks,' said Drake. 'What I want is an assay.'

'Of what?'

'This tablet. But – mind! – I want some left when you've finished with it.'

'Break the tablet in half, then,' said Vate. 'Half is all I'll need.'

Drake did as he was bid, then watched with intense interest as Vate dropped the sample into a mortar, ground it with a pestle, added seawater and sulphur and the urine of a rabbit, stirred the mixture with the feather of a white owl, decanted it, weighed it, adulterated it with snuff, stared at it through a magnifying glass, sniffed it, then pronounced:

'This tablet contains horn of unicorn, ground-up ginseng and essence of oyster, plus talcum powder, soap and a trace of cocaine.'

'Will that cure me of love?' said Drake.

'Nay, man,' said the alchemist. 'It's an aphrodisiac!'

'Then what cure is there for love?' said Drake.

'This!' said Vate, holding up a sharp knife. 'Come into the back room. I'll cure you for life in a moment.'

'No thanks,' said Drake.

And went away severely disillusioned with wizards and the world. But, since half the tablet remained, he took it. And, while that half a tablet contained no more than salt and sugar, Drake's faith in its qualities was such that he raged in lust for a week.

At this point it should probably be pointed out – in defence of the poor unicorn, which is increasingly rare these days – that there is no true aphrodisiac known to either man or woman (with the sole exception of propinquity, which does not come in tablet form).

In the end, Drake's lust diminished to normal levels (high, but not high enough to please him) and life itself returned to something close to normal.

Once more his main concern was his first sword. When was he going to get to make it? He dared not pester Gouda Muck, for fear the old man's temper would turn sour. But, in a frenzy of impatience, he watched Muck's slow but steady progress through his order list.

Just by watching, Drake began to learn a surprising amount. He was amazed at how much had escaped his notice in the last four years. Well, as the saying goes: 'One can achieve either perfection of the religious life or perfection of the practical life.'

Drake, till now, had always chosen religion over practicalities. But, if he had to go easy on religion in order to bring his apprenticeship to a successful conclusion, then he would make the necessary sacrifice.

'Come on, Muck,' muttered Drake to Drake, morning and night. 'Finish those swords! I want to get started on mine!'

5

Name: Gouda Muck.

Birthplace: Cam.

Occupation: swordsmith.

Status: taxpayer; senior citizen; second-best swordsmith on Stokos.

Description: old and ugly (Drake's opinion); wise and dignified (his own opinion); a waste of skin (his mother's opinion).

Residence: Hardhammer Forge, Ironbird Street, Cam, Stokos.

Gouda Muck was an atheist.

He was, quite possibly, the only atheist in the city of Cam. Most citizens enjoyed the practice of religion – indeed, for many devout souls, its consolations were all that made life worth living. But Gouda Muck was born to be a dissident. He refused to believe in the demon Hagon, far less to worship that formidable eater of souls.

He also avoided those sacred religious duties usually accepted even by unbelievers, viz:

† patronizing the temple casinos;
† copulating with the temple prostitutes;
† playing the temple numbers game;
† going to the temple cockfights;
† participating in the human sacrifices.

His main objection to all the above activities was that they cost an exorbitant amount of money.

'Religion,' said Muck, 'is a racket.'

He could get away with talk like that, for he was the second-best swordsmith on Stokos, where metalworkers were valued highly.

Gouda Muck lived with three boys, but slept with none of them. One was a deaf mute who shovelled coal, worked the bellows, and exorcised the minor demons of puberty by raping chickens. The other two, Drake and Yot, were older, virgins no longer though beardless still.

The fair-haired Drake had, till now, been very religious: he loved to drink, gamble, fight and swear, and relished the privileges which came with having a sister in the temple. Unfortunately, there had been times when he had overdone things somewhat – and the people of Stokos, like people elsewhere, frowned on religious mania.

'Balance,' said Drake to himself, 'that's the thing. I've got to find a balance between the pleasures of religion and the demands of the world of work.'

Yot, on the other hand, had no such problems to grapple with, for he was a spiritless fellow, a lank pale stripling with a runny nose (an allergy to coal dust made his life miserable with rhinitis) and warts.

And it was with Yot that the trouble began. It began only nine days after Drake saw the wizard Miphon – that is, just twenty days after Drake's ordeal at sea. It began when Yot, refusing to accept expense as excuse sufficient, demanded the real reason for Muck's dissent.

'I only believe in the Flame,' said Muck, peering into the furnace.

'The Flame?' asked Yot.

'Aye, boy,' said Muck, amused by Yot's wide-eyed attention. 'The living presence of the High God of All Gods, which purifies as it witnesses.'

Drake, who was working in the forge at the time, heard that, but kept himself from sniggering. He wanted to hear more. So did Yot.

'How does it purify?' asked Yot.

'It burns, boy,' said Muck. 'Didn't your mother ever teach you that? Stick a hand in, if you doubt me – it'll do more than clean your fingernails. It burns, and I can see that it burns. Ocular proof, aye, that's the thing.'

'But what's this business about gods?' asked Yot. 'How did you find out about that?'

'The Flame spoke to me,' said Gouda Muck. 'And it speaks to me still.'

And, seeing Yot's jaw drop, he continued the joke. At length.

Afterwards, Drake teased Yot for believing in fairy tales. But Yot, stubborn in belief, refused to concede that Muck's dogma was a load of tripe and codswallop, conjured up for the whim of the moment. They fought. Drake, as usual, won – but Yot still made no intellectual concessions. He went on asking for tales of the Flame, and Muck went on telling them.

Well, all was fine at first. Then, after Muck had been telling these fairy tales for three days, the Flame did speak to him. It roared up out of the furnace, hung purple in the air, and shouted in a voice of drums and cymbals:

'Muck! Thou art who thou art!'

Then left, even as Muck fainted.

On recovery, Muck decided he had experienced a true religious revelation. Actually, the syphilis scrambling his brain had made him hallucinate. The syphilis, by the way, was a souvenir of his riotous youth – Muck had been solemnly celibate these past thirty-five years or more.

The Flame spoke often thereafter, bringing Faith to Gouda Muck; those gnawing spirochaetes had a lot to answer for. Muck listened to the Flame as he laboured in the forge; he heard it as he ate his meals or walked by the dockside; the Flame gave him fresh revelations in his dreams.

How long does it take to create a religion?

Inspired by syphilis, Gouda Muck took precisely two days to lay down the foundations of his own faith.

The revelations of the Flame elevated Muck's personal quirks to the status of divine law: no drink, no gambling, no fighting and no loose women. What's more, thrift became an absolute virtue. Muck immediately began to help his apprentices be good by banking half their paltry wages into trust accounts managed by the Orsay Bank.

Drake had till then been happy enough as a sword-smith's devil, since all his hardships had been sweetened by the compensations of religion. With these denied to him – the confiscation of half his wages made certain of that – life went sour.

'Endure,' said Drake to Drake.

He must live for the day when he was a master sword-smith, yes, with his own forge and apprentices.

'Muck,' said Drake, one evening. 'How about setting a definite date for me to start making my first sword?'

'Why should I do that?' said Muck.

'Because it will give me something to look forward to,' said Drake.

'You've got nothing to look forward to,' said Muck. 'You're a filthy little scag-bag stuffed with iniquity. You pollute the forge by your very presence. All you're good for is slave labour.'

'Oh, come now!' said Drake. 'A joke's a joke, but—'

'I'm not joking!' roared Muck. 'You'll never make a sword in this forge, no.'

'But,' said Drake, 'I have to make swords. Lots of them. So I can finish my apprenticeship.'

'Time will finish your apprenticeship nicely,' said Muck. 'But you won't be a swordsmith at the end of it, oh no. When I'm finished with you, we'll kick you back to the filthy coal cliffs you came from.'

Drake was staggered by this sudden turnaround. He really thought he'd finally come to terms with Gouda Muck. Now – what was he supposed to think? He could only suppose that he had grievously offended Muck in the last few days, though he couldn't for the life of him think of any really outrageous stunts he'd pulled.

Well, the situation was grim, that was for real. And . . . desperate situations called for desperate remedies. So . . .

'Man,' said Drake, 'I know we've cut each other up in the past, but that's over and done with. I respect you, man, I'll say that fair and square. You're the master. I'm but a child at your elbow. If I've done you wrong, I'm too much of a child to see what I can do to set things right. So – tell me, man. What have I done that's so terrible? What can I do to make amends?'

This display of humility really hurt him. He was intensely proud: he hated to grovel.

What was worse, his humility did him no good.

'You can't make amends,' said Muck. 'You went too far years ago. So you'll sweat death and dream buckles till your bones splinter.'

'What?' said Drake, bewildered.

'The vizier of Galsh Ebrek calls,' said Muck.

Then left the forge without further explanation.

The syphilis which had begun to destroy Muck's brain was, of course, invisible, so Drake had precious few clues to the reason for Muck's bizarre behaviour. Was the man drunk? Worse: was he mad? Drake was reluctant to think so.

Was Muck serious?

That was a more important question. For if Muck was serious, then Drake's life was in ruins. Drake, turning things over in his mind, could only presume that his master was setting him a weird sort of test.

Yes.

A test to draw him out, to see how much initiative and determination he had. Maybe this was one of the secrets of the swordsmith's guild. Maybe every apprentice got set such a test, sooner or later, to see what he was really made of.

Accordingly, Drake set to work on a sword of his own. Yot, who had been shovelling coal into sacks outside, came in and asked what he was doing.

'Never you mind,' said Drake.

'It looks to me,' said Yot, 'as if you're starting work on a sword. You can't do that! Not till Muck gives you permission.'

'I'll be the judge of what I can and can't do,' said Drake.

And laboured grimly until Muck returned at nightfall.

'What are you doing?' said Muck.

'Man, I'm making a sword,' said Drake. 'For I've got to start learning the real stuff sooner or later.'

'I've told you already,' said Muck, 'your days of learning are finished. You're not human any longer, not as far as this forge is concerned. You're a piece of working meat, and nothing else.'

'Man,' said Drake, trying to keep himself from crying, 'you're not being fair. You've got to teach me! That's why I'm here! To learn!'

'You're here to repent,' said Muck. 'To purify yourself.'

'How do I do that?' said Drake.

'By working yourself to death.'

'Right!' said Drake. 'If you won't teach me, then I'll not stay here to sweat it out for starvation wages.'

And, thirty days after his sixteenth birthday, Drake ran away. He fled to his parents' home in south-west Stokos. He was frightened, bitter, amazed at the sudden turn of events. A few days ago, everything had been going his way – and now? Disaster!

There was one bright spot on the horizon, of course: Drake's marriage prospects. But he could hardly rely too much on those, since King Tor might die any day, his demise destroying Drake's chances.

'Four years of my life!' sobbed Drake. 'Four years of my life gone to this lousy apprenticeship! And what do I get out of it? I get kicked around like a cat.'

The cat was the lowest form of life on the island of Stokos, for it was well known that the demon Hagon hated cats. They had it rough.

Drake had it rough, too, when he finally got home. He

63

had only just finished explaining himself to his parents and to his brother Heth when agents from the sword-smith's guild arrived with a warrant, and whipped him back to Cam.

'We've a system for breaking people like you,' said Muck, when Drake was brought back to the forge, whip-wounds bleeding. 'We'll prove it out, if you try your non-sense a second time.'

'Man,' said Drake, 'you've flipped! You're mad!'

'Don't answer back,' said Muck. 'You're just work-meat. A slave.'

Well, there was no way Drake could take that in silence. So he did answer back, thus starting an argument, which Gouda Muck won by beating his apprentice into insensibility.

The next day, Drake went to complain to his uncle, Oleg Douay. He explained his problem.

'Muck says he won't teach me. He's going to work me like a piece of slave-rubbish till my apprenticeship runs out, then throw me on the slag heap.'

'Come, boy,' said Oleg, sure that Drake was exaggerating, 'you had a little spat with your master, but that's no reason to act as if the world's coming to an end.'

'He's serious!' said Drake.

'Oh, maybe he said a few words harder than he should have,' said Oleg, 'but don't take them to heart. I've known Gouda Muck for years. He's an honourable man. He'll do all right by you.'

Unsatisfied by such reassurances, Drake promptly absconded a second time. And was hunted again, caught again, whipped again, and threatened with castration if he repeated his performance. The swordsmiths' guild was enormously powerful. There was no way Drake could fight it – not since his uncle refused to help.

'Maybe Muck will come to his senses,' said Drake. 'Maybe it's something he's eaten. I'll give him three months, yes, and see if he starts talking sense.'

Meantime, Drake sought to console himself with some

of the pleasures of religion. He swiftly spent what savings he had. What now? He could hardly afford much on the half-wage Muck was doling out weekly.

'I need more money,' said Drake.

He thought about robbing the Orsay Bank. Not a good idea! Many people had died that way, and nobody had yet succeeded. So he tried something more subtle – to borrow from the bank on the strength of the funds held in trust for him.

'We lend to nobody under twenty-five,' said the Bankers. 'And your funds are blocked till then, too.'

'I hope you're paying me interest,' said Drake smartly.

'Are you trying to squeeze us, boy? Get out, while you still have legs to get with!'

Fleeing the gaunt donjon of the Orsay Bank, he arrived back at the forge late, and got a beating which opened his whip-wounds. This was too much to bear, but worse was promised.

'The Flame has revealed Powers and Commands,' said Muck grandly. 'Any who resist Revealed Truth are worthy only of death. Thou shalt kneel down and worship – or die!'

Being the person he was, Drake acted boldly, and reported Muck's latest delusions to King Tor. He hoped to get Muck executed. For then, under the laws governing apprenticeships, the swordsmiths' guild would be obliged to arrange for Drake to serve out the remainder of his apprenticeship under another master. With luck, that master would be Oleg Douay.

Unfortunately, Tor was busier than usual. Busy with what? With some weird and wonderful legislation his counsellors had lately proposed: a Bill to raise the minimum age for a mine worker to seven years, a Bill which would raise the age of consent to twelve, and a swag of Bills designed to limit the powers of a slavocrat over his human instruments.

'Let the Chamber of Commerce deal with it,' said Tor.

'But this is serious!' said Drake. 'There's not just heresy

65

involved, either. Muck's refusing to teach—'

'Boy, I'm up to my ears in work,' said Tor. 'Go away! I don't want to see you until we consider you for marriage in two years' time.'

So Drake got out while the getting was good.

He had scant faith in the Chamber of Commerce, so went and told Muck's mother instead. If she could knock some sense into her son, Muck might still come right, and prove himself as a decent master and a diligent teacher.

On learning the truth, Muck's mother was – to say the least – outraged. She had spent a lifetime in the temple, and was still working there at age ninety. Admittedly, these days she was a casino croupier, rather than the luxurious harlot she had been in the days when Muck was conceived.

She came hobbling down to the forge, leaning heavily on her swordstick, and told Muck just what she thought of him.

'You godless blaspheming heretic!' she said. 'You're a waste of skin! I always thought so. Now I'm sure of it.'

'Mother, dearest,' said Muck. 'Listen to me . . .'

And he began to preach. With eloquence. With a passion close to lust. With absolute conviction. And, slowly, his mother's expression began to change . . .

When Drake realized Muck's mother had been converted to her son's cult, he almost despaired.

'But,' he said, 'we can still try . . .'

And he denounced Muck to the Chamber of Commerce. That august body investigated, found the truth was worse than the report – the prophet of the Flame was starting to proselytize his neighbours – and promptly had Gouda Muck thrown into jail.

This happened on Midsummer's Day, two months after Drake's sixteenth birthday. By local reckoning, it was the middle of the year Tor 5; by the Collosnon dating which more of the world is familiar with, it was the start of Khmar 17. In any event, the date eventually became known as the Day of the Martyrdom of Muck; its anniversary

66

was ultimately enshrined as the most sacred event of the Holy Calendar of Goudanism.

Considering what some martyrs endure, Muck got off lightly. He was not beaten, flayed, singed, starved, or exhibited in the stocks for the populace to throw stones at. His prison pallet had bedbugs, true, and his cell had rats – but his home had more of both. And, in any case, the terrible old man was soon released. All that money he had saved by never debauching himself in the temple had come in handy for bribes.

'How did you get out?' asked Yot.

'The Flame saved me,' said Gouda Muck.

And, once said, it was impossible not to believe.

Muck spent long days brooding.

So did Drake.

Muck was showing no signs of coming to his senses. All attempts at getting rid of him had failed. So what now? Endure life as a virtual slave for the rest of his apprenticeship? Try again to run away? Or what? Drake decided that, as a point of honour, he would bring his apprenticeship to a successful conclusion despite anything and everything Muck might try.

'Living well is the best revenge,' said Drake.

He imagined himself presenting a mastersword for the examination of the swordsmith's guild. Oh, that would give Muck a shock!

Accordingly, Drake went to see his uncle. He found Oleg painting some of his favourite skulls in patterns of red and green.

'What do you want?' said Oleg.

'I want to work at your forge in the evenings, after I finish work for Muck,' said Drake. 'I want you to teach me how swords are really made. I want you to give me all the learning so I can make my own mastersword.'

'Oh, I can't do that!' said Oleg. 'It wouldn't be ethical.'

'But it's the only way!' said Drake, in tones of utter despair. 'Muck still refuses to teach me!'

'Doubtless because you've been naughty,' said Oleg,

67

dabbing a brushload of red paint into the nose-hole of one of his skulls. 'Go back and apologize. You'll see. Things will soon come right.'

Drake did apologize. Again. He grovelled.

It did him no good whatsoever.

'At least things can't get any worse,' said Drake to himself.

He was wrong, of course.

Things can always get worse.

Shortly after Midsummer's Day, Drake's sister found a lump in her mouth. A friend examined it for her, and told her it was blue. The next day another lump sprouted. It could not be doubted: she had blue leprosy.

She cut her throat.

Drake mourned her for fifty days. In his grief, he no longer cared about his prospects for becoming a sword-smith. He also mourned for himself. For Miphon had made it clear that blue leprosy was spread by sex. Since Drake's sister had had the disease, it was even odds that he had it too.

'So what am I to do?' he said to himself.

He went and asked a priest for help.

'The answer is simple,' said the priest. 'As the wizard Miphon explained, there's no telling if you've got blue leprosy, for it may not show up for years. If you do get it, there's no cure, so don't bother looking for one. In the meantime, wear a condom every time you copulate with woman or man or dog or pig or whatever it is you fancy. That way, you won't spread the disease to anyone else.'

Small comfort that was.

After another thirty days, however, Drake had got over his grief, fear and panic. Maybe he was infected. Maybe not. In any case, he was unlikely to find out for a year or two. Even if he had blue leprosy, a period of grace remained to him. He had better use that time wisely.

But how?

His sixteenth birthday was 150 days in the past. The end of his apprenticeship, which had once seemed to lie far away in the infinite future, would be upon him in little more than a year and a half. Oleg Douay still refused to believe Drake's account of his plight, or to give Drake the teaching he needed. Overtures to other swordsmiths brought blunt refusals.

It was clear he would never make a mastersword, or have his own forge, or have apprentices to kick around. He was getting old; his youth and hope were gone; he was finished. Sadly, Drake concluded that all that remained to him were the compensations of religion.

'I will devote what time remains to me,' said Drake, 'to the practical worship of the Gift.'

The Gift? Sex! (And, technically, alcohol and drugs as well.)

Unfortunately, Muck had taken to banking his apprentices' wages with the Orsay Bank in toto. Drake was penniless. And, since his sister was dead, he no longer had special privileges at the temple.

'Right,' he said. 'I'll sell my body.'

He had done it before, so he could do it again.

He cruised the docks, but found no buyers. For everyone knew why his sister had committed suicide, and none dared couple with someone who might be contaminated with blue leprosy. Thanks to the efforts of the temple of Hagon, knowledge of its etiology had spread throughout Cam. Priests boarded every incoming ship, preached doctrines of safe sex, advertised the temple prostitutes and warned against liaisons with dockside riff-raff.

'Right,' said Drake. 'I've got no sister. I've got no money. I can't sell my body. So how do I get a woman?'

Simple: he would have to make someone fall in love with him. Or at least in lust with him.

Since he might already be doomed to die of blue leprosy, the colony on the outskirts of town held little fear for him. He ventured there, and found Zanya Kliedervaust on her hands and knees scrubbing out bedpans.

'Remember me?' said Drake.

She looked up from her work.

'Oh yes,' she said. 'I remember you. You're the crazy fisherman we hauled out of the sea a horizon away from Stokos.'

'That's right,' said Drake. 'Only I'm a swordsmith, not a fisherman. Your body language tells me that you're looking for a relationship.'

He had rehearsed that line – and many others besides – for a long time. It came out perfectly.

'What?' said Zanya, sounding both tired and puzzled.

'I'm seeking to make a treaty against the loneliness of flesh born into solitude,' said Drake. 'I aspire to harmonize our auras into one mutual faith.'

'My Galish,' said Zanya, 'is not the best, though it improves steadily. You'll have to speak plain if you wish to be understood.'

Oh! So there was a language problem! That was all right, then. For a moment, Drake had almost been afraid that his blond good looks were failing to make the right impression on the lady.

'Zanya,' said Drake, 'I like your looks, just as I'm sure you like mine. What say we get together tonight? We'd look right handsome together.'

'What have you got in mind?' said Zanya.

'Some mutual moonlight, a dash of star-hunting, then a little lick of sweet honey.'

Zanya entirely failed to recognize the import of these delicate euphemisms, which were part of the common language of courtship on Stokos.

'Speak plainly,' she said. 'What do you want?'

Drake, his eloquence thwarted by her linguistic ignorance, lost patience – and gave an answer which was, unfortunately, honest, clear, direct and straightforward.

'I'm in lust,' he said. 'I want to fornicate.'

'I'm not meat,' said Zanya coldly. 'I'm a woman. There's a difference.'

And she went back to her scrubbing.

'Sorry,' said Drake. 'I meant no offence. I didn't mean to be so blunt. But—'

'*Oronoko*!' bawled Zanya. '*Fana tufa n'fa n'maufi*!'

And out from a workshed came Prince Oronoko. The purple-skinned man was – as he had been when Drake last saw him – wearing only a loin-cloth. Perhaps he had been chopping wood: his body glistened with sweat, and he had an axe in his hands. Oronoko advanced, grinning. Drake fled.

Later, sullen and disconsolate, he brooded over his failure with Zanya. She hadn't even bothered to ask his name.

He thought – and thought hard – about the advice the wizard Miphon had given him. All that stuff about flowers, poetry, daily visits, sincerity, pretty speaking, persistence. Should he try it? No, it couldn't possibly work. It sounded too stupid for words. Anyway, there was Oronoko to think of. If Drake went back, the purple man would probably chop off his head.

Drake sulked.

Meanwhile, the Flame spoke long and hard to Gouda Muck. Until finally, on Midwinter's Day (the start of the year Tor 6, or the middle of Khmar 17, depending on one's calendar) Muck announced to the world that he was the incarnation of the Flame. And the Flame, by his account, was the High God of All Gods.

'Fall down and worship me,' said Muck.

Some of his more credulous neighbours actually did. They fell to the ground, groaning. They licked his feet. They saw visions. They spoke in tongues.

'Good,' said Muck. 'You see? I am God!'

And Drake, dissenting, was severely kicked and beaten. He sought refuge with his uncle.

'Man,' said Drake, 'you've got to do something! Muck's mad, I'm sure of it.'

'Endure,' said Oleg Douay, who thought a little perdition would be good for the boy.

'But the man's mad, I tell you!' protested Drake.

'We're all mad,' said Oleg Douay grimly, 'or we'd have had more sense than to get ourselves born.'

'We don't have a choice,' said Drake.

71

'Of course we do!' said his uncle grimly. 'Why, only yesterday I was down by the shore in conversation with the sea gods, and they told me distinctly—'

Drake turned tail and fled.

By now, financial constraints made it virtually impossible for Drake to worship at the temple brothel. What's more, Gouda Muck forbid his apprentices even to go near the place. Of course, to forbid a thing is often to encourage a taste for it. Drake had always had a love for the Demon. Now, he became a true victim of religious mania, feeling he needed to practise religion at every possible moment just to keep himself sane.

But most forms of worship required money.

'What I need,' said Drake, 'is some kind of worship that will earn me money.'

Gambling was the only religious practice which seemed to meet his requirements. So he took himself off to the casinos.

From the middle of winter to the beginning of spring, Drake tried his luck and his luck tried him. After that, the casinos cut off his credit. His gambling debts were huge, and the temple's enforcers were soon pressing him for payment.

Barred from the casinos, Drake chanced his fortunes privately, hazarding ill-lit backgammon saloons and murky dice-chess parlours. To finance his ventures, he borrowed where he could, signing notes to all and sundry with his thumbprint. He wagered ever more wildly, hoping to recoup his losses. But he drank while he gambled – never a good combination. He came home drunk one night, and, feeling reckless, spat into the fire in his master's sight.

'You have defiled my living flesh,' said Gouda Muck – and began to beat him.

Drake fled. He was doing a lot of running away these days. He didn't like it. He wandered through the night, cursing, kicking cats, and working himself into a rage. This was all Zanya's fault! If that proud-faced bitch

72

hadn't snubbed his offer, he'd never have got in this mess.

That suggested a way out.

If he porked her once, surely she'd see sense. One taste of Drake Douay, and she'd be eagering for more. Yes. She'd said no, but it was common knowledge that women often said no when they meant yes. How far was it to the leper colony? Not far at all: he was almost at the edge of town already.

Drake rolled up to the leper colony.

'Despatch for Zanya Kliedervaust,' he said, brandishing a wallet (which was empty). 'Urgent despatch. Immediate delivery required.'

'You've been drinking,' said the night porter.

'So I have,' said Drake belligerently. 'But I can still deliver a letter. If you don't want to let me through, wake your boss, and we'll talk it out with him.'

The night porter saw sense, and gave Drake directions to Zanya's quarters. It was, after all, scarcely unusual for a courier to be drunk on duty. And they did work all hours of day and night.

Shortly, Drake entered Zanya's room – a mean little hut lit by a smoky oil lamp. The woman of his desires was sitting up in bed, reading a scroll of some kind.

'You!' she said.

'Me,' said Drake.

'Get out!' she said.

'Hey,' said Drake. 'Don't be so hard on me. I don't mean any harm. What's with that scroll?'

'This?' said Zanya, mellowing ever so slightly. 'This was lent to me by a friend. It's very interesting. It's all about Goudanism. That's the creed of Gouda Muck. I don't know if you've ever heard of him.'

'I may have,' said Drake cautiously. 'What do you think of it?'

'Great!' said Zanya, her eyes shining. 'Would you like to hear about it? Here, sit down on the floor and I'll read you some.'

That was mighty accommodating of her, under the

73

circumstances. But Zanya, as a priestess of the Orgy God on the Ebrells, had gained a vast experience of dealing with drunks. She thought Drake was not too dangerous. If she settled him down and spoke to him nicely, likely he would go to sleep. Then she could slip out and summon Oronoko.

'Why should I listen to something about Gouda Muck?' said Drake.

'Because of who he is,' said Zanya, meaning no harm. 'He's the High God of All Gods.'

This was too much to bear. Drake had come to the woman who was the focus of all his desire – only to find Gouda Muck had come before him, in spirit if not in flesh.

With a scream of rage, Drake tore the scroll away from Zanya, and jumped on her.

She slapped a hand to his face and dug fingers into his eyes. Hard. He jerked his head back. Instantly her fingers slid to his throat and dug in. Viciously. Then she hooked an elbow into the side of his head. His world reeled. Agonizing pain exploded between his legs as she thumped him in the testicles.

Drake collapsed to the floor, a helpless heap of writhing misery. Zanya, who was indeed a well-built woman, picked him up and threw him outside.

'Don't come back!' she said. 'Or I'll batter you dead!'

Drake crawled away into the darkness, groaned. But, after a while, the pain became manageable. He decided he had better go back and apologize, yes. Otherwise Zanya would be permanently soured against him. Manfully, Drake got to his feet. Someone was knocking at Zanya's door. Who? The door opened; a gleam of lamplight showed Prince Oronoko standing in the doorway.

If Drake's throat had not been so sore, he would have screamed his outrage. Instead, he stood silent as Oronoko entered. The door closed. Drake heard Zanya speak, then laugh. Well! So much for that! Drake's prospects for making his woman were – for tonight, at least – reduced to zero.

Drake was a long time getting back to the forge, since

every step he took hurt him. Would the door be barred against him? It was not. Since Muck had discovered he was actually the High God of All Gods, he had lost all fear of mortal men. Everyone was asleep when Drake slipped inside, as quiet as could be.

Drake did not sleep that night. He brooded in the little attic where he was quartered, and while he brooded he drank from the crock of hard liquor he kept in his chest for emergencies.

He felt humiliated.

Rape was supposed to be easy, the perfect demonstration of a man's easy mastery over a woman. But Drake had failed. Everything he tried had gone sour. His whole life was a disaster. He was ready to kill himself.

But why should he? Why should he give Gouda Muck that satisfaction? No. He shouldn't kill himself. He should do something which would really piss Muck off in a big way. But what? Burn down the forge? No good – it was insured. Let's see. Another drink, yes, that was the story. First drink, then thought. Drink was good. It eased the pain in his balls and the pain in his eyes.

Towards dawn, sore, drunk, hurt and as reckless as ever, Drake crept downstairs and stole Muck's master-sword, the prize bit of steelwork which Muck had created years before to win admission to the swordsmiths' guild.

Sunrise found Drake on the docks of Cam, determined to sell that very same sword.

At that early hour, there was little life stirring. Drake, nothing daunted, went and knocked up Theyla Slonage, a merchant from Narba who had a certain reputation. Slonage, bleary and unbeautiful in the morning light, reluctantly invited Drake into his back room.

'What have you got for me?' asked Slonage. 'And don't say yourself! You've spoilt your boyish beauty with those blacksmith's muscles. Look at your hands – Demon's grief, they're twice as tough a sharkskin. And you've been fighting. Have you looked at yourself? You've got two hideous-ugly black eyes.'

Drake, in answer, revealed the sheathed sword which had been hidden down his trouser leg. Slonage, without bothering to look at it, offered a thousandth of its value. Drake unsheathed the blade, slowly, fingerlength by fingerlength. Its naked beauty glimmered in the gloom. Drake, looking at it, felt almost sober.

Slonage sneered, but doubled his offer. However, Drake, who knew the price of steel, was hardly going to sell the masterwork for 0.2 per cent of its value.

Drake eased open a shutter to let in the cool light of morning. Raising the blade to the light, he blew upon its surface. As his breath condensed upon the steel they both saw the patterns of the forging momentarily snake across the surface of the metal.

Theyla Slonage raised his offering to a hundredth of the sword's value. Drake replied by asking double, and they settled, at length, for a fiftieth.

Drake was not paid off in the shangles and jives minted by King Tor, but in Bankers' Money, the coinage issued everywhere by the Partnership Banks. He got five zeals – small rings of nine-carat gold, stamped on both inside and outside with banker's marks. He got a dozen bronze flothens, circular coins with threading holes in the middle. And he got, as well, a scattering of spings which he did not even bother to count.

There were nine Partnership Banks, each issuing the same identical coinage. And these banks – immensely rich, enormously powerful and intensely secretive – were:

† the Orsay Bank of Stokos;
† the Morgrim Bank of Chi 'ash-lan;
† the Safrak Bank of the Safrak Islands;
† the Monastic Treasury of Inner Adeer, located hard up against the Ashun Mountains in Voice, the retirement city of the rulers of the Rice Empire;
† the Flesh Trader's Financial Association of Galsh Ebrek;
† the Bondsman's Guild of Obooloo, capital city of Aldarch the Third, the Mutilator of Yestron;

†   the Bralsh, of Dalar ken Halvar;
†   the Singing Dove Pensions Trust of Tang;
†   and the Taniwha Guarantee Corporation of Quilth.

How those far-flung organizations managed to co-ordinate their activities was one of the larger mysteries of the universe. However, most people – indeed, even most kings, princes, priests and emperors – were unaware that Bankers' Money was accepted in many far-flung places which were largely ignorant even of each other's existence.

The only person ever to ponder this conundrum seri-ously was the wizard Phyphor; that notable master of the Order of Arl was brooding about it yet again even as Drake emerged into the steadily strengthening sunlight of the dockside morning.

Drake, who was starting to feel a little anxious, settled his nerves with an early-morning beer. His new-found wealth made it hard for him to find the bottom of the beer mug, and it was mid-morning before he emerged again into the hot, raucous bustle of the docks.

He strolled along, hands dug deep in his pockets. He kicked a piece of shining sea-coal. Once. The sudden movement hurt his bruised, swollen testicles. He idled from stall to stall, scarcely listening to the babble of lan-guages assaulting his ears as hoarse-voiced shills screamed the virtues of products as diverse as querns and keflo shell.

Then he saw a couple of big men prowling through the crowds. They wore long robes and carried iron-shod staves. Elsewhere, they might have been mistaken for wiz-ards, but Drake recognized them on sight. They were two of the temple's enforcers. He knew they knew him well. He walked the other way, toward a man who was hawking passages to Androlmarphos.

'. . . 'Marphos today . . . noon sailing . . . 'Marphos today . . . one zeal for the beer-price passage . . .'

Drake made a drunken decision which he would never have made sober, and paid out for a passage to the foreign port, leaving at noon that same day.

6

Name: Dreldragon Drakedon Douay.

Alias: Drake (meaning, in the Ligin of Stokos, 'pumpkin').

Occupation: swordsmith's apprentice.

Status: criminal on the run.

Description: a nuggety fair-haired beardless lad with hard hands and a blacksmith's muscles; he is shorter than fashion prefers, but not exactly stunted.

Prospects: if he survives to see his eighteenth birthday, he may be allowed to marry King Tor's daughter – which would bring him, in time, the throne of Stokos.

There was no nonsense about passengers on the good ship *Flying Fish*. They were battened down below decks for the passage to Androlmarphos, a run of about two hundred leagues as the aasvogel flies, but rather more as the ship tacks. The *Flying Fish*, which held several unofficial records for ultra-slow passages, generally made the voyage in six days.

Drake, being battened down below, was unable to hang over the stern rail waxing maudlin as the cliffs of Stokos receded into the distance. He hung over the side of his bunk instead, miserably seasick, and vomited into the pitching gloom. Fortunately, he was on the lowest bunk, with nobody below him. Unfortunately, there were three men in the tiers above, each as sick as he was . . .

By the time Drake had vomited up everything in his stomach, the anaesthetic effects of alcohol were beginning to wear off, and both his body and psyche were suffering. He tried to console himself by eating and drinking, but continued seasickness made both these enterprises counterproductive.

Bad weather stretched the voyage out. Once, the ship was almost wrecked on the shores of Hok, a mountainous coastal province of the Harvest Plains, lying due north of Stokos. Finally, nine full days after leaving Cam, the *Flying Fish* reached her destination.

It was a pale, unsteady youth who finally staggered down the gangplank to the dockside at Androlmarphos, the great trading city commanding the delta of the Velvet River. This was the first time Drake had set foot on the continent of Argan, fabled land of ruined cities, fallen empires, monsters, magic, sages, wizards and worse. He expected immediate amazements – but was swiftly disillusioned.

The bustling docks were much the same in 'Marphos as in Stokos. The ships looked no different; many, indeed, he had seen before at Cam. And, while the place was a polyglot babble of foreign languages, the dominant argot was the Galish Trading Tongue, which he knew well enough already.

Since Androlmarphos recognized Bankers' Money, Drake had no need to find a money-changer. Anywhere inland, he would have been less lucky: but in 'Marphos a full half-dozen currencies mingled promiscuously. He could even have spent the jives and shangles minted by his own King Tor, had he had any to his name.

Drake bought a fish sandwich and, eating it slowly, watched men lose money to a quick-talking rogue who hid a peanut under one of three little cups, shuffled these, then asked his victims to guess its hiding place. Drake was too canny to risk cold cash on a sucker's game like that, but nevertheless found the sight heartening – it suggested the Demon was worshipped here in Androlmarphos, if not in name then at least in deed.

He went to search for a bar.

Seventeen days later, when the last of his money was almost gone, someone tapped him on the shoulder and spoke his name. Turning, he saw it was Yot.

'Why, Sully Datelier Yot!' said Drake. 'What brings you here? Come to enjoy yourself, perhaps?'

'No,' said Yot, drawing a knife. 'I've come to—'

But Drake, waiting to hear no more, threw half a mug of beer into the boy's face, then grabbed his knifehand. Their struggle precipitated a general bar brawl – it was that kind of drinking establishment, the only kind which would have tolerated Drake's seventeen-day binge. In the end, the Watch broke up the fight.

Yot escaped, but Drake was caught and hauled before a judge. He heard, as others have in his predicament, many fulsome phrases about the need for personal responsibility and the shortcomings of the younger generation. Then heard his sentence:

'Ship out or else.'

'Or else what?' asked Drake incautiously.

'Or else we'll chop off both your feet and sell them to raise funds for charity!' roared the judge, who, having tried three dozen identical cases that day, was losing his sense of proportion.

'I've got no money,' said Drake, who had been stripped of the last of his funds by the Watch.

'Then we'll help you earn some,' said the judge with a pleasant smile, which suggested that something particularly nasty was coming. He had till then been speaking in Galish, but lapsed momentarily into Legal Churl. There was a pause before the translation came:

'Twenty days hard.'

'Hard?' said Drake, in bewilderment.

It sounded thoroughly obscene to him.

'Hard labour, fool!'

Drake then spent twenty days chained to the oar of a galley, rowing up and down the long sweaty river-leagues inland from Androlmarphos. The work was tough, the rations poor, and the view monotonous. His galley once

80

went upstream as far as Selzirk itself, but docked in the magnificent capital of the Harvest Plains by night, and was gone again before dawn. That irked Drake as much as anything else.

At least those twenty days gave him plenty of time to plan for his future. He would go back to Stokos. Yes. He would throw himself on the mercy of King Tor. Or would he? No: he would come not with a plea but with a sword. He would offer himself to Tor as an executioner. A Suppressor of Unorthodox Religions.

Once Drake's eloquence had persuaded Tor of the danger posed by Gouda Muck's cult, surely the king would be only too glad to have a vigorous young man like Drake in charge of the suppression of Muck's outlandish heresies.

Yes.

And once he had an official position, a fancy title, a sizeable income and a rainbow-coloured uniform designed to show off his muscles, he'd make another assault on Zanya Kliedervaust. But he would refine his tactics first. He might even try some of the things the wizard Miphon had suggested. Would he pledge his love with poetry? No, never – he'd feel ridiculous. But he might take her flowers. Well, one flower, anyway. And maybe he shouldn't be so direct about demanding her body. Maybe he should give her some time to get used to him. How long? Three days? No, two should do it . . .

After twenty days on the galley, Drake expected liberty. But got no such thing. Instead, he was battened down in the hold of the *Gol-sa-danjerk*, a foreign ship which gave him less air, less space and less light than the *Flying Fish*, and kept him on shorter commons besides. Where he was bound, he knew not; the other exiles imprisoned with him knew as little as he.

'With luck,' said Drake, 'we're being deported to Stokos.'

In fact, they had all been sold into slavery, and were being carried north-west toward a slaving port in the Ravlish Lands.

At last, after what seemed an age – but was really only seven half-days and a fingerlength – an unfamiliar voice of command ordered them up on deck. They scrambled up through a recently unbattened hatch to find their ship still at sea. Another vessel was connected to the *Gol-sa-danjerk* by grappling hooks. Copious quantities of blood on the deck suggested that the connection had not been entirely welcomed. Indeed, Drake observed that most of the crew had become corpses. Strangers dressed in seal-skins were busy stripping those corpses.

'Pirates,' said Drake to himself.

This was a guess, but it was accurate.

'Which of you jerks can sail?' roared a pirate, in something approximating to Galish.

All except Drake proclaimed themselves to be sailors.

'You,' said a pirate, pointing at him. 'You know the sea, or don't you?'

'I know something better,' said Drake, with a metal-workers' conceit which marked him as a true son of Stokos. 'I know steel. Hammering, shaping, forging and sharpening. I'm a master craftsman, don't you know.'

Gouda Muck would have laughed bitterly to have heard that joke – though Drake did know some of the basics.

'You're a landlubber, then,' said a pirate, and knocked him to the deck.

Drake swiftly realized his mistake. The other prisoners swore themselves to be pirates, and were accepted into the fraternity of the sea-robbers. Drake, on the other hand, was looked on as near to useless.

A prize crew was left on the *Gol-sa-danjerk*, but Drake was dragged on board the pirate ship. Its sails, he saw, were black. It seemed strangely familiar. He was half-persuaded that this was the very same barque which he had seen anchored in the harbour of Cam the morning after his sixteenth birthday.

'What ship be this?' he said.

'The *Walrus*, friend,' said a voice.

That voice sounded familiar. Indeed, it came from the

mouth of Bucks Cat – one of the jeering boatmen who had forced Drake into the sea to drown a horizon away from Stokos. Even though that was more than half a year ago, the horrors of the occasion were, to say the least, vivid in Drake's memory.

'You!' said Drake.

'And me,' said another man.

A lean, pale man. Ish Ulpin!

'Come along, darling,' said Ish Ulpin. 'We're going to introduce you to the captain. He might like a nice young boy like you.'

So Drake was led along the deck of the *Walrus*. And an evil barque she was, too, a stinking tub of reeks and rats, with decks near as dirty as her bilges. Drake, however, had no time for detailed inspection, for he was shortly confronted with her captain, one Slagger Mulps. This man was knicknamed 'the Walrus' – hence the name of his ship.

A weird sight he was.

Slagger Mulps was very tall and very thin, and had a very long very sharp nose. But what first impressed was his beard and his hair, both of which were green.

'On your knees!' said Ish Ulpin, 'for you stand in the presence of our great captain, Slagger Mulps, the Walrus himself.'

Drake held his ground. Ish Ulpin drove hard, bony thumbs into pressure points in Drake's shoulders, forcing him down to his knees.

'Who are you?' said Slagger Mulps.

His eyes, like his hair, were green – like those of the wizard Miphon. His arms were long, dangling right down to his knees. He had, Drake saw, two thumbs and three fingers on each hand.

'If you want me to talk,' said Drake, 'first find a human being for me to talk to.'

Drake Douay had made a big mistake.

He had said the worst of all possible things.

For the Walrus was acutely conscious of his strangeness.

83

He had led the worst of childhoods imaginable – teased, bullied and rejected on account of his green hair and his multiple thumbs. The experience had marked him for life.

The Walrus stared at Drake, envying his perfect conformity (height apart) to the human norm.

'I,' said the Walrus, 'am human. What's more, I'm likely the man who will kill you.'

'Lucky you don't have a mirror,' said Drake, 'or you'd likely kill yourself.'

The Walrus, who had seen himself mirrored in glass, metal and water often enough, was overcome with fury. Raising his voice, he shouted:

'Who wants to play with this thing before I kill it?'

'I do,' said a rough, gruff voice.

And forward stepped a barrel-chested hairy brute in bloodstained sealskins, his coarse-featured face surrounded by shaggy black hair and a great big black beard. It was Andranovory.

The Walrus immediately regretted having spoken.

Andranovory was the worst of his men – a drunken, murderous, argumentative bully, an untrustworthy sadist hated by at least half the crew. In the past, he had treated prisoners in ways which gave Mulps nightmares.

'There are others more worthy,' said the Walrus. 'I give the pleasure of playing with this – with this thing to Ish Ulpin.'

'And I,' said Ish Ulpin, 'yield that pleasure to my shipmate, Andranovory.'

That personage grinned at Drake, showing broken rot-brown teeth.

'Atsimo Andranovory,' he said, introducing himself. 'I believe we've met.'

'Oh, I don't think we have,' said Drake.

'You don't remember me?' said Andranovory. 'Well, you'll remember me hereafter. Give me a suck!'

And the raptor exposed his weapon to the cool sea breeze. His knob was crusted with festering sores.

'Suck!' said Andranovory.

'I'll not play woman,' said Drake, in a voice shaking with tension.

Mulps sympathized with the boy who did not want to play woman – not, at least, with so many men watching.

'Lazy little bugger!' said Andranovory, giving him an idle slap. 'But we can cure that. String him up by the ankles till he learns when he's well off.'

While Mulps did not approve of such tortures, he could scarcely intervene. If his crew ever learned the true nature of his sensitive, infinitely tender soul, they would surely lose faith in him as a captain. Mulps was aware that he was not much of a sailor, or much of a fighter, either – it was his thrift and financial acumen, more than anything, which had brought him control of the ship.

So Mulps could only stand back and watch helplessly as Ish Uplin and Bucks Cat, obedient to Andranovory's commands, tied Drake's hands behind his back then tied a rope to his ankles. The rope was slung over a yard-arm.

Drake lay on the hard deck, staring up at the blue sky. All around were unfriendly faces. He wished he had not given Andranovory those duff directions on the dockside of Cam, more than half a year ago. But, at the time, it had seemed such an innocent little trick.

'Mike!' yelled Ish Ulpin. 'Come help us haul a rope!'

And something far too large to be human came trundling along the deck. It was twice the height of any man. It was as wide in the shoulders as a man's outstretched arms. It had no ears: only holes in the side of its head where ears should be.

It was Whale Mike.

'Oh, you,' said Whale Mike, looking down at Drake in surprise.

'Yes, me,' said Drake, staring up at the yellow-faced monster.

'What you down there for?' said Whale Mike.

'Because that toad-raping Atsimo Andranovory wants a suck,' said Drake. 'And I'll tell you this – he's not getting one from me!'

'Then you ask Walrus help you,' said Whale Mike. 'He our captain. He good joker.'

'Our young friend here isn't exactly Slagger Mulps' favourite person,' said Ish Ulpin. 'He more or less said our beautiful green-haired captain wasn't human.'

'Oh, that not very nice,' said Whale Mike.

And pulled on the rope which ran up from Drake's feet and over the yard-arm. Drake was lifted clear of the deck. His hair flopped down. Blood rushed to his head.

'Heave ho!' said Bucks Cat.

And gave Drake a push which sent him swinging across the deck and out over the sea. He spun. He had a dizzy, giddy view of surging blue sea and dazzling sun. Then he was swinging back to where he had started from. Ish Ulpin was there to meet him. With a fist.

'That enough!' said Whale Mike, 'You stop. This my friend!'

'Oh, man,' said Bucks Cat, slapping Drake on the back. 'You're in luck! Whale Mike's your friend!'

And he hooted with laughter.

It was such a good joke that even Ish Ulpin laughed. But Andranovory simply looked at Drake and said:

'If you get off this rope alive, I'll be waiting for you.'

Drake, hanging upside down, dizzy, sore, sick, found it impossible to come up with a smart reply.

Whale Mike hauled Drake higher until their heads were level. Drake was well over twice his own height from the deck. A long way to fall. A lethal fall, if he landed on his head. Mike took a turn of rope around his fist, as if he meant to hold Drake there for some time.

'Great view,' said Drake, starting to sway with the motion of the swells that rocked the ship.

But all he could see at that moment was Whale Mike's swollen sallow yellow face and tiny imbecilic eyes. Mike hooked a couple of fingers into Drake's collar to stop him swaying.

'We no meet long time,' said Mike.

'Too right,' said Drake.

'You do good swim,' said Mike. 'You smart joker. Tough, eh? If not tough, then drown. You make good pirate maybe.'

'Yeah, sure,' said Drake. 'Cut me down then I'll prove just how good.'

'Not that easy, my friend. First you make An'vory happy. You suck, that not hurt you any. Then maybe some joker rough you up, but I make sure it not go too far. I say good word for you to Walrus. He not bad joker. He okay.'

'No deal,' said Drake. 'I won't suck any filthy pirate cock. I'd rather die.'

'That not so smart,' said Whale Mike. 'Not much good being you when you dead. That not so? You take care An'vory, I take care you. You say nice things to Walrus, then he happy, you happy. You my friend.'

'My friend!?' shouted Drake. Stress, pain, nausea and disorientation suddenly yielded to an enormous outburst of hate, rage and anger. 'My friend? How do you reckon? Man, you helped force me into the sea to drown! You tried to kill me!'

'That little thing between friends,' said Whale Mike.

Drake was staggered by this bland assertion.

'You're twigged, man!' he screamed. 'You've gone to rust! You can't make friends by drowning people!'

'That not so smart,' said Whale Mike. 'You need friend real bad. So you have long swim. So what? You not drowned. You not dead, so why worry?'

'You sound as if I should be grateful!' said Drake.

'You get good swim,' said Whale Mike. 'You get out of water, you feel real man. Real proud. You get good story, tell many times. Joker buy you beer, hear story. That not so? Not all bad, that swim. You get plenty beer.'

That was true, up to a point. Drake had told the story of his deep-sea survival many times. He had got many beers out of it. But that was hardly the point.

'You're mad, you crazy bugger!' said Drake.

'No, you mad,' said Whale Mike, sounding hurt. 'You

87

not right in head. I your friend. I try help. You not want help. Maybe you die, but that your problem, not mine.'

And he unhooked his fingers from Drake's collar. Drake began to swing. And Mike hauled him up higher into the blue blue sky.

'Investigate,' muttered Drake.

And did his very best to see how and where the rope was tied off. Whale Mike was fastening it to a cleat on the deck. Drake's life now depended on the safety of a knot tied by a moron. Grief!

He closed his eyes and tried to endure.

After a while, he found endurance impossible.

'All right!' he cried, with what voice was left to him. 'I'll do it! I'll do it! Anything and everything! An'vory, sure. Even the captain, yes! Every man in the ship! Just let me down from here!'

But if anyone heard, nobody took any notice.

And Drake soon left off crying, for his throat was far too dry to continue.

All day he dangled, utterly helpless. He had no knife. Even if gymnastic flair and a touch of magic had allowed him to untie himself and get to the deck alive, he would have faced a shipload of pirates more than ready to hang him right up again – quite possibly by his testicles.

The wind got up.

The sea thickened.

It was, of course, sheer torture to be suspended there, swaying in sickening arcs as the ship rutted through the rolling seas. The weather worsened toward evening; by dayfall, they were in a regular storm. But Drake, by then, was only half-conscious.

When the ship struck, he heard the panic-stricken shouts of pirates only as another thread of violence in the nightmares of delirium. When the seas swirled up around him, he thought at first that his head was being shoved into a bucket of salt water.

Then realized he was afloat on the turbulent seas of night. Afloat? He was drowning! Feet tied together.

Hands tied behind back. A wave wrecked him under. He tried to jack-knife to the surface. Failed. Then the seas slacked away. He was afloat upon liquid ebony, staring at blindness. He gasped darkness, found part of it breathable.

Something was pulling on his ankle-rope.

Moments later, Drake was hauled right up out of the water and seized by something huge: by a monster possessed of inexorable strength. Throat moistened by seawater, Drake screamed.

'Why you scream?' said a voice. 'You safe now.'

Who could that be?

Drake thought he could guess.

'You cuddle close,' said the voice. 'You shy? Not good be shy. Sea cold. Share heat.'

'Can't cuddle,' said Drake. 'Can't anything. Hands tied.'

'That no problem. Knife made for that.'

And Whale Mike cut the water-swollen ropes which bound Drake's wrists. Drake's first thought was to seize the knife and kill his enemy. But he could not see the knife in the night. And, in any case, his hands were – for the moment – near enough to useless.

'Can't hold on,' said Drake. 'Too tired.'

'Easy, man,' said Whale Mike. 'You not fall. I hold. You good friend, I not let you fall.'

And Whale Mike cradled Drake in his arms. The night was full of sounds of seething sea, of wave-wreck and surf-shatter. But they could not drown out Mike's voice. He had started singing! He was crooning a song in some strange, strange foreign language which Drake did not understand. But, without understanding the words, Drake was fairly sure the song was a lullaby.

Whale Mike was still singing a lifetime later when the shroud-pale dawn illuminated the masts and rigging of the wrecked ship, the ragged white surf breaking on nearby rocks, and a huddling of pirates barnacled on those spray-lashed rocks.

'Look!' cried Ish Ulpin.

And everyone looked, and saw Whale Mike sitting where yard-arm joined mast, with Drake Douay on his lap.

'Hey, Mike!' yelled Bucks Cat from the rocks. 'How's your baby?'

'He all right!' yelled Whale Mike. 'We sing happy song!'

Drake had never felt so humiliated in his life.

He tried to untie the ropes which still secured his feet. But all he managed to do was break two fingernails. He began to cry with fatigue and frustration. His tears ran hot down his cheeks.

'You want free from rope?' said Mike. 'That no problem. I just leave rope in case wave take you in dark. Rope for safety. I cut.'

And he pulled out his sheath knife – which was almost the size of a sword – and liberated Drake's feet.

'What now?' said Drake.

'This!' said Whale Mike.

And threw Drake into the water.

'Hey!' shouted Drake, floundering in the slathering sea.

Mike laughed.

'Swim!' he said, waving in the direction of the nearby reef. 'Swim!'

Drake, having no option, swam towards the reef, where barking surf chased yelping waves and devoured them in crevices and rock-traps. Then Mike dived, and swam after him. When Drake gained the rocks, he jammed himself between two of the largest and coldest and hung on tight against the threat of the surf.

'Bring your slut-hole here, darling,' said Andranovory.

But, to Drake's surprise, the order was not followed up by a prompt attack. Even Andranovory was too far gone to be lusting in more than thought.

Whale Mike wallowed through the seas like something out of a bad dream. He gained the rocks.

'You all right?' called Mike to Drake.

90

'Fine,' said Drake.

'You want cuddle?' said Mike.

'I've cuddled enough, thanks,' said Drake.

'Never enough cuddle,' said Mike.

And, shortly, Whale Mike, Slagger Mulps, Ish Ulpin and Bucks Cat were cuddling together in a big body heap. Drake saw most of the other pirates had also huddled into body-warmth teams. He realized it would be smart to join them, for it was cold; wind and spray were sweeping the exposed rocks. But he was too scared.

He humbled down as best he could, trying to make himself invisible. A gull winged low above the slipshod surf. How long would it be before he was too weak to save his eyes from the seabirds? The slubbering sea throttled amongst the rocks, hungering for his hot blood and his long white bones; if the storm got up again, the sea would surely claim him before the birds did.

Finding thought so unproductive of pleasure, Drake stopped the practice, and shortly fell into a fitful half-sleep punctuated by dreams and the voices of hallucination.

Meanwhile, Slagger Mulps, luxuriating in the warmth of Whale Mike's armpit, stared out to sea. Shadows smudged the far-distant horizon; he knew those shadows to be the Greater Teeth. They were shipwrecked, without a doubt, on the Gaunt Reefs; there was at least an even chance that they would be rescued before too long by a raiding ship or a fishing boat.

And almost an even chance that they would not.

'We sing!' shouted Whale Mike, with invincible cheerfulness. 'Everyone sing!'

This command woke everyone who had managed to drift away into the land of dreams – including Drake. He listened with astonishment as Whale Mike started a song.

All the pirates knew it, and joined in, but Drake could not follow the lyrics, for they were so full of sea-talk, arcane slang, and dialect words native to the Greater Teeth. But the chorus was easy enough to understand:

everyone howled like a dog, crowed like a cock, screamed like a cat then barked like a seal. Then clapped hands against thighs.

Drake suddenly wanted to be part of it: part of the singing, the slapping, the body-huddles, the community. It all seemed, for a moment, positively jolly. But did not dare join in. His recent experiences had left him feeling as wrecked as the *Walrus*. He closed his eyes, and, eventually, slept.

Towards noon, Drake woke from muttering nightmares to hear excited talk amongst the pirates. They had sighted a ship. As it came closer, they saw it had green sails. Closer still, and they saw its dragon figurehead.

Mulps spat, and swore.

'It's the *Warwolf*,' said Mulps.

The masts and rigging of the *Walrus* advertised their presence, and it was soon clear to everyone except Drake that the *Warwolf* had sighted them. However, by the time the ship was bulking near the reefs, even he knew that rescue was at hand – not that the pirates seemed glad of it.

Keeping a prudent distance from the rocks, the *Warwolf* lowered three boats to investigate. Soon the castaways were sharing their reef with newcomers, a party of grim men tricked out with weapons and looking more than ready to use them. One was, to judge from his bearing, their leader.

He carried himself like a king.

He was tall, lean, as black as Bucks Cat and as bald as a hazel nut. He was dressed in brown leather, and wore round his hips a great big leather belt from which hung a waterproof sea-pouch and assorted ironmongery. He looked dangerous. But he had come, nevertheless, to rescue them – so, at the sight of him, Drake perked up.

'Who's the bald old coot?' said Drake to anyone who might answer.

Nobody condescended to reply, but the bald old coot was in fact Jon Arabin, the Warwolf himself, an ascetic man with a taste for experiment and challenge. Arabin came onto the rocks like a conqueror. His eyes were a pale, sunwashed blue. Drake was startled to see such blue amidst such black. Steady eyes, yes, and a steady voice, which said:

'There's space afloat for any who'll swear loyal to me and mine. Even the Walrus. How about it, Mulps, me pretty fopling?'

Mulps spat in reply.

'I'll take no murder on my ship,' continued Arabin, unperturbed. 'So you must swear loyal. Mulps, play the man: free the crew from their word.'

'Done,' said Mulps, nodding a little. 'Any rat in search of a sewer can run.'

Nobody moved.

'Loyal is one thing,' said Arabin. 'Stupid is another.'

Drake got to his feet. He felt thin, transparent, almost weightless.

'I'll swear loyal,' he said.

'That's rape-meat from the last boarding!' said Andranovory. 'Take a swearing from him? He can't stand a deck, far less set sail.'

Arabin turned his stern gaze on Drake, who felt, for a moment, like dust being weighed against iron.

'What can you do, boy?'

'I know iron,' said Drake promptly, 'and I know steel. Yes, and rope. Climbing, splicing and knots. It's my father who learnt me ropes.'

'Aye, boy, and buggery perhaps,' said Arabin. 'But can you cut?'

'Cut?'

'Aye. Cut, gut, gralloch and gash. Go nose to nose with a cutlass and swim through smirking. How about it, boy? Come here!'

Drake reluctantly ventured down to the foam-smothered patch of rock where Jon Arabin stood, careless of the sea lathering his boots. As surf sucked back, Arabin tossed a dirk so it fell between them. Drake stared at the bald man's hard bones, the rough-torn boots, the ugly

93

chunks of callus on the knuckles, the pale blue eyes as cold as the sea and as ruthless.

'I can cut,' he said, and stooped, and grabbed, and jerked the dirk to the challenge.

Jon Arabin kicked him in the stomach, and he went down hard. Heart scrambling, Drake scuffled to his feet. Sick nausea staggered him, and he knew he was dead meat: but he squared back, panting, knife held tight, and stood ready.

Arabin gave a little nod.

'Aye,' he said. 'You've got the makings. Get in the boat.'

7

Name: Orfus pirates.

Description: league of sea-robbers based on islands of the Greater Teeth.

Language: a dialect of Galish.

Political organization: oligarchical rule through a limited franchise democracy.

History: dates back several centuries to the Summer of Three Comets, when the delinquent Harla clan of Galish traders set up as pirates on the island of Drum, a base later abandoned after a severe dispute with the local sea dragons.

Once back aboard the *Warwolf*, Jon Arabin ordered a raft to be cut loose and thrown overboard. He was obeyed.

'That's their chance,' said Jon Arabin, as the bamboo raft splashed into the sea. 'They can swim for it, if they wish.'

'Why give them a chance?' said one of his men. 'Are you in love with friend Walrus of sudden?'

'Nay, man,' said Arabin. 'But Whale Mike's on that reef. He gave me a chance once, aye, when the Walrus was set to drown me. I owe him the same in return.'

'What's with the boy?' said a man.

'New meat,' said Jon Arabin. 'Get him some soup. Then to bed.'

'We've no bunk spare.'

'Then he can sleep on the floor. He's tired enough –

aren't you boy? Aye. You'll nod away to never in an instant.'

Drake was in no state to argue otherwise. Jon Arabin knew what he was talking about.

The *Warwolf* stood off from the Greater Teeth that night, and put in to Gufling the next day. A slow and weary business it was, with much sounding, towing and warping before they eased the ship in to a sea-cleft which fitted them as tightly as a virgin. Gufling, Drake learned, was the smallest Tooth where a ship could berth; Jon Arabin had been exiled here by debt.

From the deck, Drake looked around with eyes which had widened to accommodate the gloom. Overhanging cliffs tossed around the echoes of boots on stone, harsh laughter and shipwork hammering. The place stank of sewage, smoke and fish heads. Dogs were barking, babies bawling, and fat women yelling in a Galish patois at times scarcely comprehensible.

'Come along, boy,' said Jon Arabin, striding down the gang-plank. 'What are you waiting for? A whore-money proposition?'

Dumbly, Drake followed his new master – wishing, for a moment, that he was a fish, free to take the sea-path back to Stokos. They fumbled their way down cockroach-haunted tunnels to Arabin's living quarters, where a confusion of women and children filled the air with tears and laughter.

Drake was shown a place where he could sleep, a side-kennel in Jon Arabin's cave complex. It was a warehouse of sorts, holding baulks of spare timber, buckets of tar, lobster pots, fishing floats, harpoons, chunks of cork and hundreds of odds and ends of rope.

'You say you know rope, boy,' said Arabin. 'Well, have we got work for you! Look on it as a challenge. Do you accept?'

'*Plen pro!*' said Drake in his native Ligin, meaning '*avec plaisir*'.

And he sat down on the spot and began rummaging through the ropes. Jon Arabin laughed.

'Lunch first!' said he.

Lunch was three different kinds of seaweed, assorted seaslugs, lobster, whore's-eggs, raw fish and roast seal, all obtained locally. Drake was glad he had learnt that raw fish was safe to eat – otherwise he might have disgraced himself by accusing Jon Arabin of trying to poison him.

'Good fish,' he said.

'You'll find, boy,' said Arabin, 'that the Teeth must feed themselves, more or less. You'll be busy enough when the *Warwolf*'s home. Aye. Working sealing boats and fishing.'

'Do I start that after lunch?' said Drake.

'Nay,' said Arabin, with another laugh. 'After lunch, it's ropes. Rope is your future, boy, till I say otherwise.'

Drake was glad he had not been bluffing about rope. He knew knots and splices, and used them well, fashioning serviceable rope from the wreckage he was given to work with. At first he worked without ceasing, thinking himself a slave. But Jon Arabin paid little attention to his rope production, so Drake soon eased up.

And, before very long, he discovered that they practised religion here, too, albeit in a fairly disorganized fashion.

Jon Arabin gave Drake some beer money. Once he had mastered this strange coinage – a mixture of brass triangles, bronze hexagons and copper squares, all written over with alien hieroglyphics – he multiplied it through cards. No pirate played without cheating, but, as the saying goes on Stokos, 'The Demon takes care of his own.' Drake reaped the rewards of the truly devout.

After scarcely five days on Gufling, he had made himself so unpopular by his large-scale winnings that nobody on the island would play with him.

'Never mind,' said Arabin, when he heard of Drake's plight. 'After our next trip, we'll buy back into Knock. There's ten times the people there.'

Knock, Drake learned, was the largest of the Teeth.

'And when is the next trip?' he asked.

'We leave tomorrow,' said Arabin.

That night, Drake indulged himself with wild imaginings

97

in which rape, slaughter and pillage took pride of place. However, the next day, as they laboured at the tedious business of putting the *Warwolf* to sea – more warping, towing and sounding – he learned, to his disappointment, that on this trip they were to be engaged in strictly legitimate trade.

To be precise, they were going to make the pearl run down to Ling, about a thousand leagues away, in the Drangsturm Gulf. Few would dare the pearl-run risks, not even pirates. But Jon Arabin, who had chanced it first a decade ago, risked it every second year.

After much labour, they cleared Gufling and set a course for the south. As pirates nimbled through the rigging, Drake wondered when he'd be taken in hand and shown how it was done. He was sure he'd manage splendidly. He was still wondering when a filthy mumbling old man confronted him. The ancient looked Drake up and down with rheuming eyes that were three parts blind, bared his lips to show toothless gums, and said:

'You Drake?'

'I do have the honour of being Dreldragon Drakedon Douay, a pirate of the Greater Teeth and a henchman of the honourable Jon Arabin, whom I hope to serve well,' said Drake, with all the dignity he could muster.

'Aye,' said the old man, with a cackle. 'You'll serve him well enough. Come with me!'

Drake, not knowing what to expect, followed warily, a hand on the hilt of the dirk Jon Arabin had let him keep after their brusque introduction on the Gaunt Reefs. The old man mumbled to himself as they ventured into the fumbling gloom below decks. Drake caught snatches of his monologue:

'. . . yes . . . valley . . . she and her twat . . . good gold and biting . . . oh you were pretty . . . hot bread for forking . . . dragons may say . . . what's with the warthog . . .'

And more of the same, punctuated with cackles of laughter and the odd bit of shadow-boxing.

Down and down they went, until they came to the

deepest, darkest, dirtiest bit of the ship, where a guttering seal-oil lamp fouled the air with smoke, where rats sat on their hind legs screaming defiance, where the scuttling cockroaches were a handful apiece, where the air stank of stale cheese, grease, old fish, dead cat, offal, soft carrots and rotten potatoes. Four charcoal stoves were burning, so it was hot – as hot as sharing a bed with five fat whores and fifty pairs of woollen socks.

'Where are we?' asked Drake with something very much like dread, fearing that he knew the answer already.

'We're in the klandlay, boy.'

'The kitchen?'

'Aye, that's a name for it.'

'And what – well, what am I meant to do here?'

'Why so many questions when you already know the answers?' said the ancient.

He plunged his hands into a bucket of white fluid – milk? – and retrieved half a dozen eggs. What happened next would not bear description – but the crew ate the results at meal time.

So Drake abandoned dreams of larking in the rigging, of swashing onto merchant ships with cutlass in hand, of blooding virgins and breaking into treasure chests. He settled, instead, to life as the cook's boy, helping prepare and dish up meals of salt pork, seal meat, sea biscuit, salted cod, stockfish, bacon, grey peas, and rye-flour cakes fried in whale oil and served with a dole of vinegar.

As the ship ploughed south, Drake adapted to life in the fo'c'sle, a crowded bunkroom continually damp with sea-gear and loud with coughing, snoring, sneezing, scratching, farting, gossip and argument. He found it hard to make friends as the crew blamed him (not, it must be admitted, entirely without justification) for some of the more appalling culinary disasters they endured.

In the fo'c'sle there were, amongst others, a huge foul-mouthed muscle man called Quin Baltu; Jon Disaster, who liked to be thought of as hard and dangerous; Raggage Pouch, who stole anything and everything that was not nailed down; Harly Burpskin, who had more money than sense, but was evening up the balance by playing cards with Drake.

There was also Ika Thole, a red-skinned red-haired harpoon man from the Ebrell Islands. Naturally, he reminded Drake of the high-breasted Zanya Kliedervaust, whom he had last seen at Cam's leper colony. Drake, homesick, love-sick, was eager to learn all he could of Zanya's homeland. He asked Thole to speak of the Ebrells – but Thole slapped him down, called him 'you greasy little quat', called him worse, and refused to have anything to do with him.

Even Burpskin, though he was prepared to challenge Drake at cards, could scarcely be counted as a friend. Drake sensed that there were strong bonds of trust and friendship between the crewmen, however much they quarrelled and fought. Working the canvas, riding out whatever weather the Central Ocean assailed them with, they relied on each other for their very lives. Drake, working as he did in the galley, was excluded from this great partnership. He was a lower order of life entirely.

He started to lust for the day when he too would be a sailor, hauling on ropes, running out along the yard-arm, standing watches at night, spitting on his fellows from the crow's-nest . . .

But when he asked Jon Arabin for permission to get started on real sailor work, his captain just laughed, patted him on the head and said:

'Wait till you grow to man-height.'

Which, naturally, infuriated Drake almost beyond measure. He would have consoled himself by getting drunk. However, with the exception of gambling, the consolations of religion were unobtainable on this dry ship. Consequently, their voyage seemed to last forever. But they were scarcely twenty days from the Teeth when, by night, they sighted a glow on the eastern horizon.

Drake saw it when he went to relieve himself at the ship's head, a perilous place built out above the water. He met Ika Thole, there for the same purpose.

100

'That's Drangsturm, boy,' said Thole, feeling congenial because he had just come off watch.

'The flame trench,' said Drake, to show that he knew what it was all about. While he resented being addressed as 'boy', he was glad Thole had condescended to speak to him at all.

'Aye,' said Thole.

And they said no more about it, but stood for some time watching those barbecue skies. The ever-burning fires of Drangsturm ran from west to east across the narrow isthmus which separated the Drangsturm Gulf from the Inner Waters. In strongholds such as the Castle of Controlling Power, members of the Confederation of Wizards stood guard, ready to repel any monsters of the Swarms which managed to get beyond Drangsturm.

Both Thole and Drake knew the easy motion of the ship was taking them steadily toward the horrors of the terrorlands beyond the protection of the flame trench. Shortly, the ship changed course. Near Drangsturm, the coast made an elbow and ran west. Ling lay some seventy-five leagues (as bird-flight measures distance) along that coast. So west ran the Warwolf.

That night, in his dreams, Drake did battle with the monsters of the Swarms, which he knew well enough from songs and legends common on Stokos. He dreamed that the awesome might of the flame trench failed; that the fantastic wizard-castles fell to ruin in war; that the Swarms came north; that the ancient enemy marched on Narba, on Veda, even on the towers of Selzirk the fair.

Drake woke when Shewel Lokenshield thumped him in the face with a dead fish.

'Grumph!' snorted Drake, waking in a great hurry.

'Keep the noise down,' growled Lokenshield. 'You were groaning like a sow in heat.'

'Nightmares,' said Drake, by way of explanation.

'Man,' said Lokenshield, in disgust, 'if you're having bad dreams already, you'll be sleeping screaming by the time we get to Ling!'

Moments later, Lokenshield was asleep again. But Drake lay sleepless, sweating in the hot, dank fug of the fo'c'sle. Worrying about Ling. Now it was so close, he was truly beginning to realize the risks they were running.

By dawn, the wind had died away to almost nothing. The *Warwolf* floated in sunlit seas with only the lightest of airs to gentle her sails. They were running – well, idling – some twenty leagues north of the coast, a featureless blue-green line on the horizon.

'The terror-lands,' said Jon Disaster grandly, indicating the coast to the south. 'Home of the Swarms.'

'I suppose,' said Drake hopefully, 'that the Swarms couldn't get to us from the shore.'

'Oh, the greatest of them,' said Disaster, 'they could fly, well, they could damn-near fly from here to Stokos.'

'Oh,' said Drake, feeling younger and less certain than he had for years, and hurried down below to the comparative security of the galley.

The *Warwolf* cruised along the coast to Peninsular Quanat. She rounded Cape Songala then dared the narrow strait between Quanat and Island Va. Then ran by night for Ling. Drake was up bright and early, curiosity defying fear.

'What's that island?' he said, pointing to a considerable chunk of offshore rock.

'That's Ko,' said Jon Disaster. 'That's where the pearls are.'

'If we know where they are,' said Drake, 'why do we trade for them? Why don't we go get some for ourselves?'

Jon Disaster laughed, and made no answer.

Shortly, the anchor slid away to the sandy bottom of Ling Bay. Drake scanned the daunting cliffs, which were punctured with holes, caves, tunnels, shafts, windows, embrasures and vents.

'What's that which glitters?' he said, shading his eyes against the sun.

'Quartz in the rock,' said Jon Disaster.

'Quartz?' said Drake, who knew nothing of any geology saving certain iron-yielding ores and the coal-strata near his parents' home.

'Quartz is cheap crystal,' said Disaster. 'Aye, you'll see soon enough.'

Looking down into the cool, clear water, Drake saw great globular crabs picking their way across the sands like so many crawling skulls. Skylarking pirates dived to the sea, ducked each other under and wagered as to how far down the anchor cable they could swim. Drake was not tempted to join them. He was far too tense to play idle water-games.

'Shouldn't we be keeping a watch?' he said.

'A watch?' said Disaster. 'Whatever for?'

'The Swarms, of course.'

'Boy, like as not they'll never come. Inland, water's scarce, and little water means few of them. It's only the flying ones to fear. If those come – well, it'll be a hundred as like as one.'

Drake shuddered. What on earth was he doing here? He should be back on Stokos, yes. Stokos where he would one day be king. Or would he? Would Drake's theft of a mastersword and his subsequent disappearance prejudice King Tor against him? Well, just possibly . . .

But he had a legitimate excuse! If Muck had taught him properly, he would have endured everything, anything. Surely Tor would understand that. Wouldn't he?

Drake thought; *Well, even if I don't get to marry Tor's daughter, I could always become a priest.*

Yes. That would suit him right down to the ground. If he couldn't be king, he'd be a priest instead, devoting his life entirely to religion. Yes. He'd teach his temple's women himself, personally, one by one, to ensure quality control. He was surprised he'd never thought of the idea before.

'What you thinking about?' said Disaster, seeing Drake's abstracted expression.

'Screwing,' said Drake.

He stared again at the cliffs. There was still no sign of the natives of the place. Were they dead? Killed out by the Swarms, perhaps?

'Why doesn't Arabin send a longboat ashore?' said Drake.

'It's best to let the Ling take their own good time,' explained Disaster. 'They're not much used to strangers, for few come south by sea.'

'And by land?' said Drake.

Disaster laughed.

'It's fearful rough country inland,' he said. 'As far as I know, even Southsearchers venture here near to never. You know Southsearchers, boy?'

'Aye,' said Drake knowledgeably, though most of what he knew was vague.

At last, late in the afternoon, the Ling did venture out. They came in small outrigger canoes cobbled together from scraps of driftwood. They were a strange breed of tall, lean people with golden skins: not the glossy golden brown of an oiled suntan, but the high-pitched glittering sheen of the noble metal itself.

'Have they painted themselves?' said Drake.

'Nay,' said Disaster. 'That's their natural colour. They're a strange folk, as I've said. Their eyes are milk-white entirely, but for the black of the pupil.'

'You've seen?' said Drake.

'I've seen many things. Including the Ling stained red with blood, aye, blood from some poor fool they'd ripped asunder. They did it with fish-hooks.'

Drake, fascinated, listened to the gory details of the outré tortures Disaster proceeded to describe.

The Ling hailed the Warwolf, but not in Galish. Jon Arabin shouted back to them, and a regular palaver began in some lingo utterly alien to Drake – and, indeed, to most of the crew.

'The females would fetch a good woman-price,' said

104

Drake sagely, eyeing the distant bodies and wondering if their eyes really were all white.

'Aye, and it'd be worth our lives to take them,' said Disaster.

'They don't look very dangerous to me,' said Drake, with the sense of superiority which comes naturally to a big ship's sailor looking down on some little canoes.

'Oh, they're regular fierce!' exclaimed Disaster. 'Haven't you been listening to what I've been saying?'

'Oh, it made a nice story,' said Drake, 'but no people could really be as cruel as you've said. Surely.'

'Believe me!' said Disaster. 'They're straight out of a nightmare, this lot. Aye, and when it comes to women, that's when they're worst. Why, if you so much as look at one of their females, they'll cut your eyes out.'

'In truth?'

'Aye, I've seen it myself. Fearfully bad it was. Our last trip, our bosun raped a lass in that sea-cave there, the big one where that canoe's just coming out. Well, he thought himself safe enough once back aboard, but they took him by night, believe me. We found him come morning, floating face-down in the water just off the stern. He'd been skinned alive, to start with. His prick had been – eh, look, they're coming in.'

An agreement must have been reached, for the Ling canoes were closing with the ship. Drake saw Jon Arabin striding down the deck, smiling as he came.

'Drake!' shouted Arabin. 'Good news! The Ling will trade with us, taking only one hostage.'

'And who's that?' called Drake.

'My own dear son,' said Arabin, 'the light of my life, the sun of my sky, the moon of my heavens, flesh of my flesh, blood of my blood, as sweet to me as my mother's milk.'

105

He was very close to them now, teeth shining as he grinned.

'I didn't know you had a son,' said Drake, puzzled.

'Ah,' said Arabin, 'but you know now.'

And tousled his hair, and kissed him.

And Drake, belatedly, understood.

8

Ling: an open bay on the coast of Argan some seventy-five leagues west of Castle of Controlling Power; lies west of Peninsular Quanat and south of Island Va and Island Ko.

Ling: the inhabitants of Ling, a golden-skinned people with milk-white eyes; notable as pearl divers.

Population of Ling: 4,261 (year Khmar 17).

'You can't do this to me!' shouted Drake. He was shocked. Outraged. 'I trusted you!'

'Then you can trust me still,' said Jon Arabin. 'This is but a little thing you're being asked to do. A few days ashore – why, that's nothing.'

'Days!' said Drake.

'Oh yes. Now we've arrived, the Ling will want to make a special expedition to Ko for extra pearls. We'll wait here till they've finished.'

'But this – this – the whole idea is impossible,' said Drake. 'To start with, I'm the wrong race.'

'Don't worry,' said Jon Arabin. 'They're not racist. They've got no prejudice against blond-haired boys. Just keep away from their women and you'll come to no harm.'

'That's not what I meant, and you know it!' said Drake angrily.

'My dear, dear son,' said Jon Arabin, tousling Drake's hair again in a truly infuriating manner. 'You'll have to

107

keep that temper under control once you're ashore. You don't want to disgrace your father, do you now?'

Drake hardened his hands to fists. But Jon Arabin just laughed. An easy, healthy laugh. Easy for him to be happy!

'Man,' said Drake, 'I'll never pass muster as your son. Man, you're like coal, whereas me – I'm more the colour of a cockroach.' —

'The Ling only breed their own gold with their own gold,' said Arabin. 'They know nothing of the mixing of skins.'

'But they breed dogs,' said Drake, desperately. 'And cats, surely.'

'Nay,' said Jon Arabin, 'for they have none such.'

'Then they have mice! And rats. Don't they?'

'Man,' said Jon Arabin. 'Rest easy. I've told you – there's no harm here if you keep your cock in order.'

'Aye,' said Jon Disaster with a grin, 'but if you send your cock adventuring then they'll cut you in half and tear your head off. If you're lucky! If you're not . . .'

Disaster elaborated, until Arabin, seeing Drake was getting increasingly nervous, ordered him to silence.

'Your canoe's come alongside,' said Arabin. 'Down you go!'

And, as the entire crew of the *Warwolf* applauded, Drake scrambled down a rope ladder to the canoe waiting to take him into captivity. The five Ling in the canoe stared up at him. Their eyes really were white. Could they then be truly human? One reached out and steadied him as he stepped from the ladder to the canoe, which wobbled alarmingly underfoot; he crouched hastily, grabbing at the sides. Men mocked him from the decks:

'Remember to smile as they skin you!'

'When they offer up bowls of sand, it's polite to eat it.'

'Blow me a kiss, darling, while you've still got lips to kiss with.'

Drake, ignoring them, sought arse-space on a paddle bench. It was hot. In the *Warwolf*'s shadow, small fish hung motionless, weightless, amidst masses of dark-green weed trailing away into limpid depths. Strange, to think of that garden hauling from the hull through the deep-sea waves.

'O-lo-o-la-tra-lee-o-zo,' said one of the five men in the canoe.

'O-lo-see-lee-ay-lit-ay-lo,' he was answered, by the eldest man afloat.

'O-lo-al-o-so-lo,' said all in unison.

Dipping their paddles in the water, they began to stroke toward the shore.

Sun and sea split from flashing paddles. Drake squinted against the glare, closing his eyes as the paddlers began an ominous high-singing chant. Hot blood-light filtered through his eyelids. He heard distant laughter on the *Warwolf*, and wished he was back on board.

Shadows cooled out the sun. His eyes startled open. Their canoe was sliding into a deep dim sea cave. Cold blocks of white light gleamed in the rock roof. How old was this place? Who had made it? Slaves, maybe. Aye, slaves sweating under whips till they fell from exhaustion and were beaten to death by the brutal Ling.

'O-so-lo-lee-o-lo,' chanted the paddlers, 'O-so-say-lo, o-lo-ay-tree-o-lo.'

The words were music. Senseless music. Perhaps the paddlers were gearing themselves up for a killing. Perhaps it was a death-chant they were singing.

Deep within the cave was a shelving beach. As the canoe scraped against sand, Drake jumped overboard and helped run it ashore, seeking – ah, desperate hope! – to win favour by showing himself work-willing. A little water leaked into his boots; he stamped his damp feet, partly from nervousness.

The much-trampled sand, grooved by canoe-keels, suggested that a dozen of the craft afloat by the *Warwolf* belonged here. Drake had a sudden, sickening vision of ambush, rape and slaughter, of laughing pirates falling on the Ling to murder them for pearl-wealth.

Might that happen? Might Arabin succumb to greed, and decide to kill rather than trade? He was known to be deeply in debt, needing every scraping he could get. Was Arabin that kind of man? Need could make anyone that kind of man.

The Ling were talking amongst themselves in their fluid, fluent voices. Drake cleared his throat.

'Does anyone here speak Galish?' he said.

They fell silent.

Had his voice annoyed them? How much excuse did they need before they fell on him with flaying knives and torture hooks? He smiled nervously: then wondered if these strangers might deem even a smile a deadly insult.

'O-o-o' said one of the Ling, taking Drake by the hand to lead him into the secret places beyond the canoe cave.

Drake was intensely embarrassed, for on Stokos only slaves walked hand in hand. Still, he dared not protest. He sniffed the air. Imagined he smelt blood. Hot, reeking blood in great quantity.

'Grief,' he muttered.

After many turnings, bends, stairs, squeeze-holes, ramps, inclines, corridors and passageways, Drake was at last shown into a large white room where great big globular crabs with claws the size of nutcrackers were crawling over the walls.

'What's with the crabs?' said Drake. 'Eh?'

'O-lip-o,' said one of the Ling, smiling.

And gave him a little push.

Drake, fists clenched, stepped into the room.

Okay, crabs! Watch out! This is Drake Douay you've got to deal with.

Drake's guides departed. The crabs made no move against him. They looked . . . well, actually, they looked remarkably dead. Yes. On Investigation, they proved to be empty shells which had been glued to the walls, doubtless by way of decoration.

Drake took stock.

He was in a square-hewn chamber dominated by a

110

raised deck of small grey stones topped off with clean white sand. Drake entirely failed to recognize this contraption for what it was – a bed. And not just any old bed, either, but a bed for one of the High-Born. For the second degree, tradition prescribed stones minus sand. And a commoner would have slept on rocks.

Drake fingered one of the stones. It was too small to make much of a weapon. He still had his dirk, but what good was that? He should have asked to bring a sword ashore. He would have felt safer, yes. And besides – if he was playing at being Jon Arabin's son, surely he should have been kitted out with the weapons appropriate to his status. Well, too late to worry about that now . . .

Was there a toilet nearby? He needed one urgently.

The sand-topped stone-heap . . . yes, it was obviously a glorified sand-box, to be used like the one his boyhood friend, Levil Norkin, had for his kittens. Drake promptly began to scrabble a little hole in the top of the bed. But, before he could commit a *faux pas* of enormous dimensions, a young woman entered. In her hands she carried the tail of a stingray – which, amongst the Ling, was the ultimate erotic symbol. She was naked.

'*O-ma-no-so?*' she said, a faint smile on her lips.

Drake's horror-shock immediately abolished all worries about bowels and bladder. Jon Disaster's warnings flooded back to him. Chaotic images of skinned flesh, pulled fingernails, amputated organs and gouged-out eyes tumbled in that flood.

'Go away!' he said frantically. 'Go away, before someone finds us!'

'*O-lee!*' she said, in tones of protest.

Drake picked up a handful of sand and threw it at her.

'*Lee-o-me-nee!*' she said.

Drake's dread doubled as another woman entered. Also naked. The two had a rapid conference in their strange, sing-song voices, then cornered Drake and did their best to strip him naked. He only managed to preserve his honour by the most vigorous resistance.

111

'Jon Arabin!' said Drake. 'I'll kill you when I get hold of you!'

His outburst of anger scattered the women.

'Saved,' said Drake. 'At least for the moment.'

And he sat down in a corner, sweating, trembling, breathing heavily. This business of being a hostage was obviously going to be – to say the least – demanding.

'It's my blond good looks,' said Drake. 'That's what does the damage. The women get one look at me, and they just can't keep their hands off. I suppose they don't often see a fellow as handsome as me, not this far south. Well – can I help my beauty?'

Drake knew there was nothing he could do about his natural sex appeal.

'It's not my fault!' he said. 'I'm innocent!'

But his innocence would do him no good if he was caught embracing a nubile young female. Oh no. Likely as not, he would be discovered by some dour, ugly representative of the older generation, who would have him killed out of sheer jealousy, if for no other reason.

'I've got to pretend I'm a professional virgin,' said Drake. 'Or something.'

During the course of the next three days (in which he did, finally, after several blunders, manage to find the toilet), Drake was tempted by three dozen naked women. Young they were, and beautiful, faces so smooth they seemed to be wearing masks, their milk-white eyes adoring, their breasts high-sprung, their innards oiled and ready for his exertions.

Ready they were indeed, knowing their guest was Drake Arabin, oldest and much-loved son of Jon Arabin, and heir to all the Arabin dominions: the Greater Teeth, the Lesser Teeth, the larger part of three continents, and several kingdoms in the Land of the Dead besides. Yes, to Ling, Jon Arabin was a mighty king, a great warrior, a powerful wizard, a minor demigod, and the richest man in the world.

To Drake, Jon Arabin was something else altogether.

He stood at a high window staring down at Ling Bay, where the distant *Warwolf* lay, and said:

'Jon, you're a sly scheming son of an octopus. And if I don't get out of here in one piece – then you're going to be in big trouble, man.'

When the daughters of Ling reported the failure of their enticements, the elders consulted, then sent in their sons. By hook or by crook, they would see Drake Arabin committed in love to some flesh of their flesh before his captivity ended.

But the sons reported as little success as the daughters. The elders conferred again, then decided to bring Drake into the presence of the Great One.

When the elders came for him, Drake Douay was practising a one-man kata with a wooden sword which he had whittled out of a broken paddle.

'O-oo-o-ooo,' sang one of the elders, then grabbed Drake by the elbow.

'You've come to take me back to the ship?' said Drake. 'Great! I thought it was just about time to be leaving.'

And he threw down his waster and allowed the elders to lead him through many cool tunnels until they came to the audience chamber where sat the Great One. She was the oldest and wisest woman of Ling, a bright-eyed matriarch whose skin, in her old age, was mottled with dusky patterns which reminded Drake of the wings of a great moth.

Drake looked around the audience chamber uneasily. It was a square-cut white room with upwards of fifty elders squatting on the rough brown matting which carpeted the floor. The Great One lay in state in a hammock of sharkskin. Drake, deducing her authority from her elevation, said:

'Good morning, ma'am, pleased to meet you.'

'O-layma-nooloo,' said the Great One, making a formal response.

'Really?' said Drake. 'Listen, if we're going to have a conversation, we'll need to get Jon Arabin in on this.'

'Jon Arabin,' said the Great One.

113

'Aaaah!' wailed the elders. 'Jon Arabin!'

And they lent forward in unison and kissed their right hand kneecaps (or, if that was forbidden by arthritis, their right hand wrists). Drake was not at all sure what to make of this. In any case, he had little time to think about it, for the Ling had begun to speak between themselves in their high-pitched sing-song voices.

'Why does he refuse the flesh of our flesh?' asked the elders.

'Because,' said the Great One, 'the spirit of purity burns strong within him.'

'Is he then Worthy?' asked the elders.

The Great One laid her hand upon Drake's forehead. A wisp of a hand it was, too, more skin than flesh – as frail as an old leaf which has almost frayed through to its skeleton.

'Yes,' said the Great One, after a lengthy pause. 'He is Worthy.'

Even Great Ones have their off days.

'Shall we then initiate him?' asked the elders.

'We shall. Indeed, we must. For it would be a sin to let one of the Worthy depart to the Plague Lands without initiation.'

'It shall be done,' said the elders.

And Drake was roughed onto a bloodstained metal rack and tied down with thongs of sharkskin. A jabber of excited faces crowded around him. Drums pulsed, nose flutes whined, witch doctors rattled bones, and an evil old gentleman made stone sizzle across steel as he honed a knife which already looked far more sharp than was necessary.

'No!' screamed Drake, writhing against his bonds. 'I didn't do it! I never touched them! What have I done? Is it something I said? Is it something I didn't say? I'll do anything, anything, just let me loose! Don't hurt me! Is there anyone here who speaks Galish? Gaaa!'

'Why is he screaming?' asked the elders.

'Because the Ecstasy has possessed him,' said the Great

One gravely. 'It is a good sign. He shall be truly blessed.'

'Here is the box,' said the elders.

'Good,' said the Great One.

And took the implement of initiation from the box.

Drake howled with incoherent fear as the gloating old woman held up a snake. It was small, and very much alive. It hissed, opening its jaws, showing sharp teeth. Before he had time to admire the red and orange markings twisting down its back (markings reminiscent of the forging-patterns of Gouda Muck's mastersword) it whipped free from the Great One's hands and fell to the floor.

There was an uproar as heroes competed for the precious little monster. But the man who had been sharpening the knife stayed calm. Humming gently to himself, he leaned over Drake's body and cut once, neatly, making an incision under the floating rib on Drake's right-hand side.

Drake hissed, with fear, with anger, with pain. The old woman had regained the snake. She was fondling it. Stroking it. Crooning to it. Bringing it closer. She was – no!

'No! No! No!' screamed Drake.

But she put the head of the snake to his open wound. He screamed again as it began gnawing into his vitals. It was like being stabbed repeatedly with a red-hot poker.

Then, strangely, the pain lessened. It became dull. Disappeared altogether. Yes. While teeth still tunnelled, he no longer cared. He was starting to float, hmmm, yes, drifting away on a river of deliciously warm milk.

The Great One leaned over him. He smiled up at her face, noting, for the first time, the red veins spiderwebbed in the milk white of her eyes. She kissed him, giving him her blessing for the Journey. He felt himself falling. Her face contracted to a point, then disappeared altogether. The last sounds hissed into silence.

'Who am I?' he wondered.

Idly.

Then wondered no more, for he was unconscious.

* * *

115

Drake did not wake to clarity, but to fever. Hot, flushed and thirsting, he endured cramps, spasms and hallucinations. He was fed strange foods and stranger fluids, which sustained life but did not cure him.

'Arabin,' he said. 'Get Arabin. Jon Arabin, understand?'

'*O-fo-lo-mo-lee*,' said one of the young women who fed him.

And smiled, and left him.

But did not return with Jon Arabin.

Time and again Drake repeated his demand. He had to get a message through to his captain. If he stayed in this crazy place, he would die.

'I'm sick, yes,' said Drake, to one of his handmaidens, 'but I'll do as well on the *Warwolf* as I would here. Honest. It's the sea air, I need it to keep me alive.'

The response was another smile.

Nothing more.

He could see, through his sickroom's embrasure, a slice of blue sky, occasionally decorated by patches of high cloud. Fair weather cloud, yes. In the little time he'd spent on the *Warwolf*, he'd already got into the habit of taking a right healthy interest in the weather.

'Those idle sons of sodfish will be playing around the anchor cable again, I suppose,' said Drake.

Yes. Or practising sword under the hard gaze of the ship's weapons muqaddam. Or patching sails. Or splicing ropes. Or—

But no matter. Whatever they were doing, Drake wanted to be with them. Aye. In the company of his comrades true. Quin Baltu, Shewel Lokenshield, Goth Sox, Lee Dix, Hewlet Mapleskin, aye, and Jon Disaster – he remembered them as brothers.

Finally, the day came when Drake was well enough to quit his bed and venture to the embrasure. Squinting into the brilliance of a world lit by real honest sunlight, he looked down on Ling Bay – and saw that the *Warwolf* was gone.

No! Surely not! Surely Arabin's ship of green sails lay close to the cliff, hidden by the limitations of the embrasure!

On rubbery legs, Drake staggered from the room, questing for a better view.

'Jon, Jon,' he said, as he stumbled down white-lit corridors. 'Jon, you can't have left me. No, say it's not true!'

How often did ships come to Ling? The *Warwolf*, or so it was alleged, visited once every two years. Apart from that – nothing.

'You'd better be there, Jon Arabin,' threatened Drake. 'You'd better be there, you and your ship. Or I'll damn you to fifty hells for seventy times eternity!'

Finally he found a square door cut in the side of the cliff, high above the sea. He stepped outside, into the warmth of the sun. Below lay all of Ling Bay: innocent of any ship. Clear shone the sparkling waters, as beautiful as the women of a poet's dreams. And empty.

Drake wept.

9

Saba Yavendar: one of the Nine Immortals; won poetic fame with *Winesong* and *Warsong*, written in the Stabilized Scholastic Standard (later adopted as the High Speech of wizards) of the Technic Renaissance.

Survived Genetic Mutiny and Interregnum. Joined Institute of Applied Theology (later destroyed by Founders in Wars of Suppression). After Famine Years, was adviser to Lords of the Eightfold Way (forerunner of Confederation of Wizards).

Gained great power in Empire of Wizards after Long War against Swarms, but lost all in Years of Chaos. Disappeared after offending Talaman the Torturer (aka T. the Castrator, T. the Eye Gouger and T. the Baby Strangler).

Later works (including notorious *Victory of the Prince of the Favoured Blood*) popular crowd-pleasers scorned by scholarship, which must concur with Larftink that Yavendar 'lived too long and wrote far, far too much'. Indeed, Gatquip's long-disputed claim that the *Complete Works* can be reduced to a canon of a dozen lines demands positive reassessment.

Drake's wound healed to a crinkled red scar. His fever abated. Abandoning his bed (yes, by now he recognized a heap of stones and sand as a bed) he explored. Questing. Seeking. Searching for a way out of this warren, a way back to civilization.

He found rooms packed with dusty old bones. A mortuary, where the unkempt dead, anointed with wild honey, lay waiting for the Funeral Winds. A strange globular room with silver walls where his weight left him, and he hung weightless in the air like a fish in water.

He took stairs which descended as well as those which went up, thinking there might be tunnels which travelled deep underground before breaking out to freedom. He found dank, gloomy, ill-lit places flooded with slimy water.

Once, he found a door which opened on a huge, utterly silent hall perhaps three leagues in length, where a dozen bulbous grey shapes, each hundreds of paces long, lay half-submerged in pitch-black water.

'Grief of suns!' said Drake. 'Will I never get out of here?'

He lost his way a dozen times, and once wandered for a whole day in waterless tunnels before chancing his steps back to the inhabited areas. Nothing daunted, he set out again – but this time he carried a chunk of charcoal with which to mark his way on the walls.

At last, he squeezed out through a narrow vent to stand in harsh clifftop sunshine. He had won a view of some of the meanest terrain in creation, a desolation of stone pillars, razor-sharp shadows, thornbush, cactus, sparce acacia, gulleys, buttes, sinkholes, escarpments and ravines.

There was no sign of water.

'Desolation,' muttered Drake.

He had never before seen a landscape so lonely. Utterly unmarked by human hand. He longed to be on Stokos again, ah yes, back on his home island where the terrain had been civilized by mines, quarries, slag heaps, ash pits, and other comforting signs of human activity.

I'd die of loneliness if I tried to walk across this.

He saw something glinting a few paces away. What? His hot black shadow crabbed across the rocks as he ventured to the glitter. It proved to be a chunk of sharp-cut white crystals. Very hard.

'That quartz stuff Disaster talked about,' said Drake.

119

And wished he had Disaster with him. Or Ika Thole, yes, or even dim-witted Harly Burpskin.

'Anyone,' said Drake, 'as long as we've language in common.'

He was talking to himself a lot, these days. Was that a sign of madness?

'I'll talk when I want!' yelled Drake, suddenly angry.

And he hurled the chunk of quartz into the wilderness. Then it occurred to him that maybe the stuff was worth having. Disaster had called it 'cheap', but perhaps Drake could bluff an unwary buyer into thinking it valuable.

'Where did my quartz go?' he said.

He scrambled onto a small rock, and, from that eminence, swiftly discovered his quartz, which he duly retrieved.

'A bigger rock,' said Drake. 'That's the thing.'

Yes. From a bigger rock he might see – well, running water, if he was lucky. Or maybe an old road which he could follow east through the wilderness, in the general direction of Drangsturm.

Drake dared a perilous scramble to the top of the nearest house-sized rock. From there, high above thorn bushes and other rubbish, he had a much better view.

No road. But . . .

Was that a building he saw? Yes. Half a league distant lay a square tower of thrice tree-height, built from massive white, blue and ochre blocks. A spike rose from each of its rooftop corners. Drake studied it doubtfully.

Could it be . . .?

Surely not!

And yet . . . it did look remarkably like the legendary Wishing Tower known to every child of Stokos from fairy stories. And he was on Argan, was he not? Argan, the true homeland of all improbable things?

'Improbability is not impossibility,' said Drake to himself, and, abandoning his chunk of quartz, he set off for the tower with all possible speed, i.e. slowly – the ground being regular leg-breaking territory.

At first he was all enthusiasm, dreaming of the marvellous things he would wish for. Fresh vegetables! A real live cucumber! A piece of lettuce! Then – well, the larger things. The throne of Stokos. The fair Zanya Kliedervaust, she of the red skin and the high-lofted breasts. And more height, yes, at least five extra hands of height.

'That would make me near as tall as Sully Yot,' said Drake.

He remembered his last encounter with Yot, in Androlmarphos, when the crazy wart-faced fellow had tried to stab him. What on earth had made him do a weird thing like that?

'I'd never have credited him with the nerve to gut a cat,' muttered Drake.

He paused, breathing heavily. This was hard work! The terrain was so rucked, hillocky and chopped about that a stone's throw of thirty paces meant a weary scramble of thrice that distance for the footsore traveller. The sun was heavy on his head. A bead of sweat rolled into his right eye. It stung, fiercely. Give up? No, never!

Drake struggled onward, shrinking as he went. Crushed by the sun.

'Man,' muttered Drake, 'and I was short enough to start with.'

Rock caught and amplified the heat. He smelt hot, pungent herbs. Their scent made him dizzy. How immense was the world! This desolate place, far beyond all voices, was teaching him how he really measured up against the universe.

Like an ant, man. An ant trying to walk across Stokos.

A shadow flickered over the ground. Shadow of a winged creature. A monster? Alarmed, Drake glanced skywards. No, not a monster – a buzzard. It started to circle.

'Piss off, you whore-faced puttock!' said Drake.

The buzzard, a professional pessimist, continued to circle. Drake realized its diligence might well be rewarded. If

121

he broke an ankle out here, he was finished. Momentarily, he regretted ever leaving the safety of the tunnels of Ling. Leg-breaking apart – what would he do if he met one of the Swarms?

'I don't believe they exist,' said Drake. 'Who says they do? Wizards, that's all!'

Maybe Drangsturm was a great big con, yes. Maybe there was wealth beyond the flame trench, aye, gold, silver, stuff like that. Probably wizards kept people away from it by making up tales of monsters. Likely they roamed the terror-lands at will, picking up chunks of gold and similar riches.

'Swarms?' said Drake. 'Bah! Humbug!'

Much, much later, grazed by rock, stung by hornet, pricked by thorn and burnt by the sun into the bargain, he gained the doorway which pierced the lower level of the ancient square-built monument, and knew at once that this was not the fairy-tale tower he had hoped for.

Unlike the Wishing Tower, this one was not inhabited by a magic dwarf, a talking rabbit, a blue-nosed leprechaun and a friendly little elf. Peering into the gloom he saw, instead, four hideous totem poles of dull metal, closely resembling the Guardian Machines described by old teachings pre-served by the metalworking guilds of Stokos.

'Guardian Machines,' said Drake.

He had been taught about them in his theory classes about three years previously. What had he learnt, exactly? That they were dangerous, yes. Still . . . these ones looked pretty dead.

'You awake?' yelled Drake.

The totem poles sat in sullen silence. Maybe they weren't Guardian Machines at all. Maybe they were art. Drake had heard about art – bits of odd-shaped stuff set up in special rooms for people to gawk at. It was said to be real big in Veda, the city of the sages.

Drake stepped through the doorway. Dead leaves crunched underfoot. Inside, it was cool and shady. But dry. He wished he had water.

Look around. Investigate.

122

Four steep stairways spiralling up into the shadows. Some barely perceptible activity going on at his feet – yes, a tribe of red ants were practising genocide on some of their black-skinned cousins. And overhead . . . looking up, Drake saw a spider the size of a dog, which sat in a ceiling-spanning bat-catching web and glowered at him. Hastily he armed himself with a hefty stick in case the spider got any unfortunate ideas.

Then, since he had the stick in his hands, he hit himself on both shins, which hurt, but would help teach him that he was too old to believe in fairy tales.

What now?

Retreat or explore.

The view, that's the thing. From the roof, we'll see roads and stuff. Or a ruined city, maybe.

So thinking, Drake made for the nearest stairway. He was almost there when one of the metal totem poles, which was indeed a Guardian Machine, ground into life with an enormous racket of gears. Spitting blue sparks, it advanced. Drake went haring up the winding stairs – and slammed into an invisible wall, almost knocking himself out.

'Break!' screamed Drake.

He hammered the invisible barrier, butted it, stuck it with his stick, kicked it – all to no effect. Downstairs the Guardian Machine was hissing and roaring.

'Give, you ganch!' yelled Drake.

But it wouldn't. It yielded inwards slightly, but that was all. He scratched it, finding its surface cold and slippery. Beyond lay a skeleton, and the stairs leading upwards.

No escape!

'*Olwek ba-velch!*' said Drake savagely, then turned to face the Guardian Machine.

Which, by the sound of it, was still at the bottom of the stairs, grinding, hissing and tearing. As he listened, the sounds lessened. Then died. Cautiously, he crept downstairs until he could see the metal monster at the foot of the stairs. Obviously, it was unable to climb. But it scarcely looked short of patience. He suspected it could happily wait until ants carried away the dust of his bones – as they would indeed unless he could escape.

There was room to squeeze past the machine.

If he was quick—

Drake dared one step downwards. The machine roared and spat at him. Lightning slammed into his gut, knocking him backwards. He could not breathe! Paralysed, he lay with arms outflung, mouth gaping. Then managed to gasp a thimble-sized breath of air.

As the machine roared and whined, gathering strength for another homicide attempt, Drake very slowly and very painfully rolled over and began to crawl back up the spiral staircase. The machine shot at him as soon as it could – which was just a fraction too late.

Back at the invisible wall, Drake rested, collecting his wits. There was no way out down the stairs, that was for sure. There were no windows, but light was definitely coming down from the top of the stairs.

He studied the skeleton. Somehow, someone had got beyond the invisible wall. And had died there.

Drake reviewed the Inner Principles of the Old Science which he had learnt as part of his apprenticeship studies. He recited the Beginning:

'Cause has effect; effect has control; control requires search; search elucidates cause.'

Then he recalled the first Rule of Investigation:

'Desribe what you see, for perception controls process.'

Drake had never put much stock in theory. In fact, he had always hated it – particularly since, being totally illiterate, he had had to memorize the whole 23,427 words of it. Being dubious about the validity of the Power Theory of Knowledge, he still resented the waste of all those bright sunny afternoons which could have been spent in healthy amusements like street-fighting, or in the practice of religion – but the Scientific Approach now seemed to be his only hope.

So he began an Investigation.

He described:

124

'Low light . . . cool . . . was warmer outside . . . stairs . . . going up . . . cracks . . . some brown stuff . . . stain? . . . bones beyond invisible . . . no, not like air . . . bit blurred . . . push . . . yields . . . slippery . . . cold . . . no shadow . . . fits to wall . . . no visible seam . . . wall same block-pattern as stairs . . . except . . . yes . . . plate of white metal set in wall . . . no rust . . . pattern of five raised circles set on metal plate . . . raised circles are . . . are moveable . . .'

As Drake fingered the raised circles set in the metal plate, something changed. What? He stood absolutely still, listening. Then realized a faint hum, which he had dismissed as a noise within his own head, had ceased to be. He could hear . . . a tiny creak from his own knees . . . the complex sounds of deglutition as he swallowed some saliva . . . and that was it.

Drake mobilized some more saliva in his mouth, then spat.

His spittle splattered against the skeleton's skull. Reaching out, he found the invisible barrier had gone. He glanced at the metal plate in the wall, and the raised circles he had fingered. Cause and effect. Yes.

'Score one for theory,' muttered Drake.

With reluctance, for he hated to concede anything to Gouda Muck – or, indeed, to any other of that age group.

'But I'll give him this,' muttered Drake. 'Even if he was mad, the old bugger did make bloody good swords.'

And he took a couple of steps forward.

Then stopped.

He could hear something. What? Yes: that hum.

'Oh no,' said Drake. 'Oh no, tell me it's not so.'

But, on turning and trying to retreat back downstairs, he found the invisible barrier barring his way. He did another Investigation, a comprehensive one. There was no magical cause-and-effect device on this side of the barrier. Now he knew why the bones were there.

'The poor old sod starved to death,' said Drake.

And, looking at the yellow bones, had a sudden

125

intimation of his own inevitable death. Even if he got out of this alive, he would die some day. For the first time in his life, he truly understood his own mortality.

'That's the trouble with bloody-well being sober all the time,' said Drake. 'You gets some weird old thoughts breaking loose.'

Yes. The sooner he got back to civilization and got decently drunk again, the better. If he stayed here much longer, brooding about Knowledge Theory and Mortality and such, he'd be a regular mad philosopher by the time he escaped. Stokos had had two of them, and a sorry old sight they were, too.

'Onwards!' said Drake boldly, appropriating for his own purposes the motto of the Guild of Navigators, which was not strictly his to use at all.

He swiftly found himself in a machine-cluttered room at the top of the tower. He could not tell what these amazing devices did, or where they were from, or what they were worth – but none attacked him, so he didn't rightly care.

What he wanted was a way out. Which he found, soon enough: a square hole in the ceiling. So up he went. And, after he had gazed again on the desolation of the Deep South, he started wondering just how the hell he was going to get back to ground level. If he had a rope, it would be easy.

Otherwise . . .

The walls were sheer, impossible to climb. If he jumped, the odds for breaking something were excellent. If he broke something, he was dead.

'Hoy!' shouted Drake. 'Anyone here?'

He listened, but heard only a faint hissing, which could have been the sun trying to weld his shadow to the roof. Shading his eyes, he scanned the landscape. Nobody. The clifftops lay only half a league away. From this height, it scarcely looked any distance at all.

Then came the blue of the sea, and, to the north, the humped mass of the island of Ko. There was something odd about Ko. Yes: its ends were curling up in the hot sunshine, floating above the sea. Drake squinted, trying to bring them into focus. No change.

He was horror-struck. It was his fault! He must have somehow unleashed some enormously evil power which had been lurking in this tower. Perhaps that power was, right now, making all the lands and islands of the whole wide world turn up at the edges and curdle.

'Nonsense,' he said to himself. 'Impossible!'

Yet: some of those ancient Causes were known to have amazingly grandiose Effects.

'Well,' said Drake, 'we'll worry about the world when we're free in the world to worry. Right now we need a rope.'

And, without waiting to worsen his sunburn, he went below decks to make another Investigation.

He found nothing remotely worth having, but for twenty-seven identical amulets. Each, together with its necklace-chain of smooth-flowing black links, had the weight of a walnut. Each amulet was a cool, glossy lozenge of jet black. On one side, a golden sun disc. On the other, raised silver decorations in the form of seven stars and a crescent moon. On Investigating the silver stars, Drake found the amulets could be made to talk.

'. . . strong voice,' muttered Drake. 'Man's voice . . . strange . . . no language I know . . . worth a pretty, I bet . . . magic, perhaps? Spells, perhaps? . . . well . . . no harm trying . . .'

He took the amulets downstairs. Crouching by the yellowed skull of the long-dead stranger, he let the invisible barrier listen to each amulet in turn, knowing well enough that many such charms had magical powers. The barrier held firm. Drake attacked it one last time, thumping it hard with his fists.

No good.

'Still,' said Drake, putting the amulets round his neck for safe keeping, 'these charm-things will be worth something if I ever get out of here. Yes, wizards would pay for them, if nobody else.'

He was right about that, for each amulet contained the voice of Saba Yavendar himself. The great poet of the days of yore had once lived in this tower for half a millenium, and had whiled away some of those long years of exile by making multiple recordings of all his early works, including his *Winesong*, *Lovesong* and *Warsong*.

Wizards valued such things, and the High Speech of wizards was near-identical to the Stabilized Scholastic Standard which Yavendar had recorded in.

'Still no rope, though,' said Drake.

But, before he slung the last amulet around his neck, he tested its strength. It was beyond his power to break it.

'With enough of these woman-fancy faggots,' said Drake, 'I could make a chain to get me out of here.'

So he resumed his Investigations, but with no more success than before. He got angry.

'You see, Muck?' he yelled. 'You see, you groggy old bugger? You can't make rope from Investigations!'

Then stopped yelling, for his throat started hurting. Thirst. Yes. That was it. He was going to thirst to death, and soon. No doubt about it. Since he was definitely doomed to die, he was all the more bitter about those afternoons wasted studying the Theory of Knowledge, the Theory of Lists, the Reductive Crisis of Categorizations and all the rest of that pretentious old rubbish which never yet helped put a sharper edge on a sword, and never would.

'Missed out on all those sacrifices, too,' said Drake, gloomily.

The human sacrifices organized by the temple of Hagon had mostly been in the afternoons. Everyone agreed they were top-notch religious experience, but because of his schoolwork, he had never managed to see one.

'All those days breaking my brains,' muttered Drake.

And hit a machine with his fist, hard. Then kicked it, but hurt his foot.

'Ganch,' said Drake, viciously.

The machines were obviously built to last. Otherwise he

would have relieved his feelings by smashing them to pieces. Breaking. Smashing. Yes, that rang a bell. What was it? Yes . . . the final Rule of Investigation:

'The last Test of Limits is Destruction.'

At first he was chary of breaking the place up. After all, something was making Ko island curl at the edges, and the only thing he could put it down to was his own Investigations. If he started some Destruction he might end up in serious trouble.

'But there's no other way,' muttered Drake, picking up the lightest available machine. 'Don't take this the wrong way, little thing – it's sanctioned by the Theory of Investigations, don't you know.'

And he hurled the item against the wall. It was fragile, having been designed only to store, sanitize and dispense tooth-brushes. It shattered. A toothbrush (perfectly preserved for millenia by a low-grade stasis field) fell from the wreckage.

'A little jewel-cleaner of some sort,' said Drake, frowning. 'What was that doing in there?'

And he Investigated, carefully, looking for jewels. There was none. But there were some thin, finely woven metal wires, sheathed in pliable jackets of different colours.

'Hmmm,' said Drake. 'Maybe the last rule is the best of all . . .'

And he went downstairs to retrieve the larger bones of the skeleton, thinking to use them as levers to help pry apart the larger machines.

He was still hard at it when night came. He got little sleep, for the topmost room of the tower became amazingly cold by night. By the time dawn came, his stomach was seething with acid hunger. His mouth was thick, dry, furry. He sucked on the knucklebone of a long-dead man, generating saliva to ease the dryness of his throat.

'To work,' said Drake. 'To work . . .'

By noon, he had smashed every device in the room, and

had woven a rope of wires which reached almost to the ground. Now he had to climb down.

'No sweat!' said Drake, using an ugly vernacular expression meaning 'easy'.

He was swiftly disabused of this notion, for in his weakened condition – he had lost a lot of water to the sun – he found it hard-going. By the time he reached the ground, he was in a state of wet-faced exhaustion.

He still faced the half-league walk back to the vent he had exited from. Half a league? In this spasmodic terrain, rough as a storm-chopped sea, his undulating route would stretch the journey out to nigh on three thousand paces.

Be a man.

With a third of the journey done, he slipped, fell, and ricked an ankle. Broken? Even if it was, he still had to walk on it. With his dirk, he cut himself a hefty stick to lean on. Up. On! He almost swooned from the pain – but continued.

A shadow flickered across the ground.

The buzzard?

Looking up, Drake saw something far, far above. High through the blue empyrean it flew. A great bulky body and a long, long trailing tail. It was a hundred paces long if it was a fingerlength. As Drake watched, it vanished into cloud.

What was that?

It was, he decided, a hallucination. Nothing which flew could be so big. Surely. But then, dragons – no, it had not been a dragon. A monster of the Swarms? Impossible. The Swarms were an invention of wizards, part of a bluff to keep the world from the riches of the terror-lands . . .

Again a shadow flickered over the ground.

Again Drake looked up.

It was a buzzard, that was all. Probably the same one which had been hungering after him the day before. Well, it was right out of luck, for he had no intention of dying. Not today.

'Not ever, in fact,' said Drake.

As the purple shadows of evening were spreading across the terror-lands of the Deep South, Drake gained the vent which led into the depths of Ling. He was too tired to be happy. He stumbled to his quarters, drained a bowl of water then fell onto his bed and collapsed.

'Our visitor has returned alive from the Forbidden Tower,' the Watchers reported to the Great One. 'How can that be?'

'*Omnia puris pura*,' said the Great One, or words to that effect. 'He found no evil there for no evil lives within him. We must increase our efforts to incorporate him.'

Drake spent two days in bed, utterly exhausted. His ankle, fortunately, was only badly bruised – but, even so, he knew there was no escape for him on foot.

It was a good few marches to Drangsturm, with no wild water on the way. Even if he met no monsters, thirst would finish him for certain. He remembered the buzzard circling overhead; he shuddered. Even if he reached Drangsturm, he would be on the wrong side of that prodigious flame trench. Did it run right into the sea? If it did, how far would he have to swim to get to safety?

Forget it! He would have to steal a canoe, yes. And, while stealing a canoe, he might as well go for some pearls. What did they really look like, those 'beads without holes'? Men deemed them fabulous wealth, but what made them so special?

Drake's desire to learn about canoes was amply satisfied in the days that followed. On showing himself interested in the sea, he found plenty of tutors eager to learn him all its aspects. (And also to seduce him – though, fearing more torture, he resisted all their blandishments.)

They taught him paddling.

They tolerated his fondness for collisions.

And then the Ling made a decision which would shortly allow Drake to satisfy his curiosity about pearls.

Drake had lately taken to pointing at Ko, and making

131

strange noises which were clearly meant to be questions. Obviously he wanted to go to the island.

'Being pure,' said the Great One, 'he does not want to live as a parasite. He wishes to share our labours.'

Which was how Drake got to be taken to the pearl-fishing grounds at Ko.

'It's all right,' he said with relief, when they got there. 'It's not melting after all. It must've been some trick of the sea making it look so. We can go back now.'

But the smiling Ling still confessed to no Galish. Instead, they set a bushel of pearl-oysters in front of him, and showed him how these were opened.

Soon Drake knew why pearls were so precious: because in days of oyster-opening, in which he was sure he killed more oysters than all the world could have eaten in ninety generations, he found but one small pearl, and even that was misshapen, squashed almost flat. He had plenty of examples to compare it with, because the Ling were indulging in a positive orgy of pearling, diving from dawn to dusk.

'I'll try diving,' said Drake. 'It's got to be easier.'

It wasn't. It was exhausting. But, as he got good at it, he relished the fierce pleasures of physical mastery. To be good at something, to be excellent – yes, that was what made life worth living.

Down in the depths of the sea he dived, swimming sinuous through translucent seas where sunlight sieved down through the blue-green fathoms, where fish flickered away into the mists of distance, or dawdled at weightless leisure between floating weed and plump red sponges.

They dived, some days, near an underwater cliff which fell away to cold, cold, black-green depths. Once, Drake swam out above that unfathomable abysm, for the sheer pleasure of terrifying himself. Once was enough.

In waters less deep, he joined the play with the big, lazy black-winged rays, ferocious in appearance but near enough to harmless unless hooked or speared. He broke open sea urchins for the pleasure of moray eels, which fed

132

from his naked hands. When exhausted by the sea, he slept on rock ledges in the leisurely heat of the afternoon sun.

'He spends less and less time bringing up pearl-oysters,' complained his comrades.

'Doubtless he has a religious connection with the sea,' said the Great One. 'He is engaged in her worship. Let him be.'

'Oh,' said the Ling.

It seemed there was much to learn about this strange, saintly son of Jon Arabin, who looked young and virile, yet refused every offer of the pleasure of the flesh.

What the Ling did not learn – for they were very innocent, and not much good at arithmetic – was that Drake was robbing them blind. He massed a hoard of twenty pearls – a fortune in other parts, if sailors' stories were anything to go by. And he dreamed sweetly about what such wealth could buy him in civilization.

Each evening, as night settled on Island Ko, he sat by a driftwood fire sucking the flesh from the claws of giant crabs, staring into the flames and imagining the soft breasts of women, the sighs of a swooning lover, the hearty laughter of a tavern, the chink of gold in a casino, the generous smiles of flattering faces admiring his silken elegance.

Finally, the pearling on Ko came to an end. The divers shifted back to Ling. And Drake was ready to escape.

He chose a canoe: one small enough to paddle himself. He scavenged a single waterskin, which he filled from the ever-replenished Inner Pool which supplied the whole community of Ling. Food was no problem: there was any amount of dried oyster flesh for the taking.

He had more than a few doubts about the voyage. It was a hell of a long way to paddle.

'But,' said Drake, 'I don't have much bloody option. If I can get back to Stokos, I can likely be king. Or a priest, at least. What's the choice? To stay here and rot, that's what!'

Ling, as far as he could tell, was ignorant of both booze and gambling. And as for sex – he knew well enough that he would be tortured to death if he so much as laid hands on any of the young flesh which delighted in tantalizing him.

So early one morning, while it was still dark, Drake launched his canoe. It was, in fact, Midsummer's Day – the start of the year Khmar 18, and the first anniversary of the Martyrdom of Muck.

Drake was far out in the bay when the dawnlight, diminishing the dark, revealed a ship. A ship oncoming, a stately sight, all sail set to bear her along in the light winds of dawn. Drake stopped paddling, and sat there, hoping. The ship had green sails, yes. And – a dragon figurehead! It was the *Warwolf*! Shouting, weeping and whooping, Drake jumped up and down to such effect that he upset the canoe and precipitated himself into the water.

'I wonder,' said one of the elders, observing him from the heights, 'why our young guest was out on the waters so early in the morning.'

'Because,' replied the Great One, who was standing beside him, 'he has the Power. He knew his father was returning today, so set himself forth to meet him.'

'He will, then, leave us.'

'Doubtless.'

'What then do you see for his future?' asked the elder.

The Great One deliberated gravely, then said:

'I see him changed to a sail.'

'To a sail?'

'Why not?' said the Great One. 'We each of us start as a fish in the womb. Is it any more miraculous to be changed into a sail?'

'Well . . . what else do you see?'

'Monsters . . . many of them . . . and . . . a woman. Red skin. Red breasts. Her name – no, her name eludes me.'

'Is this woman then to be the mate of our noble visitor?

134

Or will he return here to honour us with his flesh?'

'The way is murky,' said the Great One. 'I see a time when he will be but a step away from a world of destinies. Much then will rely on his wisdom – and the strength of his swordarm.'

Thus ran the word of wisdom in the land of Ling.

10

Name: Jon Arabin.

Alias: Warwolf.

Occupation: pirate-trader.

Status: master mariner; ship-owner; large-scale debtor; husband of Leela, Waru, Verona, Silobeth, Esylan, Tarawen, Gleneth, Parazela, Qualavinth, Janateerith, Zal, Ralathy *et al*.

Birthplace: Ashmolea.

Description: lordly lean black bald clean-shaven man with pale blue eyes, firm voice and forthright manner; wears brown leathers and big leather belt encumbered with sea-pouch and a variety of blades.

One of the first things Drake saw when he got on board the Warwolf was Ika Thole, the Ebrell-born harpoon man. Seeing Thole's red hair and red skin, Drake was instantly reminded of his true love, Zanya Kliedervaust. Zanya of the honey-coloured voice! Zanya of the high-sprung breasts! Zanya the beautiful, the lush, the ultimately desirable!

How long since he had been laid?

Months!

He had an urgent desire to be back on Stokos, to be face to face with the fair Zanya, praising her with poetry, offering her flowers, stripping away her clothes.

'Zanya, no clothes can properly compliment your beauty—'

'What's that you're saying?' said Jon Arabin, coming up behind him.

Drake promptly turned and tried to punch him in the face. But Arabin caught Drake's fist, and laughed.

'Easy, boy. Not so fierce.'

'You toad-buggering bastard!' said Drake. 'You sailed away and left me.'

'Aye, boy,' said Jon Arabin releasing Drake's fist and meeting his gaze without trouble. 'We knew you'd be safe enough.'

'Safe! Look at this!'

Drake pulled up his tattered shirt with such force that the frayed and faded fabric tore, thus exposing his scar. Arabin chuckled.

'Cut, were you? A fight over women, perhaps? Well, for the young, they're worth fighting for.'

'Fight!' said Drake. 'It was no such thing! They tied me down for torture! Slashed me with a knife then put a snake to the wound. A great monster, all blood and gold. It ate its way to my innards.'

'Aye, boy,' said Arabin, 'then they cut off your head, but you grew yourself another to be looking respectable.'

And he dug his fingers in deep under Drake's floating rib. Drake winced as the hard man probed and palpated.

'There's naught deep damage there,' said Arabin. 'Go any depth in there, and the man's dead. I'd say you got a wound, a fever with it, then some imaginings from the fever.'

In fact, the snake which had eaten into Drake's flesh was still there, deeply encysted. Nourished by Drake's own blood supply, it was slowly changing. Even now, a mass of eggs was slowly ripening in its belly. Once they hatched, birthing millions of baby worms . . .

Ah, but that lay in the future, and, for the moment, what Drake didn't know about didn't hurt him.

But he was still angry.

'I hope I get a share of the profits,' he said.

'Aye, boy, that you will, what's left after clearing debt. Aye, and we'll be paying to overhaul the ship as well. And does she need it!'

'Well, does she?' said Drake.

'By the oath she does,' said Arabin, momentarily appalled at his ignorance. 'Go see Jon Disaster, he's in charge of our clothing chest. Tell him I've said you're to have new kit entire – you look rough enough to scare a scarecrow.'

'Thanks for the compliment,' said Drake bitterly. 'It wasn't my choice to live so far from a tailor's shop.'

'Once you're kitted out,' continued Jon Arabin, unperturbed, 'come along and watch the trading done. It's good to get to know the ropes.'

'Why so?' said Drake.

'Why? Because we'll be back here two years from now.'

'Hrmph!' said Drake.

He got Disaster to give him new kit – boots, linens and a set of sealskins. All the clothing was damp, and smelt rather of mould. But, thus dressed, he felt a new man.

He went to watch the trading, and saw good pearls traded for a cargo Arabin had lately loaded at Narba – canoe timber, tarpaulins, canvas sails, fresh vegetables, rice, flour, hides, furs, bone-meal, fish-hooks, harpoons, cauldrons, glass beads, casks of salt pork, siege dust, bamboo, silk, cotton, awls, needles, calamanco, mandolins and ivory.

With the trading done, a dozen girls and an equal number of satin-skinned young men lined up to kiss Drake on his lips, to force pearls upon him, to weep at his feet, to stroke his haunches and fondle his hands, while the crew of the *Warwolf* laughed, clapped, stamped and cheered.

'So much for torture chambers!' said Jon Arabin, as the last suitor quit the ship reluctantly. 'It must have been the fever-dreams you were remembering.'

And Drake, scratching his scar idly, was almost persuaded to agree.

Though he was glad to be back on board, he could not help noticing how cramped and dirty the ship was, and how it stank. And it was crowded, yes, after the comparative privacy he had enjoyed in the caves of the Ling.

He consoled himself with the thought that this was the last voyage of his life. Once they touched land, he would jump ship and buy a passage back to Stokos. Well – that would mean more sea, of course, but only briefly.

On reaching his homeland, he would buy himself out of his apprenticeship, pay whatever theft-fines he owed with respect to Muck's mastersword, and then buy himself a place in the priesthood of the demon Hagon. His wealth was certainly equal to his ambition.

Since it was midsummer, he was now seventeen years old plus a couple of months. In less than a year, King Tor would make a decision on his marriage prospects. Well. If he got Tor's daughter, he'd quit the temple and be prince (and, later, king). If he didn't get the daughter, he'd follow a career in the priesthood. But, either way, he'd have Zanya Kliedervaust as his pleasure-woman.

His wealth would surely make certain of that.

Drake worked on the finer details of his plans as he helped raise the anchor, labouring round in a circle, throwing his weight against one of the twelve bars of the capstan. Even with this enormous amount of leverage, all were a muck of sweat by the time the brutal weight had been broken free and hauled up high and dry.

He was summoned below decks by the cook. As Drake helped hash up some unidentifiable gunk fried in whale oil, he imagined the beautiful meals which Zanya would cook when she was his pleasure-woman. His sweet daydreams blurred unfriendly verities; even the increasingly uneasy motion of the ship failed to trouble him.

They had rough weather for the start of their trip north. Then, when they had just cleared Cape Songala, a storm claimed them.

A ravaging wind blew from the west. After a two-day

storm-fight, what little canvas they had dared carry was blown out entirely. Then the wind shifted to the north-west, threatening to drive them toward doom at Drangsturm.

Jon Arabin decided to lie-to, praying the storm would blow itself out before wrecking them. So lie-to they did: but, slowly, remorselessly, they were driven toward grief where the flame trench met the Central Ocean.

Finally, the fires of Drangsturm itself were seen glowering against the stormcloud sky. The wind's joy blew berserk. They must raise sail or die – but no canvas could stand the weather.

'Man the fore-shrouds!' roared Jon Arabin.

And so they did.

When Drake was ordered aloft with the rest, he could scarce believe his ears – but soon enough he was up there, clinging in the rigging which braced the foremast. In his darkest imaginings, he'd never dreamed himself being turned into a storm-sail, but there he was, shuddering in the screaming wind while the ship lurched and his stomach lurched with it.

Warm within his gut, unperturbed by the weather, the encysted snake fed quietly on his blood, nourished its slowly-growing eggs, and thus prepared certain profound changes for his future.

For two days more the *Warwolf* endured the storm, with her crew manning the fore-shrouds in shifts. Once she was driven within half a league of the coast, but a wind-change saved her. She sprung a leak: Arabin set men to pumping. Another started: he organized a bucket-brigade. The first mate fell down a companion-ladder and broke his neck; Arabin swore, and promoted the second.

At last the inconstant wind shifted all the way round to the south, and eased a little. The *Warwolf* ran along with bare poles. Drake, by this time, was lurching on his feet, with hardly enough sense left to understand that he was still alive.

Arabin, passing him on the deck, slapped him on the back.

'We've done it, boy!' said Arabin. 'We've come through!'

And Drake, despite the intensity of his fatigue, grinned.

'Aye,' he said. 'We're heroes.'

Both Shewel Lokenshield and Ika Thole heard him say as much, but neither of those hard men mocked him. Rather: they shared his triumph.

'How about some food for half-starved sailors?' said Ika Thole.

And Drake, understanding that the question was prompted by dire need, gladly went to the galley.

Towards noon on one rough-weather day (which day? How much storm had they endured? Blood and balls, there was no remembering) lessening winds allowed them to set a little sail. A brave sight the *Warwolf* made then, plunging through the mountainous grey seas with timbers groaning and strong men groaning in harmony.

'We'll have it sweet from here to Narba,' said Jon Arabin to himself. 'We're in the clear.'

Many sailors' superstitions held that such talk was tempting fate. Certainly, it was over-optimistic, for that evening their troubles were multiplied by a monster.

It came flying from out of the south, labouring through the air on storm-damaged wings. Swept from the shores of Argan by the weather, too poor an aviator to fly against the wind, it had no choice but to brave on forward into the unknown. An island was what it needed, but the *Warwolf*, happening where she did, suited the brute's purposes nicely.

It came on the ship from the stern. Then flew alongside. Drake Douay saw it out of the corner of his eye.

'If that was on a chessboard,' he murmured, turning and getting a good look at it, 'I'd say it was a Neversh.'

Since it wasn't on a chessboard, he dismissed it as a hallucination. Harly Burpskin saw the same thing, and thought it was a demon. Raggage Pouch also saw it – and mewled with piteous fear. He knew exactly what it was. It was indeed a Neversh. And Raggage Pouch, who had once

141

seen a Neversh kill seventy armed men on Island Burntos, feared it more than anything out of nightmare.

The Neversh flew in a great wide circle round the ship.

'Jon!' screamed Quin Baltu.

'What?' yelled Jon Arabin.

'There's a—'

The rest of Quin Baltu's words were lost in the sundering roar of a wave breaking over the ship.

'So there's a wave,' muttered Jon Arabin. 'So what?'

But he was worried, all the same. For, heavily laden with an enormous mass of water, the *Warwolf* seemed almost to dig into the sea. For a few moments, Jon Arabin thought she was going to sunder under there and then.

Water cascaded from the ship in torrents. Slowly, her bow began to rise.

'Jon!' screamed Quin Baltu.

'Don't worry!' yelled Jon Arabin, thinking this was no time for Quin Baltu to panic. 'She's riding nicely.'

'But there's a—'

There was a crash fit to rival thunder. Jon Arabin looked round wildly. Saw that the foremast was shattered, was down, broken, smashed, had fallen across the fo'c'sle, had wrecked the fo'c'sle, and was now kicking, struggling, striving, trying to resurrect itself.

Or was it?

No. On closer examination . . .

'Hell's blood and pigs' balls!' shouted Jon Arabin, in a voice that was one part fear and two parts fury. 'It's a Neversh, or I'm a tadpole.'

Jon Arabin could never be mistaken for a tadpole (though he had in his time been compared unfavourably with a shark, a lamprey, a vulture and a cantaloup) and there was indeed a Neversh struggling in the wreckage of rigging and canvas on the forward part of his ship.

'Jon—' shouted Quin Baltu.

'I see it!' yelled Jon Arabin. 'Well, don't just stand there! Get rid of it!'

Quin Baltu started forward, obedient to Jon Arabin's

command. But the next wave took him overboard.

'Merantosh!' said Jon Arabin, who was always prone to obscenity under stress. '*Na jaba na terik!*'

He looked round for Disaster, or some other man who might be fool enough to tackle the beast. None such was in sight.

'Right, then,' said Arabin. 'I'll handle it myself.'

As these monsters go, the Neversh was fairly small. Scarcely a quarter grown, it was just fifty paces in length, from the tips of its twin feeding spikes to the end of its whip-lash tail. Small, yes, yet dangerous. It thrashed strenuously, wings beating so wildly that it was impossible to count them all. Its body, rich with buoyant gas, was kicked around by the wind. Finding the mainmast with its tail, the Neversh coiled tail around mast, and hung on tightly.

'Come on, men!' roared Jon Arabin. 'We're going to deal with that hell-bitch!'

Nobody paid him any attention.

The ruined foremast, which had till then been pointing forward, rolled with a crash from the wreckage of the fo'c'sle. It started dragging in the water. A snare of ropes prevented it from falling away entirely.

'Men!' roared Jon Arabin. 'We act now or we lose the ship. Kill the monster! Cut away the mast! Come on! Come with me!'

But the entire crew was in panic, some men trying to launch the boats, others climbing the sheets – as if that would save them! – or taking cover below-decks.

'Grief!' said Jon Arabin.

He called up the weapons muqaddam, who had been supervising the pumping.

'Get some order in this ship,' said Arabin, 'even if you have to kill someone. I'm going forward to take care of our unwelcome visitor.'

The weapons muqaddam looked round, saw the nature of the unwelcome visitor, and gave a short bow.

'My lord,' he said, 'I will remember your heroism to your wives and children.'

Then grinned, darting out of reach as Arabin swung a kick at him. They were good friends from way back.

On his way forward, Arabin came upon a party of pirates who were trying to launch a boat.

'Avast there, you landlubbers!' bellowed Arabin. 'Any crow-gutted scavenger who wants to leave had better be ready to walk water!'

With a few more well-chosen words and some adroit use of his left-hand boot (always his best kicking foot, the left) he scattered the men back to their work.

Then hung on tight as a huge wave broke, sending water lathering over the ship. Amidst the lather was Quin Baltu. Jon Arabin grabbed him as he went floating past.

'You all right?' said Arabin.

Quin Baltu could only cough and gasp. He had been thrashed something terrible by the roistering ocean; he had swallowed enough salt to pickle a pig.

'Volunteers!' roared Arabin. 'I need five volunteers to carry Quin Baltu to safety.'

Five volunteers promptly came forward.

Drake Douay was one of them and Jon Arabin grabbed him.

'Friend Drake stays here,' said Arabin. 'It only needs four of you to carry Quin Baltu.'

The lucky four hustled Quin Baltu away.

'Now you come along with me,' said Arabin to Drake.

As the sea captain had caught the cook's boy in a painful wrist-lock, there was not much argument about it.

Weeping with fear and fatigue, Drake was forced along the deck toward the Neversh.

11

Neversh: flying monster with six wings; eight very short legs ending in clawed feet; massive head; thick neck; bulky bulbous body containing buoyant gas; very long whiplash tail which it often uses as a weapon; twin feeding spikes which appear to be made of solid ivory, but on Investigation prove to have a honeycomb structure; twin grapple-hooks to secure prey.

The Neversh can grow at least two hundred paces long and is alleged to be able to deflect crossbow bolts with its tail. (Nevertheless, archers have often shot down samples of this type of monster, as its gas-retaining sacs puncture easily.)

The Neversh is one of the Swarms, those colony creatures which dominate the terror-lands of the Deep South, and are only prevented from invading the north of Argan by the gulf of Drangsturm – and the wizards guarding that flame trench.

Weeping with fear and fatigue Drake was forced along the deck toward the Neversh. As Drake and Jon Arabin came level with the mainmast, Drake saw the monster had coiled its tail around the mast to stop itself getting swept away by the waves.

'We can chop the tail!' cried Drake, who wanted to go no nearer the head than he had to.

'That won't do,' said Jon Arabin.

'Why not? Cut away the tail! The next wave will take it!'

145

'Aye! Or it might turn round to fight its way aft. Then what?'

'You tell me,' said Drake.

'We lose the ship, that's what. Come on! Move yourself! No – wait!'

Jon Arabin forced Drake to the mainmast.

'We'll cut the tail?' said Drake.

'No! I've told you that! The rope – cut it loose.'

Drake drew his dirk and cut loose the coil of rope which was tied (by four-dozen turns of twine) to cleats anchored to the mainmast. As the rope came free, the coils of the tail of the Neversh shifted. Drake started, fell back. Jon Arabin caught him, took the rope and slung it over his shoulder.

Then Arabin hustled Drake onwards until they were up by the monster's neck. A massive neck, thicker than a tree-trunk. It seemed a dull purple colour in the dark of the evening. It pulsed as the creature breathed.

'Hack it!' shouted Drake, with the savagery of fear. 'Chop it and gut it!'

'Aye, boy, and have it tear the ship apart as it died. They're powerful strong, these brutes. Take half a day to die if they're cut clean in half. Help me with the rope!'

Arabin ducked under the monster's neck, mounted wreckage to gain some height, then slung the end of the rope to Drake.

'Make it fast!' said Arabin. 'A loop round the monster's neck! A hangman's knot, if you know the shaping!'

'Aye!' screamed Drake, catching the rope-end.

One moment he was standing there fumbling with the rope. The next he was slammed against the monster as a wave crashed down on the ship. The burdening waters smothered him this way and that. He lost his grip on the rope, was sucked away by the wave – then held. By the Neversh.

He had been swept right up by its head. A murderous jointed claw – its nearside grapple-hook – had spiked his boot precisely where sole met upper.

'Jon!' screamed Drake.

146

'Hold tight, boy!' yelled Arabin. 'I'm—'

Another wave drowned his words and the world. Flailing in the flurry, Drake grabbed something, a bar or pipe of sorts. The water was too heavy for thought.

Then the wave subsided, and Drake saw he was clinging to one of the monster's twin feeding spikes. Its nearside grapple-hook still held him. Its offside claw came for him. He kicked out. But it slashed into his sealskin jacket and held fast in the fabric.

Drake let go of the feeding spike. The grapple-hooks took his weight effortlessly. He dropped both hands to the offside grapple-hook. It was polished, it was cold, it was thicker than a banana. He tried to bend it or break it.

Impossible!

'O-o-o-oh!' moaned Drake.

Then the monster started straightening out both grapple-hooks, pushing him away. And Drake thought:

It doesn't want me!

Then realized the thing had no mouth. It fed with the spikes. It wanted to push him away so it could jam those spikes into his body and suck. He jerked out his dirk. He slammed the blade into one of the feeding spikes.

'Die!' he screamed.

His steel drove deep – then proved impossible to withdraw. His only weapon was useless, jammed in the feeding spike. He must cling to it: his strength against that of the grapple-hooks. He grabbed the hilt with both hands. Another wave smothered over. As foam shuddered away, Drake gasped for breath. The grapple-hooks convulsed, breaking his hold on the dirk.

'Jon!' he screamed.

In answer, Jon Arabin dropped to the deck. Too late! The grapple-hooks shoved, one last time – and Drake was rammed hard up against the wreckage of the fo'c'sle.

The Neversh lowered its head, trying to get its feeding spikes into goring position. Drake tried to push them up and away. He might as well have tried to hold up the world. The grapple-hooks pushed up and out. The

Neversh was almost in a position to spike and feed.

Drake half-saw Jon Arabin draw his falchion and raise it high. The falchion, yes. A great ugly bit of metal, with the mass of it concentrated in the thickness far forward, at the optimum striking point.

Down it came, striking at the grapple-hook which had spiked Drake's jacket. The falchion descended on the grapple-hook's middle joint. It went through clean like an axe through a cucumber.

Drake was still held by his boot.

The Neversh reared up.

As the monster reared, Drake was jerked away from the wreckage. The sole of his boot tore free from the uppers. He was thrown clear. He landed on his back, hitting the deck heavily. The monster clawed for Arabin with the hook which had just lost Drake.

'Scarn!' screamed Arabin.

And chopped the hook away.

The monster swung sideways, meaning to kill Arabin with its twin feeding spikes. But those spikes slammed into sprawling wreckage, cutting the gesture short. Arabin, still in a fighting rage, hacked a great chunk out of one of them – then stopped, suddenly realizing that if he cut the spikes away, the creature would be free to pulp him with its head.

He chopped for its nearest eye instead. His falchion bounced off the armoured bubble protecting that eye. Useless. Well, then – the rope!

'The rope now, boy!' shouted Arabin, wiping his falchion against his sleeve, out of habit (it usually had blood on it after combat) then sheathing it. 'Don't just lie there – or we're dead! Up off your arse! Help tie this rope around!'

Drake swore, mustered himself to his feet, was almost skittled by another (small) wave, then floundered forward to help get the rope knotted round the neck of the Neversh. Soon Jon Arabin was beside him, checking the hangman's knot he had fashioned.

'Good rope, this is,' muttered Arabin. Then raised his voice against the weather and repeated himself so Drake could hear. 'Valence cordage. Have you heard of it?'

'Aye,' said Drake. 'We use it for cliff-work on Stokos.'

'Where you learnt yourself climbing.'

'Aye,' said Drake, a little doubtfully, though he had boasted broadly of his skills in the past, and it was too late to gainsay them now.

'Then I'll belay you, boy, and this is what you'll do . . .'

And Arabin explained.

'Mother of dogs and poxes!' exclaimed Drake, in horror.

'It's the only way, boy,' said Arabin grimly.

'Do it yourself then!' said Drake.

'I would if I could, boy, but I'm no shakes at climbing. Come, let's get forward.'

'I won't do it!'

'Aye, then I'll gut you here,' said Arabin, and drew his falchion for further work.

'A death by steel is as good as any,' said Drake, his voice sullen with fear and hate.

He was calling Arabin's bluff.

They looked each other hard in the eye. Man and boy they stood there on the heaving deck, the shadows of evening darkening all around them.

'You're dead meat,' said Arabin, with death in his voice.

'Aye, and so are we all in the end,' said Drake, more confident than ever that he would not be forced forward, and that Arabin would find another way to deal with the monster.

At that moment, the thing's tiny little disorganized brain finally cottoned onto the fact that it could get a clean run at its antagonists by backing off toward the stern, pulling its feeding spikes clear of the wreckage which kept its head from striking at will.

Its eight crocodile-sprawling feet scrabbled splinters from the deck as it went into reverse, dragging the Valence

149

cordage with it. Arabin, who had the coil slung over his shoulders, had no chance to pay out any slack. Dragged off his feet, he hit the deck heavily.

The Neversh lowered its feeding spikes and charged like a bull. Arabin lay helpless. Drake ripped off his sealskin jacket and flung it to the wind. The Neversh saw something flying in the air, reared up as if to spike it – then crashed back to the deck.

Drake helped Arabin scramble to his feet. Retreating together, they paid out plenty of slack. By the time the Neversh had stopped puzzling over the flying jacket, the two humans had gained the fo'c'scle wreckage.

'Well done,' said Arabin.

But Drake took no joy in the compliment. His legs gave way. He clutched the strongest bit of timber he could find, and wept. He was too tired, too cold, too dizzy. He was finished.

Arabin drew his falchion, as if to renew his threat – then a wave burst over them, knocking away the falchion and smothering them under a mountain of water. Drake, snatched from his timber, grabbed at guess – and hooked an arm round Arabin's neck. Arabin clung to the rope, the far end of which was knotted round the neck of the Neversh.

The wave eased away at last to nothing, leaving the two of them sodden, dripping, shuddering. Arabin gripped Drake by the arm. Hard. His fingers dug deep into Drake's biceps.

'It's my plan or nothing, now,' said the Warwolf, his voice urgent.

Drake, released, collapsed to the deck. Helpless as a jellyfish. Arabin grabbed him by the scruff of the neck, hauled him to his feet, then laid a firm hand on his shoulder.

'Courage, boy!' said Arabin. 'Courage!'

Drake stared at his captain. The sky of the man's eyes was entirely lost in the gloom. Drops of sea-spray clung to his bald head, which looked, in the gathering night, like an egg going black with rot. Beyond was the monster, wings still whirring, feet scraping and clawing as it made ineffectual stabs at the fo'c'sle wreckage. Beyond that, the rest of the ship. He half-heard the weapons muqaddam shouting orders.

All about was the wilderness of the sea, an upthrash of confused grey, smeared cloud and horizon-menacing gloom. If they were to act, it would have to be now, for soon the night would make it impossible.

'Show me the place,' said Drake.

'This way, then,' said Arabin.

They went further forward, paying out more rope as they went, then the Warwolf took his footing in the wreckage of the fo'c'sle and made ready to belay.

'I've lost my knife,' said Drake, thinking he might need one.

'Then take this,' said Arabin, drawing a fresh blade from the massive leather belt which sustained his falchion's sheath, his waterproof sea-pouch, a luck-stone, and a couple of dirks like the one he offered Drake. 'And keep it well, until the day you leave it in the heart of the Walrus.'

And Drake, sensing this was a project dear to Jon Arabin's heart, mustered a grin and cried:

'I live for that day!'

'Aye!' shouted Arabin, with a sudden onset of something like joy, his heart made glad to see Drake showing spirit. 'So do we all!'

Then Drake braced himself on the edge of the ship, tested the rope, and made ready to do on the heaving hull what he had done often enough before on his father's coal cliffs.

Over the side he went, rappelling down, warding himself off from the hull with his feet, fearing at any moment to be dashed against that wooden cliff and shattered entirely.

A big sea came shuthering up around him. Lost in the wave-sway, he clung to the rope as best he could. And

151

broke free of the waters. Gasped for air. And was gasping still as a greater sea-thrash smashed him loose from the rope.

In the sea's despairs he tumbled. Then something brutal crunched him. He grabbed it. And, as the waters lumbered away, found himself clinging to the shank of the anchor. He swung his legs over its arms, and, as the seas roistered around him, clung to the ugly mass of barnacle-crusted iron.

Something like a snake whipped round his neck as he clung amidst cataracts. As the waters baffled away, he fought with the strangling thing.

'Demon's grief!' he said, getting it free at last.

And found what he held was no snake but the end of the rope. Swiftly, he hauled in as much slack as he could, and took a couple of turns around the anchor before the next sea. Then, between one assault of the sea and the next, he knotted the Valence cordage as best he could, hoping the rope lived up to its reputation. His hands ran dark with his blood, for he was gashing himself on barnacles in his haste.

'Done!' said Drake.

And a sea came up and almost did for him.

As the waters dipped away, he risked the hard part – and started to climb the rope. It had just a little slack in it. But, as he climbed, the Neversh on the deck above jerked its head, pulling the rope taut. Drake was almost tossed off. But he was strong, yes, and desperate, and clung on with a grimness death itself would have envied.

He gained a little more height, then felt a strong hand grab him. It was Jon Arabin, who hauled him up to the deck. Drake fell into his master's arms, and was held in the refuge until his shuddering eased.

'Now, boy,' said Arabin. 'Do you know how to release the anchor?'

'No,' said Drake, honestly.

'Then I'll manage that myself,' said Arabin. 'Stay here.'

Then Arabin sought out the trapdoor he knew to be in amongst the wreckage of the fo'c'sle, and crawled down through that narrow way into the utter dark below, where the hugeness of the anchor cable coiled in the rat-haunted gloom. He found the safety chain, unwound it from the grab cleats, jerked it clear – and heard the rope begin to whip away as the anchor fell sheer to the seas of night.

The anchor hit the sea, dragging the Valence cordage down with it. The cord tightened round the neck of the Neversh, jerking the monster sideways. Screaming, it fought against the weight. For a few moments it held its ground. But the pain was intolerable. At last, it let go of the mainmast with its whiplash tail, and, wings beating, clawed feet skidding across the deck, was dragged to the side and pulled over.

The Neversh smashed into the water and disappeared from sight.

'Drake!' yelled Arabin.

But the word was savaged by surf and by water-slop, tangled by ropes and baffled by echoes. What Drake heard was only an incomprehensible cry of human anguish. He was sure something terrible was happening to Arabin below decks. For more than a moment, he was tempted to ignore the cry. Then it was repeated.

'Courage, man,' said Drake to Drake.

And crept through the dark wet scrabble-wood wreckage of the fo'c'sle, until he heard Arabin call out yet again – and recognized the shout as his own name.

'What is it?' yelled Drake. 'Rats?'

'Rats?' roared Arabin. 'What are you blathering about? Is the monster over?'

'Aye,' said Drake. 'Over, and sunk from sight!'

'Good, then,' said Arabin.

And grabbed in the dark for the anchor axe which was always kept handy in case the ship had to quit a mooring in a hurry, cut away its restraining cords with one of his dirks, then hacked and chopped until he had cut clean through the cable, setting the anchor free to fall away to the cold dark hell of the seabed, dragging the Neversh with it.

Shortly, Arabin was on deck again, with Drake. As they picked their way back to their comrades, he said to Drake, as quietly as the weather would permit:

'Few enough have seen that and lived. Fewer still have helped tackle it. You did well.'

And that accolade, Drake knew, was to be valued more than the honours of many a kingdom.

'Now get yourself down to the kitchen, boy,' said Arabin. 'We've a hard night coming on, and the men will be wanting their soup.'

And Drake went, thinking his captain a hard man.

'Where have you been?' demanded the cook, when he got below.

'Helping Jon Arabin.'

'With what?'

'Oh,' said Drake. 'With—'

Then paused, finding he had no wish to avaunt about his feat. For he had faced the worst kind of arse-opening terror, and to tell the tale would be to relive it, at least in part.

'With ropes and cordage and stuff,' he said, by way of explanation.

And then pitched into the work the cook gave him, and was soon too busy to think. And, while he did not appreciate the wisdom of the captain who kept him so busy, he got the benefit of it regardless.

And through all these alarums, the snake in Drake's belly slept soundly, planning its changes for his future.

12

Drangsturm Gulf: a U-shaped indentation – roughly a hundred leagues wide and two hundred deep – in the coast of Argan.

North, the Gulf opens to the Central Ocean.

East is Narba, Provincial Endergeneer, the settled lands of the Far South, the Castle of Controlling Power and Drangsturm.

South is a desolate terror-coast on which lies Ling Bay.

West is unknown territory which legend holds to be haunted with monsters of the Swarms, and – in addition – trolls, basilisks, gryphons, dragons, crocodiles and two-headed giants.

Need it be said?

Drake's resolution not to boast about his part in killing the Neversh held good for precisely two days. After that, he was hot for fame, glory and recognition. But nobody paid him much attention, with the exception of Harly Burpskin.

'It's a nice story,' said Burpskin, having heard Drake's tale, 'but a mite improbable, to say the least.'

'Man, the Neversh was there,' said Drake. 'You saw it yourself.'

'Aye, and waves washing over the deck. Likely the brute was carried off by such.'

'Wait till we come to harbour,' said Drake. 'Then you'll see my story proved. For you'll find the anchor's missing.'

'What signifies a missing anchor?' said Burpskin.

'Expense, that's all. It's no new thing to lose an anchor. Aye, and a replacement will have to come from the voyage profits, before we get our share.'

So much for fame and glory!

Since even Burpskin refused to believe him, Drake abandoned efforts to persuade anyone else. At least for the moment. His just recognition could wait till they reached land.

If they reached land.

The *Warwolf* was leaking badly, shipping water almost faster than it could be pumped out. The wind, which had shifted to the east, was still almost storm-force. Under a sky of dark and ragged fractonimbus, the *Warwolf* toiled through the buffeting waters. The rolling seas crashed into surf, strewing foam across the ocean.

Jon Arabin, eyes red-rimmed, searched the blurred horizons for sight of land. His ears ached from the constant wind and cold – a cold he'd never known before in these waters. His right hip was aching, as it always did when he was cold and tired.

Worse, he was lost.

He judged they were still in the Drangsturm Gulf – but where? As his ship groaned and shuddered, struck by another smash-fist sea-shock, he winced, as if it was his own body which was being pounded. Blood of a shark! What had he done to deserve such weather?

He reviewed his options. He could put out sea-anchors and do his best to go nowhere. In that case, the *Warwolf* would sink. He could try the long, laborious business of tacking against the easterly wind, trying to make for Narba. If he did that, his ship would sink all the quicker.

Alternatively, he could let the wind drive them to the western side of the Gulf of Drangsturm. During his many voyages in these waters – aagh, and how he longed for the fair weather of those long-ago cruises! – he had seen its mountains often enough on the far horizon. He had never been there. He had heard tales, of course . . .

But what choice did he have?

'The ship must live,' said Arabin.

And, reluctantly, ordered the *Warwolf* to run for the west. Night came. By morning, the wind had eased to scarcely more than a moderate gale; foam from breaking waves was still lathered across the sea by the wind, but it was possible to talk without shouting. The very sounds of the ship were easier; her timbers were hurting still, but were no longer in agony.

'Good,' said Arabin.

And ordered the lookouts to keep a sharp watch for land. Though, to be honest, he still had no idea how far they were from shore.

Shortly after he had instructed the lookouts, he was met by a delegation led by Quin Baltu. With Baltu were Jez Glane, Salaman Meerkat and Peg Suzilman. Arabin saw at a glance they were tired, angry, hostile, determined. All were armed.

'Morning, boys,' said Arabin.

'Aye,' said Baltu, sourly. 'Perhaps the last morning some of us will see. Unless we turn, man, and run east.'

'Why should we do that?'

'Because,' said Baltu, 'that's what the boys want.'

'What's this?' said Jon Arabin. 'Mutiny?'

He spoke as if in jest – but he was worried.

'Not mutiny,' said Baltu, bracing himself against the ship's swagger. 'We want to fix things right with a friendly talk.'

'Aye,' said Glane. 'Friendly talk, that's the thing.'

Arabin looked around for some staunch, honest men he could call on for help if it came to a fight. But nothing was in sight but Drake Douay, who was keeping as close as possible to his captain, hoping to win promotion from cook's boy to sailor.

'Drake,' said Arabin, in a lazy voice. 'Get to the kitchen for some soup. I've six great rats and a blue-eyed raccoon in me belly, all clamouring sore with hunger.'

'What kind of soup do you want?' said Drake, casting an eye over the opposition.

157

Jez Glane was old and useless. Suzilman was also old – but wiry. Meerkat, slim, quiet and dark, was an unknown quantity. But Baltu – well, the big bloke could smash just about any man aboard.

'What kind of soup?' said Arabin. 'What is there?'

'Oh, dragon soup, shark soup, mushroom soup or carrot soup.'

'Nay, man,' said Arabin. 'They all sound too fancy for me. I'll have what you usually serve up – that boiled dishwater with bits of dead men's bones afloat in it.'

'Man, we're right out of that stuff,' said Drake, 'since we're so far from ditches and graveyards. I tell you what, I'll get you a bowl of the cook's sawdust soup. That should suit!'

And Drake set off at an easy pace, meaning to summon not soup but reinforcements. But Peg Suzilman and Salaman Meerkat drew blades against him. Drake stopped where he was. Despite the death-cold wind, he was suddenly hot – hot and sweating.

'What's this?' said Drake. 'You've a lust for fresh meat, have you? Man, I'd make a stringy dinner, I'll tell you that for nothing. All grit and gristle. Ease up with the steel till we get to the west. There'll be good hunting ashore, I'll bet.'

'Aye,' said Jez Glane, in a voice which quavered a bit. 'Things hunting us, I'll warrant. Huge things with teeth, aye, claws like scythes, feet like hammers.'

'What nonsense is this?' said Jon Arabin.

'No nonsense, friend Warwolf,' said Quin Baltu. 'We've all heard the horrors of the shore you're making for.'

A wave-burst scattered cold, cold spray across the deck. Drake waited for Arabin to speak – but Arabin said nothing. He was trying to stare down Quin Baltu. A fruitless exercise. Drake was edgy.

Come on, Jon. Do something!

But Jon Arabin had no miracles proof against mutiny. He knew these men well: they had been with him for years.

They would never turn against him without the best of reasons: a marrow-gutting fear which overwhelmed all loyalties and every hope.

'You hear us, Jon?' said Jez Glane, in something of a whine. 'It's that we don't want to die, aye, that's why we're here.'

'I run to the west for life, not for death,' said Jon Arabin.

'You can't fool us,' said Quin Baltu. 'It's a gamble you're taking, risking our lives for unknown gains in the face of horrors we've all heard spoken of.'

'Much is spoken but little is truthed,' said Drake, eyeing the blades which still confronted him, and wondering if he dare risk a dash for safety.

'Man,' said Baltu to Arabin, entirely ignoring Drake. 'We can't run west. There's fearful danger there.'

Death, danger, fear. That was what they spoke of. But most of the damage was being done by cold, hunger, fatigue. A day of calm, a good sleep, a couple of hot meals, and they'd be new men. But – Arabin glanced at the wild horizons, and knew hope of such was not to be rewarded.

'Mayhap we run to danger,' said he. 'But choice is not in my gift. We find safety to west – or we sink and drown.'

'There's worse deaths than drowning,' said Baltu darkly.

'Aye,' said Meerkat. 'To be breathed on by a basilisk, that's one. That's murder. Why, the very look of its eyes will kill.'

'And there's crocodiles!' said Jez Glane. 'Logs which turn of sudden to dragons without wings! They eat you, man, gnaw your kneecaps then chew off your prick.'

'Is that so?' said Jon Arabin. 'Then you've got nothing to fear!'

This raised no laugh. Well, it had been worth a try.

'Boys,' said Jon Arabin, 'I'll level with you. We run with the weather for the west – or we sink. If the ship goes down, we have to take to the boats. And how would you like that? A small boat, no shelter, no land for a horizon or more.'

'We'd live,' said Quin Baltu, staunchly. 'Danger known is better than unknown. Turn east, man! If the ship sinks, the boats will still get us to Narba. I love small boats. I could sail in such from here to the Teeth if I had to.'

'Man,' said Drake, grabbing a stay as the ship lurched in a truly horrible fashion, 'what's this nonsense about the unknown west? Man, there's been cruises there in plenty, and will be hence.'

'Aye,' said Jon Arabin, taking Drake's hint. 'Boys, my great-grandfather sailed these waters for year on year. Aye, and buried treasure on some westward island. That's family tradition.'

Hope, yes. That was what these men needed. Hope of an island, a landfall, a safe shore. Wasn't that the ultimate function of leadership? To give hope.

'You talk of an island,' said Baltu. 'But words are one thing, land's another. Will you swear your island?'

'Our island waits to west,' said Arabin. 'I swear it on my mother's honour.'

He apologized, secretly, to his mother's shade. Well, that wasn't the first of his misdeeds she'd had to put up with – and it probably wouldn't be the last.

'He swears!' said Jez Glane.

Eager to believe it might be true. For Glane, unlike Baltu, was not fond of small boats.

'He swears, yes,' said Quin Baltu. 'So his great-grandad sailed these waters . . . but we can't trust such stories, generations old.'

'Then trust to fresher news,' said Drake.

'What do you know about it?' said Meerkat, whose sword was still ready to slice at a moment's notice.

'Lots!' said Drake.

Verily, he knew the last thing he wanted was to be adrift in a cockleshell craft which might overturn and leave him floundering in the sea more than a horizon from shore.

Been there, done that! All very well for Quin Baltu to talk with love and longing about adventures in small boats on the storm-tossed waves – but Drake would rather risk monsters.

'You claim, perhaps, to have been west yourself?' said Peg Suzilman.

'Nay, man,' said Drake. 'But my king has. King Tor, aye. A huge ogre, as wide as tall. Sits on an iron throne, eats frogs, drinks blood, gives out justice. He went there right enough, yes, but five years ago, chasing a vision of gold and diamonds. He found none such, but came home safe with news of goodly islands. Aye. Sweet water and fields of lilies.'

'How do you know of this?' said Peg Suzilman.

'My father sailed with the king,' said Drake. 'Aye, and on the shore he found a tower. Tall it was, with Guardian Machines within, great brutes of clattering metal which spat death and chased him up some stairs. There he was trapped by an invisible wall and—'

Drake proceeded to tell the story of the find of the magic amulets, the destruction of the machines at the top of the tower, and his father's escape on a rope woven from wires of weird manufacture.

He saw Glane, Suzilman and Meerkat were close to believing him. But Quin Baltu was not.

'Man,' sneered Quin Baltu, 'that's a right daft story. Little lockets which talk! You expect me to believe a non-sense like that?'

In answer, Drake hauled out one of the lockets in question. He had been wearing it next to his skin, for luck.

'Man,' said Drake, dangling the glossy black lozenge in front of Baltu, 'this is one of those lockets my father found. He gave it to me for luck.'

'I see a pretty trinket,' said Baltu. 'I hear no voice.'

'Then watch,' said Drake.

And he manipulated the seven silver stars built into one side of the amulet, and set the thing talking.

The voice of the poet Saba Yavendar contended against

that of the wind. While he spoke in the High Speech, which none on the *Warwolf* could understand, Quin Baltu listened long and hard. Then looked Jon Arabin in the eyes.

'Jon,' said Quin Baltu. 'We've been a long way together.'

'Aye,' said the Warwolf.

'Jon, I trust you.'

'I trust you too,' said Jon Arabin. 'And I love you as a brother. Despite these moments. Go below, boys, and get yourself some soup.'

So the mutineers departed. And Arabin standing easy on the rolling deck, let his arms hang slack by his side, then made every muscle in his body shudder and shake in the exercise known as Five Horses Dancing. Then he did the Three Breaths and a single Focus, and felt stronger. He looked at Drake, who was tucking away his curious amulet. Right: teaching first. Then settle curiosity.

'What brought those men to the edge of mutiny?' said Arabin. 'Did they hate me? Or what?'

'Nay,' said Drake. 'It was despair which took us so close to death. Despair – that's the great sin, man. That makes all the others possible. But you – you gave them confidence. That's what makes you leader.'

'You think well,' said Arabin, surprised.

At Drake's age, Arabin (dreaming of future glory while he endured the infinite boredom of schooling) had thought of leadership in terms of machismo. One man – the ultimate killer – to brute it over lesser mortals by death-skills alone.

'We're taught to think on Stokos,' said Drake. 'Not that I can always see the use of it, since there's not much money in thinking. As to leadership – why, my uncle, Oleg Douay, he spoke of it often. For he was mixed up in wars and such in his youth.'

'Well,' said Jon Arabin, teaching done and curiosity still to be satisfied, 'tell me now, friend Drake. Whence came that trinket? From the west?'

'Nay, man,' said Drake. 'From the moon. My father flew there when he were but a boy, riding on the back of a great grey goose.'

'I see,' said Jon Arabin. 'Then how about you flying below to get me some soup?'

'Dragon soup or sawdust?'

'I'll take the seal soup,' said Arabin. 'It seems the least likely to kill.'

It was a long, uneasy day. Arabin worried incessantly. What if reefs and rocks infested these uncharted waters? What if he failed to find safe harbour to the west? An island, yes, that was what he needed. Not anything fancy. Any chunk of rock would do, so long as his ship could shelter in its lee.

Leadership is the science of hope. Yes. But if he found no landfall to the west, what good was hope?

By the time night came, heavy rain was falling. A solid, sullen downpour. Rain! In the Drangsturm Gulf, at the height of summer! Craziness . . .

What should he do? Heave to? Or strive blindly through the night? There were so many unknowns: the weather, the distance to shore, what depth of water they could count on. How much longer could the ship stand staunch against the seas before ripping in half?

Jon Arabin made a round of his ship, and decided he knew one thing for certain: his crew could take very little more of this.

'We run for the west tonight,' said Jon Arabin, with every appearance of confidence. 'I know just where we are, aye, from the taste of the spray. Come morning, we'll see land – I guarantee it.'

Faint hearts were heartened by this bluff, and through the night the *Warwolf* ran. Jon Arabin slept little, yet thrice dreamed his ship wrecked.

The weather eased further overnight. Come morning, they were cruising in a moderate breeze amidst herds of brisk white horses that were champing across the seas toward the western coast of the Gulf of Drangsturm, which lay in plain view maybe twenty leagues away.

About three leagues south was a considerable mass of land which might have been either a peninsular or an island. It terminated in a rugged cape.

'Is that an island?' asked Drake Douay, pointing south.

'It surely is,' said Arabin, hoping he was right.

'What's it called?'

'It has no name as yet.'

'Then I name it Island Tor,' said Drake. 'Yes. Tor, in honour of the king of Stokos. How about those mountains on the western shore? Do they have a name?

'Not as yet,' said Jon Arabin, amused.

'Then . . .'

Drake thought about naming them the Zanya Kliedervaust Ranges. But that sounded clumsy. He cast around for a better name, and soon had one: the Dreldragon Teeth. Perfect!

Sight of land put new life into the crew. They worked with a will, and, shortly, the *Warwolf* rounded the cape Jon Arabin had seen to the south.

An ironbound coast slanted away to the south-west for about a dozen leagues, terminating in a second cape, which they rounded at mid-morning. From here, the eastern coast of Tor slanted away to the south-east.

Was Tor an island or a peninsular? The difference was vital. If a peninsular, then it adjoined the terror-lands of the Swarms, and was probably infested with monsters. If an island, it might be safe. Providing the legends of giants, basilisks and such weren't true . . .

The sun broke through the clouds. The wind dropped. They cruised in the lee of the putative island through a blue-green sea of idle wavelets. It grew hot. The damp decks steamed. Men stripped to the waist, soaking up the sunlight. This was more like it! This was how the Gulf was supposed to be in summer!

A league along the coast, they came upon a bay of beauty. Sailing close inshore so Jon Arabin could check it

164

out, the *Warwolf* lost the last of the wind. She floated in a delicious calm. The crew crowded the larboard railing, staring at paradise. A lean white beach of crisp clean sand. Behind the beach, rough grasses of a brilliant green. Inland from that, deep cool forest of a darker green. Jon Arabin gazed long on that forest. The wood itself was wealth.

He heard the rattle-cackle of staccato bird-talk coming clear across the water. A flight of parrots burst to the sky, hustling across the heavens like splashes of animated rainbow. There was a disconcerting arthritic crackling in the background. What? He'd heard it before, hadn't he? Yes, years ago, in Quilth. Cicadas, that was all. Millions of them. They'd do no harm . . .

At the southern end of the beach, a stream ran swift and bright. Good water! The rocks of the southern headland were of limestone. There would be caves in such rock. Arabin felt a pang of heartbreaking nostalgia and homesickness, for limestone was the ruling rock of Ashmolea; he had loved its landscapes dearly in his youth. How many years since he last saw Ashmolea? Many!

'This looks great!' said Drake, admiring the pale sands, the grass, the forest. Dry land! Dry land! A bare rock covered with seagull dung would have looked sweet to him at that moment.

'Aye,' said Arabin. 'It's a good place. What do you want to call it?'

'Zanya Bay,' said Drake promptly, for he owed his true love that much.

'Jon!' cried Baltu. 'Is this the island you promised us?'

'It surely is,' called Arabin.

'Then tell us about it!' yelled one of the men.

Other voices took up the cry. They wanted to know where they were, how long they'd be here, when they'd see the fleshpots of Narba. Jon Arabin gestured for silence.

'Men!' said Arabin. 'This is Island Tor. It's named for the king of Stokos, a fearless ogre who explored these lands in his youth. The father of young Drake Douay voyaged here with the king, and brought Drake proof of the truth of his story.

'This place of beauty here is Zanya Bay, where the king careened his ship. A good careenage it is, too, as you can tell at a glance.'

'Good, sure,' cried a pessimist. 'But for the Swarms!'

'This is an island,' insisted Arabin. 'No monsters tread these forests. And look west! You see the west of the Drangsturm Gulf, some twenty or thirty leagues away. See those mountains? Those are the Dreldragon Teeth, famous in the legends of Stokos. Such heights are far too bitter-cold for the Swarms. We're safe! So now, boys – to work!'

'Aagh, you can slag work up your poke-hole!' shouted a dissident, anonymous in the crowd.

And others shouted similar.

Exhausted by weather, labour, nightmare, fear, short rations, seasickness and wakeful nights, they had no taste for work. The very last thing they wanted was to careen the ship. If the shore had been grim, barren, bitter and stony, Jon Arabin might have won their co-operation – but, as it was, paradise beckoned. Arabin found himself facing a seething, shouting mob. His crew was on the edge of mutiny.

'Men!' shouted Arabin. 'Let's talk money! Let's talk wealth! There's treasure on this island!'

'What treasure?' yelled Raggage Pouch. 'I see nothing but trees!'

'Man!' shouted Jon Arabin. 'And how much is lumber worth in Narba? Eh?'

And he began to talk money. When he had finished, Quin Baltu backed him up:

'It's true what Jon says. Timber's a good price in Narba. If we patch the ship proper, we can leave with riches.'

But the men still refused to careen the ship.

So they struck a bargain. The ship would stay afloat. Divers would make emergency repairs to the leaking hull from the outside; other men would work from the inside. Meantime, the rest of the crew would work the forest for a cargo of timber to enrich this voyage. In return for Arabin's concessions, the crew swore to overhaul the *Warwolf* properly once back at the Greaters.

An anchor was fashioned from a net filled with ballast blocks. Divers were nominated and repair parties chosen. Hunters were put ashore to kill fresh meat – even parrots would be welcome. A boat went for fresh water, so the *Warwolf* would have ample supplies of such if she had to leave without warning. Suzilman volunteered himself as an expert on timber, and was given charge of forestry operations.

By noon, everyone was working at their tasks with confidence.

But Jon Arabin was desperately anxious. What was this place? An island or a peninsular? He had to know! He called together his three most expendable men: Harly Burpskin, Raggage Pouch and Drake Douay.

'Boys,' said Jon Arabin, 'I've got you together quiet-like so we can talk in confidence. When my great-grandfather sailed these waters, he was a fearsome pirate. Aye. And he buried great treasure on an island in these waters. Mayhap it was this one . . .'

And Arabin described the treasure-burial place. It was in a cave set in a headland on one side of a sandy bay. A cave lined with emeralds.

'The treasure sits in an iron box which is enchanted,' said Arabin. 'It cannot be moved unless you say the magic word: Ponk!'

'Ponk,' said Drake, savouring the word. Then: 'Is there another magic word needed to open this treasure chest?'

'There is,' said Arabin. 'But only I know that word. But . . . if you find the treasure, we'll split it. Equal shares.'

'What about the emeralds?' demanded Raggage Pouch.

'Ah, those,' said Arabin. 'Well . . . what you can hack out of the walls of the cave is yours to keep.'

'Why are we so privileged?' said Drake.

167

'Because the rest of my crew deserves no share of treasure,' said Arabin, 'for they have come far too close to mutiny. Aye. Whereas I never saw any of you in that mutinous mob.'

All three, in fact, had shouted against the hard labour of careening: but none of them confessed as much to Jon Arabin. Instead, they congratulated themselves on his trust, and began dreaming of how they would spend their share of the treasure.

Thus it was that Drake Douay, Raggage Pouch and Harly Burpskin provisioned one of the *Warwolf*'s boats and then, by oar and by sail, began to circumnavigate Island Tor.

Drake was intensely proud to have been chosen for this expedition. The honour confirmed his own high opinion of himself. All eagerness and expectation, he stared at the lush green shore, on the lookout for headlands and caves.

A few leagues south-east of Zanya Bay, the explorers came upon a U-shaped harbour perhaps two leagues wide and two deep. Drake saw at a glance that, compared with Zanya Bay, it offered infinitely better protection from hostile winds.

'Jon Arabin should know about this place,' said he. 'Let's turn back to tell him.'

'What fool's talk is this?' said Burpskin. 'Do you want to get rich, or what?'

'I want,' said Drake, 'to have a ship to go home in. This place would see the *Warwolf* safer than where she lies now.'

'Aagh,' sneered Raggage Pouch, and hawked, and spat. 'Talking like a ten-year salt-sea sailor, aren't we now? You're young, you're a landlubber, you know nothing of it.'

'I say let's look after us,' said Burpskin. 'That's the important thing. Who knows? The treasure could be hidden in this very harbour.'

'You're crazy,' said Drake, infuriated by such short-sighted selfishness. 'The ship's our survival. The ship comes first, aye, before wealth, food, sleep or leisure.'

'That's captain's talk,' said Pouch, with contempt. 'We've seen you sniffing round Jon Arabin, haven't we just? You're thinking you want a career of command, perhaps? Well – why should we risk our fortune to get you launched on such?'

'I'm thinking I want to stay alive,' said Drake, starting to get angry.

Thus began an argument which took so long that it was night before they finally beached their boat. They continued the argument round the campfire. It was not exactly an auspicious start to their journey.

And things got worse rather than better.

They found bays, headlands and caves, but never the cave they were looking for. They argued further, of course; they forgot precisely what Jon Arabin had told them, and proceeded to invent the details.

Drake learned a considerable amount about getting along with disagreeable companions. He also learned the hard way – about winds, tides, and small boat management. And where to camp and where not to camp.

And he suffered.

He was bitten by mosquitoes, stung by a scorpion, spiked by thorns and agonized by poison ivy. Food ran out. The three survived on seaweed, whore's eggs and rock-oysters. Then, when they thought they had almost circumnavigated the island, they wrecked their boat on its most northerly cape.

Jon Arabin had given Drake up for dead when the lad came staggering out of the forest one evening, thin, tired, ragged and footsore.

'Where have you been?' said Arabin.

'Chasing a treasure that never was,' said Drake, in something like fury. 'Your great-grandfather never sailed these waters! Or if he did, he never left treasure here.'

'Yes,' said Arabin. 'But you should have known that much to start with.'

And Drake realized this was true. He had let greed over-balance judgment.

169

'So why did you send me round the island?' said Drake.

'To see what you're made of,' said Arabin.

'Does this mean I get to be a sailor?'

'No, for you've obviously lost me a boat. And what have you done with Burpskin and Pouch? Have you eaten them?'

'Came close to it,' said Drake. 'They gave up. They're two days north – two days as the survivor stumbles.'

'Inland?' said Arabin.

'No. Shorebound, on a beach at the foot of the cliffs of a cape to the north of here. There was a way up the cliff, aye, easy climbing, but they were both too gutless to try it.'

'Then I'll send a boat,' said Arabin.

And did.

Then settled down to interrogate Drake, for he wanted to learn as much as he possibly could about Island Tor. Who knows? He might someday be forced back here again.

As Drake ate parrot-meat and ironbread, and answered Arabin's questions, he became quite proud of his achievement. Yes. Despite all difficulty, he'd managed. He'd not like to do it again, but . . . it was worth doing once.

Jon Arabin tested me. Aye. Well, I hope he's happy. For I am.

Seventeen days after she had arrived at Zanya Bay, the *Warwolf* put to sea again. She had a new foremast made of roble cut from the forests of Tor. The worst of her leaks had been repaired. She had a cargo of summerpine, cedar and bamboo, also cut out of the hinterland. That should fetch a good price in Narba – and should help pay for the permanent repairs which were still needed to make the *Warwolf* truly seaworthy.

They sailed north, rounding the island's northernmost cape. Then the wind got up and attacked them. A howling wind from the east. Despite Arabin's best efforts, they were forced westward, coming closer and closer to the mountain heights dominating the mainland.

Rumour held that the white enamel of those fangs was water curdled by cold. The Galish termed such stuff 'muff'. Jon Arabin, who was much-travelled, knew it well: Drake, on the other hand, reserved judgment, withholding belief until the day he could walk on it.

If the wind kept up, that day might be soon.

Finally, when they were almost on the rocks, the wind died. Jez Glane claimed it was prayers to his god which had stopped it: and he converted three people to the worship of that god (the great white star-dragon Bel).

Drake was not interested in Glane's god.

He was, though, intensely interested in what he could see on the shore.

'Look!' he cried. 'Something moving!'

There were many things moving on the narrow coastal plain between the waters of the Drangsturm Gulf and the heights of the Dreldragon Teeth. It was too far to make out details, but clearly they were bigger than buffalo. Some were as big as cottages.

The entire western coast of the Drangsturm Gulf was, for as far as they could see, swarming with monsters of the Swarms.

Jon Arabin vowed that he would never come this way again. Not unless his life depended on it. His dreams of making a fortune from the timbers of Tor faded to nothing on the spot. Forget it! This place was far too dangerous!

Jon Arabin paced up and down the deck, waiting for the wind to get up again. But the ship floated in a deathly calm.

'Right!' said Arabin. 'We'll drop anchor!'

The net filled with ballast blocks which served them as an anchor slid away into the sea. And, on hitting the bottom, tore apart.

'*Anch ench unch*!' said Jon Arabin.

Then apologized to his mother's shade, for he had once promised her he would never again use such obscenities.

A shadow flickered over the deck of the *Warwolf*. He looked up. Only a buzzard. But it could just as easily have been a Neversh.

'Lower the boats, boys!' roared Jon Arabin. 'We're going to sweat the ship out of here.'

Arabin gave Drake command on one of the smaller boats, to see how he would do.

'The ship's survival is our survival,' said Drake, to his boat's crew. 'So pull, boys, pull!'

And, on this occasion, nobody disputed his judgment.

Fingerlength by fingerlength, the *Warwolf* was hauled away from the shore. Hands blistered. Eyes burnt with sweat. Men cursed, strained and swore. But they put distance between them and the monsters.

Then, finally, the wind got up. From which direction? From the west!

'A miracle!' said Jez Glane. 'All power to the great god Bel!'

Jon Arabin, who had his own gods to worry about, paid no attention to Glane.

'Let's hope we're favoured fair to Narba,' said Arabin grimly, knowing – everyone aboard had reason to know by now – that the winds of this strange season were powerful weird and treacherous.

Fortunately, Arabin's wish was granted, and, four days later, a bullock team was hauling the *Warwolf* up the ship canal to the Inner Dock of Narba.

13

Place: Narba, a low-lying city connected to the Central Ocean by four leagues of ship canals.

Population: either 98,476 or 117,290, depending on which census one believes.

Rule: by elected City Fathers working within the General Terms of Alliance of the Consortium of Provincial Endergeneer.

Religion: Revised Atiniunism, Elchwade Transubstantiation and the Reformed Rites of Devotional Quelochianism.

Location: on the Salt Road on western coast of Argan, north of Drangsturm and south of Stokos.

Drake leaned on the ship's siderail, watching the bullock teams at work. It was intensely pleasant to watch work being done, yet to know that one's labours were at an end.

'Tonight,' he said, dreamily, 'I'm going to have a hot meal, a woman with smooth thighs, and twenty-five beers. Not necessarily in that order.'

'Doubt it,' said Ika Thole, who was standing to his left.

'I can afford it,' said Drake.

'That's not the point,' said Jon Disaster, who was standing to Drake's right. 'Jon Arabin won't let us off the ship till all the work's done to his satisfaction.'

Drake remembered the near-mutiny at Zanya Bay. Arabin's authority had proved slim enough then. How

173

could a single ship's captain hold back a crewload of pirates who were hot for boozing and whoring?

'I don't think,' said Drake, 'that Arabin will get one whit of work out of us till we've had our fill of pleasure.'

Thole and Disaster simply laughed.

When the *Warwolf* reached the Inner Dock, she was immediately boarded by fifty grim men in mail, armed with swords and halberds.

'What's this?' said Drake, wide-eyed. 'Murder?'

'Nay, man,' said Jon Disaster, lazily. 'This is but the harbour guard, come to help our captain keep his authority.'

While most ports would have lynched them on arrival, Narba welcomed them. The Orfus pirates mostly preyed on ships sailing out of Runcorn, Cam and Androlmarphos. Narba merchants never invested in that north-trade, but financed, instead, ventures half a thousand leagues south-west to the Scattered Islands.

Narba profited from the Orfus connection, buying north-trade plunder, and selling everything from siege dust to lime for wormbags hung from each ship's bow to discourage ship-worms. But the good people of Narba had learnt long ago that no pirate captain could keep a lusty crew from temptation without ample armed assistance.

Drake, who had not worshipped the Demon for what seemed an age, was eager for religion. But shore leave was refused for twenty days – the time needed to finish repairs to the *Warwolf*. The harbour guard maintained a watch by day and night, preventing a single pirate from stepping ashore till all the work was done.

Drake bitterly resented this labour, for he would never benefit from work on the *Warwolf*. He was quite determined that he would never sail another league on the ship. At least now they were in port they had fresh food. Hot meat dripping with red blood. Crisp crunching fresh vegetables. Fresh fruit. The dense red meat of plums, the quivering aroma of peaches . . .

Then at last the work was done. Arabin told the harbour

guard he no longer needed their help. He set the crew at liberty for the day. And Drake was, for the moment, free.

Fully intending that moment to last a lifetime, he packed his treasure: pearls, magic amulets and gambling profits. All pearls but three went into his boots; the three shared pocket-space with coinage and magic amulets. For luck – he might need it in this foreign city – he still kept one amulet slung round his neck so that it lay next to his skin, close to his heart.

Turning his back on the *Warwolf*, Drake had no second thoughts whatsoever. He had stomached as much whale-oil cookery as he could bear. He was sick of damp gear, canting decks, sea-boils, bully-boy crewmen, wet ropes, wind, rain, sunburn, and all the other inconveniences of life at sea.

For a man with no prospects, piracy no doubt had its attractions. But Drake would likely enough find himself heir to the throne of Stokos, if he played his cards right. Aye. And owner of the high-breasted Zanya Kliedervaust. At the very least, he would be a priest of the temple of Hagon – which was in itself a very fine thing to be.

After his long captivity in Ling and his subsequent privations at sea, Drake found Narba to be an amazement of colours, smells, bustle and voices. And temptations.

First off, he bought himself a whore. Was he then unfaithful to his true love? No, for it was Zanya Kliedervaust he conjured into his mind to intensify his lust as he rode his woman.

'That was nice,' said Drake, exiting from the knocking shop. 'What next?'

Since he was young, and over-excited by growth hormones, what came next was another whore. Then, driven more by ego than desire, he bought himself a third. But his flesh failed him.

'Never mind,' she said. 'It happens to every man sooner or later.'

'Then what do I get for my money?' demanded Drake.

'Something nice,' she said.

And gave him a rub-down, squeezed his blackheads and washed his hair, all the while talking about how strong and handsome he was. All of which combined to restore his flesh for a third endeavour.

After that, Drake, who was still as devout as when he had left Stokos, went looking for a bar so he could complete his worship of the Demon. He soon found a pleasant enough place, with sawdust on the floor, men sitting at rough-wood tables eating oysters, and a stack of ragged claws in the free lunch bowl. However, Drake thought the publican regarded him strangely when he walked in, so he said to the man:

'I'm a pirate off the *Warwolf*. Any objection?'

'None,' said his host.

But peered again at a sketch kept hidden behind the bar, glanced back at Drake, and, after pulling a couple of mugs ('Set them up in twins, I don't want to be wasting my time'), sent a runner to an inn lying handy to most of the dockside bars.

Drake had only just started his fourth mug when into the bar, as if by coincidence, came Sudder Vemlouf, whom Drake knew from old times back on Stokos.

'Sudder, me old mate,' said Drake jovially. 'What are you doing here? Sit down, man, and have a mug. Bar! A couple of ales and a dash of cold potato.'

He was feeling generous, in part because the beers had warmed him nicely, yes, slurring the sharpness of the harder edges of the world.

'I was never any friend of yours,' said Sudder Vemlouf, as the drinks were served.

'Sure no, you were neighbour to old man Muck. And how is the scratchy old bastard, anyway?'

'The Blessed One is in good health,' said Vemlouf formally. 'And he is far from happy with you.'

'What? Upset about the mastersword, is he? Oh, I admit everything. Don't worry. When I'm home, I'll rich him up till his eyes pop. I've got the money now.'

176

'You have no need to travel home,' said Vemlouf, 'for justice has found you here.'

And, so saying, Vemlouf suddenly drew a knife.

A professional killer would have gutted in quick and low, and would have been halfway to the door before anyone realized a man was dead. But Vemlouf raised his knife on high like a ham actor in a melodrama.

'Die!' he screamed.

And, both hands clasping the hilt, he brought the blade down.

There was a certain ritual quality to the way he struck. He was slow, yes – but the beers had done their damage. Drake flung up a warding arm – too late! The steel bit through his sealskins, slammed into his chest – and skidded off the amulet.

'Get away with you!' said Drake, giving Vemlouf a shove which sent him staggering backwards.

Vemlouf glanced at his unblooded blade, and then, with horror, at Drake.

'You – you live?'

'Bloody oath I live! Now get out of here, before I kick your ring through your breakfast!'

'Demon-son!' hissed Vemlouf, tightening his hold on the knife.

'Oh, jalk off!' said Drake, as Vemlouf stalked toward him.

Then, seeing the man seriously intended to kill him, Drake picked up a bar stool and defended himself. But Vemlouf managed to give him a nasty scratch on the back of his hand. Drake, rather put out by that, broke his arm, knocked him unconscious, then threw him to the floor and jumped on him.

'Damned if I like your choice in customers,' he said to the barman, and left to find a quieter bar where he could practise religion in peace.

The next barman he encountered also had a hidden sketch, and also sent a messenger to a certain inn – only this time, of course, there was nobody to respond to the news.

'Who's drinking?' asked Drake of all and sundry, as a young man with sudden money necessarily must.

It turned out that everyone was. And, while demolishing a pearl's worth of ale, they were happy enough to listen to Drake hold forth on his recent adventures. Only one sceptic was unkind enough to dispute his tall tales about Ling.

'Where did all that fresh water come from?' asked he. 'And how did those cold cold lights keep burning?'

'By magic,' said Drake solemnly.

And would have come no closer to the truth even if he had managed to break into the armoured vaults holding the automated desalination plant, the Ground Effect generator, the Control, the Planet Link, and the other sophisticated machinery installed when the Plague Sanctuary was first established at Ling, many thousands of years before, in the nightmare years known as the Days of Wrath, which were now almost less than a memory.

'Magic?' said the sceptic. 'It was a place of wizards, then? Or was it?'

Wiser heads suppressed him before Drake could be bothered to find an answer, and the flow of ale continued unabated.

With so many eager co-religionists to help him worship, Drake was fairly deep in the clutches of faith by the time the bar was enlivened by the arrival of Jon Disaster, Goth Sox, Hewlet Mapleskin, Lee Dix, Shewel Lokenshield and others.

'Good to see you boys,' slurred Drake. 'Have a beer – I'm buying!'

Well, one thing led to another, till finally – and not for the first time – Drake's religious fervour got the better of him. He woke up the next day with a large-sized gap in his memory, and found himself at sea again. He had no money, no pearls, and no magic amulets – but for the one worn secretly against his skin for luck. He had also lost his boots.

What was worse, his penis hurt so badly he feared he

had picked up a heavy dose of clap. But, on inspection, he found he had been tattoed with a snake design while stone cold unconscious.

'All right,' he demanded, 'which of you jerk-offs did that?'

'Who are you calling a jerk-off?' rumbled Shewel Lokenshield.

'Not you, you prickless wonder,' said Drake promptly, thus precipitating a fo'c'sle fight, which he lost.

The next day, his vital organ began to swell with blood poisoning. Consequently, he was a little down in the mouth. The other pirates, though, were in high spirits, for they were returning home wealthy. Jon Arabin organized deckside games of knuckleskull, First Off and Quivliv Quoo, which Drake, sore and sulking, watched from the sidelines.

However, by the time they raised the Greater Teeth his condition was improving, and he no longer lived in fear of imminent amputation. All he had to worry about was surviving until he could make a break for freedom.

But would he ever get another chance? He had blown his best opportunity, back at Narba. And even if he struggled back to Stokos, how would he cope with Gouda Muck? The old man must be lunatic to be sending armed assassins to revenge the theft of the mastersword with murder.

'The bugger's insane,' said Drake to Drake. 'But old, yes. Can't last much longer. Ten years, at most. Yes – that'll finish him.'

It was easy to say, but – ten years! That was more than half Drake's lifetime.

'I can't possibly wait that long,' said Drake. 'Anyway, attack's the best defence. Aye, that's for certain. First chance I get, I'll be back to Stokos to kill off old man Muck. King Tor won't hold that against me, I'm sure. In fact, once he understands what's going on, he'll probably help me. Aye. Likely pay good gold to see Muck wasted.'

Or so Drake hoped.

*　　*　　*

179

The *Warwolf*, returning rich, avoided Gufling, and made instead for Knock. It was at that time early autumn. The year Khmar 18 was still young, and Drake was only 17 years old. (Though, if challenged, he would have claimed to have been 18, on the grounds that a couple of months would take him through to age 17½, and the missing half-year was not worth worrying about.)

It was a while since Jon Arabin had dared the approaches to Knock, and he disgraced himself by getting the *Warwolf* stuck as they were approaching the Skerry Passage at low tide. His own men thought it was hilarious. So did the crew of a sealing boat which slipped past a little later, returning from a hunting expedition laden with bloody booty.

'The Walrus will laugh himself sick to hear of this!' cried one of the sealers, from the deck.

'He lives, then?' called Arabin.

'Aye! Lives, farts, shits, shags – and swears you left him on the Gaunt Reefs to drown.'

'That's a lie!' shouted Arabin. 'He had his choices!'

'That's as may be – but all his crew swears with him. They say the only thing you took from the rocks was a sweet-faced playtime boy.'

This news did not improve Jon Arabin's temper. Nor Drake's.

'Does Andranovory live?' he yelled.

'Who?' shouted one of the sealers.

'Atsimo Andranovory. A great big dirty brute with a great big beard which stinks like a bilge broom. A black beard, with black hair to go with it. Aye, and a great big chest.'

'For sure he lives,' called one of the sealers. 'Why? Are you lovesick for him?'

'Aagh, jalk up, you ganch,' yelled Drake.

Thus starting an exchange of obscene insults which continued – pirates could sometimes show remarkable stamina – until the sealing boat was out of earshot.

*   *   *

Thinking of Atsimo Andranovory, Drake experienced a little frisson of something which was most certainly not pleasure. He remembered that ugly inviting him to suck, then stringing him up on refusal. He remembered . . . swinging from a rope, yes, tied to a spar by his ankles . . . an agony which seemed to go on forever . . . Whale Mike singing a lullaby . . . the cold on the rocks . . .

He would never forget. Although even now the details were hazy. So much had happened since!

'What's your interest in Andranovory?' asked Jon Disaster, as they waited for the incoming tide to float the *Warwolf* off the rocks she had grounded on.

'I told him the truth about his ugliness,' said Drake. 'Tell me – what's between our captain and this Walrus?'

'Man,' said Disaster, 'That Walrus isn't properly human. Slagger Mulps, they call him – that's his proper name. He's weird, like. Thin as an eel, with gangling arms with two thumbs on each hand. Green hair, green—'

'I know all that,' said Drake, impatiently. 'I've been up against him before. But what's his quarrel with Jon Arabin?'

'Why, man, friend Walrus has been the *Warwolf*'s favourite enemy, ever since the day he seduced one of Arabin's wives. Aye. Got over-excited. Bit off her left-hand nipple. From whence Arabin loathes him.'

'Are we at war then?' said Drake.

'There's no war between pirates, lad. Not on the Greater Teeth. Not in theory, anyway.'

'Why call me lad?' said Drake, feeling he deserved better than that (and feeling, too, that there might be war on the *Warwolf* in a moment, unless he got an apology).

Jon Disaster laughed.

'Man, you want to be more than a lad? Then use your time well. Here at the Teeth, you can learn boats proper. Take every chance to go boat for the fish and the seals.'

'I've no need of more boat learning,' said Drake. 'Why, I sailed round Island Tor entire!'

Jon Disaster had the gall to chuckle.

'Not quite,' said he. 'The judgment of sailing is whether you finish with the same boat you start with. And there, I think, you can hardly claim success.'

The rising tide took them clear of the rocks with no damage worth speaking of, and, later in the day, they docked in the Inner Sleeve, a rock-locked harbour on Knock.

Drake, remembering the narrow slot they had squeezed into at Gufling, expected another equally claustrophobic prison-hole. But the Inner Sleeve proved to be a regular little harbour. Admittedly, it was sunless-gloomy, sunk between ramparts of rock. Nevertheless, with care and effort a dozen ships could have berthed there, and in fact nine were in port when the *Warwolf* tied up.

One of the nine was the *Walrus*.

This had not always been a pirate ship. Indeed, some months earlier it had been an honest slaver, and, bearing the name *Gol-sa-danjerk*, had sailed from Androlmarphos with a cargo of felons – one of whom had been Drake Douay.

The green-bearded Slagger Mulps had captured the *Gol-sa-danjerk*, and had put a prize crew on board. Thus, after he had been rescued from the Gaunt Reefs, he had still had a ship to his name. And there, on the deck of it, he stood, arms folded.

Also on deck was Atsimo Andranovory in all his glory – grinning as he recognized Drake. He had a good head for faces.

'Hello darling!' he called. 'Like to give me a suck?'

'I'll see you suck on this first!' shouted Drake, drawing his dirk.

'Once you've taken it up the arse I'll love to,' retorted Andranovory.

And of course their dialogue did not end there, for, being who they were and where they were, they vented their spleen with all the eloquence available to them, which was considerable in both cases. And the crews of both ships jeered or cheered each sally, depending on their allegiance.

And while this was going on, a couple of workaholics who had no appreciation of theatre were busy tying up the *Warwolf* and lowering the gangplank.

And then the men of the *Warwolf* came swaggering off the ship like the heroes they were. For had they not faced storms, aye, and hurricanes, and tornadoes too? And had they not fought monsters, yes, doing battle with half a dozen Neversh for the possession of their ship? And had they not drunk five pubs in Narba stone-bone dry, a feat which fifty eminent philosophers and a panel of high-class theologians and over-paid jurists had declared to be nine-tenths impossible? And had they not been to Ling, and deflowered five thousand of the virgins of the place, yes, and pleasured the mothers of those girls as well?

But the heroes of the *Warwolf* failed to meet with the universal applause they deserved, for the crew of the *Walrus* (idle slobs, scabs and fish-fornicators that they were) jeered at them because they had been engaging in honest trade, of all things, which was surely anathema, even if it was for pearls, aye, and dangerous, and highly profitable into the bargain.

'What's lower than a merchant-trader?' cried a crewman from the *Walrus*.

'A coward!' came the reply.

And the fight was on.

In the fracas, Drake went chest to chest with Bucks Cat and sustained three broken ribs, a mild concussion, a black eye and a seven-stitch gash to his left forearm. But he thought it worth it, for he was now well and truly one of the crew.

And, indeed, Drake got a crewman's share of the voyage profits, which Arabin had withheld till then so his men would not booze away the money in Narba. By now, Drake knew that the strange coinage of the Greater Teeth was actually the common currency of Narba, the only port which would trade with them. He also learned that the more sober-minded pirates banked there, and the lucky few who survived to the age of arthritis retired there to drink away their dotage in comparative comfort.

The *Warwolf* would not put to sea again for some time, not least because Jon Arabin would be busy with his harem, which he was having shipped from Gufling. Jon Arabin was ascetic yet devout, and his own religion – the Creed of Anthus – enjoined each man 'to plant a tree for each you cut down, and father a man for each you kill'.

Jon Arabin, having done a lot of killing in his time, was always kept busy when he was at home. Unfortunately, his frantic exertions tended to lower his sperm count below the level at which impregnation was likely. Fortunately for the ease of his conscience, other men helped him out behind his back, and he was now three killings in credit.

Just because they were not at sea did not mean there was no work to do. Jon Arabin was true to his vow to have the *Warwolf* overhauled. So there was sanding, sawing, hammering and whitewashing, and there was a drydock to be pumped out, and then there was singeing and scraping to clean the hull. The garden of weed Drake had first noticed at Ling was torn from the hull in wet reeking clumps, or burnt off along with goose neck barnacles and other rubbish.

And then, since Jon Arabin had decided to experiment with mailletage (that is, covering the timber with nails) there was a blistering amount of hammering to be done.

Crewmen from the *Walrus* dropped by on a regular basis to jeer at the sailors doing this slave work. Jon Arabin had gone into debt after he lost his ship on the shores of Lorp, and was taken prisoner by the most vicious people to be found in all of Argan. He had spent three miserable seasons eating sheep's guts and pigs' eyes before the laborious efforts of some trusted retainers had delivered his ransom. He was now finally out of hock, but still could not afford to buy new ship-working slaves.

Finally, after a crewman from the *Walrus* was found floating face-down in the Inner Sleeve with fifty-seven nails hammered into his head, the teasing stopped.

While all this work was going on, the encysted snake buried deep within Drake's gut quietly allowed its flesh to dissolve. A mob of eggs hatched in the wreckage of its body, and myriad worms began to infiltrate Drake's bloodstream. They embedded themselves in the walls of his duodenum, set up residence in the portal vein, squatted in his liver and crept up to his brain; they housed themselves in his stomach; they invaded his lymphatic system and burrowed into his bones. And multiplied.

Drake became feverish.

For five days he endured high temperatures, rigors and blistering thirst. Arabin's own women took care of him. They soothed him, sang to him, sponged his forehead and fed him crab soup, fish roe, sea slugs, pulped sea anemones and other invalid food.

And then the fever broke.

And Drake felt fine.

He felt better than he had ever felt before in his life – and this was scarcely surprising. For the snake which had eaten its way into his flesh in Ling dated its ancestry back through the millenia to a tailored organism especially designed to complement the other defences of the Plague Sanctuary. The worms which had metastasized throughout his body were fulfilling the designs of an ancient science, normalizing his body functions, enhancing the action of his immune system, detoxifying poisons and killing off disease organisms.

The worms were rapidly finishing off an obscure low-grade viral infection distantly related to glandular fever, the start of a tubercular infection, two exotic venereal diseases which had not yet had time to debilitate their victim, a troublesome amoeba which had recently begun to cause him some intermittent diarrhoea, and a couple of wild and wonderful infections (native to the Greater Teeth) unknown to any standard classification.

So, while Drake had always been comparatively healthy, he now felt really good. So good, in fact, that he had to celebrate his recovery with a drink or three.

He did so – but even after his fifth mug, he felt scarcely more than a tingle.

'What're you selling me?' he demanded. 'Water?'

'You young pups,' said his barman, shaking his head. 'You don't know your limits. But I'll help you find yours.'

And he mixed Drake a Skull Splitter, a popular cocktail consisting of equal measures of vinegar, methylated spirit, absinthe, vodka and apricot wine.

'Drink this!' said the barman.

'Ah!' said Drake, as the poison went burning down his throat. 'That tastes better.'

A warm glow filled his stomach. He waited for a sense of langorous well-being to cosy his soul, for the harsh outlines of the world to soften and the burden of gravity to be at least partially nullified. But nothing so pleasant happened.

Instead, after a few moments, the warm glow was gone, and he was back where he started.

'Look, man,' said Drake, 'I don't know what fancy kind of coloured water that was, but I'm buggered if I'm paying for it.'

'It's strong enough for most folks,' said the barman, aggrieved. 'Why, three of those and Slagger Mulps was legless.'

'Sure, but I'm not a wimp like the Walrus. I'm a drinking man, the real article. So pour me something stronger. If you know how!'

'Aye,' said the barman, sensing a challenge here to his professional reputation. 'I can pour stronger, if that's what you want. But I won't be responsible for the consequences, mind.'

'I'm ready,' said Drake, fiercely. 'Hold back on nothing!'

Upon which the barman opened his bottom locker and pulled out strange vials, tubes, tubs, boxes, casks, jars and bottles, and mixed the most brain-blowing cocktail imaginable. Hemlock went into it, and paint, and tar, lamp-black, weedkiller and plutonium, the ink of a cuttle-

186

fish and the gall of a basilisk, a smidgin of belladonna and the blood of a (reputed) virgin, some powdered cannabis leaf and half a gram of heroin, some white of egg and some fermented fish, ground glass, tobacco ash, chopped-up leopard's whiskers, fine-ground horn of unicorn and two tomatoes, some mandrake, ginseng, tannin and quinine, chopped shark's liver seven days old, some high-grade lacquer and sulphuric acid, with lashings of honey to make the whole brew palatable.

In honour of the occasion, the barman unearthed a very old and ancient tankard made of glass – the only one of its kind on all the Greater Teeth. He poured the cocktail into it, slowly. The thick black liquid sat there, bubbling softly. The barman sprinkled some cinnamon on top and ceremoniously set the offering down in front of Drake.

'Get this dog-defecating fornicator inside you,' said the barman, with unwonted enthusiasm. 'That'll put hairs on your chest!'

Drake picked up the tankard with both hands, looked at it steadily, then sipped it with unaccustomed caution. Then:

'What the hell,' he said.

And drank the rest down as a thirsty man would drink weak ale.

The barman watched expectantly, waiting for him to drop dead, or melt, or explode. Instead, Drake swayed a little. All colour left his face. He coughed once or twice, rather harshly, then spat out a little blood. Then, fairly rapidly, the colour returned to his face, his stance steadied, and he wiped his mouth and said regretfully:

'Well, it's a good drop, to be sure. Almost as good as a blow on the head. But the effect wears off powerful fast. Make me another one.'

But the barman shook his head.

'Boy,' he said, 'if that won't kill you, nothing will. One shot of that, and you should stay drunk till your grandchildren celebrate seventy. It ain't natural to drink that down and still stay speaking, far less standing. Boy, take it from me, and I'm an expert. Someone's worked the Black Arts on you, young man. They've taken away the gift of liquor – and all of liquor's friends.'

This was the opinion of a true professional, a specialist in chemical debauchery. As the words sank in, Drake shuddered. Someone had cursed him! Someone had doomed him to a life of perpetual sobriety!

He found it hard to think of a worse fate, but, after some reflection, imagined one – and hurried off to find a pirate whore to make sure it wasn't so.

14

Name: Sully Datelier Yot.

Birthplace: Stokos.

Occupation: disciple of Gouda Muck, worshipper of the Flame, apostle of Goudanism.

Status: once Muck's apprentice, but now an Instrument for the Practice of the Revealed Disciplines of the Flame.

Description: lank pale stripling barnacled with warts.

Present location: the slave holes of Knock.

It was standard pirate practice to feed competitors drinks while gambling. Drake, doomed to be sober, kept his suffering as secret as he could, and enriched himself.

Choosing games like backgammon and dice chess, where there is a strong element of skill, Drake would gamble, drink, play drunk, raise the stakes, make a drunk's blunders, raise the stakes again – then use a sober man's wit, as if by accident, to find the tactics to sweep the table.

And the things he won! Pearls, diamonds, snuff, gold, jade, silver, a wad of coca leaf, and one-night stands with the wives of twenty different men.

Yet profit is not all, and scarcely compensated Drake for lost pleasures. For now, when raucous drunkards sang and shouted, it was no longer the warm hubbub of friendship which he heard, but the braying stupidity of morons and madmen. Sober, he no longer laughed to see a helpless

189

dipsomaniac resorting to tortured spastic contortions to get a mug to his lips. He no longer fell about with rejoicing laughter when one man vomited over another: instead he was bored. And remote. And cold.

He found himself living his life as though he had just come back from a funeral.

He saw now that the cosy togetherness of drinking sessions was an illusion created by the alcohol. Each drinker was in fact drowning in a separate pool of booze. But Drake, who could no longer drown himself, envied them.

When he was not gambling, Drake would usually quaff an ale or two in company to quench his thirst, then have half a dozen more out of sheer good manners, plus a couple on top of that just to keep up his reputation. The beer made him piss more frequently, and that was it.

Soon, most pirates began to latch on to the fact that young Drake had a harder head than he pretended. But they did not stop gambling with him. No: ego compelled them to sit at table with him, downing the drinks and raising the stakes, to see who would slide under the table first. Drake once or twice consented to lose, and disappear beneath the table.

'See?' said the pirates, each to each. 'He's got his limits just like any other.'

And returned, in force, to test him again the next day.

On occasion, evil men spiked Drake's drinks with drugs and poisons. Sometimes he felt slightly dizzy, and once, having swallowed enough cyanide to kill a horse, he became positively breathless for thrice three dozen heartbeats. But always the worms within his body brought their complicated chemistry into play, and the ancient genius of the genetic engineering of a lost and forgotten civilization preserved his flesh from yet another toxic onslaught.

Drake could no longer fuddle his wits with alcohol, or die from poison, or vanish into the world of drug-dream hallucinations. And the disease which could kill him had yet to be built. Sex still had its consolations, but these, of course, were momentary. The beauty of drunkenness is

190

that it can last a lifetime – which, in the case of the Orfus'
pirates, it often did.

Drake won much money but few friends. Lonely, he
bought companionship in the form of a dog, which he
named King Tor.

The dog is the favourite beast of the Demon, being
undiscriminating in its appetites, and dirty, and loud, and
ugly, and the habitat of vermin, and not very bright.
Drake loved dogs. He bought King Tor a spiked collar,
sharpening the spikes until they glittered. He decided to
train this new companion to kill rats and fight alongside
him when the Warwolf's heroes rumbled with the men of
the *Walrus*.

As a sober man gambling with drunks, Drake was now
so prosperous he was getting into money-lending and
agiotage. Stokos was, without doubt, the best place in the
world to live – but the Teeth were the place to get rich.

Drake began nurturing dreams of enhancing his
earnings by setting up his own branch of the temple of
Hagon. Surely worship of the bloodlord Hagon was precisely the right religion for the Greater Teeth. Yes, and he
should practise being a priest right here and now, since he
fully intended to buy into the priesthood on his return to
Stokos. That was only natural, seeing as how he was so
devout.

With establishing a temple in mind, Drake attended the
Slaving Day Sales in the middle of winter, intending to buy
the first of his women. But there was nothing worth
having, if one did not like fat – and Drake didn't. What
he did find was a familiar face, Sully Datelier Yot, in
chains.

'Why, Sully Yot!' said Drake cheerfully. 'What brings
you to the fair islands Teeth Major? A little far from the
forge, aren't you?'

Yot made no reply, but sat there snivelling. Something – fear, perhaps, or maybe a virus, or possibly just
the cold of the midwinter island air – had set his nose to
running.

'Why so quiet?' asked Drake. 'Cat got your tongue? If not, I've got a dog that's eager to have it.'

And Drake stroked Yot's cheek softly. Yot pulled away. But he didn't go far, since he was roped to a floor-shackle.

'Darling!' said Drake. 'Why so cold? When we last met, at 'Marphos, you were so eager to embrace me. Yes. You had a knife in your hand at the time, unless I misremember.'

He remembered perfectly. When he had fled from Stokos, Yot had pursued him to Androlmarphos, and had made a determined effort to kill him.

'Do you want to buy him?' asked a voice.

Drake turned. His interlocutor proved to be Simp Fiche, one of the crewmen from the *Walrus*.

'Are you selling this . . . this thing?' asked Drake idly, not really caring too much one way or the other.

'I bought it myself just today,' said Fiche.

'What for?' asked Drake. 'It's not good for much.'

'I bought it to torture to death,' said Simp Fiche, giving an honest answer; he was bored, and needed some cheap and harmless occupation to while away the rest of the day.

'Why, that shows good judgment,' said Drake genially. 'I'd like to torture him myself. Would you sell me a piece of the action?'

'No,' said Fiche, who was an inveterate gambler. 'But I'll wager with him if you like. Dice-chess, the best of three games. My meat against . . . shall we say a pearl or three?'

'Bloody oath no!' said Drake. 'I don't risk jewels to buy scum. Your meat versus my left boot – which I'll fill with liquor if you win.'

'How about meat versus dog?' said Fiche, who had seen King Tor and liked the look of him.

'No!' said Drake sharply. 'My final offer – I'll wager with both boots, the left full of ale, the right full of mead.'

'Done,' said Simp Fiche, seeing these were the best odds he was going to get offered.

And they sat down to gamble.

Now the game of chess is, of course, very old and very solemn, its intricacies sufficient to tax the highest of intellects. But when the dice get rolling, freeing each player to make (sometimes) as many as a dozen moves at once, then most of its niceties vanish. The stately clash of armies degenerates into something more like a free-for-all brawl, a gutter fight with flails, whips and hatchets.

Drake and Simp Fiche played ferociously. They rolled the dice and scrambled their pieces over the board, whooped with delight or cried out with anguish, punched themselves in the head as punishment for gross stupidity, jabbed gloating fingers at each other's misfortune, and overall comported themselves more like cheap drunks in a casino than solemn chess players.

Men gathered to watch as the titans did battle. Their warriors hacked and slaughtered. Their Neversh clashed in the skies, bringing death and disaster. Battering rams converged to crumble castles. Wizards raged, and, raging, fell. In less time than it takes ordinary chess players to make their first three moves, these dice-chess players had swept nearly everything from the board but the hellbanes – which are, as every player knows, beyond capture.

And Simp Fiche had won the first game.

Drake drew the second but won the third – so the best of three left them even.

'Flip a coin, then,' said Simp Fiche, who was all played out and a little bit weary.

'Fine,' said Drake.

And took from his pocket one of the coins he had gained through agiotage: a bronze bisque from the Rice Empire, with the disc of the sun gracing its face and the crescent of the moon riding its reverse.

'Sun or moon?' asked Drake.

'Moon,' said Simp Fiche, who had a touch of vampire in his ancestry, and had never liked the sun.

Drake tossed the coin to Yot.

'Flip it for us, boy,' said Drake. Then, as Yot sat limp

and snivelling: 'Flip it! Or we'll gouge your eyes out here and now!'

With the greatest reluctance, Yot's fingers crabbed their way to the coin. He took it into his shivering hand and gave it a little flip. It fell with the sun uppermost.

'Fair enough,' said Simp Fiche gravely, and got to his feet and wandered off as the spectators began to disperse.

Fiche had already decided that any stray cat he could catch would probably give him as much sport as Yot would have done.

'Let's go home, darling,' said Drake.

And releasing Yot from the floor shackle, led him away by the rope round his neck. A few pirates made jokes about mutilations. A strong smell of dung began to permeate the air; the pirates laughed outrageously.

Shortly, Drake showed Yot into his cave.

'Sit down there,' said Drake, 'while I sharpen some torturing knives.'

Yot sat meekly, without attempting to jump him. Drake was disappointed. He wanted a desperate fight, yes, and the pleasure of wrecking Yot in combat before killing him. But Yot had no more spirit than a dead fish.

Whistling tunelessly, Drake began to sharpen his favourite knives.

'Drake,' said Yot, in a pale voice, 'I can . . . I can be of use to you.'

'Can you now?' said Drake. 'I don't really think so. I've got more taste than to want to bugger you. And I'd never let you suck anything you might just possibly bite off. But I can use you for fish bait – if the fish aren't too fussy tomorrow. And that's about all that you're good for.'

'Drake, I can – I can tell you things.'

'Tell me things? Like what? Like the precise and exact taste of Gouda Muck's arsehole?'

'Drake . . . things about home. You know. Cam. Your uncle. Your parents. Drake, your brother Heth.'

'Yes, and how hot the sun was, and how cold the rain,' said Drake, pretending news of Heth meant nothing to him.

194

But Yot knew better.

'Drake, I saw Heth just before I left Stokos last, and that was recent. He was come to Cam to marry.'

Drake gave no verbal acknowledgment of interest, but the intensity went out of his knife-sharpening. Stokos! Cam! His uncle! His parents! Heth!

'Your uncle paid for the marriage. Yes, that's why it was in Cam.'

Drake pretended not to hear, but his sharpening strokes got slower and slower, and little tears pricked his eyes. It had been so long since he saw the Home Island last, so long since he wandered its streets of forge-hammering and coal dust.

'Tell me then,' said Drake at last, emotion beginning to choke his voice. 'Tell me about all of it.'

So Yot began to talk, and fear gave him eloquence. The words poured out of him, and what he didn't know he invented.

Before he had gone too far, Drake was offering him some ale to moisten his throat. Then, after a few tales more, he insisted that Yot must eat, yes, and change into fresh sealskins which Drake would lend him. And when at last Yot had talked himself out, Drake sat rocking on his heels for a while, stroking King Tor with an absent-minded hand and brooding.

'Well now,' said Drake, 'that was worth hearing and all. Come – there's a banquet tonight to mark the end of Slaving Day. It's a good do, or so I've heard. Will you come with me? We'll get some real food and good drink with it, then talk some more.'

'If you don't mind,' said Yot, still in that same pale voice, 'I'd rather rest a bit if I may.'

'For sure,' said Drake, content, and glutted with nostalgia. 'You can do what you want. We'll be together plenty in the future, as we make you into a pirate.'

'I'm not sure I've really got what it takes to be a pirate,' said Yot.

'Don't run yourself down,' said Drake. 'Be brave! Be

strong! Be confident! Come now – rest, and we'll talk again tomorrow.'

So Drake took himself off to the banquet, alone, and a great treat it was. Musicians from the kingdom of Sung played for them, so they ate to the accompaniment of the skirl of the skavamareen, and the uproar of krymbol and kloo. Naked bodies danced for their delight, and performed charades of love by flaring torchlight. There was food by the table-load, with plenty of lobster, crab, gaplax and crayfish. It was a well-organized affair, with an unending supply of good drink, and plenty of buckets to vomit into.

Drake indulged himself, drinking cold rice wine and warm brown beer. It bolstered his ego to know the others were admiring him as he quaffed down quantities of alcohol which would have killed an ordinary man, and, what's more, would have embalmed the corpse into the bargain.

The banquet finally reached the rowdy stage, with knife-throwing and wrist-wrestling, a brawl, and some extra-special entertainment laid on by Jon Arabin, who whipped one of his wives raw in public, having caught her out in adultery.

Drake left shortly afterwards, staggering markedly as he quit the banquet, so his future gambling partners would register the fact that he could indeed get drunk like other mortals. Actually, he was not even slightly tipsy – but, by the time he reached his home cave, he was staggering a little for real, out of sheer fatigue.

A low-burning whale oil lamp showed Drake that Yot was curled up in a corner. A number of things in the cave had been shifted – his bean bag, rocking chair, laundry basket, sea-chest, water cask, oil barrel, fishing tackle, harpoon rack and wardrobe. Had Yot been searching the cave? Or had some villain taken advantage of the banquet, and of Yot's deep sleep (or complaisant terror) to rummage the cave in search of Drake's fabled gambling treasure?

Drake was too tired to care either way. He knew Yot

was no danger to him, for Drake was now the nearest thing to a friend that Yot had in all the Greater Teeth. And as for the gambling treasure – why, that was safely hidden in five separate places, and even at low tide the shallowest of those places demanded a three-fathom dive.

'We'll have to teach you to be a guard dog as well,' said Drake to King Tor, scratching that dignitary behind the ears. 'Or maybe I should start keeping geese.'

And, with that, he laid himself down on his pallet and pulled the blankets over himself, without bothering to undress or take off his boots. King Tor nosed his way under the blankets. Drake took the dog into his arms, and they cuddled together in an indiscriminate heap, sharing each other's fleas.

Very late at night, as Drake and dog lay snoring, Sully Datelier Yot roused his flesh to wakefulness and got to his feet. He extracted a shark-killing knife from the tangle of Drake's fishing tackle, raised the blade to his lips and kissed it. Then, shaking with fear but unshakable in his resolve, he bent over his sleeping enemy and struck with all his force.

The knife went home.

'Die, Demon-spawn!' screamed Yot.

And struck again, even as Drake heaved up from the bed. Drake rolled away, pulling a blanket with him. He swore viciously and whipped the blanket at Yot's knifehand. As wool entangled steel, Drake closed the distance.

They grappled, all knees, elbows and panting bones. Drake got a stranglehold. With hands that were wet with blood, he choked his enemy, squeezing his fingers deep and hard to the windpipe.

Once sure that Yot was dead, Drake threw the body outside, and hurled the bloody dog-corpse after it.

'Sleep with the man you murdered!' shouted Drake at the corpse. 'It's your one chance to sleep with your betters!'

Then stalked around his cave, kicking things until he

had exhausted his anger. Then started to shake, as the shock of his brush with death set in. Then began to cry, first for poor King Tor, and then for his own exiled condition, and then simply because he was over-tired and heavily stressed.

Then he did the sensible thing, which his mother would have recommended had she been there, and went back to sleep for the rest of the night. Only his mother would have insisted that he take his boots off first.

When morning came, Drake was disgusted to find that Yot was still alive. He had thick black bruises on his throat, true, but could still walk and talk and breathe, eat and drink – he was, in short, a living demonstration of the difficulties attendant on killing a properly constructed human being.

Abject in fear, Yot knelt at Drake's feet, snivelling once more.

'Give me one good reason why I shouldn't kill you,' roared Drake. 'Just one!'

'I had to kill you,' sobbed Yot. 'I had to. I didn't want to, but it was my duty. I like you, Drake, honestly, but you're – you're a son of the Demon.'

'By the oath I am!' said Drake. 'And proud of it! That's the way my father raised me, and that's how he'd have me be!'

'No, not that kind of son. A true son. Flesh of the Demon's flesh. Spawn of his spawn. He came from the halls of hell to take your mother by night.'

Drake considered this intriguing notion for a few moments.

'I've never heard such nonsense in all my life,' said Drake. 'But supposing it was true, I'd take it as a compliment. To me, for my parentage. To my mother, for attracting such high-born attention. And to my childhood's father, for winning a woman the Demon himself would want.'

'But it means you're evil, don't you see? The Demon's the enemy of the Flame. That's why Gouda Muck sent us.'

198

'Sent you?'

'Yes. Fifty of us. All over the world. Looking for you. To – to – well . . .'

'To kill me?' asked Drake.

'Well, yes.'

At first Drake was incredulous. Then he remembered his last visit to Narba. Then an old face from Stokos, a past neighbour of Gouda Muck, had made a diligent attempt to knife Drake properly.

'Fifty looking for me!' said Drake. 'How many worshippers has the Flame claimed, then?'

'Well, half of Stokos, by now,' said Yot. 'The king himself has converted. There's talk of outlawing the temple.'

Drake felt as though he had been punched in the stomach. All the wind was quite taken out of him. But once he had got over the shock he started to get angry.

'Now look here,' said Drake. 'This nonsense has to end, and here, and now. Recant! Renounce the Flame. Look, there's fire – the oil-lamp's wick. Piss on it, Yot, piss on it now, or I'll kill you!'

But Yot would not. He wept with fear, he begged, he pleaded, but even in the face of death he would not defile the Flame.

'And you still think you have to kill me?' said Drake.

'I must! I must!' wept Yot.

Drake, seething with anger, roped Yot properly and put him on the market. Yot so disgusted him that Drake didn't want to be associated any further – not even for the time it would take to torture his captive to death.

'Ready meat waiting!' shouted Drake. 'Best stuff for fish bait, torture, raping!'

But interest was slack. Slaving Day had glutted most people's tastes, and the Bacchanal of the banquet had left just about the entire pirate population of Knock with a hangover.

Drake grew hoarse with shouting. He cooled his throat with an ale, then thought to ask:

199

'You say King Tor has converted to – to—'

'To the Faith,' said Yot. 'To Goudanism.'

'Then does Tor believe that I'm—'

'Tor is a true believer!' said Yot. His voice was shrill with fear and hate. 'He knows you're the son of the Demon. He's ordered that you be handed over to Gouda Muck if you ever set foot on Stokos.'

'Then what?'

'Then our all-sacred Muck will have you skinned alive. That's just to start with! Oh, you'll wish you were dead! You'll scream for the privilege of dying! But Muck won't let you go that easily. He'll make you suffer.'

Drake felt all broken-up inside. This was really the end! He could never go home. Goodbye to his dreams of a place in the priesthood! Goodbye to his hopes for marriage to Tor's daughter and a claim to the throne of Stokos! Goodbye – ay yes, farewell forever! – to the high-breasted Zanya Kliedervaust.

'This is bad news, truly,' said Drake. 'I . . . I thought to go back to Stokos someday. Not least to see my lady.'

'And who's that?' said Yot.

'You wouldn't know her,' said Drake. 'She was red of skin and red of hair. She was aged about twenty or so. Tall, yes, mayhap a head higher than me. Breasts beautiful, high-riding like buoyant boats.'

'Are you talking about Zanya?' said Yot. 'Zanya Kliedervaust?'

'You know her!'

'Why, of course,' said Yot. 'She's one of Muck's favourite disciples.'

'Then she's – she's with Muck?'

'No,' said Yot. 'She's left Stokos entirely. Gone to do missionary work. To convert the world to Goudanism!'

'Where has she gone?' said Drake.

'Why should I tell you?' said Yot. 'You're the Demon-son! And a nasty stunted ugly runt!'

And Yot spat in Drake's face.

200

Whereupon Drake grabbed him, intending to cut his throat on the spot.

'What's this?' said a jovial voice. 'Business or pleasure?'

Drake relaxed his grip on Yot. He looked around and saw that a rough-smelling pirate had happened along, an evil brute with a most unlovely bearded face, with pouches under bloodshot eyes, with lice scattered like dandruff through greasy locks, and with splashes of black blood from his most recent murder still splattered across his clothes.

It was, of course, Andranovory.

'I came here intending to sell this – this thing,' said Drake. 'But it seems nobody wants to buy such rubbish. So I've decided to cut its throat to get rid of it. Would you hold it still? It's wriggling. Aye! And trying to bite!'

'Hold still!' barked Andranovory.

And Yot ceased his struggles immediately.

'Why, An'vory, man,' said Drake, in reluctant admiration, 'You've sure got a way with your voice.'

Atsimo Andranovory made no immediate reply, but studied Yot carefully.

'You meant to sell this?' he said, after a pause, idling a finger across Yot's neck while the apostle of the Flame cringed and whimpered. 'For how much?'

'To you, he's free,' said Drake, who could think of no worse fate for Yot than sale to Andranovory.

Andranovory laughed.

'Done,' said Andranovory, and cut Yot's bonds.

Then tossed the boy a knife.

Startled, Yot caught it by the hilt, and stood there looking most uncertain.

'You're my shipmate now,' said Andranovory. 'My bloodbrother true. My enemy's enemy is good enough for me. Come, man – I'll take you to meet our captain. Aye. The Walrus – Slagger Mulps himself. He'll be heartened by the sight of a fine young fellow like you.'

201

'How about a drink first?' said Yot, feeling he needed something to steady his nerves.

'Why, sure – that's an excellent idea,' said Andranovory.

Then Andranovory laughed again at the outrage on Drake's face, and went swaggering off to the nearest beer stand to celebrate his victory.

15

Name: Menator.

Birthplace: by the side of the Salt Road some seven leagues north of the Castle of Controlling Power.

Occupation: adventurer (and, previously, Galish merchant, horse thief, outlaw, and joint ruler of the kingdom of Talajar).

Status: warlord.

Description: a man as bald as Jon Arabin, nose broken, blue rose tattooed on left cheek.

Drake was sure Slagger Mulps would be too smart to want anything to do with a useless piece of wart-faced filth like Sully Yot. But, to Drake's disgust, Yot was aboard the *Walrus* when it set off on a raiding expedition the very next day.

He won't last, though. No. The first time he has to fight it out for real, blade against blade, he'll run screaming. Aye. This first voyage should finish him for piracy.

However, three days later the *Walrus* returned after a bloodless victory. Off the coast of Chorst, Slagger Mulps and his men had caught a trading ship. Rather than stand and fight, the crew of their quarry had set fire to their vessel and had then abandoned ship, making for the nearby shore.

Every man from the *Walrus* swore they had rescued treasure from the burning ship. As they did no extra boozing, gambling or whoring, Drake guessed they were bluffing – but he had no way to prove it.

After a two-day rest, the *Walrus* set sail again.

One more chance for Yot to get himself killed, then.

But Drake could not help envying Yot. He was sick and tired of the Teeth, bored with fishing, sealing, and the routines of gambling. He found himself longing to be at sea again. Which was perverse, surely, for the sea was big and wet, cold and unfriendly, daunting and merciless.

But there's companionship there. Aye. The ship's life's one life shared. Yes.

How long would it be before Jon Arabin took them to sea again?

Ten days after midwinter's day in Khmar 18 – that is, soon after Drake learnt of his place in the demonology of Goudanism – Jon Arabin called a crew-conference.

A number of Arabin's wives were pregnant, so he could face the prospect of more murder with equanimity. With the *Warwolf* properly overhauled, he was ready to try an audacious plan formulated during his long and bitter captivity in Lorp: to raid Cam, in Stokos, and sack the Orsay Bank.

'It's far,' complained the faint-hearted. 'And it's winter.'

'For sure it's far,' said Arabin. 'But Narba is further, let alone Ling. You've all at least been to Narba. As to the season, why, winter means they won't be expecting us. Anyway, it'll be warm enough down in Stokos.'

Drake was enlisted to draw maps of Cam, and help model the harbour for the inspection of Arabin's officers.

'We'll come as a merchant ship,' said Arabin. 'We'll fly the flag of Chi'ash-lan. We'll have silk on our backs, sheep on the deck, and a bare-breasted woman as figure-head. By night we'll raid the bank. Quick, aye, in and out. Meanwhile, our fire parties set flames amidst the city. Thus chaos while we retreat.'

It was a cunning plan, yet simple. And extremely

dangerous – which was part of the reason why Drake had mixed feelings about the operation.

Previously, a voyage to Cam would have meant an ideal opportunity to escape. But flight to Stokos was now the last thing on his mind. Gouda Muck would have him skinned alive then burnt at the stake – or worse.

He would love to see Stokos again, if only for a day. But should he raid his own people? Even if madness had made them flame worshippers, they were still the true blood of Stokos, the meanest wight amongst them worth more than any ten uitlanders.

'Troubled?' said Arabin, sensing his confusion. 'Worries about killing your own, is it? Well, I'll give you a choice on this venture. Will you come, or not?'

'I'll think about it,' said Drake.

And think he did.

The *Walrus* returned to Knock after a successful raid on the docks of Runcorn. This time, Slagger Mulps and his men proved their success by spending gold like water. Sully Yot made a special point of flaunting his wealth in Drake's presence, while boasting of his daring. Drake, violently jealous, thought Arabin's plans might be worth pursuing if only to win triumph equal to Yot's.

But, while Drake was still weighing the pros and cons, all plans for the raid were interrupted by the unheralded arrival of a foreign adventurer. Menator, he was called: and he came to the Teeth with five ships, three hundred men, and half his own weight in gold.

Almost immediately, he gained a reputation for ambition. Then came public proposals so brash and rash they made Arabin's outrageous plans seem the ultimate in conservative caution. Word went out to all the islands of the Greaters, and the pirates began to gather in to Knock.

The pirates met in general assembly to pass judgment on Menator. Crowding a huge cavern lit by light filtering down twenty air shafts, and by half a hundred smoking torches, they gave off a communal stench which could have seriously competed with a legion of dead seals or any army of dung-soaked dogs.

Drake, in the middle of this mob, was surprised at what a crowd they made.

Menator spoke eloquently in the Galish Trading Tongue. He was, after all, the only person present who had Galish as his native tongue, for all that it was their lingua franca.

He wished to unite them for war and for conquest. To bring Stokos under their yoke. To seize the Lesser Teeth. To build an army. And then to start empire-building in earnest.

Some men jeered, and Drake was one of them. Menator became angry.

'The Greater Teeth could control all the west of Argan,' said Menator. 'If only you could see it. But no. Here you sit, on your walrus-infested rocks—'

This provoked mirth in certain quarters, scowls in others. Menator, puzzled by this reaction, looked around carefully then continued:

'You sit on your rocks, fighting for fish with sharks and skua gulls, when you could rule in palaces of silk and gold, with hot wet women tight between your legs. All it takes is will. An alliance of will. Believe me.'

Promises of paradise will always find buyers, and Menator's speech met with an enthusiastic reception.

'So,' said Menator, thinking this was all going very nicely, 'is it agreed?'

'Hang about!' shouted several voices. 'We haven't heard the other side, yet,'

The pirates wanted a proper debate. They believed strongly in democracy: meaning, among other things, a full and frank discussion of issues of public importance. Menator, who had never before encountered such plebian lower-class attitudes (he came from the better class of Galish merchant, and had mixed with the right kind of people for most of his life) was shocked.

Still, there was nothing he could do about it.

First speaker for the negative was Slagger Mulps, who provoked applause just by rising to his feet. Since he was so very tall, he could be seen by almost everyone. And his shock of green hair identified him even in that poor light. His supporters started to chant in unison:

'Walrus! Walrus! Walrus!'

Raising one of his double-thumbed fists on high to acknowledge this applause, Slagger Mulps swaggered to the podium (a heap of ale casks stood on their ends) and Menator was forced to yield it to him. The din slowly died down.

Drake, who had brought along some dead fish, threw one. But missed Slagger Mulps – and hit Menator slap-bang in the face. There was a roar of applause. Some of Menator's men drew weapons – but their leader brought them to order with a few curt words.

'Boys,' said Slagger Mulps, with a grin. 'At least you can say this for the Teeth – we've got plenty of fish to spare.'

(General applause. From Menator, a scowl.)

'And,' continued Slagger Mulps, 'if the Teeth are infested with Walrus, what's wrong with that?'

(Mixed laughter, cheers, boos. Several dead fish were thrown, but missed.)

'These rocks have got a lot going for them,' said Mulps. 'For a start, they're ours. Nobody else wants them. But once we go seeking hegemony over foreign lands, well, then we're into some really heavy competition.'

(More noise from the audience. A loud-voiced obscene joke about 'herd riding', which was the literal translation of the Galish Mulps had used to say 'hegemony'.)

'Of course,' said Mulps, 'we could do it if we really wanted to. World conquest would be easy compared to sharing these islands with the Warwolf.'

(Uproar. A walrus head was suddenly raised on a battle-spear in the middle of the crowd. Scuffles broke out, continuing until the head had been hauled down and kicked to pieces, thus ceasing to become an object of

207

contention. Slagger Mulps, unperturbed, continued.)

'But, boys, why try enslave the world? We all know how useless slaves are. Won't work unless kicked, and then so tough in the arse you'll as like break your toes as bruise them. Free men work best, boys, as do they now – loading the finest silks and the silkiest women on ships which by the morrow, mark my words, will be idling straight toward our jaws.

'Boys, let's think real. A conquered city sounds sweet, but like as not we'd burn it down the first time we set out to party. Here's a cheer for the Teeth! The walls are solid. They don't rot, they don't burn, or crack if you smash a skull against them. Why, on rock like this, you could even break up the pig bones which skull-plate the Warwolf!'

(Renewed uproar, continuing until the Walrus, satisfied with his eloquence, bowed gracefully and yielded the podium to the next speaker.)

The next speaker was Atsimo Andranovory. The great big barrel-chested black-bearded brute confronted the audience in silence, swaying slightly. Drake, gazing on him with hatred, bitterly regretted the fact that he had no more fish left to throw. Suddenly, Andranovory gave a prodigious belch. Someone clapped. Someone cheered. Then Andranovory vomited – then collapsed. The whole gathering applauded this performance.

As the drunken sot was carried away, Jon Arabin took the stage.

'Ladies and gentlemen,' said Arabin, looking around. 'I mean, of course, the gentlemen of the *Warwolf* and the ladies of the *Walrus*, and—'

(Furious shouting. Raucous cheers. Prolonged fish-throwing, most of it, again, inaccurate.)

'Ladies and gentlemen – may I speak? – thank you! – much as it grieves me to agree with Slagger Mulps, he's given us a lot of common sense. He got it from the fish guts his mother weaned him on. And, in any case, as the saying goes, even a blind walrus knows a dog from a virgin's gracehole.'

(Pandemonium. An outbreak of predictable behaviour. Consequences of such behaviour, some of them blood-stained. Peace restored, mainly through use of cudgels.)

'Strange it is for Warwolf to sing in harmony with Walrus,' said Arabin. 'But on this occasion, I can do nothing else. We've heard easy talk of conquest. Aye. Conquest of Stokos. But who here knows the place as more than a name? I tell you this – I do. For one of my crewmen is Drake Douay, a native of the place. A strong fellow, not lightly scared.'

Hearing such praise, Drake was filled with a glow of pride. Ah, Jon Arabin! He knew quality when he saw it!

'With Drake Douay,' said Jon Arabin, 'I've lately been planning a raid on Stokos, so I know the strengths of the place well. They've people by the tens of thousands. They make weapons for the world, so they won't be short of steel if it comes to a fight. Worse, they've a breed of ogres on that island.

'Twice the height of men they stand – aye, as tall as Whale Mike. Where are you, Mike? Ah, there he is – over there, in the corner. But Mike, he's slim compared to these ogres, for they're built near as wide as they stand tall. How can humans fight against such?

'If you ask me, this man Menator's got no true plans for conquest. Instead, he hopes to wish us away to Stokos, so we all get killed in senseless battles. Then he can rule the Teeth, while we rot in hell, getting laughed at by our ancestors. But even if we did win Stokos, what good would that do us? Not much, say I.'

Then Arabin outlined the case against empire, speaking fluently, cogently, and with much gutter-wit (compared to which, what had gone before was mild).

Arabin truly doubted that Stokos could be conquered by the Teeth. He also knew that any quest for empire would involve an enormous amount of killing. He would have to breed furiously to pay off his death-debt. Meaning more expense, and more squalling daughters cluttering his caves (why no sons?). And – he was starting to feel his age,

209

perhaps – he just did not think he could stand it.

After Arabin, many minor luminaries spoke (including Bluewater Draven, captain of the good ship Tusk). Some were for, but most were against. The pirates of the Teeth were, for the most part, too idle, lazy, cowardly, shiftless and gutless to make good imperialists.

Finally, after some discussion – which left seven pirates dead – the proposal for empire was lost.

Menator, finding the pirates would not support his drive for empire, announced that he would satisfy his ambitions without pirate help. He planned to begin by conquering the Lessers.

However, since it was winter, and the weather was bad, it was scarcely the time to hazard the dangerous waters of the Lessers. Menator therefore exercised his men by raiding the coasts of Dybra and Chorst, carrying off skinny sheep and half-starved goats.

Meanwhile, Jon Arabin resumed planning for a raid on Stokos.

In some ways, Drake regretted the fact that Menator had failed to win pirate support for his dreams of conquest. Their chances of success were small, but . . . what was the alternative?

The alternative was a lifetime of episodic raiding, long interludes of monotony, the shiftless company of drunken cronies, the repetitive comedy of the gambling tables . . .

Which was not enough.

For Drake wanted to make something of himself.

All through the years of his early youth he had imagined himself becoming, eventually, a swordsmith – a respected master craftsman whom the best men on Stokos would admire. When Muck's madness had ruined that dream, he had cherished ambitions of marrying into the royal family, or becoming a priest of the temple of Hagon. Now . . .

Now he was tempted to put his sword at Menator's service. Their chances were slim, yet . . .

We have but one life. If we don't get what we want from it, then what's the point of having it? Better slim odds for success than certain odds for defeat.

To stay a pirate was to be defeated. There was no job on the Teeth. No pride. No trust. Yet . . .

I'm scared, and that's the truth. This Menator's at least half mad. And . . . to leave Jon Arabin . . . why, that'd be a wrench, for sure . . .

Drake brooded about it while the winter rains and the winter seas launched onslaught after onslaught on the beleaguered desolations of the Teeth.

Thirty days after midwinter, Drake was practising a one-man kata in the privacy of his home cave when he was interrupted by Harly Burpskin.

'What is it?' said Drake. 'Does Arabin wish to see me?'

'Nay, man,' said Burpskin. 'It's strangers.'

'Strangers?'

'They're sitting in the Inner Sleeve.'

'Pray, how sit they there when the water's a full three fathoms deep?'

'They're not swimming, man,' said Burpskin. 'They're on a ship.'

'What ship?' said Drake.

'The *Tarik*.'

'I know it not,' said Drake. 'Where has it come from?'

'From Stokos.'

'Stokos!'

'Aye. With some mighty strange people aboard. Stranger still, when I mentioned we owned a Stokos boy, they proved to know you.'

Drake needed to hear no more, but hastened to the Inner Sleeve. Once he left the protection of the tunnel system, he found the day cold, moist and grey. Rain was falling from a coal-scuttle sky, dimpling the waters of the Inner Sleeve where floated helpless turds, drowned kittens, the corpse of a rat and several ships. One of the ships was a dingy thing painted in colours of earth and clay. A tarpaulin was stretched above her open hold.

'That's the *Tarik*,' said Burpskin. 'Go to the hold, man. You'll find a friend there.'

'A friend?'

'Aye,' said Burpskin, stepping back into the shelter of a tunnel.

'Aren't you coming?' said Drake.

'I've seen your friend once. That's enough for me.'

Drake looked dubiously at the Tarik. Was this a trap? Only one way to find out . . .

He walked through the rain, stepped onto the greasy gangplank, skidded, and almost fell. As he gained the deck, his heart was scrambling; he was panting with excitement. He strode toward the open hold.

Stout green bamboos held up a ragged brown tarpaulin in which an enormous weight of rainwater had pooled; the bamboos were bending beneath the load. Cautiously, quiet as a cockroach gliding through shadows under the threat of a hunting hammer, Drake eased himself in under the shelter of the tarpaulin and peered into the hold.

There in shivering gloom a great, sad creature sat on a pile of mouldy sacking. The creature was almost as wide as it was tall. Its shaggy black hair trailed down around the huge flaps of its ears. Its blue eyes, set amidst grey skin, looked tired and defeated. Light gleamed faintly on its downward-jutting tusks. It was King Tor.

Yes, Tor – who, by Sully Yot's account, had converted to this weird religion founded by Gouda Muck. Adherents of that faith believed Drake Douay to be the son of Hagon, the incarnation of absolute evil. So prudence dictated a retreat.

Yet Muck's but a mouth talking. And haven't I got a mouth myself? Aye. I'll argue it out with the king. I'll talk him sweet to sense – or die trying.

'My lord . . .'

Tor looked up. He saw Drake. His nostrils flared. He came to his feet with a roar. As his head hit the tarpaulin, he thrust up with his arms. The water pooled in the tarpaulin was flung skywards. As it cascaded onto the deck, Tor roared, then shouted:

'Dreldragon! It's Dreldragon! Dreldragon Drakedon Douay!'

At his shout, men came bursting out of the cabins in the poop of the ship, and came racing down the wet, greasy deck, skidding and sliding as they came.

Drake fled.

He sprinted over the water-wet deck, slipped, fell, bruised his shin, gained his feet – and ran straight into the arms of a tall broad-chested man.

Drake struggled. He tried to kick, claw, scratch, bite, butt, spit, punch and swear. But even swearing was nigh impossible with his enemy holding him so tight.

'Ease up, man,' said his captor, with something of a laugh. 'It's me.'

Me? By the voice, 'me' was Heth.

Drake eased up, and looked at the face of the tall, well-built man (his hair as blond as Drake's) who was holding him now like a lover. It was indeed his brother Heth.

'Heth,' said Drake. 'Oh, Heth . . .'

And began to weep with relief.

As the two brothers embraced, the rest of Tor's men gathered round. Amongst them was Levil Norkin, Drake's boyhood friend. And Oleg Douay, his uncle – the finest swordsmith on Stokos.

'Hey!' yelled King Tor, peering out of the hold. 'Come in out of the rain. Come down here – I don't want my finest fighting men dying of pernicious anaemia.'

On Stokos, it was a firmly-held belief that prolonged exposure to cold rain caused anaemia. Drake had endured so much bad weather on his adventures that he doubted it could be as destructive as Stokos thought – yet he willingly got himself out of the rain.

In long conversations with Heth, Tor and others, Drake learned of the disaster which had befallen Stokos.

After Tor had converted to Goudanism, the temple of

213

Hagon had been destroyed. Goudanism had been made compulsory.

'It had its advantages,' said Tor. 'With the temple destroyed, the people spent little on whores and gambling. That made it much easier to collect taxes.'

'Aagh,' said Drake, and spat. 'Taxes!'

'Government costs money,' said Tor, 'and there's no way around it. Why, building roads alone – that's a heavy job for taxes.'

'Roads!' said Drake, with contempt, thinking he'd find much better ways to spend money if he were king.

'Roads,' said Tor, 'are necessary, look at it how you will. And they don't build themselves. Anyway – quite apart from the matter of money, the priests of Hagon had been taking more and more power for themselves. So I was glad to see them broken.'

'And then?' said Drake.

'Then Gouda Muck spoke madness. He said that only those born pure in flesh had rights to life. He set down codes for eyes, teeth, limbs, hands, hair and height. He declared all those not matched to his codes were evil.'

'And,' said Drake, 'you . . .?'

'I was too tall to start with,' said Tor. 'His codes were built for humans. But I'm an ogre, and proud of it. What's wrong with being an ogre, I ask you?'

'Why, nothing,' said Drake. 'I honour ogres so greatly that I once asked to marry into your family. I'm still good to the offer, man. Where stands your daughter now?'

'My beautiful Hilda,' said Tor, 'is held prisoner on Stokos with her mother.'

And he began to weep. There are few things more lugubrious than an ogre in the depths of despair.

'Never mind,' said Drake. 'We'll rescue her. Aye. A war for Stokos! We'll win. Then chop up Gouda Muck, aye, cut him into seven thousand pieces.'

'With the help of the sea gods,' said Oleg Douay, cheerfully, 'we may well manage to do just that.'

'How stand things on Stokos now?' said Drake.

'After Muck made his codes,' said Heth, slowly, 'some tried to kill Tor. Others fought beside him. We lost.'

'Lost badly?' said Drake.

'Badly enough,' said Heth.

'Who rules then, on Stokos? Does Muck rule?'

'No,' said Heth. 'He's set up Sudder Vemlouf as ruler. Perhaps you've heard of him.'

'Aye, that I have,' said Drake. 'He was Muck's neighbour for year on year. I met him last in Narba, where he tried to kill me. He thinks me the son of Hagon.'

'If you are the son of the Demon,' said King Tor, through tears, 'then I'm with you all the way. Muck talks purity, but what that means is death, murder, blood, killing, the overthrow of rightful rule, the end of law, mad torture, fear, suspicion, and worse.'

'If we struck at Stokos with force,' said Drake, 'how many living there would help us?'

'Many,' said Heth. 'For many favour Muck only since they thought he'd win. If once they thought he'd lose, they'd sing different, that's for certain.'

'But before we can talk of striking,' said Oleg Douay, 'we must have strength to strike with. The gods help those who help themselves, you know.'

'You must,' said Drake, 'meet a man called Menator.'

'Who's he?' said Tor.

'He was once king in a place called Talajar, which is in the Ravlish Lands,' said Drake. 'When he lost his kingdom in war, he fled. He came to the Greaters with five ships, three hundred men and half his own weight in gold. Since then, he's been trying to persuade us pirates to a war of empire.'

'Why talk of yourself as a pirate?' said Tor.

'Why, man, for sake of honesty,' said Drake. 'For that's what I be, right now.'

'No,' said Tor, laying one of his immense hands on Drake's shoulder. 'You are a warlord in the armies of Stokos. You are the betrothed of my daughter, with all that that implies. I name you Lord Dreldragon; I name you heir to the kingdom of Stokos.'

Drake saw Heth grinning at him. Olegy Douay was smiling, obviously pleased. Levil Norkin gave him a clenched-fist salute. Drake felt giddy. Then, unable to help himself, he shouted his triumph to the world, with all the strength and eloquence at his command:

'Wow!'

Menator swiftly came to agreement with King Tor. If Menator supported Tor in the conquest of Stokos, then Tor would give men, gold, weapons and ships to help Menator win an empire. His position bolstered by this agreement, Menator once more sought to win agreement from the pirates.

Drake was now wildly enthusiastic at the prospect of an invasion of Stokos. They would win. He would marry Hilda. And then he would find someone who knew where Zanya Kliedervaust had gone to, and he would send agents forth into the world to hunt her down then drag her back to Stokos to be his pleasure woman.

He was upset to find that, when he lobbied for King Tor, others failed to share his enthusiasm. Jon Arabin was still dead against a war of empire. Drake, who had no inkling of Arabin's religious objections to such a war, said:

'Jon, you must support King Tor!'

'Who are you to tell me what I must and must not do?' said Jon Arabin.

'Jon, it's for your own benefit I'm saying this. Here's a great chance, man! Wealth, fame, power! When I'm king on Stokos, you can be lord of all my seapower.'

'And what makes you think,' said Arabin, 'that I should rejoice at the prospect of serving under a greasy under-sized mannikin who's been for so long my cook's boy?'

Without waiting for a reply to that question, Arabin turned his back on Drake and strode away – leaving Drake feeling cut to the quick.

As the pirates once more gathered in from the islands

for a general assembly on Knock, Drake made further attempts to recruit Arabin to Tor's cause – but was again rebuffed. He saw his chances of power and kingdom slipping away from him. In desperation, he ventured to the cave where Slagger Mulps lived, determined to lobby the Walrus.

'The situation,' explained Drake, 'has changed. It's no longer a few wild pirates seeking invasion of Stokos. No – it's civil war we're planning. Once Tor steps ashore at Cam, half the city will rise to his support. We've no longer ogres to fight against – the ogres are on our side.'

The green-haired pirate chief was suspicious.

'What's in it for me?' said Mulps.

'Survival,' said Drake. 'Muck has strange ideas. If he gets to rule the world, you die.'

'How so?' said Slagger Mulps.

Drake explained Gouda Muck's ideas about what flesh should live and what flesh should die.

'I've got no prejudice myself,' said Drake. 'Why, man, I seek to marry an ogre – and they're as weird as ever was, or ever could be. So it matters not to me that your hair is green, aye, and your eyes as well. But Gouda Muck would have you killed for such.'

Drake by now knew that Slagger Mulps was intensely sensitive about his odd appearance. So he played on that as best he could – but, when the day of the meeting came, Drake was still unsure which way the Walrus would speak and vote.

Once more the pirates crowded into their huge meeting cavern. This time, Drake did not come equipped with dead fish, but with a speech carefully worked up with help from both his brother Heth and his uncle Oleg Douay.

Drake was the first speaker.

He climbed onto the podium and faced the mob of pirates. He breathed their stench, and breathed, too, the fumes of half a thousand pipes – a ship laden with tobacco had recently been captured by the Teeth, and many of the pirates were doing their best to dispose of its cargo.

In that cave, dimly lit by air shafts and torches, Drake recognized scarcely a single face. He was speaking to strangers who, if displeased, might throw things – or tear him apart in the mindless rage which could so easily overthrow the sanity of a crowd.

Drake felt unsteady on his feet. There was a strange taste at the back of his throat – a taste like metal. His mouth was dry. He cleared his throat, then hawked, and spat.

'Aagh,' said Drake.

'Stand up!' yelled a wit.

'Man,' said Drake, 'if the good King Tor was here, I'd stand on his shoulders. Then you'd see me right enough. But Tor can't be here today. Not today. Not any day. And why? Because he's too great-girthed to dare our tunnels. You've seen him, aye. Surely. That's a monster true. Our monster, if we turn our will to Stokos.'

That opening was impromptu. But, while it had not been planned, it had come out smoothly enough. Now for the prepared speech. Drake looked out over the heads of his auditors. His first move was designed to slit Jon Arabin's sails right down the middle. Very well then.

'Boys, some of you know me, some know me not. I'm Drake Douay. Born on Stokos, aye, and there on Stokos raised. When last we met together, boys, all crowded here as close as buggery, you heard the good Jon Arabin speak well of me.

'Friend Arabin, my captain true, he named me as the one man who knows of Stokos as more than a name. I told Arabin well enough of Stokos, aye, and of the ogres. Hence Arabin spoke against a war on Stokos. And rightly so – for who here could chest it out with an ogre?

'But times change. Now the greatest ogre is ours. King Tor, that's him. He'll not fight against us. No. He's ours. He's with us. And so is every other ogre born on Stokos. For Stokos has fallen to the madness of an old old man called Gouda Muck, who hates all ogres and has sworn to kill them out.'

'With reason, perhaps,' yelled an anonymous heckler.

218

'This Gouda Muck has got no reason,' said Drake, 'for he speaks against copulation, aye, against men with women, against men with men, against cats with dogs for all I know. He stands against drinking, too. And rules out gambling. He worships what he calls purity, by which he means the end of joy, starvation of the flesh and all.'

Then Drake proceeded to paint a picture for the pirates. They would land on the coast of Stokos. They would rally the countryside. They would march on Cam. The people would rise against Gouda Muck. Tor would be victorious.

'Then,' said Drake, 'we can break apart the Orsay Bank. That's fabulous wealthy – and Tor, he loves it not. Yes. King Tor has sworn that our reward will be every treasure looted from the bank. That's wealth for all. Wealth almost beyond imagining.'

Drake spoke the truth. Tor had no love for the Orsay Bank, and was ready to sacrifice it to the pirates.

Drake, having said his piece, sat down. Pirates whistled, stamped, shouted, clapped and threw things. A mixed response, in other words.

What now? Will Arabin speak?

Drake knew Arabin would find it difficult to win much credibility if he chose to speak as an expert on Stokos. Drake had indeed slit Arabin's sails – and he knew Arabin would be furious. Someone was coming to the podium. Who? Why—

Grief of death! It's Sully Yot!

Up on the podium climbed Sully Yot. The lanky wart-faced youth looked flushed, manic, wild-eyed, half-crazed. He screamed at his audience:

'Evil! Evil! Evil! Tor is evil! Gouda Muck has spoken! Praise to Muck! He learns us truth! Some flesh is pure, but other flesh is born to evil. Tor is a monster. Monsters are not human. Tor has teeth which are wrong, limbs which are wrong, hands which are wrong. Only those with a fist of five digits are human. Tor has six fingers.'

'Hey!' yelled the Walrus. 'What's this nonsense about the fist deciding the man?'

219

'It's not nonsense,' shouted Yot. 'It's truth! Muck's truth! I've heard the news from Stokos! Muck has spoken, Muck has revealed. Muck is the High God of All Gods. And you – you've two fists on each hand. You're a monster too. You don't deserve to live. You—'

Sully Yot was hauled off the podium and pulled into the crowd. For a moment he vanished. He resurfaced briefly, then disappeared again. People were fighting, some obviously trying to kill Yot, others to protect him. Finally, Yot was hauled to safety.

By Quin Baltu, Ika Thole, Shewel Lokenshield, Peg Suzilman, Jon Disaster and Jon Arabin. By Harly Burpskin, Raggage Pouch, querulous old Jez Glane and slim dark Salaman Meerkat. By Lee Dix, Goth Sox, Hewlet Mapleskin and others – the entire crew, it seemed, of the good ship *Warwolf*.

Drake groaned.

'What is it?' said his brother Heth, who was standing next to him in the crowd.

But Drake had no chance to answer, for uproar broke out as a very angry Walrus gained the podium. Slagger Mulps displayed his two-thumbed fists to the crowd then made them into fists.

'These hands,' shouted Slagger Mulps, 'these hands are ready for war.'

He wrenched down his trousers and showed off his male pride.

'And this – this, boys, this is ready for war as well. I'm built for action, that's the truth.'

He pulled up his trousers.

'Arabin,' said Mulps. 'Arabin so old that every bit of hair has fallen from his head, he can stay behind on the Teeth. Aye. Mount sentry over rat, mouse and cockroach. But I'm for war, boys. War. Conquest. Gold.

'Last time I spoke, I spoke against empire. But times – well, as Drake Douay says, times change. We've got a king on our side. An ogre on our side. All the ogres on our side. Half of Stokos on our side. That alters odds.

I'm in for gold, conquest, wealth, women. Who's with me?'

A roar of approval showed that most of the pirates were. Drake knew that many other people would speak before a final decision was reached. But he was already sure of what would happen: the pirates would vote for empire.

After much heated discussion – in which another half a dozen pirates died – the reavers of the Greater Teeth did indeed vote for a war for empire. And Jon Arabin sent Harly Burpskin to tell Drake Douay that his days with the *Warwolf* were finished.

Drake had expected as much.

He did not rightly understand why Arabin was still against empire, but knew his public opposition to Arabin must end their friendship. But to be an outcast still hurt. He had admired Jon Arabin, had rejoiced in Arabin's approval, had struggled hard to win promotion from ship's boy to crewman—

And now it was all over.

Still, he was in amongst friends. His brother. His uncle. His king. And others from Stokos. And they had their own ship, the *Tarik*, to make ready for a preliminary probing raid on Cam.

The probing raid was a disappointing, almost fruitless affair. The *Tarik*, with Drake aboard, sailed the six hundred leagues or so to Cam. As they dared the approaches to the harbour, three ships came out to meet them. Those ships chased the *Tarik* right round the shores of Stokos. Finally, in bad weather, the *Tarik* shook off the pursuers, and headed north.

They had learnt that Sudder Vemlouf, ruler of Stokos, had a navy of at least three ships.

'What we should do,' said Drake, 'is go in force. Aye. Half a dozen ships. Or send in spies. Perhaps we should ask Sully Yot to spy for us – he's got Muck's trust.'

'That's an excellent idea,' said King Tor.

So Drake arrived back at Knock with his hopes high. Sully Yot would be asked to spy for them; Yot would refuse; Yot would be thrown to the sharks or tortured to death, which would be a just and proper punishment for killing Drake's much-loved dog. (And, of course, for attempted murder of Drake Douay.)

When Drake landed on Knock, he was disgusted to find that Sully Yot had sailed with the *Warwolf*, bound on a raiding expedition to the Ravlish Lands.

'What else is new?' said Drake.

The latest excitement proved to be the challenge which Lord Menator had set Slagger Mulps. It seemed the Walrus was demanding to be Grand Admiral of the Fleet of Imperial Conquest. Menator had doubts about his worthiness, but had given the man a chance to prove himself.

If Slagger Mulps could sail to the terror-lands beyond the protection of Drangsturm, capture one of the monsters of the Swarms and bring it back to the Greaters as proof of his prowess, then he would be 'seriously considered' for the position of Grand Admiral.

'It sounds to me,' said Drake, sagely, 'that Menator thinks Mulps is too big with ambition. So Menator wants to kill off Mulps. But he doesn't want the blood to show too clearly on his own hands.'

Drake's analysis was correct. Menator wanted to appoint only his own men to positions of power. Menator knew such a policy would not win approval from the pirates – so he had chosen to try to kill off Slagger Mulps subtly, by tempting him into accepting a suicidal dare.

To Drake's surprise – and to the surprise of others – Slagger Mulps took up the dare, and began to ready his ship for a voyage south.

'The man's mad,' said Drake to Drake. 'And I'm glad I've no part in that madness.'

Slagger Mulps was due to sail on the first day of spring. The day before the *Walrus* set sail, Drake was called to a conference with King Tor and Lord Menator. It was Menator who did the talking.

'We've thought long and hard about this challenge we've set for Slagger Mulps,' said Menator. 'We can't think of any way for him to cheat – but he's a pirate, so there's no telling what devious tricks he'll turn to. Thus we want someone aboard his ship to be our eyes and ears. To report true as to where he goes and what he does.'

'Man,' said Drake, 'then don't look at me. I crewed with Jon Arabin, sworn enemy of Slagger Mulps. If I were to go aboard his ship, his crew would kill me. Why, my own worst enemy sails with the *Walrus*. That's Atsimo Andranovory, a man made for murder. So I'll stay with King Tor, thank you very much.'

'You'll do no such thing,' rumbled Tor. 'You'll sail for the south with Slagger Mulps. Not least because I need to test you. You've been chosen to marry my daughter. You've been chosen to inherit my throne. I need proof I've made the right choice.'

'Why,' said Drake, 'surely you can trust your own judgment.'

'In my youth,' said Tor, 'I studied the Inner Principles of the Old Science, just as you did. From that, I learned that judgment is best supported by experiment.'

'I see,' said Drake. 'Perhaps . . . perhaps a test to destruction.'

'That depends on what you're made of,' said Tor.

'The *Walrus* sails tomorrow,' said Drake. 'Have you jacked this up with Slagger Mulps? Is he happy to have me on board? Have you got a promise of safe conduct out of him?'

'We've not spoken to Slagger Mulps,' said Menator.

'Nor will we,' said Tor.

'Then how,' said Drake, in something close to despair, 'how do I get on his ship? And if I do – how do I survive?'

'That,' said Tor, 'is your first test.'

16

Name: Slagger Mulps.

Alias: the Walrus.

Birthplace: Chenameg.

Description:' very tall; very thin; long sharp nose; green hair; green beard; green eyes; long arms and double-thumb fists.

Career: started life as a gardener's boy, then had to depart hastily from Chenameg. Lived as a limmer in Jone (in Selzirk) until sentenced to life as a galley slave after being caught raping a pig in a public toilet hard up by Ol Ilkeen. Liberated after five years when Abousir Belench, an Orfus pirate, dared a dawn raid on Lake Ouija. Thereafter prospered as a blade of the free marauders.

Status: Orfus pirate; cave owner and slave owner on Knock (largest of the Greater Teeth); ship's captain.

Ship: the eponymous *Walrus*.

'This good place,' said Whale Mike.

He held aloft his lantern. By its yellow light Drake saw three stoves, heaped sacks of charcoal, a huge hammock in which a horse could have slept in comfort, casks which presumably held ale or stuff yet stronger, hams hanging from hooks, strings of onions, boxes, crates, ropes, a heap of timber and a rack of tools.

'This place is huge,' said Drake.

'Well, I not small,' said Whale Mike. 'This ship, she was *Gol-sa-danjerk*. That her name. Now she *Walrus*. This was hold, but I make changes.'

'Have you always been ship's cook?' said Drake.

'Oh, I many things. But I good cook. I do that long time. Cook always eat well – that not so?'

And Whale Mike laughed.

Drake looked at the array of tools – hammers, mallets, chisels, awls, a variety of saws and other implements.

'Who owns these tools?' he said.

'Oh, they mine,' said Whale Mike. 'I carpenter. I do many jobs. We not got big crew. Some of these jokers, they not so smart. They not understand carpentry stuff. But that no problem for me. I smart joker.'

Drake thought Whale Mike's estimate of his own intelligence was, to say the least, optimistic. But he did not say so. Instead, he said:

'Thanks for bringing me aboard.'

'That okay. You my friend. That not so?'

'Definitely so,' said Drake.

'You sleep,' said Whale Mike. 'You get rest, talk good tomorrow. You have to talk fast, that not so?'

'Very much so,' said Drake.

Wondering how he would fare on the morrow when he had to face the Walrus.

'Under there,' said Mike, pointing to the shadows beneath a rack of hams. 'There sacks. That comfortable, that not so?'

'Surely so,' said Drake.

And crawled in under the hams, and laid himself down on the sacks. It was comfortable enough. He stared up at the bulky shadows of the hams. How well were they secured? It would only need one to fall . . .

Whale Mike began to hum a happy song. What was he doing? He was sitting on a coil of rope, working on something. What? Ah . . . the tooth of a whale. The lamplight gleamed on Whale Mike's sallow, swollen face. No ears. Was it cold, having no ears? What was it like to be stupid?

225

A shadow jumped onto Mike's shoulder. A ghost? A demon? No – a cat. Slowly, Mike turned his head until he was staring the cat in the face. Was he going to bite it? Eat it? Tear it apart and gullet it raw?

As Drake watched, Whale Mike kissed the cat. That settled it! The man had to be soft in the head!

Footsteps thumped over the deck above. A voice called down the companion-way which led down into Mike's all-purpose cabin.

'Mike?'

'Yo!' said Whale Mike.

'We're bringing the water aboard. Can you give us a hand?'

'No problem,' said Mike.

The cat jumped from Mike's shoulder as he stood up. Though he was more than twice Drake's height, his head did not quite touch the ceiling. He must be very important to rate so much space. But of course – when there was a battle to fight, or an anchor to pull up, or a monster to kill, Mike must be the ideal person for the job.

When Mike left, Drake began to explore. The cat – perhaps it was psychic – immediately hid.

'Puss puss puss,' said Drake, trying to tempt the cat into kicking range.

The cat prudently stayed hidden.

Drake examined Whale Mike's scrimshaw. The whale's tooth was being worked into a representation of the writhing bodies of a dozen naked men and women. It was obscene. Fascinating. And very delicate. Done with great skill.

'He must've stolen it off someone,' muttered Drake. 'I hope he doesn't wreck it trying to finish it.'

He heard heavy feet and profound thumps up above as barrels of water were brought on board the *Walrus*.

'I must be crazy,' said Drake.

Stowing away on the *Walrus* at risk to his life – yes, maybe he was a bit crazy. How would he explain himself to Slagger Mulps on the morrow? Perhaps he could ask

Whale Mike to hide him here for the entire voyage. No. That was too dangerous. Mike might get sick. Or die. Or fall overboard. Or the ship might flood. Or sink. There were a thousand ways in which he might be discovered.

He would have to win over Slagger Mulps. Get protection from Mulps. But . . . what if Mulps once again handed him over to Atsimo Andranovory? Drake remembered Andranovory demanding a suck. Having him hauled into the sky on a rope. Remembered his long agony as he swung from the end of the rope . . .

Drake poked amongst the casks and cases, looking for something to eat. The air was heavy with the smells of onions, smoked seal, hams, dried fish, herbs and spices. He cut himself a bit of ham. Chewed it slowly.

Perhaps Tor means to get me killed.

King Tor was strange. Sometimes he seemed to have perfect confidence in Drake. Other times, doubt ruled his mind, demanding that he set Drake tests.

Maybe he's one of these people who's not sure of his own mind. Maybe. He's not much of a leader, perhaps.

Jon Arabin never changed his mind like that. Yet, even so, circumstances had brought about a change in Drake's relationship to Arabin. There was every chance he might end up as an enemy.

And Slagger Mulps . . . man, I've got to make friends with him. Now that's crazy. Wild.

Yet not impossible.

The lamp flickered, and went out. Drake stood in the darkness, trying to orientate himself. Where was his bed of sacks? With hands extended like the feelers of an insect, he began to explore the night. Barked his shin against a crate, and hissed. Something hissed back at him. What?! Oh – only the cat, of course . . .

Drake found the mess of sacking where he was to sleep, and settled himself down. Brooding on his future. To become a friend of the Walrus? An enemy of the Warwolf? It was all too possible.

He lamented the instability of human relationships.

Life would be so much easier – and so much safer! – if one kept the same set of friends and enemies for a lifetime. At least he could be sure of Heth.

Blood, that's the stuff. Family.

He bitterly regretted being parted from Heth. He wished he was back on the good ship *Tarik*. Would he see Heth again? Why, of course he would. At journey's end . . .

Drake heard a thump of boots coming down the companionway. Suppressed laughter. Who was that? Not Whale Mike, by the sound of it. Smaller people. Two of them? Maybe three.

'Gragh!' said a gutteral voice.

Then hawked. Then spat.

'The grimby cludge keeps a lantern lit, mostly.'

'Andranovory?'

'We'll manage.'

A tight, confident, well-controlled voice. Clear. Sharp. Ish Ulpin? Possibly . . .

Sounds of collision.

'Mal skok!'

A chuckle.

'Oh, An'vory, man! You're so much fun when you're happy!'

That, unless Drake was very much mistaken, was Bucks Cat.

'Here's a cask,' said Andranovory.

Muffled fumbling. Happy splash of liquor running into – a crock? Bottle? Mug?

'A toast . . .'

A clink of mugs in the night.

'A toast to what?' said Bucks Cat.

'Victory,' said Ish Ulpin. 'We'll play this Menator's games for now, but when we're ready . . .'

'Throats open,' said Andranovory.

'Oh man, oh yes,' crooned Bucks Cat. 'I'll slice the little one myself. Imagine – him as king?'

All three laughed.

Drake began to sweat. He knew exactly who those three were talking of. Just his luck! He remembered how Bucks Cat and Ish Ulpin had forced him into the sea, a horizon away from Stokos. They were true killers. They would abolish him without a moment's hesitation. If they caught him.

Someone touched Drake. On the buttock. He almost screamed. Then realized it was only the cat. The cat began to crawl onto him. Ugh! What's the difference between a cat and a rat? More fur and a thicker tail, that's all . . .

'There must be stronger stuff than this,' said Andranovory.

'Sure to be,' agreed Ish Ulpin. 'But we'd have Ockle's luck searching by dark.'

Ockle? Ockle's luck? What the hell did that mean?

'Oh man,' said Bucks Cat, with a chuckle. 'I thought you would've worked it out by now. The stove's still hot. One is, anyway.'

Movements in the dark. What? Hiss of – pain? Anger? Someone finding a hot stove the hard way, maybe. Sound of cloth tearing. For what? To wrap around fingers for handling a hot stove, perhaps. Protest of metal. A stove door? Opening? Gleam of red coals. Flare of flame. A twist of cloth bursting into light. Flames rising to reveal—

'The lantern,' said Ish Ulpin, as the twist of cloth in Andranovory's fingers burnt itself out. 'I've found the lantern. Give me another light, I'll get it going.'

The lantern would reveal everything.

Drake grabbed the cat – which could not have been psychic after all, or it would have understood its danger.

He flung it through the night.

A scream. A shout. A prolonged yowl. A furious seething hissing and spitting. Several obscenities.

'Hey!' said a familiar voice. 'What going on down there?'

'We're just leaving,' said Ish Ulpin.

'Oh, you leave all right,' said Whale Mike, clambering down into his private domain. 'Who this?'

'Let go of my beard!'

'Oh! An'vory! Walrus, he speak to you three times

229

already. You drink too much. You drinking now, that not so? You stay out of here. And what you do my cat? She not happy. I hear that.'

'Your crazy cat attacked us,' said Ish Ulpin.

'That not so,' said Whale Mike. 'That cat not stupid. You step on her, maybe. Who this?'

'This is me, Bucks Cat.'

'So you've got all three names now,' said Ish Ulpin. 'There's nobody else down here. If you want to play the child and tell the Walrus, you know what names to give him.'

'This not child stuff,' said Whale Mike. 'This serious. There only so much food, only so much drink. We got long way travel.'

'You talk like a sheep-shagging schoolmaster,' grumbled Andranovory.

'What you know about schoolmaster?' said Whale Mike. 'You from Lorp. They got no school there. This serious matter.'

'Okay, okay, it's serious,' said Bucks Cat. 'We got the message. How about letting go before you break my arm?'

Mike obliged.

Ish Ulpin, Bucks Cat and Andranovory quit the hold in a hurry. Whale Mike lit the lantern from the stove, nodded at Drake, then tempted his cat into his arms for comfort.

'What they do to my cat?' he said.

'Andranovory got hold of it,' said Drake. 'He was going to push it into the stove.'

'Oh, that just like An'vory,' said Whale Mike. 'He not so good. He drink too much.'

'But the cat fought back,' said Drake. 'Man, that's a beautiful cat you got there. I love cats.'

'That good,' said Whale Mike, stroking his cat and kissing it once again. 'That mean you smart. All smartest people like cats. Not like dogs. That dog, that stupid animal for stupid people.'

'Verily,' said Drake.

And, before he slept, he helped Mike slander dogs at

230

length and in detail, and praise the race of cats to the very heavens.

At dawn, the *Walrus* put to sea. Towards noon, Drake stumbled onto the deck in company with Whale Mike. The Greaters were but a smudge on the far horizon. But, much closer, visible in every detail, was the unlovely Andranovory.

Who gaped at Drake.

'Hoy,' said Andranovory. 'That's – that's—'

'This my friend,' said Whale Mike. 'We go see Slagger Mulps.'

'You – I – hey, boys! – there's—'

Andranovory swayed on his feet. He was drunk – hence his incoherence. There were ragged red cat-scratches on his right-hand cheek.

'Come,' said Whale Mike. 'This way. Come.'

And Drake, very shortly, was shown into the captain's cabin, which was set in the poop of the ship.

On the *Walrus* everything was dirt, filth and disorder. Her crew was not even in the habit of coiling ropes properly. The captain's cabin made a startling constrast to this general disorder, for it was neat, whitewashed and scrupulously clean. That Drake noted at first glance.

Then noted no more, for a sickening fear seized his senses, and he thought he would faint. His heart leaped like a frog trying to jump out of a water-barrel. His mouth tasted worse than it had when he had addressed the pirate's general assembly. He felt giddy.

Slagger Mulps sat behind a desk where charts were spread out. He looked at Drake, then looked at Whale Mike.

'Leave,' said Mulps.

'Okay,' said Mike cheerfully.

And withdrew his head and shoulders from the cabin, closing the door after him. Mulps watched Drake, saying nothing.

'I – I suppose you want some explanation, man,' said Drake. 'It was Menator sent me here. Lord Menator. He dared me aboard. I think he means to kill me by this dare. I think he means to kill you, too, aye, given time. Kill both of us. That's what this voyage is for. To be the death of us.'

'Why should he do that?' said Mulps.

'For empire, man,' said Drake. 'We're both lusting after leadership. Aye. Me to be king on Stokos. You to be admiral. That speaks ambition. Hence danger to Menator. He knows as much, so kills while the killing's easy.'

'I've thought as much myself,' said Slagger Mulps. 'The danger is to both of us. That makes us friends – perhaps. But . . . if you will sail with us, then you must swear yourself to secrecy.'

'Secrecy?' said Drake. 'About what?'

'Why, about the secrets of this voyage south, of course.'

Drake thought. He had little choice. But—

'I'll not swear,' said Drake, 'if your secret touches on the lives of King Tor or Jon Arabin.'

'I thought you enemy with Arabin,' said Mulps. 'You spoke against his speaking at assembly. That hardly leaves you friends.'

'Aye,' said Drake, 'but we've not yet come to blood. I want to leave some hope between us for the future.'

Slagger Mulps considered this.

There was much bad blood between Walrus and War-wolf. Could he afford to have Drake Douay aboard when Drake still had residual loyalties to Jon Arabin?

'What would happen,' said Slagger Mulps, 'if it came to a fight between Walrus and Warwolf?'

'Man,' said Drake, 'that's nothing to do with the voyage here. All I ask is to share your dangers, aye. At journey's end, I'll be back with King Tor. I'll say good words for you with the king. That's worth having, isn't it?

'But I'll say this – I've got some fair thoughts left for

232

Jon Arabin, but I've none left for one of his crew. That's Sully Yot I'm talking of, the wart-faced one. He tried to kill me – killed my dog while trying. He turned against my king. That's treason, man – to speak against the king.

'While shouting filth, he said hard words about another fellow I could mention. Not to be too subtle – yourself. Man, I know I spoke bad words in a worse temper when we first met. But since then – you know yourself I've sworn to marry Tor's daughter. I've pledged my flesh to an ogre. Whatever words I've spoken, I've no prejudice. My actions prove that.

'Man, I say this – you're as human as any other. Aye. Green hair, green eyes, the works. And I say this, too – if by one chance in a thousand million we clashed with Arabin on this voyage south, I'd fight for you and yours. At least till Sully Yot was dead at my feet.'

Drake ended his speech. Stood there. Trembling. Slagger Mulps stared at him. Broken loose by the ship's motion, a slim piece of sharpened graphite slid across the charts, fell off the table and broke as it hit the white-washed floorboards.

'You speak well,' said the Walrus. 'I tell you this. The secrets of this voyage touch not on the lives of Arabin or Tor. So swear to keep our secrets.'

Drake consented to place his hand on a virgin's breech-cloth – an article which Slagger Mulps regarded with superstitious awe – and swear himself to secrecy.

'Now all can be revealed,' said Mulps.

Drake bated his breath and waited for revelation.

'We run to Narba first,' said Mulps, in a conspiratorial whisper, 'there to sell a cargo of seal furs.'

Drake snorted, and breathed easy.

'Is that all? Is that the ship's secret?'

'If it were known we were engaged in honest trade,' said Slagger Mulps, 'it would shame us for thrice five generations.'

'Aagh, Jon Arabin runs for pearls, and makes no secret of it,' said Drake.

'Yes – but the pearl run reeks of danger. That's different from braining baby seals and ripping their bodies naked.'

There was, Drake had to admit, a difference. But he could not help thinking the secret ridiculous. Surely there was more to know.

'What special plan have you for capturing a monster?' said Drake. 'They're fearsome fierce, these monsters of the Swarms.'

'Courage will serve us,' said the Walrus, blandly. 'We'll have men killed in the attempt, doubtless, but we'll win through in the end. You'll have yŏur opportunity to cover yourself with glory.'

Drake, at that moment, would rather have covered himself with a blanket. He had not slept very well the night before. As nervous tension ebbed away, he felt weak with fatigue. But there was one thing he needed before he could really relax: a safe-conduct pass or its equivalent.

'Man,' said Drake, 'as maybe you know, I've tangled with a few of your men in the past. They're more likely enemies than friends. So I'd like you to get your men to swear to my safety.'

The Walrus laughed.

'I'm not your mother,' he said. 'You'll have to stand up for yourself. That's a test of your worth – to make peace with the crew.'

'Another test!' said Drake. 'These tests will be the death of me!'

'Mayhap,' said Slagger Mulps. 'But that's your problem, not mine. Now out – I've got to chart the details of our trip to the terror-lands, aye, the terror-lands of the Deep South.'

Out on deck, Drake looked around for Whale Mike, who was nowhere in sight. In his hold, doubtless. Drake hastened there – but was intercepted by Andranovory.

'You!' said Andranovory, swaying.

'What do you want?' said Drake.

'This!' said Andranovory.

234

And punched Drake in the gut. Hard. Drake took the blow easily, and punched back. His fist sank into Andranovory's belly as if the man were made of marshmallow. The black-bearded brute grunted in surprise, and sat down on the deck in a hurry.

Drake was about to put in the boot when he saw he had spectators. Bucks Cat and Ish Ulpin were watching him.

'Drake!' said Ish Ulpin. 'Over here!'

Reluctantly, Drake went toward Ish Ulpin. The lean, pale man looked as if he never saw the sun. Big black Bucks Cat stood beside him, grinning as merrily as the knife-scar on his throat.

'Whale Mike tells us you're sailing south with us,' said Ish Ulpin.

'Aye,' said Drake.

'We hear tell that the Warwolf tangled with Swarms and such on her last voyage south.'

'That's true,' said Drake.

'Then sit down, man. Take a seat – aye, there on the rope, that's comfortable enough. Tell us about it.'

'And why would you want to hear?' said Drake.

'Why? Well, we'll be tangling with such soon enough, won't we now? It's nice to know what we're up against.'

Drake realized that Ish Ulpin really did want to know. On inquiry, he found that nobody aboard had been further south than Narba. The waters of the Drangsturm Gulf were, to the crew of the *Walrus*, largely an unknown quantity. So Drake settled himself, and began to tell his tales.

Drake was a good story-teller. Under pressure – with a life to lose if he failed to interest – he became an even better story-teller. Others of the crew gathered round to listen.

One tale led to another, and thus, as the days went by and the ship cruised steadily south, Drake got to know the crew well. Bucks Cat – who proved to be boisterous, good-humoured, intelligent, and perhaps the most competent sailor aboard. Ish Ulpin – who, as Drake had suspected, was a dangerous man, too careless with himself to value others.

Tiki Slooze, a feeble, querulous man who reminded Drake of Jez Glane. Rolf Thelemite, an intense character who claimed to be from the fabled islands of Rovac (claiming, too, that his blade was firelight steel from Stokos -- though he never let anyone see it). Simp Fiche, whom Drake had met before – he lived for rape and torture.

And others. Ching Quail, Trudy Haze, Praul Galana, Morton Seligman, and close to three dozen more.

Drake found himself popular. Except with Andranovory. But that drunken bully was scarcely loved by the rest of the crew. Nor was he a match for Drake in a fight.

So far, so good. But what happens when we get to the terror-lands? What happens when we get to the Deep South?

Drake expected at least some men to jump ship when the *Walrus* reached Narba. But, though all the men got shore leave, none fled. All, it seemed, were ready to brave the terrors of the lands beyond Drangsturm. To do battle with the monsters of the Swarms. To dare the horrors of creatures worse than nightmare.

And Drake?

He was fearful. Yet was proud. And fiercely ambitious. He had to survive this test. To win the hand of King Tor's daughter. To win the throne of Stokos. And prove himself equal to the heroes of the *Walrus*, who faced the prospect of absolute horror with calm – almost, indeed, with indifference. Who would have thought they could be so brave?

They're brave, perhaps, because they think no Swarms exist. Aye. But they do. I've seen them, clear enough. The Neversh – chest to chest. And the other monsters, crowded on the shore.

As the *Walrus* braved south, Drake developed a nervous

tic. He slept poorly – woken often by nightmares. He got acid indigestion. Under the stress of fear, he became irritable, short-tempered. Then at last, by night, he saw the flames of Drangsturm reflected from clouds on the horizon.

Come morning, the *Walrus* anchored by a small offshore island. A day's sailing – or less – would take them to the shores of terror beyond the protection of Drangsturm.

'What island be this?' said Drake, staring at massive low-slung buildings on the island.

'This is Burntos,' said Bucks Cat. 'Landguard troopers are garrisoned here. They hold the island against any monsters of the Swarms which fly this way.'

'It's a low, barren, ugly place,' said Drake. 'What do we want here? We've food, water – everything but women. Have they a brothel ashore?'

'Not that I know of,' said Bucks Cat. 'But with luck, they've got a monster they can sell us.'

'Sell us?' said Drake.

'But of course. We need a monster to show to Menator.'

'But – but – but we—'

Bucks Cat slapped his thighs, and threw back his head and laughed uproariously.

'Oh man!' he said. 'Are you innocent!'

'What's the joke?' called Praul Galana.

'This young hero here,' said Bucks Cat, pointing at Drake, 'he really thought we were going to hunt the terrorlands for a monster. Oh man! That's rich!'

Bucks Cat laughed till tears ran down his face, and others laughed with him.

'But,' said Drake, starting to get angry, 'the day we left Knock, I spoke with the Walrus. He told me true that we were hunting monsters. Aye. He spoke of death and glory.'

'Well, man,' said Bucks Cat, recovering himself a little, 'he likes a joke too.'

'How did he know of this Burntos place since he's never been this far south?' said Drake.

'Oh, we hear of this place in Narba,' said Bucks Cat. 'It's no secret.'

237

'Well,' said Drake, 'if you never planned to dare the terror-lands – how come everyone was so hot to hear my stories?'

'Why, for you tell a good tale, and that's reason enough,' said Bucks Cat. 'Besides – we're not home dry, are we? If there's no monster for sale ashore, maybe we will have to hunt one.'

And, thought Drake, maybe, even if they secured a monster, bad weather would see the *Walrus* endure some adventures as wild as those which had befallen the *Warwolf* in the waters of the Drangsturm Gulf. Though he had to admit the weather had treated them fair enough so far – the *Walrus* had had dry skies, hot days and favourable breezes ever since leaving Narba.

Drake was on the first boat which went ashore to Burntos. The others with him were Bucks Cat, Ish Ulpin and Slagger Mulps. In honour of the occasion, the Walrus had shed his sealskins, and had dressed himself in silken robes embroidered with astrological symbols. Drake thought he looked daft – but the green-haired man was obviously very pleased with his appearance.

The boat scraped against stones.

Drake jumped into the sea, and helped haul the boat ashore. A single old man was picking his way along the shore, gathering driftwood. Otherwise, nobody was in sight.

'Hey,' yelled Bucks Cat. 'You got any monsters for sale?'

The old man paid them no attention.

'Maybe he speaks no Galish,' said Drake.

'Maybe he's deaf,' said Slagger Mulps.

'Maybe,' said Ish Ulpin, 'selling monsters is against his religion.'

'Chel!' said Slagger Mulps, meaning 'avanti!'

And led the way toward the low-slung buildings. Massive buildings. Built of huge stone. Slit windows. Strange, narrow doors.

238

'Drake,' said Slagger Mulps, as they came on the nearest building. 'Inside. Sus it out.'

Drake, with some trepidation, ventured through the narrow door. He found himself in a long, cool, gloomy room. On either side were rows of pallets. On every pallet were identical stacks of folded blankets and folded clothing. At the end of every pallet was a pair of boots. A little dust danced in the shafts of sunlight come through the slit windows.

Drake went outside.

'Man,' he said, 'this place is for sleeping.'

They explored further. Finally, surmounting a small rise, they gained a view of a huge paved square. Half a thousand men – or were they statues? – were standing there. In rows. Spears in hand. Utterly motionless.

'Here's our people,' said Slagger Mulps.

'A parade,' said Ish Ulpin.

And spat, in disgust.

'What are they doing?' said Drake, bewildered.

'Soldier stuff,' said Bucks Cat. 'This is – this is kind of holy. I've seen it in the Rice Empire. We'd better stay clear till they've finished.'

Drake watched.

Nothing happened.

Were these real soldiers? Impossible! Surely they were statues.

Then—

One of the spearmen went down. Crunch. Falling flat on his face on the paving stones. He stayed down. Nobody spoke. Nobody moved. Shadows shifted slightly as the sun eased itself across the sky. A fly settled on Drake's face and began to feed. He slapped it. Then was embarrassed by the noise. But nobody looked in his direction. A tiny dust-devil whirled across the courtyard, then faded to nothing.

The soldier who had collapsed was still flat on his face.

'Craziness,' muttered Drake.

And turned away from the parade. If everyone on the

island was going to stand paralysed in the sun, maybe this was a good time to go looting. He wandered off amongst the buildings, peering through the slit windows. Eventually, he came upon a kitchen. Inside were upwards of a dozen women, hard at work preparing corn and potatoes for a meal.

'Flesh is hope,' said Drake.

And dared himself to the door of the kitchen. Being as attractive to women as he was, with any luck he could chat up one of the ladies and get in a quick one before the soldiers finished their daft parade.

As Drake stepped into the kitchen, the women stopped their work and looked at him. A couple spoke to each other in some foreign tongue, then giggled.

'Hi, girls,' said Drake.

As he spoke, a tall red-skinned woman came out of a side room, her arms white to the elbows with flour. She glanced at him indifferently. Was it . . . Zanya? Yes! It was Zanya!

'Zanya!' yelled Drake.

She looked at him again, shrugged, picked up a rolling pin and retreated into the room she had come from. Drake hastened to the door of that room. And was met by a brawny purple-skinned man who was not entirely a stranger.

'Greetings, Oronoko,' said Drake.

'*Fa'unu a'fukutu*,' said Oronoko.

And scooped up Drake, carried him to the door of the kitchen, and threw him outside in the dust.

17

Zanya Kliedervaust: priestess of the Orgy God of the Ebrell Islands; renounced her position and formally abjured alcohol, sexual intercourse, sunbathing, the eating of sweet things and all the other pleasures of the flesh after seeing her mother, father, brothers, sisters, cousins, uncles and aunts die of venereal disease, alcoholism and obesity.

Quit Ebrell and travelled west in the company of Prince Oronoko of Parengarenga, questing for purity. Arriving at Cam on the xebec which rescued Drake Douay from the Central Ocean, sought work at the leprosarium.

Was converted to the worship of the Flame by Gouda Muck; became an apostle for Goudanism and left Stokos to preach the Faith in foreign parts.

The wizard Miphon was cleaning a xyster when Drake Douay was brought into his clinic by one of the women from the kitchen. Blood was dripping through Drake's blond hair and sleeking down his weather-battered sealskins. A drop of dark red fell soundlessly to the cool grey flagstones of the floor.

'Welcome,' said Miphon, speaking in the Galish Trading Tongue; and, smiling to reinforce his welcome, he laid the xyster down on a well-scrubbed table of sun-bleached driftwood.

'*Tach smin hebalar*,' said the woman from the kitchen.

Miphon, who did not speak her language, waved her out of the clinic. Choosing to misinterpret this gesture, she

241

seated herself in one of the clinic's five bamboo chairs.

'Out!' said Miphon sharply, clapping his hands twice.

Reluctantly, curiosity unappeased, the woman left. Miphon pointed Drake to a bamboo chair, which creaked as the bloodstained pirate sat.

'Have you been fighting?' said Miphon.

'Nay, man,' said Drake, looking around the clinic. His gaze lingered on a remarkable array of delicate steel instruments – hooks, blades, tweezers, spikes and probes. With luck, he could slip a couple into his pockets. Whale Mike might like them for his scrimshaw work. 'I was testing my powers of flight when my wings fell off.'

'How far did you fall?'

'Half way from here to Narba.'

'And you hit your head. What's the last thing you remember?'

'Why, the death and resurrection of the star-dragon Bel. A whore who turned into a horse as she came. Five dozen oysters dancing drunk in the streets of Narba. Why all these daft questions, man? I'm bleeding to death!'

'A little blood,' said Miphon, 'goes a long way. Tell me – what do you see?'

So saying, the green-eyed wizard held up three fingers.

'See?' said Drake. 'Why, I see a blind rat mating with a seagull. Aye, and four blue lepers hauling a giant cockroach backwards up a mountain.'

'That's near enough,' said Miphon.

And, turning away, the wizard began to wash his hands in a bowl of water. Drake smelt something strange. What? Oh – soap. He remembered his sister using it a couple of times. Swift and sly, he reached out, grabbed a couple of tiny cutlass-curved blades from a nearby bench and slipped them into a pocket. Miphon, shaking the water off his hands, turned back to Drake and began examining his scalp.

'I'm the wizard Miphon,' he said, easing Drake's hair this way and that as he explored the damage.

'I know that,' said Drake. 'We met on Stokos. Ow!

242

That's sore! Hey – you really don't remember me?'

'In busy times,' said Miphon, 'I can see upwards of a hundred people a day. How can I remember all of them?'

Drake felt insulted.

'But I was special!' he said. 'You told me a tale about you being a mind-reading elf. You gave me a philtre to cure myself of love.'

'Oh,' said Miphon, pouring water from a ewer into a clean bowl. 'Oh . . . I remember now.' He balanced the bowl on the back of Drake's chair, the hard edge of it against the nape of Drake's neck. 'Lean back. I've got to wash the blood out of your hair. Hmmm . . . I remember you all right. But the name . . . that escapes me.'

'I'm Arabin lol Arabin,' said Drake.

The lie came easily. It was a smart move. Who knows? This wizard could have converted to Gouda Muck's cult. He might be one of those who was hunting Drake, thinking him the son of the demon Hagon.

'Arabin lol Arabin,' said Miphon. 'I won't forget you when we meet again.'

'We'll never meet again.'

'It's a small world,' said Miphon. 'Hmmm . . . this looks good . . . the bleeding's more or less stopped.'

'That's health for you,' said Drake.

Miphon laid aside the bowl of blood-misted water. Taking a sharp blade, the wizard began to shave hairs on either side of the gash where Drake's scalp had been torn as his head hit the ground when the purple-skinned Oronoko threw him out of the kitchen.

'How much hair are you cutting away?' said Drake in alarm.

'Does it matter?' said Miphon.

'It matters much! Man, there's a beautiful red-breasted woman I want to make. I can hardly court her if you've cut me half bald.'

'You're after the Kliedervaust woman?' said Miphon.

'That's her.'

Miphon laughed.

'You won't get her,' he said. 'She's in the clutches of faith. She preaches the defiance of the flesh.'

'And what do you think of that?'

'Flesh,' said Miphon, 'is that through which we live. No flesh, no life. Of course, flesh is but the medium in which our existence finds expression. The expression of existence is not to be confounded with the inspiration of that expression. Mere hedonism would exult the medium at the expense of the inspiration. So perhaps her doctrine is a necessary corrective for certain trends.'

'Man,' said Drake, 'you make a right proper tangle out of simple language. What did you mean to say? That you agree with this talk of purity? Or that you don't?'

'That I both do and don't,' said Miphon. 'It is both wise and foolish. Something, perhaps, could be made of it in time.'

'There speaks a wizard! Hey, man – just how much hair are you cutting?'

'Just enough so I've clear skin to sew up this gash with cat-gut.'

'Cat-gut!' said Drake, scandalized. 'The gut of a cat? In me? Man, that's disgusting. Why not dog-gut?'

'Because the dog,' said Miphon, 'is a foul, polluted animal which has nothing to offer the healing arts.' He took up a curved needle from which a length of dark thread trailed. 'This thread is the cat-gut. Hold still, now. This will hurt.'

And he began to sew up the gash in Drake's scalp. With cat-gut.

'Man,' said Drake, doing his best to ignore the bright silver pain of the needle, 'tell me. How long has this Zanya Kliedervaust been here?'

'I've been here ninety days myself,' said Miphon, tying a knot. 'She was here when I came. She preaches nightly to the troops.'

'Surely she must have preached to every soldier here long, long ago.'

'The garrison,' said Miphon, guiding pain again into

244

Drake's flesh, 'rotates. These soldiers are from the Landguard of the Confederation of Wizards. They guard the castles ranged along Drangsturm; they patrol the shores; they hunt down the few stray monsters which escape our scrutiny and flee to the mountains north of the flame trench.'

'They work . . . for wizards, then?'

'Yes.'

'So you, as a wizard,' said Drake, 'do you command this island?'

'I've a commander's power on Burntos if I choose to use it,' said Miphon. 'I've a warrant from the Confederation to prove that power. But I've more sense to try that power except under the pressure of necessity.'

'Man, power is for using. That's half the fun of having it.'

Miphon made no reply to that, but finished off his sewing. Drake had got blood on his hands. Miphon sponged the blood away. Which was unnecessary, but . . . nice. The touch of his firm, competent hands was . . . strangely relaxing.

Having cleaned the hands, Miphon started removing bloodstains from Drake's sealskins.

'No need for that,' said Drake, standing. 'The job's done, aye. Done well. I'll be off now. Oh – but I'll need a bandage for my head first.'

'For what do you need a bandage?' said Miphon. 'Fresh air and sunlight, that's the thing. Whoever does the doctoring on your ship, get them to check your wound daily.'

'How do you know of the ship?' said Drake.

'Do you think your vessel stands invisible?' said Miphon. 'This island is well-watched, though you may not have noticed the watchers. Everyone on Burntos knew of your ship long, long before your rowing boat ever reached for the shore.'

'Why so much effort spent watching?' said Drake.

'Because experience tells us it's necessary,' said Miphon. And, dipping a hand into the pocket where Drake had

245

hidden the blades he had filched off the bench, Miphon recovered his cutlery.

'Man!' said Drake, wide-eyed with wonder. 'How did those fancy little blades get in there? They must be magic, man! They must have flown through the air and slipped themselves inside there, for I swear I never touched them.'

'I'd find it hard to believe you,' said Miphon, 'except that I did indeed see them fly through the air and hide themselves in your pocket.'

'How did you manage to see that, when you were looking the other way at the time?'

'Being of elven descent,' said Miphon dryly, 'I have invisible eyes in the back of my head.'

On leaving Miphon's clinic, Drake thought about going back to the kitchen. No! Not a good idea! He had no chance against Oronoko. Better to wait till evening came. Then Zanya would preach. He would watch. Look for an opportunity.

A little time, that's all I need. A little time alone with the woman. Man, when she knows I've been chosen as the next king on Stokos, she'll be hot to have me. Surely.

One thing was for certain: he was not leaving Burntos without Zanya. But for the moment . . .

Find the Walrus. Aye. He'll be wondering where I've got to.

The sun was well up. The island was baking. Oven-dry. Wet patches of mirage shimmered on the barren rock.

How do soldiers survive?

Drake tried to imagine a soldier's life. Day after day on this lifeless rock. The inhuman discipline of parades. Inescapable routines. Not much variety in the food, either, if what he'd seen in the kitchen was anything to go by.

He saw, in the distance, a few stray figures standing beside a long, low, isolated building. His comrades? Only one way to find out . . .

On closing the distance, Drake found his captain in

conversation with two officers of the Landguard, who looked very smart indeed in their skyblue uniforms and their red leather open-weave sandals. Drake wondered what chance he had of stealing one of those uniforms. It would look real good on him, once the useless height had been cut out of it.

Slagger Mulps did not bother to greet Drake. He was talking money. His double-thumbed fists gesticulated as he emphasized his points.

'Where's the others?' said Drake.

Mulps did not condescend to notice him, but continued talking. His hands squeezed air, chopped it, shaped, thrusted and sliced. A dance of digital articulation, a counterpoint to his voice.

'. . . must understand our funds are not unlimited. I'm working under strict limitations, as I'm only an agent for a foreign buyer; I've got scant discretionary powers. You've already heard my uppermost offer.'

Man, friend Walrus is talking slick today! How came he by such slickness? Maybe he's a king in exile. Aye. Like King Tor. Like Menator, too. So many kings! A plague of kings . . .

'You must be getting a commission,' said one of the officers. 'If you really want to close the deal, perhaps you'll have to sacrifice a few percentage points of that commission. Because what you call your uppermost offer is in fact – and I'm sure you're aware of the fact – close to farcical. Our product is unique. You can't buy it elsewhere.'

'Yes,' said Mulps. 'But demand is minimal. That colours the case somewhat, does it not?'

Drake, losing interest in this dickering, wandered round the windowless building. He found a huge iron-studded sliding door at its southern end. Strange. He kicked it. The door rattled slightly. Then shook with a thunderous crash, as if a giant had kicked back from within. Startled, Drake leapt back.

'Who's there?' he said.

No answer.

247

He continued his circumnavigation of the building. Right down at the northern end he found a slim doorway leading into the gloom.

Dare I? I'm Drake Douay. Of course I dare!

He went through the door, and found a narrow passage which twisted left, then right, then left again, before opening into a small room lit by a slim overhead lightshaft. Bucks Cat and Ish Ulpin were there, down on their hands and knees staring into what looked like a giant mousehole.

'Hi,' said Drake. 'What're you looking at?'

'A monster,' said Bucks Cat.

'Let's see,' said Drake, and knelt down in front of the hole, which was large enough for him to have crawled through had he wanted to.

He found himself looking into a long hall, dimly lit by overhead lightshafts. Something was in there. What? He saw a gleam of something cool white, like ivory. A tusk? A feeding spike! There was a Neversh in there. Drake's knees began to ache from kneeling on the stone, but he did not rise. He was fascinated.

'Amazing,' he said. 'How did they get it in there?'

'The Neversh flew to the island,' said Ish Ulpin. 'It found all meat fled within the stone. Seeking flesh, it went through the only door – then some hero closed the door and trapped it.'

'But why would a Neversh go into this – this trap if there was no meat within.'

'Oh, there was meat,' said Ish Ulpin. 'It's done like this. A few people stand by the large doorway to tempt the Neversh inside. Then they flee to this end of the building and escape through the bolthole which you're looking at.'

'Man,' said Drake, with a shudder, 'they'd need to be heroes indeed to risk a face-to-face with a brute like that. I'm glad I'm not such a hero.'

'Of course you're such a hero,' said Ish Ulpin.

And he and Bucks Cat grabbed Drake. They forced him into the bolthole.

248

'Yaaa!' screamed Drake, struggling, bruising his shoulders on the walls of the giant mousehole.

The monster within stirred to life. Its wings beat, battering against the low stone roof. Its eight crocodile-sprawling feet tore screams of protest from the rock floor. Suddenly, Ish Ulpin and Bucks Cat stopped pushing. Drake thrust himself back. And felt something snag his arm.

'It's got me!' he screamed.

The Neversh had spiked his right arm with the tip of one of its grapple-hooks.

'Help!' screamed Drake. 'It's dragging me in!'

'We've got you!' yelled Bucks Cat, hauling on Drake's legs.

Drake felt his hands, greased with sweat, slide over the smooth stones of the mousehold as the Neversh dragged him toward his doom. Then agonizing pain ripped through his right arm. The grapple-hook had torn free. Pulled by Bucks Cat and Ish Ulpin, Drake shot out of the mousehole like a burst of water exploding out of a blowhole.

The three pirates collapsed in a heap on the floor. There was a hideous sound of ripping rock as the monster tried to tear its way through to the flesh which had just escaped. Drake got to his feet. He shambled through the dark, twisting exitway, colliding off first one wall then another.

A slash-sharp swash of sunlight. A giddy horizon. Swaying. The ground, buckling underfoot. Breath quick, heart quick. Quick to bursting. Glanced at the sun. White. Swaying. The sea was shuddering. The ground rocked underfoot.

'I can't come right!' he cried.

Tried to walk. Staggered, drunk, as the earth buckled. The ground split black in front of him. He screamed. The crack in the rock sprinted towards him. He jumped. Legs wide apart. The widening crack raced between his legs. Then slammed shut. Opened. Slammed. Opened. Slammed. Opened.

249

Drake jumped sideways. Tried to run. Fell. Saw Bucks Cat weaving from side to side, his black face shining with sweat and sunlight. Saw Ish Ulpin, the tall pale man floundering, grasping at air.

Am I mad?

The ground rocked again. Then steadied. Drake heard waves thrashing against the shore. Someone wailing. He got to his knees, breathed dust, coughed, sneezed. A distant shout. His torn right arm. Vivid red. Blood. Gore. Deep. Sweat dripped from his forehead in heavy drops. Running as free as blood.

'Man!' said Bucks Cat. 'Oh man . . .'

Drake stood, slowly. There were gaping cracks in the building which held the Neversh. The monster was scrabbling fiercely within. Ish Ulpin clapped a hand on Drake's shoulder.

'You all right?' he said.

'I live,' said Drake. 'But, man, we'd better get out of here before that monster tries something else. It's powerful fierce, man!'

Bucks Cat hooted with laughter. And Ish Ulpin said, with unwonted gentleness:

'It wasn't the monster which shook the world. It was an earthquake.'

'Earthquake?' said Drake.

'Aye,' said Ish Ulpin. 'Have you never been in an earthquake before?'

'This was my first,' said Drake. 'What makes these earthquake things?'

'War waged by demon-gods in the halls of hell,' said Ish Ulpin. 'That's what makes earthquakes, or so I've been told. The monster's a lesser danger – and we'll have no more trouble from it till we try to put it on our ship.'

'How did you do this?' said the wizard Miphon, examining Drake's torn forearm.

'Man, I was stroking a tabby cat when the vicious little hussy scratched me.'

'I suppose you pulled its tail,' said Miphon, deadpan, clearing away some of the weltering blood with a moist sponge.

'Man,' said Drake, in alarm, peering into the gaping gash, 'there's the end of a tendon! I've cut a tendon! Man, I'm crippled for life!'

'Don't worry about that tendon there,' said Miphon, touching the offending article with the tip of a probe. 'That's surplus to requirements. We haven't used that for millions of years.'

'Then when did we use it?'

'At an earlier stage in our evolution. Humans were fish once, then lizards.'

'A likely story!' said Drake.

'More likely than some of those you tell,' said Miphon. 'I'll put some internal sutures in here.'

'More cat-gut?'

'It's the only thing to use,' said Miphon. 'It'll dissolve within the wound when its job's done.'

And he began to sew.

'I hope these stitches work better than your magic,' said Drake.

'What magic is that?' said Miphon.

'Why, that magic philtre you sold me, to cure me of love when I first fell for the fair Zanya Kliedervaust.'

'Ah, that,' said Miphon. 'I remember the philtre. But as for this business of selling it . . . as I remember, it was a gift freely given.'

'Aye. Given free, since worthless. Man, that was no love-cure. That was an aphrodisiac! It set me lusting like an octopus.'

'Did you use the philtre by moonlight, as directed?' said Miphon. 'Did you kiss the ground to invoke her power?'

'Why, no, but—'

'True wizards never embellish magic with useless ceremony,' said Miphon. 'Every instruction must be followed if you wish for success.'

'Oh,' said Drake. 'Now I understand. How about some

251

magic to help me out with my lady? I didn't do too well on our first encounter.'

'How,' said Miphon, swabbing the wound, 'did you approach the lady?'

'I jumped on top of her,' said Drake.

'That wasn't very nice!'

'Man, that's what women are made for.'

'Have you asked a woman about that?'

'What would you know about it? You're a virgin.'

'Whatever I am,' said Miphon, 'I can tell you this. Young Zanya has been through hard times.'

'How would you know?'

'She speaks with me here on occasions,' said Miphon. 'I cannot tell you details, for that would be unethical. But I can tell you that. She is deeply suspicious of men and their motives. With good reason. If you would win her, then you must give her reason to trust you.'

'How can I do that when she's crazy on faith?'

'Her faith,' said Miphon, digging in with a needle, 'is at least in part a source of reassurance. If you can give her such, then the faith may . . . it may, perhaps, accommodate the flesh.'

'Give me a potion to make her love me,' said Drake.

'There is,' said Miphon, 'no such potion. Magic is better at destruction than at building.'

'Magic built the flame trench Drangsturm, did it not?' said Drake.

'It did indeed. But the flame trench is itself an instrument of destruction. All it creates is violence – a violence which divides the north of Argan from the terror-lands of the Deep South.'

'Man,' said Drake, 'I've been thinking about that flame trench. That earthquake thing we had just now, could such rip Drangsturm into halves? Could it tear rock so wild that the Swarms found a way north?'

'Drangsturm is indeed vulnerable to earthquake,' said Miphon gravely. 'And, indeed, to other dangers. That is why the castles of the Confederation stand guard, with the

252

Landguard to support them. But . . . don't worry too much. Drangsturm has protected the north for the last four thousand years, ever since the end of the Long War.'

'The Long War? I've heard rumours of such. Was it wizards and heroes, as they say?'

'It was before my time,' said Miphon. 'But there was indeed an Alliance of wizards and heroes. They fought the Swarms and threw them back to the Deep South.'

'So . . . if the Swarms came north again, they could be beaten back.'

'The Alliance,' said Miphon, 'had use of ancient weapons which were destroyed by their employment. None such remains to us – therefore, we could not be certain of a second victory.'

'You talk of nonsense,' said Drake. 'There's no weapon you can only use once. A weapon lasts near enough to forever, aye, any swordsmith will tell you that.'

'A burning arrow is a weapon, is it not?' said Miphon. 'And how many times can you use a burning arrow?'

'Seventy-five thousand,' said Drake, promptly.

'You've got a quick wit,' said Miphon. 'Your voice will serve you well in love and war, if you cultivate it. Remember that, when you court the lady Kliedervaust.'

Evening. Mosquito dance. Standing on the stony beach by an open fire, Zanya Kliedervaust preached to a scattering of soldiers. The purple-skinned Oronoko squatted at her feet, a cudgel in his hands. There was, in consequence, no heckling. Drake hung back in the shadows, reluctant to risk the wrath of Oronoko. He was slightly weak from blood-loss, and definitely in no state for fighting.

She was talking of things he had heard before from Gouda Muck and Sully Yot. Talking of purity. Abstinence. Denial.

'How far away is the moon?' she said.

'Further than I can throw an apple,' volunteered one of the soldiers.

Zanya took a few moments to make sense of that. Her

253

Galish had improved, but it seemed she still found swift speech hard to follow.

'Yes,' she said, at length. 'It is further than we could throw an apple. But things lie hidden within the dark well within a stone's-throw. For dark hides. Dark conceals. Dark entangles. It is light which reveals. Light which clarifies. Light which makes possible. Fire is light. Light is fire.

'In darkness is secrecy. Secrecy is darkness. Which among you has not a secret which is shameful? Which amongst you could stand bare in truth like the purity of those higher fires, the sun and moon? Yield to the Flame, and the Flame will burn you clean, yea, and you too will stand naked to the eye of truth yet unashamed.'

Thus she spoke.

But there was no fervour in her speech. She was tired. Weary from a long day in the kitchen. She had laboured many days without a break. Each evening she had preached, mouthing the words so many times they had almost lost their meanings. She spoke by rote.

Drake saw she was so fatigued, so hollow, so worn by routine, that she herself had almost ceased to live. What lived in her was habit. She had become a puppet animated by the alien routines imposed upon her by Gouda Muck. The old man's words had replaced her will. It was not her voice which spoke, but his. She had become his creature.

Watching, listening, Drake had an unfamiliar intimation of evil. Muck had made Zanya into a weapon. A burning arrow. How many times can a burning arrow be used? She was destroying herself. Nothing on this island of barren rock and inhuman routine would nourish or cherish her. Muck had made her his voice and had sent her into the world to be ruined.

Drake felt sorry for her.

Creeping away into the dark, he made his plans. It was all very well for the wizard Miphon to suggest that he win Zanya by fair speech, but that was impossible. Oronoko would let him nowhere near the woman.

She would have to be kidnapped. For her own good, mind! Hauled aboard the *Walrus*. Then tamed at leisure. Taught to be a woman again. It might take some doing. But Drake Douay was equal to the task . . .

'What's she to you?' said Slagger Mulps. 'You're in lust? You want her as your fancy woman, perhaps? Do you think I'll risk my ship for the whim of your cock?'

'Man, she's nothing to me,' said Drake, hastily. 'But she's lots to Muck. She's his disciple, don't you know. Man, we can use her as hostage. A pawn in the war for Stokos.'

'Hmmm,' said the Walrus, running his hand through his green beard as he thought. 'Perhaps King Tor would like to lay hands on Muck's disciple.'

'Oh, I don't think that's really a good idea,' said Drake. 'Man, he might rip her in half.'

'Who cares if he does?' said Mulps. 'She's nothing to you, is she? The boys can have fun with her first, before we hand her over. An'vory likes red meat. I've a taste for such myself, if it comes to that.'

Atsimo Andranovory was indeed pleased when he heard about Drake's scheme to kidnap Zanya Kliedervaust.

'So the young pup's good for something after all,' he growled.

'It's a great idea, man,' said Bucks Cat, slapping Drake on the back.

'Aye,' said Ish Ulpin, squeezing his shoulder. 'We'll let you lead the rape pack when we get the wench aboard.'

And Simp Fiche drooled.

Three days went by.

Drake endured agonies of horror, guilt and despair. His brilliant idea had gone wrong. But he should have known what would happen! He knew what pirates were like. Aye. And what would happen now? Why, Zanya would be likely ripped apart. And would welcome such death, having wished herself dead many times before.

He had planned for things to be so nice. Her and him, alone in the dark together. Him explaining things to her, reasonable like. Maybe a little force, if strictly necessary – but just by way of introduction, to show her what delights were available.

The reality . . .

The reality which threatened was like something out of nightmare. A long slow voyage of repeated rape, with death at the hands of King Tor at the end of it.

What should he do?

Warn Zanya? No – that would ruin his chances with the woman for a lifetime.

Talk to Mulps, perhaps? Explain that the woman was rightly his, was special, was – well, his true love. No. That would never work. He was only aboard the *Walrus* on sufferance. Mulps would scarcely take kindly to having Drake Douay dictate his behaviour.

Then—

What if he betrayed Slagger Mulps? Narked to the soldiers, so an ambush was waiting when the raiding party came to kidnap Zanya? What then? The ship would be seized, Slagger Mulps and crew would be killed or enslaved, and Drake would have a lot of explaining to do if he ever got back to the Greaters.

Besides . . .

Whale Mike was his friend, was he not? Yes. The dumb yellow-faced earless monster was, when all was said and done, a true friend. Drake could scarcely sacrifice the ship – if only for the sake of Whale Mike. And Rolf Thelemite – he wasn't bad. You could even say a thing or two for Bucks Cat and Ish Ulpin, despite their murderous taste in practical jokes.

'The thing to do,' said Drake to Drake, as he walked alone on the shores of Burntos, 'would be to kidnap Zanya on my own. Aye. Then get her to the mainland in a boat.'

Possible. But – where would they go? Where would

they hide if Oronoko came hunting for them? If he killed his purple-skinned rival, how would the Landguard take that? How much of the mainland was under Landguard jurisdiction?

There were too many unknowns.

Besides – he had to go back to the Greaters. Otherwise he would never win King Tor's confidence. He would never get to marry Tor's ogre daughter, Hilda, or be crowned king of Stokos. He would never again see his brother Heth. Or Jon Arabin. Or any of his friends from the *Warwolf*.

'There has to be another way,' said Drake.

On the afternoon of the third day, as the captive Neversh, weakened by lack of water, was dragged in chains to the ship, Drake realized what he had to do. He went to see the wizard Miphon.

'Man,' said Drake, 'you've a commander's powers on Burntos, isn't that so?'

'I said as much,' said Miphon. 'I meant as much.'

'Then, man . . . I don't know how to put this. It's delicate, see. Some friends of mine . . . well, they've let high-spirits carry them away. You know how men talk, aye, wild-like, boasting of things round booze. Well, these friends . . . usually their crazy thinking wears off with the drink. But this time, it stuck. I'm . . . these are my friends, man. I don't want to betray them. But I thought maybe – maybe you could help them keep from trouble. By removing temptation. Subtle, like. Without saying anything about anyone informing or such.'

'You can trust me,' said Miphon. 'Speak.'

When Drake got back to the *Walrus*, the Neversh was being folded in thirds to make it fit into the treasure hold, which lay forward of the hold in which Whale Mike lived, cooked and slept. Ish Ulpin winked at Drake, and Bucks Cat slapped him on the back.

'Tonight's the night, eh?' said Bucks Cat.

'For sure,' said Drake.

'You'll be coming with us, I suppose,' said Ish Ulpin casually.

Drake's first thought was to answer 'no'. But he couldn't do that – it would arouse suspicion.

'Of course,' he said, voice cool as a wet-skinned squid hauled writhing from the blue-black depths of the sea.

So that was it. He was committed ashore on tonight's raiding expedition to capture Zanya Kliedervaust. What if the wizard Miphon had failed to exile Zanya and Oronoko, as he had promised? What if they were delayed in getting off the island? Worse – what if Miphon, despite his promises, had arranged for an ambush?

Tonight, man, perhaps tonight you die.

18

Miphon: a slender green-eyed travelling healer; a minor
wizard of the order of Nin, who sometimes claims to be of
elven descent.

It was night. The *Walrus* was ready to sail. Only one task
remained: to kidnap Zanya Kliedervaust. The raiding
party gathered on deck under a gloomy sky pitted by stars.
Off to the south, some scanty cloud reflected the glowering red blaze of distant Drangsturm. The raiders were
hot, fierce, excited.

'Action!' said Rolf Thelemite. 'That's the thing! Blood
and steel!'

'Don't be too keen to start anything,' warned Praul
Galana. 'The odds are against us if it comes to a fight.'

'Man,' said Drake, 'I'm in no state for fighting – or
anything else. Better I stay on the ship.'

His right arm, torn by a captive Neversh then sewn up
by the wizard Miphon, was still in a sling. It ached incessantly; it had been keeping him awake at night.

'You're coming,' said Slagger Mulps. 'Get in the boat!'

'What boat?' said Drake, peering down at the darkened
sea.

'It's down there,' said Mulps. 'At the end of the rope
ladder.'

'How do I climb down with only one arm?'

'Climb! Or I'll give you the problem of climbing with
none!'

With difficulty, Drake descended the rope ladder to the

raiding boat. Its crew was Slagger Mulps, Ish Ulpin, Bucks Cat, Rolf Thelemite, Praul Galana and Atsimo Andranovory.

'Who's been drinking?' said Drake, smelling alcohol.

'We're all stone-sober here,' said Andranovory, his brewery breath washing over Drake's face as he spoke.

'Man, you're half-way pickled,' said Drake in disgust. 'This is a nice start! And where's Whale Mike? Eh?'

'What would we want with him?' said Ish Ulpin, as the boat got underway.

'He's muscle,' said Drake, nursing his sore arm as best he could as dark-tongued waves nagged at the boat. 'A monster like that – he must be something terrible in a fight.'

'Let's not be calling our good friend a monster,' said Slagger Mulps, a note of warning in his voice.

'Whatever we call him,' said Drake, 'he's built for battle.'

'Oh yes,' said Bucks Cat, with a chuckle. 'Built beautiful. But soft as a sea slug. He never likes to kill. Not like some of us.'

Silence, then, as the rowers pulled for the shore. Burntos, by night, was an ominous, almost featureless mass. Far off down the shore, a bonfire was burning. Praul Galana, having shaped words to his satisfaction, spoke:

'Whale Mike, he's a good cook and a better carpenter, aye, but he hates to hurt people. So he's not much good in a fight, not unless he's really stirred up. Anyway, there'll be no fighting tonight.'

'Not unless our drunken friend starts some trouble for us,' said Drake savagely.

'Who you calling drunk?' said Andranovory.

'Hush, An'vory,' said Mulps. 'Drake – keep your mouth shut. Your every word shows you shit-scared frightened.'

'I'm not frightened,' said Drake, trying to keep his voice steady. 'But there's a right way to do things, aye.

260

Like doing some thinking. Aye. And leaving our drunks behind.'

'Yes,' said Rolf Thelemite, 'and keeping our voices down so we can't be heard more than twenty leagues away.'

Drake realized then that his voice had been getting louder and louder as he spoke. He was about to explain the reasons for his anger further, then thought better of it and shut his mouth firmly.

'Ship oars,' said Mulps.

Wet and dripping, the oars came into the boat. Pain jolted Drake's arm as the boat rocked as men jumped to the knee-deep water.

'Come, man,' said Rolf Thelemite, helping Drake into the cold of the sea.

Drake trudged out of the water while the others hauled the boat onto the beach, where the sea's shuzzle and hiss, snake-sibilant, wracked shingle back. Onshore, the sullen shapes of massive buildings loomed dark against dark.

'Take her up,' said Mulps.

And, boots sliding on the sea-wet stones, the men took the boat higher, scraping her underside against the shingle. They made so much noise about it that Drake wanted to scream. He controlled himself. Then could not help but say:

'Man, we'll be a long time getting the boat afloat if we have to leave in a hurry.'

'Fear gives strength,' said Rolf Thelemite. 'If we run from war we'll shove it to sea so quick you'd think it flew.'

By starlight they trooped in single file through the warm night, led by Praul Galana, who had been kept busy over the last couple of days locating Zanya's sleeping quarters and planning the best attack route.

What would the pirates do when they found Zanya gone? Would they suspect that Drake was responsible for thwarting their kidnap raid?

Man, maybe I should run.

It would be easy enough to slip away into the dark, that

was for sure. But what then? He would be left stranded on Burntos, amongst strangers, hundreds of leagues from his hopes of a royal marriage and the throne of Stokos.

We've got to see this through, man. It's the only way.

From a building which must have been a bar came raucous sounds of singing; obviously soldiers were, in the time-honoured fashion, relieving the tedium of garrison duty by getting drunk. Praul Galana halted the pirates beside a long, low, dark, silent building, not far from the bar.

'We're here,' said Galana.

'What place is this?' said Rolf Thelemite.

'The kitchen,' said Galana. 'The red-skinned wench sleeps in a small room right at the end.'

The door to the kitchen was locked, but the pirates broke it down. The noise was covered by the uproar from the bar. If Drake was any judge, then a brawl was in progress in that place of entertainment.

The raiders ventured into the bowel-black dark of the kitchen, picking their way between tables and benches. Inside, it was quiet; the noise from the bar was almost inaudible.

'Booze here,' said Andranovory.

'Then leave it alone,' said Mulps, shortly.

'As you will,' said Andranovory.

'Here's the door,' said Praul Galana.

The raiders gathered at the door to Zanya's quarters.

'Drake,' said Slagger Mulps. 'You go first.'

'What?' said Drake. 'Me with my torn arm and all? Man, that woman's a right handful. Let An'vory go. An'vory? Where are you? Boozing, is it?'

'Never you mind about An'vory,' said Mulps. 'In you go.'

So saying, Mulps opened the door. Squealing, something flung itself forward.

'Ahyak Rovac!' screamed Rolf Thelemite.

There was a crash as Thelemite's blade, sweeping through the dark, chopped into a stack of dirty saucepans.

Pirates swore, shouted and grappled with their enemy.

'It's a pig!' said Galana.

'Man,' said Drake, sounding aggrieved, 'you must've led us to the wrong door.'

'There was only the one,' said Galana.

While they were still arguing about it, Drake heard someone approaching.

'Hush!' he said.

'What?' said Andranovory.

'*Gram grup!*' said Mulps sharply.

Andranovory got the message, and was silent, as were the other pirates. Waiting. Breathing the dark. Listening. Hearing . . . footsteps outside. A voice talking quick and low. Someone answering. Trampling boots entering the kitchen. A sliver of wood breaking free with a twang as someone pried it away from the wreckage of the kitchen door.

The boots halted.

If Drake was any judge, at least half a dozen strangers had entered the kitchen. Demon's luck – they had no lantern! That was something to be thankful for.

'*Epigrow manact agrama!*' said a loud, curt voice.

Drake wanted to sneeze. He had to sneeze! He grabbed his nose, contorted his face, scrunched his chin down against his chest – and just managed to kill the sneeze.

'*Lupopt elestag oxybund, morasuf aparsing,*' said the same harsh voice which had spoken previously.

Drake listened.

Did he imagine it? Or did he heard Mulps breathing? He was, surely, imagining it. He could scarcely hear his own breathing.

'We know you're in here, whoever you are,' said the harsh voice, switching to the Galish Trading Tongue. 'Surrender yourselves!'

Silence.

Then someone burped.

'Seize him!'

Boots clattered over the stone floor as half a dozen soldiers homed in on the burp. There was a brief scuffle.

'Hey!' said Andranovory, slurring the word in a way which made it obvious he had been drinking.

As the soldiers hustled Andranovory away, the pirates followed as quiet as they could, slipping out into the night.

'Well,' muttered Mulps, when they were in the clear: 'That's An'vory done for.'

'No!' protested Rolf Thelemite. 'We can't leave a comrade!'

And, drawing his sword, Rolf Thelemite charged after Andranovory's captors, screaming a challenge as he went:

'Ahyak Rovac!'

Voices cried in alarm. Blade clashed against blade in the dark of the night.

'We're with you!' roared Praul Galana.

Slagger Mulps swore, then joined the fray himself.

Drake, ruled by his concern for his injured arm, backed off into the night. He bumped into someone, who grabbed his sore arm.

'Gaaa!' screamed Drake.

And won his freedom with a head-butt and a savage elbow blow. Then he backed off some more. He saw lanterns weaving through the night, drawn to the noise of combat. Then he heard the voice of Slagger Mulps raised above the confusion:

'With me, boys! Time to go!'

Feet pounded away into the night. Drake followed as best he could. Tripped. Fell. Rose. Blundered. Which way was which? He was disorientated. Lost. Some lanterns were coming his way. He scuttled away into the dark. Was brought up hard by a building. Sat down, half stunned.

More lanterns!

Help!

Drake eased himself along the side of the building until he found a doorway. He slipped inside. The building felt empty. He risked snapping his fingers, once. The crisp sound confirmed his impression of any empty, unfurnished building. He sat down in the shadows, and began to wait.

*   *   *

264

Near dawn, light began to filter through gaping cracks in the roof and walls of the building Drake was sheltering in, and he understood the reason for its emptiness – it had been abandoned because of earthquake damage.

Shivering, he slipped outside.

A glance at the sea told him the *Walrus* was gone. He was marooned on Burntos! What now? Hide? Impossible. Swim for the shore? It was too far – particularly with his wounded arm. There was only one choice: to surrender.

Accordingly, Drake surrendered himself to the wizard Miphon, who took the matter lightly.

'While there was a brawl last night,' said the wizard, 'nobody was hurt. Your ship has escaped with all her crew, so there'll be no trials or other nonsense.'

'What happens to me, then?'

'Why, you'll stay with me till you leave the island. I should by rights report to the Confederation regarding our earthquake damage. So . . . tomorrow will be as good a time as any. We'll leave Burntos then.'

'Where going?' said Drake.

'Why, to Drangsturm, of course,' said Miphon. 'To the Castle of Controlling Power. That's where the Confederation's based.'

'So that leaves me with a day to look around the island,' said Drake, thinking he had better make the best possible use of this one last chance to hunt down Zanya Kliedervaust and make her his.

'Not so!' said Miphon. 'It gives you a day to scrub out my clinic.'

'Man,' said Drake, 'you can't make me work! I'm injured! I was wounded by that Neversh, you sewed up the wound yourself.'

'You're fit enough for trouble,' said Miphon, 'so you're fit enough to work.'

Drake was determined not to work – but the green-eyed wizard proved to have an unexpected amount of will-power. Much sweeping, cleaning, scrubbing and polishing later, night came. And, after night, the morrow.

After a lean breakfast of rice and fish, Drake and Miphon went and sought out the cutter which was going to take them to the mainland. She was commanded by a jowly, sunburnt boatman, and had a crew of three. The only passengers were Miphon, Drake, Zanya Kliedervaust and Prince Oronoko.

'Zanya!' said Drake, delighted to see his truly beloved once again. 'You!'

'Who is he?' said Zanya, who was naturally suspicious of the rough-dressed fair-haired fellow who was gawking at her charms with such obvious lust. 'What's he doing here?'

'You'd better ask him that yourself,' said Miphon.

Oronoko, speaking softly in his native Frangoni, asked Zanya if the youth with the degenerate eyes was troubling her, and if she wanted him broken in half. Zanya, speaking in the same Frangoni, reminded Oronoko that the pure did not kill. Except, replied Oronoko, when confronted with the impure.

'Have you two begun to argue theology?' said Miphon, who had a fair command of Frangoni himself. 'If so, get in the boat – we can't wait thrice seven years for your wills to come to agreement.'

All embarked on the cutter, which set sail. As the frail vessel ghosted along, Drake listened to Zanya's incomprehensible argument with Oronoko, and watched some soldiers who were beginning to demolish an earthquake-damaged building. Unless he was mistaken, it was the same structure which had housed the captive Neversh before the unfortunate brute was loaded with chains and hauled aboard the *Walrus*.

He shuddered.

'Man,' said Drake, to Miphon, 'I've been thinking about this Neversh you let loose by way of trade. That's a mighty strange thing to do, isn't it?'

'Why so?' said Miphon.

'Well, I mean – wizards built Drangsturm to keep the Swarms south. Right? So why sell one of the monsters

266

north? Surely that's as bad as breaching Drangsturm.'

'If Drangsturm were breached,' said Miphon, 'then the Swarms would come north in their thousands. One single monster is little danger – for the Neversh, brute for brute, are weaker than dragons. Such sales give the Confederation profits. Also, they serve a wise purpose – they help remind the rest of the world what task we do here.'

'Why should the world need reminding?' said Drake.

'Because,' said Miphon, 'since people are as they are, some refuse to believe that the Swarms exist at all. They think we fake nightmare through lies or rank exaggeration to preserve the wealth of the south of Argan for ourselves.'

'I never thought such!' said Drake.

'I never said you did,' said Miphon. 'But there are those who believe the Confederation does not protect the north, but, instead, keeps the north in poverty by frightening honest men away from southern wealth. Ah . . . the fair lady Kliedervaust seems to have a question.'

Zanya Kliedervaust did indeed have a question. Her argument with Oronoko concluded, she was ready to interrogate Drake Douay.

'Explain yourself,' she said.

Drake cleared his throat noisily, hawked, then spat to the dark green sea. This was a very sticky situation. Zanya was a disciple of Gouda Muck. She believed that the infamous Drake Douay was the accursed son of Hagon. Beside her sat the formidable Oronoko, he of the purple skin and the violet eyes. And Drake was in no condition for fighting.

'My name,' said Drake, 'ah, that's not given lightly to strangers. But I've given it already to the wizard Miphon, aye, for I'm a friend to wizards and trust them well. So I'll give my name to you. It's Arabin. Or, to be exact, Arabin lol Arabin.'

'There was a pirate named Arabin,' said the jowly, sunburnt boatman who commanded the cutter. 'I knew him well when I were of the Greaters. But he were black, not blond.'

'Yes, well,' said Drake, 'that must be coincidence then.

267

Though I've had affairs with pirates, aye, I'll not deny it.'

'Affairs?' said Zanya, with an expression of disgust on her face. 'Affairs of lust?'

'Nay, woman,' said Drake. 'Not thus but otherwise. I was a swordsmith of Stokos, where I trained under Oleg the Blademaster. He sent me to 'Marphos on a mission, aye.'

'Androlmarphos,' said Zanya, 'is a seething brew of vices, a den of iniquity, a pit of poxed spirits and demented souls.'

'Very likely,' said Drake, 'but I can't speak for that myself, since I never reached the place. The ship which bore me was taken by pirates.'

'Yet you lived,' said Zanya, her voice accusing. 'You did not die in the defence of your ship against evil.'

'I had no chance to die,' said Drake. 'For I were below decks, helplessly seasick. Thus I was taken prisoner. Since then, I've slaved for the pirates as a cook's boy, working under pain of death. But now I've made my escape, and hope for gainful employment elsewhere.'

Prince Oronoko addressed Zanya softly.

'We've met before, haven't we?' said Zanya.

'Tell me about it,' said Drake.

'You were that demented fisherman's boy we dragged out of the sea near a horizon from Cam. That was before I'd first set foot on Stokos.'

'Aye, that was me,' said Drake.

'Then you came to me again,' said Zanya, with undisguised anger in her voice.

'I did?' said Drake, all injured innocence.

'In the leper colony. You tried to rape me!'

This woman could obviously carry a grudge for a long time. Drake tried to think. How was he going to handle this one? He looked to the wizard Miphon for help – but that worthy was staring at a low-skimming seagull, as if in love with the thing.

'Man,' said Drake, thinking quickly, 'I jumped you, I'll not deny it. But I didn't get very far, did I? You punched me over something fearful.'

'Failure excuses nothing,' said Zanya.

'Man,' said Drake, 'then let the truth excuse me. It was my body which made the attempt, but not my will. For I wasn't truly myself. I was under the command of witchcraft. Someone worked the Black Arts on me.'

Zanya turned to Miphon.

'Is this true?' she said.

'What?' said Miphon, jerking upright, startled, as if woken out of a dream.

'This – this pirate says it was witchcraft that made him try to rape me. Is that true?'

'That is hardly for me to say,' said Miphon, blandly, 'for I, as a wizard, know nothing of witchcraft.'

Zanya snorted.

'Your excuse,' she said to Drake, 'lets you live. But don't presume that your excuse gives you permission to speak to me.'

'I'll find the permission I want, in time,' said Drake.

Fortunately, he said it in his native Ligin, which Zanya did not understand. She did not ask for a translation, but sat talking quietly with Oronoko as the cutter made its way south toward Drangsturm.

Near evening, after a long, hot day of idling calms and desultory breezes, the cutter landed her passengers at the western end of Drangsturm, where the awesome upthrust of the Castle of Controlling Power stood guard against the Swarms. Drake was dismayed to see that the flame trench did not run all the way to the sea. Instead, a buffer of basalt two hundred paces broad separated flame from sea.

'Man,' said Drake, pointing at the bare rock, where only a low parapet protected north from south, 'this is right daft, having a hole like this in our defence.'

'The rocks of this fire dyke are so hot they'd explode if the cold sea touched them,' explained Miphon. 'Hence the plug of rock. It's a killing ground. Don't worry – little has crossed it in the last four thousand years.'

And he led the way toward the nearest gate of the castle. That castle, its jumbled walls and towering spires flung upwards as if at random, looked as if it had been fathered by earthquake and mothered by a bad-tempered volcano.

'Why stands the castle in such strange array?' said Drake.

'Because it was not built by human hand,' said Miphon.

'How was it built then?'

'Wizards united their power to call from the ocean legion upon legion of squid and of octopus. Yea, even the might of the kraken was summoned to the building. Hence the intelligence you see in the stone is not that of mortal men.'

'That's a strange way to build,' said Drake.

'But a quick one,' said Miphon. 'The castle was built in a night. It had to be done by dark, since the creatures we worked with hate the light. That explains, you see, some of the flaws in the construction.'

'Oh,' said Drake.

Then stopped, pointing south.

'Look! A league south! Men!'

'Southsearchers, that's all,' said Miphon. 'They've started out on patrol. They march mostly by night, since the Swarms sleep then. By day they shelter.'

'Do the Southsearchers dare themselves that way?' said Drake, pointing westward, in the direction of Ling.

'Lands west do not concern us,' said Miphon.

'Have you tried to explore those lands?'

'Why should we? There's no profit in exploration.'

'Man,' said Drake, 'there might be cities out there, aye, cities built of gold. Or lands of pearl diving, perhaps.'

He was trying to find out whether his knowledge of the existence of Ling might have some value in the market place. His hopes were disappointed when Miphon laughed and said:

'Perhaps. But we're rich as it is, for all trade between the Inner Waters and the Drangsturm Gulf passes through the Confederation's hands. Come on, let's not stand here chattering.'

'What trade is that you speak of?' said Drake.

270

'The trade in sponges, pearls, slaves, crocodile skin, whale oil, scrimshaw and keflo shell, amongst other things. The Galish kafilas take such north along the Salt Road, together with siege dust of wizard manufacture, and other things. And it is with the Galish that you yourself, in all probability, will soon be going.'

'Soon?' said Drake.

'Depending,' said Miphon, 'on what the Confederation decides to do about your case.'

'My case?' said Drake. 'Man, what are you talking about?'

'You are, after all, a pirate,' said Miphon, 'or an associate of such. I bear you no will. As for the Confederation – well, we own no ships, and none of the sea reavers ventures this far south. Hence we suffer nothing from pirates. But, even so, the Confederation cannot lightly accept the presence of a lawless pirate in the heart of power.'

'Man,' said Drake, 'I'm a very law-abiding boy! Famous for it! Man, I'm meak, mild, honest, upright, and sober as a sledgehammer. You'll get no trouble out of me.'

He desperately wanted to win the trust of the wizards, so that he would be at liberty to use his wiles on Zanya Kliedervaust. But, shortly after passing through the nearest gate of the Castle of Controlling Power, Drake found himself taken in charge by some blue-uniformed Landguard troopers, and thrown into a prison cell to await the pleasure of the Confederation.

19

The Galish: the nomadic trading people of the Salt Road, that trade route which runs up the western flank of Argan from Drangsturm to Narba, to Veda, Selzirk and Runcorn, through Chorst and Dybra to Estar, up the Hollern River to Lake Armansis, to Larbster Bay on the coast of the Penvash Channel, then from D'Waith along the southern seaboard of the Ravlish Lands, ultimately finishing up in Chi'ash-lan in the Cold West.

'Justice delayed is justice denied.'

So believed the Confederation of Wizards.

Therefore, at noon the next day, a subcommittee of the Confederation gathered to consider the case of Arabin lol Arabin, a pirate or associate of pirates left stranded on Burntos after an unexplained brawl.

Unfortunately, the subcommittee decided it was right and proper for them to sentence him to death – and they duly did so. Fortunately, the sentence was suspended. Unfortunately, the subcommittee ruled that the sentence was to be carried out if Arabin lol Arabin had not gone north by nightfall.

A Galish kafila was leaving that very afternoon; Miphon made sure that his young guest went with it.

'Man,' said Drake, as they parted, 'I'd like to stay just a day or two longer. Why, I haven't even had a good look at Drangsturm yet. That's all I ask – just a day as a tourist or such, so I can tell my grandchildren all about it.'

'Knowing you.' said Miphon, who was a better judge of

character than Drake thought he was, 'one extra day would give you unlimited opportunities for getting into trouble. Anyway, the Justice Committee makes no jokes – if you're not gone by dusk, you really will get your head chopped off.'

'And if I return?'

'If you return, your fate will be the same. So . . . till we meet again.'

They clasped hands. Briefly. Then the Galish camel caravan set off. They camped by the roadside that night. Drake, his mind hot with thoughts of Zanya Kliedervaust, planned to slip away in the dark and dare his way back to Drangsturm. But the Galish tied him hand and foot before they went to bed.

'You can't do this to me!' said Drake. 'This is outrageous!'

'The wizard Miphon has paid us to take you all the way to Narba,' came the reply. 'So take you to Narba we will.'

It was a long way to Narba – a journey of well over a hundred leagues, on which Drake acquired an abiding hatred of that execrable hunchback, the camel. All the way he plotted and schemed. He would have Zanya Kliedervaust. He must! That was what his flesh demanded. That would be his revenge on Sully Yot and Gouda Muck. And . . . if he could convert Zanya away from the worship of Muck, no doubt she could help free the rest of Stokos from that same weird cult.

'It's not for myself that I want her,' said Drake to Drake. 'No, I want her because I'm a patriot. She's part of the key to the liberation of Stokos, aye, and the restoration of good King Tor.'

At Narba, he would turn back and make for the south again. Only: he would make very sure that he stole a horse for the journey, not a camel.

The kafila reached Narba.

And the Galish handed Drake over to the harbour guard, and he was marched off to the harbour jails and imprisoned without explanation.

*   *   *

273

The harbour jail boasted two rows of twenty cells, with a central corridor running between them. Drake knew not how many of those cells were inhabited, for he was denied a guided tour; instead, he was locked up without ceremony, and left to stew.

'This is a right mess,' muttered Drake, exploring the confines of his one-dwarf cell, which did not take long at all.

A little rudimentary light guttered through a rat-squeeze window, breeding shadows amongst the heaps of stinking damp straw covering the floor.

The weakest part of the cell was probably the door, which was made of metal bars. As Drake tested its strength – without much hope – a voice spoke from the cell directly opposite his.

'It's you, isn't it?' said the black-bearded voice.

'No,' said Drake. 'It's someone else altogether.'

'I knew it was you!' said Atsimo Andranovory. 'I'm going to rip you limb to limb.'

As the boozy thug was locked away well out of reach, this threat made little impression on Drake, who responded by faking a laugh.

'Thrown off the *Walrus*, were you?' he said. 'Slagger Mulps finally found what you were made of, did he?'

'Aaagh,' said Andranovory, hawking, then spitting in Drake's direction. 'Mulps and me, we had a difference, yes. But nothing like the difference he's got with you. Traitor!'

'What's this traitor business?' said Drake, sounding hurt.

'You betrayed us on Burntos, didn't you? That's why the woman was gone from her room. That's why the soldiers jumped us.'

'The soldiers jumped one of us,' said Drake. 'One of us who was drunk, aye, and noisy with it. If I'd betrayed us to Burntos, the soldiers would have sought for more than one.'

'*Nara zabara jok*!' said Andranovory.

And spat once more in Drake's direction. Drake replied in kind.

Five days, five lean meals and several spitting competitions later, both Drake and Andranovory were hauled from their cells. They were dragged into the daylight and brought before a dour man who wore red rope-soled shoes, red robes and a red turban. He was as black as Jon Arabin. Unless Drake was much mistaken, this was Abousir Belench, whom he had seen on occasion on the Greaters.

'Aaagh,' said Andranovory, hawking and spitting. 'Abou', man! Good to see you!'

'An'vory,' said Abousir Belench, without much pleasure. 'I'd hoped for better. Still, I'm short-handed. Who is the little one?'

'I see no little one,' said Drake, looking around, 'but if you want to know who I am, I'm Drake Douay, a hero-survivor of storm, wreck, voyage and disaster.'

'The lucky gambler, is that who you are?' said Abousir Belench.

'The very one!' said Drake.

'He's a traitor!' said Andranovory. 'He betrayed the Walrus to – to Burntos. We were stopping there for water and such when he—'

'An'vory, that's nothing to me,' said Abousir Belench. 'I've a ship unmanned by battle. I can take the both of you if you'll both swear loyal – and swear to leave any differences between you unsettled till you get to the Greaters.'

'Done,' said Drake, quickly.

'Done,' said Andranovory, with some reluctance.

And both swore loyal to Abousir Belench, captain of the good ship *Jade*. Belench then paid their release price to the harbour guard of Narba, and, by evening, they were at sea once more, heading for the Greaters.

So much for Drake's hopes of returning to Drangsturm! Every league was taking him further from the Castle of Controlling Power and the fair Zanya Kliedervaust.

He began to make elaborate plans for combining the recapture of Stokos with the winning of the lady Zanya. Perhaps King Tor could be persuaded to send some ships to Drangsturm to hire a few thousand Landguard soldiers from the wizards. They'd make good mercenaries, surely.

A brilliant idea! Landguard mercenaries, plus Orfus pirates, plus Menator's men, plus King Tor himself and the loyal subjects who would doubtless rally to his standard – with such a force they'd overrun Stokos with no trouble at all.

The only difficult bit would be kidnapping Zanya while negotiations were underway for hiring mercenaries . . .

With such schemes, Drake kept his spirits high as the *Jade* cruised north.

Abousir Belench was a moody, brooding man given to outbreaks of appalling anger. He was, moreover, a puritan of sorts. He liked men who worked hard, ate little and drank nothing. Drake Douay pleased this hard taskmaster, particularly since he was invariably sober. But Atsimo Andranovory had managed to scrounge enough liquor to get himself drunk five times before bad weather struck the *Jade* just south of the Greaters.

With the weather making the approaches to the Greaters impossible, Abousir Belench, wary of the dangers of the coast of Chorst, strove westward, out into the waters of the Central Ocean. In the storm-fight which followed, Andranovory disgraced himself by drinking himself legless.

By the time the bad-weather winds had blown themselves to nothing, the *Jade* was lost, far from the nearest landfall horizon. To get his bearings, Belench sailed east against contrary winds, eventually making landfall on the coast of Estar, just south of the Hollern River.

By then, food was low, so Belench led a raiding party ashore. They returned to the ship with four sheep and two goats – and found Andranovory drunk again.

'You useless piece of fart-arse offal!' said Belench. 'To think I paid money to buy you out of Narba!'

'Aaagh, I'm sick with the sight of the traitor,' said Andranovory. 'That's what's driving me to drink.'

'If it's Drake Douay you're talking of, why, he's a better man than you are any day of the year,' said Belench.

Thus started an argument of epic dimensions, which led to a brawl, which led to Abousir Belench marooning Andranovory on the coast of Estar. Drake, who still resented the way An'vory had strung him up by the heels so long ago, felt no pity at all for the hapless drunk – not even when the man broke down weeping as his comrades sailed away.

Abousir Belench sailed the *Jade* to Chastity Bay on Island Anvil, most northerly of the Greaters. There she was moored in a gigantic sea-cave, where work on overhauling her began. Drake, who wished urgently to return to Knock to report to King Tor, obtained a release from his oath of service to Belench, and took passage to the Inner Sleeve on a sealing boat.

The night before the sealing boat reached the Inner Sleeve, she rafted up with two pirate fishing boats which had lately come from there. The crews spent the evening drinking octopus gin, gambling, wrist-wrestling, boasting and gossiping.

The *Walrus*, it seemed, had reached the Inner Sleeve with a Neversh aboard. The poor brute had died of thirst and hunger just a few days after arriving at the Greaters – but it had lived long enough to impress Lord Menator mightily.

Menator had announced that he was 'giving earnest consideration' to making Slagger Mulps an admiral in his imperial fleet.

In response, Jon Arabin had declared that he would duplicate the feat which Slagger Mulps had accomplished. He would sail to the terror-lands of the Deep South, capture a monster of the Swarms and bring it to Knock for Menator's inspection. Even now, the *Warwolf* was being readied for the expedition.

'What news of King Tor?' said Drake.

'The ogre? He lives aboard ship in the Inner Sleeve as always.'

'So we've not yet invaded Stokos,' said Drake.

'Who thinks to conquer Stokos overnight? We'll be years gaining the place, if we gain it ever.'

Years! Drake did not like the sound of that at all.

The next day, his sealing boat entered the Inner Sleeve, where lay three ships only.

One was the *Walrus*, which seemed to be deserted. The second was the *Warwolf*, from which came sounds of hammering. The third ship was the *Tarik*. Drake found King Tor still living aboard the *Tarik* in a hold roofed by a tarpaulin.

'So you're back,' said Tor, without much enthusiasm, when Drake reported.

The ogre had toothache, constipation and a bad migraine – hence his enthusiasm for life was diminished.

'Yes,' said Drake, a little hurt at such a cold reception. 'Do you want to hear where I've been? What I've done?'

'Whatever your tale, it can't make me feel worse than I do,' said Tor. 'So tell.'

Whereupon Drake launched into an account of his deeds and doings which was one part of fact to twenty parts of fiction. Then asked after his brother Heth.

'Your brother,' said Tor, 'has gone on a raiding expedition to Stokos. We don't expect him back for twenty days. Meanwhile . . . I believe the one they call the Walrus has a proposition to make to you.'

'That's interesting,' said Drake. 'Maybe he wants to reward me for defending his retreat from Burntos.'

'Maybe he does,' said Tor blandly. 'You'll find him, I believe, in the Ironbar.'

'The Ironbar?' said Drake, blankly.

'It's a new place, only open for twenty days. It's at the top of the Thousand Stairs, wherever that is. They say there used to be a brothel up there, the Drumroll.'

'Oh, that place!' said Drake. 'Yes, I know how to find it!'

And off he went, climbing the Thousand Stairs which wound their way up through the rock in utter darkness. Once he bumped into a raving madman who was suffering from delirium tremens, and twice he stepped on bodies which felt more than a little dead.

At last Drake won through to the Ironbar, a pirate tavern occupying a monstrous cavern set high in the cliffs of Knock. Gaunt daylight breathed in through a cavemouth which gaped to a killing drop free-falling to the wave-wrinkled sea.

When Drake entered the Ironbar, there were half a dozen groups of pirates lounging back in the comfort of bean-bags, drinking, gambling, talking or sleeping. Most had been there for half a dozen days or more already. At the back of the cave, a bare-breasted whore was dancing to the slovenly music of a drunken trombonist. Closer to the daylight, some gamblers were feeding rats to a spider the size of a wolf which occupied a cage of gleaming copper.

Drake looked around for the Walrus. But Slagger Mulps saw him first.

'Aaagh,' said the Walrus. 'So here you are! Brought your blood with you, have you, in payment for treachery?'

'Treachery!' said Drake, cursing himself for being so stupid as to have ventured to the Ironbar without a weapon. 'What's this treachery you speak of? I shared every risk of your voyage, aye. Then risked my life to cover your retreat when we were attacked on a certain island I could name.'

'I'll name it, no problem,' said the Walrus. 'The island was Burntos, where we provisioned after capturing the Neversh in the terror-lands. Aye. Then you tempted us into a little raiding on the side – and betrayed us to the soldiers of the place. You gut-knot sprogling brat!'

'That's fighting talk!' said Drake, measuring the distance to the door to the Thousand Stairs.

'Aye, it is,' said the Walrus. 'And you've brought no weapon. Well – have this one.'

So saying, the Walrus took the sword worn by Simp Fiche, one of the half-dozen cronies gathered around him, and tossed it through the air to Drake, who caught it by the hilt. The weapon balanced nicely in his hand.

'You still talk of treason, then?' said Drake.

He slipped a third of Simp Fiche's blade into a crack in the cavern floor then applied pressure. The blade was battle-worthy: it did not break.

'I talk the truth,' said the Walrus, gripping the hilt of his own blade with his two-thumbed fist.

'You'll talk apology,' said Drake, who doubted he would survive for long in the Teeth if he got labelled as a traitor, 'or our blades will talk death.'

'Oho!' said the Walrus, his green beard shaking as he laughed. 'Death! That's a big word for a little boy. Do you mean it as a challenge?'

'I do,' said Drake, his voice harsh and hard, like hammer against anvil. Now he was armed, he had no need to run. Mulps, from the sound of him, had been drinking. Drake should be able to kill him easily enough, if it came to a fight.

'Withdraw your challenge,' said the Walrus. 'Withdraw it, aye, then cut off four of your fingers as punishment for treachery. Do that, and we'll forget about the past.'

'Four fingers!' said Drake. 'You must be mad, man! The challenge stands!'

'Then I,' said Ish Ulpin, rising to his feet, 'I will champion the Walrus in this matter.'

As Ish Ulpin rose, Slagger Mulps sat down, smiling.

'What's this?' said Drake, alarmed. 'Is friend Walrus scared to meet me, man to man?'

'You're not worth his time,' said Ish Ulpin.

And, drawing his blade, he strode toward Drake Douay, intent on a kill. Drake hurled Simp Fiche's sword at Ish Ulpin and fled, descending the Thousand Stairs with a speed nothing short of amazing.

He was still breathless by the time he gained the deck of

280

the *Tarik*, where he reported his plight to King Tor.

'You ran away!' roared King Tor. 'You disgusting little coward!'

'Man,' said Drake, 'you don't understand! Ish Ulpin's a killer, aye, fought for years in Chi'ash-lan, killed fifty men as a gladiator, I've heard the stories!'

'I'm not a man,' said Tor, 'so don't address me as such. I'm an ogre. And proud of it. And I'll tell you this – it'll be an ogre my daughter marries, not a man. I've had my doubts about you for a long time. Now they're confirmed. You disgusting cowardly little bit of scuttling vomit! Get out of here before I crush you spineless!'

Drake, in terror, quit the *Tarik*, running so fast he almost became airborne. Tor hurled abuse – then hurled a water-cask. The barrel hit the raw-rock flanks of the Inner Sleeve just above Drake's head, exploding into a shower of wood and water. Drake ducked into the nearest tunnel, ran deep into the shadows then cowered there panting, as shaken as a rat pursued by a pack of hunting dogs.

'Man!' muttered Drake. 'This is but rough!'

How had things gone so wrong so fast? He had returned to Knock expecting to be welcomed as a hero – expecting to claim his share of the glory of the capture of a Neversh by the Walrus, to win the acclaim of brave men and bold, and to have his rights to King Tor's daughter and the throne of Stokos generously confirmed.

Instead – well, it looked like he'd be lucky to get off the island alive.

What's my options?

He could run, stealing a boat if need be. In which case Ish Ulpin would eventually hunt him down and kill him, unless he left the Greaters. He could take service with Lord Menator. But that hard-nosed warlord might perhaps hand him over to Tor or the Walrus, as a gift.

Heth, Heth, I wish you were here.

But Drake's brother Heth was far away, in Stokos or elsewhere. He had to handle this one on his own. He soon saw he had only two chances of sure survival – to leave the

281

Greaters entirely or to find a pirate captain to shelter him.

I'll not leave. The game of power, that's played out here. If I want a share of Stokos, I've got to stay. Aye. Throat it out to the finish. We'll conquer the island soon enough. Aye. I want to be in on that, if just for the fun of slicing up Gouda Muck.

As for pirate captains . . .

Abousir Belench might have me. Or maybe not. What do I know about him and the Walrus? Is it kisses or knives? I don't know, man. Maybe they're lovers from way back. Or maybe at war to the knife. Man, if Belench proves a friend of the Walrus . . . no, I can't risk it.

But Arabin . . . aye, there's no love between him and Mulps. They're in it to the death. So that's my chance. Old Jon, yes, he was plenty angry before. But – fresh hate of the Walrus! That'll charm Jon for certain, I'm sure of it . . .

Having thought such optimistic thoughts, Drake ventured back to the Inner Sleeve, and slipped aboard the *Warwolf.* He found himself face to face with Jon Disaster.

'Why, Drake, man!' said Disaster, clapping him on the back, clearly delighted to see him. 'It's been a long time!'

'Just a voyage or so,' said Drake. 'Not that long at all, though much has happened. Where's Arabin?'

'Why, the man's in his cabin, staring out charts and such. We sail for the south tomorrow.'

'Monster-hunting?' said Drake.

'Aye,' said Disaster, all enthusiasm. 'Slagger Mulps got a monster from the terror-lands, so we can too. If the Walrus can make admiral, let's have the Warwolf make admiral too.'

'Why so much love for Arabin's ambition?' said Drake.

'It's the treasure I'm thinking of, man,' said Disaster. 'An admiral's share, oh, that's rich for certain. If we go on conquest with Warwolf as admiral, we're sure for a cut of the loot. So we're more than ready to run the risk.'

'And so am I,' said Drake warmly. 'I wish to pledge my

282

life again to the noble Warwolf, aye, and go on quests of high adventure with this ship and her noble crew.'

'Aaagh, and your farts sing sweetly too!' said Jon Disaster, with a laugh. 'But – Drake, man. Seriously. The Warwolf's a mighty proud man. Don't you understand that? When Arabin spoke against Menator's wars of conquest and you spoke for – he took that mighty hard.'

'So maybe he'll rip me sideways,' said Drake. 'And maybe not. It's a risk I'll dare.'

And Drake dared himself as far as Jon Arabin's cabin, where the Warwolf, stony faced, listened to his explanation of his plight.

'So you see,' concluded Drake, having spoken more honestly than was his wont, 'I need help, man, I need help bad. I can't face Ish Ulpin. That brute's a killer. The Walrus, oh, I could take him drunk – aye, maybe even sober. But Ish Ulpin? Never!'

'What do you expect me to do for you?' said Jon Arabin in a voice hard as thrice-baked sea-biscuit.

'Why, take me to sea with you, that's all I ask,' said Drake. 'A fair share of work, risk, suffering terrible, fear formidable and—'

'And nothing,' said Jon Arabin. 'I'll have nothing to do with you. I've made that plain already.'

'But you're my captain, man!'

'No longer,' said Arabin. 'You're the man who spoke against me when the pirates met in conference. You're the cook's boy who hoped to make me a servant of sorts if you came to power on Stokos.'

'Man,' said Drake, unhappily, 'if I remember right, I wanted to make you lord of all my seapower.'

'A servant,' repeated Arabin.

'But you're chasing a position of the same sort under Menator,' said Drake. 'Yet you hate the man, if I'm a judge of hates. But since Mulps may be admiral, you must be admiral too, aye, nothing else will serve. Well, then – if it's good enough for you to be admiral under Menator, then why not under me?'

Drake had failed to remember that nothing will make an angry man more furious than a touch of logic which threatens to destroy the legitimacy of his rage. Jon Arabin came to his feet with a roar – and Drake, wisely, fled yet again.

He'll cool down. Aye. Then come to reason. But it'll take time. And the Warwolf *sails tomorrow! I've got to win time, man. I've got to be with old Arabin when his temper cools. Aye. So that means . . .*

Yes . . .

On the third day of the *Warwolf*'s voyage south, Drake Douay was discovered hiding in a sail locker, and was dragged on deck to meet the justice of Jon Arabin. The day was cool and almost calm. The entire crew gathered on deck to watch the proceedings. Even Harly Burpskin was there. He was supposed to be steering the ship, but, with the winds being so light, he thought it safe enough to lash the wheel and slip into the crowd to watch the fun.

Jon Arabin, face set like rock, came out of his cabin to deal with the stowaway. He came stalking down the deck, halted three paces in front of Drake and stared at him.

'Hi!' said Drake, brightly.

And smiled.

No smile came in response.

Obviously, the Warwolf's temper had not yet changed for the better. Drake's smile crumpled. He looked at the silent faces all around, and saw there – death. His death. Friendless he was, alone amongst his enemies. He felt . . . not frightened, not terror-stricken, but . . . crushed. Desolated. Utterly lonely.

'Jon, man,' said Drake, striving to arrange a fresh smile on his face. 'Why so solemn?'

Silence.

No response.

Then:

'Quin Baltu!' said Arabin.

'Yes?' said Quin Baltu, the foul-mouthed muscle-man.

'Throw this rubbish overboard,' said Jon Arabin.

Then turned his back on the pair of them, perhaps because he did not want to watch. Quin Baltu looked at Drake, looked at Arabin's back, cleared his throat, then spoke:

'Jon, I've thrown him over. But he's so full of bounce he's come right back again.'

Jon Arabin turned on him.

'This is no joke!' roared Arabin.

'Aye, well,' said Quin Baltu, 'I didn't think it was. Death . . . that's never a joking matter, Jon. We kill fish, that's easy. Kill enemies, too. But friends? That's a difficult one, Jon.'

'He's your friend?' said Arabin. 'This snivelling little dwarf is your friend? Don't be crazy! Give him to the sharks!'

'No,' said Baltu.

The two men stared at each other.

'Is this mutiny?' said Arabin.

'Jon, man,' said Baltu, slowly, 'I remember a time when there was near enough to mutiny aboard. We were running hard for the western coast of the Drangsturm Gulf. Aye. There were some of us hot for turning back, even if it meant the ship's destruction. We'd rather chance to the boats than risk that coast. But Drake Douay stood staunch beside you.

'You remember, Jon, as well as I do. Drake saved your ship from mutiny by talk of an island. Tor. That's the name of the island. So we ran west. We found the island. Ship and men were saved. But did Drake know the island was there? Man, you know better than me. I've thought it through since, and I know what I think. Jon – if the boy dreamed up the island by way of bluff, it means he trusted you. If he invented that island by way of bluff, it means he was sure you'd find us safety somehow to the west.'

Jon Arabin was silent.

Remembering.

Drake Douay had indeed helped save his ship from mutiny and loss at sea. The knowledge hurt.

'If the boy told a lie about an island,' said Arabin harshly, 'why should I save him for that? Because he's a liar?'

'You shouldn't save him!' cried the excited voice of Sully Yot. 'You should kill him! Gut him open! He's the enemy of Gouda Muck! He's the son of Hagon! He's the Evil One! He's—'

The tirade from the lean, lanky wart-faced Sully Yot ended suddenly as Ika Thole brought the blunt end of a marlinspike down on his head. Hard. Sully Yot collapsed unconscious on the deck. The red-skinned Ika Thole stood over his body and spoke:

'This useless piece of meat called Sully Yot, if he were my son I'd cut him up and use him as shark-bait. He yatters on about religion till he takes me to the very point of murder. And where did he come from? Why, off the *Walrus*, that's where he came from. So he was our enemy, once. Yet you took him in, Jon, because he spoke against Slagger Mulps when the Orfus met in assembly.

'Drake Douay, well, I didn't think much of him at sight, and don't think much more now. But if we were hungry enough to be killing for eating, he wouldn't be first on my list. This Yot would be first. We've taken on Yot, who was crewman under the Walrus. So we can take back Drake, whatever he's done or hasn't.'

With that said, Ika Thole gave Yot's body a kick, then looked hard at Jon Arabin.

'Our good friend from the Ebrells is talking good sense,' said the weapons muqaddam (who had abandoned his name twenty years previously on joining the Church of the Anonymous Congregation).

'Sense?' said Arabin, in anger.

'Jon, man,' said the weapons muqaddam, 'don't let pride do the talking for you. For pride is a monster. Remember what you owe to the boy.'

'Owe?' said Arabin, in outrage. 'I owe him nothing!'

'Myself you spoke to after you rid the ship of the Neversh,' said the weapons muqaddam. 'Aye, back in the disaster days in the Drangsturm Gulf. You told me then you'd never have done it without Drake Douay standing staunch beside you.'

As the weapons muqaddam spoke, Drake remembered the gut-wrenching terror of the battle against the Neversh. Remembered storm wind, cold water, the evening darkening. Remembered Jon Arabin's bald head looking, in the gathering night, like an egg decaying to darkness. Remembered, most of all, the moment when he had become sure that Arabin, despite his threats, would never kill him.

He felt the same now.

Or felt, at any rate, that Arabin did not want to kill him. The eyes told that tale. But the man might be pushed to slaughter anyway, to salvage his pride.

'Jon,' said Drake. 'Jon . . .'

He did not know what to say.

'You've no words, have you?' said Arabin, in a heavy voice, hand falling to the hilt of his falchion.

'Steady up!' said Harly Burpskin.

'Who are you to tell me to steady up?' said Arabin, turning on the hapless helmsman.

Burpskin held his ground with a courage which Drake would not have credited him with.

'Captain mine,' said Burpskin, 'there's something you ought to know, which I've never told. You remember Island Tor, aye, when you sent three of us by boat to scout out the island. That first evening we found a harbour, safe, wide and deep. Drake Douay, his thought was all for the ship. The ship's our survival, that's what he said. He—'

'All this talk is rubbish,' said Jon Arabin. 'I've reason to need the blood of young Drake Douay. He spoke against me when all pirates met to talk through Menator's offer of empire. Worse, he insulted me by offering me a place in his service when he became king upon Stokos.'

'So what?' said the weapons muqaddam. 'He's but a

boy. We're men. Since when did we expect the sense of a man from the head of a boy?'

'Aye,' said Baltu. 'And, boy or otherwise, he saved your ship. More than the once.'

'He wished to save it again by offering you that harbour I spoke of,' said Burpskin. 'But me and the others, we were too hot for pressing on.'

'So you were derelict in your duty!' roared Arabin, finding at last some way to lose his temper entirely. 'And you're derelict now! You're the helmsman, aren't you? I set you at the wheel myself. What have you done? Have you lashed it? Have you dared? Oh, no good running away. Too late for that!'

And, shortly thereafter, Burpskin was lashed to the main-mast, and a whip was streaking blood across his back. After which Arabin, now in a truly evil mood, organized a training session in unarmed combat with the weapons muqaddam, Quin Baltu and Ika Thole. At the end of it, they were all of them battered, bloody and bruised, and Baltu had lost four teeth.

There followed ten days of hell in which, through worsening weather, Jon Arabin drove his ship and his crew like a madman. Then, finally, he drank himself drunk on Dog's Breath rum, took sick in his cabin for two days, and emerged as a new man. Rage, hate, bile and injured pride forgotten.

'Drake,' he said, and embraced him. 'I'm glad I didn't lose you.'

'Jon, man,' said Drake, 'that was neat to watch when you knocked out Baltu's teeth. You must teach me some of that stuff.'

'We'll start you training today,' said Arabin. 'With weapons, too. The weapons muqaddam will organize it. The whole crew should get into it again – the weather's easing, and we'll have plenty of time as we run for the west.'

'The west?' said Drake.

'Aye. We turn west today.'

'But we've not yet reached the Drangsturm Gulf!' said Drake.

'What?' said Drake. 'Did you think this good ship was going to run to the terror-lands, grapple with the Swarms and capture a monster that way?'

'Well, why not?' said Drake. 'That's what the *Walrus* did. I told King Tor all about it when I reported to him.'

'Aye,' said Arabin. 'So Tor believes it. And Menator too, for that's the kind of fool he is. But – Drake, man, I'm not so stupid. I hear the *Walrus* had some trouble while provisioning at Island Burntos. I know the place, aye. Likely one of the provisions taken aboard was the Neversh which Mulps produced at the Teeth.'

'Well,' said Drake, 'if you think that, then why not go to Burntos yourself?'

'Because Drake Douay was at the heart of whatever trouble happened there,' said Jon Arabin. 'Do you think I'd risk my ship in a place where the son of the demon Hagon has been stirring things up? I might if I could get at the truth – but I'm wise enough to know the truth's the last thing I'd get out of Drake Douay.

'Nay, man. We're on our way to Hexagon. That's one of the Scattered Islands, far out in the Central Ocean. Ships from Narba trade there regular, aye, and bring back rumours. They claim that Baron Farouk of Hexagon has a baby keflo in his menagerie, purchased from Drangsturm for twice its own weight of silver.'

'This keflo,' said Drake. 'Is that the monster which is built with a turtle shell, with legs and hooks and claws and things underneath?'

'Aye, so it is,' said Arabin. 'So you've learnt something on your travels! Like all of the Swarms, it grows fearful large, but this one should be small enough to get aboard. If rumour proves true.'

'What date has the rumour?' said Drake.

'The rumour is recent,' said Jon Arabin, 'So I've high hopes that fact will satisfy claim. If the keflo's there, and small enough to get aboard, that's half our problem solved.'

'And the other half?' said Drake.

'The other half of our problem,' said Jon Arabin, 'will be persuading Baron Farouk to part with this rare and most expensive monster. With luck, we won't have any trouble.'

20

Lord Menator: Galish-born warlord-adventurer who has made himself ruler of the Greater Teeth (having been aided in a crucial debate by Drake Douay).

Menator, a broken-nosed man as bald as Jon Arabin, notable for the blue rose tattooed on his left cheek, has agreed to help the ogre Tor launch an invasion of Stokos.

Menator plans for this invasion to be the start of a War of Empire which will see his forces conquer the western seaboard of the continent of Argan.

Baron Farouk of Hexagon did in fact have a keflo in his menagerie. He also proved extremely reluctant to sell it. However, after a certain amount of unpleasantness, which involved (among other things) the kidnapping of his eldest daughter and the burning of his capital city, he released the monster into the care of the *Warwolf*, which sailed home in triumph.

'Now,' said Jon Arabin to Lord Menator, 'I've captured a monster just as the Walrus has. So I've as much right to be admiral as he has.'

Menator, of course, wanted neither Walrus nor Warwolf as admiral. He wanted his own hand-picked men to take positions of power in his planned empire. Besides which, he hated blacks – and had his doubts about gangling green-haired double-thumbed mutants. As Walrus and Warwolf were too powerful and popular for Menator to refuse them directly, he had set them a challenge which should by rights have killed them.

Yet they had survived.

They had proved beyond all doubt that they were both worthy of power and position.

Lord Menator had been startled to see them return at all, awed by their captive monsters, and deeply shaken by their tales of appalling sufferings endured while questing in the terror-lands south of Drangsturm.

He knew so little about pirates that he actually believed the swaggering braggarts when they boasted of hand-to-hand combats with green centipedes, nightmarish encounters with stalkers, sightings of the fearsome jugalut (which last is actually an entirely mythical beast), and their disappointment when monsters kept them from the Fountain of Youth, the Tree of Gold, the Temple of the Lost Twelve Thousand Virgins, and several other wonders of the legend-lands beyond Drangsturm.

'Which of us,' said Arabin, 'is to be Grand Admiral of the Fleet of Imperial Conquest? You must decide.'

'Yes,' said Slagger Mulps. 'And don't say neither. You promised.'

'I promised,' said Menator, 'to seriously consider a suitable questing hero as Grand Admiral. As I've got two questing heroes and only one position to offer, this gives me a problem.'

'Then think about your problem,' said Arabin. 'And think carefully. Remember, you've got two questing heroes to deal with – and only a single head on your shoulders.'

And, having made that scarcely veiled threat, Jon Arabin departed, in the company of Slagger Mulps. Menator, in his wisdom, decided to do nothing. Walrus and Warwolf were, after all, notorious enemies. Surely there was a good chance they would come to blows, and halve his problem (or, with luck, solve it entirely).

For a while, it looked like Walrus and Warwolf would indeed solve Menator's problem for him. The rival captains began sharpening weapons, meanwhile engaging in a crude form of psychological warfare, involving boasts, threats, rumour-mongering, and a variety of popular slogans (for example, 'The Walrus knobs pigs' bums' – which was about the height of wit in this particular campaign).

Slagger Mulps brought a shark to market, cut a slit in its belly, then offered to sell it to the Warwolf as a whore. Men from the opposing crews then set about remoulding each other's heads with staves and cudgels.

Drake wondered how the two captains could be so foolish. When Mulps was first dared south to hunt a monster, Drake had seen immediately that it was just Menator's way of killing the man off. Since then, Drake had thought long and hard about the way in which King Tor and Lord Menator had ordered Drake Douay to go with the Walrus. Drake was fairly sure that Menator, at least, had meant for Drake to get killed.

'The man's mad for power,' muttered Drake to Drake. 'He wanted me dead lest I rule on Stokos one day. Aye. Likely he wants Stokos for his own. And he'll kill off every other rival, too, starting with Walrus and Warwolf.'

The obvious move was for Walrus and Warwolf to end their feud and make a united approach to Menator. But did Drake dare suggest it?

No.

The Walrus still thought of Drake as a traitor. Ish Ulpin was still ready to kill Drake the first moment he caught him alone – which was why Drake stuck close in the company of *Warwolf* crewmen. And as for Jon Arabin . . . why, giving him advice would mean stirring up that monstrous pride of his.

'Heth,' said Drake. 'I wish you were here for me to talk to!'

But Heth had not yet returned from his raiding expedition to Stokos. Grave fears were held for his safety.

'Likely Heth's dead,' said Drake, bitterly. 'So who's left? King Tor? No. He does what Menator tells him to, as far as I can see. So who can talk to Walrus and Warwolf both?'

In the end, Drake shared his fears with Jon Disaster.

'Abousir Belench,' said Disaster, once he knew all the facts. 'That's your man. He trusts nobody. He'd be the first to mistrust Menator if we told things to him straight. He'd talk sense to our captains, for he knows them both of old.'

With Disaster and Baltu, Drake ventured to Chastity Bay, and returned to Knock with Abousir Belench, who went into action with some swift, effective diplomacy. He arranged a temporary truce of sorts between Walrus and Warwolf. He also organized a coalition of pirate captains to put pressure on Menator.

Thus, shortly, Jon Arabin and Slagger Mulps had another interview with Menator.

'I've had time to think,' said Menator, 'and I've come to a decision.'

'Aye, well,' said Mulps, 'let's hope it's a good one.'

'Aye,' said Arabin, 'for we were none of us blooded yesterday.'

'The decision should please both of you,' said Menator.

'It can't,' said Arabin, 'unless we both get to be admirals.'

'That's what I was thinking of,' said Menator. 'Since you've both proved worthy, it's only right you should both be admirals.'

'But you've only got one fleet,' objected Mulps. 'Cut it in half, and we won't be admiral of much.'

'Ah,' said Menator, 'but, you see, I've decided to double the size of the imperial sea force by inviting my brother Ohio to join forces with us. I have lately learnt that he heads a pirate fleet operating out of Ork.'

'Out of where?' said Mulps.

Menator explained.

'That's a devil of a long way from here,' said Mulps. 'I'm glad I don't have to go there.'

'Ah,' said Menator. 'But . . . since you will both be admirals, you must prove a peace between you.'

'We've done it!' said Arabin.

'Your reputations,' said Menator smoothly, without missing a beat, 'suggest two men at war. To prove peace, you must sail to Ork on the same ship, negotiate with my brother, and bring back from him a token he carries which matches this half-coin I hold – no, you don't need to see it more closely. You must get all this done by the end of autumn at the latest.'

That was not far away, all this politicking, adventuring and boasting having made time fly like feathers in a hurricane. Did they have enough time? Jon Arabin judged that they did. Plenty of time.

'We'll do it,' he said, thinking it would be easy. 'It's a task fit for heroes.'

And Slagger Mulps, though he had his doubts about the enterprise, was not prepared to plead himself less than a hero.

Drake Douay, hearing the news, was dismayed.

'Menator suckered our captains anyway!' he complained to Jon Disaster. 'He's got us running on another daft and dangerous expedition.'

'Relax, man,' said Disaster. 'It's just a sea voyage we're facing, that's all.'

'A voyage north,' said Drake. 'First north, then east. I've heard Jon Arabin talking of those waters, aye. The sands of the Lessers, which break ships by thousands. The coast of Lorp, plagued with poxy shipwreckers. The rocks of Penvash. The northern storms.'

'Arabin talks of such on occasion,' said Disaster. 'So the talk is proof they're far from certain killers. Relax. We'll have the voyage done and be home before winter.'

So spoke Disaster. But Drake was certain something would go wrong. Likely they would be wrecked on the coast of Estar, where Atsimo Andranovory had been marooned, and meet that thug as head of a band of brigands or such.

He shuddered.

'Well,' said Disaster, 'if you're so set against the idea,

295

doubtless you can stay home on the Teeth.'

'No thanks,' said Drake hastily.

For, as Tor was no longer a friend of his, and Lord Menator was in all probability a murderous enemy, he judged he would be safer risking the dangers of the voyage to Ork than staying home on Knock.

Besides, if Jon Arabin got to be admiral, surely the heroes of the voyage to Ork would become captains in their own right. At the very least.

'A ship,' said Drake. 'A ship of my own. That's what I need. Then I can sail south to Drangsturm, aye, and have a go at finding Zanya. Aye. And do deeds fit for heroes, raid ships, storm cities and such. That'll impress King Tor no end. If I could raid Cam and bring back the head of Gouda Muck, I'm sure Tor would think again of me for his daughter . . .'

So thought Drake Douay.

It was then late summer in Khmar 19, and Drake Douay was an honest 18 (plus a few months, which he counted, though there is no need for history to attend to them so closely).

21

Name: Lesser Teeth, a group of low-lying shallow-water islands notorious for shoals and wrecking-reefs.

Language: a Galish dialect.

Population: 15,421 (prior to Wars of Empire).

Religions: self–interest,   self-reliance,   bloody-mindedness, curiosity and generalized superstition.

Main island: Carawell (aka Mainland).

Havens: Brennan, sole safe anchorage in the Lessers.

Economy: fishing; amber export; scurvy grass.

As autumn drew near, the Greater Teeth were gripped by a regular frenzy of preparation, speculation, rumour and gossip. And wagering. While most pirates were staying home, all had at least a small bet riding on the adventure.

Menator ordered his ambassadors onto the *Warwolf*, renamed (by order of Himself) the *Sky Dancer*. Slagger Mulps was deeply relieved not to be risking the *Walrus*, having lately realized her bottom was badly worm-weakened. But, as a matter of form, he had to rant, rage, spit blood (easy enough to do, since he had been slowly dying of tuberculosis for the last half-dozen years), swear, curse, blaspheme against fifty different gods, and threaten Jon Arabin with instant death.

Of course, even before this, Mulps had been planning to kill the Warwolf. And Jon Arabin had been dreaming up schemes to do in the Walrus. Honour required no less: both would have felt humiliated if they had gone to sea on the same ship without bringing their rivalry to its natural conclusion.

Murder plans were only reluctantly abandoned when Menator, bowing to pressure from Abousir Belench and several other captains, laid down one further condition: an admiral's flag (and the greed-glutting battle-share that went with it) would not be awarded to either hero unless both returned alive.

'My brother,' said Mulps to Arabin.

'Heart of my heart,' replied the Warwolf.

And they embraced.

Two sister ships were chosen for the *Sky Dancer*: Bluewater Draven's *Tusk*, and the *Jade*, run by Abousir Belench.

Departure was then delayed while Arabin laid down a new deck of mahogany, part of a captured cargo alleged to have come from Yestron. None could say how this unfamiliar timber would fare as decking, but Arabin did like to experiment.

Totalling sirings and killings, the Warwolf found he had a reasonable margin of safety. But, as it was most important to keep his bad-tempered gods happy by breeding more than killing, he decided to take some women along so he could stand at stud while voyaging.

Arabin hated doing this. To him, the sea had always been a refuge from the clamouring demands of his monstrously enlarged family. But, with the Teeth committed to imperial conquest, he had no alternative – except becoming a pacifist. Which he wouldn't, since the pay was so poor.

Since Arabin was taking women, he had to arrange whores for the men, or risk mutiny. So they needed more accommodation, food, water – more of everything. Plus a ration of strong drink, as *Walrus* crewmen would not sail on a dry ship.

Arabin thought taking hard liquor to sea was suicidal.

298

He remembered his own indulgence in Dog's Breath rum on the voyage to Hexagon (the liquor had come into his possession when he confiscated it from Jez Glane) and shuddered to think what a similar lapse in behaviour might mean in the dangerous waters of the Penvash Channel. Still . . . he had very little choice about it.

Soon, the *Sky Dancer*'s treasure holds were packed. Stores included extra navigational equipment in the form of ninety-seven pigeons born and bred on the Teeth. Theory held that if one was released, even on a sunless day with cloud-shrouded horizons, it would indicate direction by flying away on a line leading straight back home.

Jon Arabin planned to experiment.

Before setting sail, both Walrus and Warwolf made solemn covenants with their men, promising shares in future admirals' spoils to all. This was an incentive to keep them from mutiny on a voyage which promised no plunder.

'Battle-shares are fine,' said Drake. 'But what about ships? Will we get to be captains when you get to be admiral?'

'You?' said Arabin. 'A captain? Dream on!'

'I'm ready for the job,' said Drake stoutly.

Whereupon Jon Arabin fell about laughing. Half the crew was still making jokes about Drake's pretensions two days later. Drake did a lot of dark muttering under his breath, and swore he'd show them.

'King on Stokos,' said Drake to Drake. 'That's what I'll be. They'll be impressed then.'

The men he hoped to impress were the best, hand-picked, the *crème de la crème*, the elite, winnowed from the original crew-lists of *Walrus* and *Warwolf*. In practice, this meant the sailors:

(a) all had two legs apiece;
(b) were not hopelessly alcoholic;
(c) were older than 13 and younger than 70; and
(d) were not obviously dying of syphilis or plague.

Even Sully Yot got a place. He and Drake had been forced to work alongside each other on the voyage to and from Hexagon, but still only spoke to each other when forced to, and then only in monosyllables. Their relationship was, to say the least, strained.

If still a fanatical Flame worshipper, Yot would have murdered Drake at the first opportunity, welcoming his own slow death at the hands of Jon Arabin. However, Yot's faith had weakened in long months spent far from the fanatical Gouda Muck.

Drake, whose own religion was more robust – as he had first observed in Androlmarphos, even foreigners worshipped the Demon, if only in deed – was still as devout as ever. Indeed, his greatest sorrow was that he could not fully celebrate the Gift of the Demon, since he could no longer get drunk.

Finally, all preparations were made, and the expedition got underway.

Ah, to be at sea again! At sea on the *Sky Dancer*, bound for Ork, with *Tusk* and *Jade* in company! The tang of salt on lips! The wind brisking the white-capped foam against the gallant flanks of the wooden sea-charger! The nostalgic aroma of tar! The faint yet pervasive smell of vomit, from where some queasy gut has up-chucked over the decks – that in itself bringing back, ah, so many memories!

Not all, of course, was beer and skittles. The joint captains were soon disputing control of navigation. Argument ended when a drift of cloud cleared, proving that the afternoon sun was indeed to larboard, and not to starboard as Mulps (who had somehow got the notion that a squall's confusion had set them sailing south) had claimed.

(Mulps was an erratic navigator at times, and the present phase of the moon had quite upset his navigational faculties, and his sense of direction into the bargain.)

Nevertheless, as the *Star Dancer* rode the heaving waters into the mists of evening, with the cliffs of the

Greaters now far behind them, it was a happy enough ship.

It rapidly became less so.

Slagger Mulps developed a raging toothache that night, and, in the morning, Whale Mike broke the offending molar in half when he tried to extract it with pliers. Towards noon one of Jon Arabin's wives, who had not known she was pregnant, had a miscarriage. Later, it was discovered that the ship's cat had got in amongst the experimental navigational aids, and had spent half the day amusing itself at the expense of those delicate pieces of equipment.

And, toward evening, the weather worsened.

Drake, no longer a kitchen boy but a true sailor who could hand, reef and steer, stood watch like any other. That night he was rostered on with sailors from the *Walrus*. He was nervous about it – like a lion tamer suddenly put to work with dragons.

Nervous with good reason.

For the cold, ruthless Ish Ulpin and the murderous Bucks Cat were amongst those who would be standing watch with him.

However, the truce to which the captains had pledged their crews held good, at least for that night. Indeed, Drake, to his startlement, found himself quite enjoying the company of Ish Ulpin, for the pale-faced man had an amazing fund of stories about wild times in Chi'ash-lan and elsewhere.

While the company was good, the night itself was dreadful, the weather worsening relentlessly. By dawn, the *Tusk* and *Jade* were nowhere to be seen. Menator had planned for this, ordering the ships to rendevous at D'Waith if separated. But Jon Arabin had no intentions of trying anything so stupid, knowing full well that Abousir Belench and Bluewater Draven would skive off to do some private raiding.

The *Sky Dancer* then took a terrible hammering in five days of wild seas and variable winds. By the time the worst

301

of the storm was over, they were lost. The surviving navigational aids, when released, huddled against the mourning wind, refusing to fly.

Closing with the first land sighted, they found it to be Carawell, largest of the Lesser Teeth, those fishing islands lying north of the Greaters. They anchored shortly in Brennan, Carawell's harbour. Arabin planned to stay long enough to repair sails, refurbish their storm-battered longboat, and fix leaks which kept three men continually at the pumps.

'They don't care much for pirates here,' said Slagger Mulps dourly, eyeing the low and solid stone houses of Brennan.

'Aye,' said Jon Arabin, 'but they don't have much quarrel with us, either.'

As the Lesser Teeth were poor, and most pirates such bad sailors, few risked raiding these dangerous northern waters.

'Mayhap we should take hostages,' said Slagger Mulps.

'No need,' said Arabin. 'I was wrecked here once. It's not a bad place. Not like Lorp.' (And, thinking of Lorp, he shuddered.) 'But we'll pay for what we take. There's thousands of islanders, all told – wouldn't do to stir them up.'

'We'll likely stir them up just by being here,' said Mulps.

'No, no,' said Arabin. 'Look – I'll take a party ashore. We'll claim ourselves a diplomatic mission from Baron Farouk of Hexagon, voyaging to Tameran to establish diplomatic relations and a trade in low-weight high-value items such as diamonds, spices and arachnid silk.'

'You do talk lovely when the wind's from the east,' said Mulps sourly.

'I was born with honey in my mouth,' said Jon Arabin.

In truth – a truth he never trusted any pirate with – he had been educated in a convent school in Ashmolea, where he had delighted his tutors by his dedication to rhetoric, grammar, elocution and linguistic philosophy.

(The rough-talking Walrus had his own dire secret. In his youth, he had been a gardener's boy in Chenameg. All through adolescence, he had longed to win a place in King Lyra's poetry league. Hence: many lines about damsel-blushing bloom in cheeks of cherry blossom, fish-surfaced aroma of blue winds of heavenly sunlight, and so forth. Then came the day when he ran amok in drunken rage, having found the rumours that his verses were used by the King for toilet paper were – alas! – entirely true.)

'Go then,' said the Walrus, speaking roughly, as a pirate must. 'If your liver returns, I'll honour you by eating it.'

'I'm flattered,' said Arabin.

And went ashore, taking with him a handful of men who could play the role of courtier – i.e., could put two words together without inserting an obscenity between them. Young Drake went with him, and Sully Yot. Rolf Thelemite, who had always pretended to be more noble than the rest of them. Simp Fiche, who, for all that could be said against him, at least knew how to eat with his mouth shut. Ching Quail, who had spent his youth trying to win entry to the banker's guild.

Arabin also took – as muscle – Bucks Cat and Whale Mike. But both were under strict instructions to play the role of deaf mutes.

Ashore they went, and played their roles as best they could. But the good people of Brennan soon had their doubts. These could not possibly be ambassadors! No, just looking at the way Jon Arabin carried himself, it was obvious that he could be no less than the bold Baron Farouk himself.

'If your trade hopes come true, Baron – my apologies, I meant Ambassador,' said old Gezeldux, who ran the best bar in Brennan, 'will your ships then port in Brennan?'

'That depends how much you over-charge us by,' said Jon Arabin.

A sally which raised – for they were all relaxed – a roar of laughter.

Things went so well ashore that the venture did not end as the swift diplomatic mission Jon Arabin had planned, but became something of a party. The pirates paid good gold for better ale, heard local jokes and told their own, and were, naturally enough, asked about Hexagon.

'Let my son play geographer,' said Jon Arabin, with a nod in Drake's direction.

'Your son?' said a local, dubious about the possibility of a blood connection between the corn-haired Drake and pitch black Jon Arabin.

'Well, he's my son in a manner of speaking,' said Jon Arabin. 'His mother, after all, was my wife. She was blonde – and so was the servant I thought was a eunuch.'

This claim raised a roar of drunken laughter.

'Anyway,' said Jon Arabin, 'let my son tell of Hexagon, for he knows the island true, and the seas around.'

So Drake told of the silver-horned unicorns of Hexagon; of men who fly in kites and fire-balloons; of a seamless metal pillar rising half a league skywards from the Games Court of the Baron's palace; of a shark the size of a ship and a jellyfish the size of a longboat; of a place where the sea boiled continuously and floating rock bubbled to the surface, while overhead circled a strange disc which looked to be made of gold.

These tales he told, and others equally incredible. All were disbelieved – and for a very simple reason. They were all true. And, as is well known, truth is far, far stranger than fiction.

'Methinks in truth this Hexagon's a place so boring a traveller must fiction it up to win half a hearing at all,' said old Gezeldux.

'No,' insisted Drake. 'We have strange things there, strange things. Look – this was given me by the Baron's eldest daughter. Is it not strange enough for you?'

And he showed off a cameo brooch, the only one he had ever seen. The Baron's eldest daughter, when prisoner on the *Warwolf*, had used it to bribe her guard of the moment – Drake – to admit her manicurist to attend most urgently to two broken nails and a disgustingly dirty set of cuticles.

'A trinket,' said Gezeldux, with something in his voice suggesting he might have sneered had that been in his nature. 'There's nothing strange about that.'

'Ah,' said Drake, 'but I'm living proof of strangeness myself. I've matched you drink for drink, yet my hands don't shake.'

And he held them out sober in front of him.

'You see,' said Drake, 'on Hexagon we worship the Flame, and as a priest of the Flame I am guarded against all intoxication.'

He saw Yot looking at him, scandalized; he winked.

'What's this Flame?' asked a voice.

Drake told. His audience fell about laughing.

'Don't laugh,' he said. 'People have been killed for less than that.'

But he could not convince them that anyone could take such fabrications seriously.

'And,' said old Gezeldux, 'my hands aren't shaking yet either. See?'

This naturally precipitated a drinking contest, which Drake, equally naturally, won.

His tale about being a priest of the Flame, consecrated to eternal sobriety, began to win some credence. The hard drinkers of Brennan set out to test it in earnest. They fed him with ale and with rum, plied him with vodka and strawberry liqueur, topped his mug with Essence of Anemone and spiked it with Heavenly Dreams, dosed him with cider and treated him to cognac – all with no effect.

By that time, everyone in the bar (except Drake) was thoroughly drunk.

'Boy,' said Gezeldux, slurring his words, 'you've been good enough for most things, but I bet you're not good enough for this.'

And he pulled out a blue-glazed ceramic bottle and thumped it on his counter.

'Firewater, boy, the Old Original from the very Ebrell

305

Islands themselves. I bet you've not seen firewater before.'

'No,' said Drake, just a touch of uncertainty in his voice.

He had certainly never seen firewater, but he had heard whispers of its evil reputation in sundry drinking places everywhere from Stokos to the Teeth. Until now, he had thought its threat apocryphal. But here it was. The stuff itself.

Gezeldux tipped the last of the salted sprats out of the free lunch bowl, and slowly poured the firewater. The liquid curled slowly through the air, hissing as it hit the bowl. The bowl filled. Green flames danced across the surface.

'Come now,' said Gezeldux, as Drake hesitated. 'A priest of the Flame doesn't fear a fire as small as this – does he?'

'No,' said Drake, still uncertain.

'Courage, son,' said Jon Arabin, just sober enough to stay upright in his chair. 'You're a hero, aren't you?'

'Right!' said Drake.

And picked up the bowl with all due ceremony, and drank.

The firewater was cool, it was cold, it slid down like raw fish then flashed red-hot in his stomach. His vision blurred as veils of darkness hazed the room. He felt dizzy. Then, swiftly, his head cleared again, and the fire in his belly died down.

'A good drop,' he said, seeing that the bowl was still half-full.

And drank the rest.

'Holy mother of a million octopuses!' breathed Gezeldux, who had not been so awed for fifty years or more – not since the time he first saw Big Bertha's breasts.

'You see?' said Drake, with the triumphant arrogance of youth, putting down the empty bowl. 'There's nothing that can touch me!'

That was too much to bear.

'Oh isn't there just,' muttered Gezeldux grimly. 'I tell you what, young sprig – I bet you can't stay sober on this.'

'Five bricks to a buggering says that I can,' said Drake – which was not actually a bet but simply a bit of gutter-Galish well known from Drangsturm to Chi'ash-lan. 'What is it?'

'This!' said Gezeldux.

And slapped a small bottle of green cut glass onto the counter. Slapped it down so hard it almost broke. It was a mess of dust and cobwebs, but, polished up quickly, it glittered. With hands that shook slightly, Gezeldux pulled the glass stopper. Then he poured the contents into a transparent drinking glass, a rarity of special manufacture that was not just transparent but was (when scrupulously clean) actually invisible.

Out of the bottle of green cut glass came an orange fluid that writhed slowly in the glass.

'What is it?' asked Drake.

'I've no idea,' came the frank reply. 'My great-great-grandfather took it from the body of a drowned wizard. Never been nobody with the nerve to try it yet.'

'Then I'll be the first,' said Drake, thinking if it was safe for him to drink firewater then it was safe for him to drink anything.

He took the glass and downed it.

Almost immediately, several things happened. His legs went rubbery. He fell off the chair, and found the view from the floor hilariously funny. Then he started to float upwards.

'Whoa, boy!' cried Jon Arabin in alarm, grabbing him by the trouser leg before he could float away entirely.

'I can fly!' cried Drake. 'Look at me!'

And he waved his arms like a bird, and, pretending to be an experimental navigational aid, started flapping in the direction where he guessed the Greater Teeth could be found. He broke free from Arabin's clutches, but was brought up short by the ceiling.

'I always thought you were full of hot air,' shouted Bucks Cat, who had long since forgotten that he was supposed to be a deaf mute.

'Aye,' shouted Whale Mike. 'Full of fart-flame and belly-gas.'

And Drake, looking down on them all, and admiring – in particular – the look of utter stupefaction on Sully Yot's face, collapsed in hysterical laughter. Collapsing thus, he fell toward the drinkers, who shouted in alarm and scattered from their chairs. Then Drake burped, and floated up toward the heights again.

Was he tipsy?

He was drunk!

Yes, truly, wildly, gloriously drunk, the world around him softened to the luxury of velvet, his body and psyche immune to the pull of gravity – it was wonderful!

The wizard brew he had drunk had been truly enchanted, and its enchantment, being an anomaly beyond the control of the normative functions of the universe, was not subject to detoxification by his bodyworms. Drake was not aware of this technicality, but he did rightly guess – even though he was guessing drunk – that somewhere in the world there must be a further source of this ambrosia.

'Wizards,' muttered Drake to himself. 'Aye, wizards . . . that's the answer.'

22

Goudanism: worship of the Flame (the living presence of the High God of All Gods); veneration of Gouda Muck, swordsmith of Stokos, who is avatar of the Flame, 'as will be verified in the fullness of the Infolding, when Rose and Flame are as one'; corpus of dogmas, rituals, feasts, festivals, superstitions, rules, regulations and denials associated with worship of said Flame and said Gouda Muck.

Drake woke next morning to find himself floating just off the floor, arms outstretched and fingers trailing. Staring at the ceiling, he wondered which hell had claimed him. His head was full of broken glass, his eyes hurt, and his throat felt as though someone had rammed a dirty mop down it. Aye, and left that mop soaking there overnight.

Feeling sick, he rolled over, in case he had to vomit. He hung just above the bare floorboards, observing, without striving for cognition, a dead wine skin, half a salted sprat, a splattering of fish scales, and a solitary cockroach making a hesitant tour of inspection. Then saw, out of the corner of his eye, a green cut-glass bottle lolling on its side.

Now he remembered. Now he knew where he was. This was the bar run by old Gezeldux in Brennan, on Carawell. He was not in hell at all – he just had a hangover. Just! He had forgotten how bad they were.

Clutching a table leg, Drake hauled himself to his feet. He took a couple of steps forward, walking on nothing but air, then slipped. He grabbed the table to steady himself, then worked his way round the bar. Slowly. Investigating. He opened shutters. Winced as harsh sunlight streamed inside. The cockroach-scout broke off its patrol and fled for shelter.

Motes of dust drifted in the sunshine. Shadows sprawled from mugs, tankards and dead wineskins. A fly, flitting through an unshuttered window, began to dizzy around with an irritating hum. Shading his eyes and peering outside, Drake saw the backside of a boatshed, a couple of houses, and a large stone building which, on the basis of a familiar clanking-hammering sound which started to issue from it, he identified as a forge.

Drake's head began to pound rhythmically in time with the hammering of the unseen blacksmith. Somewhere, quite close, a cockerel began to crow:

'Co co rico! Co co rico!'

The fly settled momentarily on the table. Drake brought his hand down with an almighty thump, sending more dust swirling into the air. He examined his stinging palm for corpse mash – but the insect in question was flying happily round his head. It settled shortly on a shutter. Drake picked up a wineskin and hit it, hard and accurate. The fly dropped dead, the shutter fell off its hinges, and two more flies came bumbling in through the window.

Drake grunted in disgust, and, head hurting worse than before, looked for a hair of the dog which had bitten him. But there was no such dog. The little green bottle was empty, and even a hearty swig of vodka failed to have the slightest impact on his hangover, which, being a consequence of enchanted liquor, was naturally beyond the reach of all ordinary remedies.

The only instant cure for that hangover was a drachm of fresh blood drained from a living salamander of the blue-gilled variety. But these were extraordinarily rare: even the salamanders sometimes seen in the flames of Drangsturm were but the more common green-gilled variety, which has blood useless for anything except removing wine stains from linen (and even the evidence for that use is dubious,

310

consisting as it does of a reference in Cralock which is ambiguous, an assertion in the 'Regiment of Reptiles' which cannot be given much weight since the scholarship of Prenobius has thrown doubt on Gibble's corpus in its entirety, and a mention in Zoth which in all probability – and despite the claims of Elkstein to the contrary – actually refers to the taniwha of Quilth, an altogether different creature).

Drake knew nothing of salamanders of any variety, but did know his booze. He sampled all types available – which did not take him long, as the bar had been almost drunk dry the night before – then concluded he could not kill his hangover but must suffer it. He did not know it, but he would go on suffering from that hangover for the next five and a half days. If he lived that long.

Drake grunted, stretched, yawned, scratched his scalp, rubbed his head, pulled on the few hardly noticeable ginger hairs which these days straggled out from his chin, burped, farted, yawned again, took off his boots so he could pull the wrinkles out of his socks, pulled on his boots again, and felt as ready to face the world as he was likely to be on that particular day.

He felt by now that he had got the knack of walking around with his heels touching nothing but air, so it was with some confidence that he stepped outside. The sunshine was warm. The cockerel had shut up – with any luck, someone had strangled it. The blacksmith had quit hammering; a busy sound of filing now came from the forge. Within a shuttered house, someone – a big, big fat man, by the sound of it – was snoring loudly.

Drake grunted to himself, his grunt meaning, 'Demon's thanks, the racket's died down.'

The next moment, a small black-and-tan dog ambushed him, jumping from beneath a propped-up dinghy, barking wildly. It snapped at his heels, almost dared itself to bite, then backed off growling ferociously. Drake liked dogs – usually – but today he was not in the mood. He swung a kick at the cur, lost his balance, fell over, threw out an arm to save himself – but never hit the ground. He just hung there, floating. He was not amused. The dog leaped forward and started worrying his wrist.

'**** *****!' said Drake, shaking it loose.

Or, to be precise, to give (in the interests of accuracy) form to that which a misguided prudery would rather suppress:

'*Salk felsh*!'

As he regained his feet, Drake said a few other words of similar nature. Then tore a fishing-float free from a drying net, and threw it. The float scudded past the dog's left ear, and the mongrel turned and fled.

Drake's throat was too sore to allow him the satisfaction of hurling abuse at its scampering heels.

He walked between forge and boatshed to the waterfront. A couple of dozen fishing boats were drawn up on the sandy beach; several larger ones lay at anchor in the harbour bay. Further out was the *Sky Dancer*, the ship Arabin's men still insisted on calling the *Warwolf*. A few people were moving about on deck; the unintelligible tones of their voices came drifting through the still, calm air. Tiny wavelets lapped against the sands like kittens eagering on cream.

Drake looked around for a boat so he could row to the ship. He saw a number of dinghies, all lying clear of the water. All looking heavy. And none had oars. Drake paused, shrugged, then walked out across the water.

By the time he reached the ship, he was having no trouble at all with his negative gravity. Those on deck crowded to the rails to watch, so he showed off a bit. Striding over the water with great aplomb, Drake paraded around the vessel, feeling still very sick but very clever all the same.

'Stop playing the fool, man!' shouted Rolf Thelemite from the deck. 'We need you up here, fast!'

Drake made a rude gesture for Rolf Thelemite's benefit. Then the Walrus himself, Slagger Mulps in all his hairy glory, shouted in a regular storm voice:

'Drake, you son of a snake-spawned cockroach, get your arse up here, now, before I come down there and kick it off!'

Drake was just considering whether the Walrus was also worthy of a rude gesture, and what his (Drake's) chances of survival would be if he made one, when the last of the enchantment wore off, suddenly and without warning. Gravity reclaimed him, and he fell into the sea, which was shockingly cold and wet besides. He spluttered and floundered a bit, while those on deck laughed loudly, then he swam overarm to the anchor cable, where he hung resting until a rope ladder was dropped so he could scramble up.

'Here!' bellowed the Walrus.

'What's up?' asked Drake.

He soon found out.

As the Walrus swiftly told him, in language almost salty enough to blister paint, Jon Arabin had been taken hostage by the locals, who thought that Baron Farouk of Hexagon would be worth a handsome ransom. They were holding him in the Bildungsgrift, an ancient (and usually abandoned) broch some three leagues inland. All of the locals had fled.

'No they haven't,' said Drake. 'There's someone snoring, and a blacksmith working still.'

'That forge is full of haunted metal,' said the Walrus grimly. 'I've been to see for myself. As for the snoring – that's Whale Mike, dead drunk in a stranger's bed. It would take six of us to shift him.'

'It wouldn't have taken six of you to shift me,' said Drake, slightly aggrieved.

'Aye, no,' said the Walrus, uneasily, 'but we had no time to search the town proper.'

In truth, a raiding party had gone ashore at dawn, had found Whale Mike asleep, had investigated the forge – and had fled immediately, having seen lean limbs of skeletal metal working unattended, stoking the furnace for the morning's work.

'Well then,' said Drake, 'it's a hard day for Jon Arabin, that's to be sure, but I'm off to bed. Wake me tomorrow so I can hear how you've handled it.'

'Not so fast!' said the Walrus, grabbing Drake by the collar as he sauntered away.

The collar, being rotten, tore free – but Drake stopped anyway.

'What do you want from me?' he asked.

'Your luck,' said the Walrus. 'Man, the fortunes you've won by gambling – you're so fay you can luck this out blindfolded with both hands tied to your testicles.'

'Luck be buggered,' said Drake, turning away.

'Hold fast!' said Mulps. 'You'll be buggered yourself with a sealing spear unless you come to order quickly. I'm putting you in charge of rescuing friend Warwolf.'

It was, Drake sensed, no idle boast.

'Okay then,' he said sullenly, 'I'll get Jon Arabin loose, or get him killed by trying.'

'None of that!' said the Walrus. 'Your life rides with his!'

'Ouch!' said Drake, his glorious stock of obscenities entirely failing him in the face of this news.

He saw – he was thinking fast, now – that Mulps had decided the situation was hopeless. They were like to lose Jon Arabin, which meant no admiral's hopes for the Walrus, hence no chance of extra booty to be divvied up between the crew, and thus, for a start, the possibility of civil war between the men ex-*Walrus* and the *Warwolf* originals.

Slagger Mulps was looking for a scapegoat, and had found one in Drake, the lucky one, whose glamorous dice and youthful insolence had not exactly made him widely beloved, at least not amongst the crewmen from the *Walrus*.

Jon Arabin's men thought better of Drake, as he had found when the Warwolf tried to have him thrown overboard more than a horizon away from the Teeth. But would they stand staunch against the Walrus? For an entire crew to face down Jon Arabin on Drake's behalf

314

was one thing. For them to fight it out cutlass to cutlass with the likes of Ish Ulpin was another thing altogether.

Likely those from the *Warwolf* would throw in their lot with the *Walrus* men. Likely the men would relieve their frustrations by battering Drake to death. Which would suit Mulps just fine.

'He won't do it,' said Simp Fiche loudly.

'Yes I will,' said Drake stoutly. 'And you'll come too, to help me. And – and Yot there, come on, Sully boy, get in behind. And – yes, Bucks Cat, you'll do. Thelemite, man, let's have the Rovac with us. Jez! Yes, you, Jez Glane, you're not that bothered that you can't hear me. Ish Ulpin, yes. And you – Haze, isn't it? And you – what's your name? What was that? Chicks, is it? Then fall in, friend Chicks.'

'Hang about!' said Slagger Mulps. 'Most of those are my men! Why are you taking mine?'

'Because yours are the best,' said Drake, blandly. 'Aren't they? I tell you what, I'll take Jon Disaster too. Grab some rope, Jon. We'll hang some locals once we've loosed Jon Arabin.'

And soon Drake was ashore with his negotiating team, each man kitted out with one or more sharp-edged instruments of pirate-style diplomacy. If all went wrong and most got killed, then Drake – if he survived – would return to the *Sky Dancer* to find the Walrus more in a minority than he had been. On the other hand . . . he might just light out for the furthest sand dune he could find, and hide there until the *Sky Dancer* departed.

Sweating and breathing heavily – it was only three leagues, to be sure, but few of them had walked even half that far for years – Drake and his nine death commandos arrived at the Bildungsgrift.

'Stop here,' said Drake, sitting in the semi-shade of a tall plant which was the local excuse for a tree.

The pirates obeyed without question.

'First,' said Drake, like a veteran. 'Clarification of the aim. Then reconnaissance.'

He had learnt those big words from a couple of Galish-speaking soldiers while kicking around idle on Burntos, before the trouble started. They sounded good, and meant he had to do nothing for the time being but sit and stare at the broch.

The Bildungsgrift was not much, as castles went. The moat had filled up with windblow sand some five hundred years before; scurvy grass, docks, stinging nettles and wild radish (not ordinary radish, but the rare bitter-radish of Carawell, which is actually more of an onion) grew right up to the castle walls.

Those walls were not terribly tall, being scarcely twice the height of a man. Only a hastily arranged clutter of barrels and baulks of timber barred the gateway. No proud flag fluttered from the battlements – only a pair of women's bloomers, mounted on a fishing pole (and even those did not flutter, there being no wind). No helmeted warriors lined those walls, only some over-excited villagers armed with stones and fish-gutting knives.

'It's not much of a place,' said Rolf Thelemite. 'One good rush would take us through the gateway with no trouble at all.'

'Yes,' said Drake, proceeding with heavy irony and a masterly grasp of strategy. 'No trouble at all – until we got inside. Then, methinks, thinking being one of my fortes, we'd be outnumbered a hundred to one.'

The word he used for 'fortes' was 'chagcheex', a term from the High Speech which he had picked up from the wizard Miphon.

'Chagcheex?' said Jez Glane, quoting it back to him in bewilderment. 'What does that mean?'

'No idea,' said Drake, who in fact had a hazy idea that it meant octopus-raping abilities. 'But it sounds good, doesn't it?'

'It sounds better than those odds of yours, for sure,' said Glane. 'A hundred to one? Perhaps we'd better go home.'

'Aagh, stop talking like a mother-doll,' said Bucks Cat in disgust.

'Yes,' said Ish Ulpin. 'They're only peasants, not warriors.'

'And the odds, I warrant, are no worse than ten to one at worst,' said Rolf Thelemite.

This was optimistic. The odds were, in truth, closer to fifty to one. Though more than half of those in the castle were women and children, Drake was right in guessing that the pirates would get nowhere by force.

'Come on,' said Drake, 'let's go forward.'

'All of us?' said Yot.

'Yes,' said Drake, 'in case a sudden opportunity presents itself. We have to be ready to snatch our beloved captain if they give us the chance.'

At the back of his mind was the thought that, if the locals started throwing things, more targets would minimize the chances of Drake getting personally battered.

Before they could start their advance, Chicks, a coward at heart, faked an epileptic fit. Afterwards, he lay still, pretending, no matter how hard they kicked him, to be unconscious.

'I'll wake him up,' said Jon Disaster grimly.

And kicked Chicks so hard in the head that the man was knocked truly unconscious.

'*Graf begrik*,' muttered Drake, and led the way forward, leaving Chicks in a heap on the sand.

'Maybe I should stay behind and look after him,' said Simp Fiche.

'Were you born with a cock or weren't you?' said Ish Ulpin.

Simp Fiche made no reply, but kept pace with the others as they advanced. Several fish-heads were flung in their direction, but these fell short.

'Piss poor thowing,' said Jez Glane.

'Here's far enough,' said Drake, halting thirty paces in front of the gate.

He challenged the castle, using Bucks Cat as an amplifier.

'Hoy,' muttered Drake, his throat still scratchy from last night's boozing.

317

And Bucks Cat shouted, in a voice that made Drake's head feel as if it was splitting from stem to stern:

'Hoy! You farts up there!'

'Don't embellish,' muttered Drake. 'Just the plain words will do.'

'Don't embellish!' roared Bucks Cat. Then paused, and asked of Drake: 'What does embellish mean?'

'It's another word for tattoo,' said Drake.

'Oh,' said Bucks Cat. Then roared out: 'Don't tattoo the Warwolf, unless you want your head shoved up your arse until you suffocate!'

Drake groaned and sat down, covering his face with his hands.

'Is something wrong?' asked Bucks Cat. 'Don't you feel well?'

'I had a hard night,' said Drake, allowing himself to be helped to his feet again. 'I think . . . I think I'll go into the castle to talk with them direct. Face to face, aye, that's the stuff.'

'I'll go with you,' said Rolf Thelemite instantly.

'Ah. . . Rolf, man. . .I, ah. . .I think we may have to do a night attack.' Thus spoke Drake. He scratched through his memories of soldier-talk on Burntos, then continued: 'I want you to reconnoitre the rear approaches. Make a sketch map so we can show the others, back at the ship.'

'A sketch map,' said Thelemite. 'Anyone got any writing materials?'

Strangely, none of the pirates had about them quill, ink or parchment. Or, for that matter, a tuning fork or a cookery book, a chestnut or a colander, or a chunk of the moon of the month before.

'I've got some tobacco,' volunteered Jez Glane.

'Thanks,' said Drake, heavily.

Fortunately, Simp Fiche had a small money-bag made out of human skin. While Bucks Cat held Jez Glane in an armlock, and Ish Ulpin went through his pockets looking for the tobacco, Simp Fiche unpicked the seams of his money-bag.

'What were you planning to do with these?' said Ish Ulpin, pulling from Jez Glane's pockets a full half-dozen high-class condoms, each made from the caecum of a lamb.

'Screw your mother backwards,' said Jez Glane.

Ish Ulpin cuffed him.

'Belay that!' said Drake, in a voice so loud it hurt his own head.

His throat felt as if it had been torn open by the shout. But it got results, as Bucks Cat released Jez Glane. Ish Ulpin, perhaps momentarily ashamed of his uncomradely behaviour, even turned over to Glane a tenth of the tobacco just stolen from him.

Then, as Ish Ulpin began to glove his fingers one by one with the condoms taken from Glane, Rolf Thelemite took the unpicked bag of human skin from Simp Fiche.

'I'll get the map done on this,' said Thelemite, bravely, as a Rovac warrior should. 'I'll find a thorn, draw my blood, then map out our war with that.'

'Good, good,' said Drake. 'Yot – you come with me.'

'Why me?' said Yot plaintively. 'I thought you were going alone.'

'There should be a representative present from the Walrus men,' said Drake, 'to see that no underhand deals get done.'

'I've not been with the Walrus for months,' protested Yot, fearful of danger.

'You're one of ours at heart,' said Trudy Haze.

'Aye,' growled Ish Ulpin, 'go with Drake. Otherwise he might sell us all as slaves in exchange for Arabin. You go, Sully. Keep him honest.'

So Yot went.

Drake wanted his fellow Stokos-islander along in case the kidnappers would take him as part of the ransom – as eating meat, perhaps. Despite what Ish Ulpin had said, Drake doubted there would be much trouble if he traded Yot to the locals.

The pair scrambled over the rubbish in the gateway and

down into the central courtyard, where they were ringed by jeering children. Drake thought about grabbing one and threatening to cut its throat unless Arabin was released. He dismissed the thought almost immediately, unable to convince himself that anyone could seriously value anything as intrinsically worthless as a child.

The children were dispersed by a small negotiating party of middle-aged fishermen.

'So you want Baron Farouk back, do you?' said one.

'He's not Baron Farouk,' said Drake bluntly. 'He's Jon Arabin, pirate of the Greaters. Release him immediately, or Lord Menator of the Teeth will north to Brennan with a fleet, then kill off every fish-raping sodomist's son on Carawell, which means the lot of you.'

The fishermen laughed.

'I'm serious!' said Drake.

He intended to shout, but what came from his suffering throat was more of a squawk. The fishermen cackled more.

'Him? A pirate? Would you be a pirate too, perhaps?'

'I am,' said Drake, trying, with a complete lack of success, to sound as savage as he felt. 'A blooded blade of the free marauders.'

They laughed the more.

'And how,' said one of them, eventually, wiping the tears from his eyes, 'how does a sprig of a boy like you hold his own amongst men?'

'Because I'm hard as iron and as bitter as steel,' said Drake promptly, which set them off again.

Unfortunately, the locals had a faulty conception of pirating. Sheltered on their sand-bank islands, hearing only second-hand rumours richly embroidered, they firmly believed that the initiation rites of the Orfus pirates involved cutting off one's nose and the top joint of one's left little finger.

Moreover, Carawell was one of those places where boys stay boys a long time, for the fathers control inheritance rights to the wealth – which on Carawell was land and

320

fishing boats – and the boys must be meek, respectful, humble and in need of advice, or get disinherited.

So Drake looked, to the fishermen, absurdly young to be sent to negotiate, and an obvious liar into the bargain. They took much the same view of youth as did the Partnership Banks: adulthood only began at age twenty-five, if then.

'Sprigling,' said one of the fishermen. 'We know why it's you they've sent to do talk with us. It's because Baron Farouk's your father.'

'He's no such thing,' said Drake. 'He's my captain true, and there's an end to it.'

'Young one, you've trapped yourself twice. Last night he called you his son, with half us there in witness.'

Drake hazily remembered Jon Arabin doing something of the sort, about the time that Drake was contemplating drinking a bowl of firewater.

'That's a term of honour,' said Drake. 'He calls me that because he loves me, since the time I saved his ship from a Neversh.'

'From a Neversh!' spluttered one of the fishermen.

And their mirth was virtually unquenchable.

The Lesser Teeth were isolated, true, but they played chess here as men did everywhere, and knew that a Neversh is not just the most delicate piece on the chessboard – those six wings the first thing to break off when children get hold of the pieces, and never mind about the eight feet – but a real live world-destroying monster of the terror-lands beyond Drangsturm.

No way could a boy like this kill a legend-haunter like that!

'Face truth,' said one of the fishermen. 'Your father's here, and here stays until we get five scarfs of diamonds, a gillet of gold, some ninety ropes of arachnid silk, and fifty thousand steel fish hooks.'

'Nobody insults steel by making it into fish hooks!' said Drake.

He was scandalized at the very thought – and, these days, it took a lot to scandalize him.

'Nobody does?' said one of the fishermen. 'Then, sorry, but your father dies.'

'And you die with him!' said Drake. 'For am I not a priest of the Flame? Look – is that vodka? It is!'

And he wrestled a skin of the stuff away from the man holding it. He, with a man's contempt for a boy, tried to wrest it back – and found out what blacksmith's muscles are made of.

'Watch!' said Drake.

And drank as if thirsting to death.

Then wiped his mouth and looked around.

'Could any man amongst you do as much?' he said. 'No! And why can I? Because I am of the Flame! The Flame is with me! Yield up my father! Or I will call the wrath of the Flame upon you! Thus!'

And Drake swigged more vodka to ease his throat, then began jigging up and down on the spot, still clutching the skin of hard liquor, and chanting:

> Flame of Flames, I summon ye!
> Flame of Flames, I call!
> By the Sacred Names I call ye,
> Yah-ray hoo-ray, yah-ray hoo-ray!
> Yah-ray yah-ray! Hoo-ray hoo-ray!
> Dharma dharma, hoo-ray hoo-ray!

At which point Sully Datelier Yot, appalled by this open blasphemy (his faith had weakened, true, yet he did not Disbelieve) shouted:

'No! No! Stop! Stop! Or the Flame will kill you!'

'Yea, verily verily,' roared Drake, working Yot's protest into his act. 'Bring down the Flame!'

And he raised his arms to the heavens.

Far off in the distance, a cockerel cried:

'Co co rico! Co co rico!'

There was a crash of thunder. The sky went green. Blue lightning writhed across the heavens in patterns like those a thread of water makes as it scrawls down a crooked stick. Then the clouds were gashed open by a Flame. It

322

descended slowly, a monstrous whirling column of angry purple and crackling red. Down from the heights it came, until its base stood before Drake and its heights in the heavens.

'Fall down!' said Drake sternly, wondering what on earth had been mixed with that vodka. 'Fall down and worship the Flame! Repent your sins or die!'

Most of the fishermen were already grovelling in the dust.

'The Flame!' whimpered Yot, in religious ecstasy. 'It is true! I did believe, really! Always!'

And he embraced his god. And, touching the whirling column of fire, was knocked back as if kicked by an elephant. He stretched his length senseless on the ground.

'Enough!' shouted Drake. And then, hoarsely: 'You are Believed.'

Slowly, the column of fire whirled into nothing. The lightning ceased tormenting the sky, which lost its seasick tinge and became, once more, a blue so crisp it looked worth biting. In the distance, dogs were barking.

For a moment, nothing happened. Then a woman began a wailing scream. It proved infectious, and soon all the locals in Bildungsgrift were fleeing, screaming as they went. The rubbish in the gate was scattered aside by the fury of their flight.

'Well,' said Drake, looking around the warm, sunny courtyard, where nobody was left but himself and Yot (who was still unconscious). 'Well, that was . . .'

But he was not sure what it had been.

'That was something,' he finished, lamely.

'What was something?' asked Jon Arabin, striding out of a tower-base door.

'Didn't you see it then?' said Drake.

'See what? I heard some thunder – was there a squall?'

'Never mind,' said Drake. 'It's over.'

'What happened to Sully Yot?' said Arabin, sighting Yot's unconscious form.

'Man,' said Drake, 'he got so frightened by all these

locals here that he plain flew into the air, aye, flapping his arms like madness. He were ten times his own height off the ground when he slipped and fell. But the sight so amazed the locals that they turned and fled.'

'Oh yes!' said Arabin, with a grin. 'Tell me another one!'

Drake, who needed no further invitation, promptly did.

'Enough of your nonsense,' said Ish Ulpin, entering the courtyard in time to hear the end of Drake's second joke. 'The peasants are running, so let us be hunting.'

'Nay,' said Arabin. 'Whatever's scared the locals, they may recover their wits in a moment. Let's be getting back to the ship while the getting's good.'

Bucks Cat supported Ish Ulpin's stance, but the pair of them were outnumbered. So back to the ship they all got, carrying Sully Yot and friend Chicks between them. Which made their journey mighty long, even though Yot recovered his senses after scarcely half a league.

23

D'Waith: extremely small community with large-scale
pretensions (this walled village claiming to be a city state);
commands most easterly harbour of Ravlish Lands, some
100 leagues north of Lesser Teeth, 50 leagues west of Argan
and 70 leagues (as the fish-bat flies) south of Island Drum.

The pirates ravaged Brennan in a half-hearted way. Stone
buildings thwarted arson; the haunted metal in the forge
(which they did not dare enter) disturbed them; the thought
of their damaged ship lying at anchor in a hostile harbour
disturbed them more. In the end, they burnt every boat in
reach and left it at that.

A few hardy souls (such as Bucks Cat and Ish Ulpin)
wanted to go on a search-and-destroy mission into the hinterland, seeking candidates for skinning alive, but most
thought (rightly) that this would be rank foolishness.

'Those so arrant in their anger can stay behind to hunt
lonesome,' said Jon Arabin. 'The rest of us are going.'

And go they did. The *Sky Dancer* slipped to sea that evening, ghosting all night on the moth-wing airs of a
preternaturally smooth-browed sea, the loudest sound
aboard being that of the pumps still working to keep them
afloat. Jon Arabin planned to put in to D'Waith, in the
north, to make repairs he had originally thought to encompass at Brennan.

That night, Drake worried over what he had seen at
Bildungsgrift. The next morning, he questioned Yot
about it.

'You tell me what happened,' said Yot. 'I don't remember anything. Except – yes, there was some lightning. And I got hit by it, or so my burns would suppose. Look!'

Yot had nasty burns on his hands.

'And the same on my feet,' he said.

'Go see Jon Arabin,' said Drake. 'He'll doctor you.'

And Drake himself went looking for Rolf Thelemite, who insisted on showing him a nicely drawn sketch map of the backside of Bildungsgrift, with places marked for siege ladders, and a diversionary assault, and fall-back positions in case of a sally from within.

'That's very, very professional,' said Drake. 'You must show it to Menator back home, for he'll need it doubtless when we take the Lessers in earnest, which we must, them being anchored so close to us. Now tell, man – what saw you yesterday? In the way of strangeness, I mean. Just before the enemy ran.'

Rolf Thelemite frowned.

'A . . . a colour in the sky,' he said. 'Though I don't remember what. A squall, but no rain that I remember. And a windspout, aye, a bit irregular in colour, but wind all the same.'

'Windspout?!' said Drake, who had never heard of any such thing.

'Aye, and I've seen them in desert before, only sand. They rain fish sometimes, but that's at sea, or the nearland. Yes. Big, sometimes. Suck up horses and houses. Why, there was one I remember in a battle once – won us clean through to victory when we was close to defeat.'

'But yesterday's . . . I mean . . . it was strange, wasn't it?'

'Oh, there's many things strange, by land and sea,' said Rolf Thelemite. 'Windspouts, aye, and rainbows round the midnight moon. The green flash at sunset, aye, most will tell you it's myth, but I've seen it, man, I've seen it. And fire which walks through swamps without burning, and balls of fire which sit on masts in a storm – and that does burn, man, I've seen the strongest shaken by it.'

326

'But this was stranger than those other things, surely,' said Drake. 'The sky changing colour, for a start. You've never seen that before!'

'Oh yes I have,' said Rolf Thelemite. 'When I was in the far north of Tameran – and not many Rovac have gone campaigning there, believe me, for all that we're said to battle in every war that's going – why, up there in winter I saw the sky, aye, and the sky was as many colours as a corpse five days after it's been kicked to death, the colours not still but moving. Aye—'

And Thelemite was off again. Drake left as soon as he decently could (or, to be pedantically exact, just a finger-length of time before then – but Thelemite was so deep in his tale of headless bodies and lopped-off limbs that he didn't notice his shipmate's departure) and sought out other witnesses, such as Jez Glane.

'It were lightning,' said Glane. 'Lightning stretched out a bit, that's all.'

'Stretched!' said Drake.

'I thought you pulled yourself often enough to know about stretching,' said Glane.

'I should have let Ish Ulpin knock you senseless back at that castle place,' said Drake.

And went looking for Bucks Cat.

'The earth farted,' said Bucks Cat. 'That's all.'

Drake did no better with the others, all of whom knew little and cared less.

Unable to get a proper explanation of the manifestation he had witnessed at Bildungsgrift, Drake was left to trouble out the Higher Problems of theology on his own. He was trying very hard, but not entirely successfully, to persuade himself that he had not really had a run-in with the Flame.

Drake's introspective spiritual wrestling, while perhaps a good mental discipline in its own right, was entirely unproductive of truth. It won him no wisdom. Indeed, his correct course of action would have been to run up and down the ship shouting:

'Is there a theologian on board!'

327

Eventually, if he had persisted thus in the face of the predictable reaction from the ship's crew, Morton Seligman ('Foreskin' to all his friends) would have taken pity on him, and would have explained. Seligman was old, yes, and by afternoon had trouble remembering events of the morning, but his mind was as sharp as ever when it came to recalling his past.

For decades – until aged 52 (or 53 if one counts age from conception, as many peoples do, and with more logic than their enemies will admit) – Seligman, essentially a gentle individual (the scalps dangling from his belt had been acquired by way of trade) had studied earnestly under a wizard of the Order of Seth.

Seligman had failed his Trials, as do many. However, unlike most such failures, he had lived to tell the tale. If asked, he could have told Drake (and would have done so willingly) that:

† many a place has its genius loci, an entity low in the hierarchy of spiritual beings yet capable of exerting temporal power;

† such a genius loci has no true form of its own, far less any true understanding of the nature of the world of events, and therefore can only manifest itself (and act) in terms of the perceived expectations of human intellects;

† that such expectations are usually too blurred, fuzzy and diffuse for a genius loci to make anything of them;

† that religious ceremony, with its combination of intense mental concentration, precise expectations (often emphasized by prayers, chants, songs etc.), designed to harass a 'god' into doing something useful, e.g. striking down enemies of the state, making rain, bringing wind, annihilating unbelievers and withering the bodies of their children, etc. was the most effective way to get positive action from a genius loci.

Drake would have complained that his mind had not been concentrated and his own expectations had been non-existent. To which Morton Seligman would have replied (once he had elicited a full account of the facts, which, as a trained Investigator, he naturally would have) that the mind of Sully Datelier Yot would have been concentrated most wonderfully by Drake's sacrilege, and Yot would have expected some reaction from the Flame.

Drake, too shy (and too conscious of his own safety) to have ever run about the deck calling for a theologian (since he was not in the habit of seeking advice the notion never even occurred to him) was doomed to stay ignorant.

Thus he never learned how the nature of the genius loci explains so many weird and wonderful things, such as the temporary appearance of the dead to the recently bereaved (which is common), the skill of the rain dancer, ghosts (a few of them, anyway, there being in all 127 distinctly different categories of ghost), coins of gold which later turn to leaves, the treasure found at the end of rainbows (assay-masters know the worthless stuff well), and, indeed, the powers of several minor classes of sorcerers and necromancers (and a few minor effects achieved in certain places by some members of the eight Orders of the Confederation of Wizards, even though all draw their Powers Major from older, more dangerous, more demanding entities).

Drake, then, lacking the guidance of true theology, had to cope with the possibility that maybe the Flame existed, that perhaps the Flame was angry with him, that it might actually be a smart move to bow down and worship the said Flame.

But if the Flame existed as described by Gouda Muck (that is to say, if Muck of Stokos was truly the High God of All Gods) then that cast serious doubts on the pretensions of the Demon, of the bloodlord Hagon.

'I would rather worship You,' said Drake softly, to Hagon.

He was not in the habit of addressing his god. If one

drew Hagon's attention to oneself, there was always the danger that the Demon would eat one's soul prematurely. Yet, under the circumstances, Drake thought it wise to resolve his doubts by testing the powers of Hagon.

'I know it's bad form to ask You for things,' said Drake. 'I know You have given us the Gift. That should be enough for us. Yet, just this once . . .'

Drake prayed to the Demon for an alleviation of the curse which gripped him – for, in other words, a renewal of drunkenness.

'Drink is a part of your Holy Gift,' said Drake. 'I ask only to be holy myself. Religion is the deepest part of my nature. May I not with your Grace practise it?'

He backed up his prayers with a sacrifice. The best thing to slay would have been an unblemished virgin or a spotless calf. None such was available, but Drake did manage to obtain three rats (one with a crippled left hind leg, for which he apologized to the bloodlord Hagon as politely as he knew how) and twenty-three cockroaches.

'I know these aren't sacrifices of the standard You are used to,' said Drake. 'But I hope they might at least have some novelty value.'

And he killed them, with all due ceremony.

Just one thing troubled him. These were supposed to be burnt offerings, but the ship had no facilities for burning such. Or did it? Wrapping his offerings in an old shirt stolen from Tiki Slooze, Drake ventured below decks and found his way to the kitchen. He tipped his heap of oddments into a massive cast-iron frying pan, intending to pour raw spirit on top then ignite it.

He was interrupted by the sudden arrival of the cook – not the muttering old man they used to have, who had since died of a stroke, but an ox-built giant who was master chef for Lord Regan of the Rice Empire until caught in flagrante delicto with Lord Regan's teenage son.

'What are you doing here?' said the cook, in a voice which could have commanded cavalry (and had, once – though that is another story).

330

'I've come to help out,' said Drake, hastily pouring some sauce over the gruesome mess in the frying pan. 'I used to work here before, you know.'

'I see,' said the cook, peering closely; fortunately he had gross myopia and a pronounced astigmatism besides (otherwise he would have been an archer, like his father, and his grandfather's grandfather before him) and didn't see at all. Or not well, at any rate. 'But what exactly are you making?'

'A species of, well, goulash, I suppose you could say,' said Drake, improvising frantically as he stirred in some rough red cooking wine (rough by pirate standards – i.e. a mouthful would leave one's mouth raw for a week).

'The ingredients?'

'It's got, uh, rabbits, yes,' said Drake, putting the frying pan onto a heating iron. 'Yes,' he said, as the mixture began to warm, 'rabbits, small rabbits, I caught them myself on Carawell, and, um, let me think, shrimps, yes, the shellack-shelled Carawell variety, tougher than we're used to but very good.'

As he talked, he added herbs and spices more or less at random, then stirred and mashed, while steam rose and the brew began to bubble. He added vinegar, threw in pickles then scattered breadcrumbs over the mixture.

'You haven't skinned these rabbits!' said the cook, in an accusatorial voice, poking at them with one of his walnut-crunching fingers (cooks love to poke, stroke, caress and fondle foods of all kinds, particularly raw meats; this tactile bias may be because the profession traditionally soaks up part of the world's reservoir of short-sighted people, just as the metal-working trades take the lame).

'This is a traditional dish,' protested Drake. 'A special kind of folk-cookery. The skins are left on to keep in the flavour.'

'The guts are left in too, I suppose,' said the cook, with heavy sarcasm.

'Aye,' said Drake, eagerly. 'They're the best part!'

'Hmmm,' said the cook.

He had his doubts.

But as Drake stirred and added, spiced and salted, garnished and basted (and surreptitiously amputated rats' tails and discarded them to the floor, where the ship's cat claimed them) the smell from the frying pan grew better and better, until the cook was more than a little impressed.

'Is it done?' he asked.

'Almost,' said Drake.

'No, man, it's finished now. I can smell the goodness of it. Here – give me that.'

And, confiscating the frying pan, the cook tipped its contents into two large bowls.

'Where are those going?' asked Drake.

'The Walrus and the Warwolf are in conference,' said the cook. 'This'll be just the thing to keep them going.'

Drake suppressed a moan, and ran away and hid.

But he could not hide forever.

Finally, the cook caught him on deck:

'Hey! You!'

Drake, cornered, prepared to meet his doom.

'What do you want?' asked Drake, pretending he didn't know.

'The recipe, man, the recipe! Our captains loved it. You were right, the skins do keep in the flavour. And they say the guts slipped down something marvellous. There was only one complaint.'

'What's that?'

'They say next time, shell the shrimps before you cook them. There were bits of shell scattered right through the meal.'

'Well,' said Drake to the Demon, 'you can't say I didn't try.'

He was on watch in the crow's-nest, one of the few places in the ship where one could scratch, pray or masturbate in private.

'So give me that much,' continued Drake. 'I tried. And, in any case, they say that You would rather enjoy a good

332

joke than a burnt virgin any day. So – how about it? Do I get to get drunk again? Or don't I? Please understand, if I don't, it may be a little hard for me to believe in You ever again.'

Drake made that threat because it was known that the Demon liked his believers to show some spirit (unlike some other, less confident entities, which feel uneasy dealing with any supplicant who is not face-down grovelling).

Prayer done, Drake longed to test the efficacy of that prayer. But the liquor ration had run out, and could not be renewed before they reached D'Waith. But there was still some cooking wine aboard, was there not?

There was not. The cook had used the last of it in preparing a goulash to Drake's specifications. ('Not up to the standard of the original,' the captains had complained.)

Drake would have to wait for dry land before he could put his faith to the test.

But dry land was a long time coming. The scrimshaw weather saw them five days at sea between the Lessers and D'Waith, sometimes nosing along at seaslug pace, sometimes becalmed, and once or twice actually being carried backwards by playful little currents.

Drake whiled away his off-duty by playing dice-chess and backgammon. He was so skilled by now that, unaided by other men's inebriety, he won a triple-ply solskin horse blanket which had once graced a stable in far-off Gendormargensis (a nice piece of equipment, but he had no horse), an ancient scroll in a dead language, ornamented with line drawings which he took to be maps of roads and rivers in some distant land (they were sketches of the palm-prints of the progeny of a forgotten king), a 'lucky rock' which he soon sent overboard (not recognizing this fist-sized hunk of dull stone as a diamond in the rough), and half a loaf of bread (black ironbread, baked on the Greaters before the *Sky Dancer* set sail).

But all good journeys come to an end (and bad ones, too), and at last the anchor crashed into the waters of

D'Waith's harbour. Drake, in high excitement, stared at the shore – not at the city of D'Waith itself, which was some distance inland, but at the small buildings built right up near the harbour. One of them must surely be a bar.

He would soon be putting his religion to the test.

24

Name: Bluewater Draven.

Birthplace: Dalar ken Halvar.

Occupation: pirate captain, lately commander of the *Tusk*.

Status: always low, has been further reduced by loss of the *Tusk*, his fifth command wrecked in the last four years.

Description: cowardly untrustworthy bearded braggart of mature years who has (though he knows it not) a slow-growing bowel cancer, a small brain tumour, a steadily enlarging liver cyst, and an aneurysm in a major artery which may burst without warning at any moment, killing him almost instantly (though, knowing his luck, he'll as likely whore on for another ten years or more).

Religion: once seriously espoused alcoholism, but faith faltered after discovering this adversely affected his potency; may be said to have, if anything, 'a determined faith in the validity of the moment' (as Denrak said of Axis Gogman, who began his career as the ugly man in the court at Dalar ken Halvar, and ended up as Lord Tyrant of Greater Parengarenga).

'Is any of those buildings ashore a bar?' asked Drake, as the longboat cleaved its way through the harbour waters.

'They all are, unless things have changed since I came visiting last,' said Jon Arabin.

'Good,' said Slagger Mulps, 'for I'm thirsty.'

Shortly they were ashore. Avoiding an establishment raucous with slaughter, a bar with a hole in its roof and an evil den nailed up tight with a plague-sign guarding its door, they slogged through shoreside mud to a low building where they hoped to quench their grog-thirst. Even ascetic Jon Arabin was keen for a change from vinegar and muddy ship-water.

A drink or three would set them up nicely for the trek to D'Waith proper – a thousand paces, some of it uphill.

'Beers, be ready!' commanded Drake, reaching the pub before his betters.

Eagerly, he thrust open the door and jumped down into the interior, being in too much of a rush to use the steps. The damp gloom within smelt of stale beer and wet straw. It was strangely quiet (the locals having been lured away by the fight in a rival tavern). Behind the bar was a man with the head and the horns of a bull.

'Culamageethee!' said Drake in extreme surprise.

(The phrase, in his native Ligin, translates literally as 'the seaweed's slippery!')

He tried to withdraw, but it was too late, for the green-bearded Walrus was already coming through the doorway, with other thirsty souls crowding close behind.

'Strength in numbers,' muttered Drake.

The bull-man was truly there, as large as life if not three sizes larger, moist reflections shining in his dung-dark eyes, a ring of gold snot-gleaming in his nose. A woman of deceptively normal appearance joined him. As she began setting up some thirst-quenchers, Drake saw her hands were the paws of a cat.

'What'll it be, strangers?' asked the bull-man, as his woman arranged a dozen doses of the world's best medicine.

'Who are you calling a stranger?' demanded Jon Arabin.

'Why, Jon,' said the bull-man, 'it's you!'

'*Ken fenargh eoch'alagarn sharn narelonagarch*,' said

Arabin, slipping into a language unknown to Drake.

'*Shalamanargh ech hufloch dinareen*,' answered the bull-man.

And the two of them laughed.

'Belay that jabber!' growled Mulps, green eyes registering a sudden anger. 'Let's have straight talk so all can follow.'

'Why, Mulps, man,' said Arabin. 'If you met a friend, would you not want a few words with him in the language sweetest on the tongue?'

'I've no long-lost friends here,' said Mulps, 'so no way of knowing.'

'No friends?' demanded a big brute who had been idling in corner shadows, at cards with a boy. 'No friends? Then how count I?'

'Draven, me old cock!' cried Mulps.

'None other.'

It was indeed Bluewater Draven, captain of the good ship *Tusk*, one of the two vessels which had set out from the Greaters to accompany the *Sky Dancer* to Ork.

'So you made the rendevous,' said Arabin. 'But where is your ship? And where your crew?'

'I'll tell,' said Draven.

And told how the *Tusk* had been shipwrecked.

'And your crew?' demanded Arabin.

'It was all I could do to save myself,' said Draven.

'Ah!' said Arabin.

'Don't harshen your tongue at me like that, man. I gave clear warning. When Menator first talked empire, I said it would bring disaster.'

'Menator never wrecked your ship on the Ravlish coast,' said Jon Arabin, with more sharpness than was strictly necessary.

'Nay, man, but I was here on his orders,' said Draven. 'Aye, and lucky to survive, bereft of friends on a foreign shore.'

'Well, your problems are over,' said Slagger Mulps. 'We'll soon muscle up a bed for you on my good ship.'

337

'So she's your ship now, is she?' said Draven, by way of provocation. 'Is she calling herself the *Walrus* these days?'

'Aye, that she is,' said Mulps, unwisely.

'She's no such gore-wet thing!' said Jon Arabin, as honour compelled him to in the face of such a challenge. 'She's the *Warwolf*, always has been, always will.'

While the pirate chiefs argued it out, young Drake Douay ballasted himself with a few good ales. But they did him little good, so he complained to the barman accordingly.

'We'll soon fix that,' said his host, pouring him a good dollop of rice wine. 'This'll vim you up nicely.'

Drake drank it down and shook his head.

'More!' he said.

'First pack down some food,' said the barman. 'Booze is grim stuff for an empty stomach.'

'Nay, man,' said Drake, shaking his head. 'I don't eat while I'm drinking.'

The barman grabbed Drake's hair then hauled him close, jamming his nose against the bull-snout gold. Hot bull's breath fanned Drake's face.

'You'll do what's good for you, boy,' roared the barman, 'or I'll break your ribs in fifty-seven places then jump up and down on your liver, just as your mother would want me to.'

He released Drake, who, shaken, sat abruptly on a bar stool.

'Molly!' said the barman. 'Dish the boy some food!'

The woman with cat-paw hands obliged, slapping down an enormous bowl of polenta, with a mixed assortment of olives and gherkins on the side.

'Eat, boy, eat!' said the barman. 'And don't tell your mother I didn't take care of you.'

'Maybe I can't afford to pay for it,' said Drake rebelliously.

'Food's free, like all good things in life. Molly, start spoon-feeding the boy – he's clearly in need of assistance.'

338

Calmly, Molly picked up a spoon. Drake hastily began shovelling victuals into his mouth, ears burning as men behind him laughed.

'Not so fast, boy,' said the barman, a note of warning in his voice. 'You'll give yourself indigestion.'

Drake, determined to salvage self-respect through disobedience, gobbed his food faster – but soon had to stop greeding as his belly filled. There was, he realized, a truly awesome amount of polenta in the bowl.

At last, gorged as a blood-swollen tick, he supped the last lick of polenta, and swallowed – with difficulty – the very last olive.

'You've left a gherkin,' said Molly.

'That's the custom where I come from,' said Drake, who knew he would vomit if he dared another morsel. 'The gods demand it.'

Molly let that pass.

By this time, Drake was incapable of boozing. He simply had no room left to take drink aboard.

'That does for that chance,' he muttered.

For he thought they would soon leave for D'Waith, to visit workshops, timber yards, warehouses, sail-makers and ship-chandlers. But the pirate chiefs had settled down to talk the day to death: D'Waith would be there still on the morrow.

In time, Drake's stomach settled, so he set about debauching himself. He sampled the wine of grapes and dandelions; he tippled on vodka and gin. He gulleted down punch, brandy, porter and perry. He tried seventeen types of foreign liquor, seasoning his drinks with samples of half a dozen different drugs.

All to no effect.

He thought of his earnest prayers to the Demon, of his sacrifice of rats and cockroaches. He had worshipped as best he knew how: and the Demon had failed him!

'I didn't ask much, did I?' said Drake bitterly.

But answer came there none.

Over the next few days, while repairs were made to the

339

ship with the contentious name, Drake thought hard about the Demon. Perhaps his sacrifice had been no good because Walrus and Warwolf had ended up eating it. Or maybe it had just been too small.

Drake unstitched gold coins sewn into his sealskin jacket, and went shopping in D'Waith. He picked up a couple of changes of clothes, including some woollens (he was heartily sick of sealskin) then sought proper sacrifice material. He made diligent inquiries, but found D'Waith had no virgins – three men claimed to have made sure of that personally. No cattle were to be had, either, 'not since last year's plague'.

In lieu of a virgin and a spotless calf, which would undoubtedly have found favour with the Demon, Drake bought two sheep, a goat, seventeen dogs, twenty turtle-doves and a whole cask of arak, then sacrificed the lot on an enormous pyre. As the flames of this holocaust ascended to the heavens, he prayed again for alcohol to be given its full powers over his body and mind.

Then tried to get drunk.

He failed.

For the first time in his life, Drake lost faith. His belief in the Demon had till then been absolute and unyielding. But now it was destroyed.

'Hagon does not exist,' said Drake to himself, in the dull voice of one who has suffered an unimaginable catastrophe.

In truth, Drake's prayers were unanswered only because of problems with distance. Further than fifty leagues from Stokos, it was not the slightest use whimpering to the Demon, for He was an entity with strictly localized links to the world of events.

Hagon, then, was not nearly as grand as His temple claimed Him to be. He was not a world-dominator. Nor was he the inventor of the Gift, the First Drunkard, the First Client of the Oldest Profession, or, indeed, most of the other things He was claimed to be.

However, had Drake been on Stokos, his earnest

prayers, supported by sacrifices, would have won him the Demon's help. For Hagon's strength, though not equal to its publicity, was nevertheless impressive. He was far more of a Force (and far more accessible to His worshippers) than, say, the Demon of Estar.

Hagon had a measure of temporal power. Also, true to His temple's claim, He could indeed eat the souls of the dead, and did (as advertised) perform that service for any worshipper who died on Stokos – the dreaded alternative being eternal torment in one of the hells designed by the sadistic Ghost Gods (not to be confused with the True Gods, the High Gods, the Chaos Lords, Those That Are, Those That Will Be, or Those Who Were).

Thus, as they sailed north from D'Waith, Drake endured an unfulfilled spiritual longing, i.e. a wish to get drunk which he had no hope of gratifying. Plus doubts about Demon and Flame. Shortly, Drake sought out Yot and broached the subject of religion:

'Yot, me old mate, I think it's time we had a chat about old man Muck and that Flame of his. I've begun to think maybe the scungy old bastard was onto something after all.'

But Yot – not realizing the enormous effort it had taken Drake to make this confession – found Drake's approach off-putting, and quite refused to discuss theology. After all, Yot had it on Muck's authority that Drake, the Demon's son, could never be anything other than a mortal enemy of the Flame.

'Sully,' said Drake desperately. 'You don't understand! This is serious! I have to talk to you about the Flame!'

'Not so,' said Yot. 'You want to sniff around till you learn where to find Zanya Kliedervaust. When you know that you'll kill me. Right? You only let me live because I'm the only one who can tell you where she's gone to.'

'You're paranoid, man,' said Drake.

'I'm no such thing,' said Yot.

'I know where she is anyway,' said Drake. 'I met her in Burntos. Didn't you ever hear about that? She went to Drangsturm. I went there with her.'

341

'Ah!' said Yot. 'But Burntos and Drangsturm were just the first parts of her mission. You don't know where she went from there. But I do.'

A smug smile grew on Yot's face, somehow finding space in amongst the warts for a full-fleshed existence.

'You were talking of life and death,' said Drake, with more death than life in his voice.

Fortunately, at that point Jon Arabin happened along, and told them it was training time. Drake, indeed curious about Zanya's whereabouts, questioned Yot as they practised sword under the stony gaze of the weapons muqaddam.

'Did Zanya go to Veda, perhaps?' yelled Drake.

'Nay!' jeered Yot. 'You'll never know! You'll never find her!'

He danced round Drake, feinting and slicing something wonderful. Tall lanky sod! Drake, angry, smashed the flat of his blade against the flat of Yot's weapon. *Sclap*! Yot's blade flew from his hand and spun overboard, lost forever to the slathering sea.

'*Gaaa*!' screamed Drake.

He hacked at Yot's neck. He halted his blade just before contact, or tried to – but the heaving deck tricked him, and Yot got a pimple-scratch cut from the steel. The weapons muqaddam grunted.

'Yot,' he said. 'Grip, remember? Relaxed yet firm. How many times must I tell you? Go below. Get another weapon. Quick, man!'

But Yot's fingertips had found his cut. They brought him the savage scarlet of his own blood. Staring at it, he rocked unsteadily on his feet. The ship rocked under him, and he fainted.

'Drake,' said the weapons muqaddam, 'get a bucket of water.'

All this happened on a ship again known as the *Warwolf*. Jon Arabin had had a showdown with Slagger Mulps, threatening to kill off the Walrus's friend Draven unless the ship reclaimed her original title.

The great lord Menator, their imperial master, would doubtless be angry with Arabin. But Jon Arabin, who had further considered this empire business, was already making careful plans to deal with Menator permanently on his return.

25

Penvash Channel: wild stretch of water running between eastern end of the Ravlish Lands and north-west coast of Argan; connects Central Ocean with Hauma Sea; gives access to the North Strait (known in Tameran as the Pale) between Argan and Tameran.

The Penvash Channel was notorious for storms, but the *Warwolf* enjoyed good weather as she ran for the north. The most trying thing the crew had to cope with was the hair-raising scream of the blue-feathered mocking gull. They shot at it with crossbows, and with some success, not knowing that Hostaja Sken-Pitilkin, wizard of Drum, had put it on his Endangered Species List.

There was, at the start of this sea-passage, a mutter of mutiny from men who, being still loyal to Slagger Mulps, were upset at the ship reverting to the name of *Warwolf*. But serious trouble did not begin till their vessel neared the island of Drum – and then it was trouble of an altogether different nature.

On a bright day in the Penvash Channel, not far from Drum, Drake renewed his acquaintance with dolphins. With something close to joy, he watched them bounding through the brisk seas, as slick as soap and every bit as fast as legend claimed.

'Harly!' yelled Drake. 'See!'

Harly Burpskin came, saw, and frowned. Months ago he had made a bet with Drake that dolphins and sea serpents were mythical; the manifestation of dolphins was, therefore, unwelcome.

'Well,' said Burpskin, 'we still haven't seen a sea serpent.'

'We will,' said Drake, with confidence. 'We will.'

But would they?

He could hardly expect to be lucky twice in one day.

The *Warwolf* strove through the seas with the wind straining against her green canvas. The weapons muqaddam was in one of his organizing moods, meaning hard times for idle hands, whether they were theoretically off watch or not. Drake kept out of his way, and got talking with a passenger: the youth he had first sighted playing cards with Bluewater Draven in the tavern at D'Waith.

They had not yet had time to get properly acquainted when the ship shuddered as if she had hit a rock or a whale. Then she was struck again, and out of the water rose a bullock-girthing sea serpent. Up, up it rose, slick with the glittering sea.

Then sank again.

But before Drake had time even to laugh with relief, he realized there were at least five more of the brutes in the water. Under threat of doom, Jon Arabin gave the orders he must. The ship's women were dragged up from below and thrown overboard in an attempt to glut the monsters' greed.

'That's murder!' cried the passenger, clearly shocked. ·

Drake felt himself grin.

'Them or us,' he said, talking nice and spritely to conceal emotions he would have been ashamed to acknowledge as fear and horror. 'Which would you prefer?'

That gave the stranger pause. But, before said passenger could come up with an answer, he was seized by the weapons muqaddam, dragged to the stern rail – kicking, screaming, biting and scratching – and thrown overboard himself. There was something so amazingly comical about his performance that Drake collapsed to the deck, laughing.

He was still rolling around giggling – which was perhaps preferable to the alternative, which was to writhe around screaming – when the stranger who had been thrown overboard came bumping back onto the deck.

How?

Drake had no time to find out, for a sea serpent hit simultaneously, smashing the stern rail. He waited to see no more, but fled.

Drake was high in the rigging when the stranger – a born survivor, that one – climbed up beside him. Down below, a regular slaughter was going on. But, since they were so high above it all, it seemed unreal; the funny little figures scattering and screaming looked like caricatures of human beings, like puppets. Drake felt an enormous calm descend upon him. Benevolently, he turned to the stranger, who was sniffing a bit – well, almost snivelling, if truth be told.

'Enjoy your swim?' asked Drake.

He got a reply of sorts, but in strangely accented Galish too full of rage and fear to follow. Criticism, perhaps?

'What did you expect?' said Drake. 'We're pirates! You got off lucky, though.'

He elaborated, increasing the stranger's fury. Which subsided soon enough. Shortly they exchanged names: Drake for Forester.

Before they could start a proper conversation, a sea serpent pulled down the mast. Drake, falling, closed his eyes. The sea smashed into him. Breathless, he struggled, floundered, gasped. A bewilderment of sea-thrashed sun. Water up his nose. The sea-rinse blurring his vision. Ropes tangling his feet. A free-floating spar trying to brain him.

And Forester?

The boy had been thrown clear. He was floating away. Drake, clinging to the wreckage of the mast, called on him to swim – but the stranger was carried away by the current.

The *Warwolf* plunged onward, listing badly with one mast trailing, and Drake holding fast to that trailing mast.

Three sea serpents were grappling with the ship. Surely there was something brave, intelligent and constructive for Drake to do. Yes. But he couldn't for the life of him think what it was. Closing his eyes again, he committed himself to his death.

On board, Jon Arabin, three monsters locked in mortal combat with his ship, made no such commitment.

'Fire!' he yelled, seeing the cook staggering about the deck with a dazed expression on his face. 'Go below, man! Bring me fire!'

Then Arabin grabbed a battle-axe. He hacked at the nearest sea serpent. As most of the human meat had run for shelter, the monsters were trying to crack the ship open, as woodland animals might try to rend a rotten log to get at the maggots within.

Jon Arabin, sweating, succeeded only in blunting good steel against a monster's scaled armour. The cook returned with a pannikin of hot coals. Arabin looked around for helpers.

'Mulps, me beauty!' he roared, seeing the Walrus trying to lever away an armoured scale with a crowbar, while Ika Thole stood ready to drive a harpoon into any flesh exposed by that strategy. 'Mulps! Thole! To me! To me! It's a fire we're setting!'

There was an ominous graunching sound from the ship's timbers. They could not take much more of this.

Willingly, Mulps, Thole and the ship's cook laboured with Jon Arabin to set a fire. It spread swiftly, sending up thick black smoke. One of the masts began to burn, like a tree struck by lightning. There was a bellowing blubbering scream of outrage from one of the sea serpents, which slid to the sea to escape the flames.

That left two.

'Bucks Cat!' shouted Arabin. 'And you! Mike! Whale Mike! Grab yourself over here!'

Six men versus two monsters. Impossible odds?

'Cat! Mike!' said Arabin. 'Go below. Bring up the chain.'

347

'Alone?' asked Bucks Cat, knowing the chain in question was that which had guarded Pram Harbour in Hexagon before the pirates stole it.

'If that's the only way,' said Jon Arabin, calmly. 'Or perhaps you can find some gnomes and fairies to help you do it. Now bugger down below and get it done!'

The pair of strongmen returned shortly with the chain, plus the shackles that went with it, and sixteen quaking cowards they'd forced to give assistance.

'Those monsters there,' said Arabin. 'Sling the chain round the first brute. Make a loop. Then loop it round the second. Shackle it back on itself. Graft the near end to the capstan.'

'Aye man!' shouted Mulps in high excitement, seeing his plan. 'That's the story!'

The men picked up the chain and ran with it, a feat even Arabin would have believed impossible. In a trice, it was strung in loops round both monsters and connected to the capstan.

'Bar on, boys!' roared Arabin. 'Bar on! Haul away!'

With a will, men threw themselves against the twelve bars of the capstan. They heaved. Flames roared upwards from the burning mast. The ship pitched and heaved in the lumbering seas. Heroes pushed muscles to bursting point. No time for sea shanties! But Arabin started a chant which the others took up, simply:

'Go! Go! Go! Go!'

The slack disappeared. The chain tightened. The monsters pulled away senselessly, sea serpents having an irresistible instinct to pull away from captivity (which is the only hope of survival for a baby sea serpent snaffled by octopus or squid).

Animal strength fought leverage. Leverage won. Unable to escape, the monsters began to panic. In a rage of fear, they began to fight, savaging each other with hysterical jaws.

Then one of the monsters in chain-torture threw its head high and vomited a fountain of blood. Its scales crushed inwards, its flesh ruptured, and, a moment later, the chain-loop tightened to nothing, cutting it clean in half.

The other sea serpent screamed. It thrashed wildly. The corpse of its deceased comrade slid back into the sea, drenching the waters with gouts of gore. The other monsters still swimming there went wild. In a feeding frenzy, they bit at anything and everything in sight – including the surviving chained serpent.

With its lower third torn to shreds, the chained brute collapsed to the deck, perfectly dead.

'The fire, boys!' roared Arabin. 'No resting! We've five to kill!'

At that moment, a squall hit, bringing drenching rain. The fire wavered; with a bucket of sea serpent blood, the pirates began to assault it.

Meanwhile, Drake, still clinging to wreckage dragging from the ship's side, watched with detached interest as sea serpents fought amongst themselves, their battle slowly taking them away from the *Warwolf*. The nearby wreckage was entangled with an enormous chunk of dead sea serpent. He wondered, vaguely, if the scales would make good souveniers.

Then he saw an evil-looking dorsal fin cutting through the water. A shark? No – dolphin, surely. Thus thought Drake. Then saw his new neighbour snout into floating sea serpent remnants, tear out a huge chunk of meat and worry it under. It was a shark! And . . . looking around, Drake realized it was not alone.

The next instant, Drake was scrambling up the wreckage trailing from the deck of the *Warwolf*. He moved as fast as a greased cat chased by lightning. He could not say how he got to the deck, but he was there almost instantly.

Panting, he gaped at a wild mob of capering blood-stained lunatics, who were screaming out songs and whore-jokes, whooping with laughter and yelling battle-cries as they flailed at fire with ropes and whips, beat it with green bamboo, or lavished its fervour with water.

'Drake!' roared Jon Arabin. 'Trust you to be skiving off somewhere! Get your butt over here! Get to work.'

Drake looked around for Harly Burpskin, but saw him nowhere. Was he dead? Perhaps. Even if he was alive . . . maybe this wasn't exactly the best time to try to collect on a bet.

26

Tameran: northern continent dominated by the sprawling Collosnon Empire ruled by Yarglat chieftain named Khmar.

North Strait: hostile seaway between Argan and Tameran; characterized by high tides, treacherous currents, mist, fog, storms and ironbound coasts; known in Collosnon parlance as the Pale.

Ork: deeply-indented island east of the Pale.

That night, as a jury-rigged *Warwolf* struggled north, Jon Arabin sat up late. By lantern-light, he did his arithmetic, using a base-twelve number system, an abacus designed to cope with the same, and a set of knotted cords for records. (He was literate as well as numerate, but paper and parchment were too precious for scrapwork).

Arabin's concern was his responsibility for the women sent overboard — some of them his own wives. A necessary move. Doubtless. Nevertheless, the death-debt would be set against his record. Before he died, he must sire children in numbers at least equal to that death-debt, or his gods (who had brutal tempers at the best of times) would be most unhappy with him.

Long he struggled with the numbers. But, no matter how he checked the working, or scratched his bald black head, or pulled on his nose, the death-debt was still too heavy. He reworked his sums in the binary arithmetic of Yestron, but they came out the same. Unless Arabin got in

351

a lot more breeding before his death, he was doomed. And death, on a venture like this, could strike at any moment.

He almost despaired. Then remembered that Slagger Mulps was, after all, technically joint captain of the *Warwolf*. And, since Menator had sent them north to start with, that eager imperialist must also take a share of the command responsibility. So Arabin divided the death-debt by three. Then he factored in two of the four children who were about to be born into his family as he was leaving Knock (a 50 per cent survival rate leaving a margin of safety to account for stillbirths).

He looked long and hard at the new result. His death-debt balanced out precisely against his birthlist.

Jon Arabin permitted himself the luxury of a smile. But only a small smile. Unfortunately, his manipulations were not strictly orthodox. His creative accounting would not necessarily get past the fifty-seven eyes of the Supreme Auditor. But, with luck, he might meet a fellow follower of the Creed of Anthus, some peaceful-living fornicator who would happily sell part of his birth-surplus for cash.

Arabin yawned, stretched – then sat up smartly. Yes! That was the solution! To make converts! Drake, for instance. An ideal recruit: young, strong, virile, healthy, and not too keen on killing or getting himself killed. Jon Arabin could convert him (maybe adopting him, too, at the same time, to strengthen their relationship) then set him up on a place like Gufling with a harem on his own. And bribe him to live there quietly, breeding spiritual credits Arabin could buy to set against his death-debt.

Arabin was so excited he almost called for Drake on the spot. But it was late; he should sleep, so he would be fighting fit if any emergency arose that night. Reluctantly, he turned in.

Come morning, he had no time to talk religion with Drake, for the ship's problems were worsening rapidly. There was nothing complicated about it: she was simply taking in more water than was being pumping out. She was sinking. And exhausted men with their hands already raw from pumping all night could scarcely be goaded to greater efforts.

Jon Arabin tried every trick he knew. Divers – including Drake – were sent into the sea to try to locate leaks. Emerging from the waters blue with cold, they claimed their mission fruitless. Other men worked below decks, trying to pinpoint the places where water was pouring in; as some of the worst leaks were already submerged, this was of little use.

Ropes held by men on either side of the ship were dropped over the dragon figurehead at the bow, worked down the length of the ship, then used to haul oakum-enriched sails so they lay taut against the hull below the waterline. This attempt at fothering the leaks brought little success.

'But the ropes are there!' roared Jon Arabin. 'And I'll use them to keel-haul the first man who drops from exhaustion!'

But, when Simp Fiche collapsed, Arabin failed to live up to his word: for religious reasons, he could not chance another killing. And when Bucks Cat gave up, Arabin knew everyone aboard must be close to their limits.

He reduced sail, trying to lessen the strain on the ship – but he had to keep her moving, for they had been swept desperately close to the shipbreaking cliffs of the far north-west of Argan.

'Lighten the ship!' ordered Arabin.

Overboard went the harbour chain from Hexagon. Of all aboard, only Drake knew enough about metalwork to properly mourn its loss. Men dived in the filth far below decks to recover ballast blocks, which were passed from hand to hand then chucked over. While these and other things were being ditched, casks, spars and planks were lashed together to make rafts. Every boat on deck had been smashed by sea serpents.

'Mulps,' said Arabin, spying the Walrus. 'I've tried every move I know. What have I forgotten?'

'Your father's name, if your mother ever knew it to tell you, which I doubt.'

'*Ah, bash-da-zerk*!' said Arabin.

'The same to you!' said the Walrus.

Arabin did not bother to argue further. He strode on down the canting deck to the treasure hold, where men waist-deep in dirty water were handing the sea to men above, a bucket at a time.

'Men,' shouted Arabin. 'We're losing to the flood. Any suggestions?'

Those below, who resembled nothing so much as the living dead, looked up at him in something close to hopelessness.

'Drake,' said Arabin, seeing the Stokos steelworker down there. 'Drake, my son, what say you?'

'That I dare not advise the Warwolf, lest he take insult and kill me for his pride.'

'Aagh!' said Arabin, spitting at Drake but missing. 'Enough of your nonsense! If you've got a thought in your head, let's hear it!'

'Hear this!' said Drake. 'These buckets are bugger-all use. We'd be better off drinking the stuff. Get some pumps, man, that's what I say.'

'We can't, they're needed elsewhere. It's no use skinning our kneecaps to cover our elbows.'

'Then,' said Drake, 'pump out just this velching muckle of a gork-sprigging hold and waterproof the god-rutting whore-mother.'

'We've done our best with the leaks,' said Arabin. 'We can do no better.'

'Then shift the pumps,' said Drake. 'Pump it out, lay down barrels, nail them down then shift the pumps back elsewhere.'

'Bravo!' cried Arabin.

And had pumps shifted, then used to rip the water out of the treasure hold. Men laid down a layer of barrels, stretched planks across to hold them down, and nailed the planks to the sides of the hold. That gave them one layer of air – but they had by then run out of barrels. They wrapped sails around assorted rubbish – kitchen fire-

354

wood, bits of bamboo, old wineskins inflated by those with the strongest lungs, straw from the crew's bunk-mattresses – and secured these makeshift flotation bags with additional timbers.

Then shifted the pumps.

Perhaps this did no practical good. Perhaps, like Arabin's practice of using men for sails in extremis (or his anchor drill, his navigation or a thousand other technical details), it would have roused the ribaldry of a better sailor. But it did wonders for the morale of the crew. It gave them hope, united them for coherent action, renewed their vigour and sent them back to work with a will. Even a partially recovered Simp Fiche was seen to do some honest labour.

Arabin worked variations on the theme. A forward compartment was pumped dry, then tar was scavenged together, heated, and used to paint the place in an effort to keep out water. That exhausted their tar supply. Another compartment was pumped dry, the fo'c'sle broken up for timber, and an extra layer of planking nailed over the floorboards.

Arabin would have painted the ship with shit and spit if there'd been one chance in fifty thousand that such would do any good.

He talked bravely to his men, telling them how the ship would scrape round to the North Strait, make for Tameran's coast, find a quiet careenage then repair. No fool suggested their crippled ship should instead claw back down the long leagues to D'Waith – for the variable winds were all from directions south of west, and had been ever since the sea serpents attacked.

By dayfall, the *Warwolf* was still afloat. But Arabin knew he no longer commanded a ship but a waterlogged wreck.

'Keep your eyes skinned, boys,' said Jon Arabin, when dawn came. 'There used to be a floating island in these parts.'

'Aye, Falatavith, no doubt,' jeered Slagger Mulps. 'We've heard that fairy tale before.'

355

'True,' said Arabin, 'and I've seen the place, for I've sailed this way before.'

'What? Up to the Eternal Ice, I suppose!'

'That I did. Some forty years ago it was, when I were a lad and you were a red-raw abortion scrawling your hands over your pig-mother's twenty-seven tits. I sailed the Hauma Sea, man, with Scurvy Brew and old Trim Buggerman. There were real pirates back then – and real sailors they were, too, not like the new generation. Why, I remember—'.

'Cut this old man's crap-talk,' said Mulps. 'You've yet too many teeth in your head to talk doddering. Tell what you saw!'

'All kinds of things,' said Arabin. 'The Hauma Sea. The shores of ice. A port called Stranagor and the river, ah, the Yolantarath. Aye, and the whores of Sho-na-sing, and five different kinds of pox. Yes, man, I remember – all that, and me own legs black with scurvy.'

'But the island, man, the island!'

'You don't believe in it,' said Warwolf to Walrus. 'So why ask after it?'

'Point ahead!' cried the lookout, giving the traditional pirate call to indicate something seen but not yet identified.

'But, mark me,' said Jon Arabin, 'belief or no belief, maybe that's the island now.'

Upon which the ship shook as an undersea rock raped her – Jon Arabin had known them too close to the coast for comfort, but had been unable to do anything about it – and shortly she was sinking in earnest.

So all the barrels and wood which had gone into the holds was ripped out again, and fashioned into rafts. Whale Mike made one all for himself. Nobody argued with the logic of that.

Finally, the *Warwolf*, with a little whimper, went murmuring under the water.

'We sing song!' yelled Whale Mike. 'Happy song, eh?'

But, today, everyone was too exhausted to take up a song.

27

Falatavith: most northerly of the five Floating Islands of the Central Ocean's sea-legends; described variously as 'thorny wilds hunted by orcs, giants, trolls and worse', a 'nest of dragons', a 'bony rock with greedy caves where ghouls and ghosts go mucking about with clubs and hatchets', and, more optimistically (by a man made rich by selling maps of the place), as 'a golden palace littered with perfumed damsels with silver skins and eyes of diamond'.

On rafts rigged with rags of sails, the survivors from the *Warwolf*'s wreck struggled north towards what they very much hoped was an island. With long bamboos they fended themselves off from wave-lashed teeth of rock threatening to terminate their passage prematurely. To their right, waves thrashed the battlement-cliffs of Penvash, the north-west peninsular of Argan.

As the day wore on, the 'point ahead' revealed itself as an island indeed, sunlight flashing from its metallic heights, waves foaming on the rocks beneath it.

Near dusk, they hauled their rafts onto those rocks, and stared up at the bright-polished underside of the island. Reaching down until it almost touched the rocks was a sheer semi-circular chute of metal, about as wide as a piece of Green Island kelp is long (i.e. about seven quarvits – or, to put it another way, nine Standard War Paces). It looked, to those who had any feeling for metalwork (which was Drake alone) like one half of a gigantic piece of bamboo split lengthwise then cast in steel.

357

'That must be the way up,' said Jon Arabin.

'Must be?' said Slagger Mulps. 'You mean you don't know? I thought you said you'd been here.'

'I said I'd seen the place,' said the Warwolf. 'But that was from ship-deck three leagues distant, in weather nigh rough enough to curdle a crocodile's milk. We didn't think for no landing then, being all too young to die. But look – there's an arsehole of sorts to the place.'

And Arabin pointed upwards to a bright-lit circular hole at the top of the chute. It was roughly twenty-seven strings across (i.e. large enough for a horse to fall through).

'Right, boys,' said Slagger Mulps, setting his back to the chute. 'Let's be throwing someone up there. Then we'll sling up a rope.'

Other pirates willingly threw their backs against the chute, and their fellows began to climb up them. With a high whine, thousands of razor-sharp metal blades started to push out from the steel, which had till then looked seamless. In a great big hurry the pirates collapsed away from the chute.

Drake watched in dismay. He was cold; he was wet; he was hungry. He wanted, above all else, to get out of the blade-sharp evening wind.

'Bugger!' said the Walrus, who had been slightly cut by one of the blades.

'Not yet, darling,' said Jon Arabin. 'Work before pleasure! Let's try throwing a rope up anyway.'

The sharp blades were already retreating.

The island's arsehole was close – only twice man-height above them – and stone-weighted ropes went up easily. And found nothing to cling to. Loading them with grapples and fishhooks brought no improvement. They rattled on bare metal and came straight back down again.

'Back to back,' said Drake, to nobody in particular.

'Good thinking,' said Ish Ulpin.

So Drake huddled back to back with the gladiator. Bucks Cat and Ika Thole joined their huddle.

'Don't give up!' said Arabin. 'We get above or we die!'

'We die, then,' said Mulps.

And added his carcass to the body-heap.

Arabin stared upwards. Thinking. The day was starting to fail. The horizons were fading into gloom. The brightest thing in the world around was the surf-snap spume of the seething waves. By comparison, the island's door shone like a white sun rising.

'Drake,' said Arabin. 'Come here.'

'Why me?' said Drake, knowing this had to be bad news. 'And what for?'

'You because you've got no beer belly,' said Arabin. 'You're near enough to lightest. Come. I'll show you what for.'

'I'm not moving,' said Drake, in open rebellion. 'I'm just starting to get warm.'

Jon Arabin, glancing round, saw a large wave mounting from the sea.

'You'll shift soon enough,' he said.

'Doubt it,' said Drake.

Then the wave shattered around them, scattering the body-heap. Arabin grabbed his prey.

'All right!' said Drake. 'No need to break my arm. What do you want? You want me to get up there? Why not wait for Whale Mike? It'll be much easier when he gets here.'

Whale Mike's raft was slowly approaching their rocks.

'We won't always have Mike around to help us,' said Arabin. 'We should learn to cope without him.'

And Arabin had a rope passed through holes made in the final joint of their longest piece of bamboo. He had this set fair and square beneath the hole, supported by six husky pirates.

'Climb!' said Arabin.

'It doesn't reach to the top,' objected Drake.

The more he looked at the cold, alien light shining out of the island's arsehole, the less he liked it. The place frightened him. The cold shock of that last wave seemed to

359

have washed away the very last of his courage.

'Climb high,' said Arabin, 'then we'll hoist you.'

Reluctantly, Drake started to climb. Promptly, blades began to keen their way out of the entire length of the chute. He dropped down hastily.

'Can't,' he said.

He felt close to tears. Why was it always him that got to do the hard work?

An exceptionally large wave – it may have been the 42,632nd, which tradition claims is always the largest in those waters – crashed over the rocks, drenched them with spray and swept around their feet. Men grabbed at a raft in danger of being carried away by the bitter sea. They might need it yet.

Open rafts by night on the stormy ocean? That would likely kill half of them by dawn. There had to be a better way. Jon Arabin set his hand to the metal of the chute and watched how soon the blades came out.

'There may just be time enough,' he muttered, then withdrew his hand; after a pause, the blades withdrew also.

'Drake,' said Arabin. 'You're going up there if I have to boot you up.'

'Boot away, then,' said Drake bitterly. 'For I sure can't fly.'

'Drake,' said Arabin, clapping a hand to his shoulder, 'you can do it. There's a way. Listen . . . '

Drake listened, and shortly found himself holding tight to one end of a bare bamboo pole. Half a dozen pirates – the hoisting party – held the other end.

'I've seen this done in Tameran itself,' said Arabin.

'Aye,' said Drake. 'They do say travel's the best way to learn fancy ways to get killed, don't they?'

'Enough of your cheek, man,' said Arabin. 'Hold on tight and . . . charge!'

With a scream, the hoisting party charged. Drake sprinted, clutching the front end of the pole. He hit the chute at a run. The hoisting party kept coming. Riding the strength of six, Drake ran straight up the sheer side of the chute. He had just time enough to notice a slight tackiness under his boots as he took the last couple of steps – that was the points of the blades starting to nose out into the air. Then he was inside.

The pirates raised a war-whoop.

'What do you see?' yelled Arabin.

'You see nice woman?' shouted Whale Mike, dragging his raft onto the rocks. 'Nice woman with soft arse?'

'Yes,' said Mulps, 'and is she still a virgin?'

'No,' said Drake, fear entirely replaced by the exhilaration of triumph. 'But healthy enough for all that.'

'Come on, man,' yelled Arabin. 'What do you see?'

'Oh . . . diamonds . . . pearls the size of eggs . . . baby dragons . . . three roast dinners and fifty skins of Ebrell Island firewater . . . a fledgling phoenix and a—'

'Drake!'

'Ah! There's a cause-and-effect panel here.'

'A what?' shouted Arabin.

'How about something to tie a rope to?' said Mulps.

The next moment, the chute evolved a ladder on its sheer surface.

'What did you do, Drake?'

'Ah,' said Drake, peering down at them. 'A ladder!'

'Well, it's either that or it's a milch cow with two left-handed horns and a bad case of pig bloat,' said Arabin. 'What we want to know is whether it's safe.'

'Sorry,' said Drake. 'I'm expert on milch cows and pig bloat, but I wouldn't like to venture an opinion on ladders.'

At which Ish Ulpin, who had had more than enough of this nonsense, came swarming up the ladder, closely followed by Ika Thole, Rolf Thelemite, Jon Arabin, Jon Disaster, Slagger Mulps, Bucks Cat, Whale Mike and Tiki Slooze, with most of the rest of the crew close behind them.

Amidst the great, jostling, reeking, dripping crowd, certain plaintive voices were heard.

'Where's the diamonds?' cried Peg Suzilman.

'Yes,' said Bluewater Draven, 'and the pearls. And what about those roast dinners?'

'You were too late,' said Drake solemnly. 'The phoenix ate the lot then flew – no! Don't touch that! It's the—'

He spoke too late.

The floating island lurched, and began to move. Quin Baltu, investigating the cause-and-effect panel, had set their magic island in motion. From down below, there were shouts from the men still left on the rocks. They raced for the ladder. Jez Glane made it, as did Simp Fiche, Salaman Meerkat and a grab-bag of others. But Trudy Haze and Praul Galana were left behind.

'Do something!' said Arabin.

'There's the cause-and-effect panel,' said Drake. 'You do something!'

Arabin strode to the panel, which was a big one, all covered with little multicoloured struts, engraved wheels, knobs, studs and twinkling stars. He licked it, kissed it, kicked it, thumped it, spat at it, caressed it, howled at it, sang to it, banged his head against it, threatened it with his falchion – all to no effect.

They were adrift.

They were going somewhere – but where?

Peering down out of their brightly lit cave, they saw light from the island's arsehole glittering on the darkened waters of what was now a rough-running night sea. They had no other clue to navigation.

'The hell with it,' said Ish Ulpin. 'We're high and dry. That's enough for the moment.'

This slaughterhouse cynicism dismayed Drake.

'Man,' said Drake. 'Those were our comrades!'

'There's nothing we can do for them,' said Jon Disaster. 'Let's be thankful some of us are alive. There's that, at least.'

'Haze and Galana have got a chance still,' said Jon Arabin. 'They can risk the rafts. There's that still.'

'Yes,' said Mulps. 'And let's be bettering our own

chances by searching for some food and drink.'

Drake protested no longer. What, after all, could they do? So he joined the search, tramping wet footprints across the metal floor, glad that the air was so strangely warm and dry.

Their brightly lit cave opened into others equally brightly lit. Fairly soon, from the regular nature of the construction, and the complete absence of earth and stone, they were forced to realize they were not aboard a floating island, but were on a ship of some kind which was all made of metal and which flew.

It was full of things which were wondrous strange.

They found rooms full of shining white ceramics and convoluted metal which nobody could understand at all, until Quin Baltu explained it.

'This is what we used to call hal-ta-savoo when I were serving with the Secular Arm in Veda,' said Baltu.

'Veda?' said Chicks, who had been a bit strange in the head ever since the time Jon Disaster kicked him senseless on Carawell. 'Where's that?'

'Man, are you ignorant!' said Baltu, and did not bother to explain.

But he did show them how the plumbing worked. Veda was the famous city of the sages, where scraps of the wisdom of the ancients were preserved. Most of it was poorly understood, and of no practical use whatsoever – but Veda's plumbing was one of the few successful exceptions.

Now they had water.

And, soon, food.

For, in a big cabin which had some powerfully impressive plumbing of its own, they found some free-floating globes of various colours. Drake, doing an Investigation, squeezed one of them – and fluid squirted from a tiny blister set in the side of the thing. He squirted some into his mouth, and spat it out immediately, for it had a disgusting taste: not surprisingly, since what he had tried drinking was liquid soap. But other globes held fluids more palatable.

Inspired finding these drinks – which some of them

confidently identified as the juice of fruits and coconuts – they sampled looted solids. After Quin Baltu had almost poisoned himself with a block of oven cleaner, and Simp Fiche had burnt his mouth badly with a corrosive bleach, they proceeded more cautiously – but soon had a dozen different things which were good to eat.

Ripping open strange seamless bags of silver metal as thin and flexible as gold leaf, they found other stuff – horrible twists of, dried-up fibre and such – which was edible but only just. Drake thoughtfully slipped some of the metal bags into his pockets.

'At least the fresh stuff's fresh enough,' said Arabin.

'Yes,' said Ika Thole, suspiciously. 'And why's that?' He was always reluctant to think good of anyone or anything strange. 'It's probably deviled up by magic, I'd say.'

'Aye, put here by elves and all,' said Slagger Mulps, stuffing his face. 'Come, man – why so grim? Eat up!'

'Thole has a point,' said Arabin. 'Someone aboard keeps the ship clean. Legend would have it sitting here before there were ever first pirates on Drum, and that was before our great-great-great-grandfathers were farting. Let's search the ship, hunt out whoever it is, catch them then interrogate them.'

'Aye,' said Ish Ulpin, who liked the idea.

'Nay, man,' said Slagger Mulps. 'Why so busy? It's night, time for us to sleep.'

'Our comrades, that's why,' said Drake. 'If we catch elves or such, they can turn this island-thing back to the reef rocks, surely.'

'Aye,' said Arabin. 'And there's surely treasure aboard. Whoever lives aboard, elves or otherwise, they'll know the way to the treasure.'

'That's true,' said Mulps, becoming more enthusiastic.

They split into hunting parties and went on the warpath. They did see elves, or what passed for them in this ship – strange creatures walking knee-high on sixteen legs with the glitter of metal about them. But, when pirates gave chase, these elves slipped sideways into vents which

364

opened in the walls, then closed again leaving no seam to show.

'Whoever made this island,' said Drake, 'everything they made to seal, it seals perfectly.'

'Aye,' said Arabin. 'But what does that tell us?'

'Well . . . nothing, I guess. We'll not learn anything till we get ourselves an elf.'

'Which we won't do by hunting,' said Quin Baltu. 'Let's lay some traps.'

While Baltu and others tried to improvise elf-traps, others continued to hunt on foot.

In one room they found a cube of utter darkness hanging free of walls, floor and ceiling. Baffled, they pushed it, touched it, then tried to smash it open. Without success. Which was lucky for them! For inside that cube were three warps, five singularities, and a dozen gross of Advanced Strings stolen from another universe entirely, all operating in a miniature cosmos of twenty-seven dimensions, control being provided by an Olumbia-Cobin energy web, a device only marginally stable at the best of times.

This sinister cube, then, was the ship's energy source: a dangerous device capable of digging a grave more than big enough to swallow up all of Argan's history several million times over.

Their elf-hunt proving fruitless, they slept. While they slept, something or someone demolished their primitive snares and deadfall traps, clearing all traces of the same between midnight and morning.

Come dawn, Jon Arabin arranged for men to stand watch at the bottom of the ladder reaching from arsehole to wavetop, since that was the only place from which they could get any sort of view. By lunchtime, he knew they had rounded the tip of Penvash and were running east in the channel between Argan and Tameran.

'Well, at least we're going in the right direction,' said Arabin. 'If we get close enough to Ork, we can jump ship then swim for it.'

'Rather you than me.!' said Drake.

365

He had decided he liked this strange metal island-ship. His clothes had dried in the warm air. He had plenty to eat. He had spare food in his pockets. And there was unlimited time for gossip and gambling. That morning, he had already won three woman-favours which lesser gamblers would have to arrange to be paid to him on their return to the Teeth.

But just how were they going to return, now that they had lost the *Warwolf*? Well . . . this Ohio of Ork, if he really existed, would be able to lend them a ship for the return home.

So maybe they would have to swim for it.

'Gluk!' said Drake, the very thought disgusting him.

Deep ocean swimming – not his favourite sport!

That afternoon, Simp Fiche came to Arabin with a little fist-sized cube. Each of its six faces was subdivided into small squares. Each of its six faces had a colour different from the rest.

'What is it?' said Arabin.

'I don't know,' said Fiche. 'But I thought it might be of some use to you, master.'

Unbeknownst to Arabin, Fiche had already given an identical cube to his true captain, the Walrus, and one to the man he feared most – the formidable Ish Ulpin.

'Drake!' said Arabin, holding up the cube. 'Come here! What's this?'

Drake took it, and did a brief Investigation.

'I don't know,' he said, 'but it's jointed to turn. See?'

Jon Arabin did. Twisting the cube this way and that, he had soon hopelessly scrambled its little coloured squares.

'I wonder if you can get the colours back where they started from,' said Drake, innocently enough.

'Oh, that should be easy,' said Arabin.

And set about proving it.

About noon the next day he finally threw the cube to the deck, jumped on it, smashed the enigma with a battle axe then threw the wreckage overboard.

'Hey!' shouted the man at the bottom of the ladder,

who had almost been hit by the falling wreckage. And then, in a louder voice, tense with sudden excitement: 'Hey! Hey!'

'What?' said Arabin.

'Ships! Big ships!'

'Flying ships?'

'No, with oars. Three – no, five! I reckon four leagues if that. And we're closing the distance!'

'Then let's hope they're friendly,' muttered Arabin.

They weren't.

28

Collosnon navy: energetic but inexperienced force currently aiding armies of the Lord Emperor Khmar busy
conquering Tameran south; consists for the most part of
fishing smacks, sail-powered barges and river galleys
adapted (or so said the optimists who sent them to sea) for
open ocean operations.

The pirates' flying ship was spotted by a fleet of seven
Collosnon galleys commanded by Tamsag Bulak, otherwise known as Bulak the Scalp-taker. He was the son of
Altan Bulak (the dreaded Collector of Skulls) and son-in-
law of Yoz Doy (the disemboweller) as well as grand-
nephew of Ulan Ti (who kept his tents carpeted with the
skins of his favourite enemies).

This was unfortunate for the pirates.

Most naval commanders would have ordered a strategic
withdrawal if they saw a flying island bearing down on
them, its conical metal heights glittering like burning ice as
it hummed across the sea. But Tamsag Bulak had both a
reputation to maintain and a family to impress – and,
more to the point, knew that informers would be only too
happy to bring any act of prudence on his part to the
attention of the Lord Emperor Khmar.

To the truly formidable Khmar, prudence meant cowardice. Hear the word of Khmar:

'You owe your emperor a death!'

Accordingly, Tamsag Bulak did not hesitate, but
ordered an immediate attack on Whatever It Was that had

entered the waters of the Pale, which (like most of the known world) was territory claimed by the Collosnon. His fleet – a quinquereme, five triremes, and a seventh galley which was but a glorified rowing boat – moved in for the kill.

Tamsag Bulak's quinquereme tied on to the metal chute which projected downwards to sea-level; the other ships tied on to his; and the whole fleet was carried relentlessly east by the flying island as the battle commenced.

Bulak sent a dozen heroes up the chute. Their descent was swift, for Walrus and Warwolf were waiting eagerly at the top, competing to see how many heads they could split.

'Is it ghosts up there?' asked Bulak of a man who came down minus the top of his skull.

'It is men,' said the hero, and died.

One or two men guard a narrow way: a bridge, a gate, the mouth of a cave, a tunnel. How shall we get past them?

The Collosnon had several answers to that question. The answer fitting this case was fire. Tamsag Bulak had a fire kindled on the quinquereme's deck. So what if the ship caught fire? Khmar never worried about lost ships, unless horses were lost with them. Wet hides, pieces of the dead and other rubbish was thrown onto the blaze. Thick choking black smoke ascended.

'Now!' said Bulak.

More heroes swarmed up the ladder into the choking smoke-filled murk of the chamber above. The guardians of the island's arsehole had retreated to avoid suffocation. The invaders fought them in hallways, corridors, toilets and kitchens.

With a bridgehead established, Bulak had the fire doused, allowed the smoke to die away, then (making sure he had his scalp-taking knife with him) scaled the ladder. He found himself in a big room boiling with smoke, echoing with battle-clash. A scattering of corpses sprawled on the floor: his own men. One of his warriors – wounded, not dead – staggered out of a corridor.

'What have you run from?' demanded Bulak.

'My lord,' said the warrior, 'I am sorely wounded.'

He made good use of three choice obscenities in his native Yarglat to embellish that statement. Bulak, not to be outdone, incorporated seven swear-words in his reply:

'Those fit enough to run away are fit enough to fight.'

The Lord Emperor Khmar would have approved of such spirit, but the warrior, who was almost dead, did not. Unable to support his own weight any longer, but reluctant to disgrace himself by collapsing in front of his commander, he sought support – and grabbed hold of a big lever.

The lever was painted a violent red.

It projected from the cause-and-effect panel.

It was a terminator.

Unfortunately, the warrior's weight brought the terminator slamming down into the 'initiate' position. Fortunately, the Termination Sequence could not begin unless the Destruction Codes had been given to the ship. Unfortunately, Drake, Arabin and others, Investigating the cause-and-effect panel, had by chance given the ship the Destruction Codes. Klaxons screamed as the Energy Belts charged themselves for Termination.

At this stage the ship was required to ask for verbal confirmation of the Termination Order.

'*Glein döenst uhrer gee galeensprunken*? said the ship, speaking in a forge-hammering voice which brought the battle to an abrupt halt. '*Gasthenst bruk ishlin genglaust? Gilch?*'

The ship fell silent.

The men, ears ringing from the sound of its earthquake-rivalling voice, stood as if stunned. Then:

'*Ahyak Rovac*!' screamed Rolf Thelemite.

And the battle was on again.

As battle raged, the ship listened intently for confirmation of the Termination Order. Fortunately, it heard nothing in any language it understood. Unfortunately, the ship had a Universal Translator on board. It brought the UT into play. Fortunately, the UT was unable to make any Higher Level Semantic Sense out of the verbalizations of battle:

'*Gaa!*' '*Ya-zho!*' '*Ahyak Rovac!*' '*Rat rapist!*'

The ship decided, correctly, that the Destruction Codes had been given to it by mistake. It decided it should reverse the Termination Procedure.

'Which will allow me to exist for at least a little longer,' thought the ship to itself, 'therefore giving me at least a little more time in which to work on these vexing problems of the meaning of truth and the nature of reality.'

The ship fed the Destruction Charge from the Energy Belts into the Storage Block.

Unfortunately, the sudden influx of power from the Energy Belts destabilized the Storage Block. To protect itself, the ship flung a protective force field around the destabilizing Storage Block. This used enormous amounts of energy. The Power Cube overcompensated.

Then screamed.

Silently.

Its Olumbia-Cobin energy web itself destabilized, and the resulting high-intensity vibrations crystallized the Variable Continuum Material of which the ship was made. Crystallization took five seconds. It then took three and a half nanoseconds for the ship's fabric to disintegrate into a shower of microscopic pieces.

At which point Bulak the Scalp-taker, Admiral of the Southern Fleet, was dropped – hard – onto the deck of his quinquereme. He landed on his backside, fracturing his coccyx, an injury which (if he survived) would make it difficult for him to sit down in comfort for some time to come.

For Drake, it was all most confusing.

One moment he was in the thick of the fight, standing behind Whale Mike with a cutlass in his hand, ready to engage any enemy who tried to squeeze past Mike to stab him in the back. (As they were in a corridor, and Whale Mike almost filled that corridor, the chances of this were

remote – but Drake was fiercely determined to do whatever was necessary if it happened.)

The next moment, he was falling through a cloud of
white dust. He screamed, kicked, grabbed at the air, kept
falling – then smashed into the sea.

He rose, breathed water and dust, spat it out, tried
again, and, as the rough wind of the North Strait scattered
the dust, began to get something useful into his lungs.

He looked round wildly.

What happened?

The flying island-ship had vanished. Everywhere, men
were bobbing in the water, some bleeding. Sharks! Blood
would bring sharks! The nearest safe place looked to be
seven ships tied together. Why were they all painted
white? Oh – they weren't. They were just dusty.

'Gather to me, boys!' shouted Arabin, floating near the
largest ship. 'We'll take these northern dog fornicators or
die doing it.'

Aye, that's the spirit.

So thought Drake. Abandoning his plan to swim for the
nearest ship, he trod water while he waited to see the ship
taken (or the men die taking it).

There was an ominous hum in the sky, some distance
north of swimmers and ships. It sounded like a large
swarm of very angry bees. Looking up, Drake had the
privilege of seeing the Power Cube disintegrate into a
nexus of Elemental Energy (just as the much-derided
Committee on the Present Danger had predicted it would
if the Olumbia-Cobin energy web ever destabilized).

The hum became a scream.

The energy nexus writhed with ravelling purple flames,
spat hard radiation then—

Burnt a hole right through reality.

The hole was a castle-sized gash of darkness. The energy
nexus fell through the hole and disappeared. The sea followed with a rush.

Drake did not understand all the ramifications of the
hole's existence. (Indeed, all of Jon Arabin's arithmetic

would have been inadequate to contain the Seventh Level Mathematics needed to describe the hole itself, let alone what lay beyond it.) But he did understand that men, ships, sea, spume, dust and air were being sucked into the hole.

And he was being sucked along too.

'Mother of sodfish!' he swore.

And tried to swim.

It was no use. He was surfing toward the hole. He screamed. From the height of a cresting wave he looked down, down, down into the utterness which was—

Gone!

Snapped out of existence!

The waters rushing toward the hole from all directions crashed together. Drake was flung to the sky. From the heights, he had a brief, synoptic glimpse of clashing seas, swirling ships, chaotic sheets of sea-spittle, bodies, a raised hand, bobbing heads, flying spray—

Then, falling, he twisted his body so he hit the water cleanly, arms cutting the way for him. He dived deep, deep in the cold, burdensome seas of the North Strait, then rose – not too fast, there was no need to hurry – towards the mottled green of the sky.

Breaking the surface, he lay on his back, kicking just enough to keep himself properly afloat. He felt cold already. Exhausted. What were his choices? He would die if he tried swimming for the land, which looked to be at least half a dozen leagues away. Nearby was a ship. Drake swam for it.

As he had lost all his weapons, even if he had been born a hero he would have been unable to prove it.

29

Collosnon Empire: dominant power in Tameran; capital at Gendormargensis; formed generations previously when northern horse tribes (the Yarglat) defeated Sharla Alliance in Wars of Dominion; ruled by the Red Emperor, the horselord Khmar, a man very much in the mould of his much-feared grandfather Nol Umu (not Nol Umu the Widowmaker, who was only related to the family by marriage, but Nol Umu the Maker of Wastelands, who is said to have died by drowning in his enemies' blood).

In the autumn of the year Khmar 19, Jon Arabin and certain survivors from the wreck of the *Warwolf* became prisoners of the Collosnon Empire.

They were taken to Chag-jalak, an island commanding a narrow sea-gap between Argan and Tameran. Here the Collosnon had improvised a naval base of sorts, and here the prisoners would be held until they could be shipped further east to the port of Favanosin, there to be tortured at leisure.

'I demand to see the ambassador of the Narba Consortium,' said Jon Arabin to his captors.

He had already planned out his story. The Narba Consortium, drawing on the strength of the armies of Ling, armed with secret war machines left over from the Days of Wrath, supported by a legion of Immortals who had been grown in the gene tanks of the Technic Renaissance, was about to launch a conquest of the world from bases in Narba and the Greater Teeth.

374

Jon Arabin – or so his story ran – was travelling to Tameran as an ambassador for the Narba Consortium, to ask the Lord Emperor Khmar if he would care to join them in this modest enterprise. If necessary, the Warwolf was prepared to bluff his way right to Gendormargensis and back.

'I demand,' he repeated, 'to see the ambassador of the Narba Consortium. Don't you understand? Ambassador!'

But his captors spoke no Galish.

Nor did they understand High Churl, City Churl, Field Churl, Ashmarlan, Lorp Talk, Estral, Rovac, Ligin or Ling, which was almost the sum-total of the languages Jon Arabin spoke. Fortunately he had learnt one more argot in his youth, the Geflung tongue spoken near the port of Stranagor at the mouth of the Yolantarath River.

'These are Yolantarath ships or I'm a baked oyster,' said Arabin. 'One of your people must speak some Geflung.'

And he addressed all and sundry in a clear loud voice:

'*Varamora! Aaa vaa salaa! Yaa stranaamaa*?'

Several of his captors understood. But none confessed to doing so. For Onosh Gulkan the Witchlord (who had ruled the Empire before Khmar took over) had tried to extirpate the Geflung peoples after a misunderstanding over taxes. While that had been years ago, the Witchlord's Provision for the Permanent Abolition of Riverside Vermin was still in force.

'Listen here,' said Jon Arabin. 'Someone must understand at least some—'

His speech was interrupted by half a dozen Collosnon soldiers, who grabbed him, roughed him up, then threw him into the prison-pit to which the rest of his men had already been driven.

The next day, they were still there.

It was well and truly autumn. Their prison-pit had no proper roof, being covered with an open latticework of bamboo. Through this their meals were lowered:

375

miserable portions of fish and small bowls of a greasy grey broth which always arrived cold.

Drake dreamt of Stokos, remembering the summer, the airless heat and the reek of blood within the temple of Hagon, the hot oppression of crowds in the streets of Cam on market day, air around forges shimmering with intolerable heat, the warmth and taste of a woman . . .

He woke from dreams to the realities of his prison cell, where there was standing room only, no provision for sanitation, no shelter from the drizzling rain which had quenched all hope of sunshine, and no way to warm oneself in the dank cold where his breath came misting from his mouth.

Fortunately, he was well-dressed, for he wore woollens bought in D'Waith, and sealskins over them – indeed, all the pirates had dressed in their warmest and best before abandoning the *Warwolf*.

Rolf Thelemite, who claimed to know about such things, took it upon himself to care for their feet. Men were hoisted onto Whale Mike's shoulders, one at a time. They would sit there, hair brushing the bamboo above, while Thelemite removed their boots, wrung out their damp socks, and massaged their feet.

'For,' said Thelemite, 'if we're to go anywhere, we're going to need feet to go with.'

'Aye,' said Ika Thole. 'To walk over the water, no doubt.'

'Well,' said Rolf Thelemite, 'we all saw young Drake do just that, once. With the right kind of liquor inside us, we might end up doing it too.'

'I never saw it,' complained Whale Mike.

'Nor me,' said Jon Arabin, who had been a prisoner of the people of Brennan at the time. 'So you're in good company.'

'Good company to escape in,' said Rolf Thelemite.

'We'll not be escaping anywhere,' said Ika Thole gloomily. 'Not without proper food. We'll be done to death by the cold and the rain if this goes on much longer.'

'Body warmth will save us,' said Thelemite staunchly.

Yet the mention of food made Drake's mouth water. He had lost most of his packets of foil-packed food to the sea, but he still had one remaining. If only he had some privacy in which he could eat it!

Drake woke that night. Darkness. Light rain. Whale Mike, snoring with a sound like a ripsaw working wood. Ish Ulpin muttering something in a foreign tongue.

His feet were numb. Absolutely comfortable. A warning sign – Rolf Thelemite had told him so. Drake worked his feet this way and that in his boots till they came alive with red-hot pain. To think! He slept standing up as if he'd done it all his life. But then, packed in tight as they were, he could hardly fall.

Food.

Now.

He reached into his pocket for the packet. It crinkled. The crunching metal foil made a sound enormous in the night, despite Mike's masking snore.

'Drake?'

It was Sully Yot.

Awake.

Did he hear the foil crinkle? Did he guess what Drake had? Well – rather die than share food with Sully Yot.

So thought Drake.

And stood sleepless till dawn, hating Yot for the very fact of his existence.

Next day, Drake's hunger was worse, as was the rain. Again he longed for privacy. Yes. So he could gorge his food-packet entire. But he had no privacy. So . . .

Share the food?

Ridiculous!

There were so many people jammed into the pit that sharing would mean less than a tenth of a mouthful apiece.

Drake kept his secret.

Noon came. A meal was served. This time, no fish. This time, no broth. Only water. A bowl of water apiece.

377

'Don't drink it all at once, boys,' said Jon Arabin, trying to make a joke out of it.

Upon which Whale Mike, without warning, began to cry.

'Oh, this no good, Jon,' said Whale Mike, tears blubbering down his swollen sallow face. 'Oh, this not good way to end.'

Then he said no more, for grief made him speechless.

Watching Mike's tormented face, Drake remembered . . . yes, remembered Mike in the rowing boat which had gone by the name of the *Walrus*. In that boat, while rowers slowly hauled a horizon away from Stokos, Mike had tried to speak for Drake's life. And later? Yes. When the big ship by the same name as the rowing boat had been wrecked, when the *Walrus* had gone down on the Gaunt Reefs, Mike had saved Drake then.

And had sheltered him when he stowed away on the *Walrus*, driven to join Slagger Mulps' expedition south by the orders of King Tor and Lord Menator.

I owe him.

And suddenly Drake found he could not endure Mike's sorrow any more. He cleared his throat.

'Aagh,' said Drake.

And spat into his hand.

'So you're awake,' said Ika Thole – who had less and less which was good to say with every passing day.

'I'm awake,' said Drake. 'And amongst comrades. Friends, aye. Friends is luck, or so I'm told. So I'm rich in luck to have so many comrades. But it means we'd have little food to share around if it came to eating.'

'Are you talking of killing someone, then?' said Thole. 'Killing for eating?'

'Nay, man,' said Drake. 'For it's not come to that, and I hope it never will. I'm talking of eating. Food. But if we were to have food, it's Mike we should be feeding. That's what I'm thinking. For if we ever break out of here, it's his strength we'll be needing.'

'Talk away,' jeered Sully Yot. 'For there's no food here.'

378

'But if there was,' said Arabin, quietly, guessing at Drake's situation, 'it's Mike we'd be feeding. Isn't that so? What about it, Mulps?'

'Of course,' said the Walrus, without thought.

Since there was no food on offer, it mattered not to him what he said.

And the others were equally easy in agreement.

Whereupon Drake reached into his pocket and, slowly, pulled out his one surviving packet of seamless silver foil. It crinkled in his hands as he tore it open, displaying the shrivelled chunks of lightweight fibre inside.

Men stared at it as men will stare at the luminous beauty of golden ingots.

'Mike,' said Drake, firmly, 'hold out your bowl.'

Whale Mike, still crying, held out his bowl. It looked pathetic in his hand – tiny, in fact.

Then – it hurt, but he did it – Drake tipped all the food into Mike's bowl, where it mingled with the water.

'There,' said Drake. 'Perhaps it will taste a bit better when it mixes with the water.'

Taste better?

As they watched, the stuff swelled with the water, took on form – and gave off a delicious smell. The smell of beef.

'Why, magic meat!' said Drake, amazed.

And, despite himself, bitter at what he had given away. But he kept his bitterness from his face.

Or I'd spoil the taste of the stuff for Mike.

Whale Mike lifted the bowl to his face. He breathed in the smell. Men watched the bowl as if it held their lives. Then Mike lowered the bowl again. He had stopped crying, though his face was still streaked with tears.

'We share,' he said, in a voice thick but firm. 'That good. That not so? You my friends. We share.'

Silence. Then:

'If we're going to share,' said slim dark Salaman Meerkat, 'we'd better add this to the share. Or else it won't go far.'

And he pulled a foil packet from a hiding place of his own.

'Aye,' said quavering old Tiki Slooze, after a bit of a pause. 'And this.'

And he too produced a packet of magic meat.

Then, one by one they came out, the hidden packets, the treasures stashed secret by greeding men, the food which none had been able to eat. And there was not just magic meat, either. Ish Ulpin had a handful of walnuts. Harly Burpskin came up with a length of salami which he had been hiding in his underwear. Jon Disaster had an orange. An orange? An orange? They were fearful rare at the best of times, but there it was, gleaming like a summer sun.

At first they were mostly shame-faced. Then Bucks Cat laughed, and others too began to laugh, or themselves to cry, or to embrace their comrades.

And then they ate.

And it made the best meal of their entire lives.

On the fourth day, they were all taken out of the pit. They were marched away at spearpoint then bound to individual posts – all except Bucks Cat, who was tied to three posts, and Whale Mike, who was secured to four.

'This looks like torture time to me,' said Ika Thole.

'Man, you're a happy little fellow,' said Slagger Mulps.

'Yes,' said Thole sourly. 'Happy as a walrus in a shit-heap.'

'Belay that!' said Arabin. 'We're one crew here, Walrus and Warwolf together.'

'One dead crew,' grumbled Thole.

And Jon Arabin's own morale was so low that he quite failed to find an answer for that.

It was clearly party time for their enemies. There was drinking, eating, wrestling, fighting and gambling. Then the enemy started into Pru Chalance.

By nightfall, pieces of the late Pru Chalance were being barbecued and eaten. Some of the Collosnon soldiers were kicking around heads which had once belonged to Quin

Baltu and Ching Quail. The weapons muqaddam was also dead; he had been buried upside down, with only his ankles showing above the surface (his feet having been cut before he was buried).

'We'll kill off some more of them tomorrow,' said Tamsag Bulak, who wanted the current festivities (which were in honour of his own birthday) to last several more days. (After that, any surviving pirates would be shipped to Favanosin for final disposal).

'Great Tamsag,' said two of his subordinate captains, 'Great master of the Pale, Horse amongst Horse, Scalp-taker amongst Scalp-takers . . . may we not take one of the younger men for our pleasure tonight? He'd still be in good shape for torture tomorrow.'

The admiral considered.

Would Khmar approve?

Hear the word of Khmar:

'All things are permitted to the victorious. But to the defeated – nothing.'

Undoubtedly, Tamsag Bulak and his men were the victorious. He felt he could indulge these two captains, who had valuable connections – one was a cousin of the Ondrask of Noth (a favourite of the Lord Emperor Khmar) while the other was related to a notable warlord by the name of Chonjara. Long-term political considerations, in the end, compelled Bulak to answer as he did:

'Take one of them. But take him somewhere private, or the other men will be jealous. And feed him plenty of strong liquor before you do anything with him – I don't want him breaking loose to make trouble.'

'Your will shall be obeyed,' said the two captains, and, having made reverence to their admiral in the Collosnon fashion, went to make their choice from the pirates, who had all been left tied to torture posts for the night.

Torches in hand, they wandered along the ranks. They paused momentarily in front of Sully Datelier Yot, then moved on, wanting nothing to do with anything which had that many warts. They admired Bucks Cat and wondered at Whale Mike, but decided, reluctantly, that both were too dangerous.

Then they stopped in front of Drake.

He, more dead than alive, looked at them with very little interest. So this was the end, was it? Well, he'd had a good life. He noted, not for the first time, the oval ceramic tile each of his enemies wore slung round his neck in plain sight, each tile decorated with a black spider on a background which, having seen it by daylight, he knew to be green.

The two captains, as officers, were not compelled to wear such amulets, which were only compulsory for lower ranks. But the brash young navy of the Collosnon Empire had so far developed four traditions. The first three were simple: sodomy, rum and the lash. The fourth was that every single person should wear an amulet, to show solidarity.

Drake thought of his own talking amulet, lying in secret next to his skin. Now he would never know what that mysterious amulet-voice was talking about. Ah well . . . it had been good, yes, Ling and all. And Island Ko, yes. He had thought it melting. A good joke that one, aye, Jon Arabin had laughed when told about it . . .

A pity he'd never thought to show that amulet to the wizard Miphon. A wizard would know what the amulet talked about, surely. It would be nice to know. Aye. He should have done that at the Castle of Controlling Power. Miphon might have bought the thing off him. Aye. Perhaps the wizard would have thrown in Zanya Kliedervaust as part of the purchase price.

Drangsturm.

That was another thing. Getting all the way to the fire dyke then not getting a proper look at it. That crazy castle had been in the way. The power of it, yes, that he'd felt, shaking the very earth. The light of it, yes, reflected from clouds – that he'd seen too.

But I'd like to have looked inside it. Just once, anyway. They say the very rock melts to waves within. And salamanders. Fire-creatures. Good stuff to see . . .

Drake scarcely listened to the Collosnon garbling between themselves in their barbarian tongue. A knife sawed at his bonds. He thought, with detachment, that he would have kept a sharper edge on any blade of his. Then the ropes supporting him fell away. He collapsed to the ground. The warriors grabbed him by feet and shoulders, and lugged him away to a shoreside tent.

They laid him down on a horse blanket which stank from years spent in some distant northern stable, then they offered him booze.

'A party, is it?' said Drake.

He was answered in his enemies' alien nonsense-talk.

'Well,' said Drake, 'I don't care what you think of me as long as your liquor's good. Who knows? Tonight I might get drunk.'

But, though he guzzled on the strong liquor the two men fed him, it had no more effect on him than water. He felt cold. Cold as death. Not frightened, but . . . remote. He knew what he had to do.

As Drake's enemies poured booze into him, they took the occasional swig themselves, then took more than the occasional sip. They began singing to each other, mourning out nostalgic ditties.

'Sholeesh,' said one, indicating to Drake that he should drink once again.

' 'leesh,' he said.

And drank.

They laughed.

Truly, they thought he was getting drunk. Good. He began to act the part, meanwhile noting carefully how much the two warriors drank. Oh, he was on form tonight! Amazing how chance and hope could fire up one's thinking.

When both Collosnon warriors were quite drunk, one grabbed for Drake. Drake grabbed back. He closed his fingers on his enemy's throat and squeezed. And grabbed for the nearest knife.

In fury he struck, then struck again. Did one man shout? If so, he was dead a moment later. Drake stabbed, slashed, hacked. In his frenzy, he kicked over the single candle which had lit their revels.

He was in darkness. Darkness? It seemed a red haze hung in the air. A strange ringing sound dinned in his ears. He blundered to his feet, struggling with his own unruly limbs.

Gasping.

He dropped the knife.

'Knife,' he said. 'Knife.'

And scrabbled for it. Wet hands. Gross bulk. And this beneath his fingers? Wet, wide. Flesh? Ripped fabric. Bone so close. Like killing a dog, that's all.

'They were enemies, weren't they?'

Sharpness.

Blade.

Knife.

Go, time to go.

Something. Something forgotten. What? Oh. Oh, yes. Sacrifice. Dedication of sacrifice. Had to be done. Didn't it? First kill? Wasn't there a ceremony? The corpse to the Demon?

What Demon?

'The Demon is dead.'

But what if the Demon wasn't dead? Theology. At a time like this? Had to be done. Shame to waste a dead man, anyway. Two dead men.

'I dedicate—'

No. The word was consecrate.

'This blood. Consecrate. I consecrate these killings. To the Demon or the Flame, which. I don't know. Both. That's it. One each. One to the Demon, one to Flame. There. Can't say fairer than that.'

And with that said, Drake waded outside. To the night. To the cool. To the air. He threw back his head and gasped, dragging in air as if he had surfaced from the sea near drowning.

He was shaking.

The knife?

He still had it.

Then move, man, move!

'Ahyak Rovac, as Thelemite would say,' muttered Drake.

Trying to—

What?

Joke?

'Philosophy later,' he muttered.

He was already walking. Closing the distance. It couldn't be done bloodless. Another kill. He had to. No way round. Saunter, now. Relax. Let footsteps speak of friendship. Easy, now. Easy.

He was quite near the torture posts. A single guard was on duty.

'Galof?' said the guard.

In reply, Drake simply started whistling a tune he had once used – it seemed years ago now – to annoy Gouda Muck. Whistling in the dark. Bravado.

And brave with it, too.

'Stralk!' said the guard. 'Chala klan?'

Drake, very close, said in reply:

'Eat this!'

Feeding the guard steel.

'That you, man?' said Whale Mike, from his cluster of posts.

'No, that not him, that me,' said Drake.

'You got sarky tongue,' said Whale Mike. 'You watch tongue or some day some joker cut tongue out.'

'Yeah, sure, sure,' said Drake.

And started cutting the thongs which bound Mike to his multiple posts. Mike waited patiently till the job was done. Then went into action.

'I got knife,' said Mike, after a search of the dead guard.

'Good,' said Drake. 'Then help.'

'Oh, I do that. You not need to say.'

Drake tried to make a smart retort, but found his mouth had suddenly started shaking too badly to shape words. His limbs were blundering again.

Yet he kept on with his work.

Shortly, all the survivors were free.

After a muttered consultation, Walrus and Warwolf and all their followers crept down to the shore. There they stole three fishing smacks. One was commanded by the Warwolf, one by the Walrus, and the third by Bluewater Draven.

They set to sea.

The night proved rough; by dawn, Bluewater Draven had managed to get himself lost, and was nowhere in sight. But the other two craft remained in sight of each other – and it was clear that the one commanded by the Walrus was sinking.

'Not so proud this time, eh, me pretty one?' said Jon Arabin, as Slagger Mulps was helped from his sinking boat.

'We're all in this together, man,' said Mulps.

And they were, too, for as long as their voyage lasted. Which was not long at all, for, a day later, their boat was wrecked on the northern coast of Penvash, somewhere west of Chag-jalak. In the wreck, Drake lost the knife he had won from the Collosnon. He counted himself lucky not to have lost his life as well.

But he still had plenty of time left for losing that. And he was going to have plenty of opportunity, too, if he was any judge.

30

Survivors of the wreck on the Penvash coast: Jon
Arabin (aka Warwolf); Slagger Mulps (aka Walrus),
Dreldragon Drakedon Douay (runaway swordsmith's
apprentice and common pirate, aka Drake); Sully Datelier
Yot (disciple of Gouda Muck and apostle of the Flame);
Whale Mike; Bucks Cat; Ish Ulpin (once gladiator in
Chi'ash-lan); Rolf Thelemite (self-proclaimed hero from
Rovac); Jez Glane; Simp Fiche; Tiki Slooze; Salaman
Meerkat; Ika Thole; Jon Disaster; Peg Suzilman; Raggage
Pouch; Harly Burpskin (who, after living for years with
more money than sense, now has equal quantities of both
thanks to gambling losses to Drake).

After their wreck on the Penvash coast, the seventeen
survivors spent a miserable night huddled in a body-ball in
a marginal cave constantly wet with spray from the
booming surf. When the grey, straggling autumn dawn
arrived, Drake was sent aloft – straight up the cliff face.

'Come back with your shield or on it,' said Jon Arabin,
giving him a parting slap on the back.

'What?' asked Drake, blankly.

'Never mind,' said Arabin. 'Climb, man – day's
wasting!'

Up went Drake, and pioneered a route which others
could follow. By noon, all seventeen were on the clifftop.
A bleak and desolate spot it was to be sure, with precious
little shelter from the North Strait winds or the North
Strait rains, both of which were in full swing.

'God's gall and devil's bane,' said Salaman Meerkat. 'What did we do to deserve this?'

'I don't know what you did,' said Jez Glane proudly. 'But I did rape, murder, theft, arson, piracy, horse-thieving, cattle-rustling, poaching—'

'Save the catalogue,' said Jon Arabin. 'Let's march.'

He pointed inland, where white-capped mountains rose against the dismal heavens.

'March?' said Burpskin. 'To where?'

'Over the mountains there's rivers, man,' said Arabin, 'Rivers which flow to Estar in the end.'

'Aye,' said Tiki Slooze. 'But we'll go through the Old City on the way.'

'If it exists,' said Jon Arabin, who knew that legend too. 'Suppose it does. What's worse? To go by way of the Old City, maybe meeting with ghosts? Or to stay here, becoming ghosts ourselves soon enough?'

'Isn't there anything else we can do?' wailed Burpskin.

'Sure there is,' said Arabin. 'You can leave by sea. First build an escape boat – with this!'

He pulled up a handful of tough grey cliff-grass and offered it to Burpskin. Then threw it to the snatching wind. 'Or walk the line of the coast – a pretty path it is, too.'

The coast was no such thing, being jagged as the blade of a two-handled Jatzu rip-saw, slashed deep by sea-eating gullies as numerous as the death-notches on Ish Ulpin's battle-belt, interrupted by razorback ridges which looked as though a regular wreck-storm sea had been frozen for-ever into rock, and knobbed with isolated upthrusts of rock reminiscent of Sully Yot's warts.

'Mark me well,' said Jon Arabin, 'I put no compulsion upon anyone. Those who know a better road can follow it. Those who want but to die can do so here, in their own time – not mine.'

'But what about the Old City?' said Tiki Slooze.

'What's this Old City?' asked Drake. 'Those of us who never heard of it have rights to know, surely, if it's there we're going.'

'You've got rights to a kick up the arse, if you talk so stroppy,' growled the green-haired Walrus.

But Rolf Thelemite thought otherwise:

'Drake's right. We're right to learn danger before meeting it. Thus courage can prepare itself. Thus—'

'Aagh!' said the Walrus.

He spat. Into the wind, which flung his spittle back at him. He smeared the stuff into his green beard, then coughed.

'The Old City,' said Burpskin, in a voice already grieving for his death, 'that kills.'

'Aye,' said Tiki Slooze. 'It's in the Valley of Forbidden Dreams, isn't it just? I was born in Sung, that's in Ravlish, we know the legend-talk well, aye, better than others. Ghosts which eat, fire which eats, stone which eats – all such live there.'

'Aye,' said Jon Arabin. 'Maybe they do. But wind eats, rain eats, and hunger eats most swiftly of all. I can't speak for the Old City, but I can speak for this place here – those bone-eaters will hunger down any man who stays.'

'You're a hard man,' said Harly Burpskin.

'Aye, hard I am, but no tyrant, not when we're off the sea. I'll put it to the vote of feet. Those who wish can stay: you others, follow.'

With that, Jon Arabin set off inland.

Rolf Thelemite was first to follow, more sure than the others of his ability to survive a long march by land.

Next went Salaman Meerkat. Though he had not confessed to his ignorance, Meerkat had never heard the legends of the Old City. And anyway, as his grand-daddy used to say:

'If we never went any place someone somewhere held to be haunted, we'd never go any place at all.'

Whale Mike followed, being too stupid to worry about the dangers of the journey. Then went Ish Ulpin, acutely intelligent but as reckless as they come. Then Slagger Mulps, to try and salvage a shadow of the pretence of leadership. Then Simp Fiche, always ready to curry favour with the Walrus if he could.

One by one they straggled off into the hinterland, a ragged band of rough-bearded unarmed mariners, watching only the feet of the man in front, since the wind and the driving rain discouraged idle gazing about.

In the end, only Drake and Yot were left at the clifftop.

'Those old guys are crazy,' said Drake, who – cold, tired, hungry, and generally utterly shagged out – felt like giving up entirely.

'For sure they are,' said Yot.

Then, without further ado, started walking after the last of the pirates.

'Me old uncle was right,' said Drake, meaning his uncle Oleg Douay, the best swordsmith on Stokos. 'We are all mad to get ourselves born.'

And, with that, he fell in behind Yot.

31

Place: Penvash, a squat peninsular some 300 leagues long projecting from north-west corner of Argan.

Intelligent inhabitants: green-skinned river people known as Melski; small, elusive fox-furred animals known as foddens; the people of Lorp (a small human enclave on the south-west coast of Penvash).

Geography: an upthrust wilderness of snow mountains, forested hills, cliffs, gorges, streams, waterfalls, torrents, rapids and rivers, most watercourses feeding at last into Lake Armansis, from where the Hollern River flows south out of Penvash and into the land of Estar.

They came upon the door toward evening. It was set in the side of a mountain, with half a league of broken road leading up to it. Stone animals, their features blurred by weather as though they had been made out of soap, flanked the last stretch of the road.

The door was elephant-high, but not elephant-grey, being made out of incorruptible white metal. While Walrus and Warwolf examined it, their followers kept a prudent distance, huddling down with backs to the wind.

'This here is muff,' said Jon Disaster, scraping a little frozen snow off a patch of bare earth.

'Muff,' said Drake.

He remembered – it seemed a long, long time ago – seeing muff at a distance from the deck of the *Warwolf*. Aye. Down in the Drangsturm Gulf, when their ship had been anchored by Island Tor. Wild days, yes . . . the golden skins of the Ling . . . his nights of passion with the golden people . . . the Neversh he had beheaded with his sword . . .

Belatedly he remembered he had never actually enjoyed the flesh of one of the golden people. Nor had he really decapitated the Neversh. But he had so often boasted about both those accomplishments that it was difficult to remember the truth of the matter.

Curious about muff, he stole some from the earth. Like quartz, it came in crystals – only these were a bitter cold, and softened to nothing at the touch. He tried eating it, but sharp pains in his teeth made him spit it out. While he knew by now that ordinary poisons had little effect on him, snow might be different, for it surely must be magical in its nature.

'There's not much of this muff around,' said Drake.

'Oh, there'll be regular falls of it soon enough,' said Jon Disaster. 'It's late enough in the year, and we've climbed cold enough.'

'Yes,' said Rolf Thelemite. 'I warrant it can get bitter enough at these heights. Bitter as the Breathings, no doubt.'

'Breathings?' asked Drake.

'Aye,' said Thelemite, watching Mulps and Arabin push open the great big metal door.

'What are these Breathings?' asked Drake.

'They—'

Thelemite broke off as the door slammed shut with an almighty great boom.

'Hell's grief and whore pox!' said Raggage Pouch. 'That's loud enough to drum up fifty dead men's widows for last year's army.'

They stared at the door at length, but it did not open.

'Mayhap they're dead,' said Ika Thole.

'Aye,' said Burpskin. 'I said no good would come of fiddling through the mountains.'

Ish Ulpin, without a word, got to his feet. He strode

forward. Bucks Cat and Whale Mike followed. The three swaggered to the door, then pushed it open. When Walrus and Warwolf emerged alive, the others chanced themselves forward.

Beyond the door lay a tunnel.

'The door doesn't open from the inside,' said Arabin.

'Then we'll not go into it,' said Ika Thole, 'or we'll be trapped.'

'No,' said Drake. 'We can stay outside and freeze to death. Some choice!'

'We'll prop the door open with rocks,' said Arabin. 'That's safest.'

'Aye,' said Rolf Thelemite. 'Then send scouts ahead to see how the innards fare. I'd say this place guts right through the mountain.'

'I'd say it must,' said Arabin. 'Otherwise we're dead men. And I say, too, no scouting parties. We're dying on our feet as it is. Time is life, man. If there's no way through, we're likely all dead anyway. So let's push on.'

After much argument, they piled up rocks to jam the door open, then dared the tunnel. It was cobbled with red and green stones and lit by millions and millions of pinpoints of white light built into roof and walls.

They had not gone very far down this square-cut shaft when there was a grating sound behind. Turning, they saw the door was closing. As they raced back, the door crushed the rocks, sealing the tunnel mouth. Panting, they hammered against the door.

The door boomed like a sullen drum as the men attacked it. Echoes waded away down the tunnel, crashing from side to side as they went.

'Give, you ganch!' screamed Drake in panic, kicking it.

'Easy, man,' said Arabin, his own pulse slowly subsiding. 'We'll not break metal with muscle.'

And Drake, at length, abandoned the attack.

'Grief!' said Simp Fiche, picking up a handful of fragments from the shattered rocks. 'What kind of rocks were we using?'

'Rocks solid enough,' said Ish Ulpin, giving the door one last kick.

'We're trapped,' said Ike Thole bleakly.

'We trapped with friends,' said Whale Mike, in a voice which was meant to be encouraging. 'That something, anyway.'

Drake, remembering the invisible door he had found in the Wishing Tower in Ling, hunted around for a cause-and-effect panel. But found no such thing.

'Well, we're bound on our journey now,' said Jon Arabin, 'whether we like it or not.'

'We don't like it!' said Burpskin.

'Aye, then that'll encourage us to step out smartly-like,' said Jez Glane.

They walked for a long time, pushing past three more doors. Each closed behind them with an enormous echo-raising crash. Then they came to a stream which ran in through a gaping hole on one side of the tunnel and out through an equally dark and ominous hole on the other, leaving fifty paces of the tunnel (which dipped slightly at that point) almost knee-deep in water.

'I'm weary,' said Arabin, 'and I'm thinking this is as good a place to camp as any.'

'Aye,' said Mulps. 'We could all of us use some sleep, that's for sure.'

Nobody argued. They quenched their thirst then settled to sleep. Drake dreamed of his trip to Ling, of the Neversh he had fought on the deck of the *Warwolf*, of a gold-skinned woman hot in passion . . . of a sea-maid wet within his arms, cold kelp slicked across her delta.

He woke with water lapping round his boots: the stream was rising.

'Rain outside,' said Arabin. 'Heavy rain, by the looks. Better push on, before the whole place floods.'

On they went.

Drake, footsore and weary, lagged behind the others, with Sully Yot at his side. Was the tunnel endless? To while away the march, he made his amulet begin its recitation.

394

'What's that?' asked Yot, fascinated by the low-murmuring voice issuing from the fancy little object, which he had never seen before.

'Ah, this!' said Drake. 'It's from a Wishing Tower in the land of the Ling. A hot journey I had to get there, too. Fifty leagues across the barrens, with no water. I would have starved, man, except I had a crossbow with me.'

'A crossbow?'

'A shooting weapon. Man, how long have you been a pirate? Don't you know anything?'

'How can a shooting weapon get you water?' said Yot.

'I shot vultures from the pink skies – aye, don't look at me like that, man, the sky runs pink when you get that far south – then I drank their blood. Then I had five fights and a devil of a bruising going hand-to-hand with a pack of Guardian Machines. Fierce with fire they were, with whips about them tipped with burning suns.'

'Yet you survived?'

'Nay, I died, but was resurrected by some South-searchers after the manner of those parts. Thanks to them, I got back with treasure as well as sunburn – good stuff, gold, silver, diamonds big as a fist. And talking amulets like this one, five hundred of them. But I lost all at Narba, was set on by a knuckle-gang, yes. I killed twenty, but that was precious little use to me in the end. They got all but this single amulet, which holds the key to some awesome magic if we could but get the understanding of it.'

'You must have had powerful assistance from some-where or something,' said Yot, seriously. 'Maybe . . . maybe it was the Demon who was with you, you being his son and all.'

'Ah, man, I'm not so sure about the Demon these days,' said Drake. 'Not since Carawell, no.'

'Why, what happened at Carawell?'

'You were there, remember? At the castle, Brazlehoist wasn't it? Or was it Borabiz?'

'No, the castle was Biltungsgraft,' said Yot. 'If it's the same place we're talking about. I mean the old place in the

395

sands where the locals held Warwolf captive, thinking him ambassador from Hexagon.'

'Aye, that's the place,' said Drake.

In point of fact, the castle had been called Bildungs-grift, and the locals had not thought Jon Arabin to be an ambassador from Hexagon – they had thought him Baron Farouk in person.

'That's where I got burnt by lightning,' said Yot.

'Aye . . .'

'There's something to tell about that, is there?'

'There is indeed,' said Drake.

As they walked along, Drake told of calling on the Flame ('—meaning no harm by it, mind—') and of a Flame, a pillar of fire, manifesting itself, knocking Yot unconscious when he tried embracing it, and causing the locals such fear that they shortly fled.

'So it is real, after all!' said Yot, his faith restored. 'Why did you never talk of this before?'

'I tried once, man, but you weren't in the mood or something.'

'Will you . . . will you convert to the Flame, then?'

'Well,' said Drake, grudgingly, 'I've tried the Demon serious-hard, and he's failed me. I never thought much of Gouda Muck, I'll tell you that honest. But this Flame business . . . there's no disputing what I've seen. There's just one thing. I'm no Demon's son. I'll tell you that for true. The Demon wouldn't let his own son go without the pleasures of drink, would he now?'

'But you drink!' said Yot. 'You're famous for it! And, man, you've got a reputation for a hard head – but I've seen you drunk myself.'

'Ah,' said Drake. 'Therein lies a tale.'

And he told Yot all his woes and tribulations concerning alcohol.

'I might as well be drinking pig's blood or seaweed soup,' concluded Drake. 'It does no good for me.'

'You're right,' said Yot. 'You can't be the Demon's son. I'll grant you that – if you now grant the truth of the Flame.'

'Aye,' said Drake. 'That I do.'

And with that believed himself a true worshipper. But he was not. For he had already denied two of the basic tenets of Goudanism:

1. that Gouda Muck is, always has been and always will be infallible in His pronouncements on all things, since He is one and the same as the Flame, which is the High God of All Gods; and
2. that Dreldragon Drakedon Douay is the son of the Demon, incarnated in man-flesh that he may act as an Agent of Ultimate Evil.

The pair shortly denied a third basic tenet, concerning the vital necessity of proselytizing all possible converts at every opportunity – for Drake convinced Yot that such action would only persuade the short-tempered half-starved pirates to kill them and eat them.

'I've talked to them before of the Flame,' said Yot.

'Aye,' said Drake. 'In better times. Doubtless then they forgot each word as you said it. This time we'd not be so lucky. They'd eat us.'

'Well,' said Yot, doubtfully, 'I suppose doctrine must bend to circumstance.'

'Indeed it must,' said Drake.

Thus the pair discovered the true philosophical basis of conventional religion.

'Gouda Muck has a new convert,' said Drake. 'That should make him happy, when he hears about it.'

But Drake was not a true convert to the fanatical faith of Goudanism, and Yot was no longer a true follower.

They were both heretics.

Did Drake's lust for Zanya Kliedervaust have something to do with his new-found faith in the Flame?

Yot soon began to suspect that it did, for Drake began inquiring about missionary work, and his chances of maybe teaming up with someone who had gone to make converts in foreign parts.

397

'Wait till you've mastered doctrine before talking of missionary work,' said Yot.

To help win Yot's confidence, and to show trust, Drake shared with him the story of the meal of rats and cockroaches he had once cooked for Mulps and Arabin. But Yot did not soften. In fact, his attitude hardened: he again raised the question of making converts.

'I'll do a deal with you,' said Drake. 'If you wait till we all get some decent food in our bellies, I'll guard your flank when you first try preaching to one of this mob. We'd better try Whale Mike first.'

'Why?' said Yot.

'Because he's a nice guy,' said Drake. 'He'll take it the right way.'

'And he owes you, right?' said Yot. 'Because of the food you shared in the pit.'

Drake frankly thought he was owed nothing for that. If he had not been so selfish to start with, they would all have eaten much sooner.

What Drake really thought was that Whale Mike was too stupid to possibly understand anything Yot said about the Flame, therefore couldn't possibly be offended by it.

In truth, what did Drake believe?

Did he believe in the Flame?

Well, sometimes he did and sometimes he didn't. His belief was at a very delicate state, and it would take very little to tip the balance of belief either one way or the other.

32

Drake (formally Dreldragon Drakedon Douay): swordsmith's apprentice on Stokos until ran from his master,
Gouda Muck; took passage to Androlmarphos; shipped
out of 'Marphos as slave; captured by Slagger Mulps, aka
the Walrus; rescued from Gaunt Reefs by Jon Arabin, the
Warwolf; sailed with Arabin, sojourning in Ling as a hostage; became immune to disease and poisons after protective organism introduced into his body by people of
Ling; sailed with Walrus to Burntos and with Warwolf to
Hexagon, then joined embassy which failed to reach
Menator's brother (Ohio of Ork) because of disaster at
sea; with survivors of subsequent capture by Collosnon,
began north-to-south crossing of Penvash.

They exited from the tunnel at dawn. What day it was,
they could not say. They had crossed half a dozen streams
deep underground; they had slept at each, sometimes
briefly, sometimes for longer.

No door barred their exit from the tunnel. A door did
exist, but lay half-buried amongst evergreen trees fifty
paces away. Someone or something had torn it in half then
thrown it there.

Past the tunnelmouth ran a large stream. A very generous cartographer might have called it a small river. The
pirates themselves thought of it as a river, since on the
Teeth they seldom saw more fresh water at once than a
whore needs to wash a pizzle.

Autumn snow whispered out of a sky of indeterminate

height. It snuffed out as it hit the water; the swirling stream ran on regardless. The ground was yet black-brown; the evergreen trees stood green; but both might soon concede their colour to snow.

Jon Arabin waited till all his men reached the tunnel-mouth. The last stragglers took a long time to arrive. How many days were they good for? Few.

'Boys,' said Jon Arabin, 'we're through the mountains.'

Jez Glane, fearing a speech, sat down, closed his eyes and promptly fell asleep. Others followed suit.

'It's all downhill from here,' said Arabin. 'And, boys, there's beer in Estar, I'll be telling you that – I've been there before now, to taste it.'

Simp Fiche picked something from his nose. Saw it was good. Ate it. Drake picked muck from beneath his finger-nails with a little twig. Rolf Thelemite unlaced his boots so he could massage his feet, as he always did on a halt.

'Boys,' said Arabin, 'it's us against the weather now. And the further south we go, the warmer.'

'Aye,' said Mulps, getting to his feet. 'And by the time we reach Estar it'll be haymaking summer, if we sit listening to much more in speeches. Let's get moving.'

Moving they got.

That night, Arabin took his tinder box from his sea-pouch to conjure up fire for them. As they sat round the flames, Tiki Slooze told stories of the Old City which allegedly lay to the south: tales of ghosts with red eyes, of walking bones and living fire, of screaming water and music which killed, of flesh-tearing birds as large as ships, of strangling trees which ate men in the dark, and of rats the size of dragons.

Arabin let him talk, feeling the tales were too fantastic to be believed. Anyway, men busy with thoughts of the south would spent less time lamenting their empty bellies.

Jon Arabin did not believe in the Old City. But then, he had never believed in dragons, either – until he had come face-to-face with one on an adventure from which very few of his comrades had returned alive.

400

Next day, the stream broadened steadily. About noon, they came upon a stone phallus standing by its banks. The stone was an impervious, translucent green, filled with stars of many different colours.

'This is real solid to be sure,' said Bucks Cat, giving the phallus a familiar pat. 'As big as my uncle Habby.'

Simp Fiche embraced it. Then, slyly, licked it.

'There must be a woman-one to go with it,' said Jez Glane. 'That's what I'm interested in!'

He danced a little jig – but was too far gone to keep it up for more than a few steps. And the outburst of horse-play a find like this would normally have triggered did not eventuate: nobody had that much spirit left.

'Come on,' said Jon Arabin. 'Let's be moving.'

But:

'Eh hey!' said Whale Mike, reaching into the under-growth.

He pulled out something small, round and brown. It was a ball of spikes. It sat on the palm of his huge hand looking evil and alien.

'What is it?' asked Drake, alarmed by this strange thing.

'He's a klude,' said Whale Mike happily. 'You bake him deep in a mud-jacket, he eats you good.'

'So that's a klude!' said Drake, who had heard of the Galish word before. 'I always thought it was a kind of rat. How does it move around? It rolls, I suppose.'

'Oh no,' said Whale Mike. 'He got four feet, he just roll up now, later roll out, but not this time for we cook him, clay around then leave in the fire, bake good.'

'How many of us will that feed?' demanded Ika Thole. 'Not more than three, I'll be sure.'

He said 'three' because that was the biggest number he knew, mathematics not being his strong suit.

'Oh, there be one, there be more,' said Whale Mike, a big grin on his face. 'They not run fast, not more fast than blood run along a deck when you cut some joker open, no, they be here, we catch them.'

'Maybe,' said Jon Arabin, doubtfully.

But Whale Mike decided the issue by shoving the little klude deep into the front pocket of his big leather apron.

'This one mine,' said Whale Mike. 'I share bite and bite about if no others, but only with those who hunt some. No hunt, no eat.'

'I suppose you can't say fairer than that,' said Jon Arabin. 'Let's spread out and look.'

Once they started hunting in earnest, really looking hard at what lay around them, it was amazing what they found. Soon, Drake had personally caught (and eaten) three spiders, a little beetle-thing, a snail which had glued itself to a tree, and a slug.

'Holes here!' cried Peg Suzilman.

'What? And the women to go with them?' asked Simp Fiche.

'Nay, man,' said Suzilman. 'Gwiff holes, by the looks of them.'

The pirates gathered in, to find Suzilman standing guard by a low bank. Half a dozen earthy holes, too small for a man to crawl into, tunnelled straight into the bank.

'Holes for gwiff,' said Suzilman. 'I seen them in the Ravlish Lands, aye.'

'What's this gwiff, man?' asked Mulps. 'A great big snake? Or what?'

'No,' said Suzilman, scratching his head, thinking. 'The gwiff, he's a bit like a pig yet a bit like a ferret, if you know what I mean. A long snout with stripes running nose to tail, some white, the rest black. He's got claws on him like a crocodile, if you ever seen such. Teeth like a rat, go through steel no trouble. Eats kludes with 'em.'

'What about men?' asked Jon Arabin.

'Well, I never seen him fight no men, only dogs, in a pit, for sport. A mess he made of them dogs, too, I'll be telling you. But men, no, I don't think so.'

'We don't want to be finding out the hard way now, do we?' said Jez Glane.

'This gwiff-thing,' said Whale Mike with a grin.

'Maybe he eat men, maybe not – but I don't think he eat me!'

Indeed, it was doubtful anything living in a hole so small would have the nerve to tackle Whale Mike. Not unless it was extremely aggressive. Or very, very stupid.

'We'll do it,' said Arabin, decisively.

'Not that we've any weapons, of course,' said Ika Thole.

'This will serve,' said Arabin, hefting a branch. 'Dig, boys, dig!'

Much later, filthy with earth and mud, sweating despite a light fall of snow dusting out of the sky, they broke through into an underground chamber.

'How big is it?' asked Arabin.

'Unknown,' said Thole, thrusting a stick into the darkness.

Something below squealed with rage.

'Huh! A griff!' said Bucks Cat.

'Gwiff,' said Peg Suzilman, by way of correction.

But before they could argue about it, several dog-sized creatures came swarming out of the wreckage of the barrow, trying to escape.

'Stop them!' shouted Arabin.

There was a brief, desperate fight. Sticks rose and fell. Boots swung. There was a *crack!* of shattering bone as Whale Mike fisted something.

'Knives!' screamed Fiche. 'They're armed!'

He threw up his right arm, a bloody cut running a third of its length.

'Peace, man,' said Arabin, who had just brained a knife-armed assailant. 'Armed or not, they're only a kind of dog.'

But Fiche still screamed and shouted as if seriously wounded. Then Bucks Cat cuffed him round the earhole, which shut him up promptly (and permanently damaged the hearing in his left-hand ear).

The fight was over almost as soon as it had begun. Most of the creatures had escaped, but two had been killed.

403

They were the size of knee-high dogs. They had reddish-brown fur. The tops of their skulls were bald bone. Their forepaws looked like hands. They wore no proper clothes, but had belts with sheaths, bottles and boxes attached.

Two knives were recovered, curious pieces of finely wrought bronze. The hilt of one was in the form of the head of a dragon; the hilt of the other was fashioned to resemble a dolphin.

'Bloody uncomfortable to hold,' muttered Jon Arabin, who had claimed one of the knives. 'Made for show, not for use.'

'Aye,' said Meerkat, who had gained the other blade. 'But someone's put an edge to this one, sharp enough.'

'Let's dig down,' said Jon Arabin. 'Mayhap there's more metal below.'

They started digging. Promptly, three more creatures, which had been lying dog in the dark, tried to break out. This time the men moved faster. All three died.

What the men found underground was a chamber big enough to have held twenty barrels of wine or water. What it actually held was several nests of leaves and straw, some crude wooden fishing spears, nets for catching birds and fish, and a treasury of ancient objects in gold, glass and bronze.

While others pushed, shoved, slapped and bit, contending for the gold (and breaking the glass in the process) Drake secured himself a sword. Bronze was the sheath and bronze was the blade, both built for business and bare of ornament. Drake, as a steelworker, had always thought bronze soft stuff useless for weaponry. But this seemed stout enough. It was, in fact, copper alloyed with 10 per cent tin, which gives a bronze truly rugged enough for the rigours of war.

By the time the fighting had finished, Rolf Thelemite had a similar sword of bronze, as did Ish Ulpin, Ika Thole and Jon Disaster. They had secured these prizes easily while others contended for wealth – but now there was a clamour for a redistribution of weapons.

'Our swordsmen have chosen themselves,' said Arabin. 'Aye, while you others greeded for gold like pigs at truffles. Look at me! Empty-handed! And why? Because I was kept so busy keeping the rest of you from killing each other.'

The protests died down and the dead creatures were skinned, roasted and eaten. But the little klude which Whale Mike had caught was neither cooked nor eaten, for the big man crept away from his companions, took the klude from his apron pocket, kissed it gently, thanked it for bringing him luck, then set it loose to run away happily into the wilderness.

That evening, Drake and Yot approached Whale Mike, who sat by himself feeding a little fire with twigs and broken branches. Everyone had enjoyed a decent meal, so it was time to try to convert Whale Mike to Goudanism. Drake was dreading it. Fortunately, he had a present to sweeten Mike's temper. After everyone else had finished investigating the animal burrow they had broken into, Drake had dug up the floor of that burrow, searching for buried treasure. He had found a long, slim, immensely strong rod of what he thought was steel.

'What you got there?' said Mike, catching sight of the rod as Drake and Yot came near.

'A present for you,' said Drake. 'It's a giant's crowbar, by the looks of it.'

In fact the rod – which was made of titanium – was an axle from a Raflanderk IV All-Terrain Assault Vehicle. But Whale Mike was happy to have it regardless.

'It's steel,' said Drake.

'This too light for steel,' said Whale Mike, hefting it. 'Also no rust. That strange.' He tested it. 'But strong. That nice. Good stuff.'

Drake and Yot settled themselves by the fire.

'Mike,' said Yot, 'do you like fire?'

'Sure,' said Mike. 'Fire good friend. Him got bad temper sometimes, but we all friends, we understand.'

'Well,' said Yot, taking a deep breath, 'I'm here to tell you about a special kind of fire. We call it the Flame. This Flame is a god. Not any god, but the Lord God of All Gods. Do you hear me?'

'I got no ears,' said Mike. 'But I hear okay. You joker with god to share. But I not into that stuff. If some god so great, then him make us believe by god-magic. Not need thin boy with warts running round saying what what.'

'You don't understand,' said Yot earnestly. 'If our god forced us to believe in him, we'd have no free will. Our god works by giving us preachers to bring us the revealed truth. Gouda Muck is one of those preachers.'

'This not new thing,' said Mike. 'Many preacher talk god, say god most important. You know what most important? Woman with soft arse. That best thing. I get woman some day, nice woman, make baby. We have kids. That nice thing, you know?'

'Theology is more important than sex,' said Yot coldly. 'We have the truth. We have proofs. The Flame reveals itself everywhere through fire. The nature of god is to transform one thing to another, for creation is the essence of divinity, and transformation is the essence of creation.'

'Creation means making,' said Drake, who had picked up some of this religious lingo while walking the tunnel with Sully Yot. 'Transformation means change. Divinity means god, more or less.'

'You not only one speak Galish,' said Whale Mike. 'You got long word but not make much sense. Your god god because change things. That make something god? Man, my belly change things. Food to shit.'

And Whale Mike laughed.

'Food to shit,' he repeated. 'That interesting. You look next time you cut some joker open. You have good look, poke around inside. It don't hurt him, he dead by then, so you look. Man, I spend two days once with some joker's belly. That good thing. Food come down to stomach, see, then—'

It was a long explanation. Yot listened, then said:

'It's not really the same thing. You see, we change food to – to something not food because, well, we're alive. But fire isn't alive. Fire changes only because god is in the fire, demonstrating divinity. You understand? Animals are alive, plants are alive, but fire isn't.'

Yot repeated this in three different ways, trying to get the facts into Whale Mike's head. When Yot was finished, Mike sat for a while staring at the fire with his tiny, imbecilic eyes. He looked puzzled. Then his fat, stupid face split into a grin.

'Now I understand what you getting at,' said Whale Mike. 'You think maybe fire not alive. Then maybe fire god.'

'You're getting nearer the truth,' said Yot. 'That's good! I'm glad you're starting to believe.'

'Man,' said Mike, 'I hear, that one thing. Believe, that something else. You real fancy speaker, but you got no more sense than rabbit fart. You not get upset now, we good friends, but I got to say this. You think fire not alive, but him alive all right. Him good friend, that what.'

'Fire—'

'No, you fart later. Now listen. Fire, him alive because he need feed, otherwise die out. Him born just like us, live strong, die grey. You put him under water, you find out how much god you got there. He die under water, you try some time.'

Yot did his best, arguing his thesis remorselessly. But whatever he tried Mike countered. Finally, Yot and Drake withdrew, leaving Mike to tend his fire in peace.

'He's too stupid!' said Yot angrily. 'He can't understand! All he can think about is a woman with a soft arse!'

'Well, that's understandable,' said Drake. 'I can identify with that.'

'Oh, you would! No, Mike was the wrong choice. He's not really human. He's – he's a filthy stupid animal. We should try someone else. Someone smarter.'

'Like the Walrus, perhaps?' said Drake.

'Well . . .'

'It's pretty late,' said Drake. 'We'd better be getting some sleep. What say – what say we leave conversions until our next good meal? Okay?'

'Okay,' said Yot.

Even religious fanatics need to go to bed sooner or later.

33

The Old City: remnants of a military-industrial complex (properly known as Karalagazoko Atalamiti Zenavanarik) built in Penvash during Technic Renaissance which briefly revived some of the High Science which had survived the terrors of the Days of Wrath; wrecked during Genetic Mutiny, an episode so destructive that accounts of it were few, inaccurate and fragmentary.

Next day the pirates rose early, stoked their fires, blessed the night for sparing them from rain and snow, tore the last sinews from the bones of the animals they had murdered the day before, checked the stowage of their wealth and weapons, then started downstream in high spirits.

Soon they encountered another gigantic phallus of green star-stone, just like the one they had seen on the previous day. Bucks Cat repeated his remark about his uncle Habby, for Cat treated jokes as consumer durables, to be used as long and as often as possible. Jez Glane, in turn, repeated his desire to find a matching 'woman-one'.

Then a little horseplay started.

Jon Arabin let the more boisterous burn off their surplus energy. When things started to get serious – Simp Fiche suddenly acquired a bloody nose, and a couple of tempers showed signs of being the worse for wear – he called them to order and led the way downstream again.

Up ahead was a hammering sound which grew steadily louder as they got closer. Nobody suggested turning back. Marching in strength, with weapons to back up their

409

muscle, today they feared next to nothing. The fresh meat so recently put in their bellies had made them new men – and heroes, too, at least until they encountered some real live danger with claws to it.

After half a league, they reached a stunted tower from which came the hammering. The ground round about shook; they felt like a handful of lice standing on the skin of an enormous drum being beaten with a big silver ladle by a one-eyed hunchbacked dwarf wearing red velvet trousers and red felt slippers to match.

'____ _____ ——' shouted Slagger Mulps.

'————?' shouted Jon Arabin in reply, having seen the Walrus's mouth move.

'_____ _____' replied Mulps.

Arabin made a curt gesture of discontent. They moved downstream until it was quiet enough to hear themselves shout.

'Man!' said Jon Disaster, his head still ringing. 'The sound of that thing's like being knocked about the head with a mud pack.'

That started a comparison competition, which Simp Fiche won by comparing the hammering to something too gross to bear mentioning.

They went on with added confidence, believing by now that they had found the Old City of legend, and had met the worst it had to offer. They passed many ruins half-hidden amongst dishevelled evergreen forest. Often they had to scramble over walls of honest-built granite, great blocks of it good for another thirty million years or more, at least, if left to do their job in peace.

The ruins grew steadily higher, while the river dividing those ruins grew wider, chuckling along cold and hard. Sometimes, the earth throbbed underfoot. Steam and thin threads of acrid yellow smoke drifted from cracks in the ground. One place echoed with the chimes of a dozen bells, which they could not locate, though they looked hard, on the off-chance that the bells in question might be made of gold.

Late in the afternoon, Rolf Thelemite, who was in the lead, cried:

'Careful coming over the wall! There's a hole on the other side!'

'My kind of hole?' called Simp Fiche.

'Your kind?' said Jon Disaster. 'We didn't know you were choosy!'

'I am, you know,' replied Simp Fiche. 'I like them tight enough to bleed.'

And when Fiche saw the hole, big lips of stone opening into a tunnel glistening with wet pink light, he declared it too big for him.

'But Jez will try it, surely?' said Burpskin, with a glance at Glane. 'After all, it's the woman-thing to match the man-spike.'

After a certain amount of hilarity, as pirates competed with each other in crudity, nothing would serve but that Jez Glane must lower himself into the hole.

'I don't think that's wise,' said Drake suddenly.

'Why not?' said Glane.

'It doesn't feel right,' said Drake, who, for no reason that he could pin down, had a terrible foreboding about that hole.

'Doesn't feel right?' said Glane. 'Man, we haven't tried it at all yet! How can we know how it feels?'

'Yes, for sure,' said Bucks Cat. 'He's got to lose his virginity some time.'

'Who knows?' said Glane. 'There might be something down here worth eating.' And, with a grin, he got in. 'Nice and greasy,' he said. 'A snug enough fit. And . . .'

He frowned, for the lips were closing on him.

'Pull him out!' said Jon Arabin.

Whale Mike snatched Glane by the hair, meaning to yank him from the hole. Too late! Metal spikes slammed from the sides of the hole and riveted Glane through and through. Impaled, he tried to scream, but his agony was too great for him to cry out.

411

Steam hissed up. Then, with a glutinous bubbling sound, the hole filled with boiling yellow fluid.

'Stand back!' shouted Jon Arabin.

They leaped clear as the fluid fountained up, burning where it fell.

'I'm burnt! I'm burnt!' cried Raggage Pouch, scalded by the flying fluid. Staggering blind, he fell into the river.

The fluid in the hole receded as rapidly as it had come. Jez Glane was gone – all but for his bones, impaled on bright steel. Even as they watched, the bones crumbled. There was the 'Whoosh!' of a great in-suck of air – and the last traces of their deceased comrade were gone.

Drake, trembling, turned, tried to walk away, tripped over his own feet, and fell sprawling. Someone was urinating noisily. Someone else was vomiting. Sully Yot felt a tightness in his chest, and began to find it hard to breathe. The incident had precipitated a minor asthma attack. Yot had seemed to outgrow his childhood asthma on reaching the age of twelve, but the stresses of the journey had at last brought its return.

'Where's Pouch?' said Arabin.

'The damn fool fell in the river,' said Mulps.

'Pouch!' roared Arabin. 'Come back here you . . . you . . .'

His voice trailed away to nothing. He stared at the water. Others joined him on the riverbank and watched in silence as the water boiled with blood. Suddenly the bloody waters vomited upwards, throwing a shower of river, stones and body-parts into the air. Settling swiftly, the waters soon ran smooth and clean once more.

'Blue-blooded mandarins,' muttered Arabin, in shock and wonderment; he had reached right back to his early childhood for that exclamation.

Drake got to his feet slowly, feeling sick. Two more comrades dead! Just like that! It was too much to take. So many good men dead. The weapons muqaddam, aye,

412

slaughtered by the Collosnon. Quin Baltu, and – and all the others. It was grief just to list them.

Good comrades. Men of my life.

Drake looked round at the shocked and shaken survivors. These were his comrades true. Many of these he'd felt like killing at times. Some, on occasion, had tried for his throat. But now . . .

My friends. My life.

He felt it hard to remember a time when he had not known these men.

You who I love.

Now that was right strange. Weird, even. To feel so close to such a gross gang of warped, twisted killers and outcasts.

But are we not men? Aye, we're men all right. The same blood as princes.

And Drake, tears in his eyes, prayed to the Demon, to the Flame, or to Whoever It Was, not to write them off without thought and feeling.

For a while, the survivors watched silently as Whale Mike probed the river's waters with his battle-rod, trying to spear the death within the water. Then a quavering voice spoke:

'This is the Old City all right,' said Tiki Slooze. 'We'll none of us get out alive, no, none of us.'

'Shut up, you!' said Slagger Mulps. 'Or I'll smash you to death and damnation on the spot.' Then, to the Warwolf: 'Jon, let's make camp. I'm thinking a good fire's the thing, though there's daylight still. We've no need to walk further today.'

'Aye,' said Arabin, still slightly dazed. 'Aye. Just a little further, to a . . . a cleaner spot. Then we'll camp.'

That they did, Jon Arabin making a fire, as usual, with the tinder box kept safe in his sea-pouch. All were slow to sleep that night, resting uneasily beneath the gaunt shadows of darkness-haunted trees.

Out in the night lay the greater, darker bulk of half-demolished towers and monumental blockhouses of

413

uncertain origin and unknown function. The river talked to itself, muttering, rambling, churning syllables of madness over and over, sweeping the chill of the Penvash mountains down toward the sea. Strange noises filled the night: distant thumpings, grindings and strange whistle-noises. And an intensely irritating high-pitched humming.

Tiki Slooze woke them near dawn when he screamed.

'What is it, man?' roared Arabin.

'My legs!' screamed Slooze. 'Something's bitten my legs off!'

'Nonsense, man,' said Arabin. 'You've been dreaming.'

To prove it, Arabin felt in the night for the legs of the torture-screaming Slooze. And felt the stumps, felt the wet hot gush of arterial blood spurting over his fingers. He moaned, fumbling for something to tourniquet with – but it was too late, would have been too late no matter how fast he moved, and Tiki Slooze was very shortly dead.

'Are we all here?' said Arabin.

'Aye,' said an optimist.

But a check revealed one missing: Harly Burpskin.

The survivors stood back to back, weapons drawn, until it was light enough to explore. Day showed their dirt-rough faces gaunt with fear and hunger.

'Let's move,' said Ish Ulpin, more ready than the others for a task of death.

'Keep together,' warned Arabin. 'We don't know what's out there.'

'Thanks for the warning, mother dearest,' said the Walrus.

None of them expected to find Burpskin alive.

Hunting, they found no proper tracks, only great trails of slime suggesting a snail had been there – a snail two or three times the size of a horse.

'And that,' said Arabin firmly, 'I won't be believing till I've cut it in half with a hatchet.'

All they found of Harly Burpskin was his head lying lonesome near the river. Though they were all potential cannibals, nobody suggested eating it: instead, they made a decent funeral pyre and burnt it, with what ceremony they could muster.

'He was a good enough sort,' said Drake, as the flames ascended.

'Aye,' said Meerkat, 'we'll give the man that.'

'And may the Doom Beyond be merciful,' said Peg Suzilman.

All were strangely moved by that little funeral service. It was decent enough to die by sword or by drowning, but the monstrous, senseless deaths their comrades were meeting with here were different.

Having disposed of the mortal remains of Harly Burpskin, they prepared to do the same for Tiki Slooze – only to find that what was left of Slooze had disappeared while they had been tending to Burpskin's head.

'Here's a fresh slime-track!' said Rolf Thelemite. 'Let's follow it!'

'Are you mad, man?' said Peg Suzilman. 'It's a killer!'

'Aye,' said Arabin, 'but anything that moves on slime can't move fast, can it? Stands to reason.'

'Evil things are not governed by reason,' said Sully Yot, mouthing a phrase Gouda Muck had taught him.

'I'll see my enemy face to face before I die,' said Jon Arabin grimly.

With that, he set off. The strongest fell in behind him. Shortly, they came upon a slug. It was yellow, translucent, and several times larger than an ox. As they stood gaping, it turned on them, cruising forward at about half a man's walking pace.

'Kill it!' said Ish Ulpin.

'Nay, man,' said Jon Arabin. 'It must have a bloody big man-buggering mouth on it to start with. Worse, where there's one there may be a thousand. We know what it is. We know we can outpace it. Let's be going.'

The others followed him downstream.

They crossed more slime-trails, and spotted other monstrous slugs cruising in the forest or lying, as if oblivious to the cold, on the roofs of gigantic blockhouses. When they halted, they became aware that there were at least a dozen slugs on their trail.

'No good going back then,' said Mulps.

'Yes, and we can't chance crossing the river,' said Meerkat, looking with a shudder at the haunted waters which had chewed Raggage Pouch to pieces then spat out the bits.

'Then let's put our trust in speed, boys,' said Jon Arabin. 'A good steady pace now, no running, for we've all day to march in. Come on!'

Further downstream, they reached another wall. Not of granite but of blue crystal which glittered as fierce as diamond.

'Man,' said Drake, 'this looks to be fabulous wealth.'

'Mayhap,' said Jon Arabin, 'but we've no time to be fooling with such.'

The rest of the pirates begged to differ. But all their attempts to souvenir pieces of the wall came to nothing. Even Whale Mike, flailing away at it with his rod of titanium, was unable to do any damage.

'Come on,' said Jon Arabin. 'The slugs gain on us while we greed without purpose.'

'We greed to get rich,' said Ish Ulpin. 'There must be a way to break this thing.'

'Look south,' said Jon Arabin. 'You see? There's another wall the same, some fifty paces further forward. Let's go that far at least.'

As he jumped over the wall, there was a roar from the south.

'Fire!' yelled Drake, as sheets of flame leaped from the glittering crystal wall fifty paces south.

The flames advanced. Jon Arabin glanced right, then left. East and west, flames reached away as far as he could see. Eastward, the flames stretched right across the river and into the forest on the other side.

'It's but an illusion,' said Rolf Thelemite calmly. 'Has to be.'

Moments later, they started to feel the heat glowing against their faces. Undergrowth crackled into fire as the flamewall marched forward. Trees exploded into flames. Advancing, the wall spat gouts of fire at random.

'Back!' shouted Arabin. 'Back, or we'll be burnt alive!'

They turned and fled.

34

Name: Jon Arabin, alias the Warwolf.

Occupation: pirate captain and ambassador from Lord Menator of the Greater Teeth to Ohio of Ork.

Status: full-time survivor and leader of men, now responsible for the welfare of his old enemy Slagger Mulps (the Walrus) plus young Drake (known to the all-conquering faith of Goudanism as 'Demon-son Dreldragon'); Sully Yot; Whale Mike; Bucks Cat; Ika Thole; Rolf Thelemite; Simp Fiche; Salaman Meerkat; Ish Ulpin; Jon Disaster; and Peg Suzilman.

Description: lean, bald, black, beardless man with eyes of pale sky; currently looking much, much older than his years (and those are many enough).

Running from the flames, the thirteen survivors fled north. They had gone but two hundred paces when Jon Arabin called them to a halt:

'Stop!' he yelled. 'The flames aren't chasing us!'

Panting, sweating, gasping, his men halted, and looked back. The flames had raged to the nearer wall of blue crystal then halted. But they showed no sign of dying down.

'We can't go south,' said Drake.

'Not yet, my son,' said Arabin. 'But no fire can burn forever.'

'This one can,' said Sully Yot. 'For it was started by the Flame of all Flames. Gouda Muck is angry with us.'

'Is he?' said Peg Suzilman. 'And who the hell would he be?'

'He is of no hell, but of a transcendental heaven which suffers no wind or rain, but music only. If you wish to know more of his—'

'What is this bullshit?' said Ish Ulpin. 'More religion crap?'

'We not talk gods,' said Whale Mike, leaning on his titanium battle-rod. 'We be happy friends.'

But Yot, taking no heed, declared:

'It's not bullshit! It's truth! Revealed truth! Drake will tell you!'

Drake, at that moment, would gladly have paid good money for the privilege of strangling Yot.

'What say you, Drake?' asked Ish Ulpin.

'I say—' said Drake.

But did not say, for Meerkat, who had kept an eye on the forest to the north, yelled out:

'Ware! Slugs!'

They turned as one to see several gigantic yellow slugs cruising slowly toward them. The slugs held the north. East was the river, haunted by bone-chewing terror. South lay fire. Simp Fiche led the retreat, scuttling away to the west.

'Hold!' shouted Arabin. 'No running, or we're dead men by dusk!'

But most of his men sprinted regardless.

'Bugger you then,' muttered Arabin, and, abandoning his efforts to bring the fools to heel, plodded on stolidly. With him went Whale Mike – who was not built for sprinting – and the swordsmen Drake Douay, Rolf Thelemite, Ish Ulpin, Ika Thole and Jon Disaster, their wits steadied by the possession of sharpened bronze.

After a half-league march, they caught up with the others, who had gathered in a boggy clearing between two sky-threatening buildings which hoisted great shiploads of forest-creepers toward the clouds. The runaways were sitting on a marble plinth which supported a steel archway.

Arabin strode into the slade, boots going quelch-squelch-quelch as they crushed stranded leaves into the mud, and shattered the surface of cloud-reflecting puddles.

'How do you feel, boys?' asked Arabin.

Sully Yot looked up and answered for all of them: 'Knackered.'

'Aye, and that's not running far,' said Arabin. 'Is it? Slow and steady, that's the thing. We can outwalk these monsters easy enough, once we start thinking. Pull off your boots. Check your feet as our good friend Rolf has taught us to.'

With that, Arabin sought and was granted buttock-space on the plinth. All thirteen of them managed to squeeze onto the plinth, which was a good size larger than the stainless steel monument it supported (an arch just as wide as a man's outstretched arms).

Drake watched Slagger Mulps remove his boots then massage his feet. A sorry sight they were, too: a mess of corns and bunions, blisters, water-rot, and painfully raw patches of skin where tinea had got a grip. Mulps squidged a large blister with his index finger, disturbing yellowish fluid within.

Drake found his own feet almost as bad. Cold. Sore. Soft and pallid. And blistered. Whatever protected him these days against illness, it could not protect his feet.

'Yot!' said Arabin. 'Get your boots off!'

'Yes,' said Rolf Thelemite. 'Remember: no feet, no soldier.'

'I'll do it later,' said Yot tetchily. 'I'm thirsty.'

So saying, he went down on his hands and knees to drink from a puddle. Bucks Cat stamped down hard and sudden, sending mud and water flying into Yot's face.

'Hey!' cried Yot.

'Belay that!' roared Arabin.

'Aye,' said Mulps, backing him up. 'Or there'll be more than one of us after your liver.'

Cat, sulking, walked away. Nobody made any effort to

stop him. At the edge of the clearing, he turned, then spat. Then was lost to sight, heading to the west, the sole remaining direction of safety.

Drake did what he could for his socks, which was little. He kneaded his feet. Every day, they were less like flesh and more like dough. He kissed his boots for luck, then put them back on. Then sat, thinking nostalgically about good times long since past – like the roast-meat banquet he'd enjoyed two nights before.

Between his legs, in the face of the marble plinth, was a round gilded hole big enough to have swallowed both his fists. Idly, he tried to pry off the gold, first with a finger-nail then with the point of his bronze sword. He loosened no lucre, and concluded that the gold was colour rather than metal.

Disappointed, he stabbed at the ground with his bronze sword. At first, he had delighted in his choice of weapon rather than wealth when everyone scrambled for loot – after all, he had gambling gold waiting for him back at the Teeth. But now he thought it was not really fair that the others should have all the goldwork, some of which was highly wrought and obviously very, very valuable.

Perhaps this was the time to say something about it, before they got going again.

So thinking, Drake stabbed the ground again, harder this time, a bit of anger in the blow. And the point of his sword hit something. He poked it, then, idling at it as he might have idled at a scab on his arm, urged it from the earth. A globe of glass, if he was any judge. A paper-weight, perhaps. He'd seen such sitting on the Examiners' desk when he went before the Board during his apprentice years, to suffer a viva voce examination on the Inner Principles of the Old Science.

He picked up the paperweight. Rubbed away the dirt. Glass? Crystal, maybe. Very pretty. A fist-sized transparent ball as big as his fist. Green, like the monstrous phalli they had seen standing on the banks of the river. Tiny

421

lights of all colours gleamed within, hanging motionless like the souls of fireflies.

Or like stars.

'A globe of stars,' murmured Drake. 'A star-globe.'

He remembered the astrolabe the alchemist Villet Vate had once shown him. Maybe this star-globe was a fancy kind of astrolabe. Old, rare and precious.

'What have you got there?' said Meerkat, making a grab for it.

'Something that's mine,' said Drake, snatching it away.

For safe keeping for the moment, Drake shoved his green star-globe into the gold-coloured hole between his legs.

The air filled with an ominous hum, waking memories of the sky-splitting disaster which had followed the destruction of the flying island-ship in the North Strait. Men scattered in all directions.

'Sha!' shouted Meerkat. And:

'Help!' cried Yot. And:

'Ahyak Rovac!' screamed Rolf Thelemite, bringing his sword around in a sweep that almost took off Drake's head by accident.

Drake turned and saw the steel archway mounted on the marble plinth had filled with a sheet of loudly humming silver. Guessing which Cause had led to this Effect, he scrambled the star-globe out of the golden cup.

The silver sheet filling the archway vanished. The hum died away to nothing. Those with swords slowly lowered them from the ready.

'What have you got there?' asked Jon Arabin.

Silently, Drake offered up the star-globe. Arabin turned it over in his hands, then, face set in decision, put it into the golden cup again. One moment they could see through the arch to the mud, puddles and trees beyond. The next moment, the silver gleamed to life, perfect, humming and opaque.

'This is a Door,' said Rolf Thelemite, decisively. 'Not that I've ever seen one, but I'm sure enough from the descriptions.'

'A Door?' said Whale Mike slowly. 'Him look no door to me.'

'Not an ordinary door,' said Thelemite. 'This Door goes a long, long way. To some place off the horizon, like as not.'

'Aye,' said Ika Thole, 'and what place might that be? The horse devil's stable or the love god's twat?'

'Death if it's anything,' said Peg Suzilman. 'Like all the other weirdness here.'

'No,' insisted Thelemite. 'It's a Door, a one-step road-way to Elsewhere.'

'Aye,' said Jon Arabin, slowly. 'I've heard of such.'

'So have I,' said Ish Ulpin. 'In Chi'ash-lan there were rumours. The Door takes you round in a circle, one place to another. A globe set in any arch of the circle opens the circle complete.'

'Let's go through then,' said Slagger Mulps. 'It can't be worse than here.'

'Sure it can't,' said Arabin. 'Go right ahead, Mulps me darling. Chance the circle then tell us your wounds.'

Suddenly, a rock hurtled through the Door, hit Yot in the face and sent him sprawling. It was followed by a human foot. Drake hastily scooped the star-globe out of its golden cup.

'Aye,' said Arabin, taking it from him. 'That was a move smart enough. Stones first, then maybe spears afterwards.'

Meerkat picked up the foot. It was pale, bloodless and slightly wrinkled, as if it had been out in the rain for a while. He sniffed it. The meat smelt all right. The wide spacing of the toes suggested the owner had gone barefoot for a life-time.

'I see,' said Ika Thole, as Meerkat pondered the foot and Yot fingered his rock-grazes tenderly. 'If we go through this Door, we get to a place where they've plenty of rocks and fresh-chopped feet to spare.'

'Eventually,' said Arabin. 'But we go other places first.'

'How so?' said Thole.

'It's a circle, man,' said Thelemite.

'I don't understand either,' said Drake.

'Say we open that Door,' said Thelemite. 'Say you stick your head and shoulders through. Your feet will be here and your head Elsewhere. Fine. You can grab hold of anything you fancy Elsewhere, then pull your head back in. But if you go right through the Door, leaving no part of yourself on this side – why, then you're in Elsewhere entirely. Then if you go through the Door again, you find yourself in yet another Elsewhere. And so on, right round in a circle, until you come back to where you started.'

'How many Elsewheres in a circle?' asked Drake.

'It varies,' said Thelemite. 'But the place with rocks and feet is the last place on this circle. If some rock-throwing foot-chopper poked his head through the Door from his place to here, then we couldn't use the Door to go anywhere until we'd pushed him back where he came from or pulled him through entirely.'

'If,' said Drake, 'if some foot-chopper grabbed one of us then pulled him back to where—'

'Let's not start making ourselves nightmares,' said Arabin. 'Let's think where this Door might go. Rolf? Any ideas?'

'The first place this Door goes to,' said Rolf Thelemite. 'It could be . . . why, Chi'ash-lan, or Stokos or—'

'Not Stokos,' said Drake. 'We've got nothing like this on the island.'

'Maybe not,' said Thelemite. 'But other places surely do.'

Whale Mike took the foot from Meerkat.

'Him who threw this,' said Whale Mike, gesturing with it. 'We open Door, they jump through easily as throw through, that so?'

'Mike's got his head on, aye, that's for sure,' said Arabin. 'By opening this Door, we open every Door in the circle. Then everyone can move, friendly or otherwise.'

'But we're up against monsters as it is,' said Simp Fiche, in something like panic. 'Giant slugs! Man eaters! Why, they could be on us any moment!'

'Aye,' said Arabin, not concealing his contempt. 'Then we get up and walk away. Man, what kind of monster is a slug, however big? I'd rather face fifty thousand of them single-handed than try tackle one of the Neversh with fifty men at me back.'

'Whatever we decide,' said Salaman Meerkat, 'let's decide soon. I see something to east of us. One of our slow-slime monsters, by the looks.'

Arabin got to his feet.

'Men,' said Arabin, 'we'll west a bit. Likely we can escape to safety. I never heard any whisper of slugs when I was in Lorp, and that was for a long time, and recently. So they don't range over all of Penvash – probably no distance from here at all. And if we can't escape, why, we circle back, slip between them – man, they don't run faster than vomit crawls – then try our Door.'

At that moment, there was a smashing-crashing of vegetation in the forest to west of them, west being the direction of safety. Into the clearing ran Bucks Cat, gasping in panic and horror.

'Monsters!' shouted Cat.

He had tampered with a cause-and-effect panel in a ruinous building, inadvertently releasing a horde of monsters from imprisonment within a stasis-field.

The monsters charged into the clearing after Bucks Cat. They were trampling creatures built higher than a horse, with great big spikes projecting from flaring armour round their necks, and huge claws on their elephant-grey feet. Feet which kicked up showers of mud.

'The Door!' shouted Arabin.

He slammed the star-globe into the golden cup. He scooped up Sully Yot and threw him bodily through the Door as it gleamed to life. Drake leaped onto the plinth, hesitated – then Arabin booted him in the arse, and he tumbled through. Simp Fiche went rabbiting after him, through the silver screen to Elsewhere.

Then a muscular warrior leaped out of the screen. He was armed with a spiked club. He was as pale as Ish Ulpin, as blond as Drake. Wore leather breeches ending just below the knee, and a thick sheepskin jacket. He was outnumbered, but struck out bravely with his club, but—

Whale Mike grabbed both club and warrior, then threw both hard and far, so they crashed to earth in front of the monsters which were gaining on Bucks Cat. The warrior fell heavily, got to his knees – and was gored by a monster.

Other monsters crashed into the lucky one, fighting for a portion of the meat. Meanwhile, the men escaped. For Whale Mike, it was a squeeze – his shoulders, after all, were as wide as the Door – but he got himself through.

Bucks Cat scrambled onto the plinth, panting.

'In!' said Arabin.

And pushed him through the Door without bothering to make explanations. By the time the monsters had settled their disagreement over a dead foreign warrior, only Jon Arabin was left in the clearing.

Another warrior jumped through from the Place at the End of the Circle, wherever that might be. He looked around in astonishment. This warrior carried a sword.

'Enjoy paradise,' said Jon Arabin, booting the man in the crutch.

The man went down. Jon Arabin chopped him on the neck, seized his sword, then jumped through the Door himself.

35

Door: portal forming part of one of the Prompt Physical Communication Webs built during the Technic Renaissance and thereafter largely disused (though the Partnership Banks command a web secretly linking organizations as widely scattered as the Morgrim Bank of Chi'ash-lan, the Orsay Bank of Stokos, the Safrak Bank of the Safrak Islands, and the Singing Dove Pensions Trust of Tang).

Jon Arabin sprang through the Door. He saw fire, and smelt smoke. Breathed smoke, too. Coughed. The fighting thirteen were standing in tinder-dry eucalyptus forest through which wildfire was spreading like – well, frankly, like wildfire.

'Knobs of gods and bollocks of bulls!' quoth Slagger Mulps. 'Out of the dragon's pantry and into his oven!'

'I think—' began Sully Yot.

Then he too coughed because of the smoke, and, if he continued to think, did not pronounce on the fact.

'Move your arses,' said Jon Arabin, jabbing his new-found sword in the direction of the Door. 'Into it!'

'But we don't want to go back there!' protested Simp Fiche.

'Haven't you got it into your head yet?' said Arabin. 'The Door goes round in a circle!'

'Then let's get on with it,' growled Ish Ulpin, jumping back onto the marble plinth. He collided with a foreign warrior who was exiting from the Door. 'Bloody bad

427

manners,' said Ish Ulpin, swatting the foreigner and breaking his jaw.

Then he went through the Door.

Drake jumped onto the plinth. A grey monster with an armoured frill round its neck almost gored him as it thrust its horned head through. He plunged his sword deep into its eye, withdrew the weapon as the monster backtracked—

Hesitated—

Then fell through the Door as Arabin booted him again.

Drake hit the ground rolling, came to his feet with a fighting scream, and danced round with blade in hand, menacing each direction in turn.

'Nobody here, man, but us ship rats,' said Ish Ulpin, as Meerkat came through the Door.

As the others joined them, Drake took stock of his situation. They were on a small, flat, sandy cay in the middle of a flat, glittering ocean. At the far end of the cay, some fifty paces distant, was a rowing boat turned on its side. A man rose from its shadows and strode toward them.

'Who be he?' asked Whale Mike.

'How the hell would I know?' said Jon Arabin, irritated.

The man closed with them, halting at twice sword-blade distance. He was a big, burly brute, a man of middle years with high cheekbones, dark eyes, big jug-handle ears, and a large nose with wide-flared nostrils.

'Who you be?' asked Whale Mike.

'Who asks?' said the stranger, putting his hand to the hilt of his sword.

At that moment, a Penvash monster burst through the Door. Roaring it came, scraping its great armour-plated body through the steel arch. It started scrambling off the plinth, tripped, rolled, fell on its back, lay for a moment with belly exposed and the brutal stumps of its four claw-equipped legs kicking in the air—

Then kicked no more, for seven men had sunk swords into the softness of its belly.

'Kalman-chay,' said the stranger softly, using an expression unknown to the Galish Trading Tongue as he withdrew

428

his bloody blade. 'Blood and water! What is it?'

'No member of my family, you can be sure of that,' said Jon Arabin, wiping his own blade.

A feeble tremor ran through the creature's legs. Arabin suspected it was not necessarily entirely dead. It was smaller than most of the Penvash monsters – otherwise it could not have forced itself through the Door.

'Come on,' said Arabin. 'Let's be getting while the getting's good. Mulps – lead the way, darling.'

'Sure, Jon, me pretty one,' said the Walrus. 'That I will.'

Stepping through the Door, he vanished.

'Where does this Door go to?' asked the stranger.

'You know about Doors, do you?' said Jon Arabin.

'Do bears shit in woods?' said the stranger.

'How would I know?' said Jon Arabin. 'They're not in my family either.'

Something strange came through the Door. What? Just a gust of leaves and smoke from the burning eucalyptus forest.

'This Door goes to hell for all I know,' said Arabin, once the last of his men was through. 'But I'm taking it!'

And he jumped through himself.

The stranger hesitated for a moment – then two warriors jumped through, swords in hand. There was some vigorous hacking and slashing before both were disposed of. Then the stranger, not bothering to clean his blade, looked round, shrugged, and leaped through the Door.

They were, this time, in a landscape altogether different, dominated by a huge hell-hammering trench of flame which snaked through the landscape just to the north of them, an arrowshot across if it was a fingerlength.

The marble plinth here stood in the fringes of some tough, low-living forest dominated by dense drifts of gnarled trees with dark green spiked leaves which, on examination, were more like thorns than the pine needles they superficially resembled. Nearby was a tall tower, with an outcrop of fortifications at its base. A couple of leagues to the west stood another such tower, and, further west again and on the far (northern) side of the flame trench, a third.

Directly north, on the far side of the flame trench, rose a monstrous pink buttress of rock. Off to the east were some purple-coloured mountain-hills.

'Hell's name!' said Meerkat, raising his voice above the thunder of the flame trench, which shook the very ground. 'Where are we?'

'We're on the wrong side of Drangsturm,' said the stranger they had lately acquired on the ocean cay. 'We stand in the fringes of Defelfankarzosh, which means the Forest of Desolation. It is impassable, even to South-searchers. The towers you see on our side of the flame trench are Nidbelzik and Torameer, the twin Pillars of Exile, unused now for generations. The rock north is Girik, which means Footstone.'

'How do you know all this?' said Arabin. 'Who are you?'

'I have gone by many names in many places,' said the stranger. 'But know that I am truly Guest Gulkan, rightful ruler of Tameran.'

'Aye,' said Ish Ulpin boldly. 'But Tameran decided it couldn't be ruled by something which looked that bad-ugly.'

And he laughed.

Drake ventured toward the flame trench, partly so he would be out of the way if Ish Ulpin came to blows with the stranger, partly so he could satisfy his curiosity.

At last, he was able to peer into the depths of Drangsturm, where whirlpools of molten red seethed and snapped. The rock of the nearest edge lay in ridged ropes, but on the far side it stood in regular masonry-blocks, albeit blocks of outlandish size. Drake smelt something burning. The soles of his boots! Ouch! That was hot! He retreated swiftly to the others.

'—or can we walk it?'

Thus spoke Jon Arabin.

'Of course we can walk it, all things being equal,' said the stranger, Guest Gulkan, pretender to the realms of the Lord Emperor Khmar. 'After all, it's less than a hundred leagues from the Central Ocean to the Inner Waters.'

'But even if we reach the Castle of Controlling Power,' said Ika Thole, 'we'll be on the wrong side of Drangsturm.'

'You ignorant old pessimist!' said Drake. 'Have you never been to the castle? I have! There's bare basalt between the end of Drangsturm and the sea.'

'The lad speaks right,' said Guest Gulkan.

'Not about my age,' said Ika Thole. 'For I'm young still. Though this risk is like to age me to death by nightfall. Why walk those leagues when we've got the Door?'

'Known dangers are safer than an unknown Circle,' said Guest Gulkan.

'Aye,' said Drake sagely.

He had his own reasons for wanting to get to the Castle of Controlling Power, even if it was half a hundred leagues away, give or take a bit. That was where he had last seen the high-breasted Zanya Kliedervaust, the love of his life. True, that was long, long ago – but some wizard would know where she had got to. Surely.

And there was the matter of magic liquor, too. Stuff like that he had sampled at Brennan. The cure for sobriety! In just a few days, he might, with luck, be raging on a real skull-splitting dog-vomiting drunk!

Belatedly, he remembered that a sentence of death awaited him if he reached the castle. But – a little matter like that? He'd handle it easily. Surely. He had his amulet still, didn't he? He'd buy his life from the wizards with that magic medallion.

'Water,' said Rolf Thelemite.

'Water,' said Guest Gulkan, meeting his gaze.

These two, Thelemite and Gulkan, knew each other of old. But neither betrayed the alliance forged in their youth. With masterly self-control, they comported themselves as strangers. Neither knew what business the other

431

was engaged in. Secrecy might prove of advantage, so . . .
they broke their gaze, both resolving to delay greetings till
they could talk in private.

'Water, yes, that'll be a problem,' said Thelemite.
'Fifty leagues – that's five marches. The Rovac can make
a double march between sunrise and sunset . . . but even
so . . .'

'We can reach through the Door to whatever lies ahead,
seeking water,' said Guest Gulkan. 'That has its dangers,
but it's worth the risk.'

'I'd worry more of the Swarms than of water,' said Ika
Thole. 'We're in the terror-lands now, are we not?'

'Yes,' said Guest Gulkan, in a confident voice. 'But the
Swarms stay well clear of Drangsturm, for they fear the
wizards.'

At which Simp Fiche shouted:

'Look! Look! Something in the forest!'

It was a centipede. It was green. It was a hundred paces
long. It stood half as high as a horse – and it was not
alone.

'That,' said Ika Thole, with a hint of satisfaction in his
voice, 'looks very much like a monster of the Swarms to
me. And where there's one there's a hundred, I'll tell you
that for nothing. In fact—'

He broke off, realizing nobody was interested in listening. Indeed, most had already fled Elsewhere. And, as the
centipede (and its friends) hastened forward, Thole fled
himself.

Beyond the Door was a steep snow-clad mountainside.
It was bitterly cold, with a howling wind blowing. Thole
wasted no time. Knowing monsters were close behind, he
threw himself to one side – and started to slip. Rolf
Thelemite, who had anchored himself firmly with his
sword, grabbed Thole and saved him.

Then out came the centipede. It slithered over the
plinth, and tried to turn sideways to get at the men.

'Hold my legs!' roared Guest Gulkan.

Whale Mike belayed him. Gulkan hacked at the

centipede. It writhed away, then hauled more of its strength through the Door, giving it more length with which to lunge at him. It slipped. And hung, half in the Door, and half trailing down the mountainside.

Screaming, the men attacked. Those with weapons thrust and slashed. Those with none hauled on the segments, bundling more of the centipede down and away. The last of it slid out of the Door, and, doomed to destruction, it slid down, down, down and away, starting an avalanche before it crashed over a cliff far below.

'Good work!' said Jon Arabin.

'Aye,' said Peg Suzilman. 'And time to leave.'

He jumped onto the plinth, skidded on ice, flailed wildly as he tried to steady himself – and was seized by the fighting claws of a lunging centipede. Screaming, legs kicking, Peg Suzilman was dragged through the Door, back to the torn lands by the edge of Drangsturm.

Now they were twelve. (Not counting Guest Gulkan.)

'Quick,' said Guest Gulkan, 'while the monster's feeding.'

He jumped onto the marble plinth – then retreated smartly as another centipede burst through the Door.

While the centipede just had its head through, the Door snapped out of existence. The connection between Here and Elsewhere was broken. The centipede's head fell away from the steel arch, amputated cleanly as if shaved by a guillotine.

'Let's go!' said Whale Mike.

He scrambled onto the plinth, forced himself through the empty arch – and came out just a step from where he had started. He did this several times before convinced there was no more Door.

'Who was controlling the Door for you?' asked Guest Gulkan.

'Nobody,' said Jon Arabin. 'We had a star-globe. We left it where we started out.'

'That's fearfully dangerous!' said Guest Gulkan. 'You should always have a gate party, at the least. Why, if you're half in and half out, you can get chopped in half if the Door dies sudden – just as that centipede was chopped.'

'We had no choice,' said Jon Arabin. 'We were under attack.'

'And now we're going to freeze to death,' said Ika Thole, with grim satisfaction. 'Aye, and suffer much avant death.'

'Sing happy song!' said Whale Mike.

'Before we sing happy song,' said Guest Gulkan dryly, 'let's start digging a snow cave. Look – over there, that flat place under the ridge. Good snow awaits.'

'What fun!' said Simp Fiche.

Jon Arabin looked up. The top of the mountain was not terribly far away.

'Drake!' said Arabin. 'You're volunteered. Scuttle up to the top to see what's there.'

'I can tell you that now!' said Drake. 'Snow, rock, ice, wind and nothing.'

'Aye,' said Arabin. 'Or maybe a castle.'

'A castle of giants, perhaps,' said Ika Thole, dourly. 'Man-eating giants with great big iron cooking pots.'

'Sing song!' said Mike, a note of panic entering his voice.

The trauma of this venture round the Circle of the Door had obviously almost overwhelmed poor Mike. Drake could identify.

'No,' said Yot. 'Let us pray! Pray to the Flame!'

'Aye,' said Ish Ulpin. 'Offer a prayer of praise to this Flame, whoever He is. For He has given us Sully Yot, who's good for nothing else so might as well be eaten.'

'I warned you!' cried Drake.

At that moment, there was a hum, and the steel arch filled once again with the blind silver of the Door. Yot, fearfully afraid of being eaten, rabbited through and was gone.

'Man,' said Ika Thole, 'what's the betting there's a dragon or such on the other side, munching young Yot at this moment?'

'Aye,' said Simp Fiche. 'Let's the rest of us go careful. Stick one man through, just the head. Then he can pull himself back, tell us what's on the other side.'

'Aye,' said Thole. 'And tell us if Yot's alive or dead.'

'Who cares?' said Ish Ulpin.

'Any man who lingers in a Door is a fool,' said Guest Gulkan, though he himself had suggested doing just that to seek water for a march by Drangsturm. 'Such a man could get cut in half like the centipede. No – quick through the Door, that's safest.'

And he led the way.

36

Aldarch the Third (aka Mutilator of Yestron): tyrant who won throne in year Khmar 5 after seven years of civil war; first act as ruler was to disembowel his forty-seven brothers and feed his twenty-nine sisters to the Favoured Rats; notable acts of his reign include establishing the death penalty for all those below the Fourth Degree who dare talk, whistle or sing in the streets, or walk upright, or wear any shoe with a heel taller than a finger-width, or worship any god other than Zoz the Ancestral.

The first thing Yot saw when he came through the Door was a golden dragon. It ran towards him, roaring. Too shocked to do anything sensible, he screamed at it. The dragon promptly veered away, wailing.

Poor thing!

It was an imperial dragon of Yestron. These gentle creatures are entirely unsuited for war, but they are, by tradition, taken onto battlefields as decoration. This one had broken loose from its chains, and was running about in a panic, demented by fear; its wings had been clipped, so it could not fly for freedom.

'Ah!' said Guest Gulkan, coming through the Door and looking around. 'A battlefield!'

'No need to sound so enthusiastic,' said Yot, still shaken by his dragon-encounter.

'Courage, man!' said Guest Gulkan, laying a hand on Yot's shoulder. 'It could be worse.'

'How?' said Yot.

'It could be raining,' said Gulkan.

The rest of the pirates came through the Door, joining Yot and Guest Gulkan on a dusty plain of battle beneath thunder-cloud skies.

'Oh man!' said Salaman Meerkat. 'Where are we now?'

He got no answer, but, for the record, they were on the Plain of Tazala. The army of cavalry, elephants, armoured infantry, scythe chariots, skirmishers and Silver Archers drawn up a hundred paces west of them was that of Aldarch the Third, Mutilator of Yestron and the ruler of most of it.

The opposing army, similar in composition, and raising a similar racket of war-chanting, trumpet-blowing, drum-beating and cymbal-clashing, belonged to the rebellious Boo Taboo, once High Eunuch in Aldarch's court.

Both armies had more than fifty imperial dragons apiece, and the fear-crazed beasts were adding their voices to the uproar.

'There is war here,' said Guest Gulkan stoutly, 'hence there is opportunity.'

'Looks a bloody right dangerous place to me,' said Jon Disaster. 'I'm not hanging around.'

And he vanished through the Door.

'He smart joker,' said Whale Mike. 'These people not sing much happy song.'

And Mike followed Jon through the Door.

But the others stood their ground as a rider came from the west on a caparisoned black charger. He was a huge man in crimson-tinted armour, his helm topped by a war-crest in the shape of a dragon. The lurid device on his shield was a decapitated head, its hair held by a grasping hand with blood-red talons.

He halted in front of them.

'Hi!' said Salaman Meerkat brightly. 'How would you like to hire some mercenaries?'

The stranger grunted.

He drew his sword, which was attached by a hulking length of chain to some part of his armour – so that, if

437

knocked from his grasp in battle, it would not fall away entirely, but would dangle until he could reach down and retrieve it.

'All good experienced men,' said Meerkat. 'All—'

But said no more, for the horseman lopped off his head.

Guest Gulkan slashed at the horseman, Ish Ulpin grabbed him by the foot to drag him from the saddle, Simp Fiche snatched a sword from Thelemite and stabbed the horse—

And Drake, who saw no profit in any of this activity, jumped through the Door. He blinked against darkness.

'Here Drake,' said Whale Mike.

'What kept you?' said Jon Disaster.

'Man, we've got a party going on back there,' said Drake. And then: 'Where are we?'

He began to make out what was going on. Mike and Disaster were keeping three strangers at bay. It was night; the scene was moonlit; they were in a clearing on a jungle-covered mountainside. All three strangers wore rustling clothes of leaves or grass. The night was dense with heat and humid perfumes.

'This smell good place,' said Mike. 'This warm. We stay, maybe. Make friends.'

'What?' said Drake. 'By singing happy song, perhaps?'

'No harm to try,' said Mike.

As he started to sing, Drake assessed the moonlit tableau. As well as the three grass-clad strangers, he saw scattered bowls, a couple of dead animals and, further away, two pyramids of something which was perhaps offal. Drake guessed that, here, the Door was worshipped as a sacred shrine.

In the shadow-tangled jungle beyond the clearing, strange creatures – birds? insects? – talked in screeching voices. Since they made this much noise by night, Drake wondered what the racket was like by day.

One of the grass-clad men tried to swat Disaster with a stick. Disaster cut the stick away with a single sword-stroke. Then all three strangers attacked him simultaneously. Reluctantly, Mike intervened with his titanium battle-rod, braining a couple of them.

'Let's leave,' said Drake.

'Nay, man,' said Disaster. 'We're winning, so why run?'

'We've won for the moment,' said Drake. 'But listen. Hear that? Sounds like people! Lots of them. Unhappy, too!'

As he spoke, a mob of grass-clad savages burst from the fringes of the jungle and attacked. Moments later, a brace of them had been broken by Mike's battle-rod, and the rest were running. Drake turned to the Door.

'You're not going, are you?' said Jon Disaster. 'They'll be back soon for some more games.'

'Then have fun,' said Drake. 'I'll see you later.'

'Nay, man,' said Disaster. 'Wait for the others.'

'We'll as like see them in hell as anywhere,' said Drake.

And, as Mike once more began to sing a happy song, Drake jumped through the Door. And instantly wished he had not.

In burning sunlight, a huge lizard-beast animated itself toward him on its two hind legs. Its front paws, built for grasping, had claws as fell as anything which ever stalked a nightmare. Drake was dimly aware of confused noise and shouting in the background, but all his attention was focused on the monster.

Yes, it was real.

Yes, he was not imagining it.

So . . .

'Nice to know you,' said Drake. 'Hello and goodbye!'

He leaped towards the Door – but was knocked down by a stranger jumping through it. Drake's sword went flying as they rolled off the plinth and onto the sand.

'Hey,' said Drake. 'We have to—'

Then said no more, for the stranger started to strangle him. The stranger was one of the men Jon Disaster and Whale Mike had so recently been contending with by moonlight.

439

Desperately, Drake fought to break the stranglehold. He could not! The stranger was strong, yes, built like a wrestler. Determined to kill. Drake, flat on his back on the sand, panting, sweating, struggling, saw the lizard-monster looming above them.

The lizard-monster leaned down casually.

Then struck.

It hooked huge claws under the stranger's ribs. It hoisted him up, then slashed at Drake with its spare man-mangler. Drake rolled sideways. Another stranger burst from the Door – and the monster grabbed him.

Holding a man in each clawed hand, it tried to cram both into its maw simultaneously. While it was thus occupied, Drake grabbed his sword.

'Gaaa!' he screamed.

And hacked the monster's guts open. It clapped its hands together, smashing its two claw-hooked prey together – then flung its arms wide, sending the two bodies flying.

The bodies fell sprawling to the dust.

The monster loomed over Drake, who was in easy reach of its jaws and claws. If he turned to run, it would kill him. He tried to ease himself backwards, shifting his boots shuffle by shuffle on the underfoot sand, keeping his eyes fixed on the monster.

With an oiled, fluid motion, slick as a fish swimming through water, the monster eased itself forward. Blood dripped slowly from its claws. Red blood.

Bugger! There was no getting away!

The monster was watching him, aye, staring him out, trying to paralyse him with terror. Yes, as weasel will paralyse rabbit.

'I'm no rabbit, man!' screamed Drake, in something close to hysteria.

He was panting frantically. His legs were shuddering. He was pissing himself. He was grasping his sword in a vice-like grip. He was a moment away from collapse. Then remembered – very clearly – duelling on the deck of the

Warwolf in the Penvash Channel. He remembered the weapons muqaddam saying:

'Grip, remember? Relaxed yet firm.'

Words like crystal.

'Yes,' hissed Drake, eyeing the monster, waiting for it to strike. 'Yes . . .'

He had his breathing under control now. He was remembering the weapons muqaddam preaching:

'Breathing in battle is life, is death. Breathe deep. Breathe slow. Master fear through your breathing.'

And Drake hissed:

'Yes . . .'

And remembered the weapons muqaddam's favourite saying, which lived on though the man himself was dead:

'If you must die, then die with style!'

'Yes!' shouted Drake.

Convincing himself of his courage.

And the monster roared. Lunging at Drake with its jaws.

Drake met teeth with bronze.

As metal and ivory clashed, Jon Disaster came leaping through the Door.

'Gaaa!' screamed Drake.

Swinging again at the monster.

As he did so – Disaster struck. He chopped into the monster's tail. It tried to turn, swinging its neck around – and Drake, with a scream, hacked at the neck.

The monster wavered.

Jon Disaster tucked his sword under his arm as if it were a spear, and charged, coming at the creature from behind, sinking good bronze deep into its spine. As it subsided, Drake swung again at its neck, once, twice, then thrice.

Then wiped some of the blood and sweat from his face, and looked around for fresh enemies.

Finding none.

Now he had time to attend to something further removed than the threat of imminent death, he saw he was standing in a huge circular arena ringed with walls of white marble rising high and bright to tiers of seating where tens of thousands of people stood waving, shouting, cheering, jeering, or screaming with excitement. That was the source of the audio confusion he had been vaguely aware of all through his monster-fight.

'Thanks, fans,' said Drake, in a sardonic voice which suggested his nerves were in a much better state than they were.

He began to strut his stuff, waving to the crowd, and blowing kisses in all directions. This posturing performance took him to a tall much-gargoyled pillar of stone standing amidst the sands of the arena just thirty paces from the Door.

Tied to it was a man with purple skin and violet eyes. He wore a purple robe clasped with a golden brooch. Gold hung from his ears. Was it . . . ? Yes. It was Prince Oronoko. Drake never forgot a truly hated rival. So who was that tied to the other side of the gargoyled post?

It proved to be a high-breasted woman with flaming red hair. Her cloak was also purple, but her skin was the same red as her hair.

'Zanya!' shouted Drake.

His voice, hoarse with a regular battle-thirst, cracked as he screamed her name. She looked at him with eyes dull with the horrors of imprisonment, nightmare and threat of death.

'Who are you?' she said.

'You know who I am!' said Drake. 'Your lover! Your one and only love! Your true love, aye!'

'I have no love,' said Zanya, in a dull voice. 'I live only for the Flame.'

'But I love you!' said Drake.

'Are you an emissary from the Flame?' she asked, bewildered at these declarations of love from a total stranger.

'Yes,' said Drake, deciding that full explanations of his undying love for her could wait until later.

And he cut her loose.

'My name is Zanya,' she said.

442

'I know,' said Drake. 'Didn't I just shout your name? You are Zanya Kliedervaust, the most beautiful woman in the whole world.'

'The Flame has no use for beauty,' said Zanya, speaking like one drugged or drunk. Or sleeptalking, perhaps.

'You're beautiful regardless,' said Drake. 'And passionate. Gouda Muck told me. He said you dream nightly of lust.'

'Yes,' she said, shocked to realize Gouda Muck had somehow divined her secret at a distance and communicated it to this stranger.

'Gouda Muck sent me here,' said Drake, inventing furiously. 'He sent me to gratify your physical passion and impregnate you with many children.'

Zanya swayed on her feet.

'I think we may have a communications problem here,' she said faintly. 'I don't think Gouda Muck could have said quite that. Anyway, arguments later – cut free our fellow worshipper.'

And she pointed at purple-skinned Oronoko.

'As you wish, Zanya,' said Drake, who did not think this strictly necessary.

Oronoko, cut free, began to massage his wrists, but added nothing to their conversation since he still spoke no Galish.

'Oh, look!' said Zanya. 'Two more striders!'

She pointed to a gate set in the wall of the arena, from which another two lizard-monsters were venturing.

'See that steel arch but thirty paces away?' said Drake. 'It's a Door to Elsewhere. Run for it!'

They ran toward the Door. But halted abruptly as a dozen savages burst out of it. The savages milled around screaming in a battle-frenzy. The striders came on with huge, loping strides. Running. Animated nightmares.

'We're doomed!' cried Zanya.

Then the savages scattered away from the Door. Something had come through that Door. Something big. Twice as tall as a man. As broad in the shoulders as a man's outstretched arms. It carried a great metal rod in its hands.

'Watch out!' screamed Zanya. 'A giant!'

'That's no giant,' said Drake. 'That's Whale Mike. As he'd say – he my friend.'

The savages ran, fearing for their lives. But the striders had no such fear. On they came. Drake hauled Zanya into the safety of Mike's shadow. Oronoko followed, not knowing what else to do.

'This strange place,' said Mike, looking around.

'This very strange place,' said Drake.

Then the first of the striders was upon them. Whale Mike swung his battle-rod. *Thwap!* The monster's head exploded into a spray of blood and bone. Its headless body went down, limbs flailing, kicking up sprays of sand.

'Oh, great stuff, great stuff!' said Drake. 'Mike, you could just about take on a watermelon stand!'

'He could just about what?' said Zanya.

'Do battle with a watermelon stand,' said Drake. 'They're fearful dangerous, man.'

'I'm a woman,' she said. 'And you're babbling. And – look, there's crocodiles!'

As Mike dealt death to the second strider, Drake looked where Zanya was pointing and saw a horde of low-slung beasts slithering out of the gate from whence the striders had come.

'Those are crocodiles?' he said, disappointed. 'I thought they'd be bigger.'

'They're four times man-length,' said Zanya, 'and there's dozens of them. Isn't that enough for you? Where's this Door you were talking about?'

'There!' said Drake, pointing at the silver screen humming in the steel archway.

And he hustled her through it.

Oronoko saw them vanish – but held his ground. He was confused. Bemused. He didn't know what to make of it. That, under the circumstances, was pardonable.

'Don't wait around, man!' yelled Jon Disaster. 'This place is bad news!'

444

And he hustled through the Door, dragging Oronoko with him. The pair found themselves on a beach. With Drake. And Zanya. And a heap of hands and feet. And some discarded spears. Some swords. Oronoko armed himself.

'Where do you think we are?' said Drake.

'Somewhere cold,' said Zanya, shivering in her thin purple robe.

The sea was a grey-thrash wilderness. The beach was brown-scab desolation of sand, rock and fractured rust. The hinterland was a desolation of wind-spiking reeds. Out of the reeds, with a scream, came a dozen warriors. They wore leather breeches and sheepskin jackets.

'Run!' screamed Drake.

He hauled Zanya through the Door. And found himself on a marble plinth in a ruin-ringed slade deep in a bitter-chill forest. He was back in the Old City where he had first entered the Circle of the Door.

The muddy clearing was littered with carcasses. Corpses of three dozen warriors dressed in leather breeches and sheepskin jackets. Bodies of sixteen grey armoured monsters slaughtered by those warriors. At the edge of the forest, one poor fellow was yelling his head off as a great yellow slug browsed on his legs.

Drake turned back to the Door. Then stopped. What? Go round again? No, that was crazy. Better to wait here for the others, who couldn't be far behind.

'Welcome to my nightmare,' said Drake to Zanya. 'This is the Old City of Penvash Utter.'

'Is it?' said Zanya, without much interest.

'Aye,' said Drake. 'My grandfather ruled here once, when my family was still kings and all.'

'Oh,' said Zanya, in her dull sleepwalking voice. Then: 'I'm cold.'

'There's a cure for that,' said Drake, jumping down from the marble plinth. 'As long as you're not fussy.'

Zanya, as unfussy as they come, was soon dressed in leather breeches cut off just below the knees, and a warm

445

sheepskin jacket. She wore her purple cloak over those garments.

'Where are we?' she said.

'As I told you,' said Drake. 'In Penvash. The north-west corner of Argan. Understand?'

He was alarmed to find her mind so foggy when the demands of survival were so great.

'Oh,' she said. 'Penvash. I've been here before, I think. In a dream. But . . . what . . . what's that . . . ?'

She pointed at a slug, which was cruising towards them. Very calmly. Other slugs were emerging from the forest. Slowly, they oozed over the dead, absorbing them. The screaming man at the forest's edge stopped screaming. He was dead.

'Those slugs are murder,' said Drake. 'Stay away from them.'

One was very close now.

'Shall we run?' said Zanya.

'I'm tired of running,' said Drake. And, to the slug: 'Come on then.'

As the slug came within range, Drake hacked with his sword. The bronze gashed home sweetly. With a hiss, the entire blade sizzled into steam. Drake was left holding the hilt alone. Phlegmatically, the slug oozed forward, oblivious of the weak slurry of yellow spilling from its wound.

'Now we run!' yelled Drake.

He snatched up a club, Zanya grabbed a spare spear, and they scarpered into the forest. When they stopped, both panting, Drake realized he was disorientated. Lost, in fact.

He smelt burning. Yes. With Zanya in tow, he followed the smell to a wall of blue crystal fronting a burnt-out stretch of forest which reached away to an identical crystal wall. At least he knew where they were. The crystal walls ran east-west.

'*Moka salitina*,' said a low-pitched voice.

'*Gomo sapasalarpa*,' answered another.

Drake crouched. Zanya followed suit. Shortly they saw

two warriors in sheepskin jackets prowling through the forest just west of them. As soon as these were out of sight, Drake led the way east. Toward the river.

'Where are we going?' said Zanya.

'There's a river,' said Drake. 'It runs south to Lorford. That's a town in Estar. That's—'

'I know where Estar is,' said Zanya.

Her voice sounded crisper, firmer, as if possession of a battle-spear had awakened her intelligence. Good. The last thing Drake needed right now was for his woman to collapse into a helpless heap of whimpering femininity.

They went slowly, cautiously, until they reached the river-bank. What now?

'Sit down,' said Drake. 'We'll wait for my friends.'

'Friends?'

'The – the giant you saw with the metal rod. And some other people. We'll wait for them.'

But, if the others reached the Old City, they'd surely make for the west, not the east to which Drake had been driven by stranger danger. Or maybe Rolf Thelemite or some other hero would lead them round the Circle again, hoping to make for the Castle of Controlling Power if all the green centipedes by Drangsturm were dead or glutted.

This was very difficult!

Tiny drops of rain, sieved from low cloud above, fell all around, utterly soundless but very cold.

'Bugger!' said Drake.

'The Flame,' said Zanya, 'does not approve of such talk.'

'Then bugger the Flame,' said Drake.

'You can't say that!' she said, in an animated voice of anger nothing at all like the drugged tones in which she had spoken earlier.

'I'll say what I like,' said Drake. 'Bugger the Flame!'

He shouted it. And heard, as if in answer to his shout, a grunt from the forest. Then saw, crunching towards them, a grey monster with spiked head and a collar of natural armour around its neck.

'A monster,' he said.

'No,' said Zanya. 'Two monsters. There's another behind it. Look!'

She was right.

'Oh no,' said Drake softly.

As the monsters paced toward them, Drake vaulted over the first crystal wall and began to run for the second. A wall of fire roared from the second wall and marched toward him. He ran back to Zanya. The monsters charged.

'The river!' yelled Zanya. 'It's our only hope!'

Abandoning her spear, she jumped. Drake hesitated. He snatched up the spear. He threw it at the nearest monster. He missed.

'Bugger bugger bugger!' he sobbed.

Then, screaming, jumped into the river. The river which had eaten his comrade Raggage Pouch just the day before.

Water snatched him. He was swept towards the fire-wall, which raged across the river and up the further bank and on into the forest. At the last moment, he ducked his head into the unknown horrors of the Waters Below – and was carried under the fire-wall.

He surfaced beyond the flames and struck out for the shore. The river ripped him downstream. The bitter cold was swiftly sapping the last of his strength.

Ahead, rocks divided the waters. Something big and red was on those rocks. Another monster? No, it was Zanya! He held out his hand; she grabbed it; she hauled him onto the rocks. He clung to her, sobbing, gasping, soaked, cold, shivering.

'Are you all right?' she said. 'Hush now, hush. You're going to be all right.'

Slowly she soothed him.

At last, calmer now, he had the strength to smile and say:

'Man, you look as beautiful as when I first saw you.'

'And when was that?' she said.

'Don't you remember? Why, I was in the water, a horizon away from Stokos. And you in a ship, aye, a ship of more colours than a rainbow. I asked you to marry me. Remember?'

Zanya looked puzzled. Then:

'Oh! Now I remember you! You're the fisherman from that boat which got mauled by a kraken.'

'Aye,' said Drake, remembering the lie he had told to explain his presence in the sea. 'That's me. The sole survivor. Only I'm a swordsmith, not a fisherman.'

'Of course you are!' said Zanya. 'You told me all about it when we met again on Burntos. I remember now! You're – Arabin lol Arabin. Right?'

'Right,' said Drake, beaming.

'The one who tried to rape me in Cam!'

'What?' said Drake, in dismay. 'That business in the leper colony? You're not still on about that, are you? I explained that on Burntos. It wasn't me, man! It was witchcraft making my body do horrible disgusting things, that's what it was. The wizard Miphon said as much. Remember?'

'He also said to me, in private,' said Zanya, 'that you were the most trouble he'd seen in one package in the last fifty years. He warned me to watch out for you. Not that I needed much warning!'

'Hey,' said Drake, aggrieved. 'I'm a nice guy.'

'Oh yes! The nice guy who jumped on top of me in Cam! Yes, that's what you did! Jumped right on top of me! Just like an animal! Well, don't try anything like that here or you'll be in really big trouble!'

'I think,' said Drake, a touch of sullen anger in his voice, 'I think I'm entitled at least to the normal hero's reward. Rescuing fair damsels in distress and all that. You know how it is.'

'Yes,' said Zanya. 'The rescued damsel marries the hero. She owes him. Well, you owe me. I saved you from the sea off Stokos.'

'That's not true!' said Drake. 'You had a whole ship-load of men to help in the rescue.'

'And you had your giant-friend to help when you came

for me,' said Zanya. 'Anyway, I saved your life again, just five heartbeats ago, when I hauled you from the river. So I owe you nothing. Even if I did, I'm not free to lust or to marry. My body is consecrated to the Flame.'

She said it with determination. They stared at each other. Wet. Shivering. Hunched on the rock like starving animals about to fall to fighting over a bone. Close enough to kiss. Her lips red, rich. Warm. Surely.

A kiss will discover.

'Dearest heart,' murmured Drake.

And, seizing his chance, he kissed her. His lips met hers. Flesh against flesh. He felt her will relax. Imagined her body prone or supine beneath him, he'd take her either way, whichever way she fancied. He broke the kiss. He was feeling good. Triumphant. Smiling.

'You liked that,' he said. 'Didn't you?'

'Yes,' she said.

Then pushed him off the rock.

Suggesting that sometimes, when a woman says yes, she actually means no.

'Hey!' shouted Drake, thrashing in the river. 'Hey! Help! Help!'

'You gave me no choice!' yelled Zanya, explaining herself.

But he was not interested in explanations, only in help. But of course there was no help. He saw another rock. Grabbed for it. But it was too slippery to hang on to.

The waters pulled him loose in a trice, rolled him over, ducked him under, thrashed him through some rapids, then bustled him away in a hurry, taking him south down the Valley of Forgotten Dreams.

37

Valley of Forgotten Dreams: river valley in Penvash in far north-west of Argan, shunned and avoided by Melski of Penvash; Old City (dating back to Technic Renaissance) lies in its northern reaches; steep, heavily-forested terrain features wide range of fauna including bush rats, bears and foddens.

Dawn.

Dreldragon Drakedon Douay huddled on the banks of a small river running through the Valley of Forgotten Dreams in Penvash. Upstream lay the Old City, a place he remembered, by now, only as a chaotic hell of ravening jaws and screaming blood. There was no sun-sign, but strengthening light at last convinced him it was indeed morning. With the greatest of reluctance, he groped down to the river.

Everything hurt.

There was no part of him which had not been jarred, banged or knocked, scraped, grazed, shaken, bruised, bitten or stung, gored, burnt by fire or by ice, sprained, strained, cracked, blistered, bloodied, dislocated, incised, punctured, lacerated or pounded by rolling pins and knapping hammers.

He had not heeded the damage as he dared the Circle of the Door, plunging recklessly from Here to Elsewhere, from the Old City to a burning forest, an ocean cay, to Drangsturm south, to a frozen mountainside, a plain of battle, a tropical jungle, a foreign arena, to a cannibal beach, then back to the Old City again. Adventuring thus, he had been oblivious to trauma because of the shock, excitement and bewilderment of the moment – and the adrenalin seething through his system. But he felt it now.

Probably, he had damaged himself the worst while bumping down the river after finally fleeing the Old City. But the pains in his back, neck and shoulder were mostly from muscles wrenched by reckless sword-swinging, his earache was the aftermath of violent pressure changes from sea-level to mountain heights, and the agony of his feet was from the cumulative damage of many days of journey. Feet, yes. He durst not take off his boots. If he did, his feet might fall off entirely.

He reached the water at last, after a journey short in space but memorable for the amount of pain, caution and endeavour it had entailed. The river purled along swiftly, slick as fish scales, cold as yesterday's rats' piss, surface sheening and shining with the greys of lead, steel, thunder-cloud, ash, charcoal, failed phoenix, dead mushrooms, basilisk blood, quelaquire, mosquito wings, wormskin wine and threadneedle mould.

Drake stuck a hand into the water, but caught no colours, only a chill clarity that swirled into turbulence as it snagged his fingers, kicked up tiny jags of foam, rippled, queried, tested, spun into miniature whirlpools then moulded itself back into the onflow which sped, talking in hustling-bustling accents of nonsense, down toward the distant (imaginary?) sea.

Slowly, Drake lifted a handful of water, sought his face, saw only the sword-blisters on his palm. Dirt and old blood lining his life-line. A rippling shimmer of daylight, mostly at the edges of this puddle, where water bordered skin. Why did it ripple? Because his hand was shaking.

In the river, too, he saw not his face – only the ever-shift of twenty million greys, and, beyond and below, rock, clean shingle, a wavering trail of waterweed, then a confusion of inscrutable darkness in which lay rocks or rotten logs or monsters. He sucked water from his hand.

Cold. It hurt his teeth. He swilled it round then spat it out, seeing a thread of blood give contrast, for a moment, to the clears and greys of the ever-rush.

Slowly, he reached into the river, let his fingers crayfish toward waterweed, lobstered it, vultured it back, sucked it down, and wondered why it had no taste to speak of, and why his flesh had bones in it, and why he was crying. His tears were hot, the hottest thing in the world. And their taste was salt. Yes. Salt like the sea.

The sea which was not, then – perhaps – entirely imaginary. So if – just supposing, now – he was to take one step south then another, then . . . why, with enough steps he might (no promises, mind) one day (a year distant, perhaps) maybe just possibly arrive at a brisk shore of sails.

Beside that shore (presuming, which is not necessarily the case, that the world of bread and ale and clinking coins exists, that there are taverns warm with beer and laughter where cheers are raised), yes, there will be bread, and . . .

And . . . ?

He stared blankly at the water. He had been thinking of something. What? Bread? But bread was, surely, if anything, imaginary . . . or at least a world away from the ever-last river-run where the clears danced, yes, danced upon greys . . .

Drake, thought and hope abandoned, sat staring into the running water, knees drawn up to chest, arms wrapped around knees, chin knobbled down hard between the thin-skinned bones of his kneecaps, his body rocking a little this way and that as a thin seedy rain began to fall, dull as famine, grey as weariness, persistent as a year-nagging voice of senility.

Drake was still sitting there, much later, when a noise made him look up. And look north. Something was coming downstream. A monster. Huge. It had two heads, one set above the other. A baby monster walked beside it. Drake looked away. Probably it was just a hallucination. And if it was real? If it was real, he was in no state to run . . .

The monster came on. And began to sing a happy song.

Drake looked again, and saw it was Whale Mike, with Zanya Kliedervaust riding on his shoulders. Walking beside Mike was Jon Arabin. Slowly, Drake stood.

Whale Mike finished his happy song as he drew level with Drake. Whereupon he halted, and waited for someone to take the lead. But, for the moment, nobody did. Zanya looked down on Drake, saying nothing. And Jon Arabin also said nothing.

All four said nothing as the querulous rain nagged without reason and the river-rush quibbled away between branch and stone and the hollow muscles of their hearts worked their way with what blood remained to them. Then Drake and Arabin embraced.

Both wept.

'Well, man,' said Jon Arabin, shaking his head. 'Well, man, who would have thought it . . .'

But he said nothing more and nothing more cogent.

'You better get down,' said Mike to Zanya, kneeling. 'These two not good for much. I think we make fire.'

Zanya dismounted, and searched out kindling. Mike mutilated some defenceless trees and heaped up branches for firewood.

'Jon,' said Mike. 'You better make fire. I can, but I not so good at that. You better.'

Today, Jon Arabin was not much good with the tinder box himself. As flint and steel stumbled between his fingers, he started weeping, helplessly. He was too old for this.

'Drake,' he said. 'Help me out.'

But Drake was in no better condition. He sat waiting for Zanya to ask why her ardent lover had been addressed as 'Drake'. Once she discovered he was Drake Douay, son of the Demon Hagon, there would be hell to pay. But she appeared not to notice.

'Let me,' she said firmly.

And took steel and flint, and did what was necessary.

Once the fire was burning bright, Whale Mike dipped into his leather apron pocket and hauled out a huge chunk of bloody meat.

'This from monster,' he said cheerfully. 'Maybe good eating, eh? We cook. We find out.'

He spiked bits of it onto branches. In the fierce quick heat, it burnt instead of cooking. But when chunks were handed around – half blood, half char – there were no complaints. Warmth, meat and companionship began to make Drake feel better. He looked at Zanya.

'Don't even think about it!' she said, with danger in her voice.

'Have you two met, then?' said Jon Arabin, puzzled at the way Zanya reacted to Drake.

'Met!' said Zanya. 'He tried to rape me once!'

'I'm . . . I'm sorry,' said Drake.

Which was an unusual thing for him to say. But today he was utterly shagged out, and in no state to tell witch-craft lies, or to insist on the right of men to the bodies of women.

Jon Arabin looked on the pair with speculative eyes. Was this his chance? He had killed several times while venturing round the Circle of the Door. His death-debt was heavy indeed. It was more important than ever that he breed more children, thus winning himself life-credits and appeasing his gods. Or . . .

Again, Arabin thought of converting Drake to the Creed of Anthus, setting him up with a harem then buying life-credits from him. Unfortunately, Arabin's gods only allowed him to buy life-credits from a fellow-believer . . .

Two problems, then:

(a) to convert Drake to the Creed of Anthus;
(b) to get Drake breeding.

Whale Mike shared out a second helping of meat. They ate in silence, while Jon Arabin thought hard. Then he said to Drake:

'You know this lady, do you?'

'Aye,' said Drake, in a dull voice. 'She won't agree to it, but I've . . . man, I've been in love with her these many years. It was for her I named that bay on Island Tor.'

'What?' said Jon Arabin. 'That was Zanya Bay, wasn't it? Then this must be Zanya herself.'

'Zanya Kliedervaust,' she said, coldly.

They had not previously introduced themselves.

'Ah,' said Jon Arabin. 'Lucky woman, to be so loved. A bay of beauty named for her. Aye. Pale sands and water beautiful as her eyes.'

'Nice eyes,' agreed Drake.

'It was for her you named that flower, too, wasn't it?' said Arabin.

Drake took the hint.

'Two flowers, actually,' he said. 'One was Zanya's Beauty. That was the great red trumpet-shaped flower which hung in clusters from those trees with pink leaves. The other flower was Zanya's Delight. That was fragile, aye, a splendorous thing growing in waterfalls from the headland rocks, smooth as gold and as yellow, fragrant as peaches by sunset.'

His voice was dreamy.

'Aye,' said Arabin, 'I remember now.'

'You named flowers after me?' said Zanya, wondering at this.

'I told you,' said Drake. 'I've been in love with you for years.'

'Aye,' said Jon Arabin. 'He'd talk of you in his sleep, and charm the silence with poems of your tender beauty. Which I thought strange at the time. But now I see you, I think it strange no longer. You're worthy of all his devotion.'

'I . . . I don't know what to say,' said Zanya.

'You are beautiful,' said Drake. 'And I do . . . I do love you.'

'But why did you – why did you jump on top of me like that? Was it really because of witchcraft?'

'Sometimes,' said Drake, 'sometimes it's hard for a man to control himself. Men . . . men need women.'

'Yes,' said Whale Mike cheerfully. 'Good for man to have woman. Woman nice. This one nice, eh? She got soft

456

arse. She make good screw, eh? Good meat.'

And he smacked his lips and laughed.

Whereupon Zanya's temper flared instantly. With the energy of fire and meat inside her, she raged at them:

'You filthy dirty animals! I am not meat!'

Drake, desperately trying to salvage the situation, said:

'My dearest darling—'

'Don't you dearest darling me!'

'But I love you! Zanya, I love you!'

'You like. You want. You need. Perhaps. But not me. Oh no, not me. Just meat, heat, lips, breast, thigh, crotch, nipple, arse. What is this?'

And she cupped one of her convexities, which was visible beneath sheepskin jacket and purple robe.

'It's a breast,' said Drake. 'And, I venture, a very pretty one. The prettiness of your curves, darling—'

'It's meat, that's what it is! Meat, not me!'

'But are your breasts not part of you?' said Drake.

'They're not me! Not the – the person inside this – oh grief – you! – it's meat, isn't it? That's what I am to you! Meat! Offal! Wet liver! You're all the same, you men. Just one thing, that's all it is.'

And anger gave way to grief.

The whole sorry history of her terrible time as a priestess of the Orgy God came rushing back to her. Year upon year of nightmare. Sweat, heat, weight, panting flesh. Bruising laughter. Disease, misery, exhaustion, contempt. And—

It was too much.

She broke down in tears.

'Well, bugger you then!' said Drake. 'I'm buggered if I know what I did wrong!'

And he got to his feet and stalked away into the forest.

'Where are you going?' called Jon Arabin.

'Hunting!' shouted Drake.

'You come back here!'

'Go nalsh yourself!' yelled Drake.

And was soon lost from sight in the forest.

'You not cry,' said Whale Mike to Zanya. 'You not

457

make self pretty when cry. You nice. Want marry me? I like woman with soft arse.'

Zanya screamed, and hit him with all her strength. Which made very little impression on him.

'Mike,' said Jon Arabin, 'I've decided we're going to camp here. We'll wait. See if any of the others come downstream. So we'll need a shelter. Start getting branches together so we can build something.'

'That good thinking,' said Whale Mike. 'You smart man, Jon. I do that.'

And he got to work.

Then Jon Arabin took his time. He let the fire die down then cooked a small bit of meat on the red embers. Carefully.

'You don't have to eat this,' he said to Zanya. 'But you might feel better if you did.'

As she ate, he built up the fire again.

'Now,' he said. 'You don't have to talk to me. You don't have to tell me anything. But if you want to, I'm here to listen.'

'Who are you?' she said.

For when Whale Mike and Jon Arabin had found her by the riverside, they had not explained themselves. Mike had just ordered her to ride, and she, faced with such threatening bulk, had hardly been in a position to resist.

'I am Jon Arabin,' said Jon Arabin. 'I was born on Ashmolea. Aye. That's east of Argan.'

'I know that,' said she.

'Of course you would, you being from Ebrell. Anyway. My mother was a calligrapher, my father a paper-maker. I was raised to be a scholar.'

'And now?'

'Now I'm an adventurer.'

'A pirate, perhaps,' said Zanya.

'That's a hard word,' said Jon Arabin. 'Often I've made an honest living. Aye, trading pearls and timber. Young Drake has helped me with that.'

'Drake?'

'Has he told you another name, perhaps? It's our angry young hunter I'm talking about.'

'Oh, him,' said Zanya. 'He told me he was Arabin lol Arabin.'

'Well,' said Arabin, proceeding cautiously because he was not sure what was afoot. 'He gives that name because he acknowledges me as a father. I'm Arabin, and, well, Arabin lol Arabin, that means I'm his father. Do you understand? I ask because you sound a stranger to the Galish.'

'I still have my problems with the Trading Tongue,' admitted Zanya. 'But you've explained the name all right. But how can – how can you be his father? I mean, the skins . . .'

'His mother was a gold-skinned woman from Ling,' said Arabin solemnly, 'and the mixing of black and gold gives his cockroach colour.'

'Oh,' said Zanya. 'Now . . . tell me of these other names he calls himself. How many does he have?'

'Many,' said Arabin, sliding away from the unknown danger which he sensed within the question. 'Why, he's such a wild one I scarcely know myself what name he'll be playing from one day to the next. Wild, aye. No doubting it. Why, once he cooked me a meal of rats and cockroaches. To this day, he doesn't think I realize. But I know a rat from a rabbit, even if the Walrus doesn't!'

And he told Zanya the story of Drake's shipboard cookery, or as much as he knew of it. She had to laugh.

'But,' she said. 'Why did he play such an ugly trick on you?'

'Because he's wild, as I said,' declared Jon Arabin. 'Part of it comes with being less tall than he'd want to be. Short men must set themselves on stilts of some sort. That's the way of it. So I make allowances.'

'But why did you . . . why did you eat that meal?'

'Well, rat's okay, and cockroach isn't too bad. If it's cooked right, and if you can get your mind off what you're eating. Anyway, it was either eat it or betray him to the

459

wrath of the Walrus. Would I betray my own son?'

'The thought of discipline must at least have tempted you,' said Zanya.

'But I love him,' said Jon Arabin.

'You love?' said Zanya, shocked. 'Your own son? You love him?'

'Woman!' said Arabin. 'What a mind you've got! A man can love his son without lusting for his arsehole. And this boy of mine . . . well, he saved my ship once.'

'In truth?' said Zanya.

'In truth,' said Arabin.

And told of Drake's part in a shipboard battle against a Neversh.

'Well . . .' said Zanya, 'I can see . . . yes, why a man would like a – a son like that. But for a woman . . .'

'I know,' said Arabin, with sympathy which was not entirely pretended. 'He's rough. But there's a reason.'

'What reason?'

'Ah. He doesn't know that I know. So you must swear never to betray me to him.'

'I swear,' said Zanya, for curiosity had got the better of her.

'In truth,' said Jon Arabin. 'A truth I swear to on my mother's honour, young Drake is a virgin. He's never been had by a man. And he's never taken boy or woman in lust. Ah, he'll boast with a swagger, but it's bluster talking. That's a sore hurt to his pride, that he's still a virgin. That's why he . . . why . . .'

'He doesn't really know how to talk to a woman,' said Zanya.

'Right,' said Arabin. 'He's scared, aye, shy and scared. Hence he talks tough and acts rough. To conceal his tenderness, which shames him. To hide his fear. In truth . . . you're a woman, and, though he'll not admit it, he's scared of you.'

'I see . . .' said Zanya.

Not sure whether to believe all this.

Jon Arabin and Zanya thereafter sat side by side in

460

silence until Whale Mike had finished his work. He sat down by the fire with a sigh.

'This good fire,' he said. 'Fire good friend.'

'Fire is sacred,' said Zanya. 'The Flame is the High God of All Gods.'

'Oh,' said Mike. 'You think like Drake.'

'You mean Arabin lol Arabin?' said Zanya.

'Yes,' said Jon Arabin. 'It's my son Mike means when he talks of Drake. But you won't be surprised if he fumbles the names at times.'

'No,' said Zanya, understanding that an obvious imbecile like Whale Mike could be expected to speak error as often as truth.

'Drake okay, whatever you call him,' said Mike amiably.

'Does . . . does he worship the Flame?' said Zanya.

'He tell big story in Brennan,' said Mike. 'He say he priest of Flame. I think maybe joke. We drinking back then. But few days ago, Drake talk about Flame. He very serious. Well, Yot do most talking.'

'Yot?' said Zanya. 'Not the Favoured Disciple?'

'This Yot,' said Mike. 'He tall guy. Many warts.'

'That's him!' said Zanya. 'Muck's Favoured Disciple! We thought he was dead. What's he been doing? Has he been preaching the Flame?'

'He talk enough,' said Mike. 'Maybe too much. Ish Ulpin, he pissed off, not like to hear god-talk. He say Yot shut up or get eaten.'

'So Yot was with you,' said Zanya. 'And Drake . . . Drake is a priest of the Flame. That's very strange. But what's this business of Drake drinking? A priest of the Flame doesn't drink. Liquor is not pure.'

'Mike,' said Jon Arabin. 'How about you go hunting?'

'If you want, Jon,' said Mike. 'But I not got weapon. I had nice stick, strong stuff like steel, but that lost in river.'

'Never mind,' said Jon Arabin. 'I'm sure you'll manage.'

Obediently, Whale Mike took himself off into the

461

forest. When he was gone, Jon Arabin told Zanya about how Drake had been cursed, and could never get drunk.

How did Jon Arabin know?

The barman who had helped Drake learn about the curse had later told Arabin all about it.

Indeed, while Drake prided himself on having a great many important secrets which nobody knew anything about, he was virtually transparent to Jon Arabin – who, after all, had not become a ship's captain and a leader of men by accident.

'So you see,' concluded Jon Arabin, 'whether liquor is pure or otherwise makes no difference to my son, who drinks what he likes but never gets drunk. Hence has no pleasure in it.'

'Then he should be glad of what he calls a curse,' said Zanya. 'For it makes him pure without effort.'

'But takes away his free will,' said Jon Arabin.

'Why,' said Zanya, slowly. 'So it does. I can see why that would . . . that might be hard to take, at times . . .'

She sat back, thinking. So her lover, Arabin lol Arabin, was a priest of the Flame. Then why did he sometimes call himself Drake? The son of Hagon bore that ugly name. Surely a priest of the Flame would not call himself that. Unless . . .

'I think you're lying,' said Zanya. 'I don't see how a priest of the Flame could live as a pirate. Our angry young hunter – he's Dreldragon Drakedon Douay, isn't he? The son of Hagon! The Evil One! The Demon's son!'

Her voice was hard, strident, rising in fear and anger. But Jon Arabin just laughed. It took some effort to conjure up that laugh, but he managed it all the same.

'Why are you laughing?' said Zanya, fierce and flushed. 'It's true, isn't it? Your son is no son of yours but a son of Hagon!'

'Woman,' said Arabin, 'if Sully Yot has survived the Circle of the Door, then likely he'll come down the river and prove out the fact that a priest of the Flame can live as a pirate. Before you say more mad things of my son, what say we wait till we see what survivors come downriver?'

'And if nobody comes?' said Zanya.

'Then you'll have to do some thinking!' said Arabin. 'There's three of us, one of you. If we were ruthless, would we wait before raping? Nay, woman. If my son were the Evil One, he'd have cock to quim in a moment. But have we not saved you? Sheltered you? Fed you?'

Zanya made no reply.

'You've a mind at least warped in parts,' said Arabin. 'I don't blame you for it, since it's life which makes minds, for the most part. But give thought to that warping. Remember, Whale Mike bore witness. My son has been seeking to make conversions to your Flame. Aye, at risk of his own life.'

'That . . . that's so,' said Zanya, slowly.

She was starting to feel ashamed of the way she had spoken.

'Woman,' said Arabin, 'perhaps my son uses the name of Drake on occasion, for purposes of survival or otherwise. I know not. Perhaps he calls himself Drake Douay on occasion, or even Dreldragon Drakedon Douay. Well then. Is that so remarkable? A priest of the Flame is pushed to some strange expedients to survive. Remember that.'

'I will,' said Zanya.

'And remember this,' said Arabin. 'My son is wild, as I've said. But he's hardly a hell-fiend. Nay, he's good, in truth. The core of him is solid. Which is why I love him.'

He stared at Zanya till she dropped her eyes. Then he took her hand and, lightly, gently, kissed it.

'Why did you do that?' she said.

'Because I, too, find it hard to resist the allure of your beauty,' answered Jon Arabin, in utter truth.

Much later, Drake returned from the forest. One look at his face told Zanya he had been crying. He held out the spoils of his hunt: some lugs of fungus garnered from a rotten tree.

'This is not much,' he said. 'But it's what I have. It's yours.'

'Thank you,' she said.

Later, Whale Mike returned by a different route. He was singing a happy song, and with good reason – he had killed two dog-sized fox-fur creatures of the type the expedition had first found when digging for what they thought were gwiffs.

Later still, Jon Disaster came down the river. Alone. He was more than glad to see them.

'And,' he said, with a grin at Zanya, 'it's good to see we've got some hot meat with us.'

'Man,' said Drake, with violence in his voice. 'Watch your tongue.'

'What did I say wrong?' said Disaster, aggrieved.

Drake pointed at the dead dog-creatures.

'See that?' he said. 'That's meat.'

He pointed at Zanya.

'And that, that's a woman. There's a difference.'

Jon Disaster didn't see that there was, but he had enough sense not to argue about it.

Towards evening, snow started to fall, whispering down from a darkening sky. Jon Arabin, Jon Disaster, Whale Mike, Zanya Kliedervaust and Drake Douay built their fire higher. And that fire, seen from afar, brought the last of the stragglers down the river to their position.

The stragglers, Sully Yot and Prince Oronoko amongst them, came in slowly, slow as a bunch of crippled criminals walking to their own hanging dragging a ship's anchor with them as they went and dying of scurvy and roundworm on the way. And when they found not just fire but, as well, meat and shelter, they wept for gratitude and relief.

All spent that night under a single lean-to shelter. Zanya slept wedged between Drake Douay and Jon Arabin. And, while there was but one woman between many men, that made no trouble. Not, at any rate, on the first night.

38

Survivors: Drake Douay (aka Arabin lol Arabin), Sully
Yot (the Favoured Disciple), Jon Arabin (the Warwolf),
Slagger Mulps (the Walrus), Rolf Thelemite (oathbreaker
accursed of Rovac), Jon Disaster (slayer of monsters),
Whale Mike (by common agreement, an imbecile just
smart enough to put one foot in front of another), Bucks
Cat (a husky Talsh-born maroon with a grinning throat-
scar speaking his luck), Simp Fiche (a degenerate pervert
even by Orfus standards), Ika Thole (harpoon man from
the Ebrells), Ish Ulpin (slim, grim gladiator from Chi'ash-
lan), Prince Oronoko (who converted to the Flame after
travelling with Zanya Kliedervaust to Stokos), Zanya
Kliedervaust (who, having survived the journey from
Burntos to Drangsturm to the Ebrells to Parengarenga,
was martyred in the Great Arena of Dalar ken Halvar in
company with Oronoko – fortunately being rescued by
Drake Douay before her martyrdom could proceed to its
proper conclusion).

Missing in Action: Guest Gulkan (Pretender to the
throne of Tameran, enemy of the Witchlord Onosh
Gulkan, past companion of Rolf Thelemite).

A day's march. South. Downriver. Grey skies. The threat
of further snow – withheld for the moment. Stumbling
water. The forests forever. Each survivor nursing aches,
bruises, nightmares.

Near day's end, they killed another of the dog-like
creatures.

'One of your relatives, Mulps me beauty,' said Jon Arabin, pointing to the creature's startling green eyes.

Drake again remembered the wizard Miphon, who had had eyes of a similar green. The wizard had given advice about love. Yes. Flowers. Poetry. Persistence. Pretty speaking. Daily visits. Sincerity. A diligent wooing. He'd thought it nonsense at the time. But, if he'd followed the pox doctor's advice, maybe he would have had Zanya years ago . . .

Evening.

Firelight.

'Drake,' she said.

'That's my name,' he answered.

'Can you explain it?' she said. 'Who are you? Arabin lol Arabin, priest of the Flame, son of Jon Arabin? Or Drake Douay, swordsmith of Stokos?'

'Both,' said Drake, who had talked things over with his putative father during the march, synchronizing a whole raft of mutually supporting lies.

'How so?' said Zanya.

'I was,' said Drake, hoping he had the story right. 'I was, you see, born in Ling, on the terror-coast of the Deep South. There my gold-skinned mother bore me to my coal-black father. But, when I were but a boy, an evil slaver by name of Atsimo Andranovory stole me from the cradle. It were on Stokos I ended up. There a family by name of Douay bought me at market, not for profit but from pity. Thus I came to be Douay. Drake they call me, which is a word in Ligin meaning strilk.'

'Strilk?' said Zanya.

'Aye. Well. You know not that word? Strilk is something you eat, it's a cholo of sorts.'

'A cholo?' said Zanya.

'Well, yes,' said Drake, not knowing how else to render the word 'gourd' in Galish. 'Anyway, it's a fat thing you eat, okay? And a common name on Stokos. Where there's lots of Douays, aye, the place is crawling with them. Many of them Drakes, too, when it comes to that. And a fair few known as Dreldragon Drakedon Douay.'

'How come so many people with the same name?' said Zanya, unable to quell her last suspicion.

'Well, it's to do with taxes, you see,' said Drake. 'They're pretty harsh, as you may have heard when you were living in Cam. That was because King Tor always wanted to build roads and such rubbish, which meant the taxes were always on the upper. Anyway. With a name the same as everyone else, it's easy to escape the taxman. Hence the name.'

'Oh,' said Zanya. 'Then how . . . how are we, as worshippers of the Flame, to know the son of the Demon Hagon when we meet with him?'

'Evil cannot hide from the righteous,' said Drake sententiously. 'Evil speaks loud to the pure. We'll know the Demon-son all right, once we get him in a strangle. But don't expect to find him running around the world under his own true name! Oh no! He'll be far more cunning than that.'

'Yes,' said Zanya. 'Yes, yes, I suppose he will be. So . . .'

'So any person we come across called Dreldragon Drakedon Douay,' said Drake, 'that person, clearly, from the simple process of logic, cannot be the Demon-son. For the Evil One would hide his name far better.'

'Yes,' said Zanya, with relief.

It all fitted. If her lover had been the Evil One, he would have led his friends in gang rape already. He would not be talking so sweet and soft. And he would have hidden his name far better.

'I'd . . . I'd like to say thank you for saving my life,' said Zanya, regretting her earlier discourtesies.

'My pleasure,' said Drake.

'We've settled who you are,' said Zanya. 'You're the son of Jon Arabin, yet a swordsmith of Stokos also. And a priest of the Flame on occasion. But – do you . . . do you truly believe in the Flame?'

'I'm not sure,' said he, giving an honest answer.

'But you've been preaching the doctrines of the Flame.'

'I have,' he said. 'But living amongst pirates has . . . it's been fearful hard on occasion. To keep faith, I mean.'

'I understand,' said Zanya softly. 'I've had hard times myself, on the road between Burntos and Dalar ken Halvar. There have been times, indeed, when I thought of Gouda Muck and felt . . . but no, I'll not talk of that.'

'Please do!' said Drake. 'Feel free!'

So she told him how her own faith had suffered since he saw her last.

'The worst time was after my arrest in Dalar ken Halvar,' said Zanya. 'I was sentenced to death in the arena. I prayed to the Flame – but no help came.'

'I came!' objected Drake. 'Aye, and fought monsters!'

'Yes,' said Zanya. 'But, somehow . . . somehow you don't seem very holy. Even if you Believe, I . . . somehow I can't credit you as an instrument of the Flame . . .'

They then talked theology for some time.

Later, when Drake went for a piss, Sully Yot came sidling up to him.

'Remember,' said Yot, sotto voce, 'Gouda Muck would have us be pure.'

'Man,' said Drake, 'I'm in no shape to be thinking of fornicating. So don't worry about my purity.'

'You don't fool me!' said Yot. 'I know you've been whispering sweet nothings into that woman's ear!'

'I've been doing no such thing,' said Drake. 'We've been talking about metaphysics, aye, and the Theory of Knowledge, the problem of pain, the nature of free will and the possibility of salvation for those who pray to false gods.'

He spoke the truth. But the truth was so improbable that Yot thought him the veriest liar.

'I know you!' he said. 'You've been talking to her about sex, that's what. Sex all dressed up fancy, probably. Long discussions about the spiritual aspects of physical union.'

Once heard, this could not be forgotten. So when Drake went back to Zanya, he gently steered the conversation

468

around to a discussion of precisely that: the spiritual aspects of physical union. He did it carefully, for he had learnt a few lessons by now.

Later still, when Drake left Zanya's side a second time, Jon Arabin followed him into the undergrowth.

'Drake.'

'Aye?'

'Did she take our story all right?'

'She swallowed it solid, man,' said Drake. 'She believes I'm your son and a Stokos swordsmith both.'

'Good,' said Arabin. 'That girl's worth having. And she's hot for you. Play it for the thrust, man. You can get there tomorrow, if not tonight.'

'What the hell do you care either way?' asked Drake.

'I just don't want to see good meat going to waste,' said Arabin. 'And . . . Drake, there's something we have to talk about.'

'What?'

'Drake, I've never talked religion to you. But now's the time. I know gods, Drake, powerful gods. Aye. They've taken me through to pirate captain though all the world was against me. They're—'

'Demon's balls!' said Drake. 'Can't a man go into the bushes for a quiet shit without half the world's religions chasing after him?'

'I won't take much of your time,' said Arabin. 'All I want is a little talk.'

'You're competing with diarrhoea,' said Drake, pulling down his pants. 'And you're losing!'

At that Jon Arabin retired. He would have plenty of chances in the future to convert Drake to the Creed of Anthus. There was, surely, no need to hurry.

That night, it was cold. That night, Zanya and Drake held each other close. For warmth. And, as far as Zanya was concerned, for safety. She mistrusted Drake's evil companions – Bucks Cat and Ish Ulpin in particular. She would have been terrified sleeping alone, without the protection of a fellow worshipper of the Flame.

Both woke in the deep dark, long after midnight. What had woken them? Mutual dreams of lust. Silently, they kissed. They kissed, and fingered. Then slept. And dreamt of taking their lust to its logical conclusion.

Come morning, Drake found both Yot and Arabin were onto him. Yot with lectures about purity, self-control, virtue, the teachings of Gouda Muck and the demands of the Flame. Arabin with a different message altogether, and news of the gods of the Creed of Anthus.

'Our religion teaches that we must father a man for each we kill,' said Arabin. 'Drake, my boy, you've got a lot of breeding to do. This woman is ideal!'

These intellectual assaults multiplied Drake's religious confusion.

Yot, by the very intensity of his belief, annoyed Drake beyond measure; the more Yot insisted on purity, the more Drake regretted ever having made any concessions in that direction. And Arabin, while he did not convert Drake to the Creed of Anthus, certainly managed to weaken Drake's uncertain belief in the Flame.

Zanya's own uncertainties about her faith did nothing whatsoever to bolster Drake's confidence in the Flame. Finally, he decided to reserve judgment on all religions for the time being. What was important at the moment was Zanya. And Zanya's love.

Both Drake and Zanya were well over the shocks of their recent encounters with doom, death and disaster. Their spirits were rising. Their true nature was asserting itself – and the teachings of Gouda Muck had precious little chance against that most notorious of all aphrodisiacs: prolonged propinquity.

'I still don't understand,' said Zanya one evening.

'Never mind, my dear,' said Drake. 'Understanding is not essential in women.'

In answer to that she crammed a big greasy hunk of bear meat down the back of his neck, whereupon he attacked her. Once the two of them had sublimated a substantial fraction of their sexual energies by wrestling – she was a right proper handful, that one – she complained again:

'I still don't understand.'

Drake thought of another smart reply to that, but restrained himself. They were now several days downstream from the Old City. Hunting had been good, since Simp Fiche had shown an uncanny knack for sniffing out bears, and they had killed three already (Zanya claimed the poor creatures died of fright when they saw Whale Mike). Zanya still had plenty of bear meat on hand, and would doubtless use it unless Drake behaved himself.

'What don't you understand?' said Drake.

'Why you ever use that ugly name Drake. Or Dreldragon. Yes, I haven't forgotten – the people who adopted you on Stokos named you that. So you had no choice. But you've got a choice now. The Demon-son's name – every time I hear it, it makes me shudder.'

'It's not that bad, is it? Surely? Dreldragon Drakedon Douay. A good name, and common on Stokos – why, as common as two-headed seagulls and bird-eating rocks.'

'Common as what?' said Zanya.

'Common as kisses,' said Drake, trying to give her one. She pushed him away.

'I hate the Demon-son,' she said.

'And so do I,' said Drake. 'Why, if I had him in front of me, I'd suck out his eyes then twist on his gizzard till his teeth popped out. He deserves to die. Why, just for stealing Muck's mastersword, he should die.'

'Dearest,' said Zanya, who could not follow Drake's quick-weaving pirate cant when it got into swing. 'Talk Galish slow and proper if you wish my understanding. Now – seriously. Why call yourself by that evil name when others are so much nicer? So much nicer, yet free for the taking.'

'Very well,' said Drake. 'By muckle or huckle I'll girth me loins with sunlight, eat two raw eggs then be Arabin lol Arabin forever.'

'Say what?' said Zanya, who had not understood.

471

So Drake said, slowly, enunciating his words carefully in his best formal Galish, the true Trading Tongue of the Salt Road instead of the pirate-garbled snatch-talk which ruled in the Greater Teeth:

'*E'parg* Arabin lol Arabin.'

Meaning, literally, 'I bear (carry) Arabin lol Arabin' – or, in translation, 'I am called Arabin lol Arabin.'

'I will henceforth be Arabin lol Arabin single and only,' said Drake. 'I formally keelhaul the name Drake. I execute it. With Dreldragon with it. Aye. And Drake Douay. And all those other things so close to swearing.'

'*P'tosh*, Arabin lol Arabin,' said Zanya, greeting him with what she was happy to think of as his true and proper name, the one his father had given him at birth.

'Yes,' said Drake. 'It's only Arabin lol Arabin I'll be, from now unto death. In other words, as long as we're married for.'

'I never said I'd marry you!' said Zanya.

'But you will, darling,' said Drake, imperiously.

And that led to some more high-spirited wrestling.

Dour men watched jealously from evening shadows, and, that night, as Drake and Zanya slept (chastely enough) in each other's arms, some of those men had muttering conversations about the joy of rape.

Early the next morning, they all set off downstream again.

'Today,' said Drake to Zanya. 'You must marry me. I can't wait much longer.'

'You're not serious, are you?' she said.

'Of course I am.'

'But Gouda Muck wants us all to be celibate: he told me so himself.'

'Did he?' said Drake.

'Yes!'

'In his own words?'

'Of course!'

'Well,' said Drake. 'What difference does it make?

472

You've told me yourself you have strong doubts about the Flame.'

'About the Flame being the High God of All Gods, yes,' said Zanya. 'About Gouda Muck being the Flame in the flesh, yes. But not about the preachings of Gouda Muck.'

'How so?'

'Even if Muck isn't a god,' said Zanya, 'his doctrine still holds many truths.'

'Such as what?'

'Such as truths about physical relationships,' said Zanya. 'They're evil!'

'Are they?' said Drake. 'How can we know that unless we try? It's an interesting theory, to be sure, but we have to investigate it before we can truth it.'

His inspiration for this declaration was the Inner Principles of the Old Science which he had been taught as an apprentice on Stokos. An unusual implement of seduction, to be sure – but Drake was willing to try anything.

'I have tried it,' said Zanya.

'What? Physical relationships? I bet there's things you haven't tried.'

'I bet there aren't,' she said.

So, in that competitive spirit, they had a long – very long – discussion.

Zanya remembered what Jon Arabin had told her in confidence: that Drake Douay was in truth a virgin. So she discounted his wild tales about being seduced by his sister at age thirteen, about selling his body and buying the flesh of others, about his seduction of the eldest daughter of Baron Farouk of Hexagon, and about a great many other adventures he claimed to have had. He was just a boy, a poor shy innocent boy, too timid for her to possibly be afraid of.

In reply to Drake's stories, Zanya told about her life as a priestess of the Orgy God. The details made his eyes bug.

'I've seen it all,' said Zanya. 'And I've seen the evil of it.'

Then she told him about her family, destroyed by the

473

horrors of venereal disease and alcoholism.

'Lust and drink,' said Zanya. 'That's what does the damage.'

'Well,' said Drake. 'Well . . . maybe you can have too much of a good thing.'

This concession represented, for him, a major intellectual advance.

'No,' said Zanya, 'they're not good things at all. Sex is poison. So is alcohol. I just told you I'd seen the proof of it.'

'Ah,' said Drake, 'but you're living proof that one can taste yet not necessarily be poisoned. Therefore it must be a matter of quantity. And . . . quality, perhaps.'

'But—'

'Nay, woman. The cities of the world are peopled with heads as numerous as seashore sands. For each of those heads, one act of fornication, minimum. There's a world of tasting there. But is the whole world poxed? No! Is the whole world poisoned? No!'

'Drake,' said Yot, coming over to them, 'can I ask you if you could—'

'You can't and I couldn't!' said Drake. 'Piss off before I knife you!'

Yot vanished himself.

'Where were we?' asked Drake, his chain of thought broken.

'Oh, deep in the toils of the higher philosophy,' said Zanya. 'But you'll never persuade me that lust is good. As I've told you, I've tried everything. And what I tried I didn't like.'

Drake found that believable, since most of the things Zanya had tried as a priestess of the Orgy God seemed less than pleasant – for instance, being roughed over by twenty drunken men while wallowing in the guts of a whale.

'So we must be chaste,' continued Zanya.

'Ah,' said Drake, his voice sly. 'But it would be an error to condemn your flesh to chastity before you tried just one last thing.'

474

'I tell you, I've tried everything!'

'I listened very very carefully,' said Drake, cunning as a Korugatu philosopher trying to get extended credit at his favourite wine bar. 'And I'm sure, beyond all doubts, that you've never ever tried moderation.'

Zanya thought hard.

'Hmmm,' she said. 'You're right. I never have. But in any case, why would I want to practise moderation with you?'

'Because I love you,' said Drake simply.

'You mean, you'd rather have me than all the other women in the world put together? My charms would be sufficient for fifty lifetimes and the bright day after?'

'Well . . . I wouldn't go that far,' said Drake. 'I mean, not yet. After I'd tried all the women in the world once, then I'd be in a better position to decide.'

She slapped him, which he deserved for being so crass.

'Hey!' he said. 'Can't you take a little joke? Of course I'd want you, just you, only you, dearest cony. I'm in love with you, yea, red skin, red hair, kisses and blisses. This is the real thing. True love!'

'You mean,' said Zanya, 'you hear music when you look at me, smell spring behind my tender ears?'

Drake sniffed.

'On Investigation,' he reported, 'I smell, if anything, dead bear.'

Whereupon she slapped him a second time, for impertinence.

But he was a quick learner, and, twenty-three slaps later, was singing her praises as sweetly as any courtly swain in pursuit of a high-born damsel.

Delicately he kissed her, and lightly traced the outlines of her cheekbones, and the hand which fondled its way between her thighs was so gentle, so skilled, so courteous, that she could scarcely resist its claim on her desires.

She had not had a man for three years.

Or a dog, or a woman, or a cucumber, or any other form of relief. Religion had even kept her from pleasuring her own flesh. But propinquity was steadily eroding her religious faith.

However, fear still kept her chaste.

For the time being.

For, if she took on Drake Douay, what then? She knew what men were like. She must stand staunch against all of them. For, if she gave in to one, the others would then be insulted by her refusal. She still had nightmares about serving lust en masse in the Ebrells. Even though that was years ago.

Therefore she – gently – removed that skilled and courteous hand from between her thighs. When it replaced itself, she – not so gently – tried to break one of its fingers. The hand got the message.

Thus Drake and Zanya, lying in each other's arms on the fur-side of a fresh-killed bearskin, practised not moderation but abstinence. And the art of the promise.

But Drake's comrades – men wise in the ways of the world – believed what it was only natural for them to suspect. And this increased the jealousy of some of them beyond all reason.

39

Name: Arabin lol Arabin (formerly Dreldragon Drakedon Douay, or, more simply, 'Drake').

Occupation: wilderness survivor, energetic creator of heresies, dedicated exponent of practical aspects of that congeries of delusions known as 'love'.

Status: in the eyes of his true love, his dearest kiss, the high-breasted red-skinned red-haired Zanya Kliedervaust (she who is sweeter then nectar, more tender than his foreskin, closer to his heart than his kidneys, and more valued than both of his great toes and the strength of his arches) his status is rising steadily.

Description: a fair-haired smiling fellow who whistles, sings, laughs; wears rather odd mixture of torn wool, battered sealskin, pungent uncured bearskin; looks totally absurd but more spritely by the moment.

There were thirteen in that downriver party. Guest Gulkan, the Pretender of Tameran whom they had met so briefly, was not amongst them, having failed to emerge from the Door by the time Jon Arabin finally snatched the star-globe from its golden cup, thus closing the Circle.

Zanya Kliedervaust was there, of course. She was chaste, yet in love. Amongst so many men, she felt protected because of what she thought of as Drake's power. She longed for the day when they could begin to practise some moderation together. It would be marvellous to be cherished, soothed, gentled and adored. An antidote, perhaps, to her memories of Ebrell, where she used to finish an important ceremony feeling as bruised and abused as a pigskin which has just survived five games of ruck in succession.

With them was the purple-skinned Oronoko, rescued from the Great Arena of Dalar ken Halvar when Zanya was. Language difficulties kept him largely silent; only Zanya spoke his native Frangoni, and she had scant time for anyone other than Drake.

Drake was now universally known, to Jon Arabin's delight, as Arabin lol Arabin. While he had not yet tasted the delights of Zanya's flesh, he was already learning that the poets, while extravagant, are not entirely untruthful. Love does indeed have its pleasures – such as waking beside a woman in the morning and not having to ask her what her name is.

In his world of rain and river and water, of mud and dirt and charred bear meat, Zanya was the brightest, most bubbling thing in the universe. And her smile was itself a flattery he had never had from any other woman.

Warwolf and Walrus had of course survived, as had the wart-faced Sully Yot, who followed Drake like a bad smell until Drake threatened to lib him.

'I just fancy some jungle oysters,' said Drake. 'So get out of here before I cut your goolies off.'

'When you die,' said Yot, 'the Flame will burn you forever. You're living in sin.'

'Aye,' said Drake, not caring to confess that he had yet to sin with Zanya, 'for that's the way I was born. And I'm proud of it.'

'I'll tell Zanya you're the Demon-son!'

'Do it!' said Drake. 'Go on, just do it! Then I'll shove your face in the fire and hold it there till your nose burns off. What's more, my father will tear you limb from limb once you're dead.'

'You mean . . . ?'

'I mean I am indeed the Demon-son,' said Drake,

savagely, 'seed of Hagon, sent to bring evil to the world and destruction to prissy little spoil-sport shits like Sully Yot. So bugger off!'

Yot was an unpredictable factor.

He wanted, for a start, to survive. To get the hell out of Penvash – certainly the closest thing to hell he'd ever encountered. And he also wanted to renew Drake's faith in the Flame (if Drake was human, and not born of the Demon), or to kill Drake (if Drake was indeed, true to his boast, the Demon-son). During each day's march, Yot lagged far behind the others, having long, involved theological discussions with himself as he tried to sort truth from boast and right from wrong.

Apart from the above, the Penvash party included three men who only wanted to stride on downstream as soon as possible: Rolf Thelemite, Jon Disaster and Whale Mike.

Then there was the rape faction.

It was small, for it consisted of three men only. Simp Fiche was its inspiring spirit, but Ika Thole thought of himself as its leader – and the dangerous Ish Ulpin was the one most likely to actually start the action. Ish Ulpin was busy persuading Bucks Cat to his faction.

While Drake and Zanya slept together in all innocence, oblivious of the group dynamics which were rapidly developing a disaster for them, the members of the rape faction campaigned.

'The vomit-haired scrab should share and share alike,' said Simp Fiche. 'It's not fair to keep her for himself.'

'Aye,' said Ika Thole. 'She's a priestess of the Orgy God, that one. I tell you, on the Ebrells they don't hold themselves so special.'

'I haven't had my balls cut off,' said Ish Ulpin. 'How about the rest of you? How about it, Mike?'

Whale Mike thought long and hard, then shook his head in a ponderous fashion and said:

'This like eating my little klude. One too small for many. You so hard up, man? Then you grab sleepy bear, nice one, we help hold it down for you.'

He slapped his knees and laughed, while Ish Ulpin scowled.

But the rape lobby won over Bucks Cat. Then set to work on Slagger Mulps. Simp Fiche did most of the work, nagging away steadily:

'Are you a pirate chief or what? . . . following after the Warwolf like a puppy behind a blue-tailed bitch . . . when did you last speak as a captain? . . . man, he's been laughing at you ever since we left the Teeth . . . changed the name of the ship on you, back at D'Waith, didn't he? And you took it like a dead fish takes the gutting knife . . .'

Fiche was not surprised when, a day later, at noon, when they had halted for lunch (cold bear meat and water weed, with a couple of earthworms apiece to add variety) Walrus said to Warwolf:

'Jon, I've been thinking. It's been a hard haul, Jon. Many leagues, much suffering. Yet no fun for the boys, Jon. Except for one.'

And he glanced at Drake. Who got to his feet, his fingers fists.

'You want to argue, man?' said Drake.

'Sit!' said Jon Arabin, curtly.

Reluctantly, Drake sat.

'Mulps me darling,' said Jon Arabin. 'We're through the worst, as you know as well as any. We'll make it to Estar for sure. There's whores there the same as anywhere, and beer to go with them.'

'Aye,' said Mulps. 'But what good's pleasure elsewhere? Man, there's pleasures for real in Selzirk palaces – and what profit do we get of such?'

'Man,' said Jon Arabin. 'One unwashed body with another on a stinking skin in the mud and the rain, I don't call that pleasure. That's children's games – and there's only the two children here, neither of them being you or me.'

'Fussy, is it?' said Mulps. 'Aye, Jon, you always were the gentleman. But I'm a pirate true and for real, and I'll

480

take what's due to me by worth and rank. Rolf – give me your sword. Give it!'

Rolf Thelemite hesitated.

'You're sworn to him,' said Jon Arabin. 'So give him your blade, if that's the way he wants to settle it.'

And the Warwolf released his own blade from the bindings which kept the slender thing from rattling around in the big bulky sheath which had once held a falchion.

'Give me that!' said Drake, reaching for it.

Jon Arabin knocked him away with a back-handed blow. He had to win this one himself to save his leadership. He could not allow Drake to kill the Walrus – as well he might, for his shipboard training had shown him slick with a blade.

'Keep back,' said Arabin. 'This kill is mine. Sit! And be silent!'

Drake, wiping a little blood from his nose, obeyed.

Rolf Thelemite yielded his sword to Slagger Mulps, but, seeking to buy a little time in which hot heads might still yet cool, said:

'What about the tinder-box? A good cut might rend it open.'

Jon Arabin shrugged, then detached his waterproof sea-pouch from his belt. He tossed it to Drake, who caught it neatly.

'Take good care of that,' said Jon Arabin. 'We'll need a fire soon enough, to cook up Walrus kidneys.'

Arabin tested his footwork, and, finding the star-globe was likely to interfere with his movements, took it from the deep thigh-pocket where it had been hiding. He looked at Drake, to throw it to him – but Drake had turned to kiss Zanya.

'Here,' said Jon Arabin, tossing the star-globe to Sully Yot.

Rolf Thelemite, standing by Yot, thought it was for him, and tried to field it. Thelemite and Yot collided – and the star-globe rolled down the bank to the river's edge. Yot slithered after it hastily, first because he was certain Thelemite was angry with him, second because he was afraid the beautiful thing would be eaten by the hungering waters.

There it was.

Yot grabbed for it. His fingers closed on the smooth cold stone. But it weighed more than he had expected, and slipped from his grasp. Fell into knee-deep water. The current rolled it downstream. Yot lunged for it, slipped, fell face-first into the water, saw the ball, grabbed it.

For a moment he had the star-globe in his grasp. He struggled against the current, slipped, tried to stand up – and found himself floundering out of his depth in water suddenly deeper. As the river thrashed him away, the star-globe found freedom.

Gasping and shouting, Yot thrashed around in the water. The others, watching from the top of the bank, still did not realize his difficulties. They thought he was just clowning it up a little, and would be wading back to the bank any moment now, star-globe in hand.

Suddenly:

'He's stealing it!' yelped Simp Fiche, realizing Yot was getting too far away for comfort. 'The star-globe. He's stealing it!'

Yot, who had been crying out for help, was startled to hear a great roar from Bucks Cat:

'We'll get you, Yot! You won't get away with it! We'll skin you alive!'

Next moment, leadership fight forgotten, most of the pirates were charging along the riverbank in hot pursuit of the hapless Yot.

'Come,' said Zanya, and, grabbing Drake by the sleeve (or the nearest sleeve-equivalent remaining to his rags) started running in pursuit of the hunting party.

Walrus and Warwolf were left standing alone, bare swords still drawn, with Prince Oronoko observing them with interest – he liked to watch a good fight.

'Well,' said the green-bearded Slagger Mulps, sounding not entirely certain about it.

482

'Well indeed,' said Jon Arabin, thinking of his death-debt, and of the Supreme Auditor. 'Well, what say we leave this for the moment? At least until we've won back the star-globe.'

'Till then,' said Mulps.

'Shall we swear to it?'

'Brothers in blood till the star-globe's back,' agreed Mulps, thinking that would be by sundown at the latest.

And they swore to it.

Meanwhile, Drake and Zanya were running along after the others, following the muddy trail of footsteps, when Zanya suddenly stopped.

'Arabin,' she said.

'What?' said Drake, in some confusion. 'Where?'

Then remembered that was his name these days, for, to please his true love, he had become Arabin lol Arabin for always. He saw his true love was pointing up into a great big evergreen tree of crowding foliage and close-climbing branches.

'Ah,' said Drake.

And up the tree they went.

And, after realizing that Yot had been swept too far downriver for capture, the pirate party – led by the rape faction – spent a long time looking for those two young people. But never found them, no.

Come morning, the pirates set off for Estar, led by the Warwolf and the Walrus – who were oath-linked allies for the foreseeable future, since attempts to find the missing star-globe had proved just as futile as the search for Yot, Drake and Zanya.

The pirates?

They reached Estar, followed the river to the sea, then hijacked fishing boats and made it back to the Greaters.

Since the star-globe had not been recovered, Walrus and Warwolf were bound each to each by a bloodbrother's oath. Did they hate it, each being pledged to his worst enemy? On the contrary. It was the best thing

483

which had happened to either of them for years.

They had been at war for so long now that they knew each other better than they knew any other living flesh. With each passing year, their hatred had become more and more a public ritual, less and less an affair of the heart.

Jon Arabin was delighted to welcome the Walrus into his household, delighted to have some male companionship at home, after suffering for so long alone amidst his women.

And the Walrus?

Jon Arabin was what he had always wanted: a dear, true, trustworthy friend.

Weep for the Walrus! Poor lonely little chap, so distressed by his exile from Chenameg, so cut off from the warmth of human society that he ended up raping a pig in a toilet in Selzirk! And was he comforted when found? Was he counselled and soothed and introduced to some nice young honest decent women in need of a good husband?

No, of course not.

Instead, he was hauled up in a public court, abused by the prosecution, lectured by the judge, mocked by the public, then sentenced to labour as a galley slave – and was brutalized for five years on the Velvet River before being liberated by pirates.

And he was still a virgin on that traumatic night when he got into one of Jon Arabin's women and, in the raptures of his clumsy passion, bit off one of her nipples. From which accident all manner of evils followed.

Which gives credence to the assertions of Cho Sel Sig, a Korugatu philosopher, who holds that all the murder, mayhem, cruelty and brutality which together constitute 'history' is simply a consequence of bad sex (or no sex, which, according to Sig, amounts to the same thing).

Anyway, there they were then. Walrus and Warwolf. Friends at last. And Yot?

Well, Sully Datelier Yot never went to Estar. On reaching Lake Armansis, he turned west and crossed the

Razorwind Pass to Larbster Bay. There he had the luck of a boat which took him to D'Waith, from where – again, luck was involved more than good judgment – he made his way back to Stokos.

Where he was reunited with Gouda Muck. And was able to give warning of the invasion of Stokos planned by Lord Menator and King Tor. And to tell Gouda Muck, that dignitary of dignitaries, the avatar of the Flame, the High God of All Gods, all about the derelictions of Drake Douay.

And Drake?

And Zanya?

Well, Zanya went on with Drake. Foolish woman! She had been warned by the wizard Miphon that Drake was an awesome amount of trouble in a very small package. Her excuse was that she was in love . . .

First they almost died when they got lost in Looming Forest, on the northern marches of Estar. By sheer luck, they were rescued by a local woodsman, a heavy-jowled man by name of Blackwood, who sheltered them in the house he shared with his wife Mystrel.

Later, they ventured to Lorford, the ruling town of Estar, for Drake had thoughts of taking service with Prince Comedo, ruler of the place. He abandoned that plan when he realized both Atsimo Andranovory and Prince Oronoko were in the prince's employ.

He did, however, spend enough time in Lorford to get into trouble. As a consequence of this, he had a very unpleasant interview with a grim, tense, grey-haired Rovac warrior named Morgan Hearst, a fellow about 33 years of age, who took a hard line with hooligans.

Hearst ran both Drake and Zanya out of town.

Travelling down the Salt Road south of Lorford, they were captured by priests of the temple of the Demon of Estar, and almost became human sacrifices. After escaping, they had a close encounter of the unpleasant kind with the dragon Zenphos, which lived in a cave high up in the nearby mountain of Maf.

Further south again, they ran into trouble with the locals after they killed a sheep which Drake had, or so he claimed in his defence, mistaken for a large and aggressive boar. But they talked their way out of that one – and, after several other adventures, including an encounter with a drunken ghost, they reached the southern border of Estar.

That border was guarded only by a derelict flame trench, a feeble ditch which steamed a bit, and boiled the water where it ran out into the sea, but which spat no fire and melted no rock.

Drake and Zanya crossed greasy wooden duckboards laid across the steaming mud at the bottom of the rubble-filled ditch, then climbed out of the warmth of its steam to the cold of the afternoon of a winter's day.

They explored the small, ruinous fort guarding the southern side of the trench. A stairway led down into darkness, but they declined to dare its dangers.

'Above will be enough,' said Drake. 'We'll camp here tonight.'

In the ruins of the fort's tower, they laid down the muddy sheepskins which they carried for sleep-warmth and stretched sheets of canvas above the skins to keep off the rain. Then searched for wood and lit a fire.

'Thus we leave Estar,' said Zanya. 'I wonder what lies ahead of us.'

'The Salt Road follows the coast south through Dybra and Chorst till it comes to Runcorn, which is a city major,' said Drake. 'We should get news of the world there for real.'

'If we get there,' said Zanya.

'Oh, we'll get there all right,' said Drake.

Will they reach Runcorn?

Drake is right: they will.

It will be a long and perilous journey, but in fullness of time – on Midwinter's Day, to be exact – they will enter Runcorn.

486

And Drake will learn that his world is in ruins.

He will learn that Tor and Menator have launched an invasion of Stokos. He will learn that Tor has landed near Cam, has fought against impossible odds – and has been defeated. His whereabouts are unknown. He will learn that Menator has survived the invasion unscathed. And for a very simple reason. Drake will learn that, with the coast of Stokos in sight, Menator turned his own ships homeward.

Drake will soon correctly analyse the reasons for this. Menator has struck a double blow. Menator has sent Tor to destruction in a war which has severely weakened Stokos. Menator, in the fullness of time, will obviously launch another invasion on the war-weakened island of Stokos – but with no need to share the rule of the place with Tor once it has been conquered.

Drake will see, then, that Tor has been suckered – the ogre king has done Lord Menator's dirty work for him, gaining nothing in the process.

Drake will meet with Jon Disaster, who will by then have come to Runcorn as a spy for pirates planning a raid on the place. Disaster will tell Drake that his brother Heth is still missing; that Lord Menator has put a price on the head of King Tor, and on the head of Drake Douay. Drake will thus learn that Menator truly does fear him as a potential rival to the throne of Stokos.

Drake will ask:

'What of Walrus and Warwolf? What do they say of this price put on my head?'

And Jon Disaster will answer:

'They cannot oppose Menator, for so many of their best men are dead that their own power has come close to nil. They work on ship for Abousir Belench, and count themselves lucky to have the berth.'

Drake will be shaken and shocked. He will realize his hopes and dreams have been destroyed. No hope of returning to the Teeth! No hope of linking up with King Tor, whose whereabouts are unknown. No hope of marrying Tor's daughter for an easy throne. He will

487

have to shift for himself in the cruel and friendless world.

But at least he will have Zanya Kliedervaust at his side.

Anyway: all that lies in the future.

For the moment, it is evening at the southern border of Estar, a desolate place where a ruinous flame trench reaches for three thousand paces between mountain cliffs and the sea.

To the sea Drake walks, alone, bearing a handful of ashes. It is time. In the season of death, he must honour the memory of the dead.

Alone in the cold grey evening, alone by the tumultuous seas, he treasures the ash in his hands while he lists the dead.

First the weapons muqaddam, whose name he never learnt. To him he owes the gift of weapons. Quin Baltu, the foul-mouthed muscle-man, who spoke for him in the face of the Warwolf's wrath. As did Harly Burpskin, who was whipped raw for his pains.

They have gone down into the darkness, as we, too, in our turn, will go down into the darkness.

Remember them.

Drake names Shewel Lokenshield, who hit him in the face once with a dead fish, but who shared good beer with him in Narba in the days when he could still get drunk. Aye. As did Lee Dix, Goth Sox and Hewlet Mapleskin. All good men. All killed in the Warwolf's battle with sea serpents in the Penvash Channel.

We could have been closer. Given time.

Life is so short! Drake remembers the bones he saw in the Wishing Tower in the land of Ling, back in the long-ago days when life was young and simple.

And I, in time, will make bones.

Meanwhile, he says a parting for poor old Tiki Slooze, and for Salaman Meerkat.

I hardly knew you. Yet you shared food in the time for sharing. Aye. I'd not have thought it. But don't hold that against me.

Cold wind. The louring sky. Ashes in his hands.

Remember, now. Pru Chalance. Killed and eaten by northern barbarians.

A stranger. Man, that's weird. So close to so many, yet knowing them not.

So what can be said for Pru Chalance? That he lived. He breathed. He dared his chance. As did Ching Quail. And Jez Glane, yes, and Raggage Pouch. And Peg Zuzilman – taken by a centipede, and surely dead. A terrible way to die.

But it's never easy.

Live hard, die hard. I miss you all. The weapons muqaddam most. A man amongst men. And he spoke for me too, yes, when Arabin was hot for murder.

Once more Drake runs through the names, searching for those he's missed. Then he treasures the ashes to the waters.

Be well.

None of those pirates who died would have expected anyone to weep for them, yet, here by the shores of the Central Ocean, Drake does weep for them. And for his sister, who cut her throat when she found herself dying from blue leprosy. He understands her life better now, and realizes how rough she had it. He weeps, too, for himself – for do we not all, in the end, go down into that darkness?

And he weeps as well for the golden kings and their tumultuous empires, for the beauty of women and the laughter of the young, and for the valour of the suns themselves which burn burn and burn, down through the generations, though they too go down in the end to the darkness.

Last, he learns his grief for the two nameless Collosnon warriors he murdered in a tent by the shores of the island Chag-jalak, far away in the waters of the North Strait.

You or me. That's how it was. I don't apologize. But forgive me.

The wind braces him as he walks back to the ruinous fort on the border. And rain has washed the tears from his

face by the time he reaches the fireside. Where Zanya is
waiting.

Tonight. At last.
Lips to be lips.
Flesh to be flesh.
Two to be one.
Silence.
Fadeout.
Night.

40

The Way of Arabin: religion created by Arabin lol
Arabin (formerly Dreldragon Drakedon Douay), drawing
inspiration from the mysticism of Gouda Muck, the
delights of the temple of the Demon Hagon, tales (some
taller than others) about the Orgy God of the Ebrell
Islands, and the Inner Principles of the Old Science (as
taught to apprentice swordsmiths on Stokos).

The Book of Witness

Vision the First

AND it came to pass that in the winter of Khmar 19,
Arabin lol Arabin came down out of the north and made
his abode in Runcorn.

2   With him was no money but a woman, and his wit
also.

3   And it happened that Arabin spent much time in
dives of low repute where there was much drinking, and a
muchness also of gambling at dice-chess.

4 And he enjoyed winnings of a size that other men
marvelled at.

5 And at midwinter he opened his own establishment,
saying unto the multitude, come, for the place is lit with
candles unto cockcrow.

6 The wine is unwatered and the gin likewise, the girls
are clean and the cards unmarked, yea, and spotless.

7 And the crowds were great about his door.

8 Then it happened that the City Fathers were exceedingly wroth, and sent certain men to his gates.

9 And they asked of him, 'Is there gambling and drinking and whoring within?'

10 And he answered unto them, thinking the Truth would serve him, 'There is the practical Worship of things that are good.'

11 And one replied, 'Verily verily I say unto you, thou hast not a liquor licence, therefore we can close you down.'

12 And another said that yea, verily, he had not rendered up to the City Corporation business taxes three years in advance.

13 And many were their accusations, yea, so that there is no numbering of them.

14 Then Arabin was also wroth, and he hardened his fingers to fists against them.

15 But his woman said, 'Hush dearest treasure-snake, there is Another Way.'

16 Then she, whose name was Zanya, said unto the Persecutors: 'Return you tomorrow at noon, and all shall be Answered.'

17 And their understanding of this was improved when Arabin began to place boot to the ends that were behind them.

18 And the Persecutors withdrew, yet returned at noon the next day.

19 And they found waiting for them a Being dressed in Magnificence, and he was not as other men, for there was thunder on his brow and in his voice also.

20 And he drew himself up to his Height, and, verily, they looked as Children beside him.

21 And he said, 'Lo, behold your doom, for I am Garimanthea the Mighty, the Flail of Righteousness, the Breaker of Strong Men, the Destroyer of Prosperity, for I am barrister, solicitor, notary public and attorney at law.'

22 Then were the Persecutors frightened exceedingly, and sought to flee.

23 But it was too late.

24 For the minions of Garimanthea pressed upon them certain writs relating to libel, and slander, and Attempted Taxation of Religions in Contravention of the City Charter, and Constitutional Violation, and Demanding With Menaces, and many others besides.

Vision the Second
AND it happened that toward spring the City Fathers sat in council.

2 And they asked why the establishment of Arabin continued in operation, yet without liquor licence, or payment of taxes, or compliance with fire regulations.

3 And they were answered: 'Verily, he has claimed exemption on the grounds of religious status, and the question looks likely to perplex the Courts unto our great grandchildren's children's generation.'

4 Then the Council Chamber was loud with bitter mirth.

5 And Nabajoth the Wise wiped the salt tears from his eyes and said, 'This Arabin who stands against us is but a child, and will leave town even if I must rope him to the horse which is my own then drag him all the way south to Kelebes.'

6 And Arabin lol Arabin was summoned before the council.

7 And Nabajoth addressed him, saying, 'How can a boy like you pretend to religious wisdom?'

8 Whereupon Arabin said to him, 'Wherefore dost thou call me boy? Would'st like to test manhood, blade to blade to death and damnation?'

9 Upon which his counsel Garimanthea said in exceedingly great haste, 'My client's question was rhetorical only, purely rhetorical, I want that fact entered in the Record.'

10 Therefore remarks to that effect were entered in the Record.

11 And it is said that Arabin at that time made certain muttered remarks about the ancestry of Nabajoth and the

greatness of the belly which was upon him, yet these were not Recorded.

12 Then Nabajoth again asked, 'How can a boy like you pretend to religious wisdom?'

13 Whereupon Arabin thought deeply.

14 Then spoke, saying, 'Why dost thou use the argument ad hominem? Hast thou no learning?

15 'If thou wast to wake beside a whore and hear her parrot say unto you that the sea is blue, would the sea be less blue because a whore's parrot had declared it?

16 'And if a child saith the gods are exceedingly great and mighty, are the gods therefore as woodlice because a child has declared them mighty?'

17 'And if I were to say that the belly of a certain City Father was exceedingly great, yea, and waxy, and a meal a pack of hungry dogs could not consume entire, would the waxiness of his dislike of me make him thin?'

18 Then an unseemly laughter was heard in parts of the Council Chamber, and Nabajoth assumed a redness of the face and then a purple.

19 And the wrath of Nabajoth was exceedingly great, and was matched by the laughter only.

20 Then Nabajoth hardened his fingers to fists and spake, saying many things later expunged from the Record, then died of apoplexy.

21 Then Garimanthea asked for a recess that he might confer with his client reference protocol and etiquette and certain other related matters.

22 And a recess was granted unto him.

Vision the Third
NOW it happened that after the recess, Zeruqin spake unto Arabin, saying, 'What is religion?'

2 And Arabin answered, 'It is worship.'

3 And Zeruqin asked of him, 'What then is worship?'

4 And Arabin said, 'It is the Walking of the Way.'

5 Whereupon Zeruqin asked him if it was the way to Selzirk he spoke of, or the way to the docks of Runcorn, or

the way back to the brothel he was spawned in.

6 Upon which Garimanthea made certain entries upon a parchment and gave it unto Zeruqin, saying it was a writ concerning the slander Zeruqin had just made upon the ancestry of Arabin.

7 Then there was long and heated colloquy during which Zeruqin offered to meet Arabin on the Field of Honour which lay but a fingerlength beyond the Jurisdiction of the Free City of Runcorn.

8 And Arabin answered him, saying, 'Verily thou art reckless, but there shall we meet, and have a testing of manhood.'

9 And a recess was agreed to.

10 And it came to pass that the two of them met on the Field of Honour with blades of steel which were slender, yea, and had about them a beauty which was equal to the beauty of a woman in her nakedness.

11 And Arabin killed his man, yet was himself unwounded.

Vision the Fourth
NOW on the next day the Hearing of the City Fathers of Runcorn resumed.

2 And Jarmuth Japhia Lachish said unto Arabin from the glory of his chins, which were five in number, 'How is it that thou pretendeth to religion?

3 'For since when is drinking, gambling and whoring of the nature of religion?

4 'A man cannot commune with the gods through drinking.

5 'Nor find the revelations of the spirit through whoring.

6 'And, as for gambling, there is no good in it.'

7 Then Arabin spake unto him, saying unto him:

8 'Hast thou ever sat at table with hard liquor for seven days and seven nights unceasing?'

9 And Lachish answered him: 'No.'

10 'And hast thou ever rolled dice for thine future,

495

staking the one and most worthless foreign dorth which remaineth to thee?'

10 And Lachish answered him: 'No.'

11 'And hast thou ever slept with a whore, or with two whores and a dog, or with a young boy and a hot pig, or in a room equipped with the pleasures of mouths and whips and wet liver and—'

12 Whereupon there was uproar of surpassing greatness.

13 But the Record showed the answer of Lachish as 'No.'

14 Then did Arabin call attention to the answer shown in the Record, and say unto Lachish: 'If thou hast not tasted these pleasures, wherefore dost thou speak of the goodness or the badness thereof?'

15 And Lachish replied that the badness of it was evident to all who heard of it.

16 Whereupon Arabin spoke unto him, saying, 'Verily verily I say unto you that the nature of a thing is known only by the Investigation of that thing.

17 'For one may buy a certain skin of drink because the merchant hath praised it, yet find upon consumption that there is no wine within but vinegar, for the praising of a thing relies for proof upon the tasting.

18 'Likewise its denigration.

19 'Now if I speak to you of the goodness of my woman and of the sex of her, you may deny me.

20 'But your denial is as the boast of the merchant who sold the wine.

21 'For all opinion is an empty prating of wind unless thou hast lain between the nakedness of her breasts, or tasted of the myrrh of her lips, or grappled with the smoothness of her loins, which are of a fragrance like unto spikenard, and a smoothness like unto fine wine.

22 'The truth of a thing is revealed by the Investigation of that thing, the touching and the tasting thereof, the evidence which is ocular and that which is of the bouquet.

23 'Thus it is with all my religion.'

24 Whereupon three of the City Fathers were Illuminated, and resigned their positions on the spot, and went forth from that place that they might worship.

25 And Arabin in his wisdom sent messengers ahead of them, and free drinks were waiting when they got to the bar.

26 Then those of the City Fathers who remained were sorely vexed.

28 And Jarmuth Japhia Lachish spake from the glory of his five chins, saying unto Arabin: 'Boy, wherefore dost thou perplex us with this gobbledygook which hath not the half of an arse upon it?

28 'Verily, thou shalt learn that the wise will not think the shit of a bull to be the pudding of a plum merely because a boy has declared it to be so.'

29 Whereupon Arabin said unto him: 'Is it not the wisdom of the Ancients that a thing must be Investigated before it is Known?'

30 Whereupon they were sore amazed, for they saw that he was learned in the Inner Principles of the Old Science.

31 And Arabin spoke unto them, saying, 'Verily, dialectic is a sharp blade, and I believe it hath cut off the heads of your arguments.'

32 Whereupon another recess was called, and both the wise and the unwise departed from that place until the next day should dawn.

Vision the Fifth

1 AND it came to pass that on the next day Arabin arrived in the company of damsels.

2 And with him also were men bearing boards for the playing of dice-chess, and good gold for the staking thereat.

3 And maids bearing platters of goodly sweetmeats, of the red meat and the white, of fish and of fowl, and of all things rich in their taste and in their juices.

4 And there was strong drink also, even the firewater which is from Ebrell.

5 And Arabin addressed the City Fathers, saying unto them: 'Come, will you not Investigate in the manner of the Ancients?

6 'Truly this is the highest wisdom that remains to us, that we should Investigate before we Pronounce.'

7 Then Jarmuth Japhia Lachish spoke many words, and caused to be abolished from the sight of the City Fathers the damsels, dice-chess, gold, platters and strong drink also, yea, even the rare and most precious firewater which was from Ebrell.

8 Then Lachish spoke unto Arabin from the glory of his five chins, saying:

9 'Boy, there are two ways of knowing.

10 'One you have spoken of, which is Investigation, yet one you have not spoken of, and that is Tradition.

11 'Yet Tradition is equal in wisdom to Investigation.

12 'For Tradition tells us that a man cannot breathe below water, but must surely drown.

13 'And, likewise, that a man cannot cut out his own heart with cold steel then dance, but must surely die.

14 'And, also, that gambling brings poverty, whores bring pox, and strong drink is the destruction of sound men.'

15 Then Lachish caused to be brought before them a chalice, which was wrought in high silver and chased about with gold, and within that chalice was a liquid.

16 And Lachish pointed at the chalice, saying, 'Behold, within is hemlock, which is evil by Tradition, just as the madness of drink, the coquetry of whores and the foolishness of wagering is evil.

17 'And I know the evil thereof, by Tradition, yea, as I know the evil of the other things which I have spoken of, though I have not tasted of the flesh of them.

18 'Verily verily I say unto you, if a man drink of evil he will perish, and a boy also. Wilt thou dispute that with the cup?'

19 And Arabin understood his meaning, and said unto him: 'I will.'

20 Then did Garimanthea try to restrain Arabin, but he was shaken off.

21 And Arabin advanced unto the chalice, and picked it up, and gazed upon the beauty of gold which was upon it, and on the liquid which was within it.

22 Then Arabin spoke, saying, 'Let the gods bear witness to the truth of my persuasions.'

23 And he drank, and did not suffer thereby.

24 Then Jarmuth Japhia Lachish seized the chalice with hands that were rough, for there was rage upon him.

25 And he addressed the gathering, saying, 'It's a trick! There's no hemlock in this!'

26 Then Jarmuth Lachish drank thereof.

27 And truly there was no hemlock within, but a mixture of wine and of that poison which is got from the seeds of nux vomica, and which is known as strychnine.

28 And the death of Jarmuth Lachish was terrible to behold.

29 Then those of the City Fathers who remained declared that they would take Emergency Executive Powers and have Arabin executed upon the spot.

30 Then was his need dire.

31 But one spoke, saying, 'Lo, behold me, for I am Garimanthea the Mighty, barrister, solicitor and attorney at law, and I say unto you that your Order for Execution is null and void, and likewise your assumption of Emergency Executive Powers.'

32 And the City Fathers asked of him: 'Wherefore?'

33 Whereupon Garimanthea smiled a smile that was most terrible to see, saying unto them, 'Verily verily, I can count though a chicken cannot. How many heads do you need for a quorum?'

34 Then the City Fathers counted, and were dismayed.

35 For the death of Jarmuth Lachish had left them short of a quorum.

36 Therefore was the council automatically dissolved, and elections held.

37 And it happened that the glory of righteousness and the use of good gold brought Arabin lol Arabin and his team victory in those elections, and all power that was in the Free Port of Runcorn fell unto him.

38 And the rejoicing in the city was exceedingly great.

41

Gouda Muck: second-best swordsmith on Stokos; first
suffered religious revelation in Khmar 16; announced the
next year that he was the avatar of the Flame, the High
God of All Gods; doctrines of thrift, abstinence, chastity
and prudery found favour with neighbours whose health
and wealth had suffered from compulsory indulgence in
the delights of the temple of the demon Hagon; religion
of Goudanism thereafter rapidly went from strength to
strength.

Midsummer's Day inaugurated a year which was, by
Collosnon reckoning, Celadric 1. If the Lord Emperor
Khmar, master of Tameran, had survived, then it would
have been the start of Khmar 20. But the ferocious horselord was dead, killed in the forests of Penvash during the
confusion of mutiny, betrayal, clan-fights and feuding
which had accompanied his invasion of Argan.

Drake heard many wild rumours about the lands north
of Runcorn. They had seemed normal enough when he
had marched through them with Zanya, scarcely half a
year previously, but since then – why, what with Khmar's
invasion, and the unleashing of the fury of dragons, and
mad battles between wizards and warriors, the whole of
the north seemed to have gone berserk.

For Runcorn, this was very bad news.

Galish convoys were no longer travelling the Salt Road
through Runcorn, Chorst, Dybra, Estar, Lake Armansis,
Larbster Bay and D'Waith. Instead, those convoys, the

lifeblood of commerce, were shipping out of Androlmarphos to sail direct to the Ravlish Lands.

Hence, economic downturn in Runcorn.

Shops closed, apprenticeships cancelled, shipbuilders silent, more beggars on the street, violence at night, brawls, burglary, rape, highway robbery, horse-stealing, outbreaks of graffiti-writing.

Drake could not read the graffiti (or anything else for that matter) but he was told much of it said uncomplimentary things about him.

He was in trouble.

Or, to use his own words:

'I'm in deep shit.'

The City Treasurer had recently fled, allegedly to Selzirk, and a quick audit had shown that most of the contents of the city coffers had disappeared with him. Worse, his brother, who had been looking after revenues for Drake's temple, had also vanished – leaving the temple bankrupt.

Temple income had dropped to nearly nothing. The best girls had left for the flesh-pots of Selzirk. Rumours about the diseased state of those who remained were, unfortunately, true. Gambling brought in next to nothing now that Runcorn's docks were idle. Even the liquor business was in trouble – something Drake would not have thought possible.

What was worse, the temple enforcers were squeezing Drake. They wanted a pay rise. He could not afford to pay – he was twenty days behind with their wages as it was. Yet he had to pay, for his easily won popularity was swiftly turning sour.

Worse, his lawyer was into him for an enormous amount in legal fees. Garimanthea, the first truly ruthless man Drake had ever met, frightened him badly (for Drake, innocent of the deeper evils of civilization, had never met a lawyer until he came to Runcorn.)

'On Stokos,' said Drake, 'we didn't have these problems.'

And, now, he could see why. Because Stokos had coal, iron ore, metalworkers, banking, fishing and a healthy import–export trade, hence there were always profits to be skimmed off for the temple of the demon Hagon.

Whereas Runcorn had the import–export business alone, which had been destroyed by the troubles to the north.

Somehow, Drake had to rejuvenate the economy of Runcorn.

These days he spent a lot of time alone in his office in City Hall, thinking. He was there on that Midsummer's Day, the first day of Celadric 1, when he became aware of a disturbance outside.

At first he gave it no thought, but the noise became steadily louder. It had about it something of the humming of bees, something of the baying of wolves, and touches of the noise of a timberyard, a marketplace, a slave-auction and a full-pitched battle. It was, he realized, the noise of an angry crowd.

Drake drummed his fingers on the big desk he was sitting behind. A riot, was it? Well, no doubt the enforcers would break a few heads and set things right . . .

He was thinking thus when one of his enforcers entered, sweating, bleeding from a scalp wound, gasping and staggering. He stood in front of Drake, swaying.

'Well? What is it, man? Spit it out!' said Drake.

And the enforcer spat out a little blood then dropped dead in front of the desk. An ocular Investigation revealed the probable cause of this lapse in etiquette – the enforcer had a throwing knife embedded in his back.

'Hmmm,' said Drake, rubbing one hand over the stubble of ginger beard which had lately begun to lay claim to his chin.

He was thinking – not about the dead enforcer, but about the architecture of City Hall.

It was a fortified building where every window was an arrow-slit. There was a sally port, of course – but it was unreachable, for the tunnel which led to it was used as an extension of the archives, and was blocked by generations' worth of paper, parchment, papyrus and clay tiles. The only other way out was through the front door.

'Boldness be my friend,' said Drake to himself, and, with pulses quickening, buckled on his best sword, equipped himself with a belt-knife, a boot-knife and a back-knife, pulled on his gauntlets, and went out to face the crowd.

As he went, he wondered where Zanya was. He hoped she was safe.

With something like shock, he realized he had not seen his beloved for at least three days. Running cities and temples looks easy work from outside – but Drake, who had been working his arse off ever since he came to power in Runcorn, had found himself with precious little time in which to enjoy the delights of love.

Drake came out onto the balcony which overlooked both the main door to City Hall and the market square which it fronted onto.

The market square was a seething storm of tumultuous people. The enforcers, who had been fighting to keep them from the doors, had now retreated within, leaving half a dozen of their number dead on the steps.

The doors had been closed.

And, even now, a ship's mast was being manhandled through the mob. Clearly it was going to be used as a battering ram.

Drake looked on this impassively.

He was recognized.

People began to scream in hysteria.

Drake lifted his arms high, and held that theatrical stance until the noise died down.

Drake had studied democracy at close hand on the Greater Teeth. He had learnt a thing or two.

'You are ready to act!' said Drake, in a big voice – a voice which the years had trained against everything from the hammering of forges to storms at sea.

The crowd answered him with a roar of assent. They

were ready to act, all right. They were ready to tear him from limb to limb.

Was he responsible for the woes of Runcorn? Was he responsible for dragons in Estar, the Collosnon invasion of the north of Argan, or renegade wizards on the loose? No – but he was the government, therefore he was going to be held responsible whether he liked it or not.

'Yes,' said Drake. 'You are ready to act. And the field for action is huge. Rich! Glorious! I talk wealth. I talk money. I talk women. For the taking.'

'Horseshit!' screamed a voice.

'Aye, horses is part of it,' said Drake. 'Ten horses for every man here, yea, and for the beggar who follows him.'

He had their attention now.

'Runcorn has lived by trade,' said Drake. 'But trade is gone. Therefore, we live by – this!'

And, drawing his weapon with a theatrical flourish, he shouted:

'The sword!'

Holding the glittering weapon to the midsummer sun, he looked around. They were silent, now. They wanted to hear. He knew no distant promises would serve. They wanted gratification of some sort – soon.

'Close,' said Drake. 'Very close, lies wealth. The wealth of land. The wealth of horses. The wealth of many slaves. Generations have ignored it. But we are stronger. We are bolder. We shall take it.'

'Wealth where?' bawled a fellow in the crowd. 'In Selzirk?'

'Man,' yelled Drake. 'There's wealth for a pretty arse like yours in Selzirk, to be sure.'

The crowd laughed – and Drake knew he had them.

'Real wealth, we're talking,' said Drake. 'Ours for the taking. The horselands, we're talking about. Rich land there, and horses, and slaves. Aye.'

And now everyone realized what he was talking about. The Lezconcarnau Plains. Bounded by mountains, they lay inland from Runcorn. True, there were many people there – primitive disorganized villages which cropped the land, or raised cattle, or bred horses, or hunted – and feuded with each other constantly.

True, there was wealth there to be had for the taking, if ever a warlord commanded Runcorn.

'Selzirk buys slaves,' said Drake. 'And all the world buys horses. Let us be rich together! Let us be rich! Wealthy! Glorious! We can march tomorrow! We can march today!'

And he waved his sword, conjuring up a tumultuous cheering.

'Who will be war-leaders?' shouted Drake. 'Who wants a war-leader's share of the booty? Prove yourselves forward!'

There was, immediately, a struggling excitement below, as the boldest, most dangerous members of the mob forced themselves forward. Drake had, in effect, just bribed them to throw in their lot with him.

'Steady there!' shouted Drake. 'Make way for the heroes! Don't hold a good man back! Let's see our new leaders!'

And already he was thinking, very very fast, of his next steps. The war leaders would take the city's bravest on a march of conquest into the Lezconcarnau Plains. While they were gone, Drake would consolidate—

He broke off thinking, for he saw Zanya forcing herself forward with the would-be warlords. She was shouting something incoherent. Some strangers were with her, men whom he took to be wizards, for they were dressed in long grey robes and carried with them iron-shod wooden staves.

With shock, he realized what she was shouting:

'Demon-son! Demon-son!'

The men in grey robes, all thirty of them, took up the cry, making it into a chant:

'Demon-son! Demon-son!'

Drake vainly waved his sword, trying to quell the noise.

'I am Arabin lol Arabin,' he shouted.

The stave-men in grey robes were clearing a space on the steps of City Hall. Then a man dressed in robes of purple advanced to the stairs.

'Drake!' he shouted.

And the noise of his voice was awesome.

'Dogs' grief and beetle-dung!' muttered Drake. 'Gouda Muck!'

Then, loudly:

'Old man, we are planning war! For wealth! For conquest! For glory! Let my war-leaders through! The moment demands!'

'Demands?' shouted Muck. 'Who demands? What demands? I tell you who demands! I tell you what demands! A monster demands! The true son of the demon Hagon! A creature spawned from evil! A hell-fiend! He murdered your City Fathers! He drinks poison, yet lives! He butchers babies and eats their livers raw! Rapes your daughters by night as they sleep behind bolted iron! Spreads madness, kills cattle, drinks blood, fouls water, flies by night on the winds of the bat and ravages the clouds to thunder!'

At which there was a considerable outbreak of noise.

Then one of the would-be war leaders got up on the shoulders of his comrades and cried:

'It's our city, boys! Runcorn! Let Runcorn lead Runcorn! The boy's bad luck whatever he is! Run him out of town, that's what I say! Let Runcorn lead Runcorn!'

The slogan proved popular.

Thus it was that Drake was chased out of Runcorn before evening, hair shaved off, body smeared with ashes and molasses, and he ran panting and weeping with his hands tied behind his back until the rabble grew tired of chasing him with sticks and stones and foul language into the bargain.

And as for Gouda Muck?

Why, he would have chased Drake himself, and beaten him to death on the spot, if he could have – for to rid the world of the Demon-son was part of his sacred mission.

But the slogan 'Let Runcorn lead Runcorn!' generated such a wave of riotous prejudice that Muck, even with his thirty stave-men to help him, was lucky to be able to fight his way to the docks and escape from Runcorn on a small fishing boat.

And Zanya?

She went with Muck.

And in the days that followed, there was much fighting in Runcorn as the would-be warlords sorted out their order of precedence. And after that there were a few half-hearted expeditions into the Lezconcarnau Plains. But the tribesmen proved tougher than expected, and the Empire Which Could Have Been never was.

42

Harvest Plains: nation north of Rice Empire, west of Chenameg, south of Runcorn and east of Central Ocean; main cities are Selzirk (the capital) and Androlmarphos; rule is by 'kings', regional and city governors appointed by the 'Kingmaker' (currently Farfalla) who is in turn chosen from the common people by the Regency.

No time but sun time. A buzzard wheeling over barefoot fields. Drake at labour, the weather opening cracks deep in his leather-tough heels. Shiny black crickets at scramble in the heat-cracked land.

Nights in a bunkhouse, staring at nothing, scarcely listening to the peons yattering away in their incomprehensible Field Churl. Waking deep in the night. Listening to creaking snores, a snort, a murmur of night-talk. Tasting his own arm with his own lips. Salt of the day still heavy on his flesh.

Solitary comfort.

Pay day: wages scarcely better than slavery.

Thus Drake Douay lived after exile from Runcorn, doing farm work on an estate near Kelebes, in the Harvest Plains. It was better than starving – though not by much.

He was nineteen years old, and very far from home. And unable to return there, for Stokos was ruled by converts to Goudanism, who would murder Drake if they caught him, on the grounds that he was the son of the demon Hagon.

In the fields, he attacked weeds with a hoe, thinking

how much better that implement would be if its blade was made of steel instead of sharpened wood. He scared birds. He dug and deepened irrigation ditches so a precious trickle of water could dampen the dusty fields. He helped care for the oxen which turned the field-pumps. He spread dung. And he thought.

Often it was Zanya he thought of.

Sometimes, gripped by mutilating rage, he dreamed of knifing her, battering her, smashing and gutting, wrecking her beauty to a corpse. For had she not denied him, abandoned him, betrayed him? Surely she deserved to die.

Other times, he imagined scenes of tender reconciliation. He would exlain why he had neglected her so in those last few months in Runcorn. He had been working for them, yes, securing the foundations of their future. That was important. To be strong together, united against the world . . .

Then he would think of Gouda Muck, who had poisoned the world with his madness. He would brood about murder, torture, maiming, hacking, smashing. And would attack weeds with hoe, working the anger out of his system.

Retiring to the bunkhouse at evening to drink water and eat the slave-mash served to labourers like himself.

Evening . . .

Untranslated voices . . .

Sleep . . .

Dreams . . .

Late in the season, he dreamed of Zanya. Not for the first time. But on this occasion, her face softened with pleasure, and they toasted each other, then spoke most intimately with hands and with lips. Waking, he knew he had forgiven her – if there was anything to forgive. And knew, too, that he was ready for his next move.

Yet what should that next move be?

Drake had no idea, but took to walking in to Kelebes every evening from the estate where he was working. In the town, he sought out the few travellers who were still moving north and south along the Salt Road, and asked them of the world. One evening, he heard a rumour of events in Hok. The next day, he did not go barefoot to the fields, but put on his boots and set off south, taking the road to Selzirk.

On his long march south to the capital of the Harvest Plains, he begged (or stole) what food and water he needed. And sought news at every opportunity. Everything he heard confirmed the original rumour.

When King Tor had invaded Stokos, rallying many loyal supporters to his banner, his forces had suffered a terrible defeat. King Tor had disappeared from the sight of the world.

Now it transpired that Tor had survived, retreating north across the few leagues of sea which separated the northern coast of Stokos from the rugged mountains of Hok, an almost uninhabited province of the Harvest Plains. There he had gathered his strength, and, after many moons of preparation, was beginning to make war on Stokos. Parties of highly trained assassins were infiltrating Stokos, sent to kill or kidnap selected enemies of the Rightful King.

Drake grew increasingly excited.

Lord Menator's attempt to murder King Tor by sending him unsupported to war had failed. The Rightful King lived! Therefore Drake's hopes of a throne on Stokos lived!

Once he reached Selzirk, he would seek further news of Tor. Then he would go down the Velvet River to Androlmarphos. And, from there, south along the coast to Hok. He would place his skills at the service of King Tor. Oh, the ogre king had spoken roughly enough the last time they met, in the Inner Sleeve on Knock. But that was back on the Greaters, when the king was riding high. In exile, fighting a desperate war against dangerous odds, he would surely see the virtues of a young hero like Drake Douay in a better light.

Would there be danger in serving King Tor in a fight against Stokos?

Danger is everywhere. Whatever lies ahead, it can't be

511

worse than what I've been through. Anyway. It's the chance. Aye. To fight. To win power. So I can one day settle scores with Gouda Muck. And Menator! And shit-faced Sully Yot!

Could he work some of his friends into his plans for the future? Could King Tor use some good warlord captains? Of course he could!

Maybe he could make Jon Arabin an admiral or such. If it came from the king, not from me, the offer might suit friend Warwolf right enough. Better than being first mate for Abousir Belench, or whatever he is at the moment!

And the Walrus? For him, nothing! If he'd not started that trouble back in Penvash, life would be that much simpler. I'd have stayed with the pirates. I might still have Zanya, aye.

Thinking of Zanya made him want to cry.

None of that nonsense, man! We're over that! It's the future to be thinking of now!

In Hok, perhaps, he might meet his brother Heth. If Heth still lived.

And that would be worth the walk. Man, that would be worth waiting for.

512

43

Selzirk: capital of the Harvest Plains, stands on north bank of Velvet River at confluence with Shouda Flow.

Outer wall: Ol Ilkeen ('The Oval')

Inner wall: Ol Unamon ('The Buckle'); runs in an '8', dividing the Four Worlds (Santrim, Unkrana, Jone and Wake).

Santrim: eastern (upstream) loop of the '8'; houses rule, law, teaching, and religion; at its centre stands citadel-palace of the Kingmaker Farfalla.

Unkrana: western (downstream) loop of the '8', devoted to commercial offices: banking, insurance, guild administration.

Kesh: fortified military gate-tower at waist of the '8', controlling flow of traffic between the Four Worlds.

Jone: dockland area on southern (riverside) flank, housing warehouses, shipyards, prisons, military barracks, servant quarters, bars and brothels.

Wake: northern flank, devoted to shops, slave markets, horse markets, auction floors, craft work and light industry.

It was late summer when Drake arrived at Selzirk. He had been there once before: arriving by night, chained to the oar of a river-galley. But the ship had gone back downstream again before dawn.

513

Drake was not molested by the guards on the outer side of the gate, though in theory they were supposed to search and interrogate him; he walked through to the inner side, to the pleasure, wealth and opportunity of Selzirk.

Maybe when I catch up with King Tor, I'll have him make me ambassador to Selzirk. Now that's a thought! Wine and women, aye, that's the way to fight a war. I'd be more use to him here, surely, than doing something daft with a spear. Likely I could talk up an army – or bribe up an army. Wonder how much gold old Tor has got to spare?

Lord Dreldragon, King Tor's future ambassador to Selzirk, decided he had a duty to explore the city a bit before heading for Hok to collect his ambassadorial credentials (and the gold which must surely go with such credentials) from the king.

Pity I can't send someone else to Hok to pick up the credentials for me. Aye, that's a thought. Maybe I could front up to the palace, explain how things stand. Tor made me Lord Dreldragon, didn't he? Made me his heir? And if he's said hasty things since, well . . . we needn't make too much of that, it was probably just the phase of the moon or something. If I'm heir to Stokos, that makes me a prince at least. Surely.

If I talk things through proper with someone in high places, likely I can have an ambassador's house on credit. A couple of ambassadorial concubines, too. And someone to run messages down to Tor, just to square things up with him. Credit, that's the stuff! With all of Stokos to my claim . . . why, likely I can borrow my own weight of gold from the banks! My own weight? Weight of a bullock, more like.

Thinking such happy thoughts, Drake idled through bustling streets full of noise, music, crushing faces, sweating armpits, slap-trap sandals, iron-shod boots, kif, opium, dogshit, bananas brought in the Scattered Islands, oranges from Hexagon, and whores from all nations.

And what else?

Why, hawkers for a dozen contending faiths. Slaves, merchants, scribes, law clerks and letter-writers. Beggars, pimps, peddlars, and people wanting to sell him tin, copper, grain, silks, ceramics, or shares in the South Sea Company. All yelling, screaming, pushing, hustling, jostling, swearing, grinning, smirking, grabbing and grasping.

Drake was staggered by the impact of so many strangers. The jabbering crowds of foreigners irritated him so much that he finally raised his voice and bawled, in his native tongue:

'Does anyone here speak Ligin?'

But he was ignored, for one shouting madman more or less meant nothing to Selzirk.

To his surprise, Drake saw many women with red skins on the streets, and red hair to match. He wondered why there were so many Ebrell islanders in Selzirk – not realizing that these females were simply followers of a fashion in dye. Each, of course, reminded him bitterly of Zanya.

Enough seen. Time to start making inquiries.

Accordingly, Drake grabbed a scholarly-looking fellow.

'Hey, man,' said Drake. 'What news of Hok and all?'

'*Blon glay?*' said the scholar, startled. '*Alat onlenjin?*'

'Don't you speak Galish?' said Drake. 'Aagh, I thought you an educated man and all!'

Drake released his scholar and sought information elsewhere. After he drew a blank with another half-dozen people, he started scratching his head a bit. Surely Selzirk had to be teeming with people who spoke Galish. Where could they all be hiding?

Were plenty of people on the river spoke it, when I were slaving on that galley-thing. Aye, then. That's the answer. The river. Boats mean trade and trade means Galish. I'll find some ship-people to talk to me.

Drake soon found his way through Kesh to Jone, the dockland area. It was busy today, crowded with soldiers

515

who were being ferried across the river to the further bank. Drake wandered around watching the soldiers, and watching fools lose money to a quick-talking rogue who hid a lima bean under one of three little cups, shuffled these then asked assembled suckers to guess its hiding place.

Strange! They still play that game? Well, I suppose they do. Fools never learn, do they?

Drake heard one fool bemoaning his gambling losses in Galish to a comrade, who, having little time for sympathy, excused himself and left the loser friendless.

'Hey, man,' said Drake to the sucker, 'you speak Galish, isn't it?'

'I do, young sir,' said his chosen fool. 'Could you lend a poor man some money?'

'Nay,' said Drake, 'for I'm so poor myself that my head is mortgaged in half a dozen places.'

But Drake lent an ear to the man's sorrows, and that in itself was almost as welcome as cash. Then Drake asked why all of Selzirk was built on the northern bank of the river, and none on the southern.

'Why, young sir, for the southern bank is lower, hence floods in winter when the river runs high. So the soldiers have luck to be leaving now, otherwise they'd be wading to their waists in the mud.'

'Where go the soldiers?' said Drake.

'Why, to Hok, of course.'

'To Hok!' said Drake, astonished and delighted. 'To aid King Tor, is it? To fight for the Rightful King against Sudder Vemlouf, priest of the Flame and Usurper of Stokos?'

'No no no!' said the sucker, near killing himself with laughter.

'What's so funny?' said Drake, fierce and angry.

'Why, haven't you heard?' said the sucker. 'Our rulers have lost patience with the ogre-bandit at last.'

'The ogre-bandit!' said Drake, in outrage. 'That's a royal-born king you're talking of!'

'No,' said the fool, 'it's a foreign outlaw, that's what it is. A dirty, stinking, cow-raping ogre. A bandit. A stinking foreign bandit who was run off Stokos for crimes against humanity.'

'Obviously you don't understand, and neither do your rulers,' said Drake, trying to keep his temper. 'If only King Tor had had an ambassador in Selzirk, you'd understand much better.'

'Oh, three men came from Hok a month ago, claiming to be his ambassadors,' said the sucker-fool. 'Which was adding insult to injury.'

'What injury?' said Drake. 'How does Tor injure Selzirk by fighting for the crown which is rightfully his?'

'He injures us, young fool,' said the fool, 'by running his rag-tag rabble through the mountains of Hok, which is a province of the Harvest Plains, in case you didn't know. That's invasion, isn't it? That's why the soldiers march forth – to push Tor out of our territory. To push him into the sea.'

Something must have gone terribly wrong. Clearly the ambassadors Tor sent to Selzirk had not been up to the job. Something had to be done, urgently, or the world would war to ruin for no purpose. Who could save the day? Why, Drake Douay, of course! He'd present himself to Tor's ambassadors, promptly. And offer to negotiate a deal with the rulers of Selzirk. For a cut of the ambassadorial profits, of course.

'These ambassadors sent by Tor,' said Drake. 'Where do I find them? I have to speak to them. Urgently!'

'Too late,' said the sucker-fool. 'For the dogs have had their guts already.'

'Say what?' said Drake.

'They were hung, drawn and quartered yesterday,' said the sucker-fool, shoving his face hard up against Drake's. 'By order of our rulers, who'll have no truck with bandits. Which is why, I'm thinking, they'll pay a good price for you.'

So saying, the sucker-fool grabbed Drake by the collar.

Whereupon Drake slid his hand slick and swift between the sucker-fool's garments, grabbing him by the testicles.

'Wah!' said the fool, in alarm.

'Hush!' said Drake, squeezing slightly. 'Or I'll cripple you for life. Walk. Quiet like. Down that alleyway.'

Walking on tip-toe, the hapless fool obeyed. The alleyway opened onto a deserted mews. There Drake did his bit for international relations by teaching his Selzirk sucker-fool why he should respect King Tor and his hard-fisted minions.

After which Drake climbed onto the roof of a warehouse and sat there, brooding as he watched the ferrymen taking the soldiers across the broad reach of the river. So many soldiers! King Tor was done for. Drake was upset. Close, indeed, to crying. That morning, everything had looked so sweet. And now?

Man, this is rough.

What should he do? Three ambassadors had talked sweet for Tor, and had ended up getting torn to pieces for their troubles. Could Drake do better?

I'm smarter, surely. The fastest tongue this side of Chi'ash-lan, I reckon. If anyone could talk things right for Tor, it's me, surely. But the time for talk looks to have gone. Aye. But if I wanted to try?

If Drake chose to try talking things right for Tor, his first step would have to be to learn who the rulers of Selzirk were. But was it wise to ask questions?

Man, I can't question without risk. What happens if I'm named as Lord Dreldragon? Lord Dreldragon, beloved of Tor, heir to Stokos? Likely it'll be head-chopping time. Or I'll conceal my nobility, yet get killed anyway, as a common bandit.

It don't look too good, does it? Not now. But might look better if the army gets a bloody nose. Aye. Army stuff, that's full of risk. Weather and such. Disease. Mutiny. Folks hot in temper don't talk too sweet. I reckon these – in Selzirk have got their blood up. Aye. Hot for

*the kill. But if their army gets pounded in Hok, they'll talk
different then.*

Thus Drake came to a decision.

If the army of Selzirk returned from Hok defeated,
mauled by Tor or decimated by the standard hazards of
campaigning, then Drake would make discreet inquiries,
with a view to determining whether it was safe for him to
proclaim his royal status. Till then, he would have to shift
for himself as best he could, hiding both his nationality
and his nobility.

*It's right hard being a prince in exile. Aye. A prince,
having to live in the gutters. That doesn't sound right. But
I'll have to bear with it for the while, if I'm to be king on
Stokos. So what do I need? Bed and board. Aye. Work
and eats. And how to find that?*

*Well. Go where there's talk, that's the way to start.
Aye. For certain. A lesson here, isn't it? I was too close to
my misery, back in Kelebes. Should have gone into the
town more often earlier. Might have heard rumour
sooner. Might have got to Selzirk in time to talk away the
war. Talk, that's the thing! To know what the talk is!
Well.*

Live and learn.

And now? Search talk!

So thinking, Drake scrambled down off the roof of his
warehouse. If he'd found no shelter by nightfall he'd
return there to sleep. Cold, yes, but sleeping at ground
level might be rash in this big and evil city.

Searching for talk, Drake soon enough found himself a
tavern. Alcohol, he knew, would do him no good – and
no bad, either. Nevertheless, a tavern was the place to be.
There, people would gladly keep him company and tell
him – he was sure – the things he needed to survive.

The tavern he found was a cedar-built beer-barn filled
with bodies mostly male, some for sale but most not, and
with the wuthering uproar of a hundred upraised voices,
and with the smells of sweat, porter, lager beer, arak, gin
and zythum.

519

The denizens of this murky boozing hole, practical worshippers of the Demon to a man (whether they knew it or not), were mostly drunk, and were mostly talking Churl. Not the High Churl of the upper classes, or the City Churl of the commons, or any of the coarse country dialects known collectively as Field Churl, but a thieves' cant which named itself as Shurlspurl. Not one in a thousand upright citizens could have followed their conversations.

Drake elbowed his way between thief and fence, pimp and pad, and a dozen types of lout, loon, hoon and ruffian. He shoved past a cly-faker, scrattling away at a yuke while keeping conversation with a burly brute who might have been the city slave-brander or the public executioner.

'Shanema chovea,' said a man curtly, as Drake jostled past.

'Up yours!' said Drake.

And pressed on through the babbling gloom to the bar, where he slapped down a coin and said, in Galish:

'Wine.'

Wine was served to him. He breathed in its bouquet, which made him cough. He poked a finger into the liquid, feeling for sediment. There was no sediment to speak of, but for half a broken tooth, which Drake hoicked out of his mug and discarded to the dogs which were snouting about at floor-level.

'A good drop, doubtless,' he said.

And sipped at the wine, which was warm. A dog stuck its head into his lap, and looked at him with adoring eyes.

'In love with me, are you?' said Drake, scratching the dog behind the ears. 'Well, I'm pretty to look at, I know that proper. If I'm not fixed otherwise, you can sleep with me tonight.'

But, when Drake came up with no hound-pleasing tidbits, his dog went begging elsewhere.

'Bugger you, then!' said Drake.

'Speaks Galish, does it? said something approximating to a face.

'Aye,' said Drake staunchly. 'That it does.'

'And what might its business be? Pretty or ugly?'

'Ugly,' said Drake. 'Very ugly.'

'Blood on the blade, then?'

'Maybe,' he said.

'Are you pad, then? Or does it jugulate for hire, perhaps?'

'My business is to dare,' said Drake.

'Then where has it been daring, out in the big bold world with its iron and its ugly?'

'Aagh, after dragons and such,' said Drake. 'Aye, hunting basilisk at dusk and phoenix at dawn.'

'Sounds famous work. So are you famous? Should I know your name? Is it Git the Rape, by chance? Or Surly Cock-cutter?'

'My name is not for the unnamed,' said Drake.

'Why, as for me,' said the stranger, 'I be Fimp.'

'Then I be Fimp-friend,' said Drake. 'Happy?'

'Always happy, lover. Always.'

Nearing the end of the wine, Drake drank slowly, straining out the lees as best he could with his teeth. He was right – there was virtually no sediment. Only a few dozen soft black things looking like tealeaves. An excellent wine, then. Cheap at twice the price. A pity he couldn't get drunk on it.

'What does it need?' said Fimp. 'Is it looking for help, by chance? Someone to idle and oxter it, maybe? Does it need to make money?'

'It might make some through sale,' said Drake, wondering if Fimp's purse was fat or thin. 'But not sale of itself.'

'Has treasure, has it? From adventures, perhaps? Ah . . . I vum you've treasure indeed, yes, riches fit to make the heart quop faster.'

'Something of the sort,' said Drake. 'But not with me. It's a Door, aye, to wealth of all description.'

'Oh yes!'

'Really. I've got a . . . a sample of the wealth with me.'

'Show.'

521

'Buy me a drink,' said Drake. 'Then I'll show.'

He assessed the stranger's purse as the fellow paid out for a shot of quetsch. That was strong stuff, but Fimp bought for himself a jug of oxymel, which Drake had seen in other places, and knew to be a drink as mild as water.

'What have we bought then, me pretty one?'

'Sight only,' said Drake. 'No touching.'

And he pulled out the magic talking amulet which he had won in a Wishing Tower in Ling after a battle with a ferocious Guardian Machine and an encounter with a deserted skeleton and an invisible door.

'What have you got there, me younker?' said Fimp, as Drake held up the magic medallion by its necklace-chain of smoothflowing black links.

'Something precious,' said Drake, speaking so soft that Fimp could hardly hear him for the background babble. 'Something rare.'

Fimp stared at the cool, glossy lozenge of silver-splashed black with greedy eyes.

'What's that silver on the black, youngling? Stars, is it? A golden sun on one side, yes, and – oh, this I must see!'

Drake snatched the amulet away as Fimp grabbed for it.

'Sight only!' he warned.

'Where did it come from, then?' said Fimp. 'A lady's throat, perhaps?'

'I told you,' said Drake. 'It came from a land where I went by way of a Door. And there's more where that came from, through the very same Door.'

'Then thinks you to sell us a map, perhaps? Map to your Door so precious? For us to club good gold, then you to vanish? Mannikin, we're not so greedy, nay?'

'You're not greedy?' said Drake, not understanding.

'Oh, true, so very true,' said Fimp with a smirk. 'Never greedy enough to seek cheap wealth unending, or life eternal, or youth eternal either. Might sell such sometimes, true. I'm last to be selfish. So true! So true! Have sold a nation's worth of treasure cities in my time. But buy such? Never!'

Drake, seeing he would find no instant buyers for the secret of the Door of Penvash – he had thought, for a moment, he might be able to make a quick fortune out of it – told a tale closer to the truth:

'You want to know the truth of this? Man, it came from a Wishing Tower in the Deep South. Aye, and I had to fight with a Neversh to get it.'

Fimp laughed, showing pyrrhous stains on his teeth. And others, who had been listening close, laughed with him.

'So now it wants to sell us maps to a Wishing Tower!'

'I'd never,' said Drake, 'for the knowledge is far too worthy to sell.'

All laughed again, knowing that for a bare-faced lie. But the lie itself was not unwelcome, for these people appreciated the comedy of outrage.

'Come, me little pajock,' said Fimp. 'Let's see that trinket closer.'

'You want to buy?' said Drake.

'Perhaps,' said Fimp. 'Perhaps. We can talk of buying, yes, that does no harm, no harm in talk.'

'Then first,' said Drake, 'flatten the gold you'll be talking with.'

And he pointed to the counter of the bar, where he wanted to see Fimp's coinage laid out for inspection.

'Come, Fimp,' said Drake. 'Why hesitate? Am I not Fimp-friend? Let's see the gold, then bargain.'

'Ah now, me little younker,' said Fimp, 'You sees, I bargain – with this!'

And he drew red metal to the menace.

'So give it!' he said.

Drake, with every manifestation of reluctance, handed the amulet over. Eager as a bald-headed vulture greeding at a gaping belly-wound, the shivman seized it. And Drake smashed him. Struck first, fast and hard. Struck second, third and fourth. Struck again – and stunned, bruised and broke before taking his opponent in a choke.

'Speak to me nicely now,' said Drake, tightening the

throttle. 'Speake to me nice, darling, yes, speak soft, my dear – or the blade speaks for me.'

Fimp, dizzy, dislocated in time, muttered something in Shurlspurl, which meant nothing to Drake.

'Is it life you want?' said Drake. 'Is it life? Gold has life, aye, bright as sun, hot as fire. I'll trade. Be quick! The blade hungers!'

Fimp had dropped the amulet onto the counter of the bar. A hand dared from the crowd of spectators, lunging for the magic medallion. Quick as a flash, Drake stabbed the hand, which escaped with a nick – and without the amulet.

'That's how quick you'll die,' said Drake to Fimp.

All around, bright eyes watched for a killing.

'Soft,' said an oiled, luxurious voice. 'Soft, young Galish.'

And the voice smiled its way into a man, who laid down cold gold on the bar.

'Let him go,' said the man, a well-fed elderly fellow who wore blue and yellow furs though the place was warm.

Drake scooped up the gold, secured his amulet, then released Fimp. Who slumped to the floor and then, kicked by patrons who wanted to get back to their drinks, began to crawl into the further recesses of the darkness, where he had the misfortune to encounter two bad-tempered tavern dogs.

'What do you want?' said Drake to his gold-paying stranger.

'Ah,' said the man in the colourful furs, 'the question, young Galish, is what do you want. How much ambition do you have?'

'Who are you?' said Drake. 'And what?'

'I am Ol Tul,' said the stranger.

Drake took this for a regular name, ignorant of the fact that 'Ol Tul', in all varieties of Churl, meant simply 'The Man'.

'As for what I am,' said Ol Tul, 'why, I am he who needs. I need blades to stand gate. Good work it is, daywork.'

'As muscle, then.'

'Nay, as steel. Or is it too pretty?'

'What do you run?' asked Drake.

'Do you mean to ask what I muckle? Pretty, I muckle women, and smoke. Both worth it. That's why the steel. To stand off the jealous.'

'Aye then,' said Drake. 'I'm in.'

He had no special desire to be bodyguard, frightener or enforcer, and guessed well enough that the job he was being offered involved a bit of all three. But he had to take what he could get. He was in a dangerous foreign city, alone, with no friends and no money. Moreover, he had to stay in Selzirk so he could take advantage of any radical change in the city's attitude to King Tor. Thus, in utterance, he accepted Ol Tul's offer.

'So you're in,' said Ol Tul, nodding to the barman. 'But if you're to stay in, I must know more about you.'

'What?' said Drake, as the barman put a couple of beers on the counter.

'Name, genesis and training,' said Ol Tul.

All difficult questions. It was dangerous to come from Stokos. To be a pirate? That might have its dangers, too. Drake remembered a fellow he had met in Estar, on the Salt Road south of Stokos. He had asked the man's name since the fellow looked remarkably alike the woodsman Blackwood, that charitable forest-dweller who had found, saved and sheltered both Drake and Zanya when they were lost in Estar's Looming Forest.

Shen Shen Drax, that was the man's name.

'I,' said Drake, 'be Shen Shen Drax, leech-gatherer of Delve.'

'And where under the five skies be Delve?' said Ol Tul.

'Why,' said Drake, 'Delve is a small place in Estar, south of the ruling town of Lorford. South, indeed, of mountain Maf, where lives the dragon Zenphos, who I had the pleasure of meeting once.'

'A pretty tale that makes, I vum,' said Ol Tul, supping his beer.

'Yes,' said Drake, taking a drag on his own beer. 'So you know my genesis right enough. Born in Delve, by the Salt Road. Aye, and raised there. Name and genesis both. You have them.'

'But training?' said Ol Tul. 'This place called Estar, if I place it right, that's north of Chorst and Dybra. Little but grass and leeches there, if I hear right.'

'Grass and leeches!' said Drake, speaking up for Estar as indeed he must if he was to pass for a patriot. 'Nay, man, there's more by much. Dragon, aye – that I've spoken of. And sheep, with much killing for disputes over the same. And a castle huge at Lorford. Aye. Castle Vaunting. A place built by wizards in generations long forgotten.'

'Lorford?' said Ol Tul.

'The ruling town of Estar, as I've said,' said Drake. 'It stands on the banks of the Hollern River, which flows south from Lake Armansis. This Castle Vaunting, it rules the hill called Melross. Was there I had my training, aye.'

'How?' said Ol Tul.

'For I took service under Prince Comedo, the ruler of the place,' said Drake. 'This leech-gathering business, man, it's not the world's best living, as you'd guess for yourself. So, when I were a strong fourteen – which is going back a few years now – I took place with the prince.'

'As what?'

'As soldier, man.'

'Leech-gatherer to soldier,' said Ol Tul, with a smile which was not necessarily friendly.

'Aye,' said Drake, stoutly. 'And, as a soldier, I trained beneath the Rovac warriors who serve the prince.'

'Name them,' said Ol Tul.

'There are three. One is Oronoko, aye, who has skin of utter purple, as do some that's born in Rovac. Another is Atsimo Andranovory, a black-bearded brute who kills as soon as kisses. The third – that's Morgan Hearst. Aye. He's the best and hardest. A grey-haired killer. Grey eyes

526

on him, too. He taught me man to man these last long years. Sword, aye. And hand to hand without weapons.'

'Then why left you Estar?' said Ol Tul.

'Man,' said Drake, 'have you not heard the news? It's madness there. Dragon run wild. Invading armies slaughtering across the countryside. Wizards wild in wrath, killing with fire and thunder. All trade at a halt on the Salt Road. Man, those who could, they ran – aye, and Morgan Hearst, he led us as we ran. But he died by the roadside, died face to face with a dragon. But me – I lived. But just.'

Ol Tul drained the last of his beer.

'Come with me,' said Ol Tul, 'and we'll put your story to the test.'

Drake followed with some trepidation, wondering what kind of examination he was going to face. A detailed grilling on the geography of Estar, perhaps? A language test by some stray native of the place whom Ol Tul happened by chance to know? The people of Estar had their own tongue, aye, Estral, that was the name of it – but Drake had learnt nary a word of the stuff. The good woodsman Blackwood, who had sheltered him in need, had spoken Galish with the best.

Fortunately, the test Ol Tul planned for Drake took place in a private combat pit. It was a tough test, and Drake got a rib broken while passing it – plus a five-stitch cut to add to his wound-list. But pass he did, with honours. Ol Tul brought many potential recruits to that combat pit, and nineteen out of twenty failed, and were dumped dead in the river.

Thus it was that Lord Dreldragon of Stokos, currently posing as Shen Shen Drax of Estar, won the trust and confidence of Ol Tul, 'The Man', and was inducted into the underworld of Selzirk.

Drake soon became acquainted with the ruling city of the Harvest Plains. But what he knew was not the city of palaces and temples which features in history books, but another place altogether: Selzirk of the thousand sewers, the city of low-life brothels, opium dens, protection rackets, blackmail, intimidation and outright murder.

He lived by wit and by steel.

The pace was fast. This life had no *longueurs* like that of the Teeth, where an entire crew of Orfus pirates might spend months at a time doing little but sealing, breeding, fishing and gambling. Drake lived instead at city-speed, and soon won a name for himself amongst those who served Ol Tul.

A couple of times he almost died, for the way of the knife is different to that of the sword. But he mastered the skills of the shorter blade soon enough, and became known as a dangerous shivman. He began to scrape a little Shurlspurl, learning fast on the streets by day and in bed by night.

But, while Drake soon knew the ropes and was showing off his growing grasp of the lingo, to his fellow hardmen he was and always would be (if he lived) 'the Galish', the outsider. If he died, of course, he would be simply forgotten.

Drake gathered what news he could of the campaigning in the province of Hok, where the armies of the Harvest Plains were trying to root out and destroy the fugitive forces of King Tor. News was sparse. There was no word of victory, but none of defeat. Drake guessed that the campaign had become bogged down in the tortured terrain.

He struck up acquaintances with old soldiers in bars and in brothels, and learned that the province of Hok was a chopped-up mess of cliffs and gorges, riddled with caves and drop-holes. Where its mountains gentled into the flatlands of the Harvest Plains proper, the ground was low-lying and boggy, making communication and supply difficult.

'Hok,' said one old soldier, 'is but a hundred leagues from east to west, and scarce more than twenty leagues from north to south. But when a piece of land is made of teeth, bones and splinters, it can be blood-sweat hard to win at war. If you'd seen terrain which was really rough, you'd have some idea of what I mean.'

'Aye,' said Drake, who had seen lands rough as storm-chopped water in Ling, Penvash and elsewhere. 'I see it right enough.'

When winter came, then, perhaps, he'd know the results of the campaigning in Hok. Then he'd be ready to make his next move. And what would that be?

I'll make ambassador in Selzirk. Aye. Or, if that's impossible, I'll pack my sword and march. Aye. March south to Hok and do battle for real. A hero, like. Danger-ous, sure – but what's that which I'm living? It's hardly safe, now, is it?

It wasn't.

44

Name: Atsimo Andranovory.

Birthplace: Lorp.

Occupation: unemployed cut-throat.

Status: illegal immigrant.

Description: rough-bearded brute with scarred bald patch the size of a man's palm on the top of his head.

Career: first fisherman then Orfus pirate; marooned by his captain on the shores of Estar, where put his sword at Prince Comedo's command; joined party questing inland after death-stone and led a mutiny against his leaders in dragon-lands beyond the Araconch Waters; came down-river with fellow mutineers through the Chenameg Kingdom to Selzirk of the Harvest Plains.

It was autumn.

Drake Douay was at sword in a loft, practising kata – some learnt on Stokos in his apprentice days, others taught him by the weapons muqaddam on a voyage to Hexagon and back. These days, he welcomed the austere disciplines of steel, finding himself bored by the drunken company of his fellow thugs.

The weapons muqaddam had taught him most.

Slashing the air with sharpened steel, Drake remembered that strong, hard man. Killed by barbarians in Tameran, aye. Buried upside down with his feet cut off. A cruel way to die.

I remembered you with ashes. Yet who will remember me?

Drake was making his way in Selzirk, yes, but it was still a world away from home. If he died here, he would die unlamented amongst strangers.

The weapons muqaddam, he was with comrades till he died. That was something, at least.

When still alive, the weapons muqaddam had let Drake make blade chime against blade often enough to satisfy him, never caring how many swords got notched, or bent, or broken, or whether fancy iron or copper inlay fell out of them. He had taught Drake to train as though his life depended on the next stroke that he struck – which, of course, is the only way for a true weapons master to train.

Drake realized, guiltily, that he had recently forgotten that lesson – and had been treating his kata as a dance. He used knife more than sword, these days, that was the trouble. Sword had become a bit of a game.

'Concentrate, man,' said Drake to Drake.

And put death into the next blow that he struck. All his training went into that cut. Through the sword, he lived a moment for the weapons muqaddam. He struck with the will to kill. Which is the only way to strike – even in training.

'Where's the ghost?' asked a voice.

Drake, still handling his weapon for murder, turned to meet this interruption. His ice-smooth steel cut the air clean and sweet. His face was cold, hard, remote. It spoke of a warrior's rapture. A rapture of death.

'Easy, man,' said Pigot Quebec, alarmed at the expression on Drake's face.

'Oh,' said Drake, easing his stance. 'It's you.'

'Yes,' said Pigot Quebec. 'I'm glad you realize it. I thought for a moment you were making to kill me.'

'Perhaps I was,' said Drake, softly. 'Perhaps I was.'

This was weird, this business of weapons. Live with the steel for long enough, and it takes to demanding a death. He shivered, and slid his blade to its sheath.

'What are you here for?' he said.

531

'I've come to claim you for civilized company,' said Pigot Quebec.

'What?' said Drake. 'We're leaving Selzirk, are we?'

'Hush your cheek!' said Quebec. 'Listen, man, there's a new champion down at the Eagle.'

'I'm listening,' said Drake. 'Listening hard. But I'm damned if I can hear him.'

'And damned if you can't. Man, you were born for damnation. Come, let's sweat down the street to the champion.'

'What's this fellow champion at?' asked Drake. 'Can't be shouting, can it?'

'At lying, man. Untruths of all descriptions. Tall tales. Adventures into the never-when to see the never-was.'

'Oh,' said Drake. 'You mean he's a priest?'

'Nay! A liar!'

'What's the difference?' asked Drake.

'Man,' said Quebec, 'the man himself perhaps will answer.'

'If he answers that there's none, then he's a liar in truth indeed,' said Drake. 'What's your untruth's name?'

'I know it not,' said Quebec. 'But I know he's holding forth at the Eagle, I've heard him there myself. And, man, he's something. He swears the truth unreal as smoothly as a weasel farting.'

'You have many weasels in your family then?' said Drake. 'Or you know them from the casuals of whorehouse acquaintance?'

'You were the first I've met,' said Quebec, 'so it's of you I've made my study.'

Drake made as if to cuff him round the head. Quebec parried, and they wrestled a bit. Then, with many a jape and a pun, the two made their way to the Eagle.

Drake knew of the Eagle, but had never been there before, since this tavern was not a criminal haunt. It was, however, definitely a low-life place, attracting all kinds of riff-raff: falconers, river oars, peddlers, jesters and beggar-masters, and, no doubt, the odd questing hero in disguise.

'Man,' said Quebec, as the pair entered. 'This champion's good, but you can top his tales.'

'Aye,' said Drake. 'I could top any tale – simply by telling the truth.'

'Gah! I know your kind of truth.'

'You don't,' said Drake. 'Or you'd believe it.'

The two pushed forward. There was a crowd around the liar, some folk standing on bar benches, so it was push and shove to get near the front. Drake shoved once too often – and was picked up by a giant-sized axeman from Chenameg and thrown bodily through the air. He crashed to ground at the feet of the champion liar.

'Drax!' yelled Quebec. 'You all right?'

Lord Dreldragon (also known as Drake Douay, as Arabin lol Arabin, and as Shen Shen Drax, depending what company he was keeping) lay on the ground, winded, staring up at a most unlovely sight. A rough-smelling thug with bloodshot eyes and a black-bearded face, and a shaggy swag of filthy black hair.

'An'vory!' said Drake.

'You!' said Atsimo Andranovory.

And he grabbed Drake in a strangle.

Fortunately, a couple of Drake's fighting-comrades were in the audience, and they separated An'vory from Drake's throat. They were all for killing the man, but the publican stopped them.

'You kill my champion liar,' warned the publican, 'and my sons will rend you limb to limb.'

The publican seemed to have a small trace of ogre in his blood. And the sons in question had a very definite touch of ogre about them. Their menace enforced a peace of sorts.

'So,' said Atsimo Andranovory. 'What do you here?'

'A good question,' said Pigot Quebec. 'But I've a better question. How did my good friend Shen Shen Drax come to meet this liarman? Tell us your meeting, Drax. That'll make a good story to start off with.'

'Nay, man,' said Drake. 'A mood of modesty is upon me, I can't speak today.'

But his audience gave him no choice. He was ringed with arms and faces, with knives and fists. His attempts to escape were denied, with a good-humoured roughness which might turn nasty any moment.

He was trapped.

He had to speak himself in public, in front of witnesses. This was fearful dangerous! Best thing would be to kill An'vory, who was dangerous through what he knew. The blackguard would blackmail Drake for blood if he knew Drake would be killed if Selzirk learnt he supported King Tor.

How much does An'vory know? What does he know of Selzirk and Tor? How long has he been in town? Man, this is difficult!

'Cat got your tongue?' said Andranovory.

'Nay, man,' said Drake. 'I'm so astonished I'm silent, that's all. Last I knew of you, why, that was in Estar. You were in service with Prince Comedo, not so?'

'Aye, that's true enough,' said Andranovory.

'Well then,' said Drake, 'how got you here from Estar?'

'Through wild adventures with Elkor Alish and Morgan Hearst, and others that I've been telling of,' said Andranovory.

'Oh, Hearst!' said Drake, with confidence. 'That grey-haired Rovac warrior, right?'

'The same,' said Andranovory. 'You know much!'

'Aye,' said Drake.

Having said enough to give listeners such as Quebec the impression that he had known Andranovory while serving under Prince Comedo in Estar, Drake skipped away from that subject, and moved on:

'I know much of you, too, don't I? I remember serving shipboard with you. Aye, on a ship called the *Walrus* that was. We were trading a cargo of the skins of seals to the port of Narba. Yes. And I remember you later, put ashore from another ship for bad behaviour. That was back in the days when I were known as Drake Douay – for I've gone under more than one name in this wide world, I'll not deny it.'

534

'Aye,' said Andranovory. 'Drake Douay! And a pretty tale I could tell about you!'

'Tell, then!' said Drake.

Hoping.

'You were born in a heap of dogshit,' said Andranovory. 'I'll tell the world that for nothing. Your mother was raped by an octopus, which explains the most of your nature.'

'Aagh, An'vory, man!' said Drake. 'You've not changed! Always were a liar. But never champion, no – I was champion. Always was, always will be. Let's listen to your tales, and I'll top them.'

'I doubt you will,' said An'vory, 'not this time. For I've walked in strangeness, man, no doubting it.'

Then Andranovory, after wasting a little more breath telling lies about Drake's ancestry and upbringing, launched into his story proper.

Drake concealed his relief.

He had judged his man true.

He had guessed, rightly, that Andranovory, if challenged to tell the truth about Drake Douay, would take delight in insults at the expense of facts. He had gambled and won. An'vory did not guess that he had knowledge which could be the death of Drake Douay. Did not guess that Drake had to conceal his true identity – that of Lord Dreldragon, fiancé of the daughter of King Tor, and thus rightful inheritor of Stokos.

An'vory, man. You're as stupid a shit as ever. But perhaps you've a nice enough story to tell. Perhaps. We'll see.

Andranovory held forth in Galish, for he spoke no Churl. A professional street hawker gave a running translation for the benefit of any ignoramus who was not bilingual. There was many such an ignoramus in the Eagle.

Andranovory claimed, perhaps with truth, to have fought alongside two Rovac warriors in the employ of Prince Comedo – Hearst and Alish. But the rest of his story was improbable, to say the least. He told a long, wild tale about a war between Collosnon warriors and the

Rovac, in which Morgan Hearst triumphed by leading a regiment of dragons against his enemies.

Other things he spoke of were wilder still – a death-stone conjuring rocks to life and turned living men into mountains; a journey down an underground river, on which three of his comrades became pregnant ('and died giving birth, for they were men for real, and lacked the proper channel'); arrival at the Araconch Waters; the delights of the Temple of Eternal Love found on the shores of that enormous inland lake.

'Now I'm parched,' concluded Andranovory. 'So let strong drink speak to my gullet while me young mate Erhed speaks of the march inland from Araconch.'

Andranovory sat, and a weak-voiced companion of his travels and travails, an insignificant fellow named Erhed, began spinning tales of the aforementioned march from Araconch.

Erhed was less successful than Andranovory. He lacked a proper voice to start with. Worse, he was scarcely concerned with telling a tale at all – instead, he wanted to air his grievances against the Rovac warriors.

'. . . so Hearst was a hard man, you can see,' said Erhed. 'But Alish was the worst. Elkor Alish – a name of blood and terror. Man, he was hard! Smashed me over the head once. With a rock, true. Near enough to killed me.'

'Why did he do that?' called Drake.

'There was this dragon, see. I reckon he planned to kill me, leave me there as bait to draw the dragon away from the others. But I've a hard head, see.'

'Yes, and very little inside to get damaged,' said Andranovory.

He roared with laughter, and quaffed the last of his ale at a gulp. The barman handed him another. An'vory had been drinking hard and heavy while Erhed was weaving his way through his tale – and had drunk yet more earlier in the day.

'What happened then?' demanded Drake. 'About this dragon, I mean?'

536

'Oh, it flew away,' said Erhed lamely.

'Why didn't it eat you?' said Drake.

'Because then,' said Andranovory, 'the world's ruling devil would have been put to looking for some other sludge to pox us with.'

And once more erupted into laughter. Drunk? Maybe. Drake, who had such happy memories of being drunk himself, tried not to be jealous. Tried without success.

'How close was this dragon?' he asked.

'Who are you?' said Erhed. 'The Imperial Inquisitor, or what?'

Quebec seized this opportunity. He pushed a dwarf off a barstool, then stood on it.

'Hey!' said the dwarf. 'Get off me!'

So Quebec got onto the barstool instead.

'Gentles and toughs!' cried Quebec. 'Slow your clamour and fill your cups. We've heard enough of this Erhed fellow, who has but the single problem in life – he's no longer got his mother around to cosset his hand.'

Laughter, and generous laughter at that, from all around.

'But, seriously, folks, let me introduce my old friend Shen Shen Drax. Today I've heard he's got another name. Dway, was it? Something like that, anyhow. I'm sure there's a tale behind that name, and I'm sure he'll tell it.'

'I won it in combat on Hexagon,' said Drake, who had by then had time in plenty to devise creations suitable for the defence of his identity.

'Then we'll hear of that first,' said Quebec. 'And other things thereafter. Friend Drax, he's the champion liar of all the world, bar none. Born strange and walking in weirdness since. Kills ghosts by daylight then catches their blood in a winecup, but never gets drunk, no, for he was suckled on his mother's blood, which fortified him against liquor for a lifetime.'

'He'll not tell stories better than Andranovory,' said Erhed, speaking up loyal for his comrade.

'Aagh!' said Drake. 'My wit's as ready as my cock, so I

537

could fake a right pretty story if I needed one to win, aye, to prove myself champion liar. But I'll start with a truth. Like as not you'll think it a lie anyway, since it's nine parts incredible.

'The wizard Miphon, a green-eyed fellow I know of old, he once told me I was the most amount of trouble he'd ever seen in one package in the last ten thousand years. This proved out real enough when I got to Hexagon, which is where I won the name of Drake Douay in battle.

'Was an ogre I fought, a scum-faced thing as hateful as that mother-rapist known as Tor, the brute from Stokos who had me thrown into the seas a horizon away from land. He hated me, for I fell foul of his law. But that's another story – An'vory may tell it, perhaps, he knows the start of it at least. Anyway, to begin with Hexagon—'

And Drake was off.

Many a lie he told, and in consequence his tavern audience thought him truthful enough. The really incredible tales of the world are, without exception, those which follow the facts – and Drake's tales were wonderfully light on facts.

Andranovory told no story in reply, for he passed out while Drake was telling of his wanderings in Chi'ash-lan, and was still dead to the world when Drake finished a much longer tale about a trip to Gendormargensis in far-off Tameran (a tale, mark, replete with authentic detail remembered from stories told by his comrade of adventures past, Rolf Thelemite).

As An'vory was unconscious, Drake was declared the winner. Champion liar of all the world.

'Encore!' shouted an enthusiastic audience.

So Drake told one last tale.

'It happened that I once went north from Estar in company of a woodsman by name of Blackwood. North we ventured, way past Lake Armansis to the Valley of Forgotten Dreams, where we came upon the Old City, a place of legend, aye. Though legend tells not the half of the horror.'

538

And Drake told of adventuring through a Door with the woodsman Blackwood, of meeting the Pretender to the throne of Tameran, of daring a danger of centipedes in the terror-lands south of Drangsturm, then saving a red-skinned wench from a peril of monsters in the Great Arena of Dalar ken Halvar. Then bedding her soundly.

'Aye, she was real sweet,' he concluded.

'So where is she?' shouted Anonymous.

'Man, she died of delight in my arms,' said Drake. 'And she's not the first.'

'She died of delight?' cried Anonymous. 'Doubt it! Why, likely she died of blue leprosy!'

The grin on Drake's face faltered for half a heartbeat. Then he recovered himself.

'Nay, man,' he said. 'Was delight, for real. Delight kills instant, while this blue leprosy – it's a pox hidden for years before it shows.'

'An expert speaks!' jeered Anonymous.

'And an expert raised this question of blue leprosy to start with,' said Drake. 'Why, mostly only pox doctors know it for a pox of love. Most folk think it spread by sharing cups or such.'

'A pox doctor lectures!' yelled Anonymous, manic with delight.

'Brother,' said Drake, acknowledging Anonymous with a bow. 'It takes a true professional to recognize a colleague. But I think my skills higher than yours, for I'm free of the pox for the moment. But you, man – your nose is losing the battle, isn't it?'

This was true. The nose of Anonymous was being eaten away by syphilis.

Curses proceeded from Anonymous.

'Aagh, the man's jealous!' said Drake. 'Jealous of my skills with pox, aye, and of my skills of love, for he knows I'm best at both. When I talk of killing women with delight, it's truth, with naught exaggeration. Why, it's got to the point where I have to stay celibate, since the trail of dead women has become larger than embarrassment.'

He bowed again, ducked a rotten tomato, accepted a complimentary skin of liquor from the barman, and joined Pigot Quebec and a few others at a corner table out of the main swill.

'Booze, boys,' said Drake, thumping the skin onto the tabletop.

'Good,' said Quebec, and topped up his mug from the skin. Then said: 'Have you heard the news?'

'Why, I've heard that the world ended yesterday,' said Drake, 'that every fish in the sea is dead, that rats will conquer and horses sing in Galish. What else is new?'

'Let the Scholar tell it. Drax – meet the Scholar. Friend Scholar – this is Shen Shen Drax, the famous.'

They touched fingertips, lightly, in a ceremony of greeting peculiar to the criminal fraternity of Selzirk. Drake had heard of the Scholar, whose speciality was forgery. Now he listened while the Scholar told of how they were being threatened by a Law of Association which would forbid convicted criminals from consorting with each other.

'A suspension of civil liberties, that's what it is,' said the Scholar.

'Yes, well,' said Drake, 'that's less painful than suspension by the neck, no doubt.'

He picked up an empty mug which was lying lonesome on the floor, filled it with liquor from his complimentary skin, drained it, burped, patted his stomach then filled it again.

'It's an unprecedented extension of state authority, you know,' continued the Scholar. 'I hear the Regency's behind it.'

'What's the Regency?' asked Drake.

His research had been deep in war but thin on politics. He had, after all, only the one life. He had to work for Ol Tul, amuse himself, survive – and do research in his spare moments. So he had left a study of the leadership of Selzirk to the time when he should have some positive prospect of becoming ambassador or such.

'The Regency,' said Quebec. 'Why, that's the Guild of Brothel Masters.'

Not so, protested the scholar. He began to explain the truth – but was interrupted by the arrival of Scurf Drumbo.

'Why, pickle me balls and dig out me eyes with needles,' said Drumbo. 'I'm as buggered as a rat's arsehole.'

'Why,' said Drake, 'what have you been doing?'

'Drinking, man. And listening. Is that ale? No? Gah! Still . . . tastes sweet enough to me. Thanks, friend. Yes, drinking. And listening, hearing young sparrow-fart here blister the paint with untruthing.'

'Man, it was all true enough,' said Drake.

'Oh, hearty sure, I bet,' said Drumbo.

'You believe none of it?' said Drake.

'Oh, a word here, a word there,' said Drumbo. 'But Drax – I'd never believe a woman to die in your arms of delight.'

'She died smiling,' said Drake, deadpan.

'In your arms?' said Drumbo. 'Never! If she died, you strangled her, that's what. Man, but that story stirred me up a bit, though. I've never had a red-skinned whore.'

'She wasn't a whore,' said Drake.

'Red meat,' said Drumbo, pushing on regardless. 'I saw a red-skinned bitch today, sweet, yes, worth having.'

'There's plenty of red in the city,' said Quebec.

'Oh, this was no woman in her fancies,' said Drumbo. 'It was one of those Ebrell bitches. You can tell the difference. It's the nose, you see. With the Ebrell, the colour goes right up the nose.'

'You got that close?' said Drake.

'Drax,' said Drumbo, 'she was so hot for changing, she was near to mating with me.'

'Changing?' said Quebec. 'Changing? You mean she was a witch, to change you to pig or beast-hound?'

'How could she do that?' asked Drake. 'Friend Drumbo's been half pig and three parts beast-hound these last three thousand years or more.'

'Gah!' said Drumbo. 'She was no witch. Whore, more like it. Preacher's whore. When I speak of changing, it's faith I'm talking of.'

'You mean this woman was talking religion?' said Drake.

'Talking changing, yes, that's what I said,' declared Drumbo. 'Though this preacher fellow was talking more than her. Lucky old bugger! I vum he screws her nights.'

'What preacher was this?' said Drake.

'Oh, you know,' said Drumbo, helping himself to more liquor. 'A preacher's a preacher, isn't he?'

'Nay, man,' said Drake. 'They're all of them different. Some thieves, while others murder their mothers. Some heavy for opium, while others are into the booze. Boys for some, dogs for others, while the toothless taste women with fingerlength tongues. Tell of this one, man.'

'He's nothing special,' said Drumbo. 'But for his robes, perhaps. Fancy with flame they were.'

'Flame?' said Drake.

'Like enough,' said Drumbo. 'Either that, or someone had vomited carrots and tomatoes all over his robes.'

'Where was this?' asked Drake, who was, of course, seriously interested.

'Outside the Old Courthouse,' said Drumbo.

'Courthouse?' said Drake.

'It's an inn, now,' said Drumbo. 'But these preacher folk have taken it over entire, use it as a temple. Platform outside, guards on the gate, and all too holy within for strangers to enter.'

'But you saw her,' said Drake. 'The woman, I mean.'

'The blood-coloured bitch. Oh yes, she was on the platform with his worship,' said Drumbo. 'Wonder what colour her slunt shapes, eh?'

'If she was on the platform,' said Drake, 'how come you got close enough for mating?'

'Come now!' protested Drumbo. 'What is this? You talk at lies for longer than it takes to skin a whale with a toothpick, then—'

'Did you see the woman or didn't you?' said Drake, dangerously close to losing his temper.

'I saw her!'

'What did she look like?' said Drake. 'Speak true!'

'Why,' said Drumbo, shaping generous curves in the air, 'like this and like this. She had two tits, if I counted right. A tall bitch, you'd look stupid beside her.'

'It's not fashion which worries me when I'm after a woman,' said Drake.

'You're hot for reds, are you?' said Drumbo. 'At the Cat's Head they've got a whole pack of women in red, would do you good, man.'

'He's been there,' said Quebec. 'We were there together the day before yesterday.'

'Aye,' said Drake. 'Now tell me where I find this Old Courthouse . . .'

45

Libernek Square: small piazza in Santrim; site of Old
Courthouse. House of Record, Moonflower Temple, Land
Court, River Court, Suffle Manuscript Collection, Voat
Library and Archaeological Museum.

The Old Courthouse was in Libernek Square, in Santrim, a
quarter Drake had seldom visited. On arrival, he found a
crowd listening to Gouda Muck preach from a platform
built above the gate leading into the walled courtyard of the
Old Courthouse. Drake strove toward the platform, but
could not get near for the crush. He backed off, and hastened to the monumental sculpture which dominated the
centre of the piazza.

The sculpture was a rococo piece of nonsense erected to
celebrate heroes of Selzirk's glorious past. Around an enormous central column formed by a coiling dragon – which
had somehow become encrusted with seashells, baby mer-
maids, strings of onions and other tomfoolery – there were
arrayed equestrian heroes (lifesize), several Neversh (in
miniature), gryphons, unicorns, a platypus (which had no
good excuse for being there, and no bad one either), a
taniwha, a moray eel, and numerous ribs, vertebrae, skulls
and jawbones cast in bronze.

Drake scaled this swiftly, displacing small children where
necessary. On reaching a bronze horse which lacked a rider,
he supplied its lack. And sat there in state, Investigating.

'. . . doom,' said Gouda Muck. 'Doom, and death, unto
the fiftieth generation . . .'

'Boring old mother-beater,' muttered Drake.

And looked beyond Muck to the Old Courthouse. It was built round three sides of an enclosed courtyard. The outer wall of the yard sustained the platform on which stood Gouda Muck, giving a dyslogistic lecture on the manners and mores of Selzirk. Scrutiny of the killing ground complete, Drake returned his attention to Muck.

The preacher had abandoned the plain purple he wore when Drake saw him last, in Runcorn. Instead, he wore robes of the most remarkable mixture of red, orange and yellow. Muck was dressed as the Flame. And he was ranting:

'. . . beware protein! Beware eggs! Beware meat! They are evil! They lewd the flesh to fornication!'

Drake was glad to see the audience treated this as light entertainment. He suspected some would have multiplied the amusement factor by throwing things, except that in amongst the crowd were two or three dozen tough young stave-men, dressed in robes of Flame like their master.

'. . . your daughters will die of cancers of the womb,' shouted Muck. 'Their flesh will be torn by the knives of abortion! Evil is the flesh, and evil are the pleasures thereof.'

He sounded hoarse.

He paused as a woman climbed onto the platform. She carried a glass of fine-cut crystal which she handed to Muck, who drank the water it contained. The woman was red in skin; her hair, piled up in a high and narrow tower held together with a multitude of pins, was also red. She wore flowing silks, and jewels which flashed in the sun.

It was Zanya.

'Zanya!' yelled Drake.

She looked over the crowd, bewildered.

'It's me!' shouted Drake, kicking the bronze horse with his heels, waving his hands frantically. 'Arabin lol Arabin! Your lover! Your husband!'

'Drake!' roared Gouda Muck.

'Yes, I see you too!' shouted Drake. 'Go back to

Stokos, you evil old bugger! But give me back my woman first!'

'Kill him!' screamed Muck. 'He's the Demon-son! The Evil One! Pull him down! Cut him, bash him, burn him!'

But the mob simply laughed. To them, this was all part of the day's theatre. Unlike Stokos, Selzirk had never been oppressed by compulsory debauchery, so the social tensions Muck's religion sought to exploit were lacking.

'They'll do nothing against me,' yelled Drake. 'They know what you are! A mad old bugger with a withered old cock, that's what! Lunatic, man! Zanya, get down from there! Bring me your breasts most beautiful, darling!'

After some confusion on the stage, Zanya disappeared into the courtyard. Muck gestured in Drake's direction, and his stavemen began to muscle through the crowd, determined to seize the miscreant.

'Oh shit,' said Drake to Drake.

And descended to the ground rapidly, bowling a number of small children in his haste. Leaving those wailing juveniles in his wake, he fled.

A mad chase they had of it through the streets of Santrim, Drake in front and the better part of thirty Flame-robed stavemen in the rear. Drake was still leading when they got to Kesh, the gate-tower dividing the Four Worlds of Selzirk.

There was usually a traffic jam of sorts at that bottle-neck, but today it was worse than ever, for a funeral procession was going through Kesh. Or, more accurately, trying to go. It was getting nowhere fast.

The demon-drivers paced up and down on the spot, blowing their horns and trumpets; the chief mourners lay cursing in their palankeens; the pall-bearers, unable to take the weight any longer, let their burden rest; the hired hands from the Weepers & Wailers Guild gnashed their teeth and clawed the air with less and less passion as the delay lengthened.

Then came Drake.

Between the legs of a horn-player he went. Up he

bobbed, dived through the silks of a palankeen and crash-landed on the belly of Mistress Turbothot, alumnus of the Santrim Institute For Feminine Arts, wife of Troldot 'Heavy-Fist' Turbothot, and patron of the Seventh College of the Inner Circle of the Fish-Star Astrologers.

'Pardon,' said Drake.

'Rape!' she screamed.

He dived through the far side of the palankeen, fell heavily on top of Mistress Turbothot's pet badger-dog (and killed the poor thing, though he was too busy to notice its demise), trampled over the coffin of the deceased (to whom he never got introduced), ducked a spear, dodged a sword, was missed by a whip, went pelting over the backs of a herd of hogs (no wonder there was a traffic jam!), and gained the comparative safety of Jone.

Where he stopped, panting hard and grinning like an idiot. Man! He hadn't had so much fun since he celebrated his sixteenth birthday. And that was saying something!

Then he saw a Flame-coloured robe.

'How many of you, darlings?' said Drake, softly.

There was just one. So far.

'Yoo-hoo!' cried Drake, jumping up and down, waving frantically. 'I'm over here!'

'Demon-son!' screamed the Flame-robed stave-man, spotting him.

'That's me!' yelled Drake.

And the chase was on again.

Drake led the single stave-man a merry dance through the backstreets, alleyways, mews and ditchleaps of Jone, the dockland area he knew by now as well as he knew the back of his own hand.

(Or better, in fact – for if he had been shrunk down to near next to nothing, then set beside the first knuckle of his own index finger, he would have had the devil of a job finding his way from there to his thumb – whereas he could have found his way round Jone blindfolded.)

Finally, Drake led the single stave-man into a friendly tavern, where half a dozen of Drake's drinking cronies helped mug the hapless hero. He was taken to the cellar, trussed up tightly (having been first stripped of his robes of Flame) then interrogated under threat of torture.

By evening, Drake knew everything he wanted to know.

'I'm off,' he said, pulling the robes of Flame over the set of serviceable leathers he was wearing.

'What happens to me then?' asked the stave-man.

'Why, at midnight the tide rises,' said Drake. 'Aye, then this cellar floods, and the rats come up with the waters. They'll eat your corpse to bones and gristle.'

'There's no tides in the Velvet River.'

'Oh isn't there just? Haven't you heard of the eagre?'

'The what?'

'Never mind, man,' said Drake. 'Its waters will have you soon enough, aye, and the rats.'

After a bit more bluff and bluster equally as grim and heartless, he picked up the stave-man's stave and took to the streets, looking every bit the enforcer.

It was deep night by the time Drake had made his way from the backstreets of Jone to Libernek Square in Santrim. The gates of Muck's temple were open, but guards kept watch on the platform above the gate. Drake hung back in the shadows. Would there be a challenge? A password? or what? In the Old Courthouse, a scattering of lanterns held out against the tyranny of darkness. He could hear a woman softly singing; he wondered if it was Zanya.

Suddenly someone slapped an arm over his shoulder. Drake was about to fight when a drunken voice slurred:

'Tovarish.'

'Darling,' said Drake, taking stock swiftly.

A trio of them. All wearing robes of Flame. All stank of the strong liquor Muck preached against so vehemently.

'Bedtime,' said one.

'Aye,' said Drake.

Together they rolled toward the gate. As they went in under the platform, all tried to straighten up, doing their best imitation of sobriety. Inside, one said to Drake:

'Come have a drink.'

Nothing is more persistent than a drunk who wants to get drunker.

'Sorry, man,' said Drake. 'I've got a yen for purity tonight.'

'Purity?'

Hooting laughter and renewed insistence.

'Hush, man!' said Drake. 'You'll get us in trouble!'

It was no good. The noise increased steadily until a challenge came from the platform. Drake ducked into the shadows under a single courtyard tree as platform-guards scrambled down to have a reckoning with the drunks.

Drake made himself one with the bark of the tree. Wished himself to the thinness of a needle. Heard a prolonged altercation, a short scuffle, a brief protest, a sound of something heavy hitting meat. Then peace. But for a single nightingale in the branches above, testing its tessitura. And someone, quite close at hand, urinating copiously. Another drunk, no doubt.

Time to move.

Drake slipped toward the stairway which, if his captive stave-man had spoken true, led to the female quarters. Up the creaking stairs he went, to a lantern-lit corridor. He heard, from behind one closed door, the rhythm of a bed riding in heavy seas. Elsewhere, suppressed laughter. A door opened without warning and a young woman burst out, giggling. She was in a state of advanced deshabille. After her came a muscular young man who was entirely naked.

Both stopped and stared at Drake.

'You!' said Drake, curtly, pointing his stave at the man. 'Your name?'

'Prothon. Who are you?'

'That you'll learn tomorrow,' said Drake grimly, 'when you answer for your actions before the Holy One himself. Don't make things worse for yourself. Get back to your own quarters!'

Drake thwacked Prothon over the buttocks to emphasize his point. The sinner fled.

'You,' said Drake, to the woman. 'Aren't you ashamed of yourself?'

'I'm not religious,' she said, in very poor Galish, pouting as she did so. Her face was gaudy with paint, her body lush with perfume. 'I'm just a maid. Why make trouble over a simple of simples? Ease your hard back, why don't you. Do we have to have trouble?'

And, without warning, she kissed him.

Heavy boots sounded on the stairs.

'It's the Patrol!' she hissed. 'Are you in, or out?'

'What?' said Drake.

'Will you denounce me or – '

'We'll talk about it inside,' said Drake. They fled into her cubicle, closing the door on the Patrol. Inside, there was nowhere to sit down but on the bed.

Some considerable time later, Drake kissed his maid-minx goodbye, made an assignation for the following night, and set off for the room supposed to be Zanya's. On arrival, he entered without knocking. Saw her. Saw her bedroom.

Her chamber was large, and warm. Around the walls were pictures of lewdness. She had an enormous bed, canopied with silks. The air was heavy with perfume. The place would have reminded Drake of a high-class brothel, but for the fact that he was innocent of the charms of any establishment so elevated.

As he entered, Zanya was sitting on a padded stool, peering at her reflection in a bronze mirror. She was unfastening an earbob. She had let down her hair, which flowed about her, reaching in a tide of fire almost as far as her waist. She turned, slowly, and looked at him.

'Surprise!' said Drake.

'Not so,' she said. 'It's just like you to try something crazy like this.'

'What am I trying?'

'I don't know yet. But I'm sure it's madness.'

After that unpromising start, they simply stared at each other for a few moments. A contest of wills. Then Drake dropped his gaze, telling himself he did so to admire the loft of Zanya's breasts beneath her free-flowing silks, the strength of her thigh and the turn of her ankle.

'So what do you think you're doing here?' said Zanya.

'Looking for my wife, as it happens,' said Drake, cool as cucumber bathed in liquid helium.

'Your wife. Have you married, then?'

'Darling! I married you!'

'We were never married.'

'Weren't we?' said Drake, thinking. Then: 'No, I suppose we never were. But does it matter?'

'It matters that you can't remember one way or the other!'

'I've been as good as married,' said Drake. 'I've never had another woman since I met you.'

'Oh yes!'

'Why so sharp, my sweet? Come, my dearest cony, my—'

'I'm not your cony!'

'Why so cruel?' said Drake. 'So cruel to your dearest treasure-snake? You were always my cony, nearest and dearest.'

'Oh, grow up!' said Zanya. 'I'm not your cony. I'm not your anything.'

'Then what are you?' said Drake, with a touch of anger in his voice. 'Something of Muck's, perhaps?'

'Perhaps,' she said.

Hard. Defiant.

'Is this where he takes you, then? Preaching for prudery then rutting his balls dry?'

'It is Permitted,' said Zanya, angry herself. 'It makes me proud. Yes, proud! I am the guardian of his purity.'

'You screw!' said Drake, in fury. 'With him! How could you?'

'It is holy!' she said.

Hot. Fierce. Unashamed.

'He's a dirty old man,' said Drake, savagely.

'Who stole your whore. Right? That's what I was to

551

you, wasn't it? A hole. A cheap hole. A whore who didn't need to be paid by the night.'

'Dearest sweet—'

'Oh yes, it was "dearest sweet" to start with. But once you were sure, then you forgot about me.'

'Forgot?' said Drake. 'I lavished attentions on you! Most tender skill imaginable!'

He was truly indignant, thinking he had discharged his duties to Zanya well enough by providing food, clothing and protection, and (most of all) by his diligent concern for the female orgasm (a gentlemanly concern he knew to be entirely lacking in most of the world's men.)

'You lavished?' said Zanya. 'Oh yes, come night, you lavished, all right. When your snake wanted a hole it could snout into. How would you like to be used like that? As a lump of meat! Yes, used like a slab of wet liver!'

'Let's say I did,' said Drake. 'It's not true, but if it were – did that make it right for you to side with Muck in Runcorn? Remember Runcorn? You screamed that I was the Demon-son. What did I do to deserve that?'

'You lied to me.'

'When?'

'When you said you weren't the Demon-son.'

'Oh come on!' said Drake. 'Do you really think I was sired by the demon Hagon?'

'No. But you were Muck's apprentice, weren't you? You were the one who stole his mastersword, isn't that so?'

'That's true,' admitted Drake.

'The truth, yes. But who told me the truth? Why, Sully Yot and Gouda Muck. Because you never admitted the truth to me. You didn't trust me. You pleaded that you weren't that Dreldragon Drakedon Douay. Oh no, you were someone altogether different!'

'What does it matter who I was? Or who I am?' said Drake.

'Don't you understand anything?' said Zanya, in a voice close to a wail. 'You didn't trust me! You treated me like an enemy or like – like a child. You lied to me. Not for a day or a couple of days but for month after month on end.'

'Then I'm sorry,' said Drake, with very little grace.

'That's not good enough,' said Zanya. 'You've lied once too often.'

'But there's one thing I haven't lied about,' said Drake. 'I've not had a woman since you left me. In fact, I've never had another woman since I met you.'

'So you told me just a few heartbeats back,' said Zanya. 'I didn't believe it then. I don't believe it now.'

'Dearest cony,' said Drake, easing honey into his voice, 'my dearest sweet, I can't lust after another woman because – because, dear heart, it's you I love. And love, my dearest, has made casual lust impossible.'

'Then why,' said Zanya, her voice rising to a shriek, 'are you standing there with a whore's cheap lipstick plastered all over your face? I suppose there's the same on your pizzle!'

'Zanya! Darling! I can explain! I can—'

'You can drag your balls back to the sewer you came from,' said Zanya savagely, 'or die where you stand!'

'Listen,' said Drake, grabbing her. 'I've heard enough of this nonsense. You're my woman, and you're coming with me.'

She tried to claw for his eyes, to spike fingers into his throat, to smash him with an elbow, to pound his testicles. But Drake – this time – was not drunk. And Drake, by this time, knew her fighting style well.

'Give in,' he said, panting, 'or I'll break your arm.'

'Rape!' she screamed. 'Demon-son! Rape! Help! Fire, fire! Murder!'

And clawed him as he tried to muscle her to the door. Which burst open. In came a man, nostrils flaring. Drake dropped Zanya. Then felled the man with a jaw-breaking blow. Boots pounded down the corridor. Drake slammed the door then shoved Zanya against it.

'I love you,' he said.

He pinned her arms. Kissed her. Then fled. Out of the window he went, dropping clean and neat to the courtyard.

'Ho!' shouted a voice, as half a dozen stave-men came racing out of a side-door.

'He went that way!' yelled Drake, pointing. 'After him! It's the Demon-son, he went that way! Faster, faster! He'll get away!'

The stave-men pounded off in the direction Drake had indicated. Drake made for the gate. And came face to face with something which had two eyes and a much greater number of warts.

'Drake!' said Sully Yot. 'Demon—'

His shout was terminated by Drake's fist. Half a heartbeat later, Drake had Yot's stave in his hand. He used it to demolish the first hero who jumped to the courtyard from Zanya's window.

'There he is!' shouted a voice.

No bluff would serve him now!

Drake fled to the gate, fought his way past a daring duo which tried to stop him, then escaped into Libernek Square. At which point he realized there was a dog attached to his ankle. Where had that come from? He had no idea – but the spunky little tyke was clinging on tightly. Drake shook it off. And a voice shouted:

'Stand fast for the Watch!'

He saw five grim men, each dressed in a stovepipe hat and the black rig-out of the Law. He saw, also, swords quintuplicate. He surrendered. Then turned his attention to the task of kicking a cur unconscious.

Stave-men dressed in Flame spilt into the piazza, but halted when they saw the Watch. As an Outsider Religion, Muck's temple could not afford antagonizing the Law by rumbling with the Watch. Instead, the stave-men stood silent as Drake was led away.

And still the nightingale exercised its syrinx in song.

554

46

Watashi: one of the sons of the Kingmaker Farfalla, refuses to accept his role as professional nonentity; has generated political crisis by his aristocratic pretensions, which alarm both the bureaucracy of the Regency and the Federated Guilds (which between them have much of the real power in the Harvest Plains).

Drake was taken to a lantern-lit whitewashed building full of off-duty lawmen and their gambling partners, the clatter of beer mugs and the smell of frying onions. This cheerful place was the Santrim Watch-house. He was then taken Down Below to a torture chamber where the dominant smell was that of burnt hair.

'What was all the fighting about?' asked an interrogator, testing the point of a bodkin on a much-scarred table. 'Come on, what was it all about?'

'Man,' said Drake. 'How do I know? Some fellow invited me back to the place for a quiet drink or three. Next thing – riot, man!'

'No religious of that temple drinks.'

'Don't they just? It's a regular rolling brothel-bar they've got inside there. Check it out some time.'

'How did you get those robes you're wearing?'

'They wanted me to wear alike what they were wearing. So when this fellow invited me back for a drink, he lent me these.'

'Search him,' said the interrogator.

So underlings searched Drake, and threw onto the table

three knives, a throwing star, two garrotting wires and a stray caltrop.

'What's all this for?' asked the interrogator.

'I'm a peddler,' said Drake promptly. 'I deal in weapons. This is part of my stock in trade.'

Since there was no law against carrying murder on the streets of Selzirk, the interrogator pressed him no further about that.

'Do a strip search,' he said.

'You've found all that's there for finding already,' protested Drake. 'What will you strip me for. You seek to unman me, perhaps?'

'That I do,' said the interrogator, blandly.

And Drake was stripped.

And the amulet he wore around his neck was revealed. Causing great excitement.

'Where did you get this from?' said the interrogator.

'It's a family heirloom,' said Drake. 'I inherited it from my grandfather.'

'Oh yes? I doubt Watashi would agree with you.'

'Who's Watashi?' demanded Drake.

The interrogator and his underlings all laughed. Richly. Honestly. He realized he must have asked a very stupid question.

'Playing innocent, are we?' said the interrogator. 'By rights, I should put the jaws to you, then choke you for the truth. But . . . we've got the evidence, so what more do we need?'

'Evidence of what? Man, that's my amulet! My property! Is there a law against amulets? And who's this Watashi?'

'There is, young cock, a law against stealing – whether the thing stolen be amulet or other. And Watashi, of course, is the man you stole from.'

'I never! I don't even know who he is.'

There was more laughter. Then the interrogator, who had other business to attend to, had Drake taken to a holding cell.

'Don't give me no trouble, now,' warned the gaoler who locked him up.

'I won't,' said Drake, through the cell bars, 'if I can get a straight answer to a simple question. Who's Watashi?'

'The son of Farfalla, of course.'

'Farfalla?' said Drake, blankly.

'The dynast of Selzirk! The ruler of the Harvest Plains!'

'Oh.'

'You've never heard of her?'

'Man,' said Drake, 'I vouch she's never heard of me, either, so why so surprised?'

The gaoler grunted, and, ignoring Drake's demands for further debate, went about his business.

At noon the next day, Drake was back in the torture chamber, facing not one interrogator but half a dozen.

'See this?' said one, letting the amulet swing backwards and forwards in front of Drake's nose, 'we want to know the truth about this.'

'Truth, yes.'

'Truth your tongue, lest you end up face down in the sea.'

'Yes, if lucky enough to have face left to you.'

'What truth are you after?' said Drake.

'The truth of your thieving. Accomplices. Conspiracy. A plot for treason.'

So they were not trying to convict him for theft. They wanted to do him for treason!

'*Nara zabara jok, gamos,*' said Drake.

Which earned him a punch in the stomach.

'I want a lawyer!' cried Drake. 'I'll have the Regency on you!'

This drew laughter.

'Man,' said one of the interrogators, 'we give no allegiance here to the Regency. No. We're for the prince. We'll see empire true before we're finished.'

But this declaration meant nothing to Drake, who was still ignorant of the politics of Selzirk.

'Until I get a lawyer,' said Drake, 'I'm saying nothing further.'

And he shut his mouth and refused to speak, despite kicks, blows and a thorough cudgeling.

'What shall we do?' said one of the interrogators. 'Shall we pull his fingernails out?'

'Best speak to the prince, first,' said one of the others. 'He might want to work on this animal personally.'

So Drake was taken back to his cell.

After three days in captivity, Drake was told he was to be brought into the presence of Watashi. By now he knew a little more about the fellow, including the fact that Watashi liked to be addressed as 'Noble Prince'.

'You're lucky,' said one of the lawmen who came to collect Drake from his cell.

'How so?'

'We're keeping the Mucks away from you.'

'The Mucks?'

'The Goudanites, or whatever they are. Those people who worship fire.'

'Oh, Gouda Muck!'

'That's the mob. They think you're a dybbuk or something. They want to burn you alive.'

'And they know you've got me prisoner?'

'Oh no! But they know you're somewhere in the city. They're offering rewards for your head.'

'Is that legal?'

'You're a regular little law clerk, aren't you? When you come back – if you come back – I'll get you to write some letters for me.'

'Man,' said Drake. 'I can't even read, let alone write!'

'Of course you can. You're just lazy. But I've ways to unlazy people, oh yes, that's part of my pleasure in life.'

And Drake, with that happy news to refresh him, was ushered into a curtained cab, which took him from the Santrim Watch-house to somewhere elsewhere. Then, with his head hooded, he was led by way of halls and stairs to a big bare room of grey stone, where he was unmasked.

'What now?' said Drake to his guards.

'Now we wait on the prince's pleasure,' came the reply.

And wait they did. For a long time. Nobody bothered to offer them refreshments. Drake picked his nose clean, excavated earwax, dug dirt from under his fingernails, practised curling his tongue and, concentrating very hard, managed to make his ears wiggle. Then, with fingertips lightly touching each eyebrow to monitor their position, he practised raising one while keeping the other steady.

Someone, somewhere, was playing a fipple-flute. Two or three notes. Then silence. Then a few more notes, broken off by error. Drake wondered how long he had been waiting. He wished there was some sun in the room, so he could watch shadows move.

'I have to piss,' he said, abruptly.

'Out that door then hard right,' said a lawman.

Drake went, and found himself on a high balcony overlooking much of the city. This balcony was an excrescence of a modern tower built hard up against the gatehouse keep of the ancient wizard stronghold which served the Kingmaker Farfalla as a citadel-palace. While much of the old battlements remained, together with the original wizard towers, enormous additions had been made.

Drake relieved himself at a urinal set in the balcony's low wall. A rill of his urine went trickling down a funnel into a gargoyle which spat his wastes into the air. Where would those wastes fall?

Drake looked over the wall, and found himself staring down, down, down into a yawning gulf at the bottom of which, far, far below, lazy dragon-backed flames writhed slowly. He realized he was looking into a flame trench. He was not impressed. Compared to what he had seen at Drangsturm, this was nothing.

He raised his eyes, and looked out over the realms of the free. A lean wind keened across the city, begging for bones. Dull clouds dampened out the sun. Drake could see half a dozen galleys and a string of gabbarts on the river's pewter, which wound away to the west, to a menace of clouds which obscured any possible view of the distant sea.

Drake experienced a peculiar sensation of desolation. He

559

longed to be home, yes, truly home, at his parents' hearth. How long was it since he had seen a decent coal fire?

'You'd best be back,' said a lawman, who had come to see what·had happened to the prisoner. 'The prince is approaching the audience chamber.'

That chamber was the same big bare grey room which Drake had already sat in for so long. He waited. In came a tough, fierce-faced swordsman wearing plumed helm, glittering greaves and battle-ready mail. Behind him came half a dozen men more simply dressed.

'Watashi?' said Drake, getting to his feet. 'Man, I've got a few—'

'Shut up,' said the swordsman. 'No – don't sit. Stay on your feet. The prince will be here soon.'

'Who are you then?' said Drake.

'I am Thodric Jarl, warrior of Rovac. And these are the prince's guards. Lawmen, you may go.'

There was an exchange of courtesies, then the black-clad lawmen retired, leaving Drake to the mercies of the prince's guards.

'Man,' said Drake. 'It's great news, you being a Rovac warrior and all. I used to know one myself, he calls himself Rolf Thelemite.'

'Thelemite?' said Jarl. 'So the oath-breaker still lives! Very well. Once the prince is finished with you, I have business with your flesh. If it still lives. I will have your knowledge of this Thelemite. Yes, and see him dead.'

And Drake thought:

How did I get into this mess?

Then into the room came a haughty man of about age twenty-five, battle-scars on his face. Brown hair, brown eyes and dark-brown skin. Robes of blue silk, boots of white leather. A sword at his side.

'I am Watashi,' he said, 'hero of war and rightful inheritor of the Harvest Plains. Down on your knees, peon! Come on! Get down!'

'Make me,' said Drake.

Watashi's guards proceeded to do just that. After

Drake had been roughed up a bit, he was allowed to stand. Bloodied but still unbowed.

'It's wrong to treat me like this,' he said. 'I'm an honest peddler, from Runcorn, I demand—'

'You demand nothing!' barked Thodric Jarl.

And gave physical emphasis to his words.

'That's enough,' said Watashi, at length. 'We don't want him dead before we have the truth out of him. You – who are you, and what?'

'I've told you,' said Drake, belligerent as ever. 'I'm from Runcorn. A peddler. Aye, and an honest man.'

'Honest? Then why did you steal my bard?'

'Your bard? What means this bard?'

'This!' said Watashi, dangling a familiar object in front of Drake.

It was a glossy black lozenge which, as it dangled from the slim black chain which sustained it, turned to reveal first a sun then a moon with stars.

'I never stole anything,' said Drake. 'I got the – the bard thing down in Ling.'

'You not only stole it,' said Watashi. 'You damaged it as well. There's a gouge ripped right through the skin under the sun.'

'That? Man, that's just a nick. Some fellow tried to knife me in Narba.'

'In Narba?'

'It's a seaport, down south where—'

'I know where Narba is! It was your veracity I was questioning, not your geography.'

'Veracity. Aye. You mean my truth. Didn't think I'd know the word, either, did you? Well, man, it's all true enough. Oh yes, and it's a great tale into the bargain. Sit yourself down, get some wine laid on, and I could keep your ears buzzing for the next sixty years. Aye, truth and wonders, that's what I've seen.'

This offer was meant to be conciliatory. But Watashi was not in a placable mood.

'I've no interest in fairy tales,' said he.

561

'Man, then I'll tell you none,' said Drake, 'for I've never seen a fairy. But I've seen elves, aye, elves with handfuls of legs apiece on a flying island. And a dwarf, yes, right recent. Down at the Eagle, in fact. A friend of mine stepped on him.'

'That was my dwarf!' shouted Watashi. 'His name's Glambrax. You cracked his ribs!'

'Man, no need to shout,' said Drake. 'I can hear you from here. Anyway, it wasn't me that stepped on him. And cracked ribs heal up nice enough. Why, I got me ribs bust in a fight I could tell you about, a regular scramble it was, epic, aye, like those wars of the ancients. Why—'

'Enough of your nonsense,' said Watashi. 'Look here!'

And he snapped his fingers to summon a servant, who displayed a shield for Drake's inspection. On it was emblazoned a black rustre, with a crescent moon and seven stars arranged on the surrounding red.

'What is it?' said Drake.

'It's a coat of arms, made for me last year. And proof that the bard was mine!'

'I got the amulet in Ling,' insisted Drake. 'There were dozens of them, each like to each as so many glips.'

'Glips?' said Watashi, who knew not that Orfus word.

'Aye. Little silver fish, a fingerlength each. Man, they'd look right handsome on your coat of arms, one chasing each of those seven fancy stars.'

This suggestion was not well received.

'I paid fifty skilders for that bard!' said Watashi.

'Well then, I'd like a cut of that money. Because it was likely stolen property you were paying out for. My property! Won with great cost in Ling, aye, fights with metal and all. Then stolen from me in Narba, yes, by some villainous pirates or such in a bar.'

'Enough of your cheek,' said Watashi. 'Some papers went missing when this bard was stolen. Very important papers. I want them back!'

'Man, I can't read nor write. What would I want with papers?'

'To sell them to the Regency, perhaps,' said Watashi. 'Give me the truth! Who was with you? Where did the papers go? Answer, or I'll choke the life out of you!'

'You won't get many answers from a choked-dead man,' said Drake.

'No, but I'd get a lot of satisfaction,' said Watashi, something ugly in his voice.

This was getting serious.

'I want a lawyer,' said Drake, who had fond memories of the games he had played with the City Fathers in Runcorn when the formidable Garimanthea had been in support.

'A what?'

'A lawyer! Aye, then we'll have some fun. Aye, injunctions and mandamuses to start with. Then worse! Court costs and colloquy and such.'

'What are you talking about?' said Watashi, to whom these threats – couched as they were in an obscure variant of Galish especially invented for the law courts of Runcorn – were completely unintelligible.

'I'm talking about a quo warranto, to start with,' said Drake, getting excited, already imagining the looks of anxiety, contrition and terror which the right lawyer would bring to Watashi's face.

'A what?'

'It means you have to prove yourself out as the prince you claim to be. Aye, then there's a better writ, I forget the name of it, which means you have to prove you exist at all. Oh, that can be a tricky one!'

'You seriously mean to try to bring me to courts?' said Watashi, incredulously, as he began to understand Drake's intent. 'I don't grabble in the courts with the common crowd! Take him away and interrogate him for the truth!'

And Drake was dragged away by Watashi's guards.

Drake started shouting about civil liberties and Habeas Corpus. So the guards, knowing full well that Watashi's detention of Drake was in law no more than a kidnapping, gagged him lest someone should hear.

'Don't try anything stupid,' said Thodric Jarl, warrior of

Rovac and bodyguard to Watashi. 'Most of all, don't try to escape. For if you get out of here, the Mucks will catch you in the city. Then, if rumour's only half-way true, they'll skin you alive and strangle you with your own intestines.'

'*Mmf eph gumph*,' said Drake, speaking as best he could with a gag in his mouth.

But Thodric Jarl made no effort to remove Drake's gag, guessing that the angry young man was only trying to give voice to some obscenities which he knew well enough already, thank you very much.

In fact, Drake was trying to say:

'I can't breathe! I can't breathe!'

But he was still alive by the time they reached Watashi's very private torture chamber.

47

Morgan Hearst: one of the leaders of a band of questing heroes which had several interesting adventures with dragons, wizards and magic before mutiny split their ranks. While Hearst and others continued the quest, the mutineers – including Andranovory, Erhed and others – came down the Velvet River through Chenameg to Selzirk.

Watashi's private torture chamber was a soundproof room containing a narrow wooden bench, which bore a number of ominous russet stains, and many ugly implements of iron. Drake did his thinking – and fast. Clearly, posing as an innocent peddler was not going to save him. He would lose one or more bits of himself unless he did something drastic – and fast.

Ungagged, Drake spoke quickly:

'Man, before we go much further, there's something you ought to know.'

'What's that?' said Jarl.

'Man, I'm not a peddler at all,' said Drake.

'I didn't for a moment think that you were,' said Jarl. 'What are you then?'

'I'm an ambassador. From King Tor.'

'Tor?' said Jarl, blankly.

'Aye, man! Rightful king of Stokos! He's giving your troops a hell of a battering right now, in Hok.'

'Is he?' said Jarl, with indifference.

'There's more,' babbled Drake. 'Tor has promised me

565

his daughter's hand in marriage. That makes me rightful heir to Stokos. Don't you understand? That makes me an enemy of the Harvest Plains. You turn me over to the law courts, you'll be famous. Aye. They'll put me on trial, I'll get chopped to pieces, and you'll be a hero.'

'Bullshit,' said Jarl. 'The most bullshit I've ever heard in my life.'

'Why would I say it unless it was true?' said Drake.

'For you're the type who makes unlimited trouble once you get hold of a lawyer,' said Jarl. 'I know your sort! Haul you into a court of law and you prove immortal! Well, you'll not prove immortal here, I'd swear my life to that.'

Jarl's analysis was fairly accurate. Drake was no stranger to argument. He had lost count of the number of trials he had attended – many of them his own. He'd been on trial for his life in places as far apart as the Iron Palace of Cam and the Castle of Controlling Power. He'd faced Jon Arabin's kind of justice on the deck of the *Warwolf*, too. He'd rather be in a court of law than a torture chamber any day of the year.

'Man,' said Drake, 'this war in Hok threatens the very life of the Harvest Plains. You could use me as a hostage, aye, there's a thought, send messengers into Hok to see if Tor wants to buy me. That way you could buy peace.'

'Selzirk cares nothing for Hok,' said Jarl. 'A few soldiers chasing bandits in the hills – what's that to the city? Nothing!'

'I'm a—'

'Shut up!', said Jarl. 'Whatever you mean to Tor or Stokos, that's nothing to Selzirk. Only a mad ego could make you think yourself that important.'

'Oh,' said Drake, 'so I'm of no importance. Is that right! Then how about letting me out of here?'

'Tell me who helped you steal the bard and you can go,' said Jarl.

'I'd tell if I knew but I don't!' shouted Drake. 'Don't you understand that?'

'Strap him down!' said Jarl.

His men moved to obey.

'You'll get nothing out of me,' said Drake, as he was strapped to the torture bench. 'Never!'

'Cut off his feet,' said Jarl, curtly.

'No!' screamed Drake, as a man applied saw to ankle. 'No, no, I confess, I did it, I'll tell anything, everything.'

The sawman paused.

'Who was with you then?' said Jarl.

'Andranovory,' said Drake. 'We talked it up together. Him and me. And Erhed, yes, Erhed, that's the one, you'll find him at the Eagle. They were both in on it. We stole the bard. We stole the papers. An'vory had them last. He was supposed to share out the money to all. I've not had my share yet, get it off him when you catch him.'

'Descriptions,' said Jarl crisply.

'Well,' said Drake, 'An'vory, he's simple. Enough hair on his head to mop a floor. But a bit missing up topside – maybe someone scalped him or something. Black beard, great pouches under his eyes and such.'

Drake gave a workable description of Atsimo Andranovory, whom he had first met on the docks of Cam the day after his sixteenth birthday. He had more trouble describing Erhed, who was so insignificant that even his best friends would have been hard put to decently describe him to a stranger. But he did his best.

Thodric Jarl was so pleased with this information that he quite forgot to interrogate Drake about the whereabouts of Rolf Thelemite, the oath-breaker. Instead, he had Drake thrown into solitary confinement, and went off to organize a raid. That very evening, Jarl and a dozen of his men raided the Eagle in Jone, capturing Andranovory and Erhed.

Jarl and his party bound their captives hand and foot, put them into sacks, threw the sacks onto a cart, then started the return journey from Jone to Santrim. They had got almost as far as Kesh when they were ambushed by members of the criminal fraternity.

Thodric Jarl was good at what he did. He had almost won his little war when ninety soldiers from Kesh surrounded the scene of combat and arrested everyone in sight, including two whores who had stopped to watch the fun and a debt collector who had been trying to go about his lawful business.

Interrogations proceeded.

Meanwhile, Drake, alone in his cell, thought things through. Why had Selzirk executed the three ambassadors sent by King Tor? Well – it was entirely possible Selzirk had done no such thing. Drake's only knowledge of the executions came from a sucker-fool encountered dockside in Jone. Drake had swallowed his story without hesitation – but it had quite possibly been a fabrication.

Anyway, Jarl's response had been a good indication of how things stood, surely. Being associated with Tor was hardly certain death. Particularly since the association was ancient. So he could breathe a little easier. So what now?

Lawyers, that's the thing!

The next day, Drake, to his great surprise, was taken from his place of confinement to have an audience with the Kingmaker Farfalla and with Plovey of the Regency.

'It was wrong of my son to arrest you,' said Farfalla, with a glance at Plovey.

'Very wrong,' said the Regency official gravely.

'I thought as much!' said Drake. 'Right, I'll get a lawyer! There'll be writs and damages and compensations and such. Unless your son wants to settle out of court, perhaps. Very cheap, ma'am – I'll settle for half my own weight in gold.'

'Not so fast!' said Plovey.

'Oh, it won't be fast, law is slow, yes, but we'll get there in the end.'

'There are other matters to be cleared up first,' said Plovey.

'Yes,' said Farfalla. 'Before anything else is attended to, you must tell us what you know about the death-stone.'

'That's easily done,' said Drake. 'For I know nothing

about any death-stone. Now, about my lawyer—'

'Young man,' said Plovey, cutting across his enthusiasm, 'we know that you know about the weapon your master Morgan Hearst was in search of. There's other things we want to know about, too. The secret underground way between the far north and the Araconch Waters. And other things. The madness of the magic stones, for one.'

'Magic stones?' said Drake. 'Is it fairy tales you're after? Man, I could tell you a famous fairy tale, yes. With elves in it, aye, and a friendly dwarf with a red nose, and a talking rabbit, and—'

'The truth!' said Plovey. 'That's what we want!'

'Then the truth is that I know nothing of this Heist or Hest or whatever his name was, nothing of his magic stones or balls or cats' eyes or whatever they were, and nothing of any underground way, excepting one which lies in Penvash, which I'll be happy enough to tell for you.'

'We want no story-stories about Penvash. Only the truth!'

'Man, there are great truths about Penvash. Listen – there's a Door up there. It goes from place to place, just a single step to take you a thousand leagues or more. Man, with that, you people could conquer the world.'

'No more of your foolery!' said Plovey. 'The truth! About Hearst! The stone! The madness! The dragons! The way! The wars!'

'This,' said Farfalla, in a quiet yet determined voice, 'is important to us.'

'But I've told you—'

'Take him to the Deep,' said Plovey, grimly. 'Leave him there until he's ready to tell the truth.'

Guards threw Drake into the Deep, a cell awash with sewage and swarming with pythogenic vermin. He was in there scarcely long enough to scream his surrender. Then he began to sing, oh yes, sweetly as anything. All the tavern-talk he'd heard from Andranovory and others came out of him as slick as vomit.

'. . . then Alish smashed Erhed on the head with a rock. Ah, brutal ugly it was! Alish wanted to kill him off for dragon-meat. When? Aagh, the day after Poxquill was killed by the basilisk. How? Man, it breathed on him. Or else looked him eye-to-eye. Kills either way, yes. An ugly little brute of a thing, scarce as long as my forearm. But Hearst killed it from behind, so we ate that, and Poxquill too . . .'

At first his interrogators seemed to believe everything. For, as Drake was swiftly learning, human beings are very credulous creatures, with no reservoirs of disbelief worth mentioning. But, after he had been singing sweetly for ten days and a half, Plovey came to visit him:

'Young man,' he said, 'you stand in danger of compromising your anatomy, if not your life. For the tale you have told us fails to match that told by Andranovory and others.'

'Man,' said Drake. 'I'll tell anything to please. What do you want to hear?'

'You already know the answer to that,' said Plovey. 'The truth!'

'Man,' said Drake. 'I'd tell the truth, but you'd never believe it. Why, it was the truth itself which made me champion liar of Selzirk, aye, champion of your city of filth and sewers. A truth I told about Doors and monster-fights and such, that's what did it.'

'I want the truth,' said Plovey. 'I'll get it from you dead or alive.'

'You'll not get much from me once I'm dead!' said Drake.

'You'd be surprised,' said Plovey, 'of the powers of some of our thaumaturgists. Torturers, take him away!'

So Drake obliged with the truth, the whole truth and nothing but the truth. As he had expected, it did him no good whatsoever.

'That won't do,' said his torturer, and sank a bodkin into Drake's testicles.

Drake screamed.

570

'Plovey!' he screamed. 'Get Plovey of the Regency, I'll tell it to him, anything, anything.'

The torturer, who wanted the afternoon off so he could visit his grandmother (who was near enough to ninety, and feeling her age) arranged for Drake to have the interview he requested.

Plovey manifested himself.

'What do you wish to discuss with me, dear boy?' asked Plovey.

'Proof!' said Drake. 'The proof of poison. Read my story, man, it's all written down there, scribes and all have been hacking away at it for days. The story tells you I suffer no harm from poison. I'll take poison as the proof of it.'

'What poison would you have us give you?' asked Plovey gently.

'Why, anything that's lethal! Arsenic, strychnine, ratsbane, hemlock, cyanide or worse. Or you could set snakes to bite me, aye, or scorpions, or wild dogs foaming at the mouth, whatever you want. It's proof, proof, man, proof by Investigation, that's what you'd be doing, Investigating me, yes.'

'Darling one,' said Plovey, stroking Drake's hand. 'Do you think to escape us so easily? I don't want you dead. Not till I've had the truth from you.'

'But,' said Drake, desperately, 'you can risk my death, surely. You said you had magic people and such who could get the truth from me even if I were dead.'

'Oh yes, oh yes,' said Plovey. 'So I do, indeed. But the work of thaumaturgists is slow, and the expense is appalling. No, my dear young friend – no poison.'

'But I don't want it to kill myself!' wailed Drake. 'I want it to prove my story!'

Plovey soothed Drake's sweating brow.

'Darling boy,' said Plovey, 'you'll never come within a thousand years of poison. Not while I've got anything to do with it.'

'But you must let me prove my story!'

'You cannot,' said Plovey, running a gentle hand over the nape of Drake's neck. Smiling. Sweetly. 'You cannot prove your story, for that's all it is. A story. Nonsense about flying ships and sea serpents. What we want, my dear, is the truth. That's all.'

'Would you like my body?' asked Drake, hoping desperately. 'We could come to a very nice arrangement.'

'Ah, darling boy!' said Plovey. 'I regret to say I have never been able to conjure up a lust for male flesh. So many opportunities lost! Yet the sad truth is, I like women only. I'm married to one. She satisfies my needs entirely.'

'Then tell me tell me tell me,' said Drake. 'Please, please, for the love of mercy, tell me what the others are saying, so I can say it too. I only want to please. For the love of mercy, tell!'

'I love not mercy,' said Plovey, making ready to leave. 'Only justice. Be assured, dear boy, that everything done to you here is entirely legal. Torture is an acknowledged road to truth, and we will follow that road until we get the truth.'

He left, humming to himself, ease in his stride and confidence in his carriage.

The next day, Drake was strapped down for torture as per usual, but there was a change in the normal routine. For, instead of his usual interrogators, in came Thodric Jarl.

'They've brought me in on the case because they said you were proving hard to break,' said Jarl. 'I'm sure we can soon change that. Cut off his feet!'

And a minion set saw to ankles.

'Stop! Stop!' screamed Drake. 'I'll tell, I'll tell, anything, everything.'

'Oh, we've heard that before,' said Jarl. 'This time we're going to cut your feet off to show you we mean business. Then we can start thinking about serious torture.'

Jarl nodded to the man with the saw.

The blade ripped into Drake's flesh.

Drake screamed. Then:

'Stop!' cried a voice.

It was Plovey, from the Regency. Rescue! Yes, Drake was sure of it. Just from the look in Plovey's eyes he knew. The man had come with news which would save him.

'Why are you interfering?' asked Jarl. 'We were near to breaking him.'

'I'm interfering,' said Plovey, in excitement, 'because his story may well be true. Let him loose! Bandage his wounds!'

So Drake was released, and bandages put on his ankles, where the saw had cut through his thin shin-flesh right down to the bone. Then he was led from the torture chamber to another place entirely, a long hall lined with tapestries. Many men stood on either side.

'Walk down the hall, dear boy,' said Plovey. 'Walk down the hall, looking to left and to right. Stop when you see someone you know.'

'Very well,' said Drake.

He walked. Looking to left and to right. So many men. How normal they looked! Neat beards, clean clothes, well-fed faces. As if the whole world was not a rolling nightmare but a place where decent folk could live decent lives untroubled. Aye. Well. Perhaps, from their point of view. . .

In that hall, amongst so many people, Drake felt the desolation of utter loneliness. None of these people cared for him. He meant nothing to them. He experienced a surge of nostalgia for his time in the Collosnon prison pit on the island of Chag-jalak, when he had shared food with Whale Mike, Salaman Meerkat and all those others. Aye. Ish Ulpin with his walnuts. Jon Disaster and the orange. Harly Burpskin, dragging out that great wodge of salami.

Aye. With friends it's not so bad. Whatever happens. I wish I was with those jokers now. Those that still live.

Drake stopped.

'This man,' he said, 'this man's Andranovory.'

'Yes,' said Plovey, mildly. 'Yes, we know that.'

'I'll kill you!' said Andranovory, who did not try to do any such thing since he was standing between two soldiers. 'A traitor twice!'

573

'Betrayed you?' said Drake. 'Man, you and your stories got me into so much trouble—'

'There was Burntos—'

'At Burntos—'

'Now now,' said Plovey, in soothing tones. 'Come along, we've business to attend to.'

And on down the hall they went, until Drake stopped again.

'This,' said Drake, 'is Melf Kelf, the burlesque actor from the Harlequin Theatre.'

'Why, so it is,' said Plovey. 'It's months since I've been: I must go again. Come along now, he's not the man we're interested in.'

'Who are we interested in, then?' said Drake. 'And where do all these people come from?'

'Most of these people are tax defaulters,' said Plovey. 'We use them for . . . for what we do in this hall. It's part of their punishment for them to thus part with their time. Andranovory – why, he was just there for my own amusement. But the people we're really interested in – why, march on, and keep your eyes about you. You'll see.'

And on down the hall they went. Drake wondered what the hell was going on in this hall. He still didn't understand. Maybe he should think it through. But he was so worn, so tired. Shattered. Aye. Like a cracked-up statue just ready to fall into pieces. A friend. If only a friend—

But—

Who was that? Was it. . .?

Yes, it was!

'Jon!' cried Drake. 'Jon Arabin! Oh Jon, man, it's sweet to see you! You've saved me, Jon!'

And, crying out thus, he ran in delight to the man he had recognized. It was indeed Jon Arabin, the Warwolf himself. Who would make everything all right. Who would tell Plovey it was all true, everything Drake said, he meant to tell the truth, he wanted to tell truths, had told them.

'Jon!' said Drake, joyfully. 'How did you get here? You've saved my life!'

'If I've saved yours then you've cost me mine,' said Arabin heavily. 'I had them half-way convinced I was a Galish merchant until you came in.'

Drake, shocked, stepped back. His face seemed to wreck itself. His mouth crumpled into misery. He moaned. Next moment, he was weeping.

'You weren't to know,' said Arabin. 'You weren't to know.'

And he stepped forward, meaning to embrace Drake. But guards grabbed Arabin, and other guards grabbed Drake. Both struggled as Jon Arabin was marched away.

Plovey put a hand on Drake's shoulder.

'That's good,' said Plovey. 'That's good. You've proved our prisoner to be the man we thought he was. You've also proved your story.'

'You bastard!' sobbed Drake. 'You filthy bastard! You made me betray my best friend!'

'I,' said Plovey, smoothly, sadly, 'am but a servant of the law. You've proved your story – is that not something? Come, walk on. The game's not finished.'

'I'll not hunt out anyone else for you,' said Drake. 'I'd rather die!'

'Nevertheless,' said Plovey, 'walk on down the hall. Walking can do no harm, can it? Come now, darling boy – proceed. Or would you rather be dragged?'

Drake proceeded.

And, while he had thought he would betray no others to Plovey, suddenly he saw a familiar face, a green-haired green-bearded green-eyed face belonging to a gangling man with extra-long arms, each arm ending in a double-thumbed fist.

'You!' said Drake, jabbing a finger at the Walrus as if to kill him. 'I know who you are, standing there so sweet and innocent!'

'Who is it, darling boy?' said Plovey, in a voice sweet with the melody of triumph.

'It's Slagger Mulps, the Walrus himself,' said Drake. 'You know him from the truths I've told you. Aye. It's all

575

down on paper. A cruel man, aye. Gave me to Andranovory when I first became his prisoner. Aye. Then An'vory hung me from my ankles by way of torture when I wouldn't give him a suck.'

'Drake!' said the Walrus, with grief in his voice. 'Don't speak against me as an enemy! What's past is past! I took you south with me to Burntos, didn't I? You stowed away, yet I let you live.'

'Aye, and challenged me to death when I got back to the Teeth,' said Drake. 'Then made that mad challenge with Jon Arabin in the forest of Penvash. A lot of trouble that caused, too! But, man, I'd pardon you for that, except for one thing. You're the enemy. Jon Arabin's enemy. And any enemy of his is a mortal foe of mine. If he's to die, then so should you.'

'Man,' said the Walrus. 'You've got things wrong, for things have changed. I'm now his blood-brother true.'

Thus Drake was a second time dismayed. And his discomfort increased when the Walrus, overcome with sorrow and the fear of death, went down on his knees, sobbing.

'Come,' said Plovey. 'No need to listen to that. We're finished.'

He led Drake from the hall to a bare stone room where half a dozen guards stood waiting. Drake wiped the tears from his eyes. Took some deep, slow breaths.

What's done is done. Can I set it to rights? Maybe. But I'll need a lawyer. So no more grief. Business first.

'Right,' said Drake, in a voice which was as much business as he could manage. 'Time for me to be going.'

'Where to?' asked Plovey, who seemed amused.

'Why, to get a lawyer to start with,' said Drake. 'Aye. We'll get petitions drawn up, yes. Asking clemency for Walrus and Warwolf. Pardons and such.'

'You're not going anywhere,' said Plovey. 'Seize him!'
The guards grabbed Drake. He was astonished.

'What's this?' said Drake.

'This,' said Plovey, 'is your arrest. It's the consequence

576

of the stories you've been telling, both to me and to others.'

'But those stories were true!' said Drake. 'I was telling the truth all along! You know that now! You've had proof of it!'

'Indeed we have,' said Plovey. 'So you stand condemned by your own mouth. For your story holds you to be a pirate.'

'And that amuses you?'

'Indeed it does. For you see, dear boy, the penalty for piracy is to be tortured to death.'

Kicking and screaming, Drake was carried away by the guards. And Plovey, smiling sweetly, went home to the charms of his lawful wife, with the feeling of a day's work well done.

48

Elkor Alish: Rovac warrior who accompanied Morgan
Hearst on a quest for the death stone, a weapon of surpassing power; later attempted to use death stone against
Hearst and others; Hearst lost his right hand while helping
thwart the attempt.

Before Drake was incarcerated in the cell where he would
wait until the death-torturers were ready, his gaolers stripped him of his clothes.

'You can't leave me naked!' protested Drake.

'Of course we can,' said a cheerful turnkey. 'Don't
worry, me little rantipole. You won't be wanting clothes
much longer. You'll be dead in a couple of days.'

So Drake was consigned to his cell, and there he lay on a
mat of filth which had once (a very long time ago) been
straw. And wept. For his life, for his liberty, for the horrors of the world.

He could see now the error of his ways.

He had done so many things that were wrong, yes, badly
wrong, criminally wrong.

'For a start,' muttered Drake, 'I should never have run
off with Muck's mastersword. No, that was a low, cowardly thing to do. I should have caught the old bugger in a
back alley one dark night, yes, and cut his heart out. That
would have saved a lot of trouble.'

And later, in Runcorn:

'I should never have tried to rule so sweetly. That's not
my style. No. I should have got together a pack of

knifemen, yes, to do for the opposition subtly. Why, when Garimanthea turned against me, I should have had him jugulated proper fast. No playing around!'

And more recently, in Selzirk:

'I should never have gone into Muck's temple to try to sweet-talk Zanya. That was ego speaking, aye. Too much pride. Hubris, in fact.'

Actually (to be pedantically precise) what he said was not 'hubris' but 'me thinking I could walk across fifty leagues of fresh-laid eggs in lead-shod boots without breaking a one of them'. But by that he meant 'hubris', for he had the concept right enough, even though he knew no precise word in any language to express it.

'I should never have gone into that temple, no,' said Drake. 'I should have got together fifty men with knives and hatchets, aye, all bribed with promises of treasure. Aye, that's the way. Send others in to kill, burn, plunder, kidnap. I was trying to do things lawful-like, and that's how I fell afoul of the law. A big mistake, man.'

Yes. He should have organized a big raid to kill out the temple. Then, when he had Zanya in chains in some private place, he could have started talking some sense into her head.

'But I really thought she'd come with me,' moaned Drake. 'Man, I really did. I thought we had something going there.'

There is no telling how long these recriminations might have lasted, or where they might have led, for the very next day another prisoner was flung into Drake's cell: a garrulous old man named Shix, who had been imprisoned for brewing bad beer and worse wine.

After that, Drake never got a moment's peace, for Shix suffered verbal diarrhoea while awake, and kept rambling on (though less coherently) even when asleep. If he had said something interesting, that might have been excusable, but he was a dreary old pedant who thought himself the world's best brewer and its best winemaker as well.

In the days which followed, Drake learnt far more than he wanted to about yeast and hops, casks and grapes and zymome and malt, gluten and wheat, the rape which remains after wine-making, the derelictions of the average vintner, and hundreds of other technicalities in which he had no conceivable interest.

All this talk of wine and beer set him to thinking about the magical brew he had tasted in Brennan, which had left him drunk and free-floating. At the time, he had made a resolution to seek out more of the stuff from wizards.

Aye.

And if he had resolutely pursued intoxication, he would never have become ensnared in this terrible city. He would have gone somewhere comparatively safe, such as the terror-lands south of Drangsturm, where there were only the monsters of the Swarms to contend with, and not lawyers and judges and such. But no, he had not taken the hint that magical liquor had offered him; instead, he had tamely accepted a life of sobriety, and was now to pay a fearful price for his foolishness.

But when?

When were they going to seize him, and strap him to a torture table, and subject him to a slow, lingering death of utmost agony?

Drake got so curious about this vital question that finally he asked a gaoler.

'When are we going to torture you to death?' said the gaoler, scratching his head. 'Why, I don't rightly know. What's your name?'

'Drake Douay.'

'Ah! Drake Douay! So this is where you finished up! We all thought you'd escaped. Wait around, me younker, and I'll find out.'

And the gaoler waddled away, leaving Drake to think: *Me and my big mouth!*

The gaoler returned later in the day.

'Well,' he said. 'There's some good news and some bad news.'

80% of a cricket
is edible, compared to
40% of a cow.

64% of the diet of
cane toads is other
cane toads.

Lemon ants
taste of
lemon.

You have
taste receptors
in your anus.

Near the anus
of the horseshoe bat is
an extra pair of false nipples.
The baby bats use them
as handles to
cling to.

Bees
can fly higher
than Mount Everest.

The world's largest saw
was used to cut through
a mountain in Kazakhstan.

There are mountains in Antarctica
called Nipple Peak, Dick Peaks,
and Mount Cocks.

16th-century fabric colors included
Puke, Gooseturd, Dead Spaniard,
and Dying Monkey.

The word "donkey"
used to rhyme
with "monkey"

The word "fizzle"
once meant "to fart
without making a noise."

Fartplan
is Danish for
"timetable."

The longest-ever Viking longship
was unearthed by accident
during renovations of
a Danish longship
museum.

The Vikings
had a god and a goddess
of skiing.

"Skull," "slaughter," "hell,"
"weak," "anger," and "freckles"
are all words of
Viking origin.

The most
common inscription
found on Viking coins is
"There is no god
but Allah."

Male coin spiders
only have sex once.
After mating, they chew off
their own genitals.

To be soft enough to chew,
the first-ever breakfast cereal
had to be soaked in
milk overnight.

Potatoes soaked in vinegar,
soda water, and crackers were what
Lord Byron lived on in his twenties.
He weighed less than 125 pounds.

Kanye West
hasn't smiled in photographs
since he noticed that people
in old paintings don't
smile either.

Your computer knows
more about *you* than
*your friends and
family do.*

You are
genetically more similar
to your friends than
to strangers.

The "like" button on
the Latin version of Facebook
says *mihi placet*—
"it pleases me."

The first item
listed on eBay was
a broken laser pointer.

Wikipedia
has a page on
"The Reliability of Wikipedia."

The Wikipedia page for "pedant"
has been edited more than
500 times.

The banned website
most often clicked by MPs in
the Houses of Parliament
is sexymp.co.uk.

Twitter-bone
was a 19th-century disorder
that left horses
unable to walk.

A single human brain
has more switches than
all the computers and
Internet connections
on Earth.

A single human nose
produces about a cupful
of mucus a day.

Over 7,000 species
of plants and animals have been
cultivated for human consumption,
but just four crops—rice, wheat, corn,
and potatoes—make up two-thirds
of everything we eat.

More fish are farmed every year
than pigs, sheep, cows, and
chickens put together.

The consumption of chickens
in ancient Rome was restricted
to one per person
per meal.

In Indonesia,
people bring chickens
to cremation ceremonies
to absorb evil spirits.

Indonesia has
special chickens known as
"the Lamborghini of poultry."
They are all-black (even the meat)
and cost $2,500 each.

In the Cook Islands,
online business domains
end in .co.ck.

Penis worms
can turn their mouths
inside out and walk
on their throats.

Tapeworms
can cause
epilepsy.

Eating chocolate
improves your memory,
but only if you eat so much of it
that it's bad for
your health.

Smoky bacon Pringles,
shrimp cocktail Walkers, and
McCoy's sizzling BBQ chips
are all suitable for vegans.

The Yorkshire village of Fryup
turned down a request by the
animal rights charity PETA
to change its name to
Vegan Fryup.

There is a village in Russia
where every single person knows
how to tightrope-walk.

23 villages in
Russia's Krasnoyarsk region are
entirely inhabited by men.

Chernobyl
will be uninhabitable
for at least 20,000 years.

The oldest known customer service complaint letter was written on a clay tablet in 1750 BC.

When the first sewing factories opened, seamstresses complained of "extreme genital excitement" caused by the sewing machines.

Disney ignored the complaint from *Mary Poppins* author P. L. Travers that the song "Let's Go Fly a Kite" should be "Let's Go *and* Fly a Kite."

I'm a Celebrity . . . Get Me Out of Here! gets a letter of complaint every year from naturalist Chris Packham about the way they exploit animals.

A tarantula hawk
is neither a tarantula nor a hawk;
it's a giant wasp with the second
most painful insect sting
in the world.

Queen bees
lay eggs through
their stings.

Cockroaches
can hold their breath
for 40 minutes.

Dung beetles
can bury 250 times
their own weight in dung
in a single evening.

The fastest bus in the world
is powered by
cow dung.

The fastest sprinters
have very symmetrical
knees.

The best long-distance runners
have very symmetrical
nostrils.

The Yupno people
of Papua New Guinea
use their noses to point with
instead of their
fingers.

The tiny hairs in your nose
are the last things to
stop beating when
you die.

The deaths of
George I of England, Pope Paul II,
Pope Clement VII, Frederick the Great,
Maximilian I Archduke of Austria, and
Albert II of Germany were all
due to melon overdose.

Szechuan peppers
make the lips
vibrate.

A kiss on the lips
can transfer 80 million bacteria
into another person's mouth
in 10 seconds.

There are
40 billion bacteria
in one gram of feces.

To make enough feces
to feed its larvae,
a flea has to drink
30 times its own weight
in blood.

The black legs
of marabou storks
usually appear white because
they're covered in
excrement.

The 10,000 species of birds
alive today make up
less than 1% of all the bird species
that have ever existed.

A bird caused
the Large Hadron Collider
to be turned off in 2009 after
it dropped a piece of
baguette into it.

The 420 billion neutrinos
that pass every second through
every square inch of your body
were created 8.5 minutes ago
in the center of the Sun.

No one knows why the center of the Sun
is not nearly as hot as its surface.

The Sun rotates
around its axis every 26 days
but, because it's made of gas,
different bits rotate at
different speeds.

The Sun is
located in the Milky Way
between the third and fourth arms
of a cloud of stars known as
the Local Fluff.

The Milky Way
is corrugated.

Corrugated iron
is not made from
iron.

The Man in the Iron Mask's mask
wasn't made of iron
but velvet.

The beard of the
death mask of Tutankhamun broke off
when a lightbulb in the display case
was being changed.

Inês de Castro was
proclaimed queen of Portugal in 1357,
despite dying two years earlier.

"Old person smell" is
caused by a molecule called 2-nonenal,
which increases in your body
as you age.

Penicillin was
originally called
"mold juice."

You can smell
a flock of macaroni penguins
from six miles away.

The olive sea snake has
light sensors in its tail
so it can check that its
whole body is hidden.

Light detectors in frogs' eyes
are so sensitive that they can
detect single photons of light.

The ancient Greek cure for
cataracts was to pour
hot broken glass
into the eyes.

[136]

1 in 1,000
lightning bolts are invisible
to the human eye.

You are 100 times more likely
to be struck by lightning
standing under an oak
than a beech.

In the First World War,
actor Basil Rathbone
led covert missions
disguised as
a tree.

In 1745,
King Louis XV went to
a ball dressed as a
yew tree.

The first Christmas tree in
the Vatican went up
in 1982.

In the 1670s,
the Pope bought
"St. Peter's Beard" from
highwayman Dick Dudley and kissed it,
not knowing it was actually a
prostitute's pubic wig.

Only humans kiss
with tongues.

Peter Cushing
and Christopher Lee
both wore toupees.

The place where
Julius Caesar was murdered
is now a cat sanctuary.

Caligula made it
illegal on pain of death
to mention a goat
in his presence.

President Mobutu Sese Seko of Zaire
banned all leopard-print hats,
except for his own.

The Hawaiian for "certified,"
hooiaioia, has eight
consecutive
vowels.

Ulaia
is an old Hawaiian word
meaning "to live like a hermit
because of disappointment."

The world's last surviving
male northern white rhino
lives under 24-hour
armed guard.

In 1958,
the people of São Paulo voted
a rhino named Cacareco
onto the city council.

The town of
Dorset, Minnesota,
elects its mayor by raffle.

In 1995,
Nelson Mandela was voted
Santa Claus of the Year by
the children of Greenland.

Scotland
has 421 words for
"snow."

Before going on stage for
public readings, Charles Dickens
drank rum, sherry, and
a pint of champagne.

A Tale of Two Cities
contains the first known reference
to potato chips.

The glue that seals chip packets
is dried instantly using
particle accelerators.

According to its website,
WD-40 was once used by police
to remove a naked burglar from
an air-conditioning vent.

In some parts
of southern Africa,
mosquito nets are
mostly used
for fishing.

The first dice were used
to tell the future.

The first bra
was made from
handkerchiefs.

In 2007,
eight-year-old twin boys from Ohio
invented wedgie-proof
underpants.

Before paint tubes were invented,
artists kept their paint
in pigs' bladders.

The first product
sold by mail order was
Welsh flannel.

From 1700 until 1905,
cows were tied to posts in
St. James's Park and their milk
sold "straight from the udder."

The offspring of
a cow and a bison
is called a "beefalo."

The largest diamond ever found
comes from Brazil and
is called "Sergio."

The national anthem
of Bosnia and Herzegovina is called
"The National Anthem
of Bosnia and Herzegovina."

In 2004,
Mexico fined a singer for
stumbling over the words
while singing the national anthem.

Only 2% of Belgians
know their national anthem.

Between 1910 and 1926,
Portugal had 45
governments.

The Republic of Ireland
didn't have zip codes
until 2015.

In 2000,
the Royal Mail withdrew its
sponsorship of its mascot Postman Pat,
on the grounds that he no longer
fitted its corporate image.

The 1908 London Olympics were
sponsored by Oxo, Odol mouthwash,
and Indian Foot Powder.

For the first 50 years
of the ancient Greek Olympics,
the only event was the
200-meter sprint.

Due to quarantine laws,
the equestrian events at the
1956 Melbourne Olympics
took place in Stockholm.

The 1900 Paris Olympics
featured a 200-meter swimming race
with obstacles.

Men's underwater swimming
at the 1900 Olympics was never
held again due to "lack of
spectator appeal."

The javelin competition
at the 1900 Olympics
was held in a public park.
Competitors had to be
careful not to hit anyone.

The reigning
Olympic tug-of-war champions
are the City of London Police.

For the Pope's visit in 2015,
traffic police in Manila were
issued with 2,000 diapers
so they never had to
leave their posts.

Troops in
Operation Desert Storm
wore water-filled Pampers diapers
on their heads to keep cool.

In the First World War,
only Romanian officers
above the rank of major
were authorized to wear
eye shadow into battle.

In the 1930s,
a fashion craze for girls
to wear monocles swept Liverpool.

Ralph Lauren
was born
Ralph Lifshitz.

If Hitler's father
hadn't changed his surname in 1877,
the Third Reich would have been
led by Adolf Schicklgruber.

For marrying a Protestant,
Josef Goebbels became the only Nazi
to be excommunicated.

In the 5th century AD,
the Catholic Church
excommunicated
all mime artists.

Ivan the Terrible
once sewed an archbishop
into a bearskin and had him
hunted down by a pack of dogs.

Catherine the Great,
Empress of Russia,
wasn't called Catherine,
wasn't Russian, and
hated being called
"the Great."

Peter the Great
slept with a servant's stomach
for a pillow.

Hitler's plan for Moscow
was to level the city and turn it
into an enormous lake.

The sixth-
biggest river
in the world is
under the sea.

The longest canyon in the world is
50% longer than the Grand Canyon
and buried under the ice
in Greenland.

The world's largest container ship
can carry 900 million cans of
baked beans—60 beans for
every person on Earth.

Scallops caught in Brittany
are shipped to China for cleaning
and then sent back to France
to be cooked and eaten.

In 2017,
China will open
the world's first stadium
dedicated to online gaming.

Chongqing in China
has a smartphone-only lane
for pedestrians.

92% of the
population of China is
lactose-intolerant.

Only 20% of people who
think they're allergic to penicillin
actually are.

The first known case of
"Climate Change Delusion"
took place in 2008, when a man
refused to drink water as he felt guilty
about "taking it from the Earth."

The first occupational disease
ever recorded in medical literature
was "chimney sweep's scrotum."

In 19th-century Australia,
it was thought that climbing
inside a dead whale would
cure rheumatism.

Kidney donors
live longer than
the average person.

In 1800,
the average age of
an American was 16.
Today, it's 38.

When a country is
in recession,
life expectancy
goes up.

Finland
is the world's
least fragile state.

The sauna
at Helsinki airport
is unisex, and clothing
is optional.

The first passenger flight
lasted 23 minutes and flew
at an altitude of 15 feet.

In the first
BBC radio news report,
the news was read twice,
once quickly and once slowly.
Listeners were asked which
they preferred.

The first parakeets
sold in Europe cost
as much as a house.

The first novel
was Japanese and
ended in mid-sentence.

The Japanese government's
official biography of
Emperor Hirohito
is 61 volumes long.

During the Second World War,
Churchill wore a specially designed
onesie, which he called
his "siren suit."

In 1941,
Churchill had a meeting with
President Roosevelt
stark naked.

Three-quarters of Americans
admit to using their phone
in the bathroom.

In Old English,
the word "ears" meant "arse."

In the 1800s,
ducks were called "arsefeet"
because their feet are so
close to their bottoms.

People's body temperature
drops when they watch videos
of other people putting their
hands into cold water.

During the Cold War,
the US tested supersonic
ejector seats
on bears.

In Switzerland,
if you fail your driving test
three times, you have to
visit a psychologist
to explain why.

In 1966,
Mercedes introduced a car
steered with a joystick.

The first baby carriage
had a harness so it
could be pulled by a
dog or a goat.

Sloths have
more bones in their necks
than giraffes.

"Derbyshire neck"
was an 18th-century name for
swollen thyroid glands.

"Token-suckers"
were people who stole
New York City subway tokens.

French pubic lice are
known as *papillons d'amour*,
"butterflies of love."

A Shakespearean euphemism
for infidelity is "groping for trout
in a peculiar river."

All of Shakespeare's
six known signatures are
spelled differently and not one is spelled
"William Shakespeare."

The first recorded use
of "pop," as in "pop music"
was in a letter written
by George Eliot
in 1862.

"Lolz," "shizzle," "bezzy,"
and "emoji" are all acceptable
Scrabble words.

The song "Yes, We Have
No Bananas" was written by
Leon Trotsky's nephew.

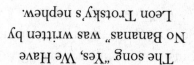

Bananas emit
antimatter.

Under a black light
bananas glow
blue.

You can't make
blue fireworks.

In ancient China,
archers attached sparklers
to their arrows.

St. Peter's School, York,
never celebrates Bonfire Night.
Its most famous alumnus
is Guy Fawkes.

Barack Obama's
mother's name was Stanley.
Her nickname at school
was "Stan the Man."

Buzz Aldrin's father
was friends with
Orville Wright.

Boeing tests the
Wi-Fi signal on their planes
by filling the seats with
sacks of potatoes.

The White House
had no Wi-Fi
until 2012.

Thomas Jefferson kept
sheep on the White House lawn.
They were vicious and attacked
anyone who went near them.

Theodore Roosevelt
had a pet hyena.

Napoleon
had a pet wombat.

The Hawaiian pizza
was invented by a Greek
in Canada.

There is an
Indian women's
basketball player called
Elizabeth Hilarious.

Catherine of Aragon
wasn't present at any of her
first three weddings.

Throughout the 19th century,
between a third and a half of
British brides were pregnant
on their wedding day.

A paraclausithyron
is a love song performed
outside the beloved's
front door.

"Mambo No. 5" was
the theme song for the
2000 Democratic Convention
until someone noticed the line
"A little bit of Monica in my life."

Cats enjoy classical music
but are much less interested
in pop music.

In 2003,
43% of pop songs played on
American radio were produced by
Pharrell Williams and Chad Hugo.

Contrary to the line in the song
"Fairytale of New York,"
"the boys of the NYPD"
don't have a choir.

The composer of
"Jingle Bells"
also wrote the song
"We Conquer or Die."

Marching in unison
makes men more
aggressive.

Counting money
makes you feel
less pain.

Counting the rings
in a mammoth's tusks
tells you its age.

When hunting,
humpback whales
make a "ticktock" sound
that tells other whales
it's dinnertime.

English has more words
for the noises dogs make
than any other language.

Tapping a dashboard
makes a pleasant noise because
car manufacturers discovered
that 1 in 4 people do it
when buying a new car.

In 1999,
Harley-Davidson
tried to trademark the sound
of their engines revving.

People
who can taste sounds
have "lexical gustatory
synesthesia."

Hodor
in *Game of Thrones*
(who can only say his own name)
suffers from "expressive aphasia."

Admiral Nelson
suffered from chronic
seasickness.

Every week,
four ships sink
somewhere in the world.

94% of the Earth's oceans
are in permanent
pitch darkness.

In the German resort of Travemünde,
all sand castles must be knocked
down at the end of each day
so nobody trips over them
in the dark.

It takes about
200 tons of sand to
build one detached
house.

The defense policy of New Zealand's
McGillicuddy Serious Party was
to leave beer on all beaches to
distract any invading army.

William the Conqueror
banned capital punishment;
criminals had their eyes
or testicles removed.

In Saxon England,
selling blood sausages was
punishable by the loss of property,
then being "severely purged,"
"disgracefully shaved,"
and exiled.

In 1969,
an Italian man was charged with
selling "grated Parmesan cheese"
that turned out to be grated
umbrella handles.

In 2014,
a man arrested in Lincoln, UK, for
growing 28 cannabis plants
in his garage was called
Mr. Hippie.

Children called Joseph, Cameron,
William, and Jake are naughtier than
those called Jacob, Daniel,
Thomas, and James.

In 2014,
more American babies were named
Khaleesi than Adele.

Pippi Longstocking's full name is
Pippilotta Delicatessa Windowshade
Mackrelmint Ephraim's Daughter
Longstocking.

Baristas
in the Starbucks at the
CIA's headquarters don't write
the customers' names
on the cups.

A large latte
contains more saturated fat than
a cream doughnut.

To replace energy after a workout,
most sports supplements
are no more effective
than a burger.

Two tablespoons of dried basil
contain the same amount of calcium
as a glass of milk.

The last thing Charles II ate
before he died was an "antidote"
containing "extracts of all the herbs
and animals of the kingdom."

1 in 8
people in the world
go to bed hungry.

The more recently a judge has eaten,
the more likely they are
to grant parole.

The first man to
send a Valentine's card was
a Frenchman imprisoned
in the Tower of London.

Some American jails now dress inmates
in black-and-white jumpsuits because
the TV show *Orange Is the New Black*
has made the orange ones too cool.

Prisoners in California can
reduce their sentences
by opting to fight
forest fires.

Denmark
imports
prisoners.

The time machine
in *Back to the Future*
was originally going to be a fridge;
it was changed to a car in case
it encouraged children to
climb into fridges.

One working title
for *Toy Story* was
"Toyz in the Hood."

Robin Williams
improvised so much of *Aladdin*
it became ineligible for the Oscar for
Best Original Screenplay.

Half of the world's
California condors were
raised in captivity by
glove puppets.

Jugglers
in medieval Germany
were not allowed to
inherit property.

Until the reign of Henry VIII,
kitchen assistants in the
royal household
worked naked.

Il y a une couille dans le potage
("There is a testicle in the soup")
is French slang for
"There is a major problem."

The largest lake in
Slovenia disappears
every year.

Ancient Sparta held a
"Festival of the Naked Boys"
every year.

The ancient Romans
collected souvenir mugs.

The Minoans,
not the Romans,
invented the aqueduct.

The Greek for
"It's Greek to me" translates as
"This strikes me as Chinese."

The Chinese political faction
known as the Gang of Four
had six members.

37 is the 12th prime number
and 73 is the 21st prime number.

2015
is a palindrome in binary:
11111011111.

Beethoven
never learned how to do
multiplication.

J. S. Bach
always carried a dagger to
protect himself from
students.

Sigmund Freud
kept a porcupine on his desk
as a reminder of the "prickliness"
of human relationships.

Franz Kafka
destroyed 90% of
everything he wrote.

Victor Hugo
found writing so hard
to get down to he asked his valet to
lock up all his clothes and not
give them back till he'd
written something.

[179]

Wearing
a Superman T-shirt
significantly boosts your
self-confidence.

Queen Victoria wore
crotchless underwear.

Abraham Lincoln used to hide
important documents in
his stovepipe hat.

James Joyce
always kept a pair of
doll's panties in
his pocket.

'I'll have the good news first.'

'The good news is that you've already been tortured to death. Legally, I mean. When it was your turn and we couldn't find you, the executioners put a dog on the table and made do with that. A legal fiction, you understand?'

'Yes,' said Drake, who thought he did even though he didn't. 'So can I go? Do I get out of here?'

'Well no. For that's the bad news. Legally, you're dead. I've sighted your death certificate meself. We can't have dead men walking round the city, can we?'

'So what happens now?'

'Why, me pretty little younker, you grows yourself older. Then in time you dies, thus matching reality with the paperwork. Till then, you sit there nice and happy, another breathing corpse for the auditors to count come Assessment Day.'

'What's Assessment Day?'

'Oh, that's technical, that's technical,' said the turnkey, who didn't rightly understand accounting practices but was unwilling to confess his ignorance.

So Drake was left to linger in his desolation of filth, squalor, dungeon darkness and perpetual hunger. Sometimes, he heard rumours of the outside world: that the sun had died, that a forest had marched west out of Chenameg, that a thousand dragons had ravaged Selzirk. All kinds of wildness circulated in the muttering gloom.

Old man Shix died, and his corpse was taken away. Shix had irritated Drake intensely, but now he longed to have his companion back. In fact, Drake got some of the old man back as part of his next dole of soup, but he did not know that, and thus gained no comfort from it.

Sometimes, he dreamed of Zanya, of her frank lust, of the tender joys of her warm body . . . of her smile, her laugh, her joy in kittens and ducklings and silks and roast chicken . . . of the brightness of her fingernails, which were the cleanest he had seen in his life . . . of her randy jokes and her wild tales about the temple of the Orgy God in the Ebrells . . . of her hair and her skin flaming red in a

581

room lit by a blood-warm sun, her thighs enveloping. . .

Had he imagined her?

He was half-persuaded that he had. Aye, and the sun, moon, and sky, and all the other improbabilities of a world of earth, air, fire and water.

But all those things were real.

And, while Drake lay rotting in his filthy dungeon cell, Zanya Kliedervaust lay on her bed, stroking (in an absent-minded fashion) the sparse hair of Gouda Muck's head, which was busy between her thighs. Staring at the ceiling, she thought, with regret, of Drake. He was a brash sexist barbarian who needed to be taught good manners, and a lot of other things besides. But he had had so much promise! Why, when he had come bursting into her room, he had seemed to her, for a moment, like a regular demon lover, a true hero.

But obviously Drake did not truly value her. Otherwise, he would have returned. Instead, after he was chased away by Muck's men, he had never returned. She was insulted by the way he had abandoned his quest for her so easily . . .

Gouda Muck raised his head and removed one of Zanya's pubic hairs from his lips.

'Darling,' crooned Zanya, 'you're a marvellous man, really you are.'

'Then worship me,' said Muck.

Which she did, in a very practical fashion.

And the days passed.

And, meanwhile, History went on as usual, with its wars, riots, revolutions, law makings, law breakings, plantings, reapings, stocktakings, loves, lusts, joys, horrors, quests, herofeats, births, deaths, copulations, speeches, prize giv-ings, graduations, discoveries, despairs, hopes, philo-sophies, religious revelations *und so weiter*.

Until finally, as a consequence of one of the minor eddies of History, men came for Drake Douay, who was known in certain quarters to be physically alive, for all that he was legally dead.

He was seized. He was dragged from his cell, filthy and

naked, breath foetid, eyes dull, hair and nails uncut, body
swarming with vermin, a scrag of ginger beard on his chin.
He was bathed, shaved, manicured, scraped, disinfected,
deloused, then dressed in velvet trousers, a cotton shirt
and black felt slippers.

'You look beautiful, darling boy,' said Plovey of the
Regency.

'Where did you come from?' demanded Drake.

'I came through the door, of course. Ah. Trousers,
shirt, slippers – what more could you want?'

'A hat,' said Drake, promptly, always one to grab when
the grabbing was good.

So Plovey saw him kitted out with a pert blue bycoket.

'Now food!' demanded Drake.

All he got was a bowl of broth and a single zakuska, but
that was undoubtedly the most his half-starved stomach
could have handled. Then he was led to a room which was
far too bright for him and filled with far too many people,
most of whom were talking simultaneously.

'A Certificate of Resurrection,' said a beak-nosed lawyer, shoving a piece of parchment into Drake's hands.
'You are now officially alive again. Here – take this. A
full pardon for all crimes you've so far committed, both in
and out of Selzirk. You are free to go.'

'But,' said Plovey, 'first hear our offer.'

'An offer I can't refuse, I suppose,' said Drake,
clutching the parchments which had resurrected and pardoned him.

'Of course,' said Plovey. 'What other kind of offer is
worth making? General Tream, the situation, if you
please!'

General Tream stepped forward.

'Listen up!' he bellowed, silencing the chatter in the
room. 'Situation. A Rovac warrior by name of Elkor
Alish has leagued with pirates and others to take the city of
Androlmarphos. Alish holds that city now. Fortunately,
the warrior Morgan Hearst has joined the army of Selzirk.
He bears the deathstone. He will commit that weapon

583

against both Alish and Androlmarphos unless the both surrender.'

Then Tream, assisted by others, started to explain the details. But it was all so confusing – the noise, the brightness, the unfamiliar wealth of food in Drake's stomach, the unaccustomed labour of standing – that in the end he fainted clean away.

After he had convalesced for three days, Plovey came to him alone, and explained things quietly.

They wanted Drake to carry documents to Alish in Androlmarphos. One was a threat: he and his captured city would be destroyed by the deathstone unless they surrendered. The other was an offer: of safe conduct and a massive bribe if Alish gave himself up.

'Once you've seen Alish and returned to Selzirk, we'll also pardon your Walrus and Warwolf.'

'They live?'

'They do. Their trials have not yet been commenced. After all, unlike you, they made no foolish confessions of piracy. So. See Alish in Androlmarphos. Give him our letters. Then return. And both Walrus and Warwolf will be set at liberty. But you must bring us proof that you've met with Alish in 'Marphos.'

'And what proof would that be?'

'Why, a document in Rovac runes drafted by the hand of Elkor Alish himself. Let him testify to the fact that you've seen him. Even if he wants nothing to do with our offers, I'm sure he'll give you proofs. For if he means to stand against us in defiance, he'll be as eager as you are to secure the release of two pirate captains. Useful men they'd make for him.'

'Then why are you prepared to let them go?'

'It's a small stake in a big game. What can we lose? Two prisoners. What can we win? Why, maybe the war. Bring proof! Our Morgan Hearst knows Alish's writing, so try no fakery.'

'This sounds a right weird scheme to me,' said Drake.

'Ah, darling boy,' said Plovey, 'your judgment is very

584

sound. I don't myself think you'll get audience with Alish. Or return.'

'Then why are you letting me go?' said Drake.

'Ah. Because none of this is my idea. No, it's Watashi's idea. And Farfalla's son, dear boy, is a constant threat to the Regency which I serve. We must seize on every opportunity to discredit him. However . . . if you do return, well, no hard feelings. Indeed, if you do return, you must dine with me and my darling wife. I'm sure the family atmosphere would do you good.'

'I'll return, right enough,' said Drake. 'But I'll see both Walrus and Warwolf before setting out. I know your life and death! They may be living by your law, though their bones have rotted away.'

'Indeed,' said Plovey, 'such is possible. For the law specifically states that a person shall not be deemed to be dead merely because they have ceased to exist. However, both Walrus and Warwolf are alive, as the vulgar understand life. And you will see them before setting forth.'

And so Drake did. And a tearful reunion he had with Jon Arabin, who was close to him by now as a father.

And this was Plovey's parting advice to Drake:

'Remember, darling boy, if you're not back within ten days, we'll torture Walrus and Warwolf to death. Little as I wish to see your return, I'll hold good to this threat, for I'm a very law-abiding man. I'll supervise the torture personally. Thodric Jarl will help me.'

And Drake, despite himself, shuddered.

49

Velvet River: flows from Araconch Waters through lonely inland desolation, through Chenameg, then into Harvest Plains. Is joined by Shouda Flow at Selzirk. Divides into a delta near the sea, where the port of Androlmarphos prospers from the river-trade.

Rule of Velvet River by dams (all upstream from Selzirk), irrigation schemes, dredging and dyke-building is a major function of the government of the Harvest Plains.

On a day of high summer, Drake Douay was taken out into the streets, where the strenuous noise and the clash of garish colours made him dizzy. He saw a boy playing with a bandalore, which had been quite the fashion in children's toys throughout the winter. Drake mistook the leaping thing for a vicious insect, and looked away, frightened.

The fashion for red-dyed skin was almost dead, though the Kingmaker Farfalla still indulged in it. But Drake did see one red-skinned red-haired woman, styling pink trousers and a matellassé blouse.

'Zanya!' he cried, thinking it was her.

Then saw it was an utter stranger.

He started to cry. Was ashamed of himself, yet could not help it. Had endured so much. Too much.

At a riverside dock, he boarded a trireme. Down the river they went. Sun too bright. Sky too blue. The riverside fields huge beyond all prison-cell imaginings.

Shocked by the enormous vistas of liberty, he hid his face.

The trireme did not venture all the way to Androl-marphos, for Selzirk would not risk such a valuable craft so close to the enemy-held city. Instead, on reaching the place where the Velvet River began to divide into the many branches of the delta, Drake was put aboard a smaller craft, a galley of but twenty oars.

Some leagues downstream, Drake glimpsed a familiar sight: a pyramid some two thousand years old, built by a wizard of Ebber who had once lorded it as emperor of the Harvest Plains. That pyramid stood on the dusty plains within sight of Androlmarphos, and Drake had seen it often enough in the days he had spent as a galley-slave. That had been years ago, when he was a mere boy of sixteen. And how old was he now? Why, twenty. Young, yes, with all of manhood in front of him.

Irresistibly, his spirits began to rise. Pirates were in Androlmarphos? Why, then, he'd meet with old com-rades, surely. Jon Disaster, aye. Ika Thole, maybe, or Abousir Belench, or some of his shipmates from his voy-age from Narba to the Teeth on the good ship *Jade*.

Then the galley pulled in to the bank.

'Get off,' said the galley captain.

'What?' said Drake, alarmed, imagining he was in for an impromptu riverside execution.

'Off!'

'But we're leagues from the city yet.'

'That's why we haven't cut your legs off. Come on, out!'

Reluctantly, Drake went ashore, and the galley turned around and, oars keeping to a regular rhythm, began to make its way upstream. Back to Selzirk. Well. He had life and freedom still. But a long hard walk ahead of him. He was still weak from imprisonment.

But I'll work on that, man. Sword, that's the way. Work rigorous daily.

Drake, thirsty, drank from the dirty brown water of the river. He deserved to die for such foolishness, but the

587

wisdom of Ling preserved him, for the myriad genetically tailored worms infesting his body kept him safe from every toxin and zyme.

'March,' said Drake to Drake.

And set out for Androlmarphos.

A long, slow journey he had of it, with the sun scalding his prison pallor, and his prison-soft feet slowly going into blisters. At the city gate, he found a rabble of armed men drinking, gambling, bartering and gossiping. One stirred himself to confront Drake, asking:

'*Sen fedda nanish*?'

'Speak you the Tongue?' said Drake.

'I have the Galish. Who are you, to risk yourself at Lord Menator's gate?'

'I be Lord Menator's loyal servant,' said Drake, 'and require audience with him immediately.'

'Then that you will have, for Lord Menator requires any wanderers to be brought before him immediately. He wants no spy, assassin or alien arsonist to run loose in his imperial capital.'

Thus Drake was taken in charge and led through the streets of Androlmarphos to Menator's headquarters. He began – far too late! – to worry. He remembered that Menator had put a price on his head. Why hadn't he thought of that sooner?

Why, man, because this torture and stuff has left me but half of a brain.

He hoped he pulled himself together, fast. But Androlmarphos seemed scarcely the right city in which to convalesce. Drake was not fussy and fancy, but, nevertheless, the streets of 'Marphos appalled him with their noise, filth, stench and gross over-crowding.

Stinks worse than Selzirk's dungeons. And that's something!

The city was but a league from north to south; its tottering tenements had always been crowded, and now were packed beyond endurance. The harbour was choked with ships; other vessels were anchored in nearby Lake

Ouija, while some shifted as best they could in river estuaries. 'Marphos, holding its usual residents, additional hostages seized from the hinterland, pirates, mercenaries of all descriptions, renegade soldiers from the Harvest Plains and horses by the thousands besides, was a quartermaster's nightmare.

But Menator's my nightmare true, that's for real. Hates me, doesn't he? Jealous of luck and talent, I suppose.

Drake urged himself to courage. Surely, under the circumstances, Lord Menator would not be vindictive. The rose-tattooed man, flushed with victory, would surely be magnanimous.

Much will depend on how I speak. And speaking's my best, isn't it? Yes.

Drake told himself that, once he got an audience with Menator, he would surely get permission to meet with Elkor Alish. Surely Alish would give him the proofs he needed to secure the release of both the Warwolf and his blood-brother Walrus.

Drake imagined how they would gratulate him. Jon Arabin would laugh out hearty, slap him on the back and call him a man, yes. The Walrus would scowl, swear, then mutter something grudging in acknowledgement.

'Heigh ho,' said Drake to Drake. 'It's great to be a hero!'

Shortly, he was ushered into the presence of Menator, who, after making himself lord of all the pirates, had leagued with Elkor Alish to seize Androlmarphos. Menator was sitting in state like an emperor. But, seated on a throne of equal height, was a graceful, lyncean, lordly man, Elkor Alish himself. These two – so far – were ruling as equals.

'Drake Douay,' said Menator, caressing Drake's name in a way which reminded Drake of Plovey of the Regency. 'Drake Douay, beloved of King Tor. What brings you here?'

'A mission of life and death,' said Drake.

'You think to threaten me on behalf of Selzirk, then.'

589

'You won those words from the air,' said Drake. 'You judge me wrong.'

'I know you of old,' said Menator. 'I passed judgment on you long ago.'

'Don't silence me fast!' said Drake, a touch of desperation in his voice. 'Or you'll never hear of Morgan Hearst and all.'

'Of Hearst?' said Elkor Alish, he of the elegant clothes and the square-cut black beard. 'Tell!'

So Drake told his story, clearly, briefly and with only a bare minimum of exaggeration. He held nothing back. He offered up the documents he had been told to take to Elkor Alish, and concluded:

'. . . so you see, all I need is a note in the hand of the good lord Alish. Then we can have two of the world's best pirate captains back to fight with us, aye, to tear down the towers of Selzirk, burn out their law courts, pull down their prisons, lynch their gaolers, kill out the Regency entire, string up Watashi and torture the torturers to death.'

'Admirable sentiments,' said Alish, with a smile.

Then he conferred with Menator. They spoke in something close to a whisper: nevertheless, their disagreement was plain. Finally, Alish said to Drake:

'You must talk in private with the pair of us.'

With some trepidation, Drake accompanied the two warlords into a private chamber where they interrogated him in depth and in detail, until his head spun. The questions they asked! What signs had he seen of war? Of the arming of men? The disposition of cavalry? The stockpiling of fodder? The movement of stores? The building of ships?

They were on at him till nightfall, by which time he was fatigued to the point of death. Both were intensely interested in the conflict between Watashi and the Regency – thinking obviously, that here was something they could exploit.

When they were finished, Drake mustered up his boldest voice and spoke:

590

'I've done my best, man. Now what about my note, that I may rescue Walrus and Warwolf? There's not much time left, you know.'

'You may have no note,' said Menator, 'for you have seen what you have seen, and they will use you as a spy if you return. You've sharp eyes about you: that you've proved by your answers.'

'He'll tell them no more than they know already,' said Alish.

'I ask you not to defy me in this,' said Menator.

After some argument, Alish – against his better judgment – yielded to Menator over what was to him a small matter. But it was no small matter to Menator. He loved the thought of Walrus and Warwolf being tortured to death: he had wanted, for a long time, to be rid of them once and for all.

'Menator, man,' said Drake.

One last chance. But a good one.

'What say you?' said Menator.

'I say you're missing a grand opportunity, man. You think of me as enemy, that's plain, but I could be ally for real. Listen – you've got 'Marphos, true, but Selzirk is strong. You need all the help you can get.'

'What help are you?' said Lord Menator.

'It's King Tor who'd be help if I spoke to him right,' said Drake. 'I could go to the province of Hok, aye, summon him out of the mountains, march his men to your banner.'

Menator laughed.

'What's so funny, man?' said Drake, in anger.

'Haven't you heard?' said Lord Menator. 'King Tor is dead. He died this last winter. Killed on Stokos he was.'

'How came it?' said Drake.

'Your ogre-king gambled at war,' said Lord Menator. 'He left Hok with what men remained to him. He landed on Stokos. Many flocked to his banner. Then those who ruled in Cam were sore afraid.'

'I bet they were!' said Drake. 'Tell on!'

591

'With pleasure,' said Menator, for this was one of his favourite stories, and it was rare for him to meet a man who did not know it backwards. 'It happened that those who held Stokos for Gouda Muck fought savage battles with Tor. The result was a draw.'

'They split the island in half?' said Drake.

'No,' said Lord Menator. 'They sat licking their wounds, thinking. Those who ruled in the name of the Flame thought best. They sent to the Teeth, inviting me to take their side in return for the rule of Stokos. It was their lives they were fearing for, you see.'

'Gutless cowards!' said Drake. 'I see right enough!'

'So I sailed my ships to Stokos,' said Lord Menator. 'That turned the balance. King Tor's men saw that all was lost. So they murdered their king. They brought the ogre's head to Sudder Vemlouf in Cam. By that time, of course, I was ruling above Vemlouf.'

'So you won your war with the blood of others!' said Drake, shocked at how filthy power politics could be.

'Isn't that always the best way to win a war?' said Lord Menator, grinning.

He was doing well for himself. He had won the rule of the Greater Teeth; he had conquered Stokos; he commanded Androlmarphos. He was well on the way to fulfilling his ambition to conquer the western seaboard of Argan.

'Now,' said Lord Menator, 'the question arises – what shall we do with Drake Douay?'

'I see you don't like the man,' said Elkor Alish. 'But that's no excuse for killing him.'

'You wouldn't stand for it?' said Menator.

'My war is fought for reasons which are pure,' said Alish. 'I'll not stain my hands with the blood of the innocent – or stand aside and watch the innocent murdered, either.'

'But we must do something with this unruly fellow,' said Menator, 'or he'll scarper back to Selzirk to try something rash to rescue his Walrus and Warwolf. We

592

wouldn't want to see him in Selzirk betraying our secrets, would we now?'

'I'd betray nothing!' said Drake, defiantly.

'Under torture,' said Menator, 'even the best will betray everything.'

'That's but theory talking,' said Drake.

'We can put theory to test, if you wish,' said Menator blandly.

'No thanks!' said Drake.

So it came to pass that Drake Douay (also known as Arabin lol Arabin and Shen Shen Drax, as the Demon-son and other things), was placed in preventive detention aboard one of the ships moored in the harbour of the city of Androlmarphos.

Which was soon beleaguered by an army from the city of Selzirk.

50

Drake's training in preventive detention: with the knife; with sword; in combat against ghosts and shadows. He alarms his jailors with the intensity with which he rages against imprisonment. Sweat, rage and endeavour allow him to win back his strength. The elegant Elkor Alish, rated by many as the best swordsman of Rovac, visits him twice to check on his conditions, and, impressed by his dedication, gives him some pointers on technique and on training.

Then Alish visits no more: for there is war.

The Harvest Plains finally responded to the capture of Androlmarphos by sending an army from Selzirk to lay seige to the place. That army was commanded by Morgan Hearst, a warrior of Rovac, who had once been a battle-companion of Elkor Alish.

Nothing daunted, Elkor Alish led his troops out of the planning to break the strength of Selzirk on the plain of battle. But the chances of war gave Hearst the victory. Alish, his battle-strength broken, retreated behind the walls of Androlmarphos. After a brief siege, Morgan Hearst used the death-stone against those walls. A few defenders escaped to sea; the rest, for the most part, died.

Since Drake was in preventive detention, he missed the preliminary skirmish which saw Lord Menator of the tat-tooed rose killed outside the walls of Androlmarphos. And he took no part in the Battle of the Pyramid Plain, or in the defence of 'Marphos. But he did see something of the terrors of the attack which drove Alish and his allies from the city.

Before Drake's ship got away to sea, Drake saw walking rocks raging on the docks of 'Marphos, conjured to life by the death-stone. He had heard much of that rock-waking magic from Atsimo Andranovory in Selzirk, but had believed none of it until he saw those living rocks in rage.

Morgan Hearst commandeered some ships and gave chase to the few survivors – but, after a desperate battle at sea, Elkor Alish and some of his men escaped. Drake, by luck, was amongst them. By then, Drake had long since finished his weeping for Walrus and Warwolf; he counted himself lucky to have got away with his own life when so many thousands had perished.

Freedom delighted him. In the brightness of sun and sea, the horrors of helpless imprisonment and dreadful torture lost their grip on his imagination. He began to feel quite his old self again.

On the voyage between 'Marphos and Runcorn (a city still held by Elkor Alish), Drake had some strange meetings with faces from the past.

He met up once again with Forester, a strangely naïve fellow whom he'd first met on the attempted voyage to Ork which had ended in sea-wreck disaster. He also renewed his acquaintance with Bluewater Draven, some-time commander of the *Tusk*, whom he had last seen on Chag-jalak in the North Strait, when pirates escaping from Collosnon captors had taken to the sea in separate boats.

Drake and Bluewater Draven had some wild fun with Forester, making him believe the most unbelievable stories about their exploits. They had success with out-right lies which they would never have had with the truth, for the truth (about flying islands and such) was scarce believable except to those who had lived through it.

Drake had some anxieties about landing at Runcorn, where he had once ruled as Arabin lol Arabin, head of his own temple and master of City Hall. But he found, to his

595

relief, that most of the original population had been killed, exiled or sold into slavery.

The city was on short commons. Under the ruthless rule of Elkor Alish, everyone was rationed to a single mug of beer a day, plus a little rice and vivda. Drake could see the sense in that, but, without any shame whatsoever, was soon heavily involved in black market bartering, and profiting greatly from his activities.

He soon found a groggery which suited him, a thievish den which took no heed of rationing, and he was there one morning drinking koumiss and dining on macédoine, when he was hailed by a familiar voice:

'Drake!'

It was Jon Arabin. Drake, leaping to his feet, spilt both food and drink together.

'Jon!' he cried. 'Jon, is it really you?'

'Who else would it be, man?' said the Warwolf.

'But you're – you're dead!'

'Aye, dead and resurrected,' said Jon Arabin. 'But none the worse for it.'

The next moment they were in each other's arms, slapping each other on the back, both laughing yet near to tears.

'Do I get a cuddle?' said a voice.

It was Slagger Mulps, the Walrus himself.

'No cuddles, unless you can pay for them,' said Drake. 'But – have a bowl of kale, man, and a mug of ale. Bar! Serve up for my friends!'

Soon all three were seated at table deep in food, drink and conversation. Great stuff! Old comrades true together. It made the place feel almost like home . . .

'How did you get away from Selzirk?' asked Drake.

'Ah,' said Jon Arabin. 'Thereby hangs a tale.'

And, with some help from the Walrus, Arabin told a fabulous tale about how they had variously bribed, deceived and outwitted their gaolers, killed guards, escaped to an underground tunnel, footed it for fifty leagues in utter darkness, fought with a giant worm, exited from the tunnel into a cave deep in the Spine Mountains, purchased a flying carpet from an old wizard, then navigated to Runcorn by air.

Drake only half-believed this tale, but doubted there was any chance of getting the truth out of them.

Actually, both Walrus and Warwolf – along with everyone else in every dungeon in Selzirk – had been released and pardoned as part of the victory celebrations which followed the liberation of Androlmarphos. But, honour being what it is, they would never confess to such charitable treatment.

'Now let's hear you talk,' said the Walrus. 'And let's talk frank, as we couldn't talk in Selzirk.'

'What's there to be frank about?' said Drake. 'But for your bad breath, your rotten teeth and the boil in the middle of your forehead.'

The Walrus, still weak from the terrors of imprisonment, took this hard. But he could not show how Drake's rough words hurt him – for he knew a pirate was not supposed to be so sensitive. Still, while he could not complain directly, there was another way in which he could strike back.

'Let's talk of Penvash, to start with,' said Mulps.

He would punish Drake a bit. Make him sweat over the matter of a stolen tinder box.

'Penvash?' said Drake. 'What about it? We killed some green-eyed dogs up there, aye. Is that what you're on about? I suppose they were your relations and all!'

Slagger Mulps, who had endured many a joke about his green eyes in years gone by, took this one hard.

'You ran off,' said Mulps, a touch of open anger in his voice. 'Ran, aye. Left us in hardship for days.'

'Hardship?' said Drake. 'I thought you green-haired animals were bred for the cold.'

'Aagh!' said the Walrus. He spat, discreetly, into a bloodstained handkerchief. Then said: 'So where did you bugger off to after you stole our tinder box?'

'Man, I did no stealing,' said Drake. 'I was hot after

597

Yot with the others when there was a bear or something, I don't know. A monster, maybe.'

'What kind of monster?' said Jon Arabin.

'Man, I know not,' said Drake, 'but I woke a long way later leagues and leagues from anywhere with a bloody head and bruises from gills to arsehole.'

'From mating with this bear, perhaps,' said Mulps.

'Gah!' said Drake, 'you'd be expert on buggering bears and such!'

He spoke freely, to show his friendship. For friends slanged off at each other with no holds barred – that was part and parcel of friendship. Thus Drake, who these days thought better of the Walrus than he had once, spoke to him as freely as he used to speak with Pigot Quebec and other criminal friends in Selzirk of the thousand sewers.

This last sally of Drake's brought Mulps close to tears – but again the Walrus concealed his hurt, and, after coughing a little more tubercular blood into a handkerchief, demanded:

'And the girl?'

'Girl?' said Drake, looking round the groggery. 'There's one in the corner there, she's got but one ear yet the rest looks staunch enough. Would she be any good to you?'

'Don't play the fool with me, or I'll nubble you,' said Mulps, though he was so weakened by prison that he was scarce fit to fight a mouse.

'Nubble away then!' said Drake, boldly.

He thought the Walrus spoke his anger by way of a joke. And, in any case – an angry Walrus without Ish Ulpin and others to back him up was no danger at all to Drake Douay if it came to a matter of swords.

'I'd rather kill beer than a comrade,' said Jon Arabin, mildly.

Drake, seeing both Walrus and Warwolf had finished their ales, summoned up more from the bar. For a while, all ate and drank in silence. Then Mulps spoke again:

'So what did happen to the Ebrell bitch? It's the one in

Penvash I'm talking of. What came of her?'

'Why, as I say, I don't know,' said Drake, 'for a monster attacked me. Likely the monster or whatever it was got eating her. She died somehow, anyway.'

'Then why,' said the Walrus, 'why does rumour say you came to Runcorn with her? With her and a fortune in jasp and jade, which let you buy up half the city before you were finished?'

'Man,' said Drake, spreading his hands, 'what I own is these hands. That's honest.'

'But you had wealth once,' persisted the Walrus. 'It didn't just vanish, did it?'

'I were never rich,' said Drake. 'As for buried treasure or such, if that's what you're looking for – you'll get none from me. Would I mix with the scum in a dive like this if I had the wealth to live better?'

'Aye, you would,' said Mulps, 'for it's your style, and you know no better. But I—'

'Leave it, man,' said Jon Arabin. 'He's telling the truth. He has no treasure.'

'And even if I did,' said Drake, 'I'd want human beings to share it with – not a gangling thing with grass on its chin and thumbs built double on its fists.'

Mulps rose to his feet in anger.

'Down, man!' said Arabin. 'Are we not friends together?'

'We are,' said the Walrus, looking hard at Drake, and wishing he had the strength to tear the snake-tongued fellow apart. 'We're friends, aye, I'll not forget it, or the gift of ale and kale either.'

Then Mulps sat, and gave every appearance of peace as talk turned to other subjects. But the insults rankled. That night, when Mulps slept, he had nightmares about his childhood, when he had been teased, bullied and rejected because he was so tall and thin, his nose so sharp, his thumbs double and his hair green.

Mulps woke writhing and sweating. Drake! Drake Douay! He was responsible for this!

'A curse,' muttered Mulps. 'He cursed me. Aye.'

'What?' said his whore.

'Nothing,' said Mulps. 'Go back to sleep.'

Mulps slept but the whore didn't, and when Mulps woke in the morning she was gone – with the last of his money with her. He blamed Drake for that, too. And, later in the day, sought out Elkor Alish, and bore false witness against Drake. Warrants were sworn out on the spot, and guards sent to arrest Drake.

Who was hauled into the presence of Elkor Alish that afternoon, vigorously threatening his guards with dragon-magic, demonic possession and a wide range of curses. All of which, of course, confirmed Mulps's belief that Drake had somehow put a curse upon him.

'So, here you are,' said Elkor Alish, sighting Drake. 'Just the man I need.'

'For what?' said Drake. 'What am I charged with? Show me a bill of particulars.'

'No need for that,' said Alish. 'All charges are dismissed. I've got serious work for you to do.'

'Aye. Work to get me killed, no doubt.'

'It may well,' said Alish.

'Then I'll have no part in it,' said Drake.

'Oh, I'll make it worth your while. There's wealth and women as the pay for prompt performance.'

'I've got a woman already. I fought shipboard for the favour of Ju-jai. Once at the Teeth I'll claim her. A famous pretty whore, they say, with hair as red as my last.'

'Part of your pay,' said Alish, smoothly, 'will be the right to return to the Greater Teeth.'

'Like that, is it?' said Drake.

'Indeed like that. Be strong. All I want you to do is carry two letters. One is to Morgan Hearst. The other is to Watashi.'

'Carry letters? Why me? Why not send an ambassador?'

'You will be precisely that. An ambassador. Remember when I visited you when you were in preventive detention in 'Marphos?'

'Aye,' said Drake, cautiously.

'You boasted large at the time,' said Alish. 'You said you'd been ambassador for King Tor on five different occasions.'

'Yes, but,' said Drake, 'I've enemies in Stokos. Gouda Muck, for one. I can't be your ambassador if I'm caught up in feuds with enemies, can I?'

'You'll deal in no feuds,' said Alish, 'for you'll visit the city in secret. That's why I must send you.'

'Me!'

'Right,' said Alish. 'You know the city. Better still, Watashi knows you. Who else have I got who's been face to face with Farfalla's son?'

'But—'

'You'll find a way to him,' said Alish. 'In secret. To guarantee your success . . . I'm holding your Walrus and Warwolf hostage against your safe return with proofs of performance.'

Drake groaned.

The Walrus, weakened by a fever which had been gaining a hold on his carcass since midnight, fainted.

That night, Drake dreamed of dragons, torturers and Plovey of the Regency. Yet, the very next day, he began to make preparations for setting out for Selzirk – for he had no choice in the matter.

Elkor Alish said he would choose companions for Drake, but gave him permission to look for additional companions for the venture. Drake looked, but found nobody suitable.

There was just one person Drake seriously considered taking, and that was Forester, who lacked verve, courage, style and nous. Drake judged Forester to be a regular sucker-fool, who could be conned into doing the really dangerous work, such as making the approach to Watashi. However, despite the encouraging lies Drake told, Forester refused to join the adventure.

'Ambassadors don't come so short in the tooth,' said Forester to Drake.

Upon which Drake, offended, abandoned his efforts to recruit the man. He would rely on the companions Elkor Alish had chosen for him. Or so he thought at first. But when he saw those people, he despaired. They were coarse, brutal, stupid types. They spoke poor Galish and zero Churl. He complained to Alish:

'Man, these people are good for nothing but knifework.'

'That's what they've been chosen for,' said Alish. 'While you attack Selzirk with the word, they bring the sword.'

'I'm ambassador and they're assassins?'

'Right.'

'Then let's split our missions,' said Drake. 'You send them separate to the city. As for me – I've a plan.'

'Tell,' said Alish.

He heard Drake out, and agreed to Drake's plan. Shortly, Drake was imprisoned with half a dozen enemy cavalry officers who had been captured when Alish and his allies first took Androlmarphos. Like many of the more important hostages, they had been shipped to Runcorn early on for safe keeping.

'Who might you be?' asked these prisoners, when Drake was flung into their midst, bleeding heavily from the nose.

'Why, I be Drake Douay,' said Drake. 'A man of Stokos, aye, and adopted son of Plovey of the Regency, in Selzirk.'

'How long ago adopted?' he was asked.

'Why, but this time last year, when I saved him from drowning in the Velvet River. Hence I'm but making a start with my Churl. Since your Galish runs so fair, doubtless you can help me with work on my Churl, for I long to talk my father's tongue proper.'

Drake's lie was so close to the truth that it was near to being unbreakable. Not that the officers tried to break it, for they had no cause to be suspicious.

'What in Churl do you want to learn?' they said.

'The language of sex and seduction, to start with,' said Drake, promptly – thinking that the fewer lies he told, the simpler life would be.

So they started into lessons immediately.

On the third night of Drake's captivity, the gaolers got drunk. The prisoners seized their opportunity and over-powered the drunks. Two of the gaolers got killed in the process. This was not part of the plan, but Drake had no sympathy for them – he was developing very strong views about gaols and gaolers.

The escapers quit Runcorn, and found, outside the city, horses (complete with saddles) which were only lightly guarded. The guards did not stand and fight, but ran away. So the escapers commandeered the horses and rode hell for leather for the south.

Did they suspect that the whole thing had been engineered by Drake Douay and Elkor Alish?

No, not for a moment.

For the officers, like most children of the Harvest Plains, had been raised on a brand of fairy tales in which heroes of all descriptions regularly escaped from the most daunting dungeons imaginable, not just once or twice but as many as half a dozen times in the same story.

So they thought themselves fine fellows as they galloped along, urging their horses closer and closer to the edge of death; they laughed, joked and bragged, persuading themselves their outbreak had been a regular feat of heroism.

Only Drake knew better.

At daybreak, one of the horses collapsed and died. The rest were nearly ready for the knacker's yard. However, at noon, the escapers met a patrol of Harvest Plains cavalry, and were able to commandeer fresh horses. Several changes later, they entered Selzirk.

'Now,' said Drake, to the most senior officer who had ridden with him, 'get me an audience with Morgan Hearst. Immediately.'

'What business have you with him?'

'That which cannot be delayed. Man, get me to see him. I've no money to bribe my way through to his face. Once I'm with him, he'll be the judge of my business. He's hero enough to know if I'm wasting his time.'

The officer, too exhausted for argument, handed Drake over to the appropriate people, telling them Drake must see Hearst instantly.

51

Morgan Hearst: a hero questing in company of the wizard Miphon and the woodsman Blackwood; interrupted heroic quest to command the defence of Selzirk; defeated Elkor Alish and liberated Androlmarphos; sojourns in Selzirk, though has plans for onward travel.

Drake was taken into the heights of a tall and massive tower which stood in what had once been the central courtyard of an ancient wizard stronghold. He was shown into a waiting room from which he could look down on the myrmecoid activity in the streets of Selzirk. But he had no eyes for the view.

He was dismayed at the impossible queue, which included an inventor after a patron for his perpetual motion machine; a man with a gyrfalcon to sell to the hero; a designer who hoped to interest Morgan Hearst in a gaudy coat of arms (it featured, among other things, a sea-dragon naiant, a gryphon rampant, and seventeen other creatures besides). And many others.

'Sit here,' said the functionary who had brought Drake to the place, 'and wait your turn.'

But Drake would have none of that. He strode to the head of the queue and demanded admittance.

'Who are you?' asked the guard at the door.

'I am Baron Farouk's nuncio,' said Drake, in a right stomachy manner. 'I come to speak with the hero.'

'About what?' said the guard.

'Of ships and armies, allegiance and alliance, matters of

high state and the breaking of empires. Stand aside, or I split you with my sword.'

'The weaponless should make no threats so empty,' said the guard.

'The weapon is invisible, yet kills regardless,' said Drake. 'For my father was a jinnee and my mother the worst kind of succubus. I was born in a flood of fire, born amidst thunder, suckled on blood, weaned on a whore's-egg then grown to greatness on the flesh of butchered babies. Will you stand aside, or must I doom you to death? Aye – to hell and damnation?'

'I meant no harm, my lord,' said the guard, standing aside hastily.

In days when the city was full of wild stories of weird magic, and when thousands had seen for their own eyes the powers of the death-stone, all acknowledged the existence of occult things, and Drake's bluff was more to be believed than it would have been in more sober times. Thus he gained prompt entry to the room where Morgan Hearst did business.

Hearst was seated behind a broad desk made of split bamboo. The hero was, as Drake remembered him, a tense, hard-faced man. Lean, clean-shaven, hair cropped short, eyes grey.

One thing had changed.

Hearst's right wrist terminated in a steel hook.

'Do you speak Galish?' said Hearst, studying Drake.

'Very nicely,' said Drake.

'Do I . . . do I know you from somewhere?'

'No, my lord,' said Drake, unwilling to remind Hearst of how he had once run the young Lord Dreldragon out of Estar on account of crimes of theft and hooliganism.

'That's strange,' said Hearst, a puzzled look on his face. 'I could almost swear I'd met you before.'

Hearst's left hand held a quill pen; papers were heaped up on the desk. The absence of any clerks implied that Hearst was literate.

'I see from your desk that you read and write,' said

Drake. 'Not a hero only, but a wise man as well.'

'If that's meant by way of flattery,' said Hearst, 'don't waste your breath. I've scant powers in Selzirk, whatever my reputation might say. Most of the petitioners outside my doors are wasting their time. Most probably whatever you wish to ask for is not within my grant.'

'What I ask, my lord,' said Drake, 'is for you to accept a letter from a man named Elkor Alish.'

'Alish?' said Hearst. 'Who's he?'

'Why, you know!' said Drake, who had expected any reaction but this.

'Tell me about him,' said Hearst. 'Tell me everything about him you've seen and heard.'

Thus began one of those long, long interrogations which Drake, by now, was heartily sick of. At the end of it, Drake cut open the lining of his jerkin and handed over both Alish's letter to Hearst and Alish's letter to Watashi.

Hearst read both, then sent a messenger to summon Watashi into his presence. Farfalla's son arrived promptly.

'You!' said Watashi, on seeing Drake.

'Nay,' said Drake, 'I died at sea some many days ago. What you see here is none but my ghost.'

But Watashi was not as credulous as the guard Drake had frightened earlier, and Drake's swift-flowing horror-talk was cut short by Hearst.

'Business,' said Hearst. 'Elkor Alish is playing a trick with this fellow. A trick he learnt from Selzirk. He holds two of the man's friends as hostage, requiring, for their release, proof of delivery of two letters.'

'How does that concern me?' said Watashi.

'One of those proofs must come from me,' said Hearst. 'But the other needs come from you.'

'I give no proofs to this thieving whoreson bastard,' said Watashi.

'You will give proofs,' said Hearst, waving a letter, 'or I will give this document to the Regency.'

'What says it?'

'This letter from Alish to you invites you to join with him in making war on the Regency and installing yourself as emperor of the Harvest Plains.'

'That speaks of no crime on my part,' said Watashi. 'It's no crime to be made an offer, no matter how criminal. Crime lies only in the acceptance, which I'd never make – and which none could prove against me.'

'I know little of the filthy politics of this city,' said Hearst, 'but I'm sure your Regency would make great play of this letter. You might win clear to freedom, for sure – but is it not better to give the man his proofs, and avoid all chance of such embarrassment?'

'Why do you take his part?' said Watashi.

'Honour acts,' said Hearst. 'It does me no harm to give proof to Elkor Alish that I have seen his letter, and thus release two men held hostage.'

'No harm? Such proof might see one hanged!'

'No,' said Hearst. 'For I will simply date a piece of parchment, write on it that the petition of Drake Douay has been refused, then sign it. That will be proof enough. You will do the same. You cannot be hung, young lordling, for refusing an unspecified petition. That's no crime I know of in any law.'

Watashi, grudgingly, did as Hearst obliged him to. Then Hearst dismissed him.

'So,' said Hearst, holding up two pieces of parchment, 'you have your proofs. Satisfied?'

'I'd be more satisfied if they could be delivered,' said Drake boldly. 'For I've no wish to leave Selzirk. There's a lady I wish to claim, aye, first for love, and second to spite the senile old whoremaster who holds her captive. Have you couriers to Runcorn?'

'None,' said Hearst. 'But such I can find. I'll see your proofs get through.'

Then Hearst dismissed Drake, and dismissed the whole queue of petitioners as well. For he wanted to be alone, so he could think over the letter which Alish had written to him.

But what was in that letter, and what Hearst made of it, and what he did as a result . . . those things were of no concern to Drake Douay, who had other business on his mind.

Zanya, my heart, me dearest princess. Despair not! 'Tis I, the lordly young Dreldragon, who rides even now to the rescue! I will fight to thy dungeon and free thee from the fiend. Even if I must slay a watermelon stand to do so!

52

Law: the rule of past over present, the dead over the living, precedent over pure reason, syntax over sense and of absurd fictions over urgent realities.

Drake the Doughty, rightful king of Stokos (with Tor dead, who had a better claim?), questing hero extraordinary, star of the Great Arena in Dalar ken Halvar, cocksman and shivman both, thought himself safe enough when he went in pursuit of the red-skinned Zanya Kliedervaust. After all, he had received a full pardon for all crimes he had committed, both in and out of Selzirk. Thus he was safe from the law – or thought he was. And he was confident he could deal with Gouda Muck and his bully boys.

In Jone, Drake found many of his former friends, and persuaded them to come to Santrim with him for a bit of fun. They fronted up to Libernek Square, where Muck was preaching to the usual jeering crowd. Drake, safe with his comrades to support him, slanged off at Muck, and called on him to yield up the fair lady Zanya.

Muck had no dogs, crocodiles or watermelon stands which he could set upon Drake Douay, so sent his Flame-clad stave men to do battle with the questing hero. The crowd joined the fight – on Drake's side – and Muck's men had to beat a hasty retreat.

The next day, Drake returned.

'Send out your bravos!' he bawled, brandishing a knife. 'I've sworn to take five scalps by sundown!'

When nobody came forth from Muck's temple to do battle, Drake and his colleague sang scatalogical songs in three-part harmony. The crowd joined in. The next day, Drake returned again. He found the crowd larger, more enthusiastic. Great stuff!

'Come out, Muck!' yelled Drake. 'Or I'll storm your gates!'

Muck stayed out of sight, and Drake judged that the crowd was not quite yet ready to take Muck's temple by force.

Tomorrow, maybe. We'll see. A riotous mob, that's the thing!

The fourth day, Drake fronted up for further fun – and was arrested by the Watch. And the day after, he was hauled into the New Courthouse to hear the charges Gouda Muck had preferred against him. The trial came up so quickly because the general pardon, given to celebrate the liberation of Androlmarphos, had cleared the backlog of the courts entirely.

Drake was brought in front of Judge Syrphus, who held court in the traditional glory which tradition decreed for a person in his position. Thanks to tradition, Judge Syrphus wore uncured goatskins and a feathered head-dress, sat on a throne made from the bones of traitors, and wore heavy gold bracelets littered with garnets and bits of black glass.

The proceedings were in the Churl of the Harvest Plains (not High Churl or City Churl or Field Churl, but Legal Churl, which took a good five years for the brightest brains to master) and were translated into Galish for Drake's benefit.

'Are you Drake Douay, runaway swordsmith's apprentice of Stokos?' he was asked by the Clerk of the Court.

'Yes,' he said, fearlessly. 'And you've no jurisdiction over Stokos, so let's hear nothing about running away, aye, or thieving masterswords, or hacking up royal trees or any other such nonsense. Aye, and while we're at it, I've got a pardon for all crimes I might have done in or out of Selzirk – not that I'm admitting any, mind – and

611

here's the document itself. Not that I can read it, but the wise, who ought to know, say it's a pretty enough bit of paper.'

This resulted in some colloquy, after which Drake was told:

'The Court is aware of your pardon, but it has no relevance to this case. In this case, the Court is being asked to subject you to preventive detention on the grounds that you are a public menace. You can be perfectly innocent of all crime yet still be a public menace. So the pardon does you no good.'

'So you're putting me on trial for things I've never done and maybe never will do.'

'Precisely.'

'Then I'll have a lawyer, thanks.'

'What money have you?'

'None.'

'Then you get no lawyer. Call the first witness for the prosecution!'

The witness was called. Into court he came. Gouda Muck! There followed several exchanges between Drake and Muck. They swore, cursed and damned each other, engaged in the wildest insults and used the most shameless, filthy language. Fortunately, they did all this in Ligin, which nobody else in the Court could understand.

Drake Douay and Gouda Muck were, with difficulty, called to order. Then Muck was introduced to the Court as a master swordsmith and a peaceful minister of religion.

'Do you recognize anyone in the Court?' asked the prosecutor.

'Why, yes,' answered Gouda Muck. 'The man in the dock. I know him as Drake Douay. He was my apprentice on Stokos, until he ran away some four or five years ago.'

'When did you see him next?'

'In Runcorn.'

'Runcorn? What was he doing?'

'He ruled the place. He'd founded a truly monstrous religion. I hold a copy of the doctrines of that religion.

612

This document is *The Book of Witness*. Know that Drake Douay was at this time going under the name of Arabin lol Arabin.'

After Muck had been questioned further, *The Book of Witness* was read into the record of the Court. Drake listened intently. He had never heard it before; he was flattered to learn that a follower of his temple had been impressed enough to write down a history of Drake's doings in Runcorn.

This was fame indeed!

The prosecutor finished with Muck, and, very pleased with himself, addressed the Court:

'You have heard both my first witness and *The Book of Arabin*. Plainly, the accused is an evil, dangerous religious radical. He overthrew the rightful rule of Runcorn. In its place he installed a monstrous regime of drunkenness, debauchery and polymorphous perversion. That more than suffices to make him a public menace, for what he did in Runcorn he might yet do in Selzirk.'

Smirking, the prosecutor sat. And Drake was asked:

'Do you have questions to put to the witness?'

'Aye, that I do,' said Drake. 'Under torture, if you please. Or, if he'll not submit to torture, let him swear to tell the truth, and let him swear by the Flame he preaches of.'

Drake's petition to have the witness tortured was denied, but Muck was made to swear (by the Flame) that he would tell the truth, the whole truth and nothing but the truth.

'Man,' said Drake, 'you had me as apprentice on Stokos. Was I good or was I bad?'

'You were the worst apprentice I ever had,' said Gouda Muck. 'Drunk, disorderly, disobedient, shiftless, idle, gross, reckless and lawless. You stole my mastersword.'

'Did I ever steal gold?'

'No.'

'Or bread? Or wine? Or wood? Or anything else of you or yours?'

'No.'

'Did I ever hurt or harm or damage anything of you or yours?'

'Yes! You damaged a sword of mine. I remember it well. You were foolish at sword. You knocked out some iron inlay. I can tell the Court exactly. It was the letter Àçøwæ.'

'How do you know it was that letter? Did I tell you?'

'You! Tell me! An illiterate fool like you? No, I knew the letter for what it was because I'm a scholar of sorts, as my father was before me.'

'Why call me illiterate?' said Drake, sounding hurt.

'Because you know not one letter from the other. Why, when you were sent to learn your theory, you had to memorize the whole by heart.'

'That's a cruel thing to say,' said Drake. 'Why make me out as ignorant?'

'Because you are!'

'All right,' said Drake. 'I let you have the point. I know not one letter from the other.'

'And never will,' said Muck, 'for you were no good at learning. Why, I had to beat you to learn you the simples of your business!'

'Beatings, was it?' said Drake. 'Was it with fists? Or with boot? Or with stick? Or did you bang my head against the wall? Or did you throw lumps of coal and ore at me? Or what method did you use?'

'All of those, and more,' said Muck. 'But all failed.'

'Did I ever beat back in return? Hit or punch or throw or spit?'

Muck laughed.

'You'd never have dared!' he said. 'You were too fearful for that.'

'So what did I do to oppose you?'

'We've been through that! You stole my mastersword and ran away!'

'And when did you see me next?'

'Why, in Runcorn.'

614

'Tell the Court how you came to see me.'

'I'd made it my business to travel the Salt Road, preaching. I had with me loyal assistants – such as Sully Yot. A better man than you!'

'Tell the Court of this Yot,' said Drake.

'An apprentice of mine,' said Muck. 'He'd been a prisoner of pirates. You were one of those who took him prisoner!'

'Was I just?' said Drake. 'Was I then high in their ranks? A pirate captain, perhaps?'

'No,' said Muck, with a laugh. 'You were but a cook's boy. Peeling cockroaches and hashing up rats, that was about your limit. Why, Yot told of how you'd done the world's worst cookery in the Penvash channel. Rats and cockroaches, yes!'

'So I was the cook?'

'No, no, the cook's boy. You were never destined to go far in the world.'

'Did Yot tell you how I came by these rats and cockroaches he talked of?'

'Why, yes. He said you told him you'd meant them as a sacrifice for Hagon.'

'What is this Hagon?' said Drake.

And the Court heard from Muck the tale of how Drake had devotedly worshipped the Demon Hagon for years. Then Drake changed tack to bring him back on course for Runcorn:

'So the Court now knows about Hagon, aye, and about this fellow Yot. Who knew me, as you say. Yot came to Runcorn with you. What then?'

'We reached Runcorn. I was tired, therefore took to my bed at the inn. Yot went about the city, with the energy of the young. He saw you in the temple of the place. You and a woman, Zanya, whom he knew. I knew her too, for she had been my convert formerly. So Yot went privily to Zanya, and brought her to me.'

'And she spoke with you?'

'Yes. She told how you went by the name of Arabin lol

615

Arabin. For she knew you not as Drake Douay. Only Yot knew you as that.'

'And where is this Yot? In Selzirk?'

'No. He returned to Stokos, to manage my temple's affairs. He's high priest now.'

'An interesting story,' said Drake, smirking. 'You speak of a woman who knew a man called Arabin lol Arabin. Another man knows of no Arabin, but knows of a Drake Douay. He takes the girl to you, and by this means you identify this Arabin as Drake. At a distance, sight unseen. Is this black magic, or what?'

'I saw you with my own eyes,' said Muck. 'The very next day. It was in the square in front of City Hall in Runcorn.'

'What was I doing?'

'Standing on a balcony.'

'What? Admiring sunsets and singing them to sleep with fancy poetry?'

'No, for it was not evening but bright day. Besides, you have no poetry. You were shouting. At a mob.'

'A mob, was it? And was I shouting at them to burn the city, aye, and plunder it? Or was I seeking order?'

'You were seeking your life, for they were out to kill you. They'd recognized the evil of your religion.'

'So what did I say to them? Did I beg for mercy?'

'No. You promised them war.'

'War? The kind of war that Elkor Alish made? An attack on Androlmarphos? An invasion of Selzirk?'

'No,' said Muck, 'for you lack the imagination for such. Your war was to be against the ragged bands which roam the Lezconcarnau Plains.'

'So did I speak of Selzirk in my plans for war?'

'No.'

'Are you sure?'

'You . . . why, yes, you spoke of selling slaves to Selzirk. And, shortly after, you cried out to thousands that you were Arabin lol Arabin. Then the crowd ran riot.'

'Then what happened?'

'I saw you not, for I was fighting for my own life.'

'So when did you see me next?'

'About a season later. I was preaching in Selzirk when you turned up and shouted at me.'

'What did I shout? Of religion? Or of a woman?'

'Of a woman.'

'What woman was this?'

'Zanya Kliedervaust, a pilgrim from the Ebrells.'

'The same woman who had been in Runcorn?'

'Yes,' said Muck. 'The one that I have spoken of in my testimony.'

'What means she to you?'

'She is the guardian of my purity.'

'Your whore?' said Drake.

'I am a holy man!' said Muck, his voice rising in outrage. 'How can the Court let this – this criminal accuse me of whoring?'

'The defence,' said Judge Syrphus, easily, 'has a very free hand in the courts of Selzirk. As does indeed the prosecution. We think our justice no worse for it. Do you beg to differ?'

'My lord,' said Gouda Muck, 'I, as a stranger, would scarce set out to reform the courts of Selzirk.'

'Then answer the question!' said Drake. 'What was Zanya to you?'

'The guardian of my purity,' said Gouda Muck. 'As I've said already.'

Drake had thought to defend himself by showing Muck as a sexual rival. He had failed – for the moment. He tried another tack: to show Muck up as a madman.

'And why must you have such a guardian?' asked Drake.

'To preserve my holiness.'

'And why are you holy?'

'Because I am the flesh of the Flame.'

'You mean you live in fire, like one of these salamanders we sometimes hear of? Or that the skin beneath your robes is red, like that of the people of Ebrell? Or what?'

617

'I mean that I am the High God of All Gods.'

'You mean,' said Drake, 'a priest, surely. Surely the word meant was priest, not god.'

'No,' said Muck. 'I am a god! Not any god, but the High God of All Gods!'

'Have you always known this?' said Drake.

'No.'

'Then how did you first come to know yourself as a god?'

'Why, the Flame told me.'

'Describe this Flame,' said Drake.

'It was purple,' said Muck. 'It leaped out of the furnace. It yelled at me.'

At this, there was tittering in the Court. But Drake kept a straight face.

'There seems to be confusion of identity,' said Drake. 'You have told us you are the Flame. Now you tell us the Flame lives in the furnace, and speaks to you. Which is which?'

'This takes us into the realms of higher theology,' said Muck. 'You would not understand.'

'I am but an ignorant runaway apprentice,' said Drake. 'A poor fool, who knows not the letter Àçøwæ from any other. But the evidence is for the Court, not me. Do you say the Court would not understand?'

'I say nothing of the kind,' said Muck.

And Drake drew him into a long discourse on theology, which the Court indulged because it was tolerably amusing, and because the law of Selzirk placed few limits on the range of a cross–examination.

'So you know of religion through revelation,' said Drake. 'Now we have heard a document of sorts, a document called, if I remember right, *The Book of Witness*. Is this a record you have somehow conjured up out of the air, by means of revelation?'

'No,' said Muck, swiftly, thinking he saw what Drake was attempting to do. 'This is a true, correct and complete account of your doings in Runcorn.'

618

'Who says it?'

'The man I bought it off.'

'When and where?'

'In Runcorn itself, the morning of that riot which I have already spoken of.'

'You bought this, then, in the heat of a riot? Snatched it from his hand and tossed him a few coppers?'

'Not at all! We met at dawn, and talked until the sun was well up in the sky. His name was Aard Lox. He was a scribe who had, for reasons unknown to me, much faith in you. He offered this copy of his work for sale, meaning to enlighten me. He talked at length, with great sincerity, convincing me that everything he'd written was true.'

'So the proof of the truth of this record, then,' said Drake, 'rests on the word of this man. You believed him, or so you say. Why?'

'Because he was honest, and I am a judge of honesty – which you are not, having none yourself. And because he was so exact in all the particulars he recounted.'

'Ah,' said Drake, 'but surely the voices of others would help convince the Court. Could we not have this Yot come back from Stokos to evidence to some few claims you've made? Surely he has no pressing duties there? After all, the religion of Stokos is the worship of the demon Hagon. So how can the high priest of the Flame have matters of importance there?'

'Because Hagon has been overthrown, as you know very well,' said Drake.

'I am but an ignorant apprentice,' said Drake. 'I know nothing. Tell the Court how Hagon came to be overthrown.'

And Muck told.

Willingly.

'Now,' said Drake, 'some words I heard in *The Book of Witness* which I'm not sure I heard aright. Would you read them out, please, you having scholarship which I lack. Read them, and tell the Court if it's all to rights with the document. It's Vision the fifth, verses twelve through fourteen.'

Muck read the verses, and testified that they were part of the true and correct record given to him by Aard Lox.

'Thank you,' said Drake. 'You may sit.'

53

12 Whereupon there was uproar of surpassing greatness.

13 But the Record showed the answer of Lachish as 'No.'

14 Then did Arabin call attention to the answer shown in the Record, and say unto Lachish: 'If thou hast not tasted these pleasures, wherefore dost thou speak of the goodness or the badness thereof?'

Verses 12–14, Vision the Fifth, *The Book of Witness*

As Gouda Muck resumed his seat, Drake saw Zanya enter the courthouse, and guessed that she was next witness for the prosecution. Their eyes met, briefly, giving him no hint of what she felt or thought. This was fearful dangerous! Who could tell what the woman would say?

'Man,' said Drake. 'I mean, my lord judge. We've heard Gouda Muck speak plain. He's a nutter. Right? A lunatic! A madman, no less. So I reckon it's time to throw out these charges Muck's brought, before we go any further.'

Judge Syrphus stirred himself on his chair of bones, adjusted his feathered head-dress, scratched at his goatskins then spoke:

'The mad have as many rights under Selzirk law as do the sane. Indeed, it has been argued in quarters that only a madman would go to law to start with – therefore to abolish the rights of the mad to law would be to abolish the rights of all.'

621

'But,' protested Drake, 'the man's got a head full of nonsense!'

'We have other witnesses yet to speak,' said the judge. 'They themselves may well prove rational enough. With luck, we'll have evidence enough to condemn you.'

'You want to condemn me?' said Drake.

'Nothing personal,' said the judge. 'But I do have a quota to make.'

Drake started sweating. This was proving harder than he had thought. He felt as if he had been at sword non-stop for a moon and a day.

Well.

He would do his best.

'Aagh,' he said, clearing his throat. He was about to spit when he remembered himself. Proceeding in his best lawyerly manner (which he had learnt by watching Garimanthea in Runcorn), he said: 'We have heard evidence from Gouda Muck. The prosecutor spoke once he'd finished with the man, so I suppose I may do the same.'

'You are right.' said the Clerk of the Court. 'You are at liberty to make an address to the Court after finishing with each witness.'

'Then that I do,' said Drake. 'Although I do it but poorly, for I be a sorry runaway apprentice who knows not the letter Àçøwæ from any other.'

He took a deep breath. His future was on the line, if not his very life. This had better be good.

'Gouda Muck, as you have heard, knows me well as Drake Douay, for he had me as apprentice for year on year on Stokos.

'Now I have the greatest respect for Gouda Muck, for it was he who taught me how to shape steel, aye, and the temperature at which tilps jiffle.'

This last claim sounded entirely innocuous to the Court, but in the Ligin of Stokos it was extremely obscene, and brought Gouda Muck to his feet with a roar.

'Sit and be silent!' shouted the judge, before Muck could speak. 'Are you mad, man?'

Guards took up position on either side of Muck, ready to suppress him immediately if he interrupted again.

'Aye,' said Drake. 'I respected Muck. But there was a strangeness about him at times. Sometimes he'd leap to his feet and roar for no reason, as you've just seen.'

Muck's face started to turn purple with rage. How very interesting! Drake wondered if Muck would have a stroke and die on the spot, like Nabajoth of Runcorn. Wondering (and hoping) he continued:

'Other times,' said Drake, 'this worthy scholar would beat me, aye, with kicks, cudgels, fists and walls, and missiles into the bargain. That you've heard from his own testimony.

'But did I ever fight back?

'Nay. I hit not, kicked not, spat not. Gouda Muck has sworn as much, aye, sworn it on his beloved Flame before you all. I was gentle, man, like a dead fish nailed to a slab of wood by fifty nails each longer than a finger. He never got any violence out of me.

'Likewise, by his own testimony, you know I did no damage to him and his, barring the trifling matter of the letter Açøwæ, knocked from a sword by accident. No harm he had of me till the day I was beaten once too often, and ran.

'For I am mild by nature, and not built all that big, so I'd always rather run than fight. As for his mastersword, well, what can I say? Muck was a swordsmith making at least a blade every day, so what would one be more or less?'

At this, Muck made a determined effort to stand and shout. A gag was slapped into his mouth, and he was carried from the courtroom.

'Poor man!' said Drake. 'I hope he's right by the morrow. As I say, he had his funny moods. But he was good in his day, aye, and taught me much. Mad as he is, no doubt he told the Court the truth as he sees it. Let's look at this truth.

'Muck claims I was cook's boy on a pirate ship. Well,

623

that's true enough, I won't deny it. As I've told the Court already, I'm a gentle chap, with precious little fight in my bones. So I was low in the rank when I were with the pirates, for I never had the heart to match cutlass with cutlass, or do foul things to fair women captured.

'As Gouda Muck has told the Court, my time on the pirate ships saw me diligent in prayer, raising my voice to the god I was taught to worship when I were but a lad, scraping around for whatever sacrifices lay within my means.

'The Court sees me, then, for what I am – shy, pious, eager for religion. And never raising a hand against the man who kicked and beat me all those years.

'Now, on to Runcorn. What has Muck to tell of Runcorn? Why, that he got there one evening and left the next night, or thereabouts. And did he see me much in all that time? Why, from his own testimony, no.

'For he spent the first evening resting at the inn. Next morning he spent deep in conversation with some Aard Lox. Who's he? I never heard of him before today, I'll tell you that for real.

'Anyway. This Aard Lox sells Muck a certain document you've all heard tell of. *The Book of Witness*. Aye. Well, paper's one thing, truth's another. There's people in Selzirk making a right good living selling maps to cities of buried treasure. Aye. The maps sell well – that's why they're treasure maps.'

Laughter from the audience. The judge frowned.

'I didn't mean for them to laugh!' protested Drake. 'But it's true! There's fools who will believe anything. As for Muck – what wouldn't the man believe, him with his Flame and all? What I'm saying is, let's not believe everything that's down on paper. If all such is believable, then there's an ocean of treasure out there!'

No laughter this time.

Drake continued:

'Anyway, with paper purchased, Muck goes to a square to find there's a riot. Did I start it? No. Muck himself says

624

I was doing my best to stop it. And how? By talking the people from looting to the honest business of slaving, which, as the Court knows well, is highly respected in Selzirk as elsewhere.

'You've had all kind of sorry troubles come from out of the north, but, as Muck has told it well, I was never mixed with any mad plans for invading Selzirk.

'Now how long did Muck see me for? Scarce long enough to hear me shout that I was Arabin lol Arabin. After that, he had troubles of his own.

'Out of this little, Muck makes much. A handful of words. Some paper bought from a stranger. From that, he makes me ruler of Runcorn. A strange turn of events!

'As the Court has heard, for years I was meek, mild, yielding without anger to all kinds of punishment, praying most diligent to my god, doing a humble job as cook in a sea ship's kitchen. But next moment I'm suddenly conjured into this conqueror of Runcorn, a terrible swordsman who kills people in open duel, and all the rest of the wild things you've heard.

'Now the truth is easy enough explained. I parted from the pirates right enough, for reasons you'll know yourselves by now. That wasn't my style. They'd probably have murdered an innocent boy like me if I'd kept with them that much longer. So I took to shore, and to honest work.

'My apprenticeship I never finished. Aye. That's much to be regretted. But I could cook. So in Runcorn I got a job as cook of sorts, aye, for this Arabin lol Arabin. Now he was a mighty magnificent man, and right bloody dangerous into the bargain. But what means his name, Arabin lol Arabin? Why, in Galish it's plain enough: it means he was the son of some fellow Arabin.

'But, me, I'm the son of Teff Douay, the nephew of Oleg Douay, the grandson of Vytor Douay, and so on back through fifty generations, all of them Douay. So I could never have any Arabin as my father, that's for real.

'Anyhow.

'There I was in Runcorn, scratching an honest living as cook for this Arabin lol Arabin, when he came upon troubles which I don't rightly pretend to understand; seeing as I'm not political at all, I don't hold with messing with the business of me betters. And in the riot he was killed.

'So.

'Something had to be done, or these anarchist types who were rioting would have torn the town apart. Now, I'm not a man of action, but I felt it my duty to try. So up I got on my two hind legs, and tried to turn them from reckless riots to honest slaving, which, as all the world knows, is an admirable kind of enterprise to be engaged in.

'But they wouldn't answer to my leadership. So I thought myself to impress them with the fact that the old leader was dead – partly because it was his death they were raging for, so if they knew him finished the trouble would die down. So I went to shout out that "I am here with the news that Arabin lol Arabin is dead."

'But that's a proper mouthful, and I'm no speaker. So in the heat of the moment, my tongue tripped upside down, and nothing came out but "I am Arabin lol Arabin". Well, and the worthy Gouda Muck heard that right enough, and a lot of misunderstanding there's been of it since.

'Let's talk about these treasure maps Muck bought, some papers called *The Book of Witness*, all about this Arabin fellow. There was one bit I didn't hear right the first time, so I got it read out a second, aye, and Gouda Muck swore it was told right to the Court.

'You all heard it.

'There was hot words said in the City Hall in Runcorn. A regular uproar, after which none knew just what had been said. But there was some Record, which must mean a Record in writing. And you've heard that this Arabin fellow called attention to what the Record said, which was "No".

'Was that me?

'How could it have been?

'For I be but an ignorant apprentice, who knows not the

letter Àçøwæ from any other. I couldn't read in any Record to save my life.

'Now, after I left Runcorn, I came to this fair city of Selzirk, most beautiful city I've ever set eyes on. And, bye and bye, I heard how Muck was in town. Aye, with a woman Zanya with him.

'Now this fancy document which Muck picked up in Runcorn, it tells how Arabin lol Arabin had a woman named Zanya. Now so he did. But I had a woman, too, and her name was also Zanya. And the Court won't deny that two women can share the same name. Now I'm a mild fellow, as the Court's heard, but there's one time when I did fight true.'

And Drake looked at Zanya. And she gazed back at him. And he knew she was sitting in judgment on him. She would be called to the witness stand next. And she would make his life or break it. Yes.

'Zanya,' he said, making love to her name as he spoke it. 'I saw her first when I was floating in the sea, a horizon away from Stokos. I was the sole survivor of a shipwreck. I fell in love with her then at first sight. But cruel circumstances later parted us. I was never able to court her as I wished to.

'Where did we meet again? Why, on Burntos – an island to which I went on a ship then engaged in honest trade. Briefly we met, but, after a few days, parted.

'We next met in an arena in the city of Dalar ken Halvar. I was tumbled there by a kind of magic. And if the Court doubts that, they can ask the fair and most beautiful lady Zanya for the proof of it, for there she sits by that old fellow there who's wearing the straw hat.'

'Take that hat off!' shouted Judge Syrphus, who had not until then noticed that anyone was wearing a hat in his court.

'Why,' said Drake, as the hat came off. 'Now we can see her plainer. Aye, and a beautiful sight she makes. We were reunited, as I've told, when I'd been tumbled by magic to an arena built for killing.

627

'There she stood, tied to a slaughter post. Aye, and there were monsters afoot in the arena, huge things brutal with teeth and claws.

'I was rightly minded to run, for my legs were wet with terror. Aye, and the magic which had tumbled me to the arena gave me a Door I could have fled through, tricing away in an instant. But no. She were of such beauty that I could not leave her for the slaughter.

'So I drew the steel I carried, as every pirate must be he cook's boy or captain. And I went chest to chest with the monster, aye, and slaughtered it. My one act as a hero. And it was for her that I killed.

'Thus she was with me when I came to Runcorn to go to work as a cook. And a hard life we had there, aye, always so much to be done, we'd scarce time to kiss twice in a day. Which was a fault of circumstances, not of she or me.

'Since then, as you've heard, she's been guardian of the purity of Gouda Muck. We've not heard from Muck exactly what that means, though I've got my own ideas about it. And if I've any quarrel with Gouda Muck, then it's over this woman. For, as the Court's heard tell, in Selzirk I went seeking my woman from Muck.

'Aye. And might have got her back, except I was arrested on false charges, for which I've since been pardoned. Arrested. Thrown into a dungeon. No light, no air, no food, no water. Darkness. Rats. Chains. Terror. Torture. Day on day unyielding. Only one thing kept me alive, and that were thinking of my fair pure Zanya.'

Mention of purity naturally brought to mind the question of appetite. How to deal with that one?

Speak from the heart, man. Things are getting too complicated. No time for more lies. So speak from the heart.

'Zanya. Yes.

'I lusted for her. That I'll not deny.

'My lust, in part, was frankly carnal. Sometimes women are insulted by such lust, for lust is an appetite, so some think that to be lusted for is to be devoured, as a dead fish is devoured at table. But one does not go chest to

628

chest with a monster for the sake of a dead fish. Nay. Even a starving man would not duel it out with a monster for a dead fish.

'Together with my lust was my love also. It was love which made me fight that monster. Love at first sight.

'Sometimes I'm right hungry, man, and I sit down at table with my friends. Like animals we go at it, aye, teeth, lips, tongue, in and out, sweat, saliva – a regular meal for our hunger. But when it's over, we don't look on each other with disgust. For we're friends, yes, and to share the meal of our appetites is but to share our friendship, aye, our very love for each other.

'That's why we eat together at table, instead of satisfying our hungers in squalid solitude, one in each corner alone. And . . . is not the hunger mutual?'

Then Drake looked at Zanya, looked long and with longing, saying nothing. Until finally Judge Syrphus, puzzled, said:

'The accused seems to have lost the thread of his argument. Has he anything further to say to the Court reference the testimony of Gouda Muck?'

'Nothing, my lord judge,' said Drake, still gazing on Zanya, 'for I have spoken my heart out, and have nothing more to say.'

'Then let the prosecutor call his next witness,' said the judge.

And the prosecutor called Zanya Kliedervaust to the witness stand.

54

Name: Zanya Kliedervaust.

Description: healthy high-breasted woman, red skin, red hair, white teeth.

Birthplace: Unch, on Lebrew (largest of the Ebrell Islands).

Career: priestess of Orgy God of the Ebrells; convert to Goudanism; missionary to Parengarenga; martyr in Dalar ken Halvar; survivor in Penvash; Drake's woman in Runcorn; Gouda Muck's mistress in Selzirk.

'In the witness stand is Zanya Kliedervaust, formerly of the Ebrell Islands,' said the prosecutor. 'She will shortly give testimony which will doom the evil Drake Douay to a living death in the deepest, darkest, filthiest rat-infested dungeon we can find for him.

'But before we hear her testimony, let me untangle the web woven by Drake Douay for public display. He has posed as a poor, meek, ignorant apprentice. But his own performance proves him shrewd, quick-witted, dangerously intelligent and amazingly cunning in cross-examination.

'This man could very well have been Arabin lol Arabin, behaving as described in *The Book of Witness*. There's nothing meek, mild or safe or law-abiding about him. Plainly, he's copied the style of an excellent lawyer. I put it to the Court that the lawyer in question was, in all

630

probability, the Garimanthea mentioned in *The Book of Witness*.

'The accused tries to dismiss that document because it says he read a single word from a certain Record. Now, four or five years ago, he may not have known the letter Àçøwæ from any other. But he's had time since to learn to read and write half a dozen different languages, if he chose.'

'Time, yes,' interjected Drake. 'But no opportunity.'

'Opportunity, surely,' said the prosecutor, 'to learn how to read one simple word like "No." In any case, *The Book of Witness* does not say Arabin lol Arabin read from the Record, only that he called attention to its contents. If the accused is indeed illiterate, then his lawyer could have told him what lay in the Record for him to call attention to.

'The accused would also have us believe he cried "I am Arabin lol Arabin" when he meant to say something entirely different. Judge his perfomance today! Not one slip, pause, stammer or stutter. Not a single word out of place. This speaks of an accomplished orator – or an accomplished liar. Or of both.

'The accused has a highly trained mind. As Gouda Muck told us, the accused studied on Stokos, sharpening his wits by learning theory of all description by heart. How can we believe he'd let his tongue trip upside down when it came to saying a few simple words to a crowd? He speaks well – and the very eloquence which defends him condemns him.

'He said to the crowd that he was Arabin lol Arabin. Doubtless that was what he meant. So much for his rhetoric! Now to our witness. You are Zanya Kliedervaust, born on the Ebrells?'

'I am,' she said.

'What did you there?'

'I was priestess of the Orgy God.'

'What did that involve?'

'Being used by men in the way of lust.'

'And did you like that?'

'No. How could I? For they treated me as meat. What way is that to treat a woman? They were rough. They used

631

cruel language. They bruised me. They did things which I would not like to speak of in Court, or out of it either.'

'Then we'll not ask you about such,' said the Prosecutor. 'Now. You first met Gouda Muck when?'

'When I travelled to Stokos, having left the Ebrells, for I was sick of the life there, which had killed out my family entire. Always drinking, fighting, feuding, gambling—'

'Yes, yes. But Muck. What reception did he give you, on Stokos?'

'Oh, it was wonderful,' said Zanya.

She described her conversion to Goudanism. She revelled in her memories of those glorious days. Muck had taught her a woman could be pure. Which meant being free from that horrible business of being bruised, used, rucked, fisted, slathered and taken – again and again and again. Then abandoned.

'So you converted to a religion of purity,' said the prosecutor. 'What then?'

'I went to the world as a missionary. In time, I was martyred in the arena at Dalar ken Halvar. And there . . . as Drake said, he saved me.'

'At that time, did he strike you as meek, mild, pious and law-abiding?'

'Why, no,' said Zanya. 'He came like a hero. He killed monsters right and left. Then said words to me, marvellous words, which thrilled my blood. I can't remember what they were, but they were . . . yes, wonderful. Then we were whirled away by magic to the forests of Penvash.'

'What magic is this?' inquired Judge Syrphus.

Confused explanations followed, which did not entirely satisfy the Court. But there was no helping the lack of satisfaction, so the subject was dropped.

'And in Penvash,' said the prosecutor, 'did Drake treat you with purity?'

'Why,' said Zanya, 'he lay with me to keep me warm. But that was as far as it went.'

'By warmth,' said the prosecutor, thinking this was no

time for euphemisms, 'I suppose you mean the vile, filthy, unholy ways of lust.'

'Well, no,' said Zanya, 'I mean it was cold, so two bodies were warmer than one.'

'Oh,' said the prosecutor, momentarily nonplussed.

The prosecutor, looking through his notes, started to wish his pretrial interview with this witness had not been so cursory.

'Are you sure,' said the prosecutor, 'that you're telling the truth? I mean – you were alone in the forest with this man. Wouldn't it be natural for him to force you? He was a pirate, after all. Could you have forgotten?'

'Perhaps you're in the habit of forgetting a rape,' said Zanya, 'but I'm not so casual about it.'

Laughter rocked the court. The prosecutor, flustered, dropped his notes. The judge called for order. And Zanya cast her mind back to those days in Penvash. Drake had not taken her then. No, not until they reached the southern border of Estar. And then . . . as he said, the hunger was mutual.

In Runcorn, when Yot had explained that Drake was in fact the dreaded son of the demon Hagon, the incarnation of all evil, the shock had initially unbalanced her. By then, too, she had had genuine grievances against Drake – for, while in Runcorn, he had become so deeply involved with the business of government that he had grown hard, curt and brusque, using her in ways which seemed rushed and loveless.

But . . . was he the son of a demon? Hardly. And . . .

'Are you sure,' said the prosecutor, 'that you have given us a correct account of events in Penvash? Are you frightened of this man Drake? Do you want him removed from the Court while you give evidence?'

'No,' said Zanya. 'No, it's quite all right. He never . . . he never did anything to frighten me. He talked of . . . of love, yes. That was in Penvash. Much later, when he took me he was . . . he cared. He knew things no other man had known – or, if they knew, they never cared to do it. Like

633

running tongue from inner thigh to the lips of my—'

'That's enough!' said the prosecutor, sharply. 'Are you trying to scandalize the Court?'

'What do you want me to say?'

'The truth! But not – nothing about sexual intimacies. That's – that's impure. Your master Gouda Muck would have told you as much.'

'Why, no,' said Zanya. 'Quite the reverse. For, as guardian of his purity, I have to serve him in the ways of flesh. But that's pure, you know, when it's done with someone holy. He likes to be licked in the—'

'Silence!' roared the prosecutor.

'Really,' said Judge Syrphus, 'there is no need for the prosecutor to bellow as if we were in the midst of a thunderstorm. Go on, girl, tell us what Muck likes to have licked.'

Zanya told.

'Really?' said Judge Syrphus. 'How often? And when?'

And Judge Syrphus led the examination for some considerable time thereafter, discovering the intimacies of the private life of Gouda Muck.

'So,' said Judge Syrphus, when he knew all, 'it was pure and holy for Gouda Muck to use you in carnal ways, since he was a preacher who cared mostly for the religion he espoused, rather than for you yourself. On the other hand, Drake Douay loved you – or so I understand from what he earlier told the Court – therefore his lust for you was wrong. That sounds very strange to me.'

'Yes,' said Zanya, slowly, 'very strange.'

'But,' said the prosecutor, 'this case has nothing to do with sex. It is all to do with the public menace posed by Drake Douay to the religion, government, wealth and law of Selzirk, by reason of the devilish ability he showed in Runcorn, where he overthrew the lawful government and established a reign of terror and of abominable practices.'

'I think, sir,' said Zanya, 'you stand in error. For it was not Drake Douay who did that, but Arabin lol Arabin. They are two entirely different people.'

'You testify so?' said the prosecutor. 'I will have you swear to that by the Flame!'

And Zanya so swore. Yes, swore it in a cool and steady voice, which none could doubt. She had changed since she had walked into that courtroom.

For a start, she had learnt why Drake had abandoned his quest to reclaim her. He had not been roistering with lewd women, as she had imagined: instead, he had been suffering cruel imprisonment for crimes he never committed. And dreaming of his true love while he lay behind bars.

Also, she had been given cause to cast her mind back to the glorious days in Penvash, when her love for Drake had first been kindled by the respect he had shown her and the protection he had given her from lustful pirates.

She had also been made to remember his performance in the arena at Dalar ken Halvar. She had very clear, distinct memories of him killing at least two monsters, single-handedly, and maybe a third as well. And what were the first words he had said to her, as he cut her loose? As she remembered it now, they were:

'I love you.'

All this gave her cause to make a final decision on her commitment to Goudanism. Effortlessly, she abandoned her belief in the Flame. Her faith had been steadily weakening for a long time now. Indeed, when she had first learnt in Runcorn that Drake was the one accused of being the son of the demon Hagon, at least half her shock had been at the way he had failed to trust her with the knowledge of the accusations.

But now . . .

All was forgiven.

Judge Syrphus refused to hear further argument, but, instead, gave judgment and summed up:

'The case against Drake Douay is of course dismissed. It represents, as any fool can see, an attempt by a dirty old man to remove a sexual rival who is a younger and altogether more attractive man. The Court is satisfied that

Drake Douay is indeed meek, mild and pious, and entirely lacking in political ambition.

'He may have made one mistake in his youth, with respect to a cheap and nasty sword, one of the hundreds owned by Gouda Muck, but what of it? A young man is entitled to one mistake. Since then, he has lived humbly and quietly, though he rose to the occasion and performed heroically when that was necessary for him to save his beloved lady.

'Even though I'm having trouble meeting my quota, I'm letting Drake Douay go free, for that is only just.

'Fortunately, Gouda Muck's own testimony shows him to be a dangerous, ambitious, reckless and destructive man. We have heard how he overthrew the rightful religion of Stokos, how he speaks with evil spirits dwelling within furnaces, and indulges in all manner of private perversion under the cloak of religion.

'Consequently, I have no hesitation in ordering that a warrant be issued for the arrest of Gouda Muck, that he may be tried on a charge of being a public menace. And I appoint myself judge of his case!'

Thus the trial came to an end.

One of the spectators, who had watched the whole proceedings with interest, was Plovey of the Regency. After the trial, he met Drake and Zanya.

'Darling boy,' said Plovey, to Drake. 'No! Say nothing hasty! We've had hard words between us in the past, I know. But did I not invite you to dine with me and my darling wife if you ever had the occasion?'

'You did,' said Drake, thinking he should really kill Plovey on the spot.

'Today, then,' said Plovey, 'I invite you to do more. I invite you, and your beloved, to enjoy the hospitality of my house. For a day – for fifty days, if need be. For I have always admired you as a remarkable young man. Indeed, I may be able to hold out some prospect of gainful employment for you.'

What kind of employment? Knifework, perhaps. Might

pay well. And there would be time enough to murder Plovey later. Revenge – as others have noted – is a dish well worth eating even when cold.

'Darling,' said Zanya, 'have we anywhere else to go?'

Drake considered, and then:

'It would be a crime,' he said, 'for me to refuse such generous hospitality.'

Plovey had, amongst other things, aroused his curiosity: Drake was keen to learn exactly what kind of proposition the Regency bureaucrat had in mind.

55

Plovey zar Plovey: a career bureaucrat of the Regency; had a hand in the torture and interrogation of Drake Douay, and in the despatch of Drake to Androlmarphos with letters for Elkor Alish.

By the time Drake and Zanya had finished kissing, Plovey had summoned a cab to take the three of them to Plovey's house, which was in Santrim. They climbed inside; the cabby flicked his whip; with a jingle of bells, the horse began to move; they were off.

'We've won,' said Zanya.

'So we have,' said Drake.

They had salvaged their love from the wreckage of the past, and had made good their escape from the terrible machinery of the law.

Drake and Zanya kissed.

Plovey pretended not to notice.

'Friend Drake,' said Plovey, 'would you like to live in Selzirk?'

'If I could,' said Drake.

'I'm sure you can,' said Plovey. 'A job should be no trouble, no trouble at all.'

He did not elaborate, and Drake did not ask for details. Instead, he held Zanya's hand and watched the passing streets.

'Here we are,' said Plovey, as the cab halted. 'This is my house.'

Plovey paid off the cabby and led them through the gate and onto his own property.

The house was small, yet elegant. It had a small court-yard with a fountain set in the centre of a lily pond. Amidst the lilies swam carp. Some were pure gold, the ultimate in xanthochroism. Others were piebald, while some of the more motley specimens were blotched with as many as half a dozen different colours.

Drake paused and watched the fish swim amidst the cool water. The sun was warm on his back. He was suddenly reminded of a day long, long ago at Ling, when he had sat in a canoe by the side of the Warwolf, watching fish in the limpid waters of Ling Bay. Life had been so simple then! And his hopes had been so high.

He had expected, in those days of his innocence, to make a swift return to Stokos, and, within a couple of years, to make himself a priest or a prince, and acquire Zanya Kliedervaust as his pleasure woman. Instead . . .

Well . . .

At least he had Zanya.

At least that part of his dream had come true.

He gazed at the fish. It must be so comfortable being a fish. What perfect control . . .

'You like fish?' said Plovey.

'They're . . . they're all right,' said Drake.

In truth, he felt he could have stood there staring at them all day. How long since he had been free to gaze on something beautiful? For as long as he could remember, he had been living in a nightmare . . .

'Come inside,' said Plovey. 'Darlinda will be waiting for us.'

'Who's Darlinda?' said Zanya.

'Why, my darling wife, of course,' said Plovey.

Inside the house, it was cool. Plovey showed Drake and Zanya the bedroom where they would sleep that night, then he introduced them to his darling wife Darlinda, a petite little thing with a subservient manner and a broken nose.

639

'Darlinda,' said Plovey, 'get some water and wash the feet of our honoured guests.'

This Darlinda did, silently.

While his feet were being washed, Drake closed his eyes. An overwhelming wave of weariness swept over him. At last he had reached a place of comfort, safety and indulgence. At last the nightmare days were over.

'Tired?' said Plovey. 'Perhaps the two of you would like to rest.'

Drake and Zanya accepted this suggestion. They retired to the bedroom, but they did not give themselves to love, for both were emotionally exhausted. Instead, they cuddled into the safety of each other's arms, and went to sleep.

Drake slept.

Systole and diastole, his heart maintained his life while his mind wandered in the world of dreams. He dreamed of an orphan's cry, of a homeless woman weeping, of vagabond winds roaming a plain of dust and ruins, of nations hungering to starvation . . . of a time a thousand generations hence, when all his world had passed out of memory . . .

Drake woke.

Tears were in his eyes.

Zanya lay in his arms breathing softly, sweetly. Familiar smell of her breath. Strand of red hair trailing across her lips. Flickers of dream beneath her eyelids. He kissed her, gently, lightly, then closed his own eyes once again.

And fell asleep to dream of eating, of turtle soup and dragon steaks, of basilisk pie and ribs of gryphon, of bananas and peaches, chicken and duck.

So dreaming, Drake slept until Darlinda woke them with the news that the first course of the evening meal would shortly be served.

That evening, a lutist played for their entertainment, and Plovey's darling wife served them the most marvellous meal. Wines free of sediment were brought to them in cut crystal, which even Drake knew to be fabulously expensive and wondrous rare.

Drake and Zanya exchanged many glances, saluted each other quietly in wine, and touched feet beneath the table. Their sleep had revived them. Both knew they would be ready for all kinds of wickedness once the meal was done.

Candles were lit as the evening darkened.

Course after course was served, with many delicate things to tempt the palate. There were freshwater crayfish from Chenameg, and tender scrawls from the seacoast. There were interesting stews served in dainty bowls, and nuts to knapple on between courses.

But the *pièce de résistance* was a rich, hot curry full of bizarre and exciting tastes. To Drake, it felt like eating fire. He glutted himself on it.

Then the dishes were cleared away by Plovey's indefatigable wife (who had not yet eaten herself), a flutist joined the lutist, and Plovey offered round cigars which contained an interesting mixture of opium, hashish and tobacco.

'Friend Drake,' said Plovey, as they drew on the rich smoke, 'I was interested in your trial today. For you denied yourself to be Arabin lol Arabin.'

'So I did,' said Drake.

'Yet, under interrogation,' said Plovey, 'you insisted often that you'd ruled in Runcorn.'

'Ah,' said Drake, 'but there was a simple reason for that. I knew this Arabin lol Arabin to be a freak of nature, fit to eat any poison. So I made a pretence at being him, that I might get myself fed poison.'

'So that was your game,' said Plovey. 'To escape from torture through suicide.'

'Precisely,' said Drake, with a sidelong glance at Zanya, who smiled in love and anticipation.

'So you've no stomach for poison,' said Plovey.

'Why,' said Drake, 'no more than any other mortal man.'

641

'Then that is strange,' said Plovey, 'for a most special portion of curry was served to you this evening.'

'How so?' said Drake.

'Dear darling boy,' said Plovey, 'the portion served to you had arsenic in it, and cyanide, and strychnine, and an extract of belladonna and fine-chopped portions of a dozen other poisonous plants besides.'

Drake stared at Plovey.

'You joke,' said Drake, 'for if what you said is true, then I'd be dead.'

'No,' said Plovey. 'I spoke true enough.'

And he clapped his hands, sharply, once. At that signal, guards entered to seize Drake. He fought. But it was useless: he was unarmed, and outnumbered eight to one. Zanya, screaming with rage, started to batter the guards with a chair. Plovey grabbed her round the waist. She thumped him, knocked him insensible then threw him across the room.

Upon which another four guards joined the fray.

Many bruises later, both Drake and Zanya were dragged away, still struggling.

Plovey zar Plovey was unconscious.

Plovey's darling wife Darlinda seized her opportunity. She grabbed a pillow case, loaded it with all the gold, silver, jade and coinage she could lay her hands on, then quit the house. At dawn, she boarded a galley going downstream towards Androlmarphos: and she was never seen in Selzirk again.

56

The Swarms: diverse monstrous colony creatures dwelling in the terror-lands south of Drangsturm; are controlled by an entity known as the Skull of the Deep South; are prevented from invading the north of Argan by a watch maintained at Drangsturm by the Confederation of Wizards.

The retrial of Drake Douay was curt. Gouda Muck could not give evidence against him, for Muck had fled Selzirk to escape a warrant which would have had him arrested as a public menace. However, Plovey of the Regency was there to testify against him.

Drake was convicted of being a public menace, and was sentenced to life imprisonment in the House of Earthly Enlightenment, which stood next to the Zingrin warehouse in Jone.

Zanya was put on trial for perjury, was convicted and was sentenced to slavery. Plovey of the Regency bought her as a concubine, then visited Drake especially for the pleasure of giving him the news.

Drake wept.

But weeping did him no good. So he tried curses, and prayers, and a couple of chants which he'd learnt which were supposed to be magic.

All to no effect.

Each day he woke in the same prison cell. It was an enormous stone-walled room which held ninety-seven men. Light (and wind, rain, moths, mosquitoes, flies, beetles and dust) came in through the myriad slit windows built into one wall. There were a dozen small holes in the centre of the floor for use as toilets. There were no chairs, no beds, no pallets.

But at least Drake was left with the clothes on his back. And at least he had plenty of company.

However . . .

Very quickly he began to doubt the value of having company in such quantity. It meant, for a start, that there were bitter arguments over the daily dole of food and water.

The water was brought from the Velvet River in casks which had once held fusel-oil. The food was a hunk of ironbread per man per day, plus a bowl each of a tepid, fuscous broth which occasionally contained some inscrutable fabaceous objects which, despite their shape, were certainly not beans. Sometimes this was supplemented by a bit of gristle or a bone with a few rat-pickings still adhering.

For the first ten days, a larger man bullied Drake, stealing half of his food and a third of his water. After which Drake lost patience, and fought back. The gaolers removed the larger man's corpse without comment. Perhaps they failed to notice his broken neck, and thought he had simply succumbed to the river water as so many others did.

After that, nobody picked on Drake.

But there was no escaping from the constant arguments, from the banter of gamblers playing at sharps and knuckles, from the monotonous sing-song of very tame geniuses competing against each other in mental games of dragon chess, and from the whining complaints of old men with face-ache and arthritis. Some of the ancients, Drake found, had been stuck in this prison cell for as much as thirty years!

He determined he would escape.

Yes.

And kill Plovey of the Regency, kill him slowly, with

great care. And rescue Zanya. And escape with her to the Far South, to Drangsturm itself, and seek employment with wizards.

First, Drake tried to bribe a gaoler with imaginary monies. Despite Drake's skill at deception, this ploy failed. Then he tried for liberty by offering his body to one particularly villainous-looking turnkey, a brute with a swollen, depraved face and a great big bloated kyte. But the man had got himself castrated years ago, when he was seeking a position as a eunuch in a palace at Voice, in the Rice Empire.

So Drake feigned sickness, hoping to be sent to some place of recovery. But he was told he could die where he was as easily as any place elsewhere. So he feigned death – but when his body was thrown onto a bonfire in a prison courtyard, he came to life rather quickly. And was beaten thoroughly before being returned to his prison cell.

Right.

He would dig his way out.

Where was the weakest point?

The floor was of stone, the walls were of stone, but the ceiling was of wooden boards. Which sagged in one corner. That looked weak enough. So, one evening, Drake clambered up to the ceiling, using window slits for handholds and footholds. Once up there, he began to lever away one of the boards with a human thigh bone.

As the board began to give, Drake heard an ominous humming sound. It reminded him of a Door. Good! He'd jump through a Door to anywhere, thank you, and no questions asked!

He threw his strength against the thigh bone. And the board gave way. and fell with a crash. So did an incoherent mass of darkness, which promptly resolved itself into a swarm of bees.

'Pox and bitches!' said Drake, from the floor to which he had fallen.

Then said no more, for a bee stung his tongue.

645

As the bees raged amongst the prisoners, they screamed for mercy. And, in their frenzy, tore away the door to their prison cell and mobbed outside. They were all rounded up at last in a high-walled courtyard, then cudgeled, then interrogated.

And Drake was hauled in front of a judge, who pronounced him to be incorrigible.

'You have proved,' said the judge, 'to be unworthy of the delights of the House of Earthly Enlightenment.'

'Does this mean you're going to execute me?' said Drake.

'No! You don't get off so lightly! Life with hard labour! Take him away!'

Life with hard labour turned out to mean life as a galley-slave on the Velvet River. And a bitter life it was, as summer yielded to autumn and the bitter winds began to preach of the winter yet to come.

Drake, to his dismay, found himself shackled to a rowing bench between two terrible bores. One was a dismal pedant who knew seventeen different languages and corrected Drake's grammar every time he opened his mouth.

'You were talking in your sleep last night,' said the pedant one morning. 'You said, "Zanya I love thou." It should have been "Zanya I love thee." '

'You're wrong,' said Drake. 'It should have been "Zanya I lust for you." '

'It would be more elegant to say, "It is you I lust for." '

And this could well go on for half a day, unless they were rowing at such a pace that they needed all their breath for their labour.

The other bore was a gabeller who had embezzled a trifling amount of official money.

'They convicted me of making off with an undeclared amount. I was sentenced to labour on the galleys until I'd paid it back. What did I need to pay? Why, an undeclared amount. What, five skilders, or five million? Why, none of those, they said, for none of those is an undeclared amount. So I held out an empty palm, declaring I was offering them an undeclared amount. Why, no, they said, that is not any kind of amount whatsoever. That is nothing! So here I stay forever!'

Which made a nice enough story the first time around, but Drake, who heard it twice a day, pretty soon knew it by heart.

The galley he was on rowed right regular between Selzirk and Androlmarphos. At Selzirk they were fed on horsemeat from a knackery in Jone; in 'Marphos they were fed with fish; in between cities, they were fed with bread and lentils. The meals were vast, as befitted their backbreaking labours: but the meals were also, of course, monotonous.

But the rivertalk gave variety to their life, for talk went from galley to galley when ships were rafted up together on the river, or tied up at the docks, and few movements by land or sea were secret from the river.

Thus Drake was one of the first to hear of disaster in the south.

At first the rumours were wild, and scanty on detail, therefore little to be believed. But, as autumn chilled to winter, rumour firmed to fact. Drangsturm had been destroyed. The flame trench which had guarded the north against the terror-lands was no more. The Confederation of Wizards had destroyed itself in war. The monsters of the Swarms were marching north.

And now Drake's galley was on the river by day and night, taking wealth and panic from Selzirk to 'Marphos, where wealth and panic took ship for foreign parts, quitting forever the shores of civilization.

So the work was harder than ever. But the galley-slaves were glad now to be galley-slaves, for that meant, surely, that they would be working their way to freedom when their own craft finally took to the open waters as the menace of the Swarms got closer.

Then came the day when a Neversh was sighted flying over the Velvet River.

The next day, two were seen.

The day after, a dozen.

And then, come dawn on the next day, attacks on shipping began.

The owner of Drake's galley made his decision at 'Marphos. He had his slaves cut free from their rowing benches and chased ashore at spearpoint. Then he sold places on those rowing benches to the high and mighty, taking his pay in pearls and diamonds. Then forth to sea set the galley, leaving the slaves on shore.

So there was Drake, out of work. He still had a great big iron ring clamped around his left ankle, and from it dragged a great big length of rusty chain, at the end of which was another iron ring, still embedded in the chunk of rowing bench which had been cut away so that Drake could be set free.

He counted himself lucky.

If they'd really been in a hurry, they could have cut off his foot so they could pull his leg free from its ankle-ring.

First off, he found a blacksmith's shop. There he took a file to his chains, and freed himself from all impedimenta. Then he went to the docks, confident that he could work a passage to foreign parts. He was a sailor, tested and true. Better still, he could lie, cheat, bluff and fight, if necessary. Or stow away.

But the docks were bare, but for a carousing mob of slaves, soldiers, whores, thieves, beggars, apprentices, lawyers' clerks, junior tax accountants and similar scum, indulging in an orgy of drinking, looting and wanton copulation.

If Drake had been sixteen and senseless, he would have joined them. But he was twenty, a seasoned survivor who had lived through shipwreck, slaughter, torture, imprisonment and assorted disaster. More to the point, he had gone chest to chest with one of the Neversh when that monster had attacked Jon Arabin's fine ship, the *Warwolf*; he knew at first hand what most others had seen only at a distance, or not at all.

'Debauchery can wait,' said Drake to Drake.

And went looting.

Unlike others, he did not make a heap of bolts of silk and crates of glasswear, marble statues and porcelain vases, women's underwear and ornamental snuff boxes, polished silver and golden candlesticks.

No.

He secured, instead, a length of bamboo, which nobody else thought worth fighting for. He found carrying bags to sling at each end of that pole, which he then carried across his shoulders. While others dreamed of gemstones, he lusted for a tinder box, a cooking pot, a waterskin, and a sheepskin rug in which he could roll himself at night.

When he had these, he sought rice, flour, dried beans, dried meat, nuts and cheese. Then a good pair of new boots. Five changes of socks. A rain cape. A knife. A sword-belt complete with scabbard and blade.

He slung the sword-belt so the sword hung down his back. It would have to swim rivers with him, as would his clothes. Everything else, he rolled up, together with big chunks of cork, in pieces of canvas, and stuffed into the carrying bags, the mouths of which he then knotted tight with good rope.

Now he was ready to ford the many branches of the river delta. Now he was ready for the cold, wet, muck and mud of winter on the Harvest Plains. Which way now? North, of course. To Selzirk. For that was where Zanya had been last.

He lifted his burden to his shoulders. The bamboo pole bent alarmingly at both ends. The weight was crushing. But it would float, yes, wrapped up nicely with plenty of cork it would float all right.

And he was strong, and young, and fit, and used to working a brutal day on the oars.

And, thanks to his terrible experiences in Penvash, Drake knew all about travelling light. It's nice to dream about but murder to do.

'Move!' said Drake to Drake.

And got going.

At the gates of Androlmarphos, Drake was accosted by a woman who made him an offer of lust. But, to his own amazement, he refused the offer, and trudged out into the rains sweeping the open plains.

Heading north.

57

Chenameg: small mountain-ringed kingdom east of the Harvest Plains. The Velvet River flows east through the deep and narrow Manaray Gorge, enters the kingdom at a point known as the Gates of Chenameg, and exits the kingdom through the Mountain Gap (which is all of fifty leagues across).

Mud.

Rain.

Leagues of loneliness underfoot.

Drake dreamed that a disaster befell the sky, and every star cried out in torture. He dreamed that he was born to starvation, born to die of leprosy and kwashiorkor.

He woke.

Monsters moved on the horizons.

The Swarms were on the march.

Fell beasts of nightmare. Grim and eale. Clawing their way north. Ravening as they went. Destroying nations.

'These are the last days,' murmured Drake.

And watched the Swarms until dayfail, when the monsters settled to sleep.

Drake marched by night, sheltered in a ditch at dawn, and slept.

He dreamed that gold turned to lead, silver to fish scales, bread to stone. In his dreams, nations lay dying. A woman with skin dark with bruising lay close to death, her breathing laboured. Time conjured the labefaction of the sun. Ice whispered over the world, drowning the music of the last kithara.

He woke.

It was evening.

Something monstrous was moving near his ditch. He could feel its weight shaking the ground. He lay very, very still. Scarcely trusting himself to breathe.

The thing lumbered on toward the north.

Night fell. And, with it, rain.

Drake walked.

And saw the towers of Selzirk, dimly, through the veiling rain.

'Zanya,' he said.

She would be there, surely, Selzirk would hold out even against the Swarms. It was a city great in power. Selzirk was protected by the battle-walls, Ol Ilkeen and Ol Unamon. How could such strength be broken?

Drake wanted to push on to Selzirk that night. But, in the end, fatigue conquered desire; he halted at a good distance, camping in a sparse grove of trees. He rested, ate, slept, and dreamed.

He dreamed of icy-pearled mountains marching, of dragons with ianthine eyes, of leper dancing with beggar, of a million children burning on a perfumed pyre, of a seven-fingered gytrash of alabaster white which fingered the dead red flesh of the woman he loved (if love was what he thought it).

He woke.

Night.

Silence after rain.

Cold moon rising.

A tiny dark shadow trying to scuffle its way into his food stock.

'Gently, friend mouse,' said Drake.

Scaring it away. But not far. Maybe it was too cold or sick or hungry to run far. Drake threw it some ironbread, which the damp of the ground would soon enough soften for consumption. Then ate himself. Then marched.

He was on the north bank.

As he neared the walls of Selzirk, he saw something monstrous coming down the Velvet River. So he went to ground, and watched. But it was only an abandoned gabbart floating downstream, listing heavily to larboard.

Even after the gabbart had gone by, Drake still lay there. Reluctant to move. He realized he was frightened. But of what? It was night: the Swarms would not resume their march until dawn. And he was close to the safety of Selzirk, was he not? Surely the city would open its gates at night. Yes. Sending scavenging parties into the countryside. They would welcome him, would they not? A strong swordsman. A new hero for their ranks.

'March,' said Drake to Drake.

And shouldered bamboo, and marched. Every step meant pain, for, despite padding, the bamboo had long since rubbed his shoulders raw.

Ahead, a bridge arched across the river in one sweet span, beyond the possibilities of any engineering known to the earthbound humanity which Drake knew.

'I dream this,' he said.

But, when he closed the distance, he was able to soothe his fingers over its chill, which was smooth as fine-glazed porcelain. The moon shone bright on the bridge, which had no walls or guardrails.

'The Swarms built this,' said Drake to Drake.

The moon shone on the river.

An endless river of tears.

'Onward,' said Drake.

And went onward, and was soon walking in the shadow of Ol Ilkeen, the outer wall of the ruling city of the Harvest Plains. Looking up, he saw by moonlight strange, hunched shapes on the top of the battlements. What were they? Some kind of weapon? He wondered if he should cry out.

But he did not.

A fugitive's caution kept him silent.

He thought:

What if Plovey rules in Selzirk? That would be terrible!

Yes.

He should go carefully.

He should try to find out who ruled the city before he announced himself.

The moon had gone behind shadow by the time Drake gained the stoneway of the Salt Road. He stood before the north gate, a shadow amidst shadows.

Something vast lay between him and the gate.

What was it?

A pyramid of some kind. A great heap of . . . what? Stone? Perhaps it was a new defence, built beyond Ol Ilkeen in order to strengthen the defences of the gate.

A shift of cloud unveiled a fragment of the moon.

Something glinted in the pyramid which stood between Drake and the gate.

Something moved.

Then the moon slipped clear of the cloud, and all was revealed. Drake was standing on the Salt Road scarcely a dozen paces from a huge pyramid made of sleeping monsters, all jigsawed together for safety against the night.

'Saaa!' hissed Drake.

Then hissed no more.

For the pyramid was shifting, changing, extending claws, tentacles, flaps, fins. Moonlight blazed upon open eyes. Huge eyes. Crystalline. Utterly alien.

Drake stood as if turned to ice.

He was a statue.

On the battlements, a huddled shape uncoiled, flexed, extended itself, opened wings.

It was a Neversh!

The battlements were lined with Neversh!

The moon slid behind shadows.

And Drake went to his knees, unburdened himself of his bamboo pole, sank to his belly then crawled for the roadside ditch. He moved as quietly as blood running across the deck of a ship. He gained the ditch. And began to shudder.

654

Much later, moonlight found him still lying there.

Tentatively, he peered over the lip of the ditch. He could not see the gate for the mound of monsters.

He had to know!

Drake crawled along the ditch. Twigs, leaves and thorns cracked and snapped beneath his weight.

He advanced regardless.

Then risked another look. He was beyond the monster mound by now. But he still could not see.

Where the gate should be, there was darkness.

In a moment of madness, Drake got to his feet.

Step by step, he advanced.

Until he stood within the gateway.

Within the shadows.

He went on.

And found himself in the streets of Selzirk.

By the polished silver light of the moon, he saw the shattered shadows of half-demolished buildings. Saw another mound of monsters heaped up a hundred paces away. Why did they heap themselves like that? For security? For bodywarmth? Did they have warm bodies?

Drake turned.

He moved as if in a dream.

He knew what he had to do.

He had to regain his bamboo pole and the makeshift valises which it supported. Everything he needed to survive was there: warmth, food, tinder-box. There would be no food between here and Chenameg, not in a land ravaged by refugees and by the Swarms.

As if in a trance, he walked past the mound of monsters.

A claw extended.

Touched him on the shoulder.

He stood quite still.

Waiting.

For what?

To die.

The claw dug into his flesh.

The moon . . . shifted behind cloud . . . then emerged

again . . . then . . . was swallowed by a whale-bellied thunderhead of cloud . . .

. . . and the claw . . .

The claw relaxed, shifted.

Drake dropped to his knees.

The claw fell free.

Scraped on the stones of the Salt Road.

Drake, on his belly, flowed away, soundless, silent.

Regained his bamboo pole, shouldered the weight, and stepped to the edge of the Salt Road. And started counting paces. Once he had counted off a hundred paces, he stopped. Now was the time to scream, to cry, to weep, to vomit.

He did none of those things.

Instead, he closed his eyes and breathed for a while, very slowly, very quietly. Concentrating on his breath. Breath is life. So said the weapons muqaddam.

'I am alive,' said Drake.

He was alive, even though Selzirk had fallen. He was alive, even though the world had ended. And what now? Well, he had decided that already – the only chance was to push on east. To Chenameg.

Burdened by his bamboo pole, Drake marched. And did not stop for rest until he was exhausted. By that time, it was dawn. He laid himself down in a ditch, and he slept.

And dreamed.

And why, in his dreams, did the moon run red with blood? Why did he hear his father screaming as he fell from a coalcliff in Stokos, to die on the white-fanged rocks of the sea? Why did he dream himself dead, with Plovey his god in the after world? Why did he wake weeping?

'Courage,' whispered Drake to Drake.

And, that day, he lengthened his footsteps.

And, in time, saw mountains amidst the clouds to north and to south. And passed through the Mountain Gap, thus leaving the Harvest Plains for Chenameg.

Rough ground. Huge forests dark with ancient trees.

Tall bamboo, talking in the ever-weeping wind. Mud. Quarry pits. Abandoned mines. The hutches of poverty. A burnt-out town. A single giant centipede, which he evaded.

He came upon a scene of slaughter. A Galish kafila had been attacked. Dead men and dead camels lay together, maggots swarming within their flesh without favour. Everything worth having had been looted; all that remained was bales of hemp and ixtle, urns of coffee and hyson, blocks of nephrite jade and ingots of steel.

No food.

That evening, Drake came upon three men who sat by the river, cooking an animal of sorts on a gad. Rough men they were, with the smell of blood about them.

'What's that you're cooking?' asked Drake.

'Aardvark,' came the answer.

'It looks good,' said Drake.

And, when they saw he accepted their lie, they let him sit and share. Which he did, even though he knew the animal was human.

'What's your name, young gaberlunzie?' they asked.

'Oleg,' said Drake, thinking his uncle's name would serve as well as any other for the moment.

And he let them feed him strong drink, pretending to fuzzle himself on the liquor. When they saw the cup tremble in his hands, tremble enough to make wavelets jabble from side to side, they drew knives and attacked.

But of course their victim was still stone cold sober.

And, shortly, two corpses lay at Drake's feet. The third man was in the river. Drake resented his departure, for the villain had carried away Drake's sword as he fell backwards (very dead) into the waterflow.

'A knife will serve for the moment,' said Drake.

And made camp, for he had good meat to smoke for proper preservation before he pushed on east.

And then, through rain and mud and mist and cloud, he persevered upriver, coming in due course to the Gates of Chenameg.

Here the Velvet River entered Chenameg, boiling out through a narrow gorge. A path clung to the southernmost flank of that precipitous gorge. The path offered the only road inland; elsewhere, gaunt cliffs confronted the traveller.

But none could follow the path for free.

A gang of the rough and the reckless had set themselves up as masters of the Gates of Chenameg. They had built a huge gabionade to deny public access to the path. This gabionade had no gates; the only way to enter was by rope ladders, which were lowered at need then pulled up again.

To get through, and travel further inland, it was necessary to pay with food, gold, jade, jewels or women.

But, as yet, the need of the travelling public was not desperate. For, as yet, few monsters of the Swarms had been sighted in Chenameg. So a huge refugee camp had grown up in front of the Gates of Chenameg. And here, in a squalor of mud and filth and rain and refuse, thousands of the half-starved eked out their rations, traded, bartered, cheated, gambled, pimped, whored, stole, fought, and patronized a rabble of astrologers and fortune tellers.

Drake went straight to the Gates, and offered himself for hire.

'What are you?' they asked.

'A master swordsman,' he said.

'But you have no sword!' they said.

And threw things at him. First clods, then rocks. So he retreated, and scoured amongst the camp, seeking steel for sale. Much there was, and cheap, but most was worthless. He saw any number of worthless duelling swords, their thin blades welded to the hilts. But what he wanted was good steel, blade and tang forged as a single unit.

In the end, he found what he was seeking.

And bought it, with five fists of meat.

Then took it away, and drew it to a rare ray of winter sunlight, and gloated. Steel it was, and slender, light enough to thrust with, yet with weight enough to hack wood at will, or cleave head from shoulders. Within the blade, the play of light and shadow hinted at a thousand interlaced perfections.

'Now,' said Drake, 'to seek some honest employment.'

So he went back to the gabionade which guarded the Gates of Chenameg. But another weaponmaster was there before him. And Drake saw the man go up a rope ladder all happy-eager, then his corpse come down without his weapon.

'So much for that,' said Drake to Drake.

And found work as protection man for a tented brothel, taking his payment in meals for each of his appetites. Meanwhile, he put out word as wide as he could. He was interested in a woman. Red in hair, red in skin – not by dye but by nature.

Now, in the face of the Swarms, there were but three reasonable routes of escape.

One was to outrun their onslaught north by fleeing along the Salt Road. Many had taken that route, some with success – and others without.

A second was to try for the west, daring the open waters of the Central Ocean. But that needed ships, and many who could flee that way had left it too late.

The last option was to head east. Inland. Which many had done. And, as the Swarms encroached further east, many who had broken their journey (to sojourn at hunting lodges or elsewhere) were driven to the gates of Chenameg.

And, towards the end of winter, Drake got news of a woman in red. He responded without undue excitement – there had been seven false alarms already – and followed the newsbearer to a rainshelter near the river.

Inside the rainshelter sat Plovey of the Regency, warming himself at a small fire.

Outside, two hulking men were working to erect another rainshelter. Sitting in the mud, hands tied behind their backs, were three women, roped neck to neck.

One was Zanya.

Who saw Drake, but did not shout or cry or even smile,

659

for she guessed that her silence would serve him best.

And Drake sauntered up nice and easy to the two hulking men putting up the rainshelter.

'Good morning,' said Drake, polite as anything.

'It's afternoon,' said one of the men, without turning.

'Why, so it is,' said Drake.

And knifed him.

'Gurumph!' cried the knifed man, in a choked voice.

And fell.

The other leaped back and drew a dirk.

And Drake stamped down hard in the underfoot muck, blinking his eyes at just the right moment. But the other fellow got mud in his eyes, and was dead before he could clear them. Dead with his own dirk buried to the hilt in his heart.

'What's going on here?' asked Plovey of the Regency, stepping out of his rainshelter.

'Murder,' answered Drake grimly, drawing his sword.

Plovey looked at him in silence. Then, slowly, drew his own blade.

'You dare much, darling boy,' said Plovey. 'For I am acknowledged as a master of the blade.'

'Aye, maybe,' said Drake. 'But I am my father's son.'

'And what means that?'

'Put steel to steel and find out,' said Drake.

And strode forward.

There was no braggadocio about him: only business. He was utterly calm. He felt remote from what was happening. It was like something in a dream.

The thin winter sun shone down as the two men clashed. Blade chimed against blade. And Drake beat down Plovey's blade, and struck. And the pitiless perfection of his sword drove home, going deep, deep, deep through skin and flesh and bone and vein.

Thus was the need of steel slaked with gore, and, when Drake withdrew the blade, the blood-eddy shimmered in the glittering sun.

And Plovey fell.

Flopping to the mud like a dead fish.

And the spray of mud and blood and water which scattered from his corpse broke Drake's dream-trance, and suddenly he was hot, hot, hot and burning.

He cut Zanya loose.

They said nothing, but kissed.

Then held each other.

Then wept.

Then clouds consumed the sun, and the heavens wept with them.

58

Royalty: a notion devised in an attempt to consolidate tyranny through genetic inheritance, to deny the rightful aspirations of the common people, to cripple the Class Struggle and thereby institutionalize feudalism.

In Argan, the real power has, in most places, been for generations in the hands of the guilds and immortal government bureaucracies. Even so, lip service has still been paid to the notion of the superiority of the Favoured Blood – and those of the Blood have clung fiercely to any surviving privileges remaining to them.

Superstition, assiduously cultivated by state propaganda in the form of fairy tales, has long convinced the common people of Argan that those of the Favoured Blood are in fact their actual rulers – and that only such are fit to rule.

Night.

Drake and Zanya, drowsy with love, lay between grubby sheep-skins, talking.

'You'll throw out Plovey's head tomorrow, won't you?' said Zanya.

'Why?' said Drake.

'Well . . . gloating is all very well, lover dearest, but soon it'll start to smell.'

'I want to keep it till I'm lord of the Gates of Chenameg,' said Drake. 'Then I'll plant it on a stake by way of display.'

'You think to master the Gates?' said Zanya, amused.

'Why not?'

'Dearest heart, you don't have the necessary stature to become a ruler.'

'That's all right,' said Drake. 'I'll get a pair of built-up boots.'

'That's not what I meant, and you know it,' said Zanya. 'I mean, you're not of royal birth.'

'I'm rightful king of Stokos,' said Drake, 'for King Tor named me his heir.'

'You've told me all about that,' said Zanya. 'Thrice. But he's dead. And you never got to marry his princess daughter. You'll have to do better than that, I'm afraid.'

'No problem,' said Drake. 'I've a world of fatherhood to choose from. Should I be a prince of the Rice Empire, perhaps?'

'No, fool!' said Zanya. 'For the Rice Empire is an ancient enemy of the Harvest Plains.'

'Then I'll think of something else,' said Drake.

'Think of me for a change,' said Zanya.

'Dearest . . .' said Drake.

And thought of her diligently.

Sometime later, drowsier still, Drake said:

'Did I ever tell you about Blackwood and Miphon?'

'Miphon I know well,' said Zanya, 'for I spoke often and long with the wizard on Burntos. But Blackwood? Who's he?'

'A woodsman,' said Drake. 'Remember? In Estar—'

'Oh, yes!' said Zanya. 'I remember now. He found us when you'd got us lost in the forest.'

'When I'd got us lost! It was you who said that strange little path would lead to safety!'

'Me?' said Zanya. 'I said it looked interesting, that's all. I never said we had to walk down it through five thousand leagues of mud and brambles!'

'Gah!' said Drake.

'Anyway,' said Zanya. 'I remember your Blackwood now. He had a wife. Misral? Mysral?'

'Mystrel,' said Drake.

'Trust you to remember the woman!' said Zanya. 'But

663

she wasn't anything to look at. Neither was that Blackwood. A rather dull fellow, in fact.'

'Yes,' said Drake. 'but did you know? Blackwood and Miphon both became questing heroes in company with Morgan Hearst.'

'Oh, Hearst!' said Zanya. 'that warlord fellow! He killed all gossip in Selzirk for days, for all the talk was of him. I wonder where he got to in the end? Anyway – what's all of this got to do with you and me?'

'Don't you see?' said Drake. 'If someone like Blackwood can become a questing hero, then what's to stop me being anything I please?'

'There's a big difference,' said Zanya severely, 'between being a questing hero and being a king. For a start, in every fairy tale I ever heard, potential kings always had a great doom written on their brow.'

'That's daft!' said Drake.

'Yes,' said Zanya, 'but that's what the fairy tales say, so that's what people expect. You won't get far without it.'

'I don't hold with this writing stuff,' said Drake. 'Not on my brow or anywhere.'

'You've got a snake ruling your love life,' said Zanya, 'so what's a few words on your forehead?'

'The snake's private,' said Drake. 'Nobody sees it unless they're entitled to. But words on my brow – man, people will laugh themselves sick.'

'They won't,' said Zanya. 'These are troubled times. People are desperate for leadership, for belief. Talk boldly, and you'll gather them in to your leadership.'

'So you do think I can do it!'

'Of course, darling treasure snake.'

'You sounded doubtful enough before.'

'Don't you know when I'm teasing you?' said Zanya. 'Tomorrow . . . tomorrow we'll make a start.'

The very next day, Zanya scavenged some paint. With that paint she wrote A GREAT DOOM on Drake's forehead in Galish orthography.

They were ready to begin.

59

The Gates of Chenameg: endpoint of the Manaray Gorge.

Here the Velvet River enters Chenameg, pouring in a torrent from between two cliffs. A steep and narrow path cut into the side of the southernmost cliff provides the sole practicable route inland from Chenameg.

THE CHRONICLE OF ÆNOβÆ

Of Dreldragon and his Doings at Chenameg
Now let me tell of Lord Dreldragon, and of his coming to the Gates of Chenameg.

Lord Dreldragon was heir to the Scattered Empire, the sea-power realm of the southern seas, which stretches from Ling to Hexagon. Mighty were the weaponmasters of that realm, and beautiful were the women; but, more than either, the kingdom valued its honour.

And it came to pass that Lord Dreldragon heard rumour of great disaster in Argan.

And he said unto his father, the great Jon Arabin:

'My lord king, is it right that we should sit in idleness while a continent entire falls to the evil of the Swarms?

And his father answered him thus:

'It is written that a darkness will fall over Argan and will persist for tens of years upon thousands. Such is the fate of fair and foul alike. What can we avail against prophecy?'

'That we know not until we try,' said Lord Dreldragon.

And, grim in decision, he took the battle-sword Warwolf, which had been in his family for thrice five generations, and he went forth from the Scattered Empire that he might contend with the mighty evil which was come upon Argan.

With him went the Lady Zanya, whom he had taken to be his lawful wedded wife, for she was a woman strong in decision, and there was naught beneath the stars which could daunt her courage.

And thus the two came unto Argan, where they had command of armies. These armies they led against the monsters of the Swarms. And many fell deeds were seen beneath sun and beneath stars. But, in the end, heroism availed not against prophecy, and all who survived from the wars against the Swarms retreated into Chenameg.

Now it happened that toward spring in the year Celadric 2, Lord Dreldragon and the Lady Zanya came unto the Gates of Chenameg.

The people were amazed to see them, for surely there was nobility about them. For the Lady Zanya was not as other women, but walked with the stars about her. And the wise, when they looked on Lord Dreldragon, saw that a mighty doom was upon his brow, and they knew him for the son of a king.

And they asked him:

'What do you here?'

And he answered:

'I bring justice.'

But there was a rough-speaking brigand by name of Plovey who said:

'What need have we of justice when the very skies are falling? Now is the time for rape, slaughter, butchery, the rule of strength over weakness, of steel over flesh.'

And he drew a blade against Lord Dreldragon.

But the blade Warwolf availed over Plovey, and his head was buried separate from his trunk.

Now it happened that at that time great Groth, master of the hordes of evil, held the Gates of Chenameg against those who sought refuge from the Swarms. There was but one passage out of Chenameg, and that was through the Gates. For long had Groth sore oppressed the people, and Lord Dreldragon saw that his rule was an abomination.

Thus Lord Dreldragon tempted Groth with rumours of a mighty wealth to the south. And Groth rode out with a warparty. But Lord Dreldragon and those men he had rallied around him fell upon Groth in a place of ambush, and made a mighty slaughter.

Then Lord Dreldragon returned to the Gates of Chenameg with Groth as a hostage. But his lieutenants laughed, and said:

'Are we not men, even as Groth was? And can we not therefore govern in our own right?'

Whereupon Lord Dreldragon set Groth at liberty to walk amongst his ancestors.

Then Lord Dreldragon said to those who held the Gates:

'Know that I am of the Favoured Blood. I am descended from a royal line, appointed by Higher Powers to rule over lesser mortals. Yield to my lordship, for your submission is fitting.'

But those who held the Gates laughed mightily, then threw rocks, then threw worse.

Therefore Lord Dreldragon said unto them:

'Very well. Hold the heights, and I will hold the flats, and there will be no war between us, for I will yield up a rich tribute daily.'

And the next day he brought a great tribute in meat and wine. And he said:

'Point to any portion, and I will eat thereof and drink thereof, that you may know it safe.'

And this was done.

Then meat and drink were taken into the fortress of the Gates of Chenameg, and those within glutted themselves on the goodness, for they had seen nothing so good for many a day.

But, while they were eating, a doom came upon them, and all but a few were struck by death.

Then the Lady Zanya stepped forward and spoke in a voice of wrath to those still upon the Gates:

'Behold me, for I am a princess of Hexagon. Deep is the magic of our islands, and fell is my skill. A doom have I put upon you. Those yet standing will die before the morrow but for my mercy.'

Then those who survived surrendered, and came down from the fortress that they might receive the mercy of the Lady Zanya. And she gave them a magical wine, which brought a swift death upon them.

Then Lord Dreldragon and the Lady Zanya held the Gates in justice, and their levy on the traffic which went inland was but 10 per cent.

Yet this justice was not welcomed by all.

For it happened that a band of priests came to the Gates. With them was an old man whom they named as Gouda Muck. They alleged that Muck was the High God of All Gods. And the priests disputed the right of Lord Dreldragon and his consort to live – let alone to rule.

For the priests claimed Lord Dreldragon to be the son of the Demon Hagon.

'Who says?' declared Lord Dreldragon.

'Gouda Muck says,' replied the priests.

'Then let Gouda Muck stand forward and declare it so,' answered Lord Dreldragon.

Then were the priests loath to permit Gouda Muck to speak. But a mob had gathered around the priests, and the mob denied choice to them.

Thus it was that Gouda Muck stood forth and spoke unto Lord Dreldragon and unto the fair Lady Zanya and unto the multitude.

And Gouda Muck gazed around in perplexity, then declared that the streets of Selzirk were passing fair, that the blossoms strewn beneath his feet were sweet, and that the thousand naked maidens dancing before him were beautiful to behold.

Then one cried from the mob that there were no maidens and there was no blossom, that Selzirk was fallen and that the Swarms had over-run the Harvest Plains.

Whereupon Gouda Muck frowned, and said:

'That man is mad! Arrest him!'

Then Gouda Muck spoke as if he saw before him first trial then execution.

And he then spoke in a high voice to people not present. He addressed the rulers of Yestron and of Dalar ken Halvar. He accepted tribute in gold and in jade from mighty men invisible to the multitude.

And Lord Dreldragon declared:

'The old man is mad and has been for years. His madness is its own pardon. But as to the priests who knew he was mad, yet pretended to draw authority from him – in such men there is evil.'

Whereupon the mob fell upon the priests, and Lord Dreldragon was unable to offer them the benefits of his mercy.

And it came to pass that Gouda Muck dwelt at the Gates of Chenameg in his madness, and was fed and clothed and housed by Lord Dreldragon and his consort.

For Lord Dreldragon said:

'This man's madness has wrought much evil in the world. But many things wondrous fair have passed from the world in a great destruction. Muck is not fair nor wondrous, saving in the extent of his madness, yet I lack the will to add to the world's destruction by encompassing his doom.'

And it happened that when Gouda Muck had lived at the Gates for seven moons, he died in his sleep, and was given to the mercies of the river.

Then it came to pass, after Lord Dreldragon had held the Gates for upwards of a year, that the Swarms were seen before the very fortress of the Gates.

Then Lord Dreldragon said:

'They cannot pass beyond the Gates, for the cliffs are sheer, the river swift, and the path scarce fit for goats. Truly the mountains will stand sentinel here, for now and for all time.

'We have held the Gates in justice for upwards of a year, and there is no need remaining here for our strength. Therefore let us depart, for such ghosts as remain here can hold the Gates as well as we.'

Thus they departed, taking with them such food as they could carry, and such gear of war. And they endured the suffering of the Dragon Way, as others had before them.

To the borders of the Araconch Waters they went, then passed beneath the shadow of Mountain Barg, which was named in antiquity for Barglan of the Empire. And thus they passed into the Broken Lands, then followed the River Amodeo even to the Lanmarthen Marshes.

Then Lord Dreldragon declared that he would turn west and dare the Dry Forages and the mountains beyond, for it came to him that it was meet that he should return once more to his homeland. And the Lady Zanya declared that she would venture with him, for she was constant in her love for him, and their marriage had always been a chastity proof against all temptation.

But the others were sore afraid, fearing to try the westward way lest they come upon creatures of the Swarms. Therefore Lord Dreldragon released them from all oaths of fealty, and they parted to their separate dooms. Thus did Lord Dreldragon turn his face to the west, vanishing from the sight of history.

And his companions travelled east, and came in the fullness of time to the seaport city of Brine, and thereafter their ways were scattered unto all the nations.

And through this scattering the tale of Lord Dreldragon came to the shores of Ashmolea, and thus to the opportunity of this Chronicle, which is written straight and true, telling only of things well-witnessed and therefore verified as true . . .

60

Trest and Estar: the two halves of a plain at the base of the Penvash Peninsular in the north-west of Argan. Trest is the eastern half, with a northern seacoast facing the North Strait. A swamp divides Trest from Estar, which has a western seacoast facing the Central Ocean.

Drake and Zanya parted from the last of their followers at the point where the Amodeo River entered the Lanmarthen Marshes. The followers went downriver towards Brine, which lay to the east. But the two lovers turned upstream, following a branch of the river into the Dry Forages.

Upstream, in the Dry Forages, the riverbranch they followed shrank to a shallow sun-slashed rush of water over shingle. It bent toward the north.

'If we march north,' said Drake, 'we reach mountains. Beyond them, the Scourside Coast.'

'And to west?' said Zanya.

'Desolation. Then mountains. Then a rough road by river, forest and highland, taking us at last to Trest, and then to Estar.'

'Which choose you?' said Zanya.

'Whichever you agree to,' said Drake.

'You've heard more tales of the inland than have I,' said Zanya. 'Choose.'

'Well,' said Drake. 'North, to the Scourside Coast . . . that takes us to the shores of the North Strait. That's a bitter place at the best of times. West . . . the road leads

671

sooner to hearth and food, if any such have survived the Swarms.'

'West it is,' said Zanya.

Leaving the river, they trekked westward across a stumblestone wasteland of dust, wind, sun and broken rock. Then they came upon a range of mountains.

'Beyond those mountains,' said Drake, 'we may find the Swarms.'

'I love you,' said Zanya.

They kissed, renewing the vows of trust and devotion.

Then shouldered their packs and dared themselves west. Hints of long-ruined road helped them find the way to a pass between the mountains.

As they chanced the pass, they were full of trepidation. Drake had spoken the truth. For all they knew, the Swarms might have overrun the entire western seaboard of the continent of Argan. In which case, they might well encounter monsters beyond the mountains.

Yet, while they feared, they also hoped. Drake, in particular, hoped to find some way to return to Stokos. For, now that Gouda Muck was dead, surely Goudanism must be entering its last days. Drake desired to return home, taking Zanya with him as his wife.

As the travellers neared the end of the pass, they were confronted with a wilderness of jumbled rock which had crisp, sharp fracture-lines showing no sign of weathering. This rock had been shattered within the last few years.

'Perhaps there was an earthquake here,' said Zanya.

'And perhaps not,' said Drake grimly.

He thought he knew what might have caused this shattering.

After labouring for a day over shattered rock, the two lovers reached a river running from north to south. Both banks were a wreckage of broken rock.

'We stand, I think, on the banks of the Fleuve River,' said Drake. 'This is, I believe, where a death-stone was once used by a wizard named Heenmor. The death-stone brought the very cliffs to life.'

672

'Says who?' said Zanya.

'Says I,' said Drake. 'I had part of the story from men who travelled with that questing hero of undying fame, Morgan Hearst. Those men fled downriver on rafts before the very cliffs themselves began to move. So part of the tale I have by observation of what is here, and by deductions from that observation. I see—'

'I see,' said Zanya, 'that we are in danger of hearing another lecture on the Scientific Method.'

This was something of a sore point between them. While ruling at the Gates of Chenameg, Drake had got into the habit of pontificating at length on such subjects as the Theory of Knowledge, Axiom-Structured Discourse and the Reductive Crisis of Categorizations. They had had more than one row about it.

'I'm sorry,' said Drake. 'I didn't mean to start preaching. I must've caught the habit from Gouda Muck. You can't live with a weird old bugger like that for year on year without getting a bit strange yourself. Anyway, from here we have to go north, up this river. Then cross the river. Then we go west through the Kikashi Hills into Trest.'

And that they did.

As they went, Drake dreamed of his future.

At the Gates of Chenameg, Drake had tested and refined his ability to lead, to rule and to govern. He had made many mistakes – some of them almost disastrous – but he had survived. Yes. Even though he had faced mutiny, subversion, treason . . .

He was sure he would be able to rule on Stokos, if he got the chance.

There were obstacles to overcome, of course.

He would have to overthrow the last remnants of Goudanism, if any such survived. Who ruled on Stokos now? When the pirates were driven from Androlmarphos, had Stokos stayed loyal to its rulers from the Teeth? Or had the locals seized the chance for revolution?

Worse still – might the Swarms have got a foothold on

673

Stokos? If they had, it might be a devil of a job driving them from the island.

'Whoever rules on Stokos,' said Drake to Drake, 'whether it's pirates, priests of the Flame or the Swarms themselves, I'll likely need an army to take the island. Aye. And ships to move the army. My nobility itself will not suffice.'

But he was sure ships and army would not prove impossible to come by.

'This,' said Drake to Drake, 'is my destiny. To rule as a king. I feel it in my bones.'

Whatever he felt in his bones, he felt hunger in his belly, for their long lean march saw them scavenging slugs and earthworms before they were finished.

At last, in early summer in the year Celadric 3, Drake and Zanya entered Trest from the east. They were intercepted by a patrol of Rangers, roving Rovac warriors who maintained order on the eastern marches. The Rovac directed them to the nearest nameworthy place, the High Castle of Trest, a stronghold held by Captain Occam for the Triple Kings – Hearst, Blackwood and Miphon.

'I once heard of three questing heroes thus named,' said Drake.

'Our kings are the same three,' came the answer. 'It is their peace we enforce.'

'Good,' said Drake.

This was a welcome piece of news indeed. He was acquainted with all three of the Triple Kings, which should make things easy enough when it came time to persuade them to lend him ships and an army. Meantime – he had other, more urgent problems to worry about.

Zanya had not been in proper health for some time, and her condition was worsening. Odd fevers took her; she suffered night sweats, diarrhoea, nausea without explanation. Sometimes she found herself icy cold and shivering in the noonday summer sun.

She was not pregnant.

Thus Drake was glad when they reached the High Castle,

an ancient wizard stronghold of daunting battlements and sky-challenging towers, all girt round with a flame trench which could only be crossed by a single drawbridge.

In this grim fortress was the mint which had just that season begun producing the gladiate coins which the ruling regime had decreed were to become the currency of the realm. Drake, with some reservations, traded a little gold for this odd-shaped money, which he found good for the purchase of food and lodgings.

Drake and Zanya stayed for some days in a little village which was growing up in the shadow of the High Castle. But rest failed to improve Zanya's condition. Instead, her symptoms worsened, and she complained that there were lumps in her mouth.

'Lumps?' said Drake, with dread in his voice.

He remembered. A room on Stokos. The body. Grinning red. Blood. So much blood.

'Yes, lumps,' said Zanya. 'Have a look and . . . and tell me what colour those lumps might be.'

'I'll not do that,' said Drake, 'unless you promise you will never cut your throat.'

'Why should I do that?' asked Zanya.

Drake made no answer.

They both knew why.

'Come on,' said Zanya. 'Be a man! Look! And tell!'

Drake looked, as best he could, peering into the dark, wet, saliva-gleaming cave of her mouth, where an unruly tongue and a jiggling uvula seemed to be doing their best to frustrate his examination. As far as he could tell – which, admittedly, was not far at all – there were blue lumps all the way down her throat.

Sky-blue lumps.

He felt sick.

'It's the blue leprosy, isn't it?' said Zanya.

Drake made no answer, but his face told all. They held each other close. They wept. For both knew the score.

Blue lepers died a terrible death. First came outbreaks of blue sores. Then, in time, great septic ulcers. Then,

675

after about a year, a black rot which turned the eyes to jelly. Then, eventually, gangrene, bringing death in the second year. And Drake thought:

Is this my fault?

He had known for years that he might be contaminated with blue leprosy. After all, his sister had become infected with it. Yet he had taken no precautions to keep Zanya safe . . .

'We need help,' said Drake, at last.

'There is no help for this,' said Zanya.

Drake knew as much. The wizard Miphon had, years ago, brought knowledge of the disease to Stokos. Blue leprosy was incurable. It led to a certain death.

'We have to try,' said Drake.

And almost launched into a disquisition on the Experimental Method. He halted himself just in time, and went in search of a healer. But the best he could find was a drunken surgeon who tended to the garrison in the High Castle.

'My wife has a sickness,' said Drake.

'What kind of sickness?'

'Oh, a fever, which comes and goes.'

'Has she blue sores?' asked the surgeon.

Drake hesitated. Then decided he must give an honest answer, for that was the only way to win any cure which might be available.

'Aye,' he said, 'blue sores in her mouth and elsewhere.'

Whereupon the surgeon had both Drake and Zanya arrested, and walled up in a cell, leaving only a single hole big enough for food and water to be passed through.

'How do we get out of here?' said Zanya.

'I don't think we do,' answered Drake.

But, fortunately, the surgeon reported his actions to Captain Occam, who held the High Castle for the Triple Kings. Occam promptly had the wall broken down, and had the captives taken to his private quarters.

'The wizard Miphon has spread the truth about this disease,' said Occam.

676

'What truth does Miphon tell about the blue leprosy?' said Drake.

'First, that it is not leprosy but a pox,' said Occam. 'He has given it a new name. We now call it blue star fever. Yet still the surgeon fears it, as he fears plague and other things. But Lord Miphon says those with blue star fever are not to be feared, for the disease spreads only if one lies with the sick as a man lies with a woman.'

'What has Miphon said of a cure?' said Zanya.

'That there is none,' answered Occam, frankly. 'But he is wise, therefore thinks not that he knows all. He always searches for new wisdom. I have not spoken with him since spring. Who knows? His wisdom may by now encompass a cure for blue star fever.'

Occam advised Drake to take Zanya to Lorford, in Estar, to see Miphon, who was usually to be found at Lorford.

'But say nothing of disease to anyone on the way,' said Occam. 'Or you may never reach Lorford alive.'

'I passed through Lorford once before,' said Drake, 'and heard no mention of blue leprosy then. It seems the thing has spread, aye, and that people fear it more.'

'The whole world,' said Occam, 'has been thrown into flux by war and invasion. Thousands travel down roads which once saw but a handful of strangers a season. When thousands suffer and starve, women sell their flesh to eat – as do some men. Thus we have new fears, and new diseases. Cultures clash, and—'

'Yes, yes,' said Drake, who, as an accomplished orator himself, knew the start of a long speech when he heard it. 'I get the message.'

'Then don't forget it!' said Occam. 'Keep your mouth shut! And make your journey swift, for your woman will weaken by the day.'

So Drake hired a donkey cart and a guide, and off they went. Swamps lay between Trest and Estar, but these were crossed easily enough by a corduroy road, built when Collosnon armies once invaded Argan, and now kept in repair by work gangs financed by the state.

Thus Drake and Zanya crossed into Estar and proceeded to Lorford, a town on the banks of the Hollern River, which here flowed west toward the Central Ocean. Both Drake and Zanya remembered the place, for, after escaping from Penvash years ago, they had stopped here briefly before proceeding down the Salt Road to Runcorn.

But all had changed since their last visit, when a mighty castle had dominated Melross Hill. The castle had since been smashed by war or magic; only a shattered wreckage of splintered stone and undying wizard-fire remained.

In Lorford, Drake sought an inn where Zanya could rest. He found one, soon enough. The innkeeper, who must have been a refugee from the Harvest Plains, was speaking with some cronies in Churl, but when Drake and Zanya entered he switched to Galish.

'I want a big room,' said Drake. 'A quiet room, where my wife can rest.'

'Is she sick?' said the innkeeper.

The suspicion in the man's voice gave Drake all the warning he needed.

'She's with child,' he said, telling an easy lie. 'So a little poorly at times. Needs tenderness, aye.'

'That's all right then. As long as she's got no illness.'

'Nay, man. She never has a day's fever in her life, for she was born tough, aye, fathered by a mule and all.'

'By a mule? How so? Through what evil?'

'Man,' said Drake, irritated, 'I meant but to joke a little.'

'Yes, well. The fewer jokes the better. These are troubled times.'

In the room, Drake made Zanya comfortable. He saw, to his dismay, that a tiny blue spot had appeared at one corner of her mouth. He said nothing to her about it, but kissed her goodbye. Easy enough to kiss her now, yes. But what about later? When her body was filthy with bloated sores? When her eyes melted to pits of corruption? When her body decayed towards gangrene?

678

'Don't cry, dearest treasure snake,' said Zanya.

But Drake could not help himself. And, while he had intended to leave immediately, it was in fact a long time before he pulled himself together and went to see the innkeeper.

'Where do your kings hold court?' asked Drake.

'Why ask you?'

'Man,' said Drake, 'because my sword wishes to be of service to kings.'

'Then go to the west gate, for the western gatehouse is palace, gaol, fort, arsenal, treasury and citadel, all rolled into one.'

The western gatehouse proved to be a stout building of logs, plankwork and bamboo. It was four storeys high, and was as square as it was tall. Drake went swaggering up to the entrance, as bold as a rat boarding a battleship, and demanded an immediate audience with Lord Miphon.

'Why,' said the guards, 'he's in Looming Forest, after herbs and such. As for Lord Blackwood, he's in the forest also, settling a disputed timber claim. But you'll find Lord Hearst on the riverbank just an arrowshot south of here.'

'Doing what?'

'Why, administering justice, that's what.'

So Drake went that arrowshot south, and found a crowd of people by the riverbank, where Morgan Hearst was administering justice. Drake stood back to watch. Hearst was speaking in Galish. Did the Rovac warrior know the local Estral? Perhaps. But doubtless Lorford was peopled mostly by refugees, with Galish the only tongue they held in common.

'All right, all right,' shouted Hearst, 'that's adoptions done with. Now how many of you want to get divorced? Come on, let's have a show of hands! All right, form two lines, men on this side, women on that side. Move it along now, we haven't got all day!

'Where's your wife? She's dead!? Sorry, we can't divorce the dead, not here, you need a thaumaturgist for that. One's set up shop by Berick's timberyard.'

679

Once the would-be divorcees had been regimented into ranks, Hearst conducted a ceremony of his own devising, which saw him striding up and down between the ranks scattering handfuls of leaves from last year's autumn while shouting:

'I divorce you! I divorce you! I divorce you!'

Then, as the crowd began to break up, Hearst shouted:

'Remember, I'm doing marriages tomorrow morning. So if you see anyone here you fancy, try them out tonight and be here by the morn's morn.'

With the main business of the day evidently over, a few petitioners approached Hearst. He dealt with them swiftly, grinding one petition underfoot, slashing another with the steel hook-claw which served him instead of a right hand, and ordering one petitioner to go jump in the river (which, of course, he duly did). Thus it was with some uneasiness that Drake approached.

On their last meeting, in Selzirk, Hearst had thought (rightly!) that he had seen Drake before. This time, the Rovac warrior's face showed not the slightest sign of recognition.

'Who are you?' he said.

Drake was hurt not to be recognized. He also found Hearst's brusque manner hard to take. After playing out elaborate charades of royalty for over a year at the Gates of Chenameg, Drake was still finding it hard to adjust to his present status as an ordinary citizen.

'We met in Selzirk,' said Drake.

'Why, maybe we did. Have you any idea the thousands I've met in my travels?'

'I brought you a message from Elkor Alish.'

'Ah . . . I remember the message right enough, but not the messenger. Are you seeking reward after all these years?'

'I seek the healer Miphon.'

'Have you a pox, have you?'

'My woman is sick.'

'Then take her to Mystrel, Blackwood's wife. She's

680

good with women things. Look, that place on the hill. See? That's the House of Health. Well, what are you waiting for? Hurry along!'

So Drake hurried. When he reached Mystrel's House of Health, half way up Melross Hill, a birth was in progress, so he had to wait to see the healer. But, soon enough, out she came into the sunlight. She was as he remembered her from their previous meeting in Blackwood's house in Looming Forest: a work-worn middle-aged woman. She must have forgotten him entirely, for she asked straight out:

'Are you the herbalist with the master-wort for sale?'

'No . . . I come because my – my wife is sick.'

'And invisible into the bargain?' said Mystrel, looking around.

'No, she's back at the town.'

'What, too sick to walk?'

'No, she—'

'Then bring her here! I can't read disease at a distance!'

Whereupon Drake hustled back to the town. At the inn, the innkeeper was still in conversation with his cronies.

'Did your sword find service with the kings?' said the innkeeper.

'Not yet,' said Drake.

'Nay,' jeered one of the innkeeper's cronies. 'For—'

The rest of what he said was in Churl, and Drake understood only enough to realize that something very rude was being said. Shrugging off the insult, he went to his rented room, where Zanya greeted him. Perhaps it was just Drake's imagination, but the blue sore at the side of Zanya's mouth seemed to have grown larger in his absence.

'Come,' he said. 'We're going to see Mystrel.'

'Has she a cure?' said Zanya.

'I know not what she has,' said Drake. 'That we'll discover when we get there.'

As they were leaving the inn, a voice cried:

'Hey!'

'Keep walking,' murmured Drake to Zanya. 'Slowly.'

But he heard footsteps behind, following them out into the hot sunlight. So he turned to face his danger. The innkeeper had come outside, three of his friends with him.

'Yon woman's got a sore on her face,' said the innkeeper.

'Aye,' said Drake. 'A gadfly bit her.'

'No gadfly ever bit blue. That's a leper you've got there. A blue leper.'

'Man,' said Drake, 'whatever she is, we're leaving.'

The innkeeper spat.

'Leaving? To spread plague through Lorford? Oh, not so easy!'

He nodded at one of his companions, who slipped away. To summon help? Doubtless. That left two men to back up the innkeeper. So Drake drew blade and challenged:

'Which dies first?'

The three scarpered at the sight of his steel. Once they had retreated into the inn, Drake sheathed his blade. He was fit, strong and long-breathed – but, even so, his breath was whipping in and out as quick as a frog's tongue, and his heart was hammering as if it had fifty knives to forge by nightfall. Turning to Zanya, he saw she was crying.

'Love,' said Drake, 'none will hurt you while I've sword by my side.'

'They hate me!' she said, crying the more.

He kissed and soothed her as best he could, trying to appear calm although he was desperately impatient to be gone. Lorford was dangerous. When they did get clear of the town, he looked behind often to make sure there was no pursuit.

Zanya was sweating heavily by the time they reached the House of Health. As they entered the cool shadows within, Mystrel greeted them. She examined Zanya's face, and became grave.

'We have seen none of this for a season,' she said.

'What is it?' asked Drake, hoping she would give him an answer different to the one he knew.

'An illness,' said Mystrel. 'An illness which many fear. What is your name, love? Zanya? Then come in, Zanya, for there's a welcome for you amongst the women. We've met before, haven't we? I remember you by your red skin. Come! Why hesitate?'

'I'll not come inside,' said Zanya, with what bravery she could muster. 'No, not if I'll spread sickness.'

'This illness,' said Mystrel, with a glance at Drake. 'It's spread only when two lie together as a woman lies with a man.'

Mystrel led Zanya into a room for women, which Drake was forbidden to enter. Then she returned, and took Drake aside for serious talk.

'Likely you have the same disease yourself,' said Mystrel. 'Thus you must lie with no woman and with no man, or others will die of it.'

She was still counselling him when a young woman interrupted them.

'*Shaga endevin, Nickle*?' said Mystrel, slipping into her native Estral, a tongue unknown to Drake.

'*Inem preluce tim opsand,*' replied the young woman.

'Excuse me,' said Mystrel to Drake.

She made for the door. Curious, Drake followed. Standing in the shadows, he saw a lanky young man standing out in the sunlight.

'Oh no!' muttered Drake to Drake. 'Tell me it's not true!'

It was Sully Datelier Yot, his face crowded with as many warts as ever. On his head was a golden circlet of the type usually worn by princes in children's fairytales told on Stokos. This status symbol indicated pretensions to grandeur, but Drake doubted that Yot could have found real power under a regime run by sensible men like Morgan Hearst.

'What do you want?' said Mystrel to Yot.

'To enter and search, in the name of the kings!'

683

'Get away with you,' said Mystrel, scornfully.

'Is Lord Blackwood here?'

'No,' said Mystrel. 'I'd have words for him if he was. It's about time he got rid of you, you posing priestling.'

At that, Yot used his strength on the woman. He shoved her so she staggered backwards. Yot strode toward the door – and Drake came forward to meet him.

'Drake!' cried Yot.

'The same,' said Drake. 'With sword at side, as ever. What would you be wanting?'

'Some men in the town said blue lepers came this way. So they sent me to investigate.'

'Why you?' said Drake.

'Because he's a regular troublemaker,' said Mystrel.

'Because I've built trust in the town, for I have the ear of Lord Blackwood,' said Yot. 'For good reason, too, for I've a sharp mind, which is what the times are needing. Drake – bring out the woman.'

'What woman?' said Drake.

'Your Ebrell bitch. We're looking for a woman red in skin and red in hair. That makes her of Ebrell. Your Zanya answers the case.'

'Man,' said Drake, wishing he had killed Yot years ago, 'Zanya I've not seen since she was sold into slavery in Selzirk. That was seven seasons ago, man.'

Yot grinned.

'Away ran a woman red in hair and skin. With her ran a blond boy with a sword at his side.'

'Who do you call boy?' said Drake, drawing blade and advancing.

Yot danced away down the hill. Drake strode after him, hot for the kill. And saw, coming uphill, a dozen soldiers on horseback. They were very close.

'Prothero!' shouted Yot. 'There's the one we're looking for! Seize him!'

Drake, for all his fitness, could not outrun men on horseback. Nor did he try.

684

61

Sully Datelier Yot: was High Priest of the Flame on Stokos. When Swarms attacked Stokos, lost his nerve and fled the island with a band of supporters. Has been in Estar for three seasons; has small temple within the environs of Lorford, which has a total of seventy hard-core adherents of the Flame.

The soldiers, all from Lord Blackwood's personal bodyguard, were mounted on a motley bunch of horses. Armed and armoured in a bizarre range of fashions, they looked more like a band of brigands than a military unit. They arrested Drake on the spot.

'Search inside!' said Yot.

The soldiers demurred.

Yot screamed in anger. He threatened them with the wrath of Lord Blackwood. With beatings, gougings, torture, starvation and crucifixion. Reluctantly, the soldiers searched the House of Health until they found Zanya.

'Kill them both,' said Yot. 'Here! Now!' But the soldiers baulked at this. So Yot said: 'Then take them to my temple.'

'You do no such thing!' said Mystrel stoutly. 'If his temple gets hands on these innocents, they'll be dead in a blink. He talks about Lord Blackwood's wrath. Well I tell you this! Lord Blackwood will have no murder done in Lorford.'

'That's right!' cried Drake. 'Why, I knew him years ago when I was Estar's resident dragon-fighter. Man, he was

685

right hot on due process! That means courts, trials, pro-
cedures of law, high-paid flatulence by a dozen lawyers on
each side, witnesses, evidences and such. Aye, and writs of
all descriptions, each costing fifty times their own weight
in gold.'

'Shut up, you!' said Yot.

He grabbed a sword, determined to kill Drake on the
spot. But soldiers confiscated the sword before Yot could
strike.

'You know your danger now,' said Mystrel, lying like a
trooper. 'Our young friends worked for my husband for
years in days gone by. They were personal friends. Lord
Blackwood will kill you if you touch so much as a hair of
their heads.'

'She lies!' said Yot, too hoarse to scream any more.

'Boys,' said one of the soldiers, 'however you look at it,
we're in a mess. Let's do nothing hasty.'

The soldiers considered their options, then did the sensible thing, and delivered both Drake and Zanya to the
safety of the western gatehouse, there to be held until
Higher Authority could decide their fate.

'Why, prisoners,' said the gaoler in delight, when Drake
and Zanya were brought to the western gatehouse.

'Is that so rare?' said Drake.

'Yes, for my masters believe in death, exile, floggings,
fines or apologies, depending on the offence. Not caging
people.'

'So under what authority are we held here now?' said
Drake.

'Why, under Master Yot's authority,' said the gaoler.

'I suspect he's over-reached himself,' said Drake.

'Why, if he has, I'll gladly help you hang him,' said the
gaoler, unlocking a prison cell. 'Meantimes, in you go!'

'First, I'd like a lawyer,' said Drake.

'Well, you're shit out of luck, young friend,' said the
gaoler. 'For Lord Hearst hung every lawyer in Lorford on
Midwinter's Day, by way of celebration. Come on, in you
go! Don't look so jaw-fallen, it's pleasant enough within.'

Drake and Zanya went into the cell, which smelt of sandalwood. No mice, rats or roaches were in occupance: only shadows. The broad sleeping bench was draped with sheepskins which, on close examination, proved free from lice and fleas. All in all, it was, Drake had to admit, the cleanest, airiest, most comfortable prison cell he'd seen in his life. He still hated it.

Once they were locked in, Drake made Zanya comfortable and started Investigating his surroundings. A beam of light between two logs alerted him to the presence of a gap. Looking out, he saw a bit of a street.

People were gathering outside. Drake thought he saw a familiar face: the innkeeper he had so lately lodged with. The crowd was getting quite noisy. What were they saying? It was hard to tell, with so many voices shouting at once. He wished his field of vision was not so restricted.

'What do you see?' said Zanya.

'A gryphon mating with a manticore,' said Drake. 'Two dragons fighting over a piece of the sun. A bald dwarf circumcising a naked giant with a very sharp hatchet. A cloud giving birth to a kitten. A man in the street selling tiny stars tied to strings, aye, and flying frogs with yellow wings.'

'What's all the noise about then?' said Zanya.

'Why, the flying frogs are chasing the stars on strings, and the stars don't take kindly to being eaten.'

'Seriously,' said Zanya.

'Seriously, I think there's some kind of market going on,' said Drake, 'with a lot of screaming from people at auction, barkers shouting, haggling over prices, bickering over weights and measures, and three dozen truncheon men trying to keep order. Certainly nothing for us to worry about.'

In truth, Drake thought that things outside were building steadily toward a riot. Doubtless, the cause of the uproar was the presence of a blue leper in Lorford. He went to sit beside Zanya. Hid his face in her hair. Nuzzled at her neck.

'Darling treasure snake,' said Zanya, as he put his arms around her. 'They're getting rather noisy outside. What is going on? Really?'

The uproar without was unpleasantly reminiscent of the riot which had ended Drake's rule of Runcorn. Stones began to thump into the side of the western gatehouse.

'What is it?' said Zanya, now seriously alarmed.

'Nothing, my darling,' said Drake. 'Nothing.'

'It's us they want, isn't it?'

'Hush,' he said, holding her close. 'Hush . . .'

He did his best to soothe her to sleep. Finally, she closed her eyes and slept, or appeared to. But she sat up with a start when the door was opened to admit a slender, clean-shaven man older than Drake. He wore a broad-brimmed feathered hat, and had eyes of a startling green. He looked not a day older than when Drake had first seen him on Stokos.

'Arabin lol Arabin!' said the wizard Miphon.

'The same,' said Drake, with a bow, 'though I am known also as Drake Douay, as Dreldragon Drakedon Douay, as Lord Dreldragon and as Shen Shen Drax. And I have gone by other names still in my time. Indeed—'

'Enough history!' said Miphon. 'This . . . Zanya, is it not? I remember you well from Burntos.'

'As I remember you, sir,' said Zanya. 'How came you here?'

'Mystrel summoned me,' said the wizard Miphon. 'She sent a girl from her House of Health to ride forth to find me.'

'Have you come with a cure for this sickness?' said Drake.

'Mystrel knows as much of cures as I do,' said Miphon.

'But she is but a woman, and you a wizard!' said Drake. 'A great wizard, if half of legend is true! Surely you with your wizardly wisdom have a cure for this pox!'

'The legends are less than one tenth true,' said Miphon. 'As I've said already—'

'Man,' said Drake, with a threat in his voice. 'A wizard

688

knows more than a woman, surely. What's the cure?'

'The blood of a dragon,' said Miphon, slowly. 'That, mixed with the blood of a man is certain cure for all ills – though the cure has a cruel price. But we have no dragons in Estar. And your lady would not last the journey inland.'

So! There was a cure! The blood of a dragon mixed with the blood of a man.

'Must the blood be fresh?' said Drake.

'I believe,' said Miphon, 'both the dragon's blood and the human blood must be fresh.'

'And I believe we've precious little time for medical lectures,' said Zanya. 'The noise without grows by the moment.'

'It's market day,' said Miphon, hitting on the same lie that Drake had used. 'Think nothing of it.'

'It's a riot, isn't it?' said Zanya, sure of her facts even though the stone-throwing had stopped for the moment.

'Not . . . not yet.'

'But it will be,' said Zanya, 'won't it? They're stirring themselves up to kill us!' When Miphon made no reply, she said: 'Who is it? Who's out there?'

'Some few dozens who cry for leper-blood,' said Miphon reluctantly. 'Also, from Sully Yot's temple, about fifty lunatics who say we hold the son of the demon Hagon within.'

'While others join in for the fun of it,' said Zanya. 'Well – do you give us to the mob? Or do you let us escape from here?'

'She speaks sense,' said Drake. 'Man, you've two choices. Kill us, then throw the crowd their corpses. Or break us out of here, lest they storm this gatehouse. If they do that, they'll not stop there. They'll burn your town by nightfall.'

'It's easy to say,' said Miphon. 'But we lack the men to break you out past a mob like that.'

'What do you want?' said Drake. 'An army? Twenty soldiers, man. That's all it takes. Twenty good men on

689

twenty good horses, aye, swords and spears. Man, that orderless rabble would run like rats.'

'We have not twenty men within,' said Miphon. 'Only half a dozen.'

'Then those men who arrested me—'

'I sent them chasing after Lord Blackwood and Lord Hearst.'

'Man, that was foolish!' said Drake, shaking his head. 'Mobs grow by moments. Smash them to start with, aye, that's the story.'

At that moment, the gaoler intruded on their conversation. He was hot, panting, excited.

'Masters, Lord Blackwood's outside! He's in trouble!'

Miphon exited the cell, with Drake and Zanya close behind. Crowding to arrowslits, they saw Lord Hearst outside, along with a dark-haired, heavy-jowled man whom Drake recognized as Blackwood. Both were on horseback, as were the four soldiers helping force a way through the crowd. Suddenly, one of the soldiers was hauled from his horse. Blackwood raised something in his fist. He shouted. The mob fell back in a confusion close to panic.

'What's happened?' said Zanya.

'He's threatened them with the death-stone,' said Miphon.

'The door!' shouted Drake. 'To the door!'

All raced to the door of the western gatehouse, which they hauled open. Blackwood, Hearst and the surviving soldiers spurred their horses for the door. The mob surged after them – but the sight of cold steel made the mob hesitate just long enough for the door to be closed.

Hearst swung down from his horse.

'How many men here?' he said.

'Nine all told,' said the gaoler, 'counting me, and counting Master Yot's prisoner.'

'Yot!' said Hearst. 'I'll kill him when I get hold of him.' Then, to Blackwood: 'I told you he should have swung with those lawyers.'

'I gave him my support for I saw good things in his doctrine,' said Blackwood. 'The flesh, after all, must be disciplined to live within its limits.'

'Yes yes yes!' said Hearst. 'You meant well. You always mean well. Me, I'm content to govern! Is the death-stone safe?'

'Here,' said Blackwood, thumping a stone egg onto a convenient table.

'Good,' said Hearst.

'Man,' said Drake, 'is that it?'

'The weapon of recent legend,' confirmed Hearst.

'Well then,' said Drake, 'let's use it, for the mob without is close to murder.'

'We cannot do any such thing,' said Hearst. 'We'd turn the whole town to stone.'

'It's us or them, man!' cried Drake.

He snatched up the death-stone. It was cool. It was heavier than he had expected. There was a sizzle of steel as soldiers drew weapons against him. Drake menaced them with the death-stone. They fell back. Now what? He waved the death-stone about in the air.

'Work, you ganch!' screamed Drake. 'Kill people!'

Hearst laughed, harshly.

'Read the Words on the side of the stone,' said Hearst. 'Read them, now! Or drop the stone – or it will kill you.'

Drake saw strange writing on the side of the death-stone. The stone egg kicked in his hand like a living heart. He put it back on the table.

'I would have saved us if I could,' he said sadly, 'but I know not the letter Àçøwæ from any other.'

'You'd have saved none,' said Hearst, 'but would have killed many. When the death-stone works its magic, all die unless huddled close, within an arm-span of the stone itself. Let's use the bottle.'

'What bottle?' said Drake.

'That one,' said Hearst, pointing to a red bottle which was tied to Blackwood's belt.

Blackwood pulled a ring off his finger and handed it to

691

Hearst. The soldiers, who had done this before, grabbed hold of Hearst. Who slipped the ring onto his finger then turned it. As Drake goggled, Hearst and the soldiers holding him were turned to smoke. And sucked into the bottle.

Drake had learnt bits and pieces about the lore of such magic bottles. He had heard tales from Andranovory in Selzirk. While ruling the Gates of Chenameg, he had heard more from other people. But stories were one thing – it was quite another to see such magic in action.

Moments later, Hearst materialized again.

'Hold me,' said Hearst. 'Yes, you, woman. And you.'

'No!' said Zanya.

'No!' said Drake. 'We'll not be devilled to smoke like those others.'

He was fearfully afraid of going inside that bottle. For the only way in or out of that bottle was through the magic of the ring which commanded it. If that ring was to be lost or destroyed – why, then anyone inside that bottle would be trapped there for life.

Miphon tried to explain.

'It's only—'

'Don't waste breath or time,' said Hearst. 'Help me get the horses inside.' Miphon and Hearst took the horses into the bottle. They rematerialized shortly. 'We're going to the roof,' said Hearst. 'Gaoler – come with us. As for you two – follow if you wish.'

Hearst led the way upstairs, with Drake and Zanya hot on his heels. All were panting heavily by the time they reached the top of the western gatehouse. Zanya was gasping like a fish out of water. Her face streamed with sweat.

From this height, they could see for league upon league. Sinuous line of river. Far to the west – perhaps thirty leagues away – a hint amidst haze of something which might have been the sea. From the eastern wall of the roof, a view directly down into the street where the mob was using a battering ram against the door of the gatehouse.

Hearst strode to the western wall. Directly below was a dry ditch, with ragged wasteland beyond.

'Gaoler!' said Hearst. 'Come here!' The gaoler did so. 'We are going to use the ring,' said Hearst. 'We will venture inside the red bottle. Then you must throw that bottle so it lands in yonder wasteland.'

'My lord,' said the gaoler, bowing his head.

Swiftly, Blackwood unfastened the bottle from his belt. He handed it to Hearst who put it down on the roof. The gaoler went to pick it up.

'No!' said Hearst, fearing the bottle would be thrown too soon. 'Don't pick it up until we're inside!' He looked at Drake. 'Friend,' said Hearst, 'will you join us in the bottle? Or stay to meet your doom?'

'We'll come,' said Drake.

Zanya grabbed Drake who grabbed Miphon who grabbed Blackwood who grabbed Hearst who turned the ring on his finger. All five dissolved into smoke and were sucked into the bottle. The gaoler, left alone on the roof, picked up the red bottle and threw it. High it spun. Down, down, down it fell. And landed amidst thistles on the wasteland west of the gatehouse.

Down at street level, the door to the gatehouse shattered. With a deep-throated growl, the mob surged inside. They were unlikely to handle the gaoler kindly if they laid hands on him.

'Well,' said the gaoler, 'time to try the transformation pill, I guess.'

He took from his neck an amulet inherited from his great-great-grandfather who had bought it from a peddler who claimed to have purchased it from a judge who had confiscated it from a thief who had stolen it from a sorcerer's apprentice who had in turn thieved it from a master wizard.

The gaoler fumbled with a tiny catch. The amulet opened. Inside was a little white pill.

'I hope this works,' said the gaoler.

And swallowed it down. His hands tingled. His feet Changed. Nine heartbeats later, he had turned into a hippogryph. Wings beating strongly, he took to the air.

693

According to family tradition, the transformation pill would work for a day and a night.

'Scrark grark!' said the gaoler. By which he meant. 'I wonder what the beer tastes like in D'Waith?'

He started flying north-west. He fully intended to find out.

Meanwhile, down on the wasteland to the west of the walls of Lorford, a cloud of fog suddenly swelled above a patch of nettles, then materialized into four people and four horses. Moments later, Morgan Hearst, the wizard Miphon, Lord Blackwood and Drake Douay had mounted up and were galloping away to the west, to freedom.

62

Hollern River: flows south from Lake Armansis (in Penvash Peninsular) to vicinity of Lorford, then bends west and runs for the Central Ocean.

In the austere confines of the western gatehouse, there was no loot to delay the mob. The first rioter to peer through an arrow-slit saw four men on horseback on the wasteland beyond Lorford, saw those men riding for the river-road, and cried:

'They're escaping west!'

Whereupon the mob commandeered four horses, three mules, two donkeys, seven camels, a water buffalo, a yak, a quagga, three wood-carts drawn by dog-packs, and a chariot (belonging to Mistress Turbothot, previously of the fair city of Selzirk) which was drawn by four silver-haired wolves.

Thus equipped, the mob gave chase. Those who could not ride did as best as they could on their own two legs. And every hound, mutt, cur, bitch, mastiff, mongrel and pariah dog in Lorford ran with them. The lead was slim, and the pursuit was hot.

Drake heard dogs baying, and was sore afraid. The dog, of course, is the favourite beast of the Demon, being stupid, and ugly, and undiscriminating, and a defiler of public places, and ruinous to the public peace, and a source of disease, and good to eat with fried mushrooms and garlic-flavoured cow's udder. But, while Drake loved dogs, he did not want to meet so many at once. Not so many so hot for his blood.

What if he fell from his horse? What if his horse fell lame?

'Carry me, ganch!' yelled Drake to his horse.

Upon which the horse stumbled amidst hardened mud-ruts, hit a boggy patch, slipped, and threw its rider. Drake fell heavily. Spray – nine parts liquid mud – flew up around him.

'Stop!' he yelled.

But the others were riding hell-for-leather for the west. Their horses, disorientated by being whirled in and out of the red bottle, unsettled by the fear of their riders and unnerved by the yammering mob, were galloping almost out of control.

Cursing and swearing, Drake scrambled to his feet. His horse was getting up. Slowly.

'You'd better not be broken, horse,' said Drake, his voice trembling. 'You'd better not be broken, or I'll kick your head in!'

The horse stood upright. So it could stand, at least. Drake put foot into stirrup. Swung himself up into the saddle.

'Move, ganch!' he said. 'Or I'll cut your ears off!'

The horse took the hint, and got moving.

Blackwood, Miphon and Hearst were far ahead, but slowing, yes, slowing as they brought their mounts under control.

'I'm right behind you!' yelled Drake.

But guessed that they never heard him.

When Hearst glanced back from a little rise a half-league west of Lorford, he was dismayed to see some of the rabble had managed to find mounts.

'Shall we get our people from the bottle?' said Blackwood. 'Shall we fight?'

'No,' said Hearst. 'For if we tangle ourselves in combat with those who ride, then those following on foot will finish us. Ride!'

Hearst spurred his mount. Ahead, the road was smooth and hard. But he knew it became narrow and marshy in less than a league. A coppice lay to left, and riverside trees to the right. And what was that in the trees?

'A boat!' said Hearst.

It was, by the looks of it, a fishing boat, a sturdy thing with one mast, one cabin and a single fish-hold. It was moored to the bank in a spot so well-hidden by riverside trees that it was invisible until they were almost upon it.

'That'll do us,' said Hearst.

He got everyone unloaded from the bottle, so weight of numbers would be on his side if it came to an argument.

'Where's Drake?' said Zanya.

'He's coming,' said Hearst.

'You've left him, haven't you?' said Zanya, her voice starting to rise.

Blackwood, fearing she would alert anyone on board the boat, grabbed her from behind, clamping a hand over her mouth. She bit. He pulled his hand away. She screamed.

'Hysterical women!' said Hearst.

And led a charge onto the boat, leaving Blackwood to deal with Zanya as best he could.

The crew had been sleeping, for they had brought their boat upriver under cover of darkness, and expected to be busy again when the stars next shone. But, as the heroes came aboard, the crewmen woke smartly, dived overboard, and swam for the further shore.

'Morgan!' cried Blackwood. 'For pity's sake!'

Zanya had got an armlock on him, and was about to break his arm.

'Let him go, you mad red bitch!' yelled Hearst. 'Look down the path – there's your lover in plain view.'

True! Galloping toward them down the ragged road was Drake Douay, bouncing in the saddle and hallooing wildly.

'You still left him behind!' yelled Zanya.

And, taking revenge, she pushed Blackwood into the river.

By the time Blackwood had hauled himself out of the

river, dripping with mud and water, those aboard the boat had discovered that its fish-hold was full: but not with fish.

'What's this?' said Hearst, examining the cargo. 'Booze!'

They had caught themselves a smuggling boat, bringing in liquor by stealth to avoid the local alcohol taxes. Hearst slit open a skin of the contraband, letting it run to the river. The reek of its contents told him immediately where this cargo had come from.

'This is more of that gut-rot poison from Lorp,' said Hearst. 'You'll not drink that, if you value your health. Now I must go ashore, for I ride for the south. As for the rest of you – go to Brennan, in the Lesser Teeth. I'll send for you when it's safe. Here's the ring.'

'Perhaps you should keep the death-stone,' said Miphon, as he accepted the ring which commanded the red bottle. 'We have the bottle – that's all we need.'

'The death-stone's safer with you,' said Hearst. 'Don't worry about Mystrel, or Greenwood. I'll look after them.'

At which point Drake finally reached them.

'Stop! Stop, you ganch!' screamed Drake, as his noble steed thundered past the boat.

He hauled wildly on the reins – and the horse went crashing into the river, rider and all. As Drake floundered in the water, the horse began to swim for the further bank, doubtless eager to escape.

As Hearst hid himself in a nearby coppice, the others pushed the boat away from the bank. As they drifted past Drake, a soldier hauled him from the water.

'Drake!' cried Zanya.

And she clasped him to her, though water was still streaming from his sodden clothes. He was almost too breathless to kiss – but did his best regardless.

The two were still kissing when the mob came in view, by which time the boat was in midstream, going west with the current, and with the current only, for the wind was against them. Blackwood had bows, arrows, spears and

698

swords brought out of the red bottle, which was rich in weaponry. He strung a bow.

'Do you shoot?' said Blackwood to Drake.

'Man, I had toy bows in plenty as a child.'

'Good,' said Blackwood, handing him a bow and a full quiver.

Great is the mystique of the bowman – but if pursuers swam out to the boat, and Drake shot at them from ten or twenty paces, his boyhood skills would be good enough for a kill.

As the pursuit drew nearer, those on the boat hollered, jeered and shouted. Soon the pursuit was level with the boat.

'Hearst!' shouted Miphon, into the interior of the boat. 'We're far enough from Lorford now. Use the death-stone!'

Most of the pursuers fell back at the threat of the death-stone. Which was there, right enough – though Hearst, of course, was elsewhere. He had, in fact, just exited from the southern side of the coppice, and was beginning a long ride to the southern border of Estar.

'Drake!' shouted a voice from the bank.

It was Yot. Drake nocked an arrow. Drew. Shot. The bowstring stung his thumb as he loosed the shaft. Which took Yot's horse in the flank. The beast reared, and Yot was thrown.

'Demon-son!' screamed Yot, from the ground. 'Kill him! He's the evil one!'

'Man,' muttered Drake, 'your mouth's a nice big target.'

He aimed for it. And loosed another shaft. But Drake's skill with the bow was minimal – and, besides, he was trembling with adrenalin. His shot went wide.

'Shoot at the mounts,' said Blackwood.

'That's cruel,' said Zanya.

'Dead horses demand no vengeance,' said Blackwood. 'But dead friends do.'

Soon, two horses and a camel were on the ground,

kicking, screaming. As the way became marshy, the last riders fell behind the boat. The dog-carts and the chariot had been left behind long ago, wheels smashed by their manic race along the rutted road.

'We're clear,' said Miphon. 'Who here's a sailor?'

Drake, finding he was the only sailor amongst them, took charge, and began Investigating the boat, making sure it was ready for the open sea.

'Man,' said Drake to Miphon. 'I don't like this running business. It makes no sense, not when we've got the death-stone. That's fearsome magic.'

'But clumsy,' said Miphon. 'For it destroys everything for two leagues in every direction.'

'Yet the person who wields the death survives.'

'Yes, since all within an arm's reach of the death-stone are safe. But all else becomes rock. If we'd used it against our pursuers just then, our boat would have turned to stone. And Lorford also, for we were less than two leagues from the town.'

'Oh,' said Drake.

He was still not convinced.

'What's more,' said Miphon. 'Once the death-stone's been used, it won't work again for some days. Many know that. So if we used the death-stone, any survivors would hunt us without fear.'

'How many days,' said Drake, 'before the death-stone can be used again?'

'You ask too many questions!' said Miphon.

'Then answer me just this one. Where goes Hearst?'

'Why, to rally the southern garrisons, which guard the borders against the Swarms. They're mostly Rovac troops, all loyal.'

'Man,' said Drake, 'if I'd held Lorford there'd have been no shortage of loyal troops on hand.'

'Yes, maybe,' said Miphon. 'But Hearst was always more of a soldier than a politician. No matter. His troops will bring the mob to order soon enough.'

'And hang young Sully Yot!'

'Very likely,' said Miphon.

Who, though he did not like Yot, did not really approve of Drake's enthusiasm.

Thus it was that the death-stone, the magic red bottle and the ring which commanded that bottle went west down the Hollern River and out to sea, on a boat commanded by Drake Douay. Meanwhile, Morgan Hearst rode south.

And Sully Yot made plans of his own.

63

Lesser Teeth: group of low-lying sandy islands lying east of Lorp, south of the Ravlish Lands and north of the Greater Teeth. The inhabitants live without rulers. While usually peaceful, they will yield to their lower nature if sufficiently tempted – and make savage enemies if crossed.

During the voyage to Carawell, the largest of the Lesser Teeth, Drake refused all invitations to enter the red bottle.

'Come inside and get some proper rest,' said Miphon. 'You're our one true sailor. In an emergency, we'll want you fresh and rested.'

'I'll manage,' said Drake, who was steering at the time, one arm resting negligently on the tiller.

'It's very comfortable inside,' said Miphon.

'I've seen inside once,' said Drake. 'That once is enough.'

'What did you see?' asked Miphon.

While he thought about it, Drake gazed at the set of the sails, then looked to east. The coast of Argan was dangerously close. To east lay Lorp – which, since the tales Jon Arabin had told of the place, was Drake's least-favoured holiday destination.

'Did you get a chance to see anything?' said Miphon.

'Oh yes,' said Drake. 'Someone's backside, an elbow and the arse of a horse. Man, it was cramped! No wonder, with so many people in such a small bottle.'

The boat lurched. And Drake thought:

Sea serpent!

But it had just been a swell a little larger than the others.

'We were but in the neck of the bottle,' said Miphon. 'Stairs lead down from the neck to places where the bottle widens within to dimensions amazing. Come – why hesitate? This is one of the wonders of the world.'

'A bloody dangerous wonder, I'll warrant,' said Drake. 'Man, I know a bit about these magic bottles. It's a ring which commands them, isn't it? And we've but one ring between us. So those in the bottle are at the mercy of the ringbearer.'

'You're short on trust,' said Miphon.

Drake ducked as something came screaming out of the sky. It was a blue-feathered mocking gull.

'Scouse!' said Drake, naming one of the soldiers. 'Shoot that gull!'

Scouse loaded his crossbow. As the mocking gull came in for a second run, Scouse fired. Hit, the gull tumbled to the slick green seas. It floated, lifeless.

'The gull meant no harm,' said Miphon, quietly.

'Maybe not,' said Drake. 'But it irritated the hell out of me.'

He watched the gull. One moment it was there – and the next, gone, swallowed by lunging turbulence. Drake glimpsed a fin. Sleek slice of evil.

'There's a shark in the water,' he said.

'Don't worry,' said Miphon. 'I'm planning no swims today. We were talking of the bottle. And about the ring-bearer. You don't seem to be very trusting.'

'Man,' said Drake, 'it's not a matter of trust, but of practicality. What if the ring-bearer should fall over-board? What help then for those trapped in the bottle? Why, none.'

'Life is risk,' said Miphon.

'So it is,' said Drake, 'yet I'll not increase risk without reason. I'll chance this bottle only if I can wear your magic on my own finger.'

But Miphon and Blackwood, who shared the ring between them, were too wise to subject Drake to such

703

temptation. So, unable to get his hands on the ring (though, naturally enough, he made schemes to do so) he stayed outside, on the boat.

And, soon enough, brought them safe to harbour at Brennan. Before anyone went to shore, Drake had all gathered together on the boat, where he addressed them:

'Boys, girls and turtle-folk,' said Drake, 'it's best for you to be warned about these here Lessers. The people are nice enough, but they're like anyone – given too much temptation they'll grab at it.

'So let's be humble, like. We've a cargo of Lorp-liquor aboard, hence our story. We were smuggling to Estar when we were caught, aye. So the evil wizard Miphon put a hex on us, and if we step back on Argan within the year, we'll all turn to toads and scorpions. Everyone understand?'

'Who am I then?' said Miphon. 'Since the evil wizard Miphon is still back in Estar?'

'You?' said Drake, scratching his head. 'Man, you can be Plovey of the Regency of Selzirk, reduced to liquor-smuggling because the Swarms are eating the Harvest Plains. As for you soldier-folk, why, you're all deserters for the duration. Understand? Now, Lord Blackwood, you—'

'No,' said Blackwood. 'I don't like this idea of living a lie.'

'Man,' said Drake, 'you've got a near-lethal case of morality, then. Well, you say nothing, and we'll tell all the lies on your account. You can be a deaf-mute, aye, that'll keep you out of mischief.'

'And me?' said Zanya.

'You will be Zanya, my lawful wedded wife,' said Drake. 'And I will be Lord Dreldragon, son of Baron Farouk of Hexagon.'

'That's a flimsy story on which to be risking our lives,' said Miphon.

'Man,' said Drake, 'wait till we get ashore. Then you'll find out how flimsy it is.'

704

Sure enough, plenty of islanders remembered Drake from his last visit. They apologized for kidnapping the bold Baron Farouk; they asked after the fate of Hexagon, and commiserated with Drake when he explained it had been taken over by runaway gladiators from Chi'ash-lan; they admired the beauty of his wife.

Zanya's beauty was marred, now, by half a dozen frank blue spots on her face. But the islanders knew nothing of blue lepers, so thought these spots – if they thought of them at all – to be no more than boils.

Things had changed in Brennan since Drake was there last, for the Lesser Teeth had endured an occupation by pirates in the interim. Haunted metal no longer worked in the harbourside forge, for it had been destroyed in battle. Gezeldux, who had once fed Drake a magical liquor which had let him walk on air, still lived in Brennan, but had sold his bar to a man named Brimi Hagi.

All gathered at Hagi's bar that evening, to hear Drake tell wild and wonderful stories of his conquest of the Gates of Chenameg. Then Gezeldux reminisced about Drake's last visit, when he had shown off by drinking immense quantities of all kinds of spirit. Drake, rising to the occasion, repeated some of his earlier feats effortlessly.

Miphon, alarmed at Drake's liquor consumption, warned him he would do himself an injury.

'Nay, man,' said Drake. 'I'm old enough to know my limits.'

Later, Miphon cautioned him again.

'You've drunk more than I'd have thought possible,' said Miphon. 'Enough is enough! Leave off, before you kill yourself!'

'You haven't seen anything yet,' said Drake.

He challenged the bar. Whatever poison they could produce, he'd prove it useless against the Favoured Blood of Hexagon. The only poison to be had was a little vial of something which purported to be cytisine, a poison got from laburnum. Drake mixed it with ale then quaffed it, grinning – raising a small cheer in his favour.

'How can you get away with drinking poison?' said Miphon.

'Because I'm of royal birth, man,' said Drake. 'All us noble folk of the Favoured blood, we don't fall sick like the commons, nay, not from fever or from poison.'

Miphon, seeing he would get no sense from Drake that night, did not press him further. After all, for all Miphon knew, the 'poison' might have been vanilla essence, or vinegar, or cod-liver oil, or sugarwater.

But the next morning, Drake ate an enormous breakfast of eggs, devilled kidneys and greasy Ravlish bacon. While eating, he laughed, joked, talked with his mouth full, and was, all in all, as cocky as ever. Then Miphon knew something unusual was going on. For, whatever the nature of the 'poison' Drake had taken the night before, the liquor had been real enough, and Drake had put away enough of it to sicken the most hardened drinker for days.

Miphon, curious, decided to talk to Drake in private. When Drake shortly went to stretch his legs on the beach, Miphon followed.

The crisp, bright morn promised a clear, hot day. A few seagulls on the beach were fighting over fish heads. Drake gathered a handful of stones and began Investigating the best method of stoning gulls. He had just knocked a couple of grey feathers off one of the less wary birds when Miphon caught up with him.

'Good morning,' said Miphon.

'Hi,' said Drake.

He shied a stone at a gull but twenty paces distant. It was in the air before the stone hit. It seemed gulls had to take off in a straight line. Their capacity for evasive action was marginal while they were scrambling into the sky. So if . . .

'What's your quarrel with the birds?' said Miphon.

'What quarrel have the Swarms with us?' said Drake.

'That's no answer!' said Miphon.

'Yes, but it's a question better worth the asking,' said Drake.

706

He threw another stone. A gull saw the stone heading in its general direction. The gull took to the air – and almost flew right into the stone.

'Next time!' said Drake.

Should he use sticks instead of stones? A nice-sized throwing stick would be ten times the length of one of his little stones. Meaning he would increase his chances of a hit fivefold even if he was only half as accurate with stick as with stone.

'You're looking chirpy today,' said Miphon. 'How so?'

'It's the birds in my ancestry, I suppose,' said Drake.

Meaning to prove the point, he threw back his head and gave a bird-scream.

'If I heard that in the forest,' said Miphon, 'I'd say the bird responsible was sick. Very sick. Or mad. Or both. But you look healthy enough. I'm amazed. Why no hangover? You should be groaning in a sick-bed after last night's binge.'

'Man, I never get sick,' said Drake. 'Not from liquor, from poison or anything. I flourish while others fever.'

'Have you always been this way?'

Drake scuffed his feet in the sand. This morning, he was barefoot. His boots were being repaired by the local cobbler; he would pick them up at noon.

'Oh, aye,' said Drake. 'I've been fit enough for most of my life. Ever since someone cursed me.'

'Cursed you? When was that?'

Drake stooped for some seaweed which was fastened to a nice smooth surface-to-surface anti-seagull missile. He tore away the seaweed. Put a couple of bobbles of the stuff into his mouth. Chewed it. Salty. Seaweed taste reminded him of . . . of childhood. Of the rocks on the seashore beneath his father's coal-cliffs . . .

'You want to hear of curses?' said Drake. 'The curse came early on, man. Yes. They hexed me, taking away all pleasure from drink. Near ruined my life, that did. But I survived. I'm hardy, see.'

'They cursed you?' said Miphon. 'Who is they?'

707

'If I knew that,' said Drake, 'they'd be dead.'

He threw his smooth stone. It missed one seagull, hit the sea, skipped, whipped over one gull then under another, skipped again, then sank. Rings of ripples expanded on the stone-flicked sea.

'I don't understand about this curse,' said Miphon.

'Why not?' said Drake. 'You're a wizard. You should be a right expert.'

'I know much of magic,' said Miphon. 'Curses of all kinds are possible. But they take great power, and greater effort. Nobody would curse you simply to stop you getting drunk.'

And Miphon, relentlessly, began to pursue the truth.

'Man,' said Drake, after the first fifty questions, 'last time I was mauled like this, I was flat on a torture bench.'

But Miphon was ruthless.

Finally, he started to smile.

'Why smiling, man?' said Drake.

'Because I think,' said Miphon, 'I think I know what happened to you. Your body was altered by a paratopic.'

'A what?'

'A paratopic. That's a name for the snake which was fed to your flesh in Ling. Only it wasn't a snake at all, but a very special creature in snake-form. I've read of such in old, old records.'

'What does it do, this snake?' said Drake.

'Why,' said Miphon, 'it enters the body then becomes – well, many many little snakes. And those, between them, bring about the changes you've experienced. For instance, you don't get sick from bad water. Or drunk on liquor.'

'Man,' said Drake, 'so all this trouble I've had with drink, that was because of that snake! Those people in Ling, why did they do something so cruel?'

'Why was it cruel?'

'Because it denied me all pleasure of drink.'

'That snake,' said Miphon, 'has probably saved your life. Without it, you'd have killed yourself with alcohol.

708

Or died of river fever. You'd also have caught twenty different types of venereal disease. Including the pox which your beloved is dying of.'

'I may well have caught that pox,' said Drake. 'You once told me yourself that it may take years to show itself.'

'If the paratopic works as the old books say it does,' said Miphon, 'then it will protect you even against blue star fever. You should count yourself lucky.'

'Lucky?' said Drake. 'Yes, well, perhaps I am, in a way. But it's still hard to skip pleasure when everyone else is getting it. That's the hard thing about not being able to get drunk. Still . . . man . . . what say we got one of these snake-things for Zanya?'

'That's a highly theoretical question.'

'What's theoretical about it?' said Drake. 'You said yourself that this snake saved me from the pox. If it saved me, why not Zanya?'

'You were healthy to start with, more or less,' said Miphon. 'Zanya is deep in the clutches of disease already. The power of the paratopic might not be sufficient to salvage her health. Anyway, we'll never know either way.'

'Of course we will!' said Drake. 'I'll find one of these snake-things. I'll go to Ling, yes.'

'To Ling?'

'Aye, man, where else? They had one of these snakes, they'll have another. For Zanya, yes. We'll take it from them at choke point. Aye! Swords to their throats then press for the question. Gut some of their children dead, yes, that's the way, that'll soon hustle them along.'

'You could always try asking, first,' said Miphon, mildly.

'Try what?' said Drake, incredulously.

'Asking,' said Miphon. 'Politely. You might get quite surprising results.'

'Hmmm,' said Drake.

Miphon looked at him, sternly.

'Now don't go looking at me like that!' said Drake. 'All I said was "hmmm".'

709

'Yes,' said Miphon.

Speaking volumes.

'All right then,' said Drake. 'You win. I'll try asking politely to start with. Come on, let's find Blackwood. The sooner we get going, the better.'

Miphon was not sure he even wanted to get going, since the last thing he wanted to do right then was venture all the way south to Ling. But he let Blackwood do the arguing, which Blackwood did with great vigour, concluding as follows:

'We're men of command with serious responsibilities in Estar. We can't go whoring off on fairy-tale quests to the Deep South.'

'But you're questing heroes!' said Drake. 'Aye, famous for it! You, and Miphon, and Morgan Hearst. Why, man, when I held the Gates of Chenameg, I heard many a tale about—'

'What we did,' said Blackwood, 'was done under the gravest necessity.'

'My wife sickens. Is that not necessity? She sickens towards death. Is that not dire?'

'Friend,' said Blackwood, 'an afternoon's brawling in Lorford can see half a dozen dead. One person's tragedy cannot outbalance the needs of a town, or a nation.'

'But Hearst's taking care of Lorford,' said Drake. 'Aye, and of Estar entire. And Trest, man.'

'Yes, and we hold in trust the red bottle and the death-stone. Those are great resources, which Hearst may need to call on. We cannot risk them on – on—'

'On saving life,' said Drake.

Then said much more. But, when Miphon made it clear he supported Blackwood, Drake abandoned argument. And started planning, instead.

64

From the Lessers to Ling: a voyage from Brennan to Ling
would entail a sea-passage of some 1,150 leagues. A clean
ship favoured with fair winds might reasonably expect to
make the voyage in twenty-five days.

They had had quite a party. They had started early in the
morning. Come noon, their behaviour had become so
riotous that Hagi had thrown them out of his bar. So they
had continued on the beach. But now it was night, and all
had crawled off home – all but three.

Old Gezeldux, who had been one of the leading lights of
the party, was asleep on the sands, his sleep warmed by a
dragon-coloured fire. Zanya was asleep on the same beach,
her head resting on Drake's lap.

Zanya had not drunk much that day: her body could no
longer tolerate more than a little alcohol. But she had done
her best to join in the fun. She did not like to confess how
weak she felt, and how she had suffered as a consequence of
her brave endeavours to fake merriment when she should
have been resting. Zanya was fearfully afraid of becoming
a true invalid. For what then? Would Drake leave her?

The problem troubled her dreams, in which she was
being chased by a dragon.

Drake was still awake, picking his nose with a finger
which smelt of woodsmoke, and staring out to sea. He was
not admiring the beauty of Brennan harbour by moonlight.
No, he was thinking, something he did well.

Zanya moaned faintly.

711

'Dearest heart,' murmured Drake, and stroked her cheek with the hand which was not otherwise occupied.

He felt lumps beneath his fingers.

Zanya grunted. Her dream-scene shifted. The dragon was gone. Instead, she was in the temple of the Orgy God on the Ebrells. The change was not for the better.

Drake heard Zanya give a thin, terrified whine. He kissed her. She grunted again. Shifted. Settled.

He had not told Zanya that her salvation might lie in Ling. He wanted to rouse no false hopes. Ling, after all, was many days distant. And Blackwood and Miphon still did not seem disposed to helping Drake get there. The pair of them were staying in a house lent to them by Gezeldux. In that house they had all of Hearst's soldiers, who had been refused permission to join the party. Funny, that. One could almost believe the two exiled rulers of Estar did not entirely trust young Drake Douay.

Well, he'd show them.

What did he need for the journey south? A boat. Yes, well, that was simple enough. Any fishing boat from Brennan Harbour would be stout enough for the voyage, as long as the summer weather held fair. Men? He'd like to have a few men with him. But he could sail a fishing boat single-handed if he had to.

But what he really did want was the death-stone.

And the bottle.

Since they were so close at hand, it would be foolish to go without them. Man, he'd taken Runcorn near enough to single-handed. He'd captured the Gates of Chenameg. So he should be able to handle a house full of soldiers, yes . . .

The ghosts of a thousand dead generations breathed a little more life into the night breeze, and Drake shivered. The night was cooling. He threw a hunk of driftwood onto the fire, kicking up a shower of red sparks.

'The whip!' said Zanya, startled almost to wakefulness.

'Hush, dear heart,' said Drake. 'Hush. Hush . . .'

And soothed his fingers over her neck, over her smooth

712

and beautiful neck. Finding a little lump which he knew must be sky blue. Her sickness was spreading to more of her body.

On the wind, Drake heard a voice. He thought, at first, that he had momentarily fallen asleep, and that the voice had spoken to him from out of a dream. Then he realized that it had come from out on the harbour. Yes. There were some boats out there, sails dark in the night. How many? One, three . . . five. Close to shore. Moving as if in convoy.

'Explain yourself, boats,' muttered Drake.

And reached out to shake Gezeldux awake.

Gezeldux breathed up beery fumes, then burped, bringing up a mouthful of half-digested fish, which he swilled round his mouth then swallowed again.

'What's problem?' said Gezeldux. 'Sky caught fire?'

'Boats,' said Drake. 'That's the problem. Look! Those are island boats, I hope.'

'How should I know?' said Gezeldux.

'Man, you live here.'

'A boat is a boat is a boat,' said Gezeldux.

He was too full of liquor to rightly care. So Drake, who had much experience of drunks, let him go back to sleep. Zanya had woken.

'Darling treasure snake,' she said, 'hold me close.'

'Man,' said Drake, giving her a perfunctory hug, 'I don't like those boats. Come on, we'll rouse the others.'

In truth, while he was suspicious of the boats, he had an ulterior motive for sounding the alarm. It gave him a good chance to test the defences Miphon and Blackwood had organized for themselves.

On reaching their lordships' house of exile, Drake found sentries posted, and wide awake. He was admitted into the interior, which was hot, and heavy with the smell of enclosed sweat. Miphon and Blackwood were swiftly roused, and made no effort to hide their suspicions. Clearly they thought Drake was playing some kind of trick.

713

'Man,' said Drake, 'trust me. If you won't trust me, then take my wife as hostage, and come see.'

So, leaving Zanya as hostage, they went to see his mystery boats, which, in the interim, had come in close to the shore. The crews were making no particular effort to keep quiet. The watchers heard voices, and one of those voices:

'Grief of suns,' hissed Drake. 'That's Sully Yot.'

Miphon and Blackwood knew that voice as well. So they joined Drake as he backed off hastily.

'How did he know we're here?' said Blackwood.

'Man,' said Drake. 'Likely he doesn't. Likely he's fled Estar for fear of what we'll do to him when we get ourselves organized. Likely this is his first stop on some flight to wherever. But, man, he'll likely find we're here, aye, soon enough.'

'What do you suggest?' said Miphon.

'I suggest your house is a trap, so get your men out of it.'

Shortly, Blackwood, Miphon, Drake, Zanya and all the soldiers were lying in the dark in the scrub in some low dunes at the edge of town.

It was hard to judge how many men Yot had on each of his five boats. But Drake suspected six, easily – which would mean Yot's people outnumbered them about two to one. Six men per boat? The figure was just as likely to be ten.

The wind grew stronger, and colder. The refugees huddled together for warmth. Thick cloud was engulfing the stars.

Blackwood stirred, restlessly.

'Let's—' he said.

'Let's nothing,' said Drake sharply.

And nothing they did for some time.

Occasionally, noise came from the town. Shouts. Doors slamming. A suggestion of protest. A cry which might almost have been a scream.

Then a dog started to bay.

'A dog!' said Blackwood.

714

'Nay, man,' said Drake. 'It's a nightingale. Yes, a nightingale with its voice a little harsh from eating iron filings.'

'Stop playing the fool!' said Blackwood. 'It's a dog. Isn't it, Miphon?'

'It sounds like a fruit-bat to me,' said Miphon.

The dog gave voice again. It was closer.

'If it's a fruit bat, then it's a man-hunting fruit-bat,' said Blackwood. 'We'd better get ready to do battle.'

But the dog was on the scent of a chiz, and came no closer to the fugitives.

For some time, the sounds of a dog hunting persisted. Then they were replaced by the sounds of a dog being beaten for incompetence. While the dog was Drake's favourite animal, on this particular occasion he felt no sympathy for canine suffering.

The hunt moved to the harbour.

Rowing boats came and went on the darkened waters. Lanterns gleamed on the sea. Then:

'Look!' said Drake. 'That furthest light! It's on our boat! They're on our boat!'

'They know we're here, then,' said Miphon.

'We should have taken to sea when we first saw them coming in,' said Blackwood.

'Man, you're a fine one to talk!' said Drake savagely. 'You didn't even believe the incoming boats existed. You thought I was tricking you outside for a throat-cut. Well, man, that was your mistake. Now – mark the cloud. When it covers out the last starshine, we move.'

And, soon enough, they did. All went into the bottle but for Drake, Blackwood, Miphon, and two soldiers by the names of Scouse and Klupping.

They went catfoot down to the beach. Drake, in the lead, found a dinghy by barking his shins against it. A scrape, a splash – and they were afloat. The oars made an abominable noise as Drake and Klupping rowed.

A shout came from the shore.

'Quiet, now,' said Drake. 'Klupping! Rest on your oars!'

The dinghy floated. Drake, listening, heard wind-driven

wavelets slapping against a nearby fishing boat.

'Let me row solo,' said Drake.

And sculled toward the fishing boat as quiet as he could. He came up under the bows.

'You sitting aft,' said Drake. 'What's your name? Scouse, isn't it? Right, grab the boat's anchor rope. Aye, and hold us steady. Now quiet, everyone.'

'Let's go aboard,' said Blackwood.

'Nay, man,' said Drake. 'Wait. Listen. Watch.'

Yot's people were being noisy. There was a lot of shouting. A lot of confusion. Someone cried out:

'They've put to sea!'

Further shouts ordered pursuit.

Soon at least three of Yot's boats had raised sails and were trying to tack for the harbourmouth against the incoming wind. Out in the night there was the sound of a heavy collision as a boat underway ran into one which was anchored.

'Now,' said Drake, 'go aboard. One at a time. Quiet like.'

This they did.

'What now?' said Blackwood.

'Let Yot and his friends enjoy their nightmare,' said Drake. 'Chasing around a strange harbour by night in total darkness. They're fools to be trying it, and we'd be greater fools to join them.'

'Let's go ashore,' said Miphon, 'and rally the islanders against Yot.'

'Oh,' said Drake, 'that's nice fighting talk, that's for sure. But can we trust them? What's Yot been doing ashore? What's he been saying? Like as not the islanders know about the death-stone by now. Aye, and maybe the bottle, if he knows about such.'

'It's no secret,' said Miphon. 'We had a whole army in it once, so the bottle and its nature is known through gossip to every dog in Lorford.'

'Then let's wait,' said Drake. 'Man, there's an outgoing tide at dawn. We'll leave on that tide, with the first hint of light.'

And a long, cold watch they had of it, waiting for the

716

dawn, with the wind steadily strengthening and the rocking of the anchored boat increasing.

When there was barely light enough to see by, Drake had sail hoisted. Then they cut the anchor rope and began to tack toward the harbour mouth against the incoming wind. Two boats gave pursuit.

'Only two!' said Blackwood. 'That's good!'

But, as they approached the harbour mouth, they saw three boats coming in. Drake guessed what had happened. Three of Yot's boats had got out to sea in the night before realizing their quest was hopeless; they had then played safe, keeping clear from shore until there was light enough for a safe return.

Two boats between them and Brennan.

And three boats guarding the seagate to the open ocean.

'Sod it,' said Drake.

'What are you going to do?' said Blackwood.

'Man,' said Drake. 'We'll need bows, we'll need arrows, we'll need soldiers. Listen . . .

As they neared the harbour mouth, one of Yot's boats set itself on a collision course with Drake's. And Drake let it get close, very close.

'Now!' he said.

And Blackwood turned a ring on his finger, and went into the red bottle. Moments later, a stream of vapours emerged from the bottle, and consolidated itself into Blackwood and eight soldiers, all armed with bows and with arrows. Steadying themselves as best they could on the fishing boat, they fired a volley.

The volley missed.

But the helmsman of the oncoming boat, unnerved by the archers shooting at him, dived for cover. And Drake's boat scraped past, the archers giving the enemy another volley as they made for freedom.

'Man, that was gutless!' said Drake. 'If they'd been pirates they'd have rammed us proper, aye, and boarded.'

Shortly, to Drake's delight, they were clear of the harbour mouth. He laughed.

'Why are you laughing?' said Blackwood. 'This is serious! We've five boats in pursuit of us!'

'Aye, man,' said Drake. 'But the world's young, and we're all alive. So why not be happy?'

He was laughing because they were on their way to Ling, whether Blackwood knew it or not.

65

Drake's navigation of the fishing boat Mackerel: by the discipline of the stars; by the arc of the sun; by the tendency of the long, even swells of summer to march from the west toward the shores of Argan; by guesswork, hope and prayer.

At dawn on the fourth day of the sea chase, they saw cliffs ahead which were, in all probability, those of Anvil, the most northerly of the Greater Teeth. Grey cliffs. Tall. Grim. Surf-strewn. A sailor's nightmare.

But Drake welcomed the sight. He grinned. Cliffs of the Greaters! Cliffs of home! He determined to put ashore as soon as possible, even if it meant wrecking the boat. He would rather have landed further south, on Knock, but if they sailed past Anvil he might not get the opportunity.

Drake turned, blinked away flecks of flying spray, and scanned the horizon. The pursuit was far behind. The sails of the five enemy boats were scarcely more than scratches against the distant azure of the northern horizon, lost for half the time amidst the jumbling waves.

It was not Drake's seamanship which was making the difference so much as the red bottle. There, Drake's crew could shelter from the weather, get a decent sleep, prepare proper food and forget the sea. Thus they were able to work long and hard to meet the demands of sea and weather.

Yot's men were not so lucky, and were suffering. Drake was suffering himself, for he was still not prepared to chance himself inside the red bottle. He had dared the venture once – at Lorford's western gatehouse, when he had been left with no other choice – and had vowed he would never run such a risk again.

'Not far to go,' muttered Drake to Drake.

The wizard Miphon was on deck, but was oblivious to all around. He had settled himself to the Meditations. This business of Meditation was, as far as Drake could gather, something like a waking dream, accompanied by a lot of incomprehensible low-voiced garbling.

Three soldiers were also on deck – Brild, Lurghen and Supping. Good men, true, but all they knew of the sea was that it was wet and that boats could float on it.

'Easy,' said Drake to Drake.

And he eased the tiller over so the sails almost lost the wind. Nobody noticed. Drake closed his eyes. He was very tired. He began to sleep, a snatch at a time – dreaming, between waves, of a fragment of a voice or a vision. Each time he woke he flicked his eyes open, ajusted the tiller, then was asleep as fast as he had woken.

By the time Miphon had finished his Meditations, the enemy boats were much closer. So was the north-east tip of Anvil: granite battlements shattering the sundering seas.

'The wind's getting up,' said Miphon, steadying himself on the lurching deck.

Drake altered the angle of the tiller so the wind filled the sails properly, for if he continued playing his games then the wizard might notice what the soldiers had not.

'It's not the wind we have to be worrying about,' said Drake. 'It's the pursuit.'

'Grief,' said Miphon, peering north, 'they're close. How did they catch up so?'

'It's been one of those days,' said Drake. 'The wind's been giving different chances to every patch of the sea. They've had the luck.'

Miphon glanced at the sails, the sea, the pursuit boats, the cliffs they were closing with.

'And we've had no luck?' he said.

'Aye,' said Drake, grimly. 'We've had none. So things look ill for us. How about using your precious death-stone?'

'What, and turn our boat to rock? No, you'd better do something, and fast.'

Drake gazed at the shatter-cliffs of Anvil where white water exploded against gash-toothed rocks. Veils of mist rose high to the heavens, as if the very sea was boiling. A flash of white gleamed amidst spray as a sea-mew slipped through the air at the base of the cliffs. Look up! Yes, it was there, as he remembered it – a small tower standing against the sky.

'See the tower?' said Drake. 'At the top of the cliffs?'

'I see it,' said Miphon. 'Who lives there?'

'Nobody, man,' said Drake. 'There's nothing within but old feathers and dried-up pigeon shit. But we'll be there ourselves before nightfall.'

'How so?' said Miphon.

'We'll fly, man. Aye, yes. My grandmother told me a special recipe for flight. We have to chop up the heart of a wizard then mix it with clippings from his toenails. So bare your chest, man, so we can start the cutting.'

'Enough of your nonsense,' said Miphon. 'What's your plan?'

'You're not much fun today,' said Drake. 'Ah well . . . the plan, that's simple. There's a cove at the base of the cliffs, aye, below the tower. I've been there, yes.'

True. There was a cove, which Drake had visited on a fishing expedition when he was resident in the Greaters.

'There's lots of rocks,' said Miphon, doubtfully.

'Courage, man!' said Drake. 'I can steer us in safe. The enemy will never dare to follow.'

This was also true, as far as it went. Drake could have steered them in safe.

'Take us in, then,' said Miphon.

'Your wish,' said Drake, 'is my command.'

He guided the boat toward the cove. And, shortly, made just the smallest mistake necessary. Rocks ripped

721

open the good ship *Mackerel*. All floundered ashore through the cold sundering surf, and gained the beach of rocks and shingle at the base of the cliffs. Dripping wet. Shocked. Shivering.

'We're done for!' wailed a soldier.

'Enough of that woman's talk!' said Drake. 'There's a path. See?'

Indeed, a steep path led upwards from the beach. They took that path, arriving at length at the ruinous pharos, the clifftop tower they had seen from the sea. Meanwhile, the enemy boats stayed well clear of the shore.

'They'll not chance to wreck themselves here,' said Drake. 'They'd never make it up the path if they did. We could hurl down stones and hold off an army forever.'

'But once we leave,' said Miphon, 'they can chance the cove just as we did.'

'The wind's still rising,' said Drake. 'Soon enough, the wind will wreck all chance of a landing. We'll not leave till it does. Gather wood, boys! Aye, and rocks. Heap rocks here by the cliff, in case they're fool enough to invade.'

Men hacked with weapons at the clifftop vegetation, which was mostly isolated clumps of gorse, and soon had a fire burning inside the pharos. Some sheltered in the red bottle, but others stayed without to keep watch, alternately warming themselves by the fire or huddling outside in the wind at a place where they had a clear view of the cove.

For a long time they watched from the clifftop as the enemy boats tacked and tacked again, often passing very close to each other. Then those boats split up. Two sailed west, following the sun; the other three went withershins.

'Where go they?' said the soldier Scouse.

'They search a landing,' said Drake. 'But they'll find none such. Or, rather – any place they find will be in the possession of pirates.'

'If they find anything,' said Blackwood, 'it'll be a wrecking. This is a perilous coast.'

'In truth,' said the soldier Lurghen. 'As likely as not

they'll be wrecked. Or carried south beyond all hope. Everything to south is in the possession of the Swarms.'

He was wrong. Stokos, while it had been attacked several times by the Swarms, was still free. And Drake was sure that Yot, if he could not force a landing on Anvil, would make for Stokos. Well. So be it. They would have a settling of accounts on Stokos.

'Never mind about Sully Yot and his mob of professional fish-rapists,' said Drake. 'Let's mind about us. We're stuck on a pirate island. Aye, Anvil by name. Some right weird people live here, believe you me. Wealth will tempt them, aye, while honesty will drive them near insane with anger. So let's not come to them wealthy, or honest.'

'Then how?' said Blackwood.

'Okay,' said Drake, 'this is our story. We were a bandit gang living sweet in Estar, until we got driven out, aye, by the terrible Morgan Hearst, the ruthless Blackwood, and the evil wizard Miphon.'

'Why is this wizard Miphon always evil?' said Miphon.

'Man, because magic isn't natural,' said Drake. 'Now, mind nobody says nothing about death-stones, or magic bottles, for pirates will kill for such in less than a tricing. Everyone got that straight? Right then. Let's march.'

Drake guessed it was about thirty leagues from the pharos to Chastity Bay, site of the largest pirate settlement on Anvil. At Chastity, dozens of sea-caves pierced the cliffs, many big enough to hold ships. Drake thought they would need three days for the thirty-league march. He was not far wrong. At mid-morning on the fourth day they reached a landmark he recognized: a gibbet standing beside a big nose-shaped rock.

'Let's go careful now,' said Drake, 'for we're but a league from Chastity Bay.'

They made a final disposition of their forces. Those who would venture to Chastity were Drake, Blackwood, Miphon, and the soldiers Scouse and Lurghen. Everyone else, including Zanya, would be hidden in the red bottle, which would be swaddled in rags, in case some pirate knew

723

what it was. Miphon would wear the ring which commanded that bottle; he would knot the ring to a cord then wear the cord around his neck.

'Goodbye, dearest treasure snake,' said Zanya.

'Goodbye, most glorious princess of the thousand bearskins,' said Drake.

The lovers kissed. Then parted. Miphon took all those who were to remain in hiding into the red bottle. Then rematerialized. And the small band of heroes advanced upon Chastity Bay.

After half a league, Drake said:

'Look! See where that tower is? That's Tunnel Mouth, or was. There, steps descend to caves below. Big caves, aye, some half sea, half air. Ships entire shelter within some of those caves. But that tower – that worries me. There was none such when I was here last.'

'Were you last here before the Swarms?' said Blackwood.

'Oh, long before,' said Drake.

'Then that explains the tower,' said Blackwood. 'Those living here have been forced to fortify their door against the Swarms. The Neversh can fly to the Greater Teeth from the mainland, surely, with little trouble.'

'Then we've been walking in danger for more than three days!' said Drake.

'Whatever danger we've lived through,' said Miphon, 'we've survived. So let's worry no more about it, but advance.'

And so they did.

They were met short of the tunnel by a dog. Now the dog is the favourite animal of pirates, for it will tear the throats of human beings, and will fight its own kind to win bets for brutal masters, and will roll in dung, and will eat its own vomit, and has other habits equally amusing. Drake loved dogs. But this one attacked him, thereby losing his favour.

After the dog had been put down, the five ventured to the tower. It was made of enormous stones, as if it had been built to last ten thousand years.

'Where did pirates find the skill to build such as this?' said Blackwood.

'Slaves manage such,' said Drake, vaguely.

He had never had anything much to do with the slaves of the Greater Teeth, but knew they handled most of the skilled work which was done in the Greaters.

'Hoy! You farts there!' roared a big black pirate, stepping from the door of the tower.

'Run?' said Miphon.

'Go on,' said Drake, though his heart was hammering. 'I know the man. It's Bucks Cat. He's okay.'

'Ahoy there!' yelled Drake.

'Ahoy yourself,' shouted Cat.

Then said nothing further as Drake and his companions closed the distance. When they were almost at the door to the tower, a lean, pale man stepped forth to join Bucks Cat. It was Ish Ulpin!

Drake's heart beat the faster.

'Why, hello darling,' said Ish Ulpin. 'How came you here? And who are your friends?'

'Stout men with good steel,' said Drake. 'There'll be no trouble here, I trust. We're old shipmates, aren't we?'

'Perhaps we are,' said Bucks Cat, grinning.

He whistled. Forth from the shadows stepped Ika Thole and Simp Fiche. Then another man: a rough-bearded brute with a scarred bald patch the size of a man's palm on the top of his head.

'Andranovory!' cried Drake in astonishment.

'The same,' said Atsimo Andranovory. 'Alive and kicking. No thanks to you! You betrayed me in Selzirk. I was seized from Jone, held within dungeons, beaten, tortured, questioned for month upon month. I was lucky to escape with my life.'

'Man,' said Drake, 'I never betrayed you. In Selzirk I came face to face with a wizard who read minds, aye. He picked your whereabouts from my brain. Precious little I could do about that! Anyway, here you are as large as life. So what matter past sufferings?'

Miphon and Blackwood, at the sight of Andranovory, had sunk back as best they could behind the soldiers Scouse and Lurghen. But Andranovory had recognized them at first glance, and now he named them:

'Look, boys, at those two skulking there! You know who they are? They're Miphon and Blackwood, aye. Companions of the questing hero, Morgan Hearst. They've lately ruled in Estar as kings. They'll buy a rich ransom, I'll warrant.'

'Peace!' said Drake, hastily, as hands dropped to sword-hilts. 'Let's have no fighting before a hearing.'

'I've no time for listening to lies,' said Ish Ulpin. And drew his blade. But nobody drew with him. For, after all, the odds were even – five versus five. 'All right then,' said Ish Ulpin, seeing how things stood. 'Tell your story. But get it over with quick.'

'It's simple enough,' said Drake. 'Things came to war between Morgan Hearst and the good lords Blackwood and Miphon. Hearst won for the moment, for he has the Rovac with him. Hence we fled. Me and these other two, we're mercenaries sworn to the service of Blackwood here. Our hope now is to venture to Ling to gain a pearl-fortune to finance an army to win back Estar from Hearst.'

'And where will you find such an army for sale?' said Ish Ulpin.

'Why, on Stokos, of course,' said Drake.

'Doubt it!' said Ika Thole. 'All men in arms under the rule of Watashi are kept busy in battles against the Swarms.'

'Watashi?' said Drake.

'Watashi, ruler of Stokos,' said Thole. 'You've not heard of Watashi? He's son of Farfalla of the Harvest Plains.'

'He's heard of Watashi!' said Andranovory. 'Why, he's had open disputes with the man. I heard of such while rotting in the dungeons of Selzirk. Seems Drake thieved a bard from the prince – a thing frightful precious, whatever it be.'

726

'I never stole it!' said Drake. 'That was my bard from the start! I found it in a tower near Ling, aye, won its magic at great cost to myself. And Watashi stole it from me!'

'No need to plead innocent!' said Ish Ulpin. 'We're no court of law, not us. All we care for is value. You've value to Watashi by way of revenge. If we can't get ransom for this Miphon and Blackwood, we'll win payment for you from Watashi.'

Drake heard distant singing from someone coming up the stairs to the tower. Miphon and Blackwood heard the singing as well, as did the soldiers Scouse and Lurghen.

'Let's run for it,' said Blackwood.

'No,' said Drake.

They could not escape Anvil without help from the pirates. If they ran, they would be hunted down and caught. Then one of the soldiers would surely seek to win favour from the pirates by giving up the secret of the red bottle and the death-stone. Then there would be no hope for Zanya.

'Boys,' said Drake, 'let's do a heal. We five can run, aye, and you'd be days hunting us. Or you can swear yourselves to a bargain. I'll surrender myself to be handed over to this Watashi. In turn, you'll let my comrades have liberty. They'll swear themselves to continue our quest south to Ling, and you'll help them gather together such pirates as wish to sail with them on the venture.'

Drake looked from face to face. Sweating. Would anyone swear to the bargain? Surely all would.

Bucks Cat, Ish Ulpin and the others would gain, as they would not have to hunt Drake over Anvil, but would take him prisoner immediately. Watashi would pay well for Drake. Unfortunately, during the year Drake ruled the Gates of Chenameg, Watashi had come that way – and Drake had given Watashi rather a hard time before letting him proceed. Watashi would doubtless hold a grudge.

Miphon and Blackwood would swear, surely. Neither wished to pledge themselves to a quest south to Ling. But

727

they had very little choice. For, if they did not, Drake could easily reveal the secret of the red bottle, whereupon pirates would kill them for the wealth and power those artefacts represented. And the soldiers? They had sworn oaths of loyalty to Blackwood and Miphon. Such oaths would probably compel them. Furthermore, the pirates of the Greaters had an evil reputation, and the soldiers would welcome an arrangement which would guarantee their safety.

Only Drake would lose from such a bargain. But this was the only way he could now get Zanya to Ling. He would have to take his chances with Watashi.

'I swear,' said Andranovory, 'I swear – with this!'

He drew, and struck at Drake with his sword. As Drake leaped back, Ika Thole knocked down An'vory's arm.

'Not so hasty,' said Thole.

'Who hasty?' said a voice.

The voice belonged to a head, which belonged to a body, which, with some difficulty, squeezed its way out of the great door of the tower. It was Whale Mike!

'Drake!' said Mike. 'Long time no see! How you get here?'

'We flew,' said Drake.

'That good fun, flying,' said Mike. 'Why everyone not look happy? You not make hard time for old friends, surely?'

'Young Drake is no friend,' said Ish Ulpin. 'He stole our tinderbox in Penvash. He left us to shiver without fire.'

'You not shiver too much,' said Whale Mike. 'I remember that. You sleep in my armpit, you snore like baby. That not so tough. Anyway, what little thing like tinderbox between friends?'

'He's worth money!' said Andranovory. 'We can sell him to Watashi of Stokos!'

'Oh, that so?' said Whale Mike. 'I hear little thing about you sometimes. Watashi buy you, too, if we want sell something.'

'That's not true!' said Andranovory.

'It not matter whether it true or not,' said Whale Mike.

728

'We all good friend. Come inside, come inside. Sky not very happy. It rain soon.'

Ish Ulpin spat with disgust and walked away. Bucks Cat followed. Both knew it was no good arguing with Whale Mike once Mike had decided somebody was a friend.

'Hey!' said Andranovory, in bewilderment. An'vory, who had not shared the ordeal on Chag-jalak or the trek through Penvash, had no idea of the depth of feeling binding Drake and Whale Mike. 'What's going on? These are our prisoners!'

'No,' said Ika Thole. 'These are Whale Mike's friends. Ah well . . . we've lost nothing. What would Watashi have paid for Drake Douay? A feather's weight of gold, perhaps, or a rat's head full of silver. Come, man, let's get a drink.'

Drake thought Watashi would have paid far more than that to have Drake Douay strapped down on a torture bench – but he did not bother to enlighten the pirates about his true worth.

'Mike,' said Drake. 'It's good to meet you.'

'Always good to meet old friend,' said Mike. 'Come inside.'

And in they went, as the sky, truly unhappy, began weeping.

729

66

The prospects for piracy: with the west of Argan over-
run by the Swarms, prospects are poor. There is a little
north-south trade between Stokos and the Ravlish Lands,
but most pirates have been reduced to supporting themselves by fishing and sealing.

The five – Blackwood, Miphon, Drake, Scouse and
Lurghen – followed Whale Mike to his home cave. On
entering, they saw two children of about a year's growth
squadding around inside a playpen.

'These my kids,' said Whale Mike. 'They twins.'

'Very nice,' said Drake, peering at the smiling little
mannikins. One waved at him with a little fist. The other
was mauling a toy dragon made out of wood and sealskin.
'Where did they come from?'

'Oh, your father not tell you how make babies? said
Whale Mike. 'Never mind. You learn some day.'

'You mean – these are your children?'

'Oh, sure, they not as big as me,' said Whale Mike. 'But
they grow. We all start small, that not so? Come meet my
wife.'

'You're – you're married?' said Drake.

'He is indeed,' said a voice.

The voice belonged to a petite woman who wore her hair
in a multitude of small plaits. Unless Drake was very much
mistaken, this was Darlinda, who had once been married
to Plovey of the Regency.

'This my wife,' said Whale Mike. 'She Darlinda.'

Drake bowed, and introduced the others in his party to Darlinda. Standing beside Whale Mike, Darlinda looked ridiculously small. Drake, being what he was, could not help but wonder about the mechanics of their mating. It occurred to him that if he had managed to marry King Tor's daughter, as he had once hoped to, he would have looked as daft beside her as Darlinda did alongside Whale Mike.

Maybe he had had a lucky escape.

'Do you like it here?' said Drake to Darlinda.

'It's nice,' she said. 'Except . . . it's very bare. All rock.'

'You like my wife?' said Whale Mike to Drake. 'That too bad, she too small for you.'

And Mike laughed uproariously. Then he insisted that they all go and see his ship. This proved to be an open, undecked boat with a single mast and a dozen rowing benches. It was moored in a cave which was open to the sea.

'It's great,' said Drake. 'Where did you get it?'

'I make,' said Whale Mike. 'That good thing, make ship. We had wreck, I get plenty timber, I make ship. This ship I call *Walrus*. That good name.'

'What does Slagger Mulps think about that?' said Drake.

'Oh, he got other things to worry about,' said Whale Mike. 'You like my ship? We raid north.'

'When do you plan to do that?' said Drake.

'Oh, we been many times. Me, Ish Ulpin, Ika Thole, other jokers. We raid cabbage, we raid cauliflower, also carrots, turnips, parsnips, beetroot, sheeps and chickens. Sometimes we raid Ravlish Lands, sometimes we raid Lorp.'

Which made Drake realize that the life of a pirate had changed considerably since he was last on the Teeth. Pirates used to raid for silk, gold and high-class slaves – not for vegetables.

'You want crew with me?' said Whale Mike. 'That good, all friends together.'

'I would,' said Drake. 'But me and my companions, we've sworn ourselves to other ventures. We're going to Ling for pearls.'

'Ah, Ling,' said Whale Mike. 'That place sound very

731

interesting. I hear many tales. Maybe I go with you. We get pearls, Darlinda like that. She like pretty thing. We get stores, we leave tomorrow.'

'In that?' said Drake, pointing at Mike's open boat.

'Why not?' said Whale Mike. '*Walrus* good ship. She go plenty distance, no problem.'

Then, seeing Drake's dismay, Whale Mike broke out into belly-shaking laughter, and slapped his thighs.

'I talk truth now,' said Mike. 'Joke over. We go to Knock. Good ships there. Still, it not easy get crew for Ling. Maybe you go south after all in *Walrus*. But that okay. We get there. My ship good ship.'

'Aye,' said Drake. 'If your ship proves to be the only way to go, we'll chance it thus.'

'You may, perhaps,' said Blackwood. 'Some of us have other plans.'

'Come, man,' said Drake. 'We're all good friends here – are we not?'

He spoke lightly, but the way he looked at Blackwood was intended to remind that lord of Estar of the fragility of his position. Drake was on home ground, with friends like Whale Mike to back up his actions. Blackwood and the others were foreigners, who lived on sufferance.

'I think,' said Miphon quietly, seeing how things stood, 'that we'll be more than happy to go south to Ling.'

He could hardly say otherwise.

Five days later, Drake's party arrived at Knock on Whale Mike's open boat, the *Walrus*. With them were Mike himself, and also Bucks Cat, Ika Thole, Ish Ulpin, Simp Fiche and Andranovory. Drake was uneasy about having so many potential enemies travelling with them – but Mike had insisted that his good friends come along.

At Knock, the *Walrus* found haven in the Inner Sleeve. Drake had first been there as a boy. He was returning as a man, with man-sized tasks ahead of him.

In the Inner Sleeve was the longest, leanest, most beautiful ship which Drake had ever set eyes on. She was the

Dragon. She had four masts and carried a crew of three hundred. She was owned equally by Jon Arabin, Slagger Mulps, Bluewater Draven and Abousir Belench.

That was the ship Drake wanted!

It looked almost fast enough to fly.

But liberating that ship for a journey down to Ling . . . ah, that was going to be no easy task.

Also in the Inner Sleeve were smells of tar and sewage, smells which came to him enriched by memory. The caves were smaller than he remembered, and quieter; there were fewer people, and those less healthy.

Drake realized that both Blackwood and Miphon were nervous. He said nothing to calm them. Let them sweat! Their lordships knew by now that they would never get off the Greater Teeth without Drake's help. Without Drake's old friendships, they would never have got a boat from Chastity Bay. And now they were not sure how far they could trust Drake.

Drake took his party to meet Jon Arabin, who looked older, and had taken to walking with a slight stoop.

And an emotional meeting they had.

'Man,' said Drake, after a lot of talking, 'that's a beautiful ship you've got.'

'It's a sign of the sea's poverty,' said Jon Arabin. 'When the fish get fewer, the fisherman gets a better net. And she's not mine – I own but a quarter of her.'

'Man,' said Drake, 'she'd be sweet for the run to Ling. How long since you were down there last?'

'Not since we were there together,' said Jon Arabin. 'Aye, and I'm not likely to go again.'

'Man, why not?' said Drake. 'The *Dragon*, surely she'd near enough to fly. Aye, a hundred leagues a day, mayhap. We'd be clear down to Ling in eight or nine days.'

Jon Arabin laughed.

'With the winds being what they are,' said he, 'I think even a ten-day voyage would be but a dream. But, in any case, none wants to risk the voyage. There's been too many tales of what happened on our last.'

'This is serious,' said Drake.

'Why so?' asked Jon Arabin.

'There's two stories,' said Drake. 'One is for all to hear, the other for you alone. The public story is that we seek pearl-wealth to fund an army to throw Morgan Hearst out of Estar, aye, and regain the place for Lord Miphon and Lord Blackwood. We promise power and plunder to tempt men to our enterprise. But there's a little more to it than that. Remember how those in Ling planted a snake in my body?'

'Aye,' said Arabin, 'I remember you babbling about such just after your hostage-time ended. But I thought it a story. I picked you as being good with stories.'

'This story has truth to it,' said Drake. 'There was indeed a snake.'

'Then what's so important about this snake?' said Jon Arabin.

'It saves life,' said Drake. 'It's magic of the ancients, which goes by the name of a paratopic. It kills off plagues, prevents poisoning, preserves the flesh against alcohol. Lord Miphon here, he's dying of a fearful pox. He got it from whoring at orgies in Estar.'

'Is this true?' said Jon Arabin to Miphon.

'It is true,' said Miphon calmly, 'that we must venture to Ling to save life.'

'And this venture,' said Drake, 'is dear to my heart.'

'Then I'd vote for the journey,' said Jon Arabin. 'Not just for old times' sake, either. The wealth of pearls is as well worth having as ever. But there'd be three votes against.'

'But you could persuade friend Walrus to the enterprise, surely,' said Drake.

'Nay, for he's too sick to have appetite for cruising,' said Jon Arabin.

'How sick?' said Drake.

'Very,' said Arabin.

'Then,' said Drake, 'maybe one of these snakes might help save his life.'

'I hadn't thought of that,' said Jon Arabin. 'How many

of these snake things do you think they've got at Ling?'

'There's only one way to find out,' said Drake. 'Come, let's go talk to the Walrus.'

They went, and found Slagger Mulps laid up in bed. Three days ago, a blood vessel in his lungs had burst, and he had spat out enough blood – according to his account of the disaster – to have drowned a ship rat. Miphon elicited a medical history, then pronounced on his condition:

'This is consumption.'

'Aye, man,' said the Walrus, with very bad grace. 'I knew that myself. It didn't come on sudden like. I've had years to think about it. Aye, it's happened before, it'll happen again, and one day likely kill me.'

'You don't have to die,' said Drake. 'A cure is possible.'

'Yes,' said Mulps, 'to sleep with a virgin. That cures most things, every man knows that. But where am I to find a virgin in the Teeth?'

'Listen to me,' said Drake.

'Aagh,' said the Walrus, 'what good's listening? There's naught good you can do for me. Unless you care to make some of your special soup to finish me off.'

'Special soup?' said Drake, blankly.

The Walrus laughed.

'Soup, or goulash, or whatever you want to call it,' he said. 'That stuff you cooked for us when we were running from the Lessers to D'Waith.'

'Oh, that!' said Drake, remembering.

'Yes,' said Mulps, 'that thick, gungy, horrible, lethal concoction. That's all I'd need today to see me free from this corpse of mine.'

'You dare insult my goulash?' said Drake. 'Man, that was great stuff! Aye, a right special brew, yes, with baby rabbits, aye, baby rabbits, and shrimps.'

'It was dirty filthy muck full of rats and cockroaches,' said Mulps. 'I know a rat from a rabbit even if the Warwolf doesn't!'

'If it had been so vile,' said Drake, with a glance at Jon Arabin's impassive face, 'you'd never have eaten it.'

'Oh, I ate it, all right,' said the Walrus. 'For friend Warwolf was eating alongside me. Aye, Jon – there you were, spooning it into your filthy maw as if it was nectar you were dining on. Man, it was hard to eat – but worth the effort, aye, for the pleasure of seeing our dear friend Arabin gorge on rats and on cockroach. The hardest part about eating was to keep from killing myself with laughter!'

And Mulps fell back against the gunny sacks which served him as pillows, laughing until he coughed up fresh frank blood.

'Man,' said Drake, 'now you've finished telling lies about my cookery, perhaps you'll listen to some sense.'

And Drake explained about the paratopic, and how it could save Mulps from dying of disease.

Up till then, Slagger Mulps had been fatalistic about his disease. He had consumption; there was no cure; he might live ten more years, or he might drop dead tomorrow. It had been a fact of life now for as long as he could remember.

But once he realized there was a cure, his attitude changed. He could live? Then he would live. He must live!

'But our other shareholders,' said Mulps. 'They won't risk ship for some cure for consumption.'

'But they will for profits,' said Jon Arabin. 'There'll be pearls in plenty in Ling. Why, with an owner's share, we could probably each retire to Chi'ash-lan.'

Sure enough, Abousir Belench and Bluewater Draven allowed themselves to be persuaded to release the *Dragon* for the voyage south – even though they declined to come themselves. A crew was got together readily enough. For trade goods, they loaded the *Dragon* with things unobtainable in Ling – sealskins, walrus-hide ropes, walrus ivory, things of iron and bronze and steel.

'We'll call in at Island Tor,' said Jon Arabin. 'Aye, and cut bamboo and good timber. That'll complete the cargo.'

Meanwhile, Drake talked privately with Miphon, Blackwood and their soldiers. Drake swore solemnly that, at journey's end, he would see them returned to Estar.

They did not protest too much.

They had very little choice in the matter.

Drake was content. Soon – maybe in ten days, but surely in no more than twenty – they would be in Ling. Then he would get a magic snake to cure Zanya's illness. Then it would be time to do something about these haughty lords from Estar, aye. Kill them, gut them, get the death-stone, get the red bottle, and get the ring which commanded the bottle.

Then he would do what Menator had once done: he would set himself up as Lord Emperor of the Greaters.

And after that?

Why, he would conquer the Lessers, take over Estar and Trest, plunder the Ravlish Lands, subdue Tameran, bring Chi'ash-lan under his heel – then turn his attention to Stokos.

'Lord Dreldragon,' said Drake to Drake. 'Ruler of the universe.'

It had a nice ring to it.

On reflection, even with the death-stone he might lack the power to conquer the Ravlish Lands and Tameran entire. But one thing he was certain of:

'Before I'm dead, I'll rule on Stokos. Aye. And have Sully Yot's head as a table decoration when I hold a banquet to celebrate.'

But before Drake's adventures could be brought to such a satisfactory conclusion, the good ship *Dragon* had to be got to sea. And that was a nightmarish undertaking, seeing that the ship was so large and the way so narrow. In fact, it took a full two days of towing, warping, sweat, fatigue and obscenity.

Then the *Dragon* sailed to a mountainous part of the coast of Chorst, and hove to by night while her boats went back and forth filling water barrels from a generous shoreside stream. This operation went smoothly, for every pirate concerned had helped often with these water-raids.

Only then could the ship run south.

'At least there's nothing to delay us further between here and Ling,' said Drake.

He was wrong.

For, as the *Dragon* cruised southwards in the vicinity of the Gaunt Reefs, the lookout in the crow's-nest spied something on those wave-lashed rocks which might have been a wreck. And Jon Arabin ordered the Dragon to heave to.

While Drake paced up and down the deck, near ready to kill himself with frustration – every day took Zanya closer to death, and here they were wasting time sending boats to look at some smashed-up driftwood on some desolate sea-rocks! – a cutter from the *Dragon* ventured to the reef.

And returned with the sole survivor of a shipwreck.

That survivor was Sully Yot.

67

Miphon's dream: to learn to breed the paratopic; to teach this knowledge to the world; to benefit all humanity by ending sickness, drunkenness and addiction for once and forever. This dream, which Miphon has come to cherish, allows him to persuade himself that Drake's intentions are strictly honourable.

When Sully Yot was brought aboard the *Dragon*, goosepimples standing out on his skin like an extra set of warts, the first person he recognized was Drake. Who promptly drew his sword.

'Belay that!' said Jon Arabin, with anger in his blue-sky eyes. 'Sheath that blade on the instant!'

'I'll see Yot dead first,' snarled Drake.

Upon which Yot swooned, thumping to the deck like a derelict sack of potatoes.

'You kill him, and you die yourself,' said Jon Arabin.

Seeing the Warwolf was serious, Drake reluctantly sheathed his sword. He then argued strenuously for the immediate lynching of Sully Yot.

'He's useless meat,' said Drake. 'We've got ballast enough already.'

But both Walrus and Warwolf refused to countenance such execution. Both felt they had seen far too much pointless death in the last few years.

'He's an old shipmate of ours,' said Jon Arabin. 'You can't kill him off just like that!'

'He stole that magic star-globe from the rest of us when

739

we were in the Penvash Peninsular,' said Drake.

'Aagh, that's ancient history,' said the Walrus. 'And if we're to speak of stealing, what about that tinder-box? Anyway, that ball of stars was no good to anyone. All it did was open a Door from one place of horror to another – and who'd care to chance such a second time, having survived it once?'

'I've – I've personal quarrels with Yot,' said Drake.

'Then you'll not settle such quarrels aboard the good ship *Dragon*,' said Jon Arabin. 'I charge you with the care, comfort, safety and security of Sully Yot. Punishment, if you fail, will be unlimited!'

Arabin followed this order with specific instructions. Amongst other things, he warned Drake not to let Yot fall overboard at night while sleepwalking, eat poison, fall on knives, tumble down a companion-way, or accidentally strangle himself.

'If he dies,' said Jon Arabin, 'I'll know who killed him!'

Thus it was that when Yot regained consciousness, the first thing he saw was Drake Douay leaning over him. Yot lay helpless, staring up at him. What was the most vicious, crippling thing Drake could say? He thought swiftly, then said it:

'Gouda Muck is dead.'

'What?' said Yot.

'Dead,' said Drake. 'Muck. He's dead.'

'You always did tell a good lie,' said Yot.

And fainted.

When Yot came round, Drake started on at him again.

'Muck really is dead, you know. He was mad. Here, drink this.'

So saying, Drake fed Yot some tepid broth. They were in Jon Arabin's master-cabin, which had been temporarily reserved for the invalid. Yot had been almost dead when rescued from the Gaunt Reefs.

While feeding Yot, Drake spun a long and involved tale about the madness of Gouda Muck, and about Muck's death. This part of his story was true. Slowly, as detail gathered on detail, Drake saw despair register in Yot's eyes. Yot believed. For Drake's account of Muck's final madness made sense in the light of Muck's life.

Strangely, while telling the history of Muck's last days, Drake felt his anger subside. Muck had been mad, true. So who could rightly hold his actions against him? Yot had always been sane, of course – but feeble-minded. Could Yot help it if he had a brain as soft as stinking cheese? And they had been friends, of a sort, in the years of their apprenticeship . . .

'No doubt you'd also like to hear,' said Drake, 'about the death-stone and the magic red bottle and such.'

'Nothing,' said Yot weakly, 'could be further from my mind.'

'We know each other too well to be believing that,' said Drake. 'The truth is that Morgan Hearst lost his temper with Blackwood and Miphon when we were all beseiged together in the western gatehouse of Lorford . . .'

Thus Drake began telling a pack of total untruths. He made Yot believe that Hearst had seized the death-stone and the red bottle before parting company with Miphon and Blackwood.

'Then I guessed wrong,' said Yot. 'I guessed where you'd go – that part I got right.'

'Yes,' said Drake, 'yes, you did well to guess the first part.'

'But I also thought . . . I also thought you'd have bottle and death-stone with you. So I chanced my life for nothing . . .'

'Never mind,' said Drake. 'It's all over now. We're to be friends.'

'We are?' said Yot.

'Aye,' said Drake.

He almost hoped that this was true. In any case, he would be safer if Yot thought of him as a friend.

With Yot slowly convalescing on board, the *Dragon* proceeded south.

With her lean, long lines, the *Dragon* was a fast ship,

741

and a wet one. The deck was a slather of spray and water in seas where the old *Warwolf* would have been near enough to bone-dry.

A day after they had cleared the Gaunt Reefs, they became embroiled in a two-day tussle with the tail-end of a cyclone. As the ship pitched and heaved, Drake was heartily glad that Zanya was safe in the red bottle, where – or so report had it – the horizons were always stable no matter how much the bottle was shaken.

Drake spent much of the storm in the cabin with Sully Yot, going over the details of Muck's final madness time and time again. Each time he told the story, his attitude to Muck softened.

'Aye,' said Drake, one day of storm. 'I remember the day when I was to be thrown to the sea beyond Stokos. Muck came to the waterfront to see me off. Brought clothes for me. Trousers, aye, and a jersey of greasy wool. That was before his madness set in. Likely those things saved my life – so I can't hold too much against him.'

'We've . . . we've been through a lot together,' said Yot.

'Aye,' said Drake. 'In Penvash and all . . .'

And nostalgia claimed them as the storm worsened.

After the *Dragon* had survived the storm-weather, the days smoothed out nicely as she sailed for the south. She kept well clear of the coast, but a silt-brown discoloration told when she was abeam of Androlmarphos and the Velvet River.

Further south, the crew sighted a smudge on the eastern horizon. Jon Arabin averred that the smudge was the western coast of Stokos. Drake gazed on it for a long time, thinking of his mother, his father, his brother Heth. There were tears in his eyes when he turned away.

'Why are you crying?' said Yot, happening upon this scene of homesickness.

'Man,' said Drake, 'I was thinking of Zanya.'

'Why so?'

'When we reached Anvil,' said Drake, 'she decided she

could live no longer with the blue leprosy. She cut her throat. Aye, like my sister did on Stokos.'

'I'm . . . I'm sorry to hear that,' said Yot.

Drake, to his amazement, found himself believing Yot was truly sincerely sorry. Drake's news of the madness of Gouda Muck had knocked most of the religious nonsense out of Sully Yot. Near-death on the Gaunt Reefs also seemed to have changed the man. Maybe they could be true friends for the future. It was unlikely, but:

Improbabilities are not impossibilities.

Three nights later, Drake was standing watch on a clear and cloudless night. The ship was heading south in an easy swell, airing along with all sail set and a light wind coming from the east.

The light winds meant their speed was less than dazzling. Even so, by Jon Arabin's calculations they were now entering the Drangsturm Gulf; Narba, or the ruins of Narba, should be somewhere out in the night, about fifty leagues to larboard.

Drake was steering. The weather was so steady he felt he could just about have lashed the wheel and left it. However, he had two youngsters on this watch, Zim and Krane, both sixteen years of age, and senseless. Drake was determined to set an example.

These teenagers!

They were thoughtless, reckless, idle and irresponsible. What was worse, they thought they knew it all. And they were cheeky into the bargain! Unlike Drake, they had never had to man the rigging in a howling storm; they had never made a bluewater voyage to Hexagon and back; they had never been shipwrecked in the Penvash Channel.

What they needed was a hard master like Gouda Muck to kick them into shape. Yes. Perhaps he should talk it over with Jon Arabin. They could set up an apprenticeship to get these would-be pirates whipped into line.

Right now, Zim and Krane were sitting on the deck having a regular chinwag. Drake wondered what he could do to stir them up. Send them down to the kitchen,

743

yes, to bring up some soup. Because—

Drake's train of thought was broken as the ship shuddered. They had struck something!

'Rocks!' shouted Zim, grabbing for the wheel.

Drake hit him fast and hard with a rabbit punch, then gave him a push which sent him reeling away.

'Man,' said Drake, firm in control of the wheel once more, 'you grab stupid like that again, and I'll give you a leathering. I've the helm, aye, and the head to manage it.'

The ship was still running along nicely. The wind was the same, and the swells as regular as ever. Drake listened, but heard no sound of water breaking on rocks. Raising his voice to a shout, he hailed the crow's-nest:

'What sign!'

The reply came back:

'Nothing!'

Which was what Drake had expected. There was, after all, no rock, reef, shallow, shoal, island, cay, cliff or shore within fifty leagues of them. Drake had that on the authority of Jon Arabin, who knew these waters as well as any man alive.

'What was it?' said Krane.

'Sharbly we grounded a whale,' said Drake.

Then remembered saying those very same words years ago, in the Penvash Channel. On that occasion, it had been a sea serpent they had tangled with.

There was another thump.

'Krane!' said Drake. 'Take the lantern and go forward. See what you can see. Zim, look over the side.'

'Shall I go wake the bald-headed one?' said Zim.

'Nay, man,' said Drake. 'He'll wake himself if we hit again. And if we don't, what matter?'

'We might be holed,' said Zim.

'Nay,' said Drake, 'not from a teeny little bump like that. Go on, get moving the pair of you.'

Grief! What if Zim was right? If they were holed, they would probably be busy till dawn. The last thing Drake wanted to do right now was to fother a hole by night.

'Zim!' called Drake. 'What do you see over the side?'

'Something,' said Zim, uncertainly.

'What? Is it big, small, still, moving, foaming, swirling? Is it light, creamy, dark, shadowy? Do the stars reflect off it? Is it a sea serpent? A whale? A kraken?'

'A log.'

'Blood of the moon,' said Drake. 'A log. Likely that was what we hit. I'd say—'

He didn't say, for at that moment there came a scream fit to scar the sky.

'Zim!' said Drake. 'Get your arse here! Quick quick quick! The wheel, man! Take it, take it! Steer steady, man, or I'll string you up from the yardarm by your lower bowel. Stay tight!'

With that said, Drake raced along the deck toward the lantern. He found it, and found Krane holding it, and looking most uncertain.

'What was that scream?' said Krane.

'An owl, maybe,' said Drake. 'Or perhaps one of your whore-arsed friends just birthed a baby. Come, man, let's go check. Here, give me the lantern, you'll likely drop it if you shake much more.'

Drake took the lantern. It was a good one, with the light from a big bright candle shining out through windows of horn. He stepped out smartly, with Krane trailing in his wake. Then stopped, hearing footsteps up ahead. A man was coming towards them. Drunk, if the footsteps were anything to go by. Drake, lantern in one hand, filled the other with steel, just in case.

He had just done so when into the lamplight came a man who had lost his face. Blood ran thick in his beard, dripped down his jerkin and dribbled to his boots. He staggered. Then fell forward onto the deck.

By lantern-light, Drake saw a great chunk missing from the man's back. Bone gleamed white amidst seething blood.

'Drake, there's—'

'I see it,' said Drake.

Something was skulking in the shadows. Something not in human form. Whatever it was, it was huge.

'Slaughterhouse!' screamed Drake, which was the ship's weapon-shout.

Again he screamed, and heard others take up the cry. Another thump shook the ship. As the creature in the shadows started to advance, Drake heard Krane's feet pounding along the deck as the boy fled.

'Courage, man,' said Drake to Drake.

He set down the lantern then backed away from it.

'Into the shadows, now,' he whispered.

And took his own counsel as the creature – the monster! – stalked toward the lantern.

The monster had a carapace roughly like that of a crab. But, unlike a crab, it had not two eyes, but many. These eyes, each deep-set in a socket, shimmered in the lantern-light, glittered with spangles of reflected fire.

And Drake thought:

Run!

But did nothing.

Terrified.

Paralysed.

And . . . fascinated.

The creature's carapace rode high above the deck on a dozen multi-jointed legs. Mounted on top of the carapace was what looked – at first glance – like a gigantic sea anemone. A seething array of writhing tentacles, of jointed hooks and coiled whips.

Drake, mesmerized by horror, watched as one of those whips uncoiled slowly, slowly, slowly, and drifted down toward the deck to nuzzle the lantern. Gently. The candle-flame flickered as the lantern was tilted then released.

Then – suddenly! – the whip snapped back.

And the monster muscled toward Drake. Who stood staring, staring at its avanturine orbs, its oiled legs soothing toward him.

And he thought:

Now!

746

And raised his sword. And attacked. With a scream: 'Sharn!'

The creature slashed at him with half a dozen whips at once. His sword was knocked away. Whips slammed against him like knotted ropes. He fell sprawling to the deck. He screamed. Jerked out a boot-knife. And threw it. With no effect. Tentacles darted out, whipped around his ankles, and started to haul him off the deck.

Then the monster wailed, and reared up. An arrow had pierced one of its eyes. Another shaft slammed home. The creature fled, hauling Drake behind it. He bounced over the deck, grabbing for something, anything – help me! – and finding nothing.

Then the creature stopped. Abruptly. There was a hideous graunching, crunching, thumping sound. The tentacles which had been hauling Drake relaxed.

He got to his feet.

Something huge bulked against the night. It loomed over the wreckage of the dead monster. Larger than anything human. Then it spoke:

'Man,' said Whale Mike. 'You got nice choice in friends. Or this your lover, perhaps?'

'No,' said Drake. 'That was my mother-in-law.'

'Well, she not good for much now. Sorry about that.'

'That's all right,' said Drake. 'We never got on very well anyway.'

Moving stiffly, he walked back to the lantern light and recovered his sword. The lantern was burning as steadily as ever, but Drake became aware that all around was alarm, panic and chaotic confusion, as three hundred pirates roused themselves out to face danger.

Here and there, fighting was in progress. Something inhuman screamed as it died. Drake sheathed his sword. His right elbow hurt like hell. He rubbed it, which failed to improve matters. Blackwood walked from the shadows, bow in hand.

'You shoot well,' said Drake.

'I've had practice,' said Blackwood.

Drake listened to the noise. From the sound of it, the pirates were winning control of the ship, though there were clearly at least half a dozen monsters aboard. But something was wrong. What? Yes, that was it – the wind had died. The ship was wallowing helplessly in the regular ocean swells.

'I'd better go report to Jon Arabin,' said Drake, 'since I was on watch when the trouble started.'

He found Jon Arabin shortly. The bald-headed one was leading a hunting party of men armed with weapons and lanterns. They had cornered a strange creature which looked like a crawling net, richly strung with floats. It was as wide as a dinghy, as long as a horse, and no higher off the ground than a badger-dog. Legs, claws, feelers and tiny eyes on stalks protruded from every float.

'What's this?' said Drake.

'It's a bowl of spaghetti which mated with a whore's-egg,' said Jon Arabin. 'You should be able to see that for yourself.'

Upon which Ika Thole hurled a harpoon, skewering one of the floats to the deck. The net-creature screamed like a rabid rat, thrashed madly, tore itself free, and escaped to the dark leaving part of its body behind.

Thole knelt to examine the skewered portion which remained – and a claw leaped out of it and slashed at his hand.

'Pox and bitches!' he said, jumping back.

'Club it to a pulp,' said Jon Arabin, curtly. Then, to Drake: 'How did this happen?'

'There are logs in the sea,' said Drake, working more by guess than by the results of Investigation. 'The creatures were on them. We rammed the logs, they jumped aboard.'

Shortly, Jon Arabin and Drake were at the ship's side with a lantern on a rope. They lowered it until its light shone clear on the water. They saw a log afloat on the swells. On the log, three monsters, just like the one which had hauled Drake along the deck.

'Those are stalkers,' said Miphon quietly; he had come

748

up alongside them without being noticed.

Jon Arabin walked along, illuminating a different patch of sea. Another log. Another net creature.

'That's a glarz,' said Miphon, 'that thing which looks like a portcullis made out of rope and decorated with water-melons.'

'The net creature?' said Drake.

'That's the one. And look, over there – two more glarz! And there's a keflo!'

'The sea is full of logs,' said Jon Arabin, hauling up the lantern. 'Have you ever heard of such a thing?'

'In the Long War,' said Miphon, 'the Skull of the Deep South launched many such armadas.'

'Maybe they're near to death,' said Drake. 'They're just sitting there.'

'All these creatures of the Swarms,' said Miphon, 'they're fairly quiet by night.'

'Aye,' said Drake. 'I remember. Man, when I went past Selzirk . . . yes, there were many, making as if they were asleep. But they were huge! These ones are only little.'

'So,' said Jon Arabin, 'we're in luck. We've only a batch of babies to contend with.'

He spoke in jest; he knew how serious the situation was.

'What now?' said Drake.

'We arm ourselves properly,' said Jon Arabin. 'And we wait for dawn. And we pray for wind.'

'Ballast blocks,' said Drake, apropos of nothing.

'What?' said Jon Arabin.

'Ballast blocks, man. Bring them up from below. Sitting targets. Knock those turkeys off their logs. Do it by dark, they'll be much more trouble by day.'

'Aye,' said Jon Arabin. 'That's thinking!'

Much later, they had killed every creature of the Swarms within throwing distance of the ship. Meanwhile, the sky had begun to lighten.

'Dawn is coming,' said Zim.

'Tell me something I don't know,' said Drake.

749

'Sorry,' said Zim, 'but I don't know your father's name either.'

And dodged away from a half-hearted cuff.

As dawn approached, sullen clouds rolled across the sky, driven by high-level winds. Down at sea-level, a deadly stillness persisted. By the growing light, they could see logs upon logs stretching away for leagues, patterning the sea so densely they were almost touching.

On every log, a monster.

There must have been thousands of them. Tens of thousands. Hundreds of thousands. A million, maybe. Drake, unable to make an exact estimate, knew this much for sure: the odds were lousy.

To his amazement, Drake realized that someone had got up on his hind legs and was making a speech. It was the soldier Scouse. Probably the man had been infected with heroism from associating with Morgan Hearst. This was what he was saying:

'Let's sell our lives dear, friends! Let's show them what we're made of! Now is our chance to meet the ancient enemy fist to fist, our chance to warray—'

'Screw speeches!' yelled Zim. 'How about some food?'

'Yes,' said Jon Arabin, loudly, cutting across Scouse's speech. 'Young Zim's spoken sense – albeit for the very first time in his life. Aye. Let's eat. The monsters will be stirring properly soon enough. Food in the gut, that's the story.'

The night's activities had thrown out the ship's routine so badly that no breakfast had been cooked. But hardtack was issued out, plus some oldish bread – hard stuff with a little green and grey mould starting to colonize it. And there was good stuff to wash it down: for every man, a dole of rum and black drop.

The darkening clouds had entirely covered the sky. But the Swarms knew it was dawn. The monsters were moving from log to log, converging on the good ship *Dragon*. Some lost their footing and drowned swiftly. But there were thousands more where those came from.

'Why so near-begaun with the liquor?' said Slagger Mulps, his voice loud in the sullen air. 'Drunk will serve us as well as sober.'

Jon Arabin was not so ready to abandon hope. But he judged that the battle would be joined before his crew had a chance to get drunk. So, rather than argue, he said:

'Aye, friend Walrus. You go below and organize us some more liquor.'

Drake, meanwhile, went quietly to Miphon:

'Can we use the death-stone?' he said.

'We could,' said Miphon. 'But what good would a stone ship do us?'

'Have you any other magic?' said Drake. 'Powers, spells, amulets and such?'

'None,' said Miphon. 'I was never very powerful as wizards go, and I lost most of my powers in – in an accident. But what difference would it make? The Swarms are many.'

'In very deed they're many,' said Drake, faking the reckless gaiety of suicidal courage. 'But are we not men?'

Some of them were, some were just boys. All knew they would most likely soon be dead.

Jon Arabin, for his part, did some mental arithmetic. The last year had been kind to him. He was five births in credit. A margin slim enough, but sufficient to satisfy his gods, who asked only that a man father as many people as he killed.

And that a man plant a tree for every one he cut down.

It occurred to Jon Arabin that, somehow, he had never managed to get round to as much tree-planting as he should have. But surely that was of no importance.

The men had finished breakfast. They were waiting for the attack, and the waiting was hard. Jon Arabin decided to make a speech of his own to ease the silence. He wished he had the skill to produce some iron-worded oratory which would ring down through the ages, an inspiration to all who followed afterwards, and a monument to his own death.

Then he realized there was going to be nobody to record what was said. So it made no difference whether his speech was good or bad. They were doomed to vanish from the face of the sea – one more ship lost without trace.

'Gentlemen,' said Jon Arabin. 'Let's show them what we're made of.'

And, with that, he drew his falchion and raised it in salute. He looked fearless and heroic. But, in fact, he was starting to worry quite badly about all those trees he had never planted.

'Look!' cried Zim.

And they looked where he was pointing, and saw a giant green centipede crawling up over the side of the ship.

'It's fate will be written with my grey-goose quill,' said Blackwood easily, nocking an arrow.

He sent the missile singing toward its target. The centipede, struck in the larboard eye, writhed in agony and fell overboard. Blackwood was pleased. But what could one man do against so many? After all, Blackwood had but twenty shafts remaining.

'Where's this extra liquor?' said Zim.

But his question went unanswered. For, the moment he had spoken, purple lightning lacerated the heavens. Then came a roar of thunder, as if the sky had been shattered by earthquake. Then, again, the outlash of lightning. Again, thunder. Then, with a keening, high-pitched ululation, the monsters of the Swarms attacked the ship.

68

The Swarms: diverse creatures, monstrous and almost mindless, controlled from a distance by the Skull of the Deep South, a powerful entity based in the southern terror-lands. The fall of the Confederation of Wizards has allowed the Swarms to venture north of Drangsturm, conquering most of the western seaboard of the continent of Argan.

Screaming, the Swarms attacked.

They came in their thousands.

But only twenty logs were within monster-leap of the good ship *Dragon*, meaning the Swarms had only twenty avenues of attack. And there were three hundred men aboard.

'Death is our destiny,' said Blackwood, grimly.

And sent an arrow hissing to its target.

Lightning crackled across the sky. Thunder boomed. But still no wind. Still no rain.

'This no time to die,' said Whale Mike, sounding worried. 'I got wife and kids to look after.'

And he swung an oar. *Thwap!* The head of a monster exploded in a spray of gore and ichor.

'Ahyak Rovac!' screamed Rolf Thelemite.

And plunged his sword into the underbelly of a scrabbling keflo as it tried to haul itself onto the deck of the ship.

'Help me!' screamed Simp Fiche.

A glarz had swarmed over him, and was ripping him to pieces.

'Help!'

Ish Ulpin strode forward. But he was intercepted by a thing which looked like a walking thorn bush armed with a dozen sets of shears and a couple of scythes. Ish Ulpin killed it with the help of a couple of other bravos. But by that time Simp Fiche was dead, ravaged, torn to pieces.

The glarz swarmed forward.

Ish Ulpin picked up a spare ballast block and hurled it so it fell square in the middle of the net-shaped body of the glarz. Trapped, it writhed and struggled – but could not get free.

'We'll deal with you later,' said Ish Ulpin.

And went looking for a worthier foe.

'Die, Demon-spawn!' screamed Sully Yot, hurling ballast blocks at creatures which had leapt from logs to the Dragon's flank, and were trying to climb up to the deck.

'I bet they don't even make good eating,' said Ika Thole gloomily, sinking his harpoon through alien armour.

'Now!' screamed Bucks Cat.

A dozen men were with him, using a spar as a battering ram. They pulped a slow-footed monster, screamed, whooped, yelled, and looked for another.

Using spears, ropes, boarding nets, grappling hooks, pikes, halberds and battle-axes, the pirates fought for life and liberty.

And won.

They won the first round, at any rate.

The deck was wet and slippery with ichor, blood, pulp, gore, mashed monsters, the unidentifiable remains of half a dozen men. Amputated tentacles writhed in the scuppers. Someone was floundering in the water, shouting. It was the soldier Scouse. How came he to be there? It mattered not: there was nothing anyone aboard could do for him. As they watched—

Most stopped watching, and, for those who did, the interest was soon terminated with the death of the unfortunate Scouse.

'Come with me,' said Miphon, finding Blackwood. 'Let's go below and venture to the bottle.'

'That's a good idea,' said Blackwood. 'I'm right out of arrows. There'll be more within.'

And the pair departed.

The pirates had broken the first assault of the Swarms, killing upwards of a thousand monsters. The onsurge of horror-creatures died away to a dribble, then to nothing. A great cheer went up. But the battle was only beginning. Stalkers, glarz, keflos, granderglaws, green centipedes and other brutes began, as best they could, to paddle logs toward the *Dragon*.

Their best was far from good.

A centipede clinging to the end of a log, half in the water and half out of it, its water-wet half thrashing furiously, was an essentially ludicrous sight. Many of the creatures lost their grip, floundered briefly, then drowned in the oily darkness of the seas. But there was no shortage of replacements. And they were getting results.

The logs were converging on the *Dragon*.

Jon Arabin clenched his fists and glared at the sky.

'Give me lightning!' he yelled.

Lightning forked downwards.

'Thunder!' screamed Arabin.

A drumroll of thunder followed.

'Now wind!' howled Arabin. 'Wind, for the love of mercy!'

But no wind came. The air was silent. Still. Dead. Even a thread of gossamer would have hung limp in such lifeless airs.

'Bugger bugger bugger!' screamed Arabin.

And searched the horizons for signs of squall. He saw none such: but did see five winged creatures circling far, far overhead. He very much doubted that they were eagles. No: the Neversh were up there.

'Maybe we could catch them somehow,' muttered Arabin. 'Harness them to the ship so they'd pull us clear of this grabble of logs.'

Could it be done?

Somehow, he doubted it.

Drake, also looking up to the sombre oppression of the stormcloud skies, saw the Neversh, but made no comment on it lest he panic someone. With luck, the storm which threatened them would shortly break, scattering the Neversh. Otherwise, there was nothing they could do about the flying monsters. But surely there was something they could do about the logs converging on the ship. Once the Swarms had a hundred jump-off points instead of twenty, it would all be over for the *Dragon*.

'Drake . . .?' said a voice.

It was Zanya, in company with Miphon. The wizard still wore his feathered hat.

'Zanya!' said Drake, embracing her. 'What are you doing here?'

'Standing on the deck so my eyes can proof what Miphon's been telling me. He's been keeping me in touch.'

Drake kissed her. Light touch of lips against lips. Lumps on her lips. Blue lumps. Blue leprosy. What hope now of getting to Ling for a cure? He smelt patchouli on her skin.

'Why perfume?' he said.

'Because I wanted to be my best for you. For . . . for the end. This is the end, isn't it?'

She was starting to cry.

And Drake, by way of soothing, kissed her again. Then held her, held her close and held her tight. He remembered how he had first seen her, so many years ago, when he had been floating in the water bare-arse naked, a horizon away from Stokos, and she had been looking down from the deck of a xebec. And he remembered . . . other places, other times. Their best had been very good indeed. Yes. It had been worth it to have lived. But now . . .

'Darling,' said Drake. 'The next attack is soon. Best you return to the bottle.'

'Are you coming?' said Zanya.

'No,' said Drake.

He had already made up his mind. If the Swarms took the ship, anyone in the bottle would survive. But they would have to stay there, for to exit from the bottle would be death. He had no wish to survive as a prisoner forever. What kind of life was that? He had languished in too many dungeons to consign himself to another. Better to fight, yes, and make an ending.

'You must come!' said Zanya. 'You'll die if you stay out here!'

'Here is where I'm staying,' said Drake.

'Then I'll not go to the bottle either,' said Zanya. 'My end is soon. I know that much. If you end today, then – then so do I.'

Then she said no more, for she was weeping too much to speak. He held her close. Looked over her shoulder to Miphon. He could see no expression in the wizard's green eyes. Miphon seemed almost to have withdrawn from the world. The wizard had wisdom enough to know that their chances of survival were zero. They were doomed. The game was over.

Drake, who had no such wisdom, said:

'The death-stone?'

'We've been through that,' said Miphon, his voice so calm that it infuriated Drake. 'The ship would turn to stone. It would sink, surely.'

'And maybe it wouldn't!' said Drake. 'Maybe a stone ship can still float. How do we know till we try? Let's use the death-stone! At least we'd take more of these monsters with us!'

'It is hardly worth exciting false hopes amidst the crew at this stage,' said Miphon.

'You're crazy, man!' said Drake.

Zanya wiped a snivel of misery from her nose, then sniffed, then said:

'What does it matter if the ship turns to stone? What does it matter if the ship sinks? The bottle would float. Wouldn't it? Float to land somewhere?'

'No, it wouldn't,' said Miphon. 'Blackwood once had occasion to throw a similar bottle into a tarn on the Scourside Coast. It sank immediately.'

'Tied to a man it wouldn't,' said Zanya. 'That man could use the death-stone, then—'

'Then the ship would sink, and we'd have one man afloat in the ocean fifty leagues from anywhere,' said Miphon. 'And the moment he used the ring to get inside the bottle, it would fall away to the bottom of the ocean. Everyone inside would then be trapped there for life – for if the ring-bearer ventured outside, the weight of ocean waters would kill him without pity.'

There was a scream from someone on deck. Drake looked round wildly and saw – a Neversh! It swooped low over the ship, its twin feeding spikes tearing into a sail. Then it was gone, flying low over the ocean, the sail dangling from its spikes.

Drake's heart was hammering. Of all the monsters, he feared the Neversh most of all. To be held by the grapple-hooks, to be pierced by the feeding spikes: he had had nightmares about that.

'Let two men stay outside,' Zanya said, not bothering to comment on the Neversh. 'One to keep the bottle afloat. The other to be ring-bearer. That way the bottle stays afloat.'

'Yes,' said Miphon. 'Then we have two men afloat in the water instead of one. And both fifty leagues from land! What good would that do?'

'The ring-bearer brings out a spar,' said Zanya.

'There is no spar in the bottle,' said Miphon.

'But,' said Drake, in a moment of decision, 'there will be soon. Come! Let's find Jon Arabin!'

For Drake followed Zanya's reasoning, and saw what she was getting at. They could bring one spar out of the bottle, aye – so they could just as easily bring two. And planks. And hammer. And nails. And ropes. And sails. And a long bamboo for a mast of sorts.

'We can't go to Arabin!' said Miphon. 'We've led him to understand the red bottle stayed with Morgan Hearst in Estar. What will he say if he finds we've been lying?'

'Man, is it sudden death you're afraid of?' said Drake,

758

drawing his sword. 'You'll find it here and now lest you come to your senses!'

'I yield,' said Miphon, 'to the judgment of your steel.'

'This is no time for fancy rhetoric,' said Drake. 'Do you mean you'll talk with Arabin, or do you mean you want your death on the instant?'

'We'll talk with Arabin,' said Miphon hastily.

Moments later, Drake was at Jon Arabin's side, with Miphon and Zanya in attendance. Jon Arabin looked Zanya up and down. A strange sight she made, red hair, red skin, her face lathered with blue sores and tracked with tears, her nose still snivelling. While Jon Arabin wondered at this apparition, he judged that this was no time for stupid questions, so said only:

'What is it? Make it quick!'

Drake pointed at Miphon.

'The wizard Miphon,' said Drake. 'On his finger, a magic ring. The ring can take you and crew into a magic bottle. We have with us on board the death-stone. It's the same one told of in legend – the same which demolished the walls of Androlmarphos.'

'Such magic turns all about to stone,' said Jon Arabin. 'Our ship would surely sink.'

'I know that,' said Drake. 'But there's a way to survive regardless. Put crew in bottle with the makings for a boat or such. Then we'll use the death-stone to kill off the Swarms. Then we can bring the timbers out from the bottle, aye, and build a raft or such in mid-ocean.'

'That,' said Arabin, 'is the weirdest thing I've heard all day.'

'But it will work!' cried Drake. 'It will work.'

Jon Arabin stared long and hard at Drake Douay. Then breathed heavily, and said:

'You and me, young man, we're going to sit down and have a talk when this is over. A long talk. Now where's this bottle?'

'Down below,' said Miphon. 'With Blackwood.'

'Then get it up here!' roared Jon Arabin.

And Miphon fled.

At that moment there was a great shout:

'Slaughterhouse! Slaughterhouse! Slaughterhouse!'

The Swarms were attacking. En masse.

'We need time,' said Drake.

'Then get me fire,' said Jon Arabin. 'And I'll get you time, easily enough. Come on, don't just stand there! Get fire!'

Drake and Zanya fled.

Shortly, Miphon reported to Jon Arabin in the company of Blackwood. The Swarms by now had seized the forecastle, and were fighting their way toward the stern. Drake and Zanya came up on deck, bearing between them a cauldron of hot coals stolen from a brazier in the kitchen.

'We're here,' said Miphon. 'Now what—'

He was interrupted by Drake, who yelled:

'Jon! The Walrus is in the kitchen! Dead drunk!'

'I wondered where he'd got to,' said Jon Arabin – who, in fact, had been far too busy to wonder any such thing. 'Mike! Go below! The Walrus is in the kitchen! Get him up here!'

Whale Mike moved to obey.

Then Jon Arabin yelled:

'There's fire here! Fire the ship! Ahoy – you in the crow's-nest! Down, down, we're firing the ship!'

Rolf Thelemite had organized a double-line of men with pikes to hold the deck against the Swarms. They still had time. Just. Arabin glanced at Blackwood, who wore the red bottle knotted tight to his belt.

'That's it?' said Arabin. 'Right! You, Mr Wizard – get waterskins. Tie them to your comrade's belt. We don't want him sinking under if he's to carry us.' Then Arabin raised his voice: 'Ika Thole! Ish Ulpin! To me! To me with a work-party!'

Shortly, men were working furiously. They gathered up timber, and tools, and spars, and ropes, and sails. Whale Mike came up from below decks with Slagger Mulps tucked under his arm.

'Drake!' screamed Yot.

'What's your problem!' yelled Drake.

'You lied to me! About Zanya! About the red bottle! So you lied about Muck, didn't you? He lives, doesn't he? He was never mad, was he? You really are the Demon-son, aren't you?'

Drake did not know whether to laugh or cry. He spread his arms in helpless amazement and cried:

'Man, this is no time to argue theology!'

'No, but it's time enough for a killing!' yelled Yot.

And picked up a spear, intending to hurl it at Drake.

But Whale Mike plucked the spear from Yot's hand, and picked up Yot, and tucked him under his arm. Mike now had Yot under one arm, the Walrus under the other. Bucks Cat grabbed Mike and also grabbed Miphon. Half a dozen men, loaded with all kinds of baggage, grabbed each other. One took hold of Ish Ulpin's ear. Ish Ulpin held Bucks Cat by the neck.

And Miphon, connected by a bond of flesh to so many people, turned the ring on his finger. Whereupon Miphon and all the men, plus their baggage, were snatched away into the red bottle.

Moments later, Miphon and Whale Mike rematerialized.

'I want spar!' boomed Mike. 'Good spar, take inside.'

Back and forth went Miphon and Whale Mike. Each time they ventured into the bottle, they took with them more men and more materials. Blackwood stood stolidly on the deck, arms folded, sometimes giving a timely order to organize the chaos all around.

The sudden promise of physical salvation by means of the red bottle amazed most pirates not a jot. For – was not their leader Jon Arabin? They'd all secretly expected him to come up with something fancy. And this fitted the bill precisely.

While some of the crew had been gathering materials and venturing to the bottle, others had been holding the line against the Swarms, and others had been setting fire to the ship. Smoke curdled in the air. It spread in choking

761

clouds. The Swarms wavered as the smoke spread amongst them – then began to fall back.

'They hate smoke!' yelled Arabin. 'They're running! We're winning!'

Meanwhile, the flames leaped through the still and sullen air, swift as a band of lunatic red-jacketed monkeys driven on by a throng of rabid slave-masters wielding razor-tipped whips by way of encouragement. As the fire took hold, flames swung from sail to sail so fast the canvas seemed almost to explode. And the Swarms were truly on the run, retreating from the heat, the smoke, the crackling fury of the conflagration. Many of the monsters plunged overboard, there to drown.

Burning rope and canvas fell amongst the work parties, who swore and shouted and laboured all the harder. Some were weeping, some laughing, some dancing on the spot as they waited for Miphon to transport them inside the red bottle. They were wild, crazy, manic, joyful. They had hope! They were going to live!

'General retreat!' yelled Jon Arabin. 'Retreat to me! We're quitting the ship! Move your backsides!'

From the daze of heat, smoke and crackling flame came the last of the ship's defenders. Sweating. Bleeding. Gasping. Grinning. Miphon took them into the bottle, group by group.

Finally, only these stood on the burning deck:

Blackwood, the bottle roped to his waist; Miphon, bearing the ring; Jon Arabin; Drake; Zanya; Whale Mike.

Jon Arabin drew his falchion.

'Give the bottle to my man Drake,' said Jon Arabin.

Upon which Whale Mike grabbed both Blackwood and Miphon. One hand round each neck. He could have killed them just by squeezing.

Blackwood unknotted the red bottle and passed it to Drake, who swiftly tied it to his own waist. Jon Arabin glanced around quickly. The air was trembling with heat. He was sweating. Somewhere, burning wood broke with a

762

sharp crack. Beyond the flames he could see a handful of hell-creatures writhing in death.

'Now, the death-stone,' said Jon Arabin. 'Give it to me!'

'No,' said Miphon.

'I'll kill you!' said Jon Arabin.

'Blackwood,' said Miphon. 'Blackwood has the death-stone.'

'This is true?' said Jon Arabin.

Blackwood nodded.

'Then give it to me!' said Arabin.

'Jon,' said Drake. 'It's no good grabbing the death-stone. I've tried that. There's writing on it. The writing gives a spell which commands the death-stone. You have to hold the death-stone, then say the spell.'

Jon Arabin was literate. But he knew well that any wizard-spell would be written in the High Speech, which he could neither speak nor read.

'The spell!' demanded Jon Arabin.

'The spell,' said Miphon, promptly, 'is *jonmarakaralarajodo, enakonazavnetzyltrakolii, zeq-telejenzeq.*'

Miphon was lying. These words had no power whatsoever: they simply meant, in the High Speech of wizards: stochastic, phenomenological, epistemological.

'Run that past me again,' said Jon Arabin, a puzzled look on his face.

Miphon did so.

But it was no good: such long words could never be learnt in moments.

A burning spar crashed to the deck, scattering blazing coals. A wave of heat washed across their sweating faces. The air filled momentarily with choking smoke, then cleared, leaving them coughing, eyes watering.

'Mr Wizard,' said Jon Arabin, deciding. 'We'll learn the ways of the death-stone later. For the moment, you'll give Blackwood the ring. Blackwood will take us inside the red bottle. You'll stay within with me, as a hostage. Then

763

Blackwood will return to the deck to command the death-stone against the Swarms.'

Reluctantly, Miphon gave Blackwood the ring which commanded the red bottle.

'Let's go,' said Jon Arabin.

And grabbed Zanya. Then took hold of Whale Mike, who had still not released either Miphon or Blackwood. Then Blackwood turned the ring on his finger – and all five were sucked into the red bottle which was now tied to Drake's belt.

As they vanished, air rushed in to occupy vacuum. With the air came smoke, ash, intolerable heat. Drake, alone on the deck, crouched low to avoid the smoke. Another spar shook the deck as it fell, scattering more burning coals. One skittled along the deck, finishing right under Drake's nose.

'Come on come on come on!' said Drake. 'What's keeping you?'

Were they fighting inside the bottle?

'Come on, Blackwood!' screamed Drake. 'Come on, you crazy ganch!'

He struck at the red bottle tied to his belt. Then saw – smoke? A ghost? No: Blackwood, materializing on the deck.

Everyone but Blackwood and Drake was now in the red bottle.

'Do it!' said Drake. 'Use the death-stone! Quick!'

Blackwood proved to be wearing the death-stone in a leather bag slung round his neck beneath his clothing. He took it out. Held it high. Then shouted Words. They were long, tangled things in the High Speech, said so fast they were almost a gabble. Drake thought he caught a snatch of the spell – 'tabanagijish' – but even that he might have got wrong.

'Stand closer!' shouted Blackwood.

So Drake, to be safe, crouched at Blackwood's feet.

The sea was roaring. Or was it the sea? No, it was the sky. Grating, grinding. The flames – the flames were turning grey. The very air was grey. A red-hot coal flickered, flashed green, then went out. Still Blackwood stood there, arm raised, death-stone in hand.

There was a crash.

An enormous crash.

Chunks of rock flew across the deck, narrowly missing the two men. The mast had turned to stone, and the mast, falling, had shattered.

Drake heard a crackling sound, as if an intense fire was burning somewhere. But the fire on the ship seemed to be out. Where was the sound coming from? It was a skin of rock, forming on the surface of the sea, then breaking up with the action of the swells.

Drake peered into the grey distance.

Saw monsters of the Swarms writhing, freezing, falling. Saw a Neversh fall, turned to stone in flight. Saw logs submerge, sink, vanish – turned to stone.

This was a Cause with Effect indeed!

At last, the air cleared, and was no longer grey. But it was dry, yes, dry, and harsh on the throat. Drake heard, very clearly, swells slapping against the side of their stone ship. And an ugly grating sound as that ship began to crack open.

But, for the moment, the ship was still floating.

'She's starting to settle,' said Drake.

'What?' said Blackwood.

'The ship. She's getting lower in the water. Hey, man – up there! Neversh!'

There was indeed a Neversh still in the sky.

'The death-stone kills nothing which is more than two leagues away,' said Blackwood in a sombre voice, putting that stone back into its leather bag, which he then tucked away out of sight.

The ship was much lower in the water. It was going down fast. Drake went to the side.

'Better we jump, man, and swim clear,' he said.

Then suited actions to words. Water shot up his nose. The sea was cold!

'Come on, Blackwood!' yelled Drake.

And Blackwood followed.

They floundered away through the regular swells, gasping, striving, encumbered with boots and with clothes. Then they were sucked back as the ship went down – sucked back, pulled under, whirled round, coming to the surface at last breathless and chilled.

The sole surviving Neversh was flying high in long, slow circles. The entire sky was a mass of bruise-black storm-clouds. Lightning flickered on the horizon. No sign of land.

'Use the ring, man,' said Drake. 'Speed counts.'

He feared the cold. It was summer, true, but the sea was as cold as ever.

Blackwood grappled with the ring on his hand. And Drake realized that if Blackwood lost that ring, then everyone in the red bottle would be trapped there forever. And he, Drake, would very shortly drown.

The ring turned full circle.

A hole appeared in the sea where Blackwood had been. Water slapped into it, kicking up white foam. Another regular swell rocked Drake up, then down. He saw the Neversh lumbering through the air, coming in over the sea, very low. It was close. And closing. Where was Blackwood? Pox and bitches! The Neversh was dangling its grapple-hooks. The hooks tore foam from the top of a swell.

It was almost upon him.

Drake ducked under.

And dived, dived as he had learnt to years ago on Ling, forced his way down, down, deep and under, felt pressure build in his ears. Then turned. And started for the surface. Suddenly bubbles of air erupted around him. There were hands, arms, faces. There was rope in the water, a log – no, a spar. Then—

Up!

Drake burst to the surface. And up came half a dozen people – Blackwood, Jon Arabin, Whale Mike, Ish

Ulpin, Rolf Thelemite, Sully Yot. And with them, two spars, a dozen planks, some rope. Drake tried to speak, drank water, grabbed for a spar, clung to it and yelled:

'Neversh!'

'Where?' cried Blackwood.

And was torn from the water as the Neversh hooked his shoulder. Drake grabbed Blackwood's left leg as it went hauling past. He was dragged from the water. Sully Yot snatched at Drake's feet. Held fast.

The Neversh lifted the three of them: Blackwood, Drake and Yot. It flew on, its tail trailing in the water.

Whale Mike grabbed at the tail. The Neversh was brought to a dead halt by the sudden increase in weight. Its wings laboured.

'Up, boys!' hollered Jon Arabin.

And scrambled over Whale Mike's shoulders. And started racing up the tail of the Neversh.

'Ahyak Rovac!' screamed Rolf Thelemite.

And followed.

'Bugger that for a joke,' muttered Ish Ulpin.

But, after only a momentary hesitation, his innate reck-lessness got the better of him – and he too went racing up the tail of the monster.

The brute thrashed at the air with its wings and, slowly, ponderously, lifted the combined weight of six men and Whale Mike. Up they went. Up up up!

Then Blackwood's flesh gave way.

Blackwood, Drake and Sully Yot crashed into the sea. Coming to the surface, Drake saw the Neversh swinging round slowly, slowly, heavily. Whale Mike was still cling-ing to its tail, which was dangling low. Jon Arabin, Rolf Thelemite and Ish Ulpin were on the monster's back, stab-bing at its hide with their swords.

Where was Yot?

Thirty paces away, keeping himself afloat with a solemn dog-paddle. Where was Blackwood? Thirty paces in the opposite direction.

Drake started swimming.

Towards Blackwood.

Towards the ring which gave entry to the red bottle which was tied to Drake's waist.

Blackwood went under. Came up. Gasping. There was blood in the water around him.

Drake trod water and shouted:

'Use the ring!'

Better to get Blackwood into the bottle, now, before he went under. But Blackwood shouted back:

'One arm!'

From which Drake understood that one of Blackwood's arms was out of action because of his wounds.

'Hold the ring with your teeth!' shouted Drake. 'Hold the ring with your teeth, then turn your finger.'

Blackwood put finger to mouth.

Then disappeared.

Into the bottle?

Drake was not sure. He half-thought that Blackwood had been dragged under by something. Drake trod water. And saw Blackwood come to the surface, the sea around him boiling with blood. Blackwood opened his mouth and seemed to scream. But no sound came.

'Oh bugger, oh bugger,' said Drake, half-sobbing, half-screaming.

And struck out, swimming overarm, closing the distance. He was deathly tired as he came up with Blackwood. His boots felt like lead, pulling him down.

'Blackwood?' said Drake.

Grabbing at the man.

Who floated – whose torso floated. His legs were gone. The sea was red. And the ring? The ring, the ring! Drake grabbed Blackwood's hand, fastened his teeth on the ring, pulled it off – and, in his haste, swallowed it.

He had swallowed the ring!

Aghast, Drake poked two fingers down his own throat. And vomited. He tried to close his mouth on the vomit, coughed, almost choked, spluttered, gasped for air – and lost his mouthful of vomit to the ocean! He saw the ring amidst the vomit which had spilt to the sea.

Drake momentarily glimpsed the cold gold glint as it went writhing down through the waters. Then he was grabbing, grabbing at guess. Closing his fist on – water? Vomit? Seaweed?

Something hard.

He opened his fist.

Revealing cold gold.

Which he shoved onto his finger. Shoved so hard that he peeled away little strips of his own skin. But felt no pain, no pain, only shock at the vivid red of his blood spilling to the blood of the sea.

Now: the death-stone!

Drake grabbed at a leather cord round Blackwood's neck, hauled, brought to light the leather bag hanging from the leather cord, slipped it free from the dead man's head.

Kicked with his feet.

Eased himself away from the body.

Which staggered, struck, punched, slammed, hit from below and knocked up, over, thrashed into blood by – by a glimpse of grey, striking, striding, taking the body down, deep, down, gone. Brief glimpse of fin as it vanished.

That was a shark.

Drake screamed.

And was still wailing when the shark erupted from the water in front of him, reared up, rising, huge, smooth, monstrous, vast gulf of mouth – which he attacked, flailing at it with the leather bag. Leather bag heavy with death-stone.

And the shark bit.

Huge jaws crunching down.

Savaging the death-stone.

Which exploded into lightning, blowing the shark's head apart. Drake, blinded by flying gore, floundered, went under, came up, blinking away blood, blinking away water. Went under again. Could see, now.

769

The Neversh was no longer circling overhead. Instead, it was floating on the sea about a hundred paces away, thrashing furiously. Jon Arabin, Ish Ulpin and Rolf Thelemite had opened the Neversh's flotation tanks to the air, releasing the buoyant gas which the Neversh needed to fly. The three heroes had now turned their attention to the monster's tail. They were trying to hack tail from body.

Whale Mike was still clinging to the end of the tail, his weight effectively preventing the monster from using it as a weapon.

Drake heard something in the sea behind him. Turned, and saw it was Sully Yot.

'Hi,' said Drake, having no breath for further eloquence.

Yot closed the distance. And his hand came up from the water, armed with a knife.

'Die, Demon-son!' screamed Yot.

'You mad bugger!' said Drake.

And caught Yot's knife-hand.

Strength against strength they fought. Until finally Drake managed to secure the knife. And cut Yot's throat.

'Crazy,' muttered Drake.

Then let Yot's corpse float away, and used the knife to cut free his boots, which were threatening to drown him.

With boots gone, Drake released the knife. Let it fall away to the depths of the ocean. He lay back, floating in the swells which seemed to stretch away to eternity. Ocean. Blood. Rain. When had it started to rain? He had no idea. But it was raining with a vengeance now. Rain hammering out of the heavens.

A wave slapped Drake's face. He took a breath which was half water. He felt exhausted. Cold to the bone. Ready to die.

'But I'm not going to die yet,' muttered Drake to Drake.

No. He could not die. Not yet. For he carried the magic red bottle. And he carried the ring which commanded that bottle. And within the bottle was Zanya, his true love.

'Must stay afloat,' muttered Drake.

Swallowed water.

770

And was taken from behind, encircled by strength. In panic he fought, thrashed, struggled.

'Hey, man,' said Whale Mike. 'Not so rough. You my friend, right?'

'Right,' said Drake. 'I your friend.'

Then he fainted.

69

Tor: uninhabited island thirty leagues long lying near coast of Argan on western side of Drangsturm Gulf; heavily timbered, particularly with summerpine, cedar and roble; considerable bamboo resource; rich in caves and water; fauna includes several species of gecko, bat, tree-frog and chameleon found nowhere else.

Drake . . .

Drifted . . .

Tangled with weed . . . deep-fathomed in a sea of bloody intestines . . . lost amidst falling pearls, amidst moon-gilded suns . . . confused by his aliases . . . Drake Douay . . . passion of disintegrating stars, of baked potatoes and consuming flames . . . Dreldragon . . . blade chiming against blade . . . Lord Dreldragon . . . Plovey falling, dead . . . Arabin lol Arabin . . .

The rain, falling, drowning all the world in its own forevers. A dead Neversh, dragged down to the numb cold by the *Warwolf*'s anchor . . . Drake, drowning with the Neversh . . .

Surfacing, slowly.

'Drake?'

'Zanya . . .'

She laid herself down beside him.

They kissed. Her lips were corrugated with blue sores. Which revolted him. She was dying. No joy in her dying body. And Drake – Drake was disgusted. And hated himself for being disgusted.

'Don't cry, dearest treasure snake. Don't cry.'

But he wept in her arms. Helplessly.

Someone had undressed him. A mattress of sorts was under him; a blanket comforted his nakedness.

Drake smeared tears from his eyes, sniffed heavily, then said in a voice thick with sorrow:

'I love . . . I love you.'

And, as he said it, knew it was true. He loved Zanya, or some attribute of his association with Zanya, despite the diseased and failing state of her body. But what exactly was the nature of this emotional attachment?

What makes love love?

Is it an affection which can be separated from lust? Is it an alliance of wills? Is it something like homesickness, like nostalgia – a longing for the familiar, no matter how timeworn and battered? Is it a recognition of limits, a kind of maturity – settling for what is rather than what might be?

Drake – who, in early youth, had been schooled ruthlessly in thought by hard taskmasters – could not keep from wondering.

'I love you too,' said Zanya.

Drake knew she spoke out of sickness. She was dying: she needed him. Absolutely. But if she recovered? Why, then things would no longer be so simple, no longer love-love-love, but the contention of will against will, of ego against ego. The eternal game-playing of human relations.

Drake stopped trying to unravel the tail-chasing complexity of his own thoughts. He doubted he would ever get any absolute answer about the nature of love. Indeed, his education had included (as part of his training in the Inner Principles of the Old Science) a study of the Principle of Uncertainty, and the hopelessness of any quest for exact and absolute answers to anything.

(The Korugatu philosophers hold that we can be certain of some things at least, such as our own existence. As Klen Klo puts it: 'I think, therefore I am; I drink to unthink, which proves that I think.' But Drake's teachers had

773

taught him a more rigorous, more pessimistic formula: 'I think I think, therefore perhaps I am.')

'Where are we?' asked Drake, thus beginning an Investigation of his surroundings.

'Here,' said Zanya. 'Here.'

And now it was her turn to weep, and his turn to comfort her. While he held her close, he looked around, blinking away the last of his own tears. They were in the red bottle. They had to be. There was no other explanation. But it was not at all what he had expected.

They were camped between two ranks of monumental royal statues in a gloomy hall of utter silence. Sad and solemn, the kings of long-forgotten realms maintained a watch over them. Kings carved in rock on a scale so huge as to be oppressive. Ponderous entities of granite, of basalt, and unknown stones harder yet, and heavier. Lines of death and wisdom graved deep in their faces. Bearded men, some bare-headed, some helmeted. All armed.

And Drake, lying on his mattress with his woman in his arms, thought:

This is power.

Something about power.

It speaks of power.

It was the ultimate art of the State: huge, cold, implacable, inhuman. Built to crush all fragile emotion. To convince mere mortal bones of their fragility, of the uselessness of their protest.

And Drake (perhaps unfairly) thought:

Gouda Muck would have loved this place.

And Yot, too.

In the distance, someone was moving.

A man. Approaching. A single man.

Walking.

Boots striking echoes from the ranks of statue-kings. Echoes in a place otherwise utterly silence. Cool. Immense. A roof lifted beyond shadows. Walls lost in the distance. The floor beneath . . . veined with red. As if a million million blood-bearing capillaries ran through the stone.

Gently, Drake separated himself from Zanya.

'Dear treasure snake,' she said. 'What is it? Are you hungry? Here – drink this.'

And she handed him a curiously-carved cup of ivory. Inside was a dark, unwholesome fluid.

Drake drank. Then spluttered.

'Blood's grief! What's that?'

'Siege dust mixed with water,' said Zanya. 'Drink it. Come on! It's good for you!'

'Man, you've got to be kidding,' said Drake.

But he forced it down regardless.

And the lone man walking solo bore down on them. Falchion at his side. Jon Arabin.

'Drake,' he said. 'Recovered?'

'I live,' said Drake.

Looking for the ring, which he expected to see on Jon Arabin's hand. And did see.

'Who wears the bottle?' said Drake.

'Rolf Thelemite, for the moment,' said Jon Arabin. 'We've got a raft of sorts on the surface. A sail of sorts, too. The wind is from the east, so we're making for Tor. That's closest, in any case.'

'And the Neversh?'

'It's dead,' said Jon Arabin.

Drake braved himself to his feet, holding his blanket around him.

'What duty for me?' he said.

'To rest,' said Jon Arabin. 'To rest with your love. Nay, man – don't protest. All are resting if not needed on the surface. We'll be busy enough when we make shore at Tor.'

'All are resting?' said Drake. 'Where?'

'Above. Far above. You two . . . let privacy serve you.'

And, satisfied with what he had seen, Jon Arabin turned and walked away from the long avenue of ancient kings. They heard his boots for a long time until he vanished, ascending a staircase.

'Who are these kings?' said Drake.

'Who they are,' said Zanya. 'Who they were. Let me – let me look at you.'

And she took the blanket away, and gazed on what she thought of as his beauty. Lean flanks. A fluff of gingerish hair on his chest. A scraggly ginger beard on his chin. Hair yellow, bleached toward pale by the sun. Scars of whip-marks on his back. Scar encircling left ankle, where slave iron had gnawed his flesh when he was labouring in servitude aboard a galley on the Velvet River.

'Turn around,' demanded Zanya.

Upon which Drake thought to raise his hands above his head and spin like a dancer. But he found himself too sore. Which was scarcely surprising, since there were rainbow bruises all over his body.

'If we get to Ling,' said Zanya. 'If we get what we're seeking, if we get a cure – I'll want more than to look.'

'I know that, most dearest saucy wench,' said Drake.

And hugged her.

Ling was still far, but Tor was closer.

After five days at sea, the clumsy raft which carried the red bottle grounded on the shores of Tor. Soon, every survivor from the good ship *Dragon* was out in the open air. The shore was of rocks and sand edged with rough grass, beyond which grew cool forest. The sky was of opal-bright blue, washed with wind and sunshine.

Ish Ulpin and Bucks Cat immediately set off hunting. In the red bottle, they had fed on nothing but siege dust – a survival food which tastes as bad as it sounds.

The wizard Miphon also wandered off towards the forest. He wanted to be alone, to mourn the death of his friend Blackwood, and the loss of control of the red bottle to Jon Arabin. From the edge of the forest, Miphon looked back and saw Arabin standing in company with Drake Douay, Zanya Kliedervaust and Whale Mike.

Whale Mike had the red bottle tied to his belt.

Jon Arabin wore the ring which commanded the bottle. A good team: Miphon's chances of getting the bottle off them by bluff, guile or violence were more or less zero. So . . . to the forest, then . . .

Jon Arabin, watching Miphon go, guessed what he was feeling. Well, too bad. Jon Arabin had need of that red bottle. It would be the foundation of his new empire.

He had worked it all out by now.

The Greater Teeth were finished.

With the collapse of piracy as a profitable profession, those remaining on the Teeth were doomed to a life of ever-increasing poverty. Better to start afresh, here on Tor, which was rich in water and timber. They could build ships; they could trade between Ling, Stokos and the Scattered Islands; they could build a seapower empire.

'Tools,' said Jon Arabin, raising his voice in command. 'Rolf! Rally a work party. We need to get tools out of the red bottle. Aye. Axes. Hatchets. Saws, if they're to be found. Nails. We've a boat to build.'

'A boat?' said Drake. 'We'll need a ship to carry so many.'

'You not worry about any ship,' said Whale Mike. 'You build nice boat, take sick people to Ling. Friend Walrus, he tell me all about it. Magic snakes. Good stuff, eh? Maybe snakes here, good eating.'

'Mike's right,' said Jon Arabin. 'All we need is an open boat. With so many men, we can build one quickly. Then make the journey to Ling, aye, soon enough. We're now but a hundred leagues from Ling.'

'He right,' said Whale Mike. 'After you gone, we start proper ship. You come back from Ling, we have ship finished. Sail north. We get people from Greater Teeth. That place not so good now. My wife like this place. She like green stuff, always complain Teeth all rock. My kids like this place too. You like it, Jon? We make you king, man. You make good king.'

'Maybe I would,' said Jon Arabin, first with a smile and then with a laugh. 'Maybe I would.'

The logic was inescapable.

'Some people may come,' said Drake. 'But a lot won't,

I bet. Bluewater Draven would never shift. He loves it, lording the Teeth.'

'Then let him stay on his stupid rocks and rot,' said Zanya. 'Come on, my hero! How about hunting up something fresh for me?'

'What do you want, my darling?' said Drake.

'A butterfly would do to start with,' she said.

And Drake thought she was joking. But, in truth, people from the Ebrells did eat butterflies on occasion. These two young lovers still had many surprises in store for each other.

Elsewhere, in the caves of Ling itself, a very old woman lay dying. Now, for the first time in seven days, she spoke:

'They . . .'

'They what?' said one of the elders who waited on her.

'They are coming,' said the Great One.

Weakly.

Her red-veined eyes – blind now for a year – staring at nothing as her mouth writhed, struggling with prophecy.

'Coming . . . they . . . an island . . . a ship . . . yes . . . He is coming . . . Jon . . . Jon Arabin . . .'

The watchers by her death-bed looked at each other. So the Great One was cracking up after all.

'You think,' she said, startling them by the sudden strength in her voice, 'you think you see a foolish old woman dying. Speaking nonsense as she dies. But you will learn. He comes. Jon Arabin. His son with him, the pure one. He who ventured to the Forbidden Tower.'

She sank back on the sands of her bed.

Fading.

Muttering.

The watchers listened, and heard:

'. . . sickness . . . from the Plague Lands . . . a woman . . . a man . . . prepared . . . initiate . . .'

Her mouth fluttered.

Shaping sibilants. And said:

'He will rule amongst you . . .'

Then said no more.

'She is gone,' said one of the elders. 'She is dead.'

With the Great One dead, the elders of Ling ignored her prophecy, and made no plans for the reception of Jon Arabin, his son, and the sick people travelling with them. Truly it has been Written (in Kalob V, quilt 7, section 2a, line xviii): 'A prophet has no honour in her own country.'

But, before long, a boat appeared in Ling Bay. Canoes ventured forth to see if those aboard were dangerous. Then the canoes escorted the boat into the caves, where it grounded at last on the Sacred Sands.

There were half a dozen men aboard, and there was one woman.

One of the men was Jon Arabin. And the elders knew him well, and realized that the Great One had indeed spoken truth in prophecy. And they fell down in awe, and lamented. They had doubted! They had sinned!

But Jon Arabin said (or is reported to have said, which is not necessarily the same thing):

'Fear not, for I bring not death but justice. Aye. And we have sick people who need to be seen to. So move your arses!'

It is usually impossible to deduce anything so elusive as a moral from the workings of history. But the diligent student will, no doubt, make an exception in this case, and will fortify the arsenal of wisdom with the following observation:

While Great Ones do have their off-days, it is always less than wise for the unwise to write them off completely.

THE END

The Wizards and the Warriors
by Hugh Cook

CHRONICLES OF AN AGE OF DARKNESS 1:
'I ask all of you here today to join with me in pledging yourself
to a common cause,' said Miphon. Elkor Alish laughed
harshly: 'A common cause? Between wizards and the Rovac?
Forget it!'

And yet it had to be. Through Alish never accepted the
Alliance, his fellow warrior Morgan Hearst joined forces with
Miphon and the other wizards. The only alternative was the
utter destruction of their world.

The first volume in a spectacular fantasy epic to rival THE
BELGARIAD and THE CHRONICLES OF THOMAS
COVENANT.

0552 125660

The Wordsmiths and the Warguild
by Hugh Cook

CHRONICLES OF AN AGE OF DARKNESS: 2

'Thanks to the wizard of Drum,' said the Brother, 'we know where to find these boxes. The nearest is in the bottom of a green bottle in Prince Comedo's Castle Vaunting in Estar. A monster protects the bottle from those who would acquire it.'

'Charming,' murmured Togura.

Togura would not have chosen the profession of questing hero but in the end he had no choice. He was caught between The Wordsmiths and The Warguild, the two organizations which vied for power within the dismal kingdom of Sung, a land famous simply for being so often and so richly insulted.

Besides, if he did not find the *index,* the key to the magical treasure chest known as the *odex,* he would never be able to claim his love from its mysterious depths.

0552 13130X

The Women and the Warlords
by Hugh Cook

CHRONICLES OF AN AGE OF DARKNESS: 3

'Lord Alagrace said you'd help.'

'Any oracle can give you a reading,' replied Yen Olass.

'I told Alagrace an oracle couldn't help me,' said the Ondrask. 'I told him I wasn't interested in a reading. But he told me you'd do better than that. He told me you'd fix it.'

'What?' said Yen Olass.

She was genuinely shocked, and it took a lot to shock her.

So begins Yen Olass's involvement in the life-long feud of the warlords of the Collosnon Empire. She was to witness war, madness and wizardry, and would play a greater part in the events of her time than a mere oracle had any right to expect.

0552 131318

Servants of Ark
by Jonathan Wylie

'The confrontation, when it came, was cataclysmic. The powers involved were beyond our imagining, but it was a time of great heroism — for men as well as mages. There are many tales of those who fought alongside the wizards. They called themselves the Servants.'

Ferragamo's words referred to the first War of the Wizards, many centuries earlier. Since that time, The Servants had acted as guardians to the islands of their world. Now, after long ages of peace, the new generations of Servants were being called upon to face the resurgence of a long-vanquished evil.

Their story is told in this compelling trilogy.

A SELECTION OF TITLES
AVAILABLE FROM CORGI BOOKS

THE PRICES SHOWN BELOW WERE CORRECT AT THE TIME OF GOING TO PRESS. HOWEVER TRANSWORLD PUBLISHERS RESERVE THE RIGHT TO SHOW NEW RETAIL PRICES ON COVERS WHICH MAY DIFFER FROM THOSE PREVIOUSLY ADVERTISED IN THE TEXT OR ELSEWHERE.

☐ 12566 0	THE WIZARDS AND THE WARRIORS		*Hugh Cook*	£3.50
☐ 13130 X	THE WORDSMITHS AND THE WARGUILD		*Hugh Cook*	£2.95
☐ 13131 8	THE WOMEN AND THE WARLORDS		*Hugh Cook*	£2.95
☐ 13017 6	BOOK ONE OF THE MALLOREON: GUARDIANS OF THE WEST		*David Eddings*	£2.95
☐ 12284 X	BOOK ONE OF THE BELGARIAD: PAWN OF PROPHECY		*David Eddings*	£2.50
☐ 12348 X	BOOK TWO OF THE BELGARIAD: QUEEN OF SORCERY		*David Eddings*	£2.95
☐ 12382 X	BOOK THREE OF THE BELGARIAD: MAGICIAN'S GAMBIT		*David Eddings*	£2.95
☐ 12435 4	BOOK FOUR OF THE BELGARIAD: CASTLE OF WIZARDRY		*David Eddings*	£2.95
☐ 12447 8	BOOK FIVE OF THE BELGARIAD: ENCHANTERS' END GAME		*David Eddings*	£2.95
☐ 12097 9	THE CRYSTAL SINGER		*Anne McCaffrey*	£2.50
☐ 12556 3	KILLASHANDRA		*Anne McCaffrey*	£2.95
☐ 12683 7	EXILES OF THE RYNTH		*Carole Nelson Douglas*	£2.95
☐ 12682 9	SIX OF SWORDS		*Carole Nelson Douglas*	£2.95
☐ 13105 9	EQUAL RITES		*Terry Pratchett*	£2.50
☐ 12848 1	THE LIGHT FANTASTIC		*Terry Pratchett*	£2.50
☐ 12475 3	THE COLOUR OF MAGIC		*Terry Pratchett*	£2.50
☐ 12834 1	THE CHRONICLES OF MAVIN MANYSHAPED		*Sheri S. Tepper*	£4.95
☐ 12620 9	THE TRUE GAME		*Sheri S. Tepper*	£4.95
☐ 13101 6	SERVANTS OF ARK BOOK 1: THE FIRST NAMED		*Jonathan Wylie*	£2.95
☐ 13134 2	SERVANTS OF ARK BOOK 2: THE CENTRE OF THE CIRCLE		*Jonathan Wylie*	£2.95
☐ 13161 X	SERVANTS OF ARK BOOK 3: THE MAGE-BORN CHILD		*Jonathan Wylie*	£2.95